Jacob Michaels Is…
Omnibus Edition

A Point Worth LGBTQ+
Paranormal Romance
Books 1-6

Chase Connor

The Lion Fish Press

Chase Connor Books

The Lion Fish Press

www.chaseconnor.com

www.thelionfishpress.com

Book Cover Designed By: Dean Cole, ©2020 Chase Connor

CHASE CONNOR BOOKS are published by

The Lion Fish Press
539 W. Commerce St #227
Dallas, TX 75208

AUTHORS' NOTE:
This is a work of fiction. Names, characters, places, and incidents either are the product of the authors' imagination or are used fictitiously, and any resemblance to actual persons, living or dead, business establishments, events, or locales is entirely coincidental. None of this is real.

Ebook ISBN 978-1-951860-12-7
Paperback ISBN 978-1-951860-11-0

As always:

To my beta-readers and "feedback crew": I am so glad you are all here. And I am so glad you are all so blunt with me— even if I do what I want most of the time.

To all of the readers: It has been quite a journey. I've loved every second of it. Let's get to the end together, shall we?

Also by Chase Connor

LGBTQ+ YA Books

Just a Dumb Surfer Dude: A Gay Coming-of-Age Tale
Just a Dumb Surfer Dude 2: For the Love of Logan
Just a Dumb Surfer Dude 3: Summer Hearts
Gavin's Big Gay Checklist
A Surplus of Light
The Guy Gets Teddy
GINJUH

LGBTQ+ New Adult and Lit Fic

A Tremendous Amount of Normal
The Gravity of Nothing
Between Enzo & the Universe
A Straight Line (w/ J.D. Wade)
A Boy Called Never
It Means Something Different

LGBTQ+ YA & MG Fantasy

A Million Little Souls

A Point Worth LGBTQ Paranormal Romances

Jacob Michaels Is Tired (Book 1)
Jacob Michaels Is Not Crazy (Book 2)
Jacob Michaels Is Not Jacob Michaels (Book 3)
Jacob Michaels Is Not Here (Book 4)
Jacob Michaels Is Trouble (Book 5)
CARNAVAL (A Point Worth LGBTQ Paranormal Romance Story)
Jacob Michaels Is Dead (Book 6)

Erotica

Bully

Audiobooks

A Surplus of Light: A Gay Coming-of-Age Tale

Table of Contents

Jacob Michaels Is Tired

A Point Worth LGBTQ
Paranormal Romance
Book 1

Chapter 1

A hospital. That's where everything would have ended. I would have ended up in some ritzy place with a king-size bed, a private balcony, a jetted tub, a separate living room, a kitchenette, a lap pool, overlooking the ocean, with a five-star restaurant on site. I would get room service breakfast every day, massages and other spa treatments, private laundry service, satellite television, high-speed Wi-Fi, and every other amenity that I could ever want. That would have been the type of place I would have ended up at if things had continued. Of course, that wouldn't have solved the problem. But people in my industry still tend to jettison off to those types of places at least once in their career, claim "exhaustion"—or maybe Epstein-Barre—and hide away for a 30-day vacation.

I wouldn't have been the first to do it.

Hiding away from time to time over the last ten years wasn't exactly a new concept to me. I had spent time in India at the feet of Sadhus. In Tibet with monks who refused to speak but were not above a reproaching glare if I stepped out of line. I'd been to Machu Pichu, the rainforests, a retreat to see the Northern Lights, done an Ayahuasca retreat in Peru, and been on safari in what was white people's version of "wild Africa." I'm pretty sure the wilds of Africa didn't include fancy treehouse style hotels with twelve-hundred thread count sheets on the Tempur-Pedic mattresses.

Other times, I had just taken Ecstasy and danced at some of the most exclusive clubs in L.A., New York, Ibiza, Las Vegas, London, Tokyo—everywhere in the world, really. Anywhere there was hedonism and debauchery, places that helped the rich and overprivileged "relax." But a decade of using alternative forms of treatment had left me completely exhausted. Left me uncreative, unproductive, and unhappy. Exhaustion was definitely my diagnosis now—and I wasn't using the word as a euphemism for "drug problem" or "secret sex tape"—though I'd used drugs recreationally before. Nothing severe, but using drugs is still not the best choice sometimes. However, I could almost guarantee that there were no sex tapes featuring yours truly out there since I hadn't had sex in so long that I almost forgot what it was like to actually touch another man in that way.

Ultimately, I was merely exhausted. When I looked into the rearview mirror, the dark circles under my eyes were almost as dark as my pupils. Maybe that was hyperbole, but they were definitely prominent. I hadn't trimmed my stylish beard in several days, and I was desperately in need of a shower. But I hadn't dared to stop to get a hotel on my cross-country trip. Sure, if I'd had an assistant, agent, or manager with me, I would have just sent them inside to pay and get a key to a room. By myself, however, that was a dangerous idea. Being so recognizable has its drawbacks. Even stopping for gas, I put off until the very last second since I was paranoid that someone would recognize me while at the pumps.

I'd been on the road for nearly forty-two hours. Even with the Red Bulls and coffees, and several cigarettes, I'd still had to stop to take naps in out of the way rest stops along the way. The car was smelling somewhat rank, and I felt like I was getting at least one bedsore from sitting for so long. God, I'd lost so much weight. Not that I was ever more than a decent weight for my size, but I had gone from a healthy weight, well-toned, muscled, tan—to...this. I was pale, skeletal, and weak. Even the camera couldn't make up for all the weight I had lost over the last six months.

When I crossed into Ohio from Indiana on highway 90, I breathed a little easier. I had less than two hours to go before I could park my car, crawl into a bed, and pretend to be dead for as long as I could. I lit up a cigarette and cracked the driver's side window, immediately being assaulted by frigid air. Obviously, no one had told upper Ohio that Spring had sprung. I shoved the cigarette between my teeth and held it tightly as I pulled my cardigan more snuggly around me, somehow managing to keep the car on the road throughout the process. Between the frigid air and the cigarette, as well as the last half of a Red Bull in the cupholder, I'd be able to drive for the two hours I had left.

Glancing at the gas gauge, I gave a sigh of relief. A little over half a tank of gas. I could easily make it to Point Worth. Thrown out into skull-fucked nowhere of Ohio, between Toledo and Marblehead, is Point Worth, right on the shores of Lake Erie. It's a town of less than five-thousand and has all the amenities you'd expect for a population that size. A good time in Point Worth is driving into Toledo for "fine dining" and a visit to the "big ole movie theater." It's the kind of place where you see a lot of Carhartt, if you catch my drift. The coveralls and bib-overalls are particularly popular during fall and winter.

Thinking of the fashion choices in Point Worth, I glanced down at myself. My DSquared2 jeans, R13 distressed Cashmere Sweater, Brunello Cucinelli cardigan, and Buscemi sneakers would look out of place. Yeah, I looked like a bunch of designers tossed their highly pricey and ugly cookies up all over me. However, they were all the warmest items in my bags, so that's what I was wearing. I'd do some shopping when I got to Point Worth so that I'd blend in better with the locals. After I slept for days. But I'd tie cinderblocks around my ankles and throw myself into Lake Erie before I wore Carhartt. I'd done enough of that in my youth. Besides, the color of mustard-brown shit is not really the best look for me.

It's funny how the last two hours of a long trip are always the longest and hardest. The last of my Red Bull disappeared quickly, and my cigarettes were dwindling rapidly. I groaned to myself as I realized that I'd either have to slow down on the chain-smoking or stop again before Point Worth. Risking a problem so close to Point Worth, I ended up stopping at a convenience store in the middle of nowhere and grabbed another Red Bull and a carton of cigarettes. Menthol. They had the best bang for your buck, in my opinion.

When the wheels of my car first touched pavement past the city limits of Point Worth, I had smoked nearly half of a fresh pack of cigarettes, and the freshly purchased Red Bull had been drained. I was still more tired than I ever remembered being in my entire life. I put my sunglasses on—designer again—as I drove through town as quickly as I could without drawing the attention of the police. Luckily, I was driving my old Lincoln MKZ, which I had done on purpose, so the car itself didn't draw much attention if any.

Halfway through town, I hooked a left towards the shores of Lake Erie, where, on the outskirts of town, my salvation awaited. When I could see Lake Erie in the distance, I gave a sigh of relief as I took another turn down a wooded road. A few miles further and I found the driveway I'd been looking for like I had just been there the day before. I drove down the long driveway until the woods gave way to an acre-sized clearing. The American Craftsman style home, still in excellent condition, sat in the middle of the lot, forest greens and browns and majestic, looking like Heaven.

The old Chevy pickup that was always up by the house was still sitting there, clean and in excellent shape—yet ancient. The smaller Honda Civic, newer, but also in excellent condition sat next to it. I pulled up behind the Civic and threw my car into park. Immediately, I turned the car off and laid my head against the steering wheel. I had a quarter tank of gas left. Now I was safe, and I didn't have to worry about stopping anywhere. Of course, I could've filled up when I stopped for Red Bull and cigarettes, but I had just wanted to get what I had stopped for and go.

With a great summoning of will and determination, I opened my door and stepped out onto the gravel driveway onto rickety legs. The wood stacked at the side of the house still had piles of slush on it, though the rest of the acre seemed fairly clear of winter. I grabbed my bags from the trunk, as well as the overly large gift bag, and locked the car up tight. Not that anyone would be dumb enough to try to steal anything on this piece of land. I walked around the house from the driveway and started up the steps to the front porch. However, before I made it to the porch, the front door swung open, and a whirlwind made up of a housedress, slippers, and cackling voice accosted me.

"Well, if you came looking for warm weather, you fucked up, Robbie!" The crazed woman laughed loudly. "You should've brought some of that California weather with you!"

"Hi, Oma." I smiled weakly at her.

"*Hi, Oma. Hi, Oma* he says." She put her hands on her hips. "I haven't seen hide nor hair of you in two years, and the best you got is *hi, Oma?*"

"I'm sorry." I grinned. "It's been a long trip, and I'm just exhausted."

"Well, you look like something the cat swallowed whole and barfed up half-digested, that's for sure." She shook her head.

I grimaced as she marched forward and threw her arms around me, bags and all. Even being hugged hurt my bones and what little muscle I had left.

"You smell like Big Foot's asshole, too." She pulled away but didn't rub salt into the wound by making a face. "You're still smoking."

I just looked at her.

"I brought you a gift." I held up the gift bag.

"Is it chocolate?" She asked. "You know I got the sugars."

"It's not chocolate, Oma," I replied. "You can't eat it."

"Well, shit." She sighed, disappointed, then looked me up and down. "That's...well, that's an outfit."

I frowned.

"Look like something straight out of a fashion magazine. You may as well get in the house." She shrugged. "Can't get you settled in if you just stand out here looking like an idiot, can we?"

"I guess not," I said neutrally.

"Did you have any trouble driving in?" My grandmother asked me as we entered the house and she shut the door tightly against the cold. "All the roads were surely clear by now?"

"It was a little patchy in Iowa and Illinois," I answered, still holding my bags, looking in at the warm living room and the wide staircase that led upstairs. "But nothing too bad."

"Sons of bitches can't even agree on a baseball team, how the hell do you expect their infrastructure to work?" She snorted. "Now, look, I made you some Bratwurst, creamed peas and potatoes, cabbage..."

My stomach turned.

"And you look like you could use a good meal." She finished.

Her eyes were appraising the dark circles under my eyes and the sharp angles of my face. I didn't want to remove my cardigan.

"Yeah." I nodded, not wanting to admit the truth. "That sounds delicious, Oma."

My grandmother beamed at me, but her eyes looked sad.

The truth was, I didn't know if my stomach would allow me to keep down a meal made up of greasy sausage, creamy vegetables, and gas-inducing greenery. I didn't have to ask to know that there was probably also bacon in the cabbage. And, if I knew my Oma, she had made an apple pie or Stollen. But...if I didn't eat, that would bring on a whole new set of problems that I didn't want to deal with at the moment, if ever.

"Just set those bags down, then." She shoved at my arms. "We'll get them up to your room after you eat."

It was barely eleven o'clock in the morning, which is when I told my grandmother to expect me. I hadn't even eaten anything for breakfast. In fact, I hadn't eaten anything substantial in seventy-two hours. Coffee, Red Bull, and nicotine had been my sustenance for the last three days. I had only slept sporadically. My body was going to reject the food. There was no way I was going to keep it down. However, I just had to keep it down until I got upstairs. No matter how exhausted I was, I knew that I could do that.

"Just sit down there." My grandmother practically shoved me into a chair at the kitchen chair and tossed her gift bag into another chair. "I'll fix us a plate. What do you want to drink, Robbie?"

"Rob's fine." I rolled my eyes since her back was turned. "Water, please."

"I'll call you whatever the Hell I want." My grandmother waggled her head as she faced the stove, plate in hand. "I wiped your ass and nose, I'll call you Robbie 'til the fucking cows come home."

"Okay." I put my elbows on the table and rested my head in my hands.

"You must be tired from the trip." She snorted as she shoveled food onto the plate in her hand. "Giving up that easy."

I just made a humming sound in response.

My grandmother worked at the stove for a minute, doling out portions of food onto the first plate, then another. Finally, she came over to the table and slapped one of them down in front of me. Upon the plate sat a single Bratwurst, one spoonful of the potatoes and peas, and a small portion of the cabbage. Her plate held twice as much food as the one she had practically slammed down in front of me. She sat down in the seat across from me and glared at me.

"What?" I asked it more roughly than I had intended.

"Maybe you won't puke it up if you don't eat too much." She growled back. "What the Hell have you gotten up to? You look like a goddamn corpse, and that uppity looking sweater isn't hiding shit from me. It doesn't cover your goddamn face."

"It's a cardigan."

"It could be a goddamn tarp and I'd still know you weigh fifty pounds less than the last time I saw you." She snorted. "You been on that stuff?"

"That...*stuff*?"

"Don't play dumb with me." She picked her fork up aggressively. "You know what I'm talking about. You been doing them drugs?"

"Not for over a year," I replied evenly.

"Mmm." She appraised me. "Ya' sick? You got that HIV or something? Shooting up can do that. All that unprotected sex..."

"I've never shot up anything, and I've never in my life had unprotected sex." I rolled my eyes. "I've been tested every six months since I was twenty-years-old and my doctor put me on PrEP five years ago. Not that I need it right now, so that's moot."

"Now, I've heard of that." She jabbed her fork at me. "The boys over in Toledo at the center were telling me about how you can get it for free if you do this voucher program."

I nodded.

"You still volunteer at the LGBTQ center?" I asked, picking up my fork.

"Have been since before you left." She shook her head like I was an idiot for thinking otherwise. "Like an asshole in the middle of the night. And it's LGBTQIA now."

I rolled my eyes.

"But don't change the fucking subject." She skewered a potato and crammed it in her mouth. "Why the Hell do you look like Death warmed over, Robbie?"

I used my fork to cut a bite-size piece of bratwurst off and tentatively shoved it in my mouth. It was delicious. And I wanted to puke. But I chewed it and swallowed, managing to not grimace.

"I'm tired," I replied. "I'm...I'm just tired, Oma."

"Well, tired calls for a nap." She snorted once again. "You look like you're ready for the dirt."

It wasn't my intention, but I dropped my fork on my plate and put my head to the table. And then the tears came. Silent, but big and wet, rolling out of my eyes onto the wood directly beneath my face.

"Put your napkin under your face, so you don't ruin the finish." My grandmother stated blandly.

I just did as I was told and slid the cloth napkin under my face. For what seemed like forever, I cried exhausted tears, wondering how I had let myself get to this place physically, emotionally, and mentally. How was I back at my Oma's house in the middle of nowhere, looking skeletal, all of the life I had completely gone. When the tears finally stopped, I sat up, puffy faced, *surely*, with red eyes, *absolutely*, and picked my fork back up.

"I hope you didn't come here for sympathy." She eyed me. "You're welcome here as long as you want, Robbie. But I'm not going to sit here and play the 'poor pitiful me' game with you. You just had to rush off and act a damn fool, you sit there and suffer."

"Thanks, Oma." I sniffled wetly and cut off another piece of sausage. "I knew I could count on you."

"Count on me?" She scoffed. "Who the Hell got up in the middle of the night when you called last night and made up a room with fresh sheets, aired out the room, and made it livable again? Damn right, I'll take your thanks. And whatever gift's in that bag, ya' little asshole."

"Could you not..."

"No, I cannot." She stopped me. "And if you weren't so goddamn special now, you'd have remembered your manners. You left here in the middle of the night, *sixteengoddamnyearsold*, without so much as a word, and I haven't seen an inch of your skin more than three times in the decade since."

"Look, I'm sorry, Oma, but..."

"And I don't give a good goddamn how special you are in Hollywood—or all over the world. You're here. You're only going to hear the truth from me, Robbie."

"Rob."

"Thought you'd been going by 'Jacob'?" She waved me off. "Of all the dumbass things. Like Robert Wagner is such a bad name."

"Of course it's not bad." I shook my head, shoving another piece of the sausage into my mouth. "But, surely, someone of your age is aware that there's already an actor by that name?"

She waggled her head again.

"Still better than 'Jacob Michaels'." She replied. "Sounds like a goddamn rock star or porn star."

"Well, I have been known to put on a concert," I mumbled.

"Yeah, yeah." She waved me off. "I saw that on T.V. Royal Albert Hall—aren't you fancy? Okay. So, that show was pretty good. But you're not as special as you think, Robbie."

"I played Carnegie, too. Twice." I looked up at her.

She couldn't help herself, she chuckled.

"I don't think I'm *special*, Oma." I sighed, sliding my fork into the potatoes. "I'm just tired now. Nothing else."

We ate in silence for several minutes, casting glances at each other from time to time, trying to find some middle ground.

"You ever at least get your GED?" She asked.

"Yes," I said. "I got it when I was twenty-one and had a break."

"Well, a postcard or something telling me as such would've been nice." She said. "Or, ya' know, you could've called or told me on one of your brief visits."

"Oma. I'm sorry." I said, totally devoid of energy. "Can we finish this fight tomorrow? I just don't have it in me."

"I doubt you'll be up before Monday." She rolled her eyes. "But you can bet your ass we'll fight then, too."

"Great." I spat. "Can't wait."

"What's in this goddamn bag?!" She growled, yanking the gift bag out of the chair at the side of the table.

My grandmother yanked the paper out of the top of the bag and pulled out the box holding her gift. The ladies at the store had wrapped it for me. I had done the shopping myself, but I'd paid for gift wrapping. When you drop nearly so much money on one item, you may as well splurge and get the item professionally wrapped. I didn't try to get the purse for free or even at reduced cost directly from Balenciaga. If they found out I was just giving it to my grandmother, they wouldn't have cared in the slightest. My grandmother pried the box open violently, then stopped suddenly, her face going blank.

"Do you like it?" I asked blandly.

"It's a purse."

"It's a Balenciaga," I said.

"Well, I don't know what the Hell that is...but this is goddamn gorgeous is what it is." She mooned over the bag inside. "How much this set you back?"

"Don't worry about it."

"Well, if it cost more than a hundred bucks, I'll beat the Hell out of you."

"Then it cost fifty," I replied.

"Fifty my cellulite-riddled ass." She laughed suddenly, yanking the bag out of the box and turning it over and around, looking at it from every angle. "Black goes with everything."

"Balenciaga goes with anything."

"I'll tell people it's a Coach bag." She nodded, making me cringe. "No one knows what the Hell Balensiatcha or whatever is. And no one knows how to pronounce that."

"People in Spain might disagree, but whatever makes you happy, Oma."

"You went to fucking Spain for a handbag??"

"No." I laughed loudly. "There's a shop in Beverly Hills."

She waggled her head again, but her spirit wasn't in it. The bag was just too exquisite for her to pretend she wasn't impressed. My grandmother examined the bag inside and out, getting more and more impressed the longer she looked at it. Then, suddenly, she seemed to have a thought.

"The boys at the center will love it." She beamed. "You don't know him because you haven't been here in forever, but Carlos, he's a drag queen, and he's my favorite of all my boys—he loves fashion. He'll be jealous as shit. You think we could order one for him?"

"It cost over fourteen-thousand dollars," I said evenly.

"Well...*shit.*" She held the purse to her chest as she stared down at it. "Can you get him something nice—but not that nice? Maybe some nice high heels or something?"

"I'll order something for Carlos, Oma." I just agreed so that I wouldn't have to argue. "What size high heel does Carlos wear?"

"How the Hell should I know?"

"Well, I thought maybe you were loaning him some of your items."

"You've still got a goddamn smart mouth." She snapped, but there was a twinkle in her eye.

"Find out his heel size, Oma." I waved her off. "I'll order him some Louboutin heels. If they come in his size."

"Those the one with the red soles?"

"Yes."

She squealed and hugged her purse.

"You sure got over being mad at me." I cocked an eyebrow at her.

Even that hurt.

"I'm happy for Carlos and me. You're still a fucking asshole." She snapped again. "But...thank you, Robbie."

"Of course." I nodded before shoving a potato into my mouth.

After I managed to finish the scant amount of food that my grandmother had put on my plate, drank a big glass of water, and helped her put things away, I was allowed to grab my bags and make my way upstairs. Oma was on my heels as we climbed the stairs together, her steps much steadier and spry than my own. At the top of the stairs, I was slightly out of breath, and she dashed around me down the hall. She dashed past what used to be my room when I was a teenager and went to the end of the hall.

"What?" I pointed at my old door.

"Turned it into a sewing room." She answered. "I'm going to put you in your mom and dad's old room. So, you'll have your own bathroom."

"Okay."

I ventured further down the hall and let her open the door for me. Inside, the room was immaculate, smelled fresh, and there was nothing but the furniture to remind me of my parents. Not that being reminded of them was particularly hard on me. The furniture was all still the same—heavy, dark wood, well-made. But all of the linens were different, the pictures on the wall were bright and cheerful, the curtains were gauzy with heavier drapes pulled to the side. Early Spring sunlight streamed through the windows, making the room look absolutely cheerful.

Oma watched as I sauntered over to the bed and set my bags down at the foot of the bed. I looked around the room, spotting the door to the bathroom off to the side. It was a relatively small bathroom, but it was private, and it was clean. That's all that I cared about. It had a large claw foot tub and a hand-held shower head, a pedestal sink, medicine cabinet, it would be more than enough. The room itself was large, with enough room for a chest of drawers, a king-size bed, two bedside tables, and a sofa. This was almost like going for an extended stay at a B&B.

"Don't you smoke those cigarettes in here." Oma snarled.

"I'll go outside when I smoke."

"And don't do any drugs in here."

I glared at her.

"I don't do drugs." I snapped. "I'm not going to tell you again."

"Okay." She nodded. "You ain't got any on you, do you?"

"Only prescription." I squinted at her.

"Anything good?"

I rolled my eyes. "Just Paxil and Nexium."

"Damn." She shrugged.

My grandmother wasn't going to take pills that weren't prescribed to her, so I don't know why she was posturing. Of course, she might have just been curious about what good drugs she thought a celebrity from Hollywood took.

"Why the Hell are you on Paxil for fuck's sake?" She asked. "Dropping fourteen-grand on a purse take it out of you?"

"Can we discuss it later?"

She rolled her eyes but relented.

"Well, get them clothes off, and I'll get them washed." She said, heading towards the door. "Probably have to wash every-damn-thing you brought the way you smoke."

"The bags were in the trunk."

"Well, I'll wash your sweaters and jeans if you want." She said. "And your underbritches. Just leave them in the hall there."

"It'll all have to be dry cleaned." I shook my head.

"Even your underwear?!?"

"Well, no."

"Oh." She nodded. "Well, I'm not just washing a pair of underwear. Throw 'em in the hamper."

"I can do my own laundry, Oma."

"You don't know how to work my machine." She waved me off. "I don't know that we have a dry cleaner in town. But we can run your fancy ass clothes over to Toledo when I go to the center one day next week."

"Okay." I shrugged. "Or I can do it myself."

"I bet you haven't seen the inside of a dry cleaner or a washing machine since you were eighteen-years-old." She snorted. "Probably wouldn't know what the Hell to do. Probably got an assistant for all of that."

"She doesn't do my laundry."

She was waggling her head again.

"Just, leave me be, please." I waved her off. "I'll take care of my laundry."

"Fine." She turned up her nose and screwed up her mouth. "I'll bring you some dinner later."

"I just want to sleep."

"I'll bring you some fucking dinner later, Robbie." She stated loudly. "You can wake up to eat it and go back to bed. Then, in the morning, I'll bring you some goddamn breakfast if you don't feel like coming downstairs. Then you can go back to sleep. You seein' a pattern here?!? I gotta put at least ten pounds on you before I can take you anywhere or people will think I'm living with a goddamn zombie. People around here already call me a fucking witch due to all my herbs. Don't need them thinking I know fucking Voodoo."

"Fine." I held my hands up in resignation. "Wait. What?"

"Oh, those goddamn bastard kids of the Kelly's?" She rolled her eyes. "Been telling their friends that I'm a witch 'cause I live out here all alone and got my garden. One time I might've shot at 'em when they came up on my property. So, they have to spread their rumors."

"You...*shot*...at children?"

"They're fourteen, fifteen, and sixteen." She shrugged. "And they were too far away for the shotgun to do more than pepper 'em. Sonsabitches sure knew to scatter when they were being shot at, though. If you talk to Sheriff Dennard, I didn't tell you that. He's still all kinds of pissed off."

"The Kelly's are still having kids?" I asked in disbelief. "They were ancient when I was a kid."

"They aren't Clancy's and Darby's, you idiot." She laughed. "Their son took the house over when they moved down to Florida and moved his pug-ugly wife and kids into the house with him. They're all butt ugly. Hair the color of a baboon's ass. I'm telling you. If ugly was a crime, they'd all be on Death Row. I know they were trying to see if I had potatoes in my garden."

"I know they're white—but that's still racist." I frowned.

"Fuck those ugly Irish assholes."

I sputtered for a few moments, then finally gave up.

"Okay."

Oma seemed to give up as well when I didn't have anything in me to say to such things.

"Well, so, I'll see you at dinner time." She nodded.

"Okay."

Oma went to the bedroom door and exited, pulling the door shut behind her. However, before the door was closed, she popped her head back inside the room.

"Take a shower before you lay down." She snapped. "Don't stink up my fresh sheets. I don't change them but once a week. This isn't a goddamn resort at Disney World."

"Okay, Oma." I waved her away with a sigh.

Like I'd go to a resort at Disney World.

I took off my cardigan and sweatshirt and hung them on the back of the bedroom door from the ancient old clothes hook. The same happened with my jeans. Then I took off my "underbritches" and threw them in the hamper inside of the bathroom. The hot water in the house still managed to expel water near the temperature you'd need to boil eggs, but it felt good against my skin and on my joints. I used the handheld shower nozzle to knock off the first layer of filth from my body and hair, then filled the tub and submerged my body. I laid in the near boiling water until I was beet red, then scrubbed myself with the lye soap in the basket hanging off of the tub. Next, I scrubbed my hair and scalp with the lavender shampoo Oma made herself. I gave my face a good scrub with the washcloth and lye soap, then sat in the tub until it was drained.

I rinsed myself off with ice cold water, a tip I'd learned from several other people in the business. Helps close the pores and keep out dirt and grease after a good scrubbing. When I lifted myself from the tub, I looked down at my body, sighing at my knobby hips, prominent ribs, knobby knees. I got my toiletries out of my bag and brushed my teeth, brushed my hair, and applied fresh deodorant. Then I applied moisturizer liberally from the tips of my toes up to my neck. Can't have dry, messed up skin.

When I finally slid into fresh underwear and pajama bottoms, which hung for dear life from my hips, then slid into a baggy t-shirt, I almost felt better. However, when I had closed the drapes and slipped under the warm blankets of the enormous bed, I was asleep before my head hit the pillow. It was the first time I didn't dream or have nightmares in at least two years. All I knew was darkness.

It was dark when Oma shook me awake for dinner. I forgot that even during Spring in Ohio, night falls earlier than it does in Los Angeles. Oma turned on the bedside lamp as I eased myself up to a seated position in bed. She wordlessly put a tray over my lap and set a glass of water on the bedside table. She sat down on the sofa and produced a crochet project out of nowhere.

"Are you just going to sit there?" I asked sleepily.

"Eat your fucking dinner."

So, I ate my *fucking dinner.* The meal consisted of a bagel slathered in cream cheese, smoked salmon, a dish of nuts, a couple of hard-boiled eggs, and more of the cabbage and potatoes from lunch. Obviously, my grandmother was trying to put weight on me as quickly as possible. After the bath and nap, I was actually able to eat most of the food. Once I was done, I was more tired than I had been before. Oma grabbed up my tray and empty water glass and left as quietly as she had arrived. I slid back into bed.

Breakfast was similar. The sun was pretty high in the sky outside when Oma arrived with another tray. She sat with her crochet while I ate yogurt and granola, two more boiled eggs, and a fruit smoothie she had whipped up. The smoothie tasted like shit, but I managed to choke it all down. Then Oma was gone again, and I was sliding back into bed. I could feel my hair sticking up in a million different directions, but I didn't care.

This went on for three days straight. I didn't leave bed unless it was to use the bathroom off of my bedroom. Meals consisting of fatty, high protein, calorie dense foods, were brought by Oma, and she'd sit there and crochet while I ate. Eggs, cheeses, oats and grains, meats, yogurt, granola, bagels, potatoes, dark chocolate, greens...the food just kept coming. On the fourth day, when I woke up as the sun was starting to light up the world, I didn't feel tired for once. And I smiled for the first time in months without being prompted.

Chapter Two

Oma wasn't in the kitchen when I went downstairs. She hadn't been in her own bedroom upstairs, either. Her bed had been made up, and her house dress was hanging on the hook on the back of her door as well. I assumed she was downstairs in the kitchen, making breakfast, but she wasn't doing that either. When I peeked out of the kitchen window, I finally laid eyes on her. She was in her garden, hoe in hand, breaking up the earth. I frowned to myself as I pulled my robe tightly around myself and made my way to the backdoor.

I walked down the back steps and made my way across the yard to her little fenced in garden area. Oma's garden was surrounded by a white picket fence with an actual gate with a bell. It was cute—just like it had been since I was a small child. But, the sight of my whip-thin grandmother hacking at the ground with the yard implement like she was trying to bring up oil made me cringe. Surely, she was too old to be working so hard out in the yard? Of course, she didn't show any sign that she wasn't doing just fine with the work she was doing.

"What are you doing?" I asked, holding my robe tightly around me to stave off the cold. "It's still butt-early-thirty. The sun's barely up."

"You're awake, aren't you?" She didn't even stop hacking at the earth. "If you're awake, I guess I can be awake and working, can't I?"

"That...that doesn't really answer my question."

"I gotta get this ground broke up good." She replied over chops of the hoe. "Barkley's is bringing me manure tomorrow."

I wasn't sure that that answered my question either.

"Why don't you let me do that?" I didn't want to, but I would. "Or we can go rent a tiller or something and..."

"You aren't fit to dig a hole right now." She cast an appraising glance at me. "And you don't have to be so goddamn fancy all the time, ya' know. I've been doing my garden this way since before your dad made the mistake of dragging your mom home and making you."

"That wasn't hurtful at all."

"It wasn't meant as a compliment."

"Yeah." I snorted. "I got that."

"Go in there and eat something." She stopped and leaned against the hoe. "You still look like death."

I looked at her for a few moments, wondering if I should push back on my Oma not. Having not been back for more than a handful of days, I didn't know if it was my place to tell my grandmother how to live her life and run her household. However, it worried me to see her, going on seventy-years-old, using a hoe to break up her garden in early Spring.

The ground still had to be hard and resistant to her efforts. Though, she looked much more physically capable than I was currently.

"Why don't we both get ready and go into town?" I suggested gently. "I'll buy us breakfast and then we'll go rent a tiller from...somewhere."

"Barkley's, ya' asshole." She growled. "It's still the goddamn hardware store that's been here since you were too short to piss in a toilet. How could you forget that?"

"Could you maybe just get over the fact that I ran off at sixteen?" I sighed. "Cursing me out every chance you get is not going to take that back, ya' know."

"Well, you're getting at least a full day for every year you've been gone." She glowered. "So, fuck you, you still have nine days of me acting however the Hell I want."

"I've been here for four days."

"You were asleep for three of 'em, ya' prick."

That was a new one.

"Fine." I held my hands up in defeat. "Cuss me out for nine more days if it makes you happy."

"I will!" She stomped her foot.

Obviously, I was still up shit creek for having upset my grandmother a decade prior.

"What's your fucking plan anyway, Robbie?" She went back to chopping at the ground. "You planning to sleep it off, eat all my food, tell me how to live my life, then in a couple weeks, you'll leave in the middle of the night again? Because, if so, you can just stick to your damn self now that you're on your own two damn feet again."

"Jesus, Oma!" I growled back. "Could you stop giving me grief when I can't take back a thing I've done?!?"

"Would you?!" She was shaking the hoe at me. "Do you even feel a bit bad for acting like a little shit?"

"I said I was sorry right after I got here."

"Just because I told you about yourself, ya' little shit." She stabbed the hoe into the ground. "That's no damn apology."

"I'm sorry!" I bellowed for the world to hear. ***"I'm so fucking sorry that I went off to live my life and it ruined yours, okay?!? I'm a complete fucking asshole and should be shot in the goddamn face with rock salt for being such a horrible grandson!"***

"That'd be a good goddamn start." She was leaning on the hoe again.

I cleared my throat and collected myself. I never lost my cool.

"What do you want from me, Oma?" I held my hands out helplessly. "I left to live my life. I'm sorry I didn't tell you first, but we both know you would've tried to stop me. I had an opportunity, and I took it. And it worked out incredibly well, so..."

"Worked out well?" She cackled angrily. "Look atchu! You look like you've been on that stuff. Surprised you still have your goddamn teeth. Probably veneers anyway!"

"They're my own teeth."

"Yeah. I'm sure you got the receipt." She was shaking the hoe at me.

"And I was never 'on that stuff' you mean old...I've used drugs, but I've never had a drug problem. At least, not the way you mean it."

"Then why are you so damned skinny?!"

"Because!" I threw my hands up. "Because I've been working nonstop on movies, tours, T.V. shows, press junkets...I've been around the world a dozen times in the last year. Caught Dengue Fever when we were filming in the Philippines even though I got the vaccine—for all the good that did me. I've been getting three hours of sleep a night for two solid goddamn years and living on cigarettes and Red Bull and coffee...and until I came here I hadn't had a real meal in at least six months. And no matter how skinny or sick or exhausted I am, my agent and manager keep shoving projects at me. That's why! It's not because of any bad choices!"

She turned her nose up at me, but she looked less angry with me.

"Skipping meals isn't exactly a good choice." She snorted. "And them cigarettes and Red Bulls will give you the cancer—if not a heart attack. You gotta take care of yourself, Robbie. You need your three squares, water...exercise...sleep. You're not making *good* choices."

"For the record, I'm not the one with the 'sugars,' okay?"

"I don't have the goddamn diabetes." She shook the hoe at me. "Sugar just makes me have trouble sleeping."

"Then why don't you just say it hypes you up?"

"I'm old. Old people are folksy." She snarled. "Fuck off."

I couldn't help it. I laughed.

"What the Hell are you laughing at?" She picked up a dirt clod and lobbed it at me, a smile on her face.

I managed to sidestep it.

"I'm just tired, Oma." My eyes were watery. "I'm so goddamn tired."

"Well, you look it." She didn't cuss at me, she looked sad.

"I know." I shrugged pitifully.

"Well, I'm glad you're home, I guess." She sighed, looking at me like a grandmother for once. "Just wish I knew how long to expect you is all. Your record for sticking around ain't great."

"I'll give you plenty of notice when the time comes, okay?" I negotiated. "But, I don't have a plan right now. I don't have any projects lined up...I'm...I'm just wanting to rest."

"I guess we can manage that." She gave a sharp nod. "But you start acting uppity, and I'll kick your bony ass."

"Okay." I relented.

"Carlos is a women's size 41eu—whatever the Hell that means."

"What? Who?"

"Carlos. The drag queen." She snarled. "He-she wears a size 41eu—that's what he said in her text the other day. You said you'd order him some of those fancy shoes."

"Oh, right." I finally remembered. "Yeah, okay. And it's 'she' when she's in drag and 'he' when he's not. Or whatever they prefer. And I didn't know you texted."

"Maybe if you'd try it once in a while you'd know."

"I'm sorry for not texting you, then, Oma."

She waggled her head and started chopping at the earth again.

"Are we going to breakfast and to rent that tiller or what?"

"Barkley's doesn't rent them." She said.

"Then we'll buy one. You can use it every year for your garden."

"They cost a couple of hundred dollars."

"Louboutins cost more than a tiller." I snorted. "So, if you can ask me to spend that on a pair of shoes for a stranger just so you can start to forgive me, I can get you a tiller."

"Fancy, fancy, fancy."

"Look, old lady, I'm really trying here," I growled. "Could you try, too?"

"How much goddamn money you got anyway?" She wasn't angry, she was curious. "I saw those pictures on the T.V. of that house you bought."

"What T.V. show was that?" I snorted. "I've never bought a house in my life."

"That house in Bel-Air?" She waved her hand in the air vaguely. "Fancy as Hell and probably cost more than all the homes here in Point Worth put together."

"I didn't buy a house." I rolled my eyes. "I have a small condo in L.A., but I've never bought a house because I've never stayed still long enough to bother."

"You can't even afford a house—you probably shouldn't be throwing money around here."

"I can afford a house, Oma." I rolled my eyes.

"You ever been to Bel-Air?" She asked, genuinely just making conversation. "It looks really nice."

"Yes." I nodded. "I've been to parties at some...friends'...houses there. It's...it's okay I guess."

"Okay?" She snorted. "Not uppity enough for you?"

"Exact opposite."

"Mmm." She considered me. "I saw this T.V. program the other day about this really fancy and exclusive private resort in Antigua. You ever been there?"

"Jumby Bay Island." I nodded. "Yeah. I've been there."

"Where the Hell is Antigua?" She frowned.

"The West Indies," I answered, then saw that she was still waiting. "Down by Puerto Rico, high north of Venezuela. I flew down from Miami. You have to jump a lot of islands—even flying private."

Another head waggle.

"I was just explaining because you asked." I rolled my eyes. "I wasn't trying to show how fancy I am, all right?"

"Fine." She relented.

"So...breakfast?" I prodded. "A tiller?"

"I suppose." She leaned against the hoe like she was posing for an updated *American Gothic*. "Of course, if we buy a tiller, we may as well just have them deliver it tomorrow with the manure. Then you can drive me in that fancy car of yours instead of taking the pickup. We can till and throw down cow shit all in one morning."

I just nodded, knowing the car wasn't all that fancy.

"That the only car you got?" She asked another prying question.

"No."

"You got a boyfriend? A husband?"

"Neither."

"Well, you can say whatever you like, but that's just fucking fancy." She snorted. "Why does a single man need more than one vehicle?"

"You have a pickup and a car."

"That truck belonged to your Opa." She snarled. "You ain't ever been married, so you don't have an excuse."

"Thanks for opening a wound, Oma." I rolled my eyes.

"How's a handsome movie star like you never found a man?" She frowned. "The boys down at the center go through partner after partner. Well, some of them. The others couple up and stayed that way. Hell, even the lesbians are playing house down there. Surely, you have found some guy that could put up with your particular brand of bullshit."

"Wow."

"It's an honest question, Robbie." She frowned. "Why don't you have a man yet?"

"That's just…it's a big question, okay?" I shrugged. "Can we have breakfast first?"

"Fine." She shrugged back and walked over to push her way through the garden gate. "You can't be too damn picky. I saw that damn outfit you arrived in."

"That's designer clothing." I didn't mean for it to, but it came out as a whine that could only be described as *fussy*.

"The *cardigan* was nice, but that sweater and jeans looked like the moths got after 'em." She continued. "I hope you didn't pay much for that shit. Take me down to the Goodwill. I'll buy some secondhand shit and tear it up for you for ten bucks if you think it's so goddamn cute. I'll make you a whole goddamn year's worth of clothes and be able to retire in Bermuda."

"Breakfast." I groaned as we walked towards the house. "Please."

Together, we washed and dried the hoe that Oma had been using, then returned it to its place in the shed. Once inside the house again, where it was actually warm, I indicated that I'd get cleaned up and be ready within twenty minutes. Oma cocked an eyebrow at me, as though being clean before going to breakfast was "fancy" as well. However, she kept her mouth shut and followed me up the stairs. She zipped into her room and closed the door, obviously deciding that she could use a quick wash up and change.

I went down to the bedroom I was using and did the same. Shutting the door behind me. As soon as the door was closed, I noticed the old iron clothes hook in front of me. It was empty. I frowned to myself. Had Oma taken my clothes to a dry cleaner while I was sleeping over the last few days? There was momentary panic at first, but then I realized that a dry cleaner, even in Toledo would know how to handle cashmere, virgin wool, and silk. Probably.

Walking into the bathroom, I found myself frowning again. My cardigan was hanging over the shower curtain rod. I walked over and pulled it down. It looked well cleaned, and it was dry. I spun around, looking for the sweater and jeans, but they were nowhere in sight. Had the crazy old lady handwashed the cardigan and hung it over the shower curtain rod to dry? I held the cardigan to my face and breathed in deeply. It smelled of lavender soap, fresh and clean. I shrugged to myself and walked into the bedroom to toss it onto the bed.

When I was freshly bathed and clean, I dug a pair of fresh jeans—without holes—out of my bag, a plain white t-shirt, fresh underwear, and socks, and got dressed. I threw my cardigan on over the less ostentatious outfit and dug a pair of regular white Chuck's out of my bag. Other than the cardigan, I couldn't see Oma having anything to say about the outfit—

and even she had admitted that the cardigan was nice. So, I was hoping that we'd avoid any insults for at least a few minutes.

Out in the hallway, Oma was standing in the hallway by her door, her arms cross, tapping a foot. She was in a sweater, bib overalls, and a pair of old boots. But she looked freshly bathed, and her clothes were all spotless, so I guessed it was as good as anything else. Apparently, my need to not smell was just too much for her to have to put up with. However, I ignored her impatient demeanor and walked down the hallway to greet her. She just rolled her eyes and led the way down the stairs.

We exited the house, which she didn't lock behind us—and which gave me anxiety—but I did my best not to say anything. When Oma saw the look on my face, she rolled her eyes and got her keys out of her bag to lock the place up. Finally, we hopped into my car. When I started the car with a push of a button and then turned on the heated seats, Oma waggled her head in response again. I ignored her.

"You remember how to get into town?" She asked, trying to figure out the seatbelt, as though, that too, were too fancy for her tastes. "It's still where it was ten years ago if you can remember that far back."

"I remember where the freaking town is." I sighed, basically to myself. "But you'll have to show me where we're going to eat."

"Let's go to Barkley's first," Oma said. "Get that shit over with."

"Are they open at seven-thirty?" I frowned.

"Of course, they're open at seven-thirty, Robbie." She snorted. "This is Point Worth, not Europe where no one gets out of bed before ten in the goddamn morning."

"You watch too much television," I mumbled.

"How do people take you being queer out in Hollywood doing all that you do?" Oma asked as I backed up in the driveway.

"*Queer?*" I frowned at her as I turned around.

"All the boys at the center say it's coming back into style to refer to oneself as queer." She replied casually.

"I think that's if you actually belong to the LGBTQIA community, Oma," I explained as I turned around and started down the driveway. "A little old white lady from Ohio probably shouldn't use it."

"I'm an ally ain't I? But fine." She sighed. "What do they think of you being a big ole homosexual, ya' little shit?"

"I don't know if that's better." I rolled my eyes as I drove. "No one seems to care much. I can't really work in or perform in countries like Russia without security concerns—but that's a pretty damn small price to pay for being out, really."

"Who wants to go over there anyway?" She snorted. "I haven't seen any of your movies. They never play them at the theater here."

The theater at Point Worth only played movies that were older than a decade, so that wasn't too much of an insult. I found it hard to believe that Oma had never watched one of them on DVD or on cable in the last ten years, though. However, it didn't matter to me if my grandmother had chosen to go out of her way to watch one of my movies or not. I knew that she had seen my Royal Albert Hall concert on T.V., so at least I knew she cared.

"You're not missing much." I shrugged.

"What kinds of movies have you been in?"

"The kinds that made lots of money."

"You being fancy again or is that just your way of saying that you don't give a shit about your movies either?"

"I haven't won an Oscar or anything, so I'll let you take that however you want." I laughed.

"But do you care?" She leaned over conspiratorially. "Do you want an Oscar, Robbie?"

"Between you and me?" I answered. "I don't really give a shit. But don't tell anyone else that."

"You ever win any awards?"

"You seriously haven't kept up with any of my work?" I frowned.

"I saw your concert on T.V.!" She proclaimed. "And I saw you on that episode of Unsolved Criminal Files when you first started."

I had played the suspect in a horribly written police procedural television show when I first got to Hollywood—before I made it big. It was not my best work. But, it got me in the door of other auditions, and soon, I was off and running. Academy Awards be damned—I may not have won one, but I'd attended and presented before. And I made money, so who really gave a shit?

"I've been in a few things since then." I laughed.

"Your guitar playing seems to have gotten better since you were plucking away upstairs in your old room." She changed the subject. "Your singing has definitely improved."

"Thanks, I guess." I chuckled as I pulled onto Main Street.

"You write all those songs yourself?"

"Some. Some I wrote with producers and songwriters."

"What's that one about the man in the bar flipping the coin, trying to decide on his future?"

"*Heads or Tails*?"

"Yeah. That one." She nodded. "I liked that one. Only one that wasn't too damn loud."

I brayed as I drove and waited for directions from Oma. There was still some slush in some of the gutters along Main Street. The early Spring sun hadn't managed to melt everything yet, especially areas that stayed in the shade all day long.

"I mean, they were all good and all, but you do like rock 'n roll, don't you?"

I frowned a little and shrugged.

"Here." Oma grabbed a handful of the cardigan material at my elbow and pointed. "There's Barkley's. Just pull around back there. Lucas will help us real quick, and we'll get the Hell out of here and go eat."

"Okay."

I did as Oma had instructed, pulling around the building to the back where it appeared that things were loaded, unloaded, all the pallets of seed and soil and paving bricks and early Spring plants were located. It was basically the garden center of the hardware store. When we got to the back of the store, near a large area with the gates swung open to the interior, I stopped the car and put it into park.

"Come see Lucas." Oma was pulling at my elbow again. "He's just the nicest kid."

"Let me get my sunglasses." I chewed at my lip.

"No one here is going to recognize you, you fancy asshole." She scoffed. "You're so skinny you don't even look like yourself. Just come on."

"Fine." I sighed and slid out of the car as she did the same.

Oma marched away from the car right through the garden center gates, on the search for this mysterious Lucas. I scurried along to catch up to her. My bones ached. Due to my weight loss, I was probably rubbing bone against bone whenever I moved. There was nothing to pad me from regular movements. Oma moved like she was my age and I was moving like I was ready for the home.

Pulling my cardigan tightly around myself, trying to block out the cold, I finally caught up with her in the middle of the garden center. She was looking every which way, but there was no one in sight. Barkley's was basically the same as I remembered it—though, of course, I had forgotten that it was called Barkley's. After ten years away from home, some details just get expunged. I had replaced those things with song lyrics and lines from my movies. Remembering the name of my hometown's hardware store just wasn't that important in the grand scheme of things. Oma disagreed, but that wasn't something I really cared to argue about. I would pick my battles wisely.

"Lucas!?" Oma hollered even though it was evident that no one was around.

"Oma." I stopped her. "There's no one here."

"Well, obviously someone is here, or the damn gates wouldn't be opened, would they?"

"I have no answer for that."

"*Lucas?!*" She bellowed loudly.

I jumped at how sudden and sharp her voice was. Pulling my cardigan more tightly around myself, hugging my arms around my middle, I was hoping this would be over soon. Within seconds, the sliding glass doors at the back of the place swooshed open, signaling that someone had heard my crazy grandmother bellowing for help like a lunatic. An older man, probably around my grandmother's age came hobbling out, holding a cane. I chewed at my lip. Lucas obviously was a lot spryer than he appeared if he was delivering manure to little old ladies and selling tillers.

"Jackson!" Oma said. "What the Hell are you doing here?"

"It's my store, ain't it?"

"You're too damn old to be out here." Oma snorted. "You oughta be laying up in the home. Retirement or funeral, your choice."

"Shouldn't you be shooting the Irish in your garden?" He snorted as he hobbled over. "How the fuck did you miss three teenagers with a goddamn shotgun?"

"I hit the little shits." She scowled. "I just wasn't close enough to do any real damage."

"Don't let Sheriff Dennard hear you." He said as he walked right up to her. "Kelly's still giving him crap for not at least ticketing you."

"They were on my property in the middle of the night." Oma shook her head. "I can defend myself and my land as I see fit. How are you, Jackson?"

"It was seven in the evening. And fair to Midland." He shrugged and pulled her into a hug. "Yourself?"

"Eh." She shrugged back as she pulled out of the hug. "Where's Lucas?"

"He had to run over to Toledo first thing this morning to drop off a chainsaw." He explained. "That boy could run circles around ten these others."

"You're lucky to have him." Oma nodded, still holding onto the man's arms. "You remember my grandson?"

Suddenly, I flashed back to the fact that this rickety old man was Jackson Barkley, owner of the store in which we were currently standing. Mr. Barkley turned slightly to me and appraised me with bushy eyebrows and suspicious eyes. I stood there, smiling, as I hugged my cardigan around myself. Slowly, I reached out a hand, hoping to God that the man didn't remember a thing about me.

"Bobby?"

"Robbie." Oma corrected him.

"Rob's fine." I nodded as he took my hand.

He had an firm grip for someone whose legs weren't exactly in tip-top working order. Guess slinging bags of manure around kept a person pretty strong late into life.

"Yeah." He nodded with a small smile. "I guess I remember you a bit. You've been gone for a bit, haven't you?"

"Yessir." I nodded.

"Well, you look familiar, so I'm just going to assume I remember you." He chuckled.

I just smiled back.

"You might have seen him on..." Oma began.

"We're here to buy Oma a tiller, Mr. Barkley." I interrupted her.

"For that little ole garden you have?" He turned to Oma with a teasing grin. "You're getting old, Esther Jean."

"Says the man who can barely stand." She puffed up. "Lookin' like the scarecrow using his legs for the first time."

He laughed loudly.

"Got as many brains, too." She finished. "But I want one that's going to do the job quick and easy and last a lifetime."

"Most of 'em got at least a 5-year warranty—that oughta work for you, old as you are." He returned.

"I'll shove that cane up your ass, Jackson."

"Well, you won't need nothin' too fancy for that garden of yours." He shrugged, ignoring her. "I got a Troy-Bilt in stock, 208cc engine, 24-inch front-tine tiller with a 7-inch tilling depth. It should work really nicely for your garden, Esther Jean."

"Well, how much is it?" She asked.

"Right under four-hundred if I remember correctly." He replied.

"For something I can do by hand?" She scoffed. "What the Hell is wrong with you, Jackson?!"

"That's fine, Mr. Barkley," I interjected as I reached for my wallet. "It sounds great if you think it'll work."

"The Hell it does," Oma growled. "This sonofabitch is trying to grease me up. Of all the nerve, Jackson Barkley!"

"I got a sixty-dollar one back here that will break down after two uses if you want you old hateful thing." He snapped back. "Probably kick back and cut your toes off, too. If you can even feel 'em anymore with the gout."

"You know your Betty Lynn died to get away from you, Jackson Barkley?" Oma glared at him.

"And Robert the Eldest died because the Devil couldn't be worse than you." He glared back.

They stood there, glaring at each other.

"I'll give it to you for three-hundred." Mr. Barkley finally rolled his eyes.

Oma nodded once, and they both switched to smiling.

"Okay." I shook my head and dug into my wallet. "So, here's my credit card...uh, yeah."

Mr. Barkley took the card from my hand and immediately stuck it in the breast pocket of his coat.

"What the Hell are you wearing, son?" He looked me up and down.

"He thinks he's fancy." Oma waved her hand dismissively.

"It's...it's a cardigan." I shrugged with a sigh.

"Yeah. Betty Lynn used to wear one. You need you a proper coat, son." He shook his head before shambling off towards the inside of the store again.

Exhaling heavily, I turned to Oma. She was eyeing all of the bags and stock stacked on the heavy shelving around us.

"Is everyone in this damn town still rude as Hell?" I asked. "Or is it just you and him?"

"He's just feisty 'cause I've turned him down five times now." She waved at me dismissively. "After Betty Lynn died two years ago, he went into a funk. Year later he was sniffin' 'round my hems. Old pervert."

"He seemed...nice enough." I said. "I mean, you two obviously have a lot in common. The cussing and rudeness, I mean."

"You and that smart mouth."

I laughed as she started to stroll around the perimeter of the garden center, looking at this thing and that thing, as though she were actually shopping instead of just wasting time. Following her around, I felt utterly chilled to my bones. I knew that I had lost way too much weight and that was the main reason why I felt so cold. Mr. Barkley was wrong about my cardigan, but he wasn't wrong about the fact that I needed a new coat.

"By the way, I meant to thank you for washing my cardigan," I said to Oma. "Did you take the sweater and jeans to the dry cleaners?"

"Huh?" She frowned at me.

"I figured you hand-washed this." I indicated my cardigan. "Did you take the rest to a dry cleaner while I was sleeping the last three days?"

"Oh." She chewed at her lip. "Yeah. I'll pick 'em up for you."

"Well, we could do that today," I said. "That way you won't have to let me know how much it was so I can give you cash, and..."

"I can handle it you little asshole." She turned to me and put her hands on her hips. "I'll go tomorrow or the next day."

"Fine." I gave up. "Just let me know how much it costs."

"I can pay for your damn dry cleaning." She snapped.

"Well, you sure haggled over the price of a tiller," I mumbled.

Oma spun on me, but luckily, Mr. Barkley chose that moment to come out of the sliding doors, holding my credit card and a receipt. I turned in his direction, leaving Oma with no one to direct her ire at immediately. Instead of jumping around me to face me again, she just gave up. Maybe staying with Oma for a bit wouldn't be a constant barrage of insults and screaming and cursing. As long as I could adapt to the way she behaved.

"Here ya' go." Mr. Barkley handed the receipt and my card over. "Never seen a credit card look like that. I thought American Express cards were green, gold or platinum? Had Wilby look at it since it was black, but it ran through just fine, so..."

I took the card and receipt from him.

"Told you he's fancy," Oma mumbled.

"Thank you, Mr. Barkley," I said quickly. "Can you have them deliver the tiller tomorrow when they bring her...um...manure?"

He looked around me with a scowl at Oma.

"Now you're trying to get free delivery out of me, you old bat?"

"I already paid Lucas for delivery when I ordered the cow shit, ya' old bastard." She snapped back. "Just throw it on the truck with the manure."

"I hate you down to your bones." He growled at her before turning his face back to me. "Here, you need this, son."

He shoved a very familiar looking tan coat at me.

"I couldn't take..."

"Nonsense." He practically spun me around and shoved the coat onto me. "It's one of Lucas' old ones he barely wears anymore. We're going to get another cold snap or two before Spring finally settles in. You'll need this."

Oma smiled smugly at me as Mr. Barkley shoved the coat onto me and spun me back around.

"It's a bit big on you, skinny as you are, but it'll keep you warm, son." He nodded at me.

"Thank you, Mr. Barkley." I reached out and shook his hand again.

"You're welcome, Robbie." He smiled at me before scowling at Oma. "Lucas'll bring your goddamn tiller tomorrow, you old bat."

"Suck it, Barkley." She made the rudest gesture.

"H'Okay!" I spouted. "Let's go, Oma."

Mr. Barkley waved amiably as I ushered my grandmother back out the gate and practically shoved her into the car. I dashed around the car and slid into the driver's seat before anything else would happen to cause Mr. Barkley and Oma to swear at each other. Oma was still fastening her seatbelt when I pulled away from Barkley's. A few finger points and verbal commands and Oma had us parking in front of a restaurant just off of the main drag of Point Worth. My phone dinged in my pocket.

When I swiped my thumb across my phone and read the text, I simply had to shoot off a one-word response before shoving my phone back into my pocket. Oma watched the whole interaction with great interest. I undid my seatbelt as I just looked at her.

"Quickest text reply I ever saw." She snorted.

"It was just the credit card company," I said. "Making sure I really bought something at a hardware store in Ohio."

"That's...efficient." She cocked an eyebrow. "What's the credit limit on that card?"

I stared at her for several seconds.

"I'll buy breakfast," I replied as I opened my door and started to climb out of the car.

"You buy my purse with that card?" She hollered after me as she started to pull her own seatbelt off and climb out of the car.

"Let it go, Oma," I said over my shoulder as I locked the car with the fob.

"Could you buy a car with it?" She asked, hustling along to walk along beside me. "A small house?"

"Who buys a car with a credit card?" I frowned, still walking. "Or a house for that matter? That's just crazy."

"Hypothetically, could you?"

We approached the door of the café, and I grabbed the door handle.

"Are you going to drop this?" I asked.

"Probably not. No." She shook her head.

"Hypothetically I could, I guess."

She made a whistling sound.

"You buy that car with a credit card?"

"What?!" I was taken aback. "No. That's crazy."

"Is it paid off?"

"Why are you so concerned about my financial situation?" I frowned. "I mean, you've never asked before."

"Just trying to figure out why you're back here looking like you've been on that stuff and waving around a credit card instead of cash." She explained. "You got money problems?"

I braced myself against the door handle of the café, hoping no one would want in or out while I collected myself. Oma just stood there, hands on her hips and waited for me to answer.

"I bought the car outright when I went to purchase it. It's an American Express Black Card." I sighed. "I have plenty of money. The card doesn't technically have a spending limit. I use my card, and my accountant pays the bill out of my actual bank account...accounts. That way I don't have to carry cash or a debit card or anything like that. And I've already told you why I look the way I do. There is literally no motive behind me coming to visit other than wanting rest and to see you. What's made you so goddamn suspicious since the last time I saw you?"

"It's been two years since you last saw me." She snorted. "That's not 'all of the sudden,' Robbie."

"That's not really an answer."

"Because I'm pretty sure I'm going to wake up one day, and you'll have dashed off in the middle of the night." She said evenly. "It's hard to believe you're really here and planning to stay for any length of time."

"Well, I can't leave 'til I don't look like a skeleton—as you'd put it—and that'll take some time, so I don't think you have to worry yet, right?"

"I suppose." She sniffed haughtily.

"Can we just have breakfast?" I sighed. "And can you stop looking for some ulterior motive for my visit that doesn't exist? Please?"

She made a relenting facial expression, so I gripped the door handle and opened it for her. We made our way into the café, which was nearly empty, since it was after eight o'clock on a Monday morning. The waitress was behind the counter fixing a new pot of coffee, so she just announced that Oma and I should seat ourselves wherever and she'd bring us menus in a minute. Oma led us to the back and slid into a booth. I slid in opposite her and just stared at her.

"What?"

"I don't remember this place," I replied.

"It used to be the Red Rooster Tavern." She explained. "Remember? Clancy and Darby ran it? Well, when they moved, Barkley bought it for his daughter, and she changed it to a breakfast and lunch café, changed the name, redecorated it, changed the menu...”

“Ah.” I nodded as the waitress approached.

She was a youngish woman—probably a few years younger than me and still possibly in college. Pleasant and smiling, she handed us each a menu and took our drink orders. Oma turned an eyebrow up when I asked for the biggest cup of coffee that they had and water. My grandmother ordered a coffee and a glass of juice before opening her menu to peruse the options. I had a feeling that she’d been to this café numerous times—being that it was one of the few restaurants in town—but she still liked to see her options.

When I looked at the menu, I realized that Oma’s mission to quickly put weight on me would be further advanced by this café. After everything Oma had shoved down my throat over the last few days, I was hoping for something a little lighter. The café didn’t really have a lot of those options. Even though I also wanted to gain weight back and rest up, I didn’t want to develop coronary disease in the process, either.

“Their omelets are pretty good,” Oma spoke from behind her menu. “And their cinnamon rolls are the best in the state.”

“Mm.”

“You need to stop drinking so much coffee,” Oma said casually. “It’s a diuretic and can raise your pressures and cause heart disease—and someone as skinny as you shouldn’t be drinking it anyway.”

“I can’t tell you how to live your life, but you’re going to start on me?” I looked over my menu.

“That’s right, ya’ asshole.”

I sighed.

“Must be nice.” She said cryptically before the waitress showed back up with our drinks.

Oma ordered herself biscuits and gravy and sausage, and I stuck to a veggie omelet and a fruit cup, which made Oma waggle her head and mumble “fancy” to herself. The waitress ignored the movement and mumbling, gave us a smile, and darted off again.

“What must be nice?” I prodded her.

“Being somewhere you can blend in.” She said as she began putting cream and sugar in her coffee. “But then you’re wearing that goddamn cardigan and sticking out like a sore thumb.”

“I love this cardigan.” I frowned.

“It’s nice.” She nodded as she stirred her coffee. “Sure it cost a pretty penny. But it sticks out around here. Especially with a fellow wearing it.”

“That’s so sexist. And possibly homophobic.”

“Sure it is.” She nodded. “I’m just talking about reality. No one here is going to give you much grief over it or yell slurs at you—no one here is that damned ignorant. But it makes you stick out, Robbie. Guys here wear their Carhartt and flannels and regular sweaters and jeans and work boots...not designer clothes. If you’re here to escape, you’re going about it the wrong way.”

I saw her point and immediately did my jacket up all the way to my neck.

“Oh, now you just look like an idiot.” She rolled her eyes. “Take your damn coat and cardigan off and put ‘em in the booth next to you, ya’ fuckin’ moron.”

Internally I sighed, but I did as she said. Immediately, I felt a lot better.

"Better?" I mumbled.

"Yes, smartass, it is." Her head was moving about again.

"I'll go to the local Goodwill or Salvation Army and pick up some flannels and jeans if it'll make you feel better. Maybe I can just dig around in the church lost and found?"

"They won't take your fancy credit card, wiseass." She growled at me, leaning further towards me over the table. "When did you get so damn uppity?"

"When did it become a fucking crime to wear something you wouldn't plow a field in?" I snapped back.

"Oooooh, the boys at the center would love you." She waggled her head.

Her head was going to snap right off of her neck and roll halfway across the café if she wasn't careful.

"Sassy and snappy and got a fucking answer for everything." She grumbled. "And then you're good looking to boot. You ever need a date, just go with me over to Toledo one day."

I couldn't help it. I laughed.

"What's so fucking funny?"

"You." I waved a hand at her as I sat back. "I don't remember you being this crotchety all the time—and now you've got me acting the same way. I haven't had the energy to fight with anyone in a long time. I guess you just have that effect on people, Oma."

"I suppose." She appraised me carefully.

"Look—I just like my clothes," I said. "But I'll go with you to Toledo one day and grab a few things at Target."

Immediately, I felt anxious. The thought of being recognized increased exponentially with every place that I visited. At Barkley's Hardware or the Sunny Side Up Café, I was pretty safe, especially on a Monday morning. But in a Target in a larger city...probably not. Of course, I did look a little different with my cheek and jaw bones showing so prominently...

"What?" She asked, sipping her coffee again.

I picked up my coffee and took a sip.

"Like your coffee like your men, eh?" She nodded at the plain cup of coffee.

"Oma!" I gasped, realized how loud I'd been, then corrected my tone. "Don't say things like that."

"What?" She looked offended. "You got something against people of color?"

"Of course, not—but that's just...just don't."

"You ever date a black guy?" She asked, setting her coffee mug down and leaning in.

"Oh. My. God." I looked up as though I were pleading with God to end my suffering. "I don't know if this is racist or just tacky."

"That's the problem with you folks."

"You folks?"

"Hollywood uber-Liberals." She nodded. "Thinking everything is offensive when it's just a simple question."

"I don't even know what to say to that."

"Have you ever dated a black guy?"

"Why?!" I threw my hands up.

"Because one of my boys over at the center, Andrew, he's just the sweetest boy. Always so nice and kind and helpful and helps me carry things in and out. Holds doors for me. But if you got a problem with black guys..."

"I've never dated a black guy," I answered. "But that's just because I have only dated two guys in my entire life."

"Well," she nodded, "you need to meet Andrew then. You'd just love him. Sweetest boy ever."

"When you say 'boy'..."

"I'm not being racist!"

"I'm wanting to know how old he is, Oma." I rolled my eyes.

"Oh." She gathered herself. "Twenty-five, twenty-six. Same age as you or about. He has a degree from OSU. Buckeye through and through. Got a good job. Not much family in the area anymore to speak of so you won't have to worry about meeting the parents too early in the relationship. He told me he's looking to settle down, and..."

"Have you got the wedding planned out?" I snorted. "A seating chart and menu for the dinner?"

"Well, you could take him out to dinner for starters, smartass." She quipped. "He loves Indian food—but, I don't think The Trots is a great first date situation so you might want to try Italian or something."

Luckily, our food arrived, and Oma dug into her biscuits and gravy and sausage links like her life depended upon it. I ate my omelet and fruit, looking at my grandmother across the table. How did we go from her acting like she hated my guts to her trying to set me up with 'one of her boys' from the center? Instead of asking, I just ate my food and asked the waitress for more coffee, which Oma rolled her eyes at, though she kept her mouth shut for once.

Halfway through our meals, the café was empty except for us and the waitress—and assumedly, the cook in the back. Oma was onto her second cup of coffee as well, watching me in between bites of her food. I wanted to ask her what was going through her head, but I was afraid of what she might say. I didn't want to be cussed out or fought with for as long as I could delay it. It was best just to wait for her to say something herself and enjoy the peace. Of course, I didn't have long to wait.

"You ever regret not finishing school, going to college, finding you a decent man, settling down?" She asked before popping another bite in her mouth. "You definitely could've had your pick around here."

"Here? As in Point Worth?" I realized that I was being snarky again, so I corrected myself. "I mean...you mean in this area?"

"Mmm."

"Sometimes." I shrugged. "Sometimes I wish I'd stuck around. But...when I was sixteen, this place held no appeal."

"What about now?"

"It looks a little different with an extra ten years on me."

"How'd you ever get jobs out there in California being sixteen years old and no parent with you anyway?"

"You lie that you're older when you're young, and you lie that you're younger when you're old." I shrugged. "It's how it works."

"You ain't been doing the pornos have you?"

"Seriously?"

"I heard the boys make some extra money that way." She shrugged.

"I've never done a porno, Oma."

"Maybe you should try it." She snorted. "Maybe you wouldn't be so tightly wound all the goddamn time."

I sighed. "I've never done *anything* sexual for a job."

"No wonder you don't have a man." She chortled.

"Are you endorsing those types of behaviors?" I cocked my head to the side.

"Ain't nothin' wrong with a good porno." She shrugged. "It's honest money."

"I'm not disparaging porn or porn actors." I glared at her. "I'm just saying that you seem to be suggesting that I should be having sex on camera to get a man—which I don't need by the way."

"Everyone needs a man." She shook her head. "Well, gay men and straight women, I mean. Everyone needs someone to love."

"I have myself," I said.

"Yeah." She snorted. "And look what you've done with that."

"You are the rudest person I've ever met," I stated simply. "I came here because I've hit bedrock and now you're asking me to build a goddamn basement."

"I'm just saying, you've been all alone—apparently—maybe you need a good man in your life. To watch after you. To show you love. That's all."

"I need rest and food." I frowned.

"Well, that, too." Her head was waggling again. "At least come to the center when I go and meet Andrew. The least you'll do is have a good meal and polite conversation."

"Do you know what will happen if I walk into your LGBTQ center?" I cocked an eyebrow at her.

She threw her hands up.

I looked around and leaned in to whisper-hiss at her.

"You don't seem to realize that while I'm Robert Wagner, your grandson, I'm also Jacob Michaels," I said quickly. "I can't go into a goddamn Starbucks to get my own coffee in L.A. without causing a security issue. If I want to buy new clothes, stores have to close their doors for me. Or I shop online or call designers directly. If I want to go through a fucking McDonald's drive-thru, I have to make sure that it's not during a busy time, so people don't cause a fucking traffic jam in the parking lot. Maybe people in Point Worth haven't caught on to the fact that Robert Wagner is Jacob Michaels—especially with how skinny I am right now—but they'll also put two-and-two together quickly enough. I won't be able to go anywhere here, either. If I go to the center with you in Toledo, you better be ready with the goddamn National Guard to get us out of there."

"No one here gives a damn who you are." She waved me off. "You're my grandson, and that's all they need to know. You put on normal folks' clothes, stop acting so goddamn uppity, and no one will look at you twice. They might steal a peek since you're so damn handsome, but they won't realize who you are over in California, smartass."

"Yeah, we'll see." I rolled my eyes.

"So, you're going to the center to meet the boys or not?"

I laid my head on the table and stayed there. Luckily, I had finished my food and moved my plate.

"I'll take that as a 'yes,' then." Oma snarled.

I paid the bill and left a tip with what little cash I did have in my wallet, and Oma and I left the Sunny Side Up Café. On the way back to the house, we talked very little. Oma made a few comments about this or that thing changing in town, new neighbors, some idle gossip about folks in town, but for the most part, we were silent. When we got back to the house, we went our separate ways—Oma towards the kitchen, me upstairs.

Whether I wanted to admit it or not, I was still raw about the whole venture into Point Worth proper and all of the abuse that I'd been made to endure. I wasn't used to people being so blatantly...honest. I'd lived in L.A. and traveled the world and moved in circles where people talked about you behind your back. They didn't say such rude things to your face. People were polite. But then I thought of how Mr. Barkley had indirectly said that my cardigan was a sight to behold. Then he offered me a "real coat" to keep me warm. He might not have liked my cardigan, but that didn't stop him from offering genuine kindness. Oma said whatever was on her mind...but she was letting me stay with her, feeding me, inviting me to meet her friends...maybe I was looking at things the right way.

If someone in L.A. told me that my cardigan wasn't good enough, they certainly weren't going to just hand over something else. They just wanted you to know that they didn't approve of your choices. Which was real kindness? Politeness with an upturned nose, or blunt honesty followed by an offer of help? It pissed me off to no end that maybe I'd spent ten years hating a place I'd run away from...but they weren't actually as rude as they seemed at face value. Nothing is more frustrating than someone you've seen as poorly mannered doing something so kind.

I actually kicked the doorjamb as I entered the bedroom I was staying in at Oma's house. Hoping I didn't scuff the wood, I closed the door behind me and felt myself deflate. I had left this place in the middle of the night, without so much as a word, because I had looked down my nose at it. Looked down my nose at Oma and her brusque ways, but here I was regretting all of it. Well, not the running off and becoming rich and famous part—but the *way* in which I had done it. I couldn't really blame the woman for being suspicious of every little thing I'd done in the past and that I was doing in the present. I'd be wary of a person like that, too—especially if they showed up looking like a skeleton waving around some exclusive credit card no one in town had ever seen before in their lives.

I was a dick.

And my jeans and sweater were folded and on my bed.

I frowned to myself as I looked at them from where I was leaning against the closed door. Hesitantly, I walked over to the bed and examined the pile of clothes, making sure they were actually mine. That was when I realized that the bed was made. I hadn't made the bed before we left, and Oma certainly hadn't gone into the bedroom after we had left to go into town. Frowning, I turned on my heels and headed downstairs to the kitchen.

Oma was talking to herself in the kitchen, I could hear her when I was halfway down the stairs. I rolled my eyes, wondering what new words and insults she was mumbling to herself about me. Obviously, I was a total fancy asshole who needed to be punched in the throat. I stomped my way through the living room, and obviously, Oma heard me because she stopped talking to herself. Apparently, even my Oma wasn't rude enough to continue her formerly private diatribe as I approached.

"Oma?" I stomped into the kitchen.

"What?" She turned from the sink like the cat that ate the canary.

"I thought you took my sweater and jeans to the dry cleaners?"

"I did, ya' asshole!" She snapped. "I told you so, didn't I?"

I just stared at her.

"I'll pick 'em up tomorrow or Wednesday!"

"They're on my bed. Cleaned and folded." I cocked an eyebrow at her.

"They must have delivered them." She threw up her hands. "Why are you in here bugging the shit out of me? I'm trying to do my chores!"

"The dry cleaners...*delivered*...my clothes?" I frowned. "And let themselves into your locked house, put them on my bed—with no protective covering, and let themselves out and locked up behind themselves?"

"Piss off!" She waved me away.

"If you washed them in the machine, that's fine..."

"Would you just go away?" She snapped. "Your clothes are clean, ain't they? Leave me be!"

"Okay, crazy." I rolled my eyes.

Oma spun back around and immediately went about busying herself. I just shrugged my shoulders and headed back to the stairs. I didn't know why Oma didn't want to admit that she had just washed my clothes in the washer—they had looked fine. My grandmother was always the worst about going around and doing chores and fixing up and getting her nose in other people's business. Looking back, ever since I was a child—and especially after my parents died—she was always doing and going.

Never once did a bed go unmade or a floor go unscrubbed or a dish sit in the kitchen sink for long. Never did dust settle in her household. It was probably the German in her, I figured. If she wanted to sneak around washing my clothes and making beds and acting crazy, that was her own business. I'd just let her do it. She'd been doing it my whole life, so why try to change her behavior now? Especially when I'd just get cursed at for trying.

When I got back up to the room I was staying in, my underwear and pajamas were sitting, clean and folded, next to the first pile.

Chapter 3

The Carhartt that Mr. Barkley had given me came in handy the next morning. I made sure to get up at first sign of light and get changed into an old pair of jeans and an old sweater before meeting Oma down in the kitchen for a quick breakfast. All throughout our breakfast of coffee and oatmeal—and the two boiled eggs she made me scarf down—she was mostly quiet. She just shoveled food into her mouth and nodded or harrumphed when I said anything. I didn't really know how to handle my grandmother acting like she didn't know how to talk or curse.

The previous night had been the same. Lunch and dinner had been mostly silent affairs, which in and of itself was fine, but it was unnerving since this was Oma of all people. The woman didn't know how to keep her mouth shut for any length of time. I was beginning to wonder if she needed some medication or if I had done something to make her angry without knowing it. However, I decided to let the whole thing go. Eventually, she'd snap and yell at me for whatever it was that I had done, or she would stop being quiet.

We walked out to the garden together after breakfast since Oma announced succinctly that the delivery from Barkley's would be around anytime. Out on the back lawn of the property, the white picket fence around the garden shone brightly in the early morning sun. And the entire garden looked as though it had been freshly hoed. I frowned to myself, remembering that Oma had only gotten about a fourth of the garden done before she had stopped the day before.

"Did you come out here yesterday afternoon?" I asked as we approached the garden.

I had taken a three-hour nap in the afternoon, so I realized that I wasn't exactly keeping an eye on my Oma's activities.

"Yes." She snapped. "What of it?"

"Well, if you were planning to go ahead and hoe up the whole garden, we probably didn't have to buy a tiller." I shrugged. "That's all."

"It'll need to be tilled anyhow." She grumbled. "The ground's merely turned up, not tilled."

"Okay," I replied.

"What's it to you anyway?" She snapped.

"You're firing arrows into a corpse, Oma." I held my hands up defensively.

She harrumphed just as a beeping noise came from the driveway on the other side of the house. Signaling that the truck had arrived with the manure and tiller, the beeping got louder as it got closer. Within moments, I saw the back end of a delivery truck come out from behind the side of the house. Oma clapped her hands together with a "let's get to this" determination. I folded my arms over my chest, feeling like I was swimming in the Carhartt, as the truck backed up so closely to the garden fence that I started to get worried.

At the last possible second, the truck braked and the fence was spared being run over. Oma didn't seem to have the least bit of concern that the truck wouldn't stop in time to keep her fence standing, so I tried not to worry about it. Once the truck was parked, and the engine was off, the driver's side door swung open, and a pair of work-boot laden feet popped into view. I watched as the driver jumped down, landing squarely on his feet, his head down, hidden under a baseball cap that had seen better days.

The driver was dressed for the job, heavy, steel-toed work boots, jeans that were clean but obviously distressed by use and not for fashion, a flannel showing from underneath a Carhartt coat, work gloves, and the aforementioned baseball cap. He sauntered down the length of the truck towards us, and Oma clapped her hands together. The delivery driver was obviously familiar with being out in the sun, as evidenced by his bronzed skin. Even in early Spring, he was tan. His dark hair peeked out from under the sides of his cap, and his face probably hadn't been shaved in the last 24 to 48 hours. Everything about his face was masculine and handsome—strong jawline, squares and angles, with thick eyebrows and a strong nose and chin. He probably would've been the model for a Greek sculptor if he'd lived in a different time.

He kept his head down as he approached but looked up often enough to be able to navigate his way over to us easily enough. It came off arrogant and rude, but I couldn't help but believe that it was maybe shyness. Maybe if it had just been Oma waiting for him, he would have approached her differently. He shoved his hands into the pockets of his coat as he approached, looking as though he wasn't sure how to broach a conversation. I found myself incredibly drawn to the incredibly tentative, yet confident masculinity of this driver. I shook my head to clear my thoughts and waited for Oma's guidance.

"Lucas!" She held her arms out as he approached.

He gave a half smile and accepted a hug from her.

"Good morning, Mrs. Wagner." He said lowly. "Sorry I'm late, I had to run over to Toledo this morning before I came here."

"You're right on time, hon." She patted his hand as she pulled away from him. "You remember my grandson?"

She gave a perfunctory, bored wave in my direction.

"Yes'm." He nodded, then reached his hand out to me.

I smiled at, apparently, Lucas, and reached out to shake his hand. Internally, however, I was wondering where the Hell I would know this man from. Immediately, I set about shuffling through memories, wondering where I might have run into him or when we would have been introduced in the past, but I came up completely empty.

"He was a year ahead of you in school," Oma whispered out of the corner of her mouth as I shook his hand.

"He can hear you, Oma," I spoke back in the same manner to her, then directly to Lucas. "I'm sorry, I've just been gone a while and don't have the best memory. It's nice to meet you. Again, I guess."

"You look different than I remember." He gave a nod of his head, his eyes not quite connecting with mine.

"He's lost some weight," Oma interjected.

"And gained ten years." I shrugged.

Lucas just nodded at that.

It became apparent that the conversation had come to an end.

"Well, look now, Lucas." Oma was giddy as a schoolgirl around him. "We just need to get those bags off the truck there. If we can stack them over by the front fence here and then get the tiller down here, then we can get to work on getting this garden ready for Spring."

"All right." He nodded.

He seemed to size me up, as if appraising whether or not I was capable of slinging bags of manure. I wanted to be offended, but I couldn't really blame him. I had very obviously turned into a "city boy" over the previous decade—and I was so skinny that I looked like I'd break. I needed a few more weeks with Oma before I looked hearty enough to sling bags of cow shit, I supposed.

"I suppose I can stick around and help you out if you'd like." He spoke from under the bill of his cap again. "Grandpa gave me the rest of the day off since I've been working so hard and all."

"Well, we sure wouldn't mind the help, would we?" Oma smiled widely at Lucas.

Lucas was Jackson Barkley's grandson, that was apparent now. He wasn't just a regular delivery guy.

"Lucas Barkley!" I stated more loudly than I had intended. "Yeah! I remember you now."

I was so proud of the fact that a memory about my hometown had come back to me without a massive amount of pressure from Oma.

"You played football, right?" I asked.

He looked up at me for the briefest of moments, his eyes connecting with mine, before he looked down again and nodded. Lucas Barkley was weird. Hopefully in a harmless way.

"Yeah." I shrugged at Oma. "We could use help, I guess."

So, at Lucas nonverbal direction, we all started pulling bags of—thankfully—cold cow manure off of the delivery truck. The cold kept the cow shit from stinking more than I'm sure it would have during the warmer summer months. We stacked all forty of them along the front side of the garden fence. Then the three of us worked together to pull the tiller to the end of the delivery truck and lower it to the ground. Something about Lucas' build told me that he didn't really need our help, but was being gracious in letting us help him, even if it somewhat hindered his work.

"Now, Lucas," Oma frowned, "I don't know the first thing about this shit. Why don't you get it up and running for us? Robbie and I can dump bags of shit while you do the tilling?"

"You sure?" He asked, still not looking up for any length of time. "The tilling is the easy work."

"Well, you're helping us, so it's only right." She nodded. "Besides, neither one of us knows how to get that thing going. Maybe you can explain it to us as you go?"

We got a crash course in tiller operations and maintenance from Lucas—though he wasn't too keen on having two attentive people looking over his shoulder as he worked. But once it was gassed up, filled with oil, and all systems were a go, he set off tilling after Oma and I dumped the first few bags of manure on the garden.

I kept an eye on Lucas as Oma and I picked up bag after bag of cow shit and dumped them in uniform rows in the garden so that it would get tilled under thoroughly and evenly. Lucas focused on tilling, his eyes rarely moving from the ground in front of the tiller. Something about him made me anxious. He was just...*weird*. Not in a bad way. But he was definitely not a social creature and didn't seem to know how to interact with other human beings. However, after two hours, I gave up on worrying about Lucas and focused on making sure the cow shit was getting dumped in the right places, then taking turns with Oma as we used the hoe to spread it out more for the tiller.

Within four total hours, the whole garden was full of shit—literally—and the tiller had done its work. My stomach was starting to grumble, but Oma had Lucas show us the best way to clean the tiller up and get it stored away in the shed. Apparently, a water hose was the best option, then air dry, then storage. Who'd have figured that out? However, we got the tiller washed up and set alongside the shed for the "drying cycle" before Oma spoke up again.

"It's getting on lunch time." She said, clapping her hands together again. "Why don't you stay and have lunch with us, Lucas? It'd be the least we could do for all of your work."

"What are y'all having?" He asked.

"Don't worry, I got plenty of creamed peas and potatoes, cabbage, potato rolls, a good apple pie—you ain't gotta eat any meat if you don't want to." She laughed with a roll of her eyes.

I frowned, wondering what that was about. Then it dawned on me. Lucas, the ex-football playing country boy, was a vegetarian. I internally shrugged. I lived in L.A. Who was I to judge?

"That'd be all right. Thank you." He nodded, his head still staying down.

"Why don't you boys gather up all the bags and get them thrown out and by the time you get in to wash your hands, I'll have everything laid out?" Oma suggested, then turned on her heels as if the matter was settled.

I wanted to kick my grandmother in the ass as she walked away. How could she leave me alone with this obviously strange stranger? Steeling myself for the awkwardness, I walked over to the front fence line of the garden, surveying the plastic damage laying about. Lucas sauntered over, head still down, staring at the ground, and we each started picking up remnants of bags.

"So...you work for your grandpa?" I asked, picking the first topic that came to mind.

"Yeah." He nodded. "Came back here after college."

"That's nice." I agreed, though I wasn't sure that I did. "Where'd you go to college?"

"NYU." He said simply.

My eyebrows raised of their own accord.

"Very nice," I replied. "What did you major in?"

"Secondary education with a specialization in English." He mumbled. "I teach over at the high school sometimes as a sub."

My eyebrows went higher. I couldn't imagine this shy person I was picking up bags that previously held cow shit with standing in front of teenagers and teaching them anything. He didn't seem the type that could handle that many eyes on him at one time.

"You have my respect," I said. "I certainly couldn't deal with teenagers. And teaching...not many professions as noble as that."

"It's usually the advanced placement classes." He explained. "Those kids usually aren't so bad."

This was the most he had said in the last four hours that wasn't about tilling or dumping cow shit. He didn't follow up my questions with any of his own, which most people would find annoying and rude. I found it to be a relief. I didn't want to announce to anyone in town that I was Jacob Michaels, and they just hadn't put two-and-two together. And I certainly didn't want people in town calling me "fancy," and "uppity" like Oma was prone to do.

I was glad that Lucas didn't have any interest in what I did. But it made picking up the bags together a lot more awkward than it should have been. I found myself wondering if Lucas had some type of social disorder or was just terminally shy. He picked up the bags methodically, wadding them up in his rough, large hands and moved on to the next one, looking like he wished the ground would swallow him whole.

"Your guitar playing in high school really paid off," Lucas spoke suddenly, his head still down.

"I'm sorry?" I asked as I bent down and grabbed another bag.

"I saw you on T.V." He explained. "When you did that concert in England. I watched it with Mrs. Wag—your grandmother."

"Oh." I chewed at my lip.

I was an idiot. Obviously, at least one or two people in this town would know who I was upon meeting me.

"It was a really good concert." He said simply.

"Thank you."

Lucas seemed to be having an internal debate with himself before he spoke up again.

"I remember you liked being in the plays and playing guitar and singing in high school." He said. "Everyone always thought you were crazy."

I shrugged.

"They still do." I tried to laugh it off.

"Nah." He shook his head. "You really made something of yourself, Jacob."

"Rob's fine," I said. "That's…Jacob's just a stage name. No one who knows me calls me Jacob."

He nodded. And I suddenly had the realization that a lot of people called me Jacob.

"You look different than you did in your last movie."

"You watch that with Oma?" I cocked an eyebrow with a smile.

"We went to the theater over in Toledo." He said. "We go every time a new one comes out."

I looked up at the house with a grin but didn't mention to Lucas what my grandmother had said about never having seen my movies.

"She buys the tickets, and I buy the popcorn and sodas."

"You're getting the sharp end of the stick there." I teased.

He actually chuckled.

"Yeah. Anyway." I shrugged. "I've lost some weight."

"You sick?" He glanced up for a split second.

"No." I shook my head as I bent down to pick up the last sack. "I've just run myself into the ground. I'm here to rest up and get some weight back on me."

Lucas indicated that we could just toss the bags back into the truck and he'd dispose of them later.

"You're not sticking around then, I suppose?" Lucas asked once the door to the truck was pulled down.

"I don't really know," I replied. "I'll be here for a while."

He nodded again. It was annoying.

"They say you're gay in all the magazines." Lucas blurted out suddenly, then his head dipped lower.

I considered this question-statement as he kicked at the dirt and held his hands in his pockets.

"If it's going to get me a punch to the mouth—no," I said. "If it won't—then yes."

"Just a question." His head stayed down.

"Well, there ya' go." I shrugged.

We headed towards the house, Lucas trailing behind me with his hands in his pockets and his head pointed downwards. I didn't know what to make of Lucas. He seemed to be upset all the time, but his actions didn't indicate that he was actually upset about anything. Once inside, we took turns washing our hands in the sink, and we sat down with Oma for lunch.

Lunch was a pleasant, if not awkward, activity. Oma made plenty of conversation for all three of us, but Lucas was not the loquacious type. He answered most questions as simply as possible, hardly ever making eye contact with anyone. Once, during lunch, he found a piece of bacon in his cabbage and tried, as discreetly as possible, to push it to the side of his plate. I could tell from his body language that he just wanted to stop eating altogether after that, but he was too polite to do so. I knew Oma noticed as well, but she kept that to herself, unlike many other things.

When lunch was near over, and I was done with my plate, I scraped it off in the trash and took it to the sink. After giving it a quick wash, I decided that I was done making small talk with the world's quietest weirdo. Oma looked up at me as I stood by the sink, smiling like a fool, trying to find a way to politely excuse myself. Lucas stared at his plate, his hands in his lap.

"If you two don't mind, I think I'll head upstairs for a nap," I announced cheerfully, then affected a yawn. "I'm still so worn out—especially after the tilling and whatnot."

Lucas just gave a nod.

"Well, you don't want any apple pie?" Oma frowned at me.

"I'll eat a slice when I get up," I replied, then headed for the door. "It was nice seeing you again, Lucas."

He gave another nod, and I managed not to roll my eyes as I left the kitchen and headed for the stairs. Once I was up the stairs and into the relative safety of my own room, I stripped off the Carhartt and sat down on the bed. I gave a sigh of relief and suddenly realized that I hadn't been entirely lying about the being tired part. I kicked off my shoes and started to unbutton the shirt I had worn to garden in before lunch.

As I started to pull my top layer off, I stood and walked over to the window, looking out over the backyard. My eye caught movement, and I looked down to see Oma and Lucas coming down the back steps. Oma and Lucas talked animatedly for several minutes, but I couldn't hear anything. They were too far down, and the walls and windows were too well sealed and insulated. Lucas was looking my grandmother in the eyes and talking just as animatedly as she was. When he went to leave, he gave her a big hug and jumped up into his truck, pulling out slowly as to not tear up the lawn. Oma waved until he was out of sight, then she stormed back up the back steps. Less than thirty seconds later, there was a pounding on the bedroom door.

"Come in." I rolled my eyes as I stepped away from the window.

"You're a rude little asshole." Oma pushed the door open and stepped inside the room, her hands going to her hips.

"Pardon me?" My hands froze on my buttons.

"You just up and leave in the middle of lunch." She gestured dramatically with her hand. "Lucas ended up not having any apple pie because it was so damn awkward."

"I'm sorry." I shook my head with a smile. "Are you accusing me of making the world's quietest weirdo...*uncomfortable*?"

"He's not a weirdo you little shit." She growled. "He's a perfectly sweet, nice, kind young man who..."

"Goes with you to see all of my movies over in Toledo?" I cocked an eyebrow, silencing her. "You buy the tickets, he buys the refreshments?"

She just glared at me.

"If I look in the cabinet downstairs by the T.V. I bet I'd find one of my movies." I waggled my head this time then feigned to move towards the door.

"They're all in there you sonofabitch." She snarled. "So what?"

"Just pointing out that you're going out of your way to be hurtful, you big liar." I shrugged and pulled my flannel off, tossing it onto the bed. "You don't have to try so hard, Oma. You're hurtful without even trying."

"Says the asshole who was rude to company!"

"He doesn't give a damn about me." I shrugged. "I don't really think he found me rude at all. He would barely even talk unless forced."

"He's gardening and eating a meal with a goddamn celebrity, ya' fuckin' moron." She growled again. "How'd you expect him to act??"

"Ah-so." I gave an upwards nod. "So, maybe I was right about what my presence can do to a social situation? You ready to take back calling me stupid for thinking it was a bad idea for me to go to the center with you?"

"No the fuck I am not!"

"And, for the record, he could have just acted like a normal human being." I folded my arms over my chest. "He didn't have to act like he was trying to not blurt out about all the bodies in his basement."

"You're just hateful." She frowned at me. "You're just looking for a way to get out of going to the center with me. You want to act like I'm not your grandmother—that's what this is about."

I wanted to say something rude back, but instead, I walked over to the bedside table and retrieved my cell phone. Oma glared at me as I unlocked my phone with a swipe of my finger, found a name in my contacts and selected it. I slapped the phone to my ear. The phone rang once before it was picked up by my assistant.

"*Jacob!*" Jessica announced happily.

"I don't have time right now." I stopped her from anything she might want to say. "I need a pair of Louboutins that look fit for a drag queen, size 41eu sent to me."

"*Okay.*" She didn't even question me.

I spent thirty seconds on the phone with her, telling her what to do, where to send the shoes, and to overnight them immediately to my Oma's address. Then I warned her not to give a damn person that address, who they were being sent to or why. She indicated that she understood and we ended the call. I jabbed my phone in the air at my grandmother.

"We're going to that fucking center as soon as these expensive-ass shoes come in the mail." I snarled. "And I'll give them to goddamn Carlos myself, and you can stand there with your shit-eating grin and watch it. And when the goddamn police have to show up and escort us off the property, I'll rub your face in it, you mean old bag!"

I stood there, phone jabbed out at her from across the room.

"How much them shoes cost?" She asked blandly.

"I don't know!"

"You didn't even ask."

"I hope they cost a million dollars and are made out of fucking puppies and kittens so you can feel even worse about it! And we can show them to the world's quietest weirdo vegetarian and really have a party!"

"How much money you got?" She squinted at me.

"Enough to put a hit on you and get away with it!" I growled.

"And how much is that?" She crossed her arms over her chest.

"Why the Hell do you care???"

"Because I have a feeling that I don't realize what I'm dealing with here." She put her hands on her hips. "I know you're famous, but apparently you got enough money to call across the country, order someone to get you some hoity-toity shoes on a whim and have them shipped overnight and not even bother to write a number down in your checkbook."

"Who the fuck has a checkbook??" I rolled my eyes.

"People who ain't got some black piece of plastic they buy everything with, ya' asshole."

"Do you want to call my accountant?" I jabbed my phone at her again, but this time offering it. "He can give you an approximation. Is that what you want to make sure of? That I'm not here bumming off of you? That I really, *truly* don't have any malevolent reason to be here?"

"That's not my point." She responded, and for once didn't throw in a curse word.

"Then what is it, Oma?" I brought it down a notch, but just one. "Because I'm tired of all this. Either stop dragging my ass through the dirt every chance you get or say whatever the Hell it is you think of me and get it off your chest once and for all."

"Why did you choose to come *here* instead of your condo?" She asked. "Or Bora Bora? Or Tahiti? Or Antigua? You coulda just bought a house and hidden away there."

I stood there and stared at her. Slowly, the arm holding my phone lowered to my side.

"I don't know." I shrugged finally, all of my fight gone.

"Mm." She turned her nose up.

"What the Hell does that mean?"

"It means that you got your reasons." She had her hands on her hips again. "But you just don't wanna say it out loud."

"I told you, I'm not here to bum off of you and..."

"I think you've gone too long without love—and money don't solve that." She stopped me.

I just stared at her.

"You've been off running all over the goddamn world, being in movies, playing your guitar, staying in fancy ass resorts, doing drugs, smoking cigarettes—but I bet you ain't got one goddamn friend to your name. Not any real ones anyway." She said. "I noticed that the only thing you've used that fancy ass phone for is to check with your bank and call your assistant. And I bet you ain't got a boyfriend or a husband because you don't trust no one. You haven't had anyone to trust in going on ten years. You ain't got no love in your life. That's what I think. You can stand there and act all self-sufficient and grown, but you just need someone to tell you, after ten years, to take a goddamn breath. Give you a hug. That's what I think."

I just stared at her.

"And, for the record, Lucas isn't a weirdo." She snapped. "He's a good kid—and is a good friend to me. He seems weird to you because you're not used to people who are impressed by you."

"What's that even mean?" I asked gently, looking down.

"Shit." Oma waved me off. "The first time Lucas and I went over to Toledo to see one of your movies, he couldn't stop talking about how much he admired you in high school, even though you was younger than him. You got out of this town—*actually got out of this town*. You made something of yourself. All the other kids in this town—the ones that remember you and put two-and-two together—looked up to you. And look at you. Lucas didn't expect to see you standing there today when he brought my cow shit and tiller 'cause I don't tell no one your business. Calling him a weirdo for being starstruck? You're an asshole."

Then she left.

I heard her stomp down the hall.

"*Get out of my way!*" The crazy old bag growled at no one.

One door slammed.

Then another.

Then another.

Real mature.

Chapter 4

Dinner came and went, and I didn't get out of bed. I slept from straight through lunch, through dinner, and I didn't bother going downstairs. Oma didn't come upstairs and raise a stink about me missing a meal, either. She didn't bring a tray. And I was glad about it. I didn't want to look her in the face. We both knew she was right. I hadn't just come home to rest and put weight back on—to feel better physically. I'd been missing other integral things in my life over the last decade. Home is always the best place when you feel like you've been without love for too long.

It was long after dark, hours after dinner would have taken place, and I was laying in bed, wondering why the Hell I couldn't sleep any longer. Exhaustion was practically in my bones and my brain, I could feel it wearing at me. And my stomach was rumbling at me, upset that I had done something so dumb as to skip dinner due to being uncomfortable. I laid there, wondering what I could do to pass the time. I hadn't brought a book with me, and I didn't play games on my phone. My phone served three functions, as far as I was concerned: phone, text, email. I didn't even have any social media apps on my phone—that was all handled by my publicist and assistant. In all honesty, I didn't even know what all social media I was currently on. Before I had started losing weight and looking skeletal, I'd just take pictures and send them to my publicist, and they did something with them on social media.

Everything in the house was quiet as a graveyard, which only made me even more anxious and unnerved. Finally, I sat up in bed and turned on the bedside lamp. It took me a moment to find my robe, but I found it on the hook on the back of the bathroom door after a bit of searching. After sliding it on, I tied it tightly around my waist and went to the bedroom door. I peeked out into the hallway, only to encounter nothing but middle of the night darkness.

Gently, I eased out of my room and headed down the hallway, using only the light that shone from my room to find my way. I crept past Oma's bedroom, making sure to not wake her. Getting screamed at or cursed out for that was the last thing that I wanted. I eased down the stairs, trying to keep them from creaking or squeaking as I made my way. This big old house, as good of shape as it was in, was still spooky, even in my mid-twenties. As I crept through the house, I remembered being a child and being spooked by every shadow and creak it had to offer. I couldn't help but be amazed that that still hadn't changed years later.

Down in the kitchen, at the back of the house, in the dark, it still looked like a spooky old country kitchen, even though the appliances had been updated over the years. I missed the light, airy feeling of my kitchen in my condo with all of its sleek lines and bare surfaces, where nothing could hide in the shadows, even at night. Here, in Oma's kitchen, I felt like anything could jump out at any second. Of course, I was a grown man, I pushed those fears out of my mind and went to the fridge, turning on the small light that hung over the sink on the way.

Rustling around in the fridge, I pulled out leftover potatoes and peas, cabbage, sausages, and the apple pie. I set the containers on the table and got a fork and a glass of water. A smile was spreading across my face as my stomach grumbled again and I slid into a seat. Immediately, I dug in, my appetite ravenous as I ate spoonful after spoonful of potatoes, cabbage, and chunks of sausages I chopped up with the edge of the spoon. When I felt like I was almost full, I attacked the pie, eating two slices before I felt satisfied. At the rate I was going, and with Oma's cooking, I'd gain ten or more pounds back before two weeks passed.

I sat back in my chair and rubbed my belly like a pregnant woman, at once both disgusted and pleased with myself. Even when I was at my ideal weight, BMI, and muscle mass years prior, I wouldn't have allowed myself to eat so much in one sitting. So, more than disgusted, I was pleased. It was a simple indulgence, but it felt immense in the moment. It may have been the pleasantness brought on by a good meal—even though it was straight out of the fridge—I decided that when Oma and I were both awake in the morning, I'd do my best to make amends with her.

It was the creaking sound that drew me out of my thoughts. My head snapped around to look in the direction that the sound emanated from and my eyes landed on the backdoor. It was a quarter open and slowly swinging inward. Jumping up and pushing back from the table at the same time, my eyes never left the slowly swinging and creaking door. I stood stock-still, my heart pounding as the door swung all the way in and the doorknob tapped gently against the wall, stopping the movement.

Heartbeat.

Heartbeat.

Heartbeat.

The only thing that made a sound or moved was icy, early Spring wind that whistled through the open door. Tentatively, and more scared than I'd been in a long time, I stepped away from the table towards the door. My brain was telling me that the door had probably not been latched well and the wind had caught it. My imagination told me to get ready to duck when a killer started swinging axes at my head. I approached the door, creeping slowly, alert to any and every noise and movement within the kitchen. When I got to the kitchen door, nothing had jumped out at me, and nothing seemed abnormal, save for the door swinging open on its own.

Finally, I realized how silly I was being and stepped over to the doorway. The chilly air rushed inwards, slapping against my cheeks, but held nothing malevolent. I shook my head, smiling, at how stupid I had been. Reaching for the door, I grabbed the knob and began to swing the door shut. But out of the corner of my eye, I saw movement in the yard. I turned my head and looked for the signs of the movement again. My eyes scanned the dark yard, cast only in the blue-ish light the moon emitted. Nothing.

But...then...my eyes landed on Oma's garden, and I saw it again. The slightest and quickest of movements. Something small and shadowy scurried through the garden. My eyes danced wildly as I looked for it again. I frowned to myself as I caught a glimpse of the small, shadowy figure again. No taller than a large dog, it popped up along the side of the fence furthest from the house, looked around, scaled the fence, and ran away, towards the lake. I chewed at my lip as it disappeared into the shadow of the trees at the boundary of the property.

I stared in the direction it had gone, long after I lost sight of it, as the icy air assaulted me. Had it been a raccoon? A fox? I thought it had stood on two legs as it scurried away, so maybe a raccoon, weasel, or an opossum were the best bets. Frowning to myself, knowing that it was a mystery that would never be solved, I closed the door, latched it, then gave it a few jiggles to make sure it was secure. I cleaned up my mess and headed back upstairs to climb back into bed.

Chapter 5

In the morning, I felt more rested than I had in months, if not years. Starting out the day with a good bath-slash-shower seemed like the best course of action. Then I dressed in the most "normal" clothes I had, a pair of designer jeans that were not designer looking, a pullover, and socks and Chucks. When I headed downstairs, I felt that even Oma couldn't find anything wrong with what I had chosen to wear. Even if we were in northern Ohio, far away from big cities like L.A. or New York.

"I bet that's the least fancy shit you have." Oma shot a look at me from her place at the stove as I entered the kitchen, chipper and smiling.

"Good morning to you, too."

"Mm."

"Are we still fighting?" I asked innocently as I got the orange juice out of the fridge. "I'd like to know what to prepare for here."

"I don't know?" She grumbled. "Are we?"

I turned to her, carton of OJ in hand and just gave her a blank look.

"Fine." She shrugged.

So, I got a glass down from the cabinet and poured some juice and then got a mug and poured myself a serving of the fresh coffee that Oma had made. I sat down at the table and pulled my phone out of my pocket. I actually had a text message—but it was just from my assistant, informing me that the shoes would arrive sometime in the afternoon. A "thank you" text got shot off, and the phone got slid back into my pocket.

I was sipping at my coffee when Oma, for once, gently set a plate down in front of me. Eggs, home fries, bacon, and a couple of fried tomatoes. Definitely trying to put the weight back on me.

"Thank you," I stated simply.

Oma made an "mm" sound again and sat down across from me with her own plate, coffee, and juice.

"I was thinking..." I began.

"Lord help us." She mumbled.

"Look." I sighed. "Can you just not? I mean...you want me to try hard, so maybe you could give twenty to thirty percent yourself?"

She looked at me for a minute, then popped another bite in her mouth before gesturing for me to continue.

"You're right." I shrugged. "I don't have any people I consider real friends. I don't have any love in my life. Maybe that's why I'm here as much as being exhausted and needing to relax and take care of myself. I didn't really realize it until you said it. Okay?"

She nodded.

"And maybe I thought you'd give me some of the love I need," I said gently, averting my eyes for a moment. "I know I haven't been a great grandson, running away, barely calling or visiting—but I haven't gone out of my way to be awful to you, either. Nothing I've done was to intentionally hurt you. It was thoughtless and selfish—but never once have I had the thought, 'this will really hurt Oma,' okay?"

She nodded again.

"So...I'd like it if we could call a truce here," I said. "I apologize from the bottom of my heart, and I won't run away in the middle of the night again. I'm not here to mooch or bum or *anything*. I just want to be here, with my grandmother, and relax and eat and just be Robert Wagner for a while. That's all. And I hope we can use that time to become grandmother and grandson again instead of whatever we've been doing. Is that all right?"

"I suppose." She cocked an eyebrow at me. "I'm just pissed off."

"I understand."

"I love the Hell out of you, Robbie." She sighed. "But you've been a complete fuckin' asshole for a good decade now."

I held my hands out helplessly.

"I can't take it back."

She sighed again.

"Fine." She nodded and went back to eating. "I'll do my best to not be so mean. But I need you to do something for me."

"Who needs shoes now?" I teased, rolling my eyes as I picked up my fork.

She actually laughed.

"Barkley said my garden auger is in." She explained. "Will you go pick it up for me? I got some things to do around here this morning."

She looked me over.

"Maybe you could pick up some new outfits while you're out?" She snorted.

"I'm going to let that comment go." I chuckled. "But, yeah, I can go pick it up for you, Oma."

"It's paid for, don't you let that sonofabitch charge you a goddamn red cent, either." She said forcefully, jabbing her fork at me.

"Carlos' shoes are supposed to arrive this afternoon," I said. "If I'm out for too long, will you watch for them?"

She just squealed with delight. I took that as a "yes."

After breakfast was done and we had washed up the dishes and pans, I went upstairs to grab my keys and wallet. Oma said her "goodbyes" to me as I left through the front door, grabbing the Carhartt coat on the way. I drove into Point Worth proper, hoping that I wouldn't forget where Barkley's was. Not that that was likely, but if it was possible, I'd do it. And that would just provide Oma with one more thing to rib me about.

However, ten minutes later, I was pulling around the back lot of Barkley's and parking my car, praising God for not letting me do something stupid like getting lost. When I entered the garden center, I immediately noticed a guy in a Carhartt, his back to me, restocking some of the shelves with bags of fertilizer. The familiar ballcap made me cringe internally. Biting my tongue, I walked over to Lucas, affixing a smile to my face.

"Lucas?" I asked as I stepped up behind him.

Lucas smiled widely and turned to find out who was addressing him. His eyes connected with mine for a split second. The color of gilded jade. Then he was looking down, averting his gaze from mine.

"Rob." He said simply. "Can I help you?"

"Yeah," I said. "Oma said that Mr. Barkley had her...auger...I think she said...in and it needed to be picked up?"

He chewed at his lip. "Yeah, I think I heard him saying something about that."

"Where do I go to get it?" I asked.

I motioned towards the sliding glass doors, questioning.

"I can get it for you, Rob." He nodded, his eyes still downcast. "Um, I'll be right back."

"Okay, thanks, Lucas." I did my best to smile.

He nodded again and dashed away towards the store. I frowned to myself as he disappeared into the interior of the store. When he came back out, I was going to grab him by the arms and shake him and growl "*Look at me!*" Then I remembered Oma. I swallowed my frustration at someone acting so strangely. He wasn't strange—he was just shy around me. I would do my best to be nice to Lucas—even if it drove me insane.

Moments later, the sliding doors 'whooshed' open again, and Lucas came walking towards me, an auger in hand. It looked like a giant drill, the length of a shovel, with a dual handle at one end. His eyes were still downcast, but he came right up to me and held it out, like an offering. I took it from him with a smile and looked it over.

"I don't even want to know what she's planning to do with this." I chuckled.

"Um, it makes quick holes for planting seeds deeply or for planting seedlings when it's time." He mumbled.

"Well, at least I know that I'm probably safe then," I said.

"You never know with Mrs. Wagner." I could see his smile underneath the bill of his ballcap.

I chewed at my lip. I'd already apologized to one person today, what was one more? My ego could take the hit, I supposed.

"Lucas, I wanted to apologize," I said.

He looked up for a split second, then down again.

"I was rude yesterday," I said. "It was unintentional, but that's beside the point. So, I'm sorry if I was rude or hurt your feelings yesterday."

He gave a small cough, and his body language let on that he was uncomfortable.

"Oma might have pointed that out to me, so...I wanted you to know that if I did anything rude, it was unintentional, but I'm owning up to it and apologizing." I finished.

"You weren't rude." He shook his head.

I smiled. "Well, regardless, I'm sorry."

"Well, you're forgiven." He spoke from under his cap.

"Thank you," I said.

Before I knew what I was doing—maybe it was from being so apologetic all morning and trying to do the right thing—my mouth kept moving.

"I'm supposed to get some *less fancy* clothes while I'm out to appease Oma," I said. "So I don't stick out so much. Would you like to have a cup of coffee or something? Then you could tell me where the best place to go in town is for some clothes. Make me look like a local."

Lucas' feet shuffled a bit as he stood there, unsure how to answer. I realized that some gay celebrity asking out a country boy in a feed store was how this was probably being taken. Immediately, I regretted being so nonchalant and insouciant.

"I'm sorry." I chuckled like an idiot. "That probably came out weird or something and..."

"No." He interjected quickly, but only glanced up briefly. "It's just that I'm working and..."

"Oh, of course." I shook my head with a smile.

"But I could take a break for a coffee." He nodded, still looking down. "Grandpa probably won't mind. Then I could give you directions to a decent store."

"Okay," I said. "That sounds great."

"Um, why don't I meet you down at the Sunny Side Up Café?" He gestured vaguely. "I'll head down after I let my grandfather know I'm taking a break."

I gave him a nod and headed to my car with the auger in tow. Mentally slapping myself upside the head the whole way. Why did I have to invite the world's weirdest and quietest vegetarian to have a coffee just so that I could make up for rudeness? *My very slight rudeness.* I tried to just push it out of my head—we were having coffee, and that was that. I'd made my bed. I somehow found a way to put the auger diagonally in the trunk of my car so that it would fit and hopped into the driver's seat.

Minutes later, I was sitting in a booth at the Sunny Side Up Café, waiting on Lucas to show up. The same waitress that had served Oma and me was working and the place was virtually empty again. I was starting to get an idea about the café. More than likely, locals hit the café up for a quick breakfast before work. Then the lunch rush probably happened between 11 and 2, then they closed down for the day. The times between breakfast and lunch were probably pretty slow, only a few stragglers showing up here and there. That was perfect, as far as I was concerned.

The waitress had brought me a cup of coffee and was setting it down by the time Lucas walked in the door, his head going down as soon as I looked over. The waitress hollered out to him and went over to give him a quick hug before he was allowed to come and sit down. She told him that she was going to go get him a cup of coffee when she let go of him and he finally walked over to the booth. He slid in across from me, undoing his coat and letting it fall down behind him in his seat.

"Girlfriend?" I smiled over the lip of my mug before taking a sip.

"Who?" He frowned.

"The waitress." I nodded in her direction.

"No." He shook his head. "Just a friend. She was a few years behind us in school. She became a freshman the year after I graduated. Jill Bryant?"

I smiled sheepishly and shrugged.

He nodded.

This was going great.

"Here ya' go, Lucas." The waitress, whose name I now knew, showed up and put a mug in front of my coffee partner.

"Jill, you remember Rob, don't you?" Lucas finally looked up and nodded at me, then looked back down.

"You were in here with Esther Jean the other day, weren't you?" She smiled. "Mrs. Wagner?"

"Yes." I nodded. "Lucas said we just missed being in high school with you."

Lucas missed being in high school with her due to his age. I missed being in high school with her due to running away.

"Well, I don't remember you from school." She chuckled. "But I remember you were with Esther Jean, so I guess that's good enough."

She offered her hand, so I shook it, properly introducing myself. I'd been polite as Hell to two strangers in Point Worth—Oma would surely be pleased.

"You look so familiar, though." Jill looked thoughtful as we pulled away from the handshake.

I shrugged.

Lucas perked up as if to say something, then stopped himself.

"It'll come to me." Jill shook her head with a giggle. "I have a horrible memory."

"Join the club." I shrugged goofily again.

"Well, you guys just holler if you need refills." She winked at us and walked away to other things.

I waited until she was out of earshot.

"Thanks for not telling her...about me." I said.

"I figured you were probably keeping that quiet."

"Trying to." I nodded. "So, I have to be honest. I kind of have an ulterior motive for inviting you here."

That got Lucas' attention. He looked up, and his eyes actually met mine and stayed here. Gilded jade was definitely the best description for the eyes that peeked out from under the bill of his ballcap.

"Besides apologizing," I made a checkmark motion in the air, "I wanted to tell you that you can actually look me in the eyes and talk. I'm not...special. I'm not fancy, no matter what Oma says. You don't have to be...shy...or anything."

Lucas blushed and looked down. It was endearing. Maybe Lucas could be a friend. Oma was right. He wasn't weird. Just shy.

"I've never been around a celebrity." He mumbled, looking down, then forced himself to look up.

"Well, we went to high school together, so..."

He chuckled finally.

"Look," I leaned in conspiratorially, "I don't really have...I don't really have a lot of friends around here. So, if you could take it easy on me and treat me like I'm no big deal—which I'm not—I would consider it a personal favor."

"I'm sorry, Jac—Rob." He blushed deeper but managed to keep his eyes on mine. "Sorry. I just...see Jacob Michaels when I look at you."

He said the last sentence in a hushed tone.

"It's okay." I nodded. "But...try not to?"

He chuckled again.

"I'll do my best, I suppose." He nodded.

"Good." I kicked back in my seat and took a quick sip of coffee. "So, tell me about you and every—"

"I got it!" Jill came marching over to the table. "I figured out where I recognized you from!"

I froze. Lucas swallowed hard.

"You were the kid in all the plays!" Jill jabbed a fist in the air triumphantly. "My sister was in your class, and she was always dragging me to see them. No offense. And you were always the lead in every dang one of 'em!"

Lucas chuckled. I smiled up at Jill and shrugged.

"You caught me," I said.

"Thought you'd pull one over on me." She whistled. "Good try, Rob!"

She laughed loudly and dashed away again. Lucas looked over at me with a wide grin. I shrugged again.

"So...you? Everything that's changed in town?" I prompted him and grabbed my coffee mug. "Give me the gossip, man."

Lucas swallowed nervously.

"Well, um, I went to NYU—but I—I told you that already, I guess." He smiled awkwardly. "Um, not much has really changed here since college. Café changed hands. Bowling alley closed. An extra pub opened. Somehow the hardware store does good business. Everyone goes to Toledo for a movie, dinner, dancing...the usual stuff."

"Still no nightlife, eh?" I laughed as I sipped my coffee.

"Not really." He smiled, still managing to keep eye contact. "Not unless you want to go get drunk with teenagers out in the woods."

"Pass." I shook my head. "What about you? I know where you went to school and what for, where you work...what do you do around here besides all of that?"

He shrugged.

"Got a wife?" I prodded. "Kids? Any on the way? Hobbies?"

"No, none of that."

"No hobbies?" I teased.

He chuckled nervously. "I tend to just stick to myself. Kind of a homebody. I like to read."

"What are you reading now?" I turned to put my back against the wall and kicked my legs out along the booth, coffee mug in hand.

Lucas looked nervous.

"Last book I read was the *Fifty Shades of Grey* series." I shrugged. "I was on vacation, and everyone had been talking about them for so long...well, what I'm saying is, you won't get any judgment from me."

He laughed.

"Um, *Middlesex* by Jeffrey Eugenides." He mumbled.

"Not what I expected." I chuckled and sipped my coffee. "Thought maybe it'd be *Lonesome Dove* or anything by Larry McMurtry."

"English major." He shrugged.

"Touché." I winked.

"So...yeah, I mostly read." He began tentatively. "I'm working on building my own place. You remember the Owens' farmlands?"

"North of here?" I asked. "Right on the lake?"

He nodded. "The last of the Owenses moved away and sold off the land in parcels, and I bought an acre. So, I'm building my own place out there. It's nearly finished—but I still have a lot of finishing touches to do."

"A man who reads Pulitzer Prize-winning novels and can build an entire house." I nodded with a smile. "I'm surprised one of the local ladies haven't snatched you up."

He shrugged with a smile.

"What do you do?" He grabbed his coffee mug, looking less nervous. "Besides, ya' know...?"

I thought about it for a minute.

"Honestly?" I frowned, suddenly realizing the depth of a question like that to someone like me. "I really don't know. I've done...my job...for so long that I have no idea."

"Well, if you ever want to borrow a book, I have plenty." He suggested, sounding almost excited. "Just let me know."

"I might take you up on that." I tipped my coffee mug at him in a 'toast' of sorts.

"If you would ever like to come for a visit—you and Mrs. Wagner, I mean," He stammered and blushed, "I—I wouldn't be against that. I don't really have a lot of friends either."

"I'm sure it's a lack of desire on your part." I laughed. "You seem nice enough."

He shrugged and looked down again.

"It's kind of weird sitting here talking to a celebrity." He chuckled nervously.

"We're not that great." I shrugged. "I've met tons of 'em, and we're all completely insufferable. Trust me."

"Um, can I ask you something about...ya' know, being a celebrity?" He leaned in slightly, speaking lowly.

"I guess." I nodded.

Was he going to ask me how much money I had? What kind of house I had? Who so-and-so was dating? Had I slept with so-and-so? Could I get him a part in a T.V. show or a movie? I braced myself for one of the many thousands of questions I'd been asked a million times before.

"Well, I mean, I heard that you filmed one of your movies in Finland." He asked quickly. "Did you get to see the Northern Lights?"

I just stared at him as my grin grew.

"What?" He blushed.

"Yeah." I nodded. "On a long weekend, some crew members and I went into Lapland, and a guide took us out to see them. It was..."

Lucas wasn't breathing, and he was staring at me.

"Supernal." I grinned wider. "I guess that's the best word for it."

"I love that word." He breathed out, and his grin began to match mine.

We sat there, staring at each other. One of us remembering something we'd seen and the other wishing they had seen it. Suddenly, he seemed to have a thought.

"Um, sorry." He blushed again. "I need to get back to the store. I'm sorry..."

"No, it's okay." I shook my head clear of thoughts and sat back in my seat. "Thanks for having coffee with me."

"Here." He reached into his pocket, withdrew his wallet, and threw a ten-dollar bill down. "Let me at least buy the coffee."

My first impulse was to insist that since I invited him, I should buy his coffee, but I stopped myself. Oma would be screaming "FANCY!" if I did such a thing, so I merely smiled and thanked him. Lucas downed the rest of his coffee, which was now luckily room temperature, and set his mug down. He gave a final smile as he slid out of the booth. Standing at the end of the table, he looked down at me. Well, not at me, but in my general direction.

"If you and Mrs. Wagner would like to come out for dinner Friday evening, you can borrow a book." He said tentatively. "So you won't get too bored while you're here."

"I'd like that." I nodded back. "I'll tell Oma. Seven-ish?"

"Seven's great." He smiled, met my eyes, then indicated to go.

Before he took two steps, he had a thought.

"They have a Macy's and a Hollister at the Franklin Park Mall in Toledo. Monroe Street." He said. "It's probably the best bet you have for finding some clothes that won't be too...*Point Worth*...but not too fancy."

"Thanks, man." I held my coffee mug out in a 'toast' to him again.

"Anytime." He nodded and then was gone, giving Jill a wave on his way.

I watched through the window by the booth as Lucas walked away from the café, pulling his coat tightly around himself. He had walked over to the café from Barkley's. Surely he didn't walk everywhere, but it was impressive that he hadn't jumped in his car...truck?...to go a few blocks. Maybe I could make a friend while I was back home for rest. I grabbed the bill he had left and took it to Jill at the counter. We made short, small-talk, and then I left. The Franklin Park Mall in Toledo was calling.

Chapter 6

When I got back to Oma's house, I was burdened with an abundance of bags from the mall. While I didn't spend even a tenth of what I would have in a designer's shop in L.A., New York, or some other large city, I had still done quite respectably. I had ten bags—and they were all filled to the limit. Just getting in the front door had been a chore, trying to hold all of the bags while turning the knob. Somehow, I managed the task without dropping anything, hurting myself, or banging the door into the wall and leaving a hole.

Inside, in the living room, things looked even more orderly and spotless—sparkling even—than when I had left. It became clear what Oma had planned while I had been out. I frowned to myself, wishing she had told me that she was planning to clean while I was out. I would have stayed to help and then gone to get her auger for her. But, when I remembered coffee with Lucas, I was glad that I had gone into Point Worth for her when I had.

Oma was in the kitchen, which I knew immediately because she was talking to herself again like a crazy person. I rolled my eyes with a smile and closed the door gently behind myself before heading towards the kitchen. I was going to show her that I had gone and got "normal people" clothes. Then I would go get her auger out of the back of the car. If she found a reason to be mad with me after all of that, I was just going to give up. Something told me that she would be pleased, though.

"*Just don't go in his room while he's here. Okay?*" I heard Oma saying as I approached the kitchen doorway.

I stopped, holding all of the bags.

"*Leave his things alone, especially his laundry.*" She demanded gently. "*Just do it for your own sake, okay?*"

I made a coughing noise and stomped towards the kitchen, signaling my presence. Immediately, I heard a flurry of motion and movement and the slamming of cabinets. I entered the kitchen, looking expectant, my arms overladen with my purchases. Oma was standing at the kitchen sink, her back to me, washing dishes.

"Who's here?" I asked, looking around.

"What?" Oma asked in a sing-song voice.

I frowned at her back and looked around. There was nobody in sight. Was the old lady going fruitcake crazy or what?

"I guess...nothing." I shrugged, deciding to let it go. "I bought some clothes."

"Oh, good." She said in the same chipper voice over her shoulder. "You needed something not quite so..."

"Fancy." I rolled my eyes as I placed my bags on the table. "I know."

"You go to the Men's Wholesale down there on Main?"

"No." I shook my head as I sat down at the table. "I had coffee with Lucas to apologize for being rude, and he suggested I go over to the Franklin Park Mall in Toledo."

"No wonder you were gone so long." She turned to me, wiping her hands on a towel. "You had coffee with Lucas?"

"Yeah." I nodded. "I apologized, okay?"

She just looked at me.

"He invited us to dinner at his house Friday," I added.

"Well...that's...something." She seemed concerned.

"What?"

"Nothing, nothing." She waved me off. "I'm just surprised he was willing to have coffee alone with you, that's all."

It was my turn to look concerned. "He may be a country boy from Ohio, but I don't think he's all that worried about me being a homo."

"Don't say 'homo' like that." She frowned back. "And that's not what I meant at all, ya' asshole. He's just...Lucas...he doesn't warm to people quickly. That's all."

"Oh." I nodded. "Well, I let him pay for coffee, so you'd be proud."

"You didn't pay for the coffee?!?!" She squealed.

"Can't win for losin'." I shook my head at her.

"Well, it just would've been nice." She corrected herself. "Did you get my auger?"

"Yeah." I sighed. "It's in the car. Did Carlos' heels come in?"

"They're up on your bed." She gestured vaguely. "You sure bought a lot of things."

I shrugged sheepishly.

"Seems like a lot of stuff for a...short stay?"

"I see." I smiled at her.

She rolled her eyes.

"I got some things for Spring, too." I chewed my lip. "Just in case, you know, it gets a little warmer before I go."

She just stared at me.

"If that's okay?"

"Of course it's okay." She answered simply. "You're welcome here as long as you like, Robbie. I just...well, you're here. And you're welcome until you decide you don't want to be here anymore."

Her smile told me all I needed to know. Maybe she was starting to believe me that I was indeed in Point Worth to relax, spend some time with her, and not abscond in the middle of the night again.

"Maybe you'll be here for your birthday?" She suggested. "Only a month away after all."

"Well..." I didn't want to show too much of my hand, "it'd be pointless to leave before then. I can't really put on all the weight I need before a month is up, right?"

"Right." She smiled.

A slamming door upstairs made me jump in my seat. I looked up at the ceiling quickly, then looked over at Oma. She seemed perfectly calm and collected.

"What was that?" I looked back up again.

"What was what?" She turned to the fridge.

"Is someone here, Oma?" I frowned at her.

"Besides you and me?" She was being chipper again.

"Of course that's what I mean."

"No, Robbie." She smiled as she turned around, a soda can in her hand. "Just you and me."

"Someone slammed a door upstairs." I started to rise from the table. "You can't tell me you didn't hear that."

"I think we'll go to the center tomorrow," Oma stated nonchalantly. "They've got a bunch of envelopes that need stuffing and stuff that needs to be brought out of storage for the Spring activities that are upcoming, and they could sure use our help. And you can give Carlos' his shoes when you see her. They sure could use our help."

"Yeah, that's fine." I waved her off as I looked upwards.

The house was dead silent now. Only Oma and I were making any noise in the entire space of the large house.

"Good." She said. "I think I'll make Schnitzel and Spaetzle tonight for dinner, ya' paranoid asshole."

I looked down at her.

"How fucking German are you?" I snorted.

"Well, I don't have much of a sense of humor, ya' prick."

"So, pretty German?" I asked.

"Oh, fuck off." She gestured rudely. "Go take your shit upstairs and get it put away. If you just put the bags in the hall, I'll come get 'em."

"I can throw them away." I rolled my eyes with a smile.

"I save 'em." She waved me off. "We're not all from Hollywood and just throw shit out because we can't be bothered to reduce, reuse, and recycle."

"California is big on recycling—where the Hell do you get your information, lady?"

"Oh, just go." She urged me away.

With a roll of my eyes, I gathered up my bags once more and exited the kitchen as Oma went about digging through cabinets and generally trying to look busy. I went upstairs, encumbered by all of my purchases, trying not to tip over and tumble to my death. Upstairs, the hallway was completely empty—dark, but lacking any malice. I just shrugged and went down to my room and threw my bags on the made bed, next to the box containing Carlos' shoes. When I got done putting away all of my clothes, I'd check out Carlos' shoes, just to make sure there was nothing wrong with them so there'd be no surprises when he was presented with his gift.

Chapter 7

All night long, I slept fitfully. I'd sleep for an hour or two, then a loud noise would bring me straight out of a dead sleep, and I'd spring up in bed anxious and trying to catch my breath. In my slumber, I could have sworn that I heard a door slam or someone talking. I heard scurrying, almost like large animals on the floorboards. I saw shadows. But when I woke up, and sat in the bed, looking around, everything was silent and calm. Nothing was making noise, nothing was moving, and no shadows looked the least bit malevolent. Around three o'clock in the morning, however, I ended up turning on my bedside lamp, and I left it on as I went back to sleep. The next four hours of sleep were peaceful.

When I wandered downstairs the next morning, into the kitchen, Oma was making a hearty breakfast for us again. I grabbed myself a big mug of coffee and sat down at the table with a yawn. Oma glanced over at me, looking concerned. I looked back, wondering what it was that was bothering her so much. Some of us don't sleep like a log every single night. Sipping at my coffee, I just stared back, waiting for her to say something. She started to speak, stopped herself, and went back to making whatever it was that she was making. Finally, she came to the table with two plates.

Biscuits and sausage gravy and eggs. Sunny side up.

"You didn't sleep well?" She asked neutrally.

"No." I frowned at her. "I was having bad dreams all night."

"Probably all of that coffee." She snorted.

"Or critters," I mumbled.

"What?"

"Do you have rats or something?" I asked her. "Or a pet of some kind? I could have sworn that I heard...I don't know, scurrying or something."

"Of course I ain't got any pets." She waved me off.

"Okay." I shrugged.

"Maybe if you kept that room clean you'd sleep better."

"It's pretty freaking clean." I laughed. "And what does that have to do with anything?"

"Sometimes disorder can lead to trouble like nerves and anxiety." She shrugged. "If you keep your physical environment clean, it keeps the head clean. That's all."

"Okay, crazy." I rolled my eyes.

She started to curse but stopped herself.

"Just keep your room picked up." She suggested calmly. "Try it. You'll see a difference."

"Fine." I shrugged, disarmed by her calm demeanor. "I'll keep things put away. But if I still sleep like I went to bed drunk, I'll rub it in your face, lady."

It was her turn to roll her eyes.

After breakfast, I helped Oma clean up again and then we both went upstairs to get bathed and dressed. I took time to make my bed, put away things that were lying around, then put my pajamas in the hamper before I got into the bathtub and washed up. Once I was thoroughly scrubbed and dried, I trimmed up my slight beard—the way my management and publicist insisted that I keep it. But, after spending several minutes, making it look the way they had always wanted, I found a razor and shaved my face bare. When I looked up in the mirror, I smiled at my bare skin.

Instead of styling my hair into the blowout I had been instructed to do over the last year, and which is why it had been cut the way it had, I did a simple side part. Sharp angles and jawbone from losing weight aside, the bare face and restyled hair made me look even more different. I actually...and I hated to admit it to myself...I actually looked *good*. I blushed from embarrassment at thinking such things about myself, but I was starting to feel healthier. Well rested. I didn't feel like death warmed over. And I looked fresh and clean.

I found one of the heavyweight black crew-neck tees I had bought and paired it with some medium wash, classic straight leg jeans, my new boots, and a fleece-lined jean jacket that I had purchased at the mall. The overall look was that of someone from Ohio who had decided to up the ante a bit. I'd still stand out a bit—but I'd look like an Ohioan with some fashion sense, instead of a celebrity come to infiltrate the local population. When I met Oma in the foyer, Carlos' shoe box in my hands, her eyes went wide when she saw my face.

"What?" I asked.

"Well, I don't think I've seen you without facial hair since you were sixteen." She said. "You look..."

"Good I hope?"

"Well, yes." She said. "You look almost healthy."

"I'll take it." I laughed.

Together, we left the house, which Oma made a big show of locking up again, and we got in my car. Oma directed me through Point Worth, to Highway 2, and then I basically had to drive in a straight line until we got into Toledo. Less than forty minutes later and she was directing me through downtown Toledo, pointing out this thing and that thing that was new to the area—though I was none the wiser. When we finally reached the center, I suddenly got depressed. It was an old cinderblock building, flat roof, seen better days, and though it had been decorated and manicured beautifully, it felt like there wasn't much funding. For any area as large as Toledo, it just didn't feel right that the LGBTQ center wasn't nicer.

"Here we are." Oma smiled as we pulled up front and I parked in one of the diagonal parking spaces right at the front door. "Now, don't embarrass me or act all damn fancy."

"We're spending the morning with the gays and lesbians." I snorted. "I think this would be *the time* for me to act fancy."

"Not every homosexual is as big an asshole as you, Robbie." She stated simply as she hopped out of the car.

I rolled my eyes and got out of the car and then retrieved Carlos' shoebox from the driver's side backseat. Before I could even close the backdoor, I heard Oma squealing and greeting someone cheerfully. I looked over the roof of the car to see her rushing to embrace some guy, roughly my age. Something told me that this was the infamous Andrew who had stolen my grandmother's heart and she wanted to steal mine.

Whether I wanted to admit it or not, Oma had excellent taste, at least as far as physical looks went. Andrew was very good looking. He was solidly built, tall, well-groomed and manicured, looked fashionable without it looking like he had tried too hard. He had a long, elegant, yet masculine neck, close cut hair, masculine features. I glanced down. Big hands. Big hands are always good. His sparkly white teeth shone out as they pulled back from the embrace and held hands, talking animatedly to each other. When I approached, his deep tenor completed the whole package.

"Oh, Andrew." Oma schmoozed. "This is my grandson Robbie. Remember me telling you about him?"

I smiled as Andrew turned to me. His eyes betrayed him. He looked delighted. I probably wasn't the first son or grandson he'd met—and I bet his track record wasn't great as far as meeting the sons and grandsons of people who set him up went. Then there was the slight 'haven't I seen you somewhere before' flash in his eyes.

"It's Rob." I held my hand out.

"Well, it's very nice to meet you, Rob." He grabbed my hand.

His skin was velvety and warm, and he had a firm grip.

"Likewise." I smiled.

"Esther Jean has told me that you've been away working for a while?" He queried. "She's been promising me that we'd meet eventually."

"She delivers." I gave a slight bow of my head.

"Is that a gift for me?" He cocked an eyebrow playfully at the box in my hands.

"Oh, no, Andrew." Oma grabbed his forearm. "We got Carlos' some new shoes for his show."

My instinct was to snort and say *'We got Carlos some new shoes?'* But I bit my tongue and just nodded along. Andrew acted like he was disappointed, but he just smiled warmly, understanding.

"Well, I guess meeting you is a nice enough gift."

"But...just barely?" I teased.

"Plenty nice enough." His eyes went to my feet and traveled up my body lasciviously.

The look was almost...*hungry.*

I suddenly wasn't so sure how I felt about Andrew. Maybe these were just his standard facial expressions and mannerisms, but it made me want to frown deeply. A person should never be sexualized so early upon meeting a potential love interest. That's like third date territory, as far as I was concerned.

"Well, it's nice to meet you," I stated neutrally, keeping my smile tight and affixed to my face blandly.

Andrew looked me over again as I stared right at his face and Oma watched us both in our one-sided mating ritual.

"Well, why don't we get inside?" Oma, thankfully, interrupted the nearly obscene display of desire. "I'm sure Leslie already has a list of chores that need to be done. And the sooner we get started, the less there'll be for everyone else when they show up."

"That sounds wonderful." I smiled widely at Oma, wanting to hug her for breaking up the awkwardness.

The three of us walked inside, Andrew rushing to open the door, which Oma found absolutely charming. When I thought about walking in front of Andrew, I instead insisted that he go first. He smiled and entered, leaving me to enter without someone leering at my backside. Immediately, I mentally chastised myself for assuming he'd do such a thing. But, after years in Hollywood, I was too used to being treated like a piece of meat. Sometimes an appreciative look is just that—nothing more.

Once inside of the center, we met up with the aforementioned Leslie; a complete drill sergeant, though very likable. She gathered the three of us up, along with three other men and two women who had arrived and immediately put us to work. Chairs needed to be brought out of storage, envelopes needed to be stuffed, things needed to be cleaned, the center needed to be swept and mopped...and I was glad to do any of it to keep from being left alone with Andrew. When I was introduced to everyone by Oma, they all took it at face value that I was her grandson, Robbie Wagner, come to visit for a bit. I got a few looks, but they weren't quite looks of recognition. More like a feeling of familiarity and maybe appraising, but nothing that screamed: "*We know who you really are.*" I was grateful for that.

I spent the morning working with two women, Joanie and Rebecca, a couple who kept me in stitches, pulling chairs out of storage and putting other items into storage. Then we dusted and cleaned, all while the two of them talked about how they'd been married for ten years and wished they'd never met. Then they'd kiss and giggle and make me smile. When lunchtime came around, the center had sandwiches and chips to eat before we got back to work. I found a quiet space up on the stage and sat in the lotus position, eating my food, drinking a soda, and trying to make myself as unnoticeable as possible.

Halfway through my meal, a pair of sleek, shaved legs, with feet jammed into six-inch heels came to stand in front of me. I looked up, a chip halfway to my mouth, to find a Latina (Latino out of drag) standing before me, arms folded over her chest. The purple mini was belted tightly around her waist, her breasts (which looked nearly real) pushed up precariously, large hoop earrings, and a pile of hair on her head. She was looking down at me, an accusing smile on her face, one eyebrow cocked precariously high.

"Hello." I nodded.

"You're Robbie." It wasn't a question.

"Yes?" I frowned, then had a realization. "Carlos?"

"Carlita, darling." Both eyebrows raised precariously as she made a dramatic, theatrical movement with her hands. "Carlita!"

I laughed.

"Nice to meet you, Carlita." I took her hand and gave it a quick kiss.

"Ooh-la-la." She said and eased herself down to kneel beside me.

Sitting in a similar fashion to myself would have been impossible in the dress that she was practically sewn into.

"Esther Jean said you have a gift for me." She smiled evilly. "And I do love free shit. And, of course, I've been dying to meet the elusive grandson of our resident crazy old white woman."

I laughed loudly.

"Your grandmother is just a hoot." Carlita slapped my shoulder. "Mouth like a sailor, manners of a troll, and absolutely darling. And she's here at least once a week to help us out."

"She's...something." I shrugged.

I reached to my side, where I had stowed the shoebox while I was eating and presented it to Carlita.

"For you." I nodded. "From myself and Oma."

"Well, if this isn't shoes, I'll slap you." She squealed.

No one looked over at us. They were used to Carlita. She tore into the box like a kid at Christmas, opened the lid of the shoebox, and just stared. Carlita stared at the shoes for five seconds, then slowly lowered the top and looked up at me, a wicked grin on her face.

"I knew it." She said.

"That it was shoes?" I chuckled.

"You're not Robbie Wagner." She shook her head then leaned in to speak in a hushed tone. "Well, maybe you're *also* Robbie Wagner. But, I'd recognize you even clean-shaven, Jacob Michaels. I may be high from the hairspray I used thirty minutes ago, but I'm not stupid."

I chuckled nervously.

"Please don't..."

"I won't say anything." She slapped at my shoulder before lifting the box in a thanking gesture. "Thank you, honey."

"You're very welcome, Carlita." I bowed my head slightly.

"So..." She looked around surreptitiously, "who is Esther Jean trying to set you up with?"

I laughed, realizing that this was not my Oma's first time bringing a guy to the center to try and play matchmaker.

"Andrew?" I shrugged.

Carlita rolled her eyes.

"Is that bad?"

"Oh, he's harmless. I think." She waved me off, setting the shoebox to the side, right next to her legs. "A bit of a pervert, but aren't we all?"

I leaned in. "I kind of got that impression."

"Mmhm." She pursed her lips and nodded. "I told Esther Jean to stop trying to set the boys up after the last time went so badly. And she did. But then I saw that she finally brought you and I knew she was back on her bullshit again. Vieja loca."

I laughed. "Yeah. That's pretty accurate."

"Well, baby." Carlita patted my shoulder. "Your secret is safe with me—and thank you for the shoes. I'd never be able to afford Louboutins for myself."

"You're welcome, Carlita."

She started to rise, then leaned in.

"If Esther Jean keeps trying to set you up, you just come to me." She whispered conspiratorially. "I'll tell you if the idiot she has in mind is really who she thinks they are."

"You're my she-ro." I smiled.

"I do what I can, baby." She gave me a quick kiss on the cheek before grabbing my chin in her hand. "Eat two sandwiches, baby. You look skinny as shit."

She rose to her feet and wandered off, screaming at friends to come see her new shoes. I laughed to myself and finished my sandwich.

Then I had another. Drag queens are like the wise guardian angels of the gay community. They know what they're talking about—so if they tell you to eat more, you should probably do it. Of course, anytime anyone who has to fit into a skintight dress tells you that you're too skinny, they're probably not lying.

After lunch, Oma and I helped stuff envelopes with the others for a few hours. Andrew had taken it upon himself to sit next to me at the table and inundate me with personal questions the whole time. Carlita was across the table from me, shooting me a surreptitious wink or rolling her eyes when no one else would see. It was a struggle to not laugh. I just wanted to be done with the day at the center, but I had made a promise. At least Leslie, the women I had worked with early in the morning, and Carlita could be potential friends. And whether I liked it or not, when Oma and I had left the center, I had promised to go out to dinner with Andrew on Saturday night.

Sometimes you do what's asked of you, just to make your grandmother happy. And that usually leads to trouble, though you're not aware of it until it's way too late.

Chapter 8

Something was on the bed.
Something was on the bed.
Something was on the bed.
Something was on the bed!
I sat up quickly in bed, legs kicking out, gasping for breath, reaching for the switch on the bedside lamp as shadows seemed to dance in every direction. Something was on the bed with me. When the light came on, I was already jumping out of bed, looking around the room. Nothing. There was nothing there. I shivered as I stood there, my eyes dancing around the room, looking for whatever had been at the foot of my bed.

Right as I started to feel a little calm, scurrying sounds came from right by the bathroom, and I jumped, turning to look for the source of the sound. My heart was hammering within my chest, and I was breathing like I had just run a mile. There was nothing. No movement, no critters, no shadows—just nothing. I let my eyes dance around as I slowly scanned the room, looking for any sign of weird creatures in my room.

Was Oma crazy enough to have some weird pet?

Like a raccoon?

An opossum?

Something only country people have ever heard of—like a...*jackelope*...or something?

As my eyes traveled the room, they landed on the bedside table. The pack of cigarettes that I had opened on the drive into Point Worth, and not touched since sat there with my lighter. My bottles of Paxil and Nexium set next to them. I swallowed hard, forcing myself to calm down as I closed my eyes. When was the last time I smoked? When was the last time I took my Paxil? I opened my eyes and forced myself to breathe slowly and deeply, thinking back over the previous week.

I hadn't smoked a cigarette since the moment before I had arrived at Oma's. I hadn't taken a Paxil in that length of time, either. And in that time, I was experiencing weird dreams, irritability, confusion...I grabbed the Paxil off of the bedside table, violently opened the bottle, nearly emptying the contents onto the floor, and tapped a pill out into my hand. I dry swallowed the pill before going to the bathroom and dipping my head to the faucet to take a drink.

I stood from the sink and wiped my mouth with the back of my hand as I looked at myself in the mirror. I looked fine. No physical evidence that I was experiencing withdrawal or discontinuation syndrome. I held my hands up, noticing that I had slight tremors. That could be from nerves from the dreams I just had...or withdrawal symptoms. Somehow, that made me feel incredibly relieved. There was nothing weird going on. I had just been incredibly stupid and forgot about taking my Paxil. If I wanted to quit the medication, I needed to call my doctor, find out how to wean myself off of it. But I had been taking it for almost two years. Just quitting was bound to have side effects.

"*Fucking idiot.*" I laughed nervously as I held onto the edge of the sink and took a deep breath.

Cigarettes had been greedily consumed for at least six months, too. Suddenly quitting cigarettes after smoking at least a pack a day for six months, combined with forgetting my Paxil...it was no wonder I felt like a raging idiot. I went and sat on the edge of the bed and forced myself to continue breathing as the seconds and minutes ticked by. After twenty minutes, I began to feel calmer, more serene—less anxious. The pill was kicking in.

Relief.

I laid back down in bed, sliding my legs under the covers once again. Within minutes, I was back asleep.

The worst part about forgetting to take an SSRI for a week, then suddenly starting back up is the sleep. Too much of it. I didn't wake up until after ten o'clock in the morning. When I finally drifted downstairs, still in my sleep bottoms and t-shirt, Oma was sitting at the kitchen table, playing on her phone, a cup of coffee in front of her. When I wandered into the kitchen, rubbing the sleep out of my eyes and yawning, she gave me a funny look.

"I haven't taken my Paxil in a week." I didn't bother asking her why she gave me the funny look. "I remembered when I woke up in the middle of the night and took one. That's why."

"Ah." She nodded, the funny look going away. "I wondered why you've been acting so jumpy lately."

"Yeah. Sorry." I shook my head groggily as I poured myself a cup of leftover coffee. "I guess sleeping for the first three days threw me off, and...well, anyway. It's moot now."

"Well, it's going to be a cold one." She changed the subject. "I was hoping by Monday you could help me start getting the garden planted, but it looks like that'll have to wait. We're supposed to get a frost this weekend."

"What?" I groaned. "No offense, but Ohio is shit for weather."

She laughed and looked back down at her phone.

"I mean, L.A. is shit, too, but at least it's warm." I shivered. "I've been freezing my ass off since I got here."

She shrugged. "Go jump in the lake if you can."

"Um, rude?"

"It means you don't know how cold it can be." She chuckled.

"Oh." I smiled sheepishly as I sat down across from her. "Pass."

"You want some breakfast, ya' asshole?" She looked up. "I made French toast, and there's plenty left."

"I'm not really hungry." I shook my head as I sipped my coffee.

"That's the medicine." She rolled her eyes. "Probably what's made you look the way you do, and you don't even know it. You're going to eat."

I wanted to argue, but instinctively, I knew she was right.

"Okay."

Oma looked at me for a second, obviously taken aback that I hadn't argued, then rose from her seat to make me a plate. She went about making my plate, zapping it in the microwave, then set it in front of me, along with cutlery, a bottle of syrup, and a bowl of fruit salad. I gave her a smile and picked up my fork, determined to make myself eat everything. It wasn't that the medicine upset my stomach, thus making me not want to eat, it just seemed to hamper that compulsion.

"I don't know how to ask this..."

"What?" I braced myself.

"But, both Lucas and Andrew have asked me for your phone number." She gestured with her phone.

"Aren't you just the young lady?" I teased. "Texting all the boys."

"Suck it, ya' asshole." She grumbled at me. "Anyways, they both want your number. For different reasons, I'm sure."

"You can give Lucas my number," I said. "I have another number you can give Andrew."

"You got more than one number?"

"You have my real number, calm down." I stopped her. "That's the number you should give Lucas. He...he might be a real friend. But I'll give you a dummy number to give to Andrew—it goes through an app instead of my phone."

"You didn't like him?" Oma looked scandalized.

"Stop clutching your pearls." I chuckled. "He just...he seemed...well, he seemed a little...pervy. That's all."

"Well, a little." She shrugged, not offended. "But, that's okay. I mean, that's just men for you. No offense."

"I know that we've never, um, really discussed my sex life—other than my orientation, Oma." I chewed at my lip. "But I'm...*I'm not pervy.* I'm kind of traditional. Or as traditional as a gay guy can be."

She looked up at me, an eyebrow cocked.

"You're not a damn virgin are ya'???"

"Well, no." I laughed at the thought. "I just...pervy guys kind of unnerve me. That's all. I mean, Carlita told me he's harmless, and she seemed to know what's what...but I'm not great with guys that are super sexual. That's all. And I don't want him to have free access to text me any old thing he wants at any time day or night. I hope you understand."

"Well, I suppose I understand that." She nodded. "We don't all want guys sending us pictures of their dicks all day long."

"Oma!" I laughed, dropping my fork on the plate.

"I may be old as the hills, but I know what you kids get up to." She chuckled.

I looked at her for a minute.

"Well, yeah." I relented. "I don't want guys sending me nasty things to my cell phone."

"You certainly don't have to worry about that with Lucas."

I laughed loudly.

"That's why he can have my real number," I said, then rolled my eyes. "And, I'm sorry for calling him a weirdo. He seems like a really nice guy. I...I'd like it if he were my friend."

"Told you." She waggled her head at me.

"Calm down, lady, you're one and oh right now." I teased. "Andrew isn't all you made him out to be."

"He's goddamn gorgeous though, right?" She leaned in conspiratorially. "I mean...you saw 'im."

"He is that." I agreed.

Oma tapped away at her phone for a few moments, then set it down as I was finishing the last bite of my food.

"Well, Lucas said he was going to text you about dinner tonight."

I frowned for a second.

"Oh, shit!" I hissed. "I almost forgot about that. I really am an asshole."

"I told you that, too." She chuckled before grabbing my dishes and heading to the sink. "Now, he doesn't drink, so don't be taking a bottle of wine for your host gift. He doesn't smoke or do drugs either, so..."

"Did you think I was going to show up with a baggie of heroin?" I scoffed. "And I don't do drugs for the last time, Oma."

"Oh, I'm just giving you a hard time." She waved me off as she began washing up the dishes. "But he's a pretty clean-living young man, so wine, booze, lots of candy and desserts are not his thing."

"Jeez, maybe I was wrong about being his friend." I teased.

"I ain't seen you do nothing except take your prescribed medication since you got here, and I didn't even *see* that, so stop acting so goddamn special." She grumbled playfully. "But, since you gotta take something, stay away from alcohol and sugar."

"Well, we'll stop by the store before we head over to his house." I shrugged.

"I'm not going." She snorted.

"Why?" I frowned. "I mean, he invited the two of us."

"Because I got things to do." She turned on me, putting her hands on her hips. "Just because you accepted an invitation on my behalf doesn't mean that I'm going to go somewhere. Do I tell you what to do?"

"Every chance you get, yeah." I nodded earnestly. "Won't Lucas be upset?"

"Oh, hell." She turned back to the sink. "I see him once or twice a week. We get our quality time in, don't you worry."

"Fine." I shrugged as I stood from the table, coffee mug in hand. "But, if it's awkward or he's upset you didn't show up, it's on your head, lady."

"Won't be my first time getting labeled the villain."

"I have no doubt." I rolled my eyes.

I left the kitchen without another word. Instead, I went to the front door, grabbed the Carhartt that I had been loaned by Mr. Barkley, slipped it on, then went out to the front porch. I sat down in one of the Adirondack chairs on the front porch and kicked back with my cup of coffee. Even this late in the morning, the front lawn looked a little frosty from the overnight chill. I sipped at my coffee as I kicked back and enjoyed the fresh air.

On a crisp, clear day, since the house was elevated in relation to the lake, a person could see from the house, over the tops of the trees in the woods, and spot the water of Lake Erie, shimmering in the sun. I smiled to myself as I looked out over the property. A decade had gone by since I had last called Oma's house my home...and...something inside of me told me that I wanted that to change. Hollywood, movies, music...none of it held any appeal anymore. Even thinking about making another movie, singing another song, signing another autograph, giving another interview...it made my stomach do flip flops.

Whether or not I'd been specific with Oma—I had enough money that I'd never have to work again. For ten or more lifetimes. If I ever had children, they wouldn't have to work. Neither would their children. It brought me no happiness, other than the knowledge that it provided the luxury of not having to do anything I didn't want to do. And I didn't want to be Jacob Michaels anymore. I just wanted to be Robert Wagner. After a week in my grandmother's home, I was beginning to feel that it might be possible.

Chapter 9

Lucas answered the front door when I knocked, right at seven o'clock, like a good, respectable, punctual guest. He looked harried and nervous and completely out of sorts. He had missed a place shaving on his chin, his shirt wasn't buttoned properly, and something was smoking in the kitchen in the background. It was absolutely adorable. Typically, people who get nervous around me because I'm a celebrity leave me forcing myself to tolerate them. But Lucas made it seem like the friendliest thing ever.

"Your kitchen is burning down," I stated simply as he stood before me, absolutely frantic.

"I...I...oh jeez." He shook his head.

Then he ran from the door in a harried dash to go deal with whatever it was in the kitchen that was making the smoke plumes billow up.

I turned to look out at his property from the front porch. He really was right on the shore of the lake. His front porch looked towards the north of his property, the shore of the lake just twenty yards from the front door. In the setting sun, it was absolutely majestic. I smiled to myself as I entered the reasonably large, cabin-like home, gently closing the front door behind myself. The paper bag cradled in my arm went along for the walk. I went straight to the kitchen and set the bag on the counter and looked in on my new friend.

Lucas was rushing around the kitchen, turning off burners, looking here and there frantically, then he opened the oven door. Smoke billowed out, black and miasmic, smelling like something had died a painful death within its confines. I couldn't help but laugh, which didn't help Lucas' anxiety levels. He just fanned at the smoke and blew at it, trying to clear it away. Quickly, I located a couple of potholders and joined him at the oven. I reached in and grabbed the pan of...*I didn't know what*...and lifted it out.

"Get the door." I laughed at him.

Lucas rushed to the front door and swung it wide. I dashed out, carrying the pan with me. I quickly set it near the edge of the porch and joined him back at the door. Then we went about airing the smoke out of the house and out the front door of the house. When we finally shut the door, the smell lingered, but the smoke was gone. Everything on the stovetop was half-cooked or over-cooked—and I didn't know what any of it was. I don't think Lucas knew either, but it was absolutely endearing that he had tried.

"I really am a good cook." He shook his head as we stood side-by-side in front of the oven, surveying the damage.

"I believe you." I grinned widely.

"Where...where's Mrs. Wagner?" He suddenly realized that she had not entered the house with me.

"She said she had other things to do." I shrugged. "I figured she would have texted you to let you know."

"She didn't." He still looked frantic. "But okay."

"You're a vegetarian, right?" I asked simply.

He nodded.

"Do you eat cheese?"

"Well, yes." He replied.

I went over to the paper bag that I had carried in with me. Reaching deep within the confines of the bag, I pulled out a large wheel of brie and a box of crackers, a can of cashews, a tub of seedless red grapes, and a small tub of figs. Lucas' eyes lit up with each item that I retrieved.

"This was supposed to be a host gift—but it can easily be dinner, too." I gestured dramatically over all of the containers set upon the countertop.

"That's...this was really nice of you." He smiled sheepishly.

"Eh." I shrugged as I slid onto a barstool across the counter from him. "I don't even know what was in that pan." I teased. "At least this stuff is identifiable."

"Veggie lasagna." He cringed.

I reached into the bag and pulled out the bunch of carrots and held them towards him like they were a bunch of flowers.

"For the host." I smiled goofily.

He gave a weird grin and took the carrots from me.

"Flowers for a host who is a vegetarian." I laughed.

Lucas looked at the bunch of carrots in his hand.

"I know, that's...kinda weird." I chuckled nervously. "I just...I thought it was funny when I grabbed them."

"Yes...I mean—no." He shook his head. "I mean, yeah, it's funny. It's not weird at all. I get it."

"Good." I nodded.

Lucas looked over at me, holding the carrots.

"So...if you have a knife and a couple of plates, we can chow down on our little countertop picnic?" I suggested.

"Oh, yeah, of course." He shook his head with a laugh.

Lucas put the carrots in the vegetable crisper in the fridge and then went about grabbing plates, napkins, a couple of forks and knives. He looked slightly less frantic the more he adjusted to the fact that dinner was going to be okay. He gathered up the dinner accouterments from various drawers and cabinets, holding them all in his arms, and turned to me.

"I'm sorry." He seemed to suddenly deflate. "Usually, I'm not like this, it's just that, well, you're..."

"It's okay." I smiled. "I totally understand."

"You do?" His whole body seemed to sigh in relief as he set everything down on the counter.

"Yeah. I mean, the first time I met Jack Nicholson...well, we haven't talked since unless it was in a professional capacity." I laughed. "I think he still thinks I need to be sedated."

"Oh, yeah." Lucas smiled. "You've met celebrities, too."

I shrugged.

"What would you like to drink?" Lucas pulled himself together.

"Water's fine."

"I have some Riesling if you want?" He asked.

"Oma said you didn't drink."

He shrugged. "I drink a beer or a glass of wine every now and then. But, it's always by myself. I don't enjoy social drinking. But with dinner—well, that's okay."

"Riesling then." I nodded.

"I don't really know if Riesling is appropriate for everything you've brought..." Lucas began as he reached into the fridge.

"I think any wine you like goes with anything you like," I said. "I don't care about wine pairings, personally."

"Do you drink a lot?" Lucas asked as he turned around with the bottle.

I laughed.

"Is that a yes?" He cocked an eyebrow as he pulled up a stool across from me and began to uncork the wine. "Mrs. Wagner said you've been having problems."

I rolled my eyes. "I rarely ever drink."

"Drugs?" The cork was extracted with a wet pop.

"I've dabbled...but nothing serious." I said. "Not that I'm trying to minimize any bad choices, I've tried a few things...a few times...but I've never had a drug problem. I haven't done drugs in a long time."

"Then...what problems was she referring to?" Lucas asked as he fetched two glasses and poured us each a healthy amount. "I mean, if that's not too personal?"

"We can fast track this friendship if you want." I shrugged.

He stared at me.

"Um, well, I think Oma was convinced that I was on drugs when I first arrived, mostly just because of how exhausted I was and how skinny I got," I explained, bringing my glass to my lips. Crisp and fruity. It made me happy. "But, she was probably talking about personal issues that you don't want to hear about."

Lucas took a sip of his wine and popped a grape in his mouth.

"I have nothing else going on right now." He gave a crooked smile.

"It's just boring relationship stuff—or lack thereof—that you don't want to hear about." I waved him off with a laugh as I began unwrapping the brie.

Lucas followed my lead and began opening the box of crackers.

"I mean," I shrugged, "Oma is just worried that I don't have *any love in my life*—and she's not wrong—but I've been kind of happy, or at least, content, with being by myself. Sometimes it's necessary to stick to yourself. Especially if you don't really trust anyone or find anyone who fits the position. You know what I mean?"

"Absolutely."

"I've tried dating, and early in my career, it wasn't too bad." I laid the brie between us and offered the knife to Lucas. He took it and cut us each a generous slice. "But as I got a little more recognizable..."

"Famous?" He smiled.

"Yeah." I relented. "It just became apparent that some guys were trying to just hook up to say they had sex with me or date me to further their careers—or just because they could say they did. So...I don't really date at all."

"Well, casual sex isn't necessarily a bad thing I guess." He stated neutrally.

I laughed loudly.

"What?" Lucas looked at me blandly.

"There's not a casual damn thing about me." I laughed.

"You're not into one-night stands then?" He smiled widely.

"No." I shook my head as I peeled the rind off of my cheese, Lucas followed my lead. "I haven't had sex in so long that I think I've forgotten how to do it, honestly."

Lucas had just taken a bite of his cheese and cracker and almost choked in laughter.

I shrugged. "I'm sure you're killing it with the ladies...I just, I don't know, I guess people presume things because I'm a gay man and they have ideas about gay culture, but things aren't always the way people think that they are, ya' know?"

"Yeah." He nodded, taking another bite of his cracker thoughtfully. "I definitely understand."

"Maybe that'll change." I sighed.

"Yeah." He smiled. "Maybe."

He popped the rest of his cracker and cheese in his mouth. And we both took another big drink of our wine.

"So...why no wife and kids?" I started slicing us more cheese. "You've got the house. You seem to be doing well with work. I love your house, by the way. When are you going to start being a true Ohioan male and knock a gal up and settle down?"

He blushed. "Thank you. About the house and work stuff, I mean."

"You're welcome." I smiled and dropped a couple of slices of brie on his plate for him.

"Your house is probably a lot, um, nicer."

"I don't have a house," I said simply. "But don't avoid the question."

"I don't know." He shrugged and started de-rinding his cheese. "It's kind of complicated."

"Isn't it always?"

He chuckled.

"I got a feeling the other morning that Jill wouldn't be averse to sliding under the sheets with you." I teased.

He blushed again.

Nah." He shook his head and took a sip of his wine. "She's a really good friend, that's all."

"Well, darn." I sighed. "I was hoping I could be Oma and play matchmaker."

He looked up at me and frowned.

"What? Did she..."

"She's trying." I waved him off. "I promised her I'd go out on a date."

"How's that going?" He grinned.

"Not too bad." I shrugged. "I'm going on one tomorrow night. The first in probably two years, actually."

"Oh."

"Yeah." I nodded with a roll of my eyes. "She's absolutely thrilled."

"I bet."

"Maybe she can set you up?" I grabbed a fig. "I mean, it'll probably be horrible, but maybe it'll kill your dry spell. Not that I'm implying that you don't have game or anything..."

He laughed.

"Nah. That's pretty accurate." He agreed.

"Well, why not ask her?" I said, giddy from the wine. "I'm sure she knows every damn single woman in a twenty-mile radius. She looooooves being in everyone's business. And I'm sure you have no trouble with the ladies."

"I don't know." He was blushing again.

"Fine." I chuckled. "I'll let it go. But you just say the word, and I'll mention it to her. I'd help you out, but the only women I know around here are two lesbians who are married to each other and a drag queen. They're all lovely, but..."

Lucas laughed loudly as he opened the tin of cashews and shook a few out on the board with the cheese for us. Eating dinner with Lucas was comfortable and relaxed. I was smiling internally, glad that I hadn't kept the opinion that he was just a quiet weirdo. Even without Oma around as a buffer, we got along great. And that gave me hope that I would be able to make some friends while I was back in Ohio. Which was good...because I was beginning to think that the length of time I'd be in town would be longer than I had initially thought when I headed out from L.A.

"You know, being an openly gay celebrity, the magazines are always pairing you up with someone or speculating about your...love life." Lucas looked down with a grin, realizing what he was admitting to.

"You've mentioned seeing articles...if you want to call them that...in magazines twice now." I grabbed my wine glass with a smirk. "How many gossip rags do you read?"

"Just the reputable ones, of course." He teased back.

"Of course." I drained the rest of my glass.

Lucas grabbed the bottle and refilled my glass without asking. I didn't mind too much. At least I was with someone amiable if I was going to catch a slight buzz for the first time in years.

"The two guys I've actually dated...well, they weren't famous." I shrugged. "I've never dated another celebrity. I mean, I've been flirted with, asked out, that kind of thing...but I always thought it'd be too much to handle."

"How's that?"

"I'm not, well, great at dating." I shrugged, loading another cracker with brie. "I mean, I go on a date and I just get nervous and self-conscious and don't know what to talk about and paranoid that the other person knows who I am and that's the only reason that they're there...and, well, I already explained about not being casual...so, it's just odd. Dating, I mean."

"I understand." He smiled, picking up his wine glass.

I just made a vague gesture as I shoved the cracker in my mouth.

"Can I ask you a personal question?" Lucas chewed at his lip.

"We're like best friends now, right?" I chuckled.

He nodded with a smile.

"Yeah, ask away." I chuckled.

"What do you want?" He gave a one-shoulder shrug. "Someone to travel the world with you and be there for you and your career? Do you want to settle down somewhere? Have kids? I mean...what's the long-term plan for your romantic and sex life?"

I sighed and picked up my glass.

"That was pretty personal, huh?" He cringed.

"Well, yeah. But..." I took a sip of my wine. "We've established that we're tight now. So, I'm going to answer that...but you have to promise me something."

The wine was good...and it was making me feel open, honest, and...happy.

"Okay." He smiled, taking a large drink of his wine.

"Promise it stays between us."

"Of course." He smiled wider.

"Well," I tried to sit back, then remembered I was on a stool, corrected, and immediately hoped it didn't look like I was as buzzed as I was, "I...I want to just be Rob Wagner. Now. I didn't use to want to...but I'm tired of being Jacob Michaels. I was hoping that maybe Oma wouldn't be averse to me sticking around for a while...at least until I can either figure out where I want to be permanently or find a place here. Hollywood, running all over the world for work and not really enjoying it...I just can't see doing that anymore. It's exhausting, man."

Lucas just eyed me, sipping at his wine.

"So, to answer your question...yeah. I want to settle down." I took another gulp of wine and started to make a cheese and cracker sandwich. "Find a nice guy, do the whole domesticated thing. Not sure about kids, though. But also, I want to make him travel all over the world with me. But just for fun, of course. I just want someone to love me for me."

We both sat there, sipping at our wine, taking a bite sporadically, uncomfortable at how real the discussion became so quickly and easily. There was something about Lucas that made me just be open and honest. Or maybe it was the Riesling. Yeah, it was probably the Riesling. Or perhaps it was just having someone real to talk to for the first time in a long time. Someone who didn't curse and scream at me, nor want something, nor judge me. Lucas made me feel comfortable just being myself.

"Riesling sure is a lubricant, isn't?" Lucas mumbled.

"I don't know if I would have used that phrasing." I laughed loudly.

Lucas blushed until he looked like a tomato but couldn't keep himself from laughing as well.

"This is really good wine." I pretended to slur.

"Five buck chuck." He shrugged.

"Best tasting five bucks ever."

"Do you like red wine?" He grinned sheepishly and stood from his stool before heading over to the cabinet.

He opened the cabinet over his sink to show that he had three more bottles hiding out of sight.

"You naughty little bastard."

He chewed at his lip as he held onto the cabinet door, looking down at his feet.

"These bottles would last me forever." He said lowly. "I never drink much because after one glass with dinner, I'm done. I never have any...friends to enjoy them with. And I wouldn't feel comfortable anyway. But...we're best friends now, right?"

"If there's a peppery merlot up there, yes." I teased. "Hell, even if there's not, you're my new best buddy."

Lucas laughed, a little drunkenly, and pulled a bottle down from the cabinet. He popped the cork like an expert and sat back down on his stool across from me again.

"Oma will be pissed when I show up...well...*pissed.*" I giggled like a girl as I drained the last of my Riesling to make room for the Merlot.

"Shhhhhh." Lucas held a finger to his lips. "We just won't tell her."

"What she doesn't know won't get me cursed out." I laughed.

Lucas poured me a healthy serving of wine and then filled his glass in the same fashion. We lifted our glasses and clinked them together.

"To new best friends." I smiled.

"Absolutely." He smiled back.

Wine was drunk, food was eaten, secrets and dreams and desires were shared, and I lost track of how much was eaten, drunk, and how much time went by. But hours later, I found myself having driven myself home completely drunk, stumbling in the front door of Oma's house. I managed to not swing the door in so violently that it struck the wall, but that was mostly because I was holding onto it to stay upright.

Once inside the door, I steadied myself, collected all of my faculties, trying not to giggle at how loopy I was, then gently closed the door behind myself. Thinking about taking off my coat in the foyer and hanging it neatly by the door seemed like a tall order, so I decided I would just take it off in my bedroom. As steadily as my feet and legs could manage, I made my way to the stairs and started my ascent.

Lucas and I had spent hours talking about our lives, what we did in our free time, why we couldn't find our "person," and how we were obviously the best friends there ever were. When you have good wine, good food, and good company, friendship is never far behind. And life never seems all that awful. When I had left, he had insisted that I sleep it off on his couch, but I promised him that I would be just fine going home. Of course, trying to navigate the stairs made me realize that I wasn't nearly as well off as I thought. In fact, driving home had been completely irresponsible.

I promised myself quietly, as I scaled the stairs, that there would be no more driving even after a single drink. I would prepare to stay wherever I was when I drank. At least the house was dark and quiet at such a late hour, so I didn't have to worry about Oma waking up and cursing me out, or worse, just staring at me in disappointment. When I finally crested the top of the stairs, I crept past her door, probably a lot less stealthily than I felt I did in my drunken state and went down to the room I was staying in while at Oma's.

Inside my room, once I had shut the door, I began to strip. The coat got tossed on the couch, my shoes got kicked off haphazardly at the end of the bed. My jeans were unbuttoned, unzipped, and shimmied out of, left to lay on the floor a few feet from the shoes. Then my shirt was stripped off and tossed in the direction of the couch. It fluttered to the floor in a heap, which made me giggle for some reason. I chuckled drunkenly to myself as I stumbled over to the couch and picked up my shirt, somehow managing to not tumble forward myself. Once I rose, my head swam, and I giggled again as I worked to balance myself. I finally dropped the shirt on the couch, and I blinked drunkenly, trying to assess whether or not a trip to the bathroom to puke was in order or not.

Blurrily, I gazed out of the window that looked down on the backyard. Someone was in the garden. They were shrouded in a hooded cloak of some kind, hands aloft, towards the sky. Several shadowy creatures were circled around them. My head swam again as I stared down at what obviously had to be a hallucination in Oma's garden. Next thing I knew, my head was on my pillow in bed.

Chapter 10

My dreams were filled with shadowy, scurrying creatures once again. I slept like a log, however, never once waking up from sounds or thoughts of my room or bed being invaded. Even when my mind was telling me that something was curled up by my feet, I continued to sleep. When I woke in the morning, I felt well-rested, but my head was not entirely happy with me. I sat on the edge of my bed for quite a while after taking my Paxil, then slid out of bed to start my day. The room only moved a little. Surely Oma was already at the breakfast table, waiting on me, but I figured getting bathed and washing up was important before showing my face. She would know that I had been out very late, but I didn't need to give her another reason to worry, such as looking hungover.

So, I bathed. I washed my hair thoroughly. I dried myself off, styled my hair, shaved my face, put on fresh, clean clothes. I picked up my room and made everything presentable, hiding all evidence that I had come in drunk and disorderly. When I finally got down to the kitchen thirty minutes later, I looked bushy-tailed and alert. First and foremost, I was an actor, after all. I'd had plenty of practice looking ready when I was anything but. Oma was sitting at the table, a half-finished plate of food in front of her, and mine was sitting in my spot, ready to be eaten.

Eggs, bacon, hash browns.

My stomach only churned a little.

Oma eyed me stoically, looking up from her phone every now and then as I got a glass of water and a mug of coffee and joined her at the table. As I sat, she set her phone down and looked up at me.

"Good morning." I smiled.

"You may be a good actor, but you ain't foolin' me."

"I'm sorry?" I picked up my fork.

"Lucas done texted to ask if you got home safe because you forgot to text him yourself, ya' dumbass." She swatted at my arm. "What are you doing driving home drunk?"

"I was totally fine." I waved her off.

My stomach churned, and I had to shut my mouth to make sure nothing came up.

"You're so fuckin' stupid." She rolled her eyes.

"Okay." I sighed. "Maybe I had a little too much wine. But I'm here, and I'm fine. Let's not fight."

"Got a headache?" She pursed her lips.

"Not anymore." I burped slightly.

"Mmhm."

"We were just having a good time, and I lost track of time and how much I drank...and, look, let's just drop it."

"Fine." She said. "Make sure you text Lucas."

"Okay."

We sat in silence for several minutes, eating our food, Oma happily, me forcing it down. I drank my water slowly but steadily, hoping it would help everything going on with my body. Luckily, I was only in my mid-twenties. I hadn't been drunk in a very long time, but I knew I would bounce back by lunchtime. And, apparently, Lucas had already bounced back.

"Snitch," I muttered between mouthfuls.

"Who?!"

"Lucas."

"He was just making sure you were fine, ya' asshole." She swatted my arm again. "So...did you two have fun? Like I need to ask."

"Yeah, I guess." I shrugged. "I mean, yeah. Lucas is a really nice guy. I think we're blood brothers now or formed a gang or something."

Oma couldn't help but laugh.

"Lucas is...nice."

"He's more than nice." She snorted. "He's a wonderful kid, and..."

"He's older than me." I eyed her. "I don't think 'kid' is the appropriate term for what he is."

She waved me off.

"Regardless, I'm glad you enjoy each other's company."

"Can I ask you a favor?" I asked with an evil grin before shoving eggs into my mouth, suddenly feeling better.

"I suppose." She pursed her lips again. "I mean, I guess I owe you for not dying on your way home last night, huh?"

"Oma."

She rolled her eyes and gestured for me to continue.

"I think Lucas needs a girlfriend." I leaned in conspiratorially. "And I know a certain busybody who might be able to help with that. So, what do you say?"

She stood brusquely from the table and took her plate to the sink.

"Whoa." I sat back in my chair. "I didn't mean to piss you off. The busybody thing was just a joke. Don't get all testy, Oma."

"I ain't mad." She grumbled over her shoulder.

"Seems like it..."

"Well, I'm not helping you find him a girlfriend, and that's that."

"Why not?" I frowned. "I don't know anyone around here, and he's not so keen on Jill at the café, and..."

"There's not a girl around here for Lucas." She turned and glared at me.

I held my hands up defensively.

"Okay," I said. "I get it. You're protective of Lucas. Jeez."

"And don't you dare even suggest to him that I'm going to set him up on no dates." Oma glared at me. "You hear me, ya' asshole?"

"How drunk did *you* get last night?" I snorted.

"Just don't."

"Fine." I rolled my eyes.

"Good!" She growled, then calmed down. "I tried to set him up once, and it blew up in my face, and he got kinda perturbed with me, and I promised I wouldn't do it anymore."

"That's all you had to say, crazy." I shoved hash browns into my mouth. "Well, if he got mad at you...I guess me doing it would be worse."

She smiled slightly.

"Well, you are blood brothers and all now." She teased.

I chuckled.

"Worry about yourself." She waved me off. "You didn't forget you're going out with Andrew tonight did you?"

"Shit." I lowered my head to the table.

"Shouldn't've got so drunk last night, you sot." She chastised me.

I sat there, my head laid against the table, wondering if there was a way to diplomatically get out of the date with Andrew. But I knew it would offend him no matter what and Oma would absolutely disown me—if not outright kill me. There was no way that I wasn't going to be taking Andrew out for dinner, at his place of choice, probably in Toledo, but he might even insist that we drive into Cleveland.

Getting stuck in a car with Andrew for an hour or more, one way, was just too much for me to consider with the state I was in at breakfast. Maybe I could convince him to let me meet him wherever it was that we were going to meet. I considered that as an option to limiting one-on-one time with the eye-fucker but thought that might be considered rude. This wasn't a blind date, after all. We'd been properly introduced and manners most likely dictated that we ride together to wherever it was we were going to eat.

"Does Andrew live in Point Worth?" I asked Oma as I lifted my head and she cleared my plate away.

"Yes."

"Okay."

Well, I wasn't going to be able to reason that it was ridiculous for him to drive to Point Worth from Toledo to just pick me up. Oma washed up the dishes as I sat there and rehydrated and sipped my coffee. After she had placed the plates and cutlery and pants in the draining tray, she turned and looked across the kitchen, out of the window. She seemed lost in her own thoughts for a minute before turning to me.

"I have a confession."

I looked up at her with a cocked eyebrow, coffee mug held to my lips.

"I done texted Andrew and told him to be here by five to pick you up." She sighed and crossed her arms over her chest. "He's going to take you into Toledo for Indian food."

She rolled her eyes.

"That way he can get you home before dark tonight." She added.

"Um, okay?"

I didn't know if I was pissed off or relieved.

"You were out too late last night anyway, so tonight you should be home and in bed at a decent time. That's all!" She said.

"I didn't say anything." I snorted.

"Well, anyway, he'll be here at five."

"So...you didn't mind me going to dinner at Lucas' near dark and getting drunk...but you're worried about me being out after dark with Andrew?" I grinned widely. "Are you worried about my virtue?"

"Lucas is a good ki—young man." She said. "Andrew...well, I don't spend a lot of time with him away from the center except for an occasional coffee or something. I don't want him to think you're...ya' know."

"Easy?" I smiled sweetly.

"Sure. Let's go with that." She nodded. "I just don't know him as well as Lucas by a long bit, so it's different."

"You're too cute for words, Oma."

"Look—it's just—tonight—just make sure you're home before dark, damnit." She stammered.

"Calm down, crazy." I laughed. "I didn't want to go on the date anyway. This was all your crazy idea."

"Maybe we could reschedule..."

"What?" I was so confused but amused as well. "Why would I reschedule? If I'm going to go on this damn date, I want to just get it out of the way. Maybe he won't be so bad? I mean, he seemed a little pervy and all—but what man isn't to some extent, right?"

"Degrading your own gender."

"Well, I mean, it's true." I shrugged. "Most guys have a little pervert in them. Some just control it better than others."

"I guess so." She chewed at her lip. "Well, anyway, be ready at five."

"Okay." I shrugged and stood from the table. "Whatever you say, boss."

"Get the Hell out of here." She waved me off violently.

As I left the kitchen, she was typing away on her phone like her life depended upon it. I just said a silent prayer to myself that she would find whatever help she needed for her mental health issues. First, she wanted me to go out with someone, then she didn't. She talked to herself and slammed doors and acted crazy every time I turned around. Oma was definitely in need of a prescription for an SSRI herself, as far as I could tell. Possibly an antipsychotic.

Chapter 11

The drive to Toledo with Andrew had not been as bad as I had thought that it would be. Andrew had picked me up at Oma's house a few minutes until five and was perfectly respectable towards me and even more polite with Oma. He hadn't leered at me lasciviously when I had answered the door, nor had he made any inappropriate comments about my outfit or how I looked. I mean, he had said that I looked "very handsome" but he had done it with an appropriate tone and look in his eyes, so no harm, no foul.

On the ride into Toledo, he kept to his side of the car as he drove us down the highway, making small talk about his work. I made sure to steer every question and answer back to him and what he did as to avoid admitting that I was a famous actor who he just hadn't recognized yet. Andrew informed me that he was a financial manager at a corporation in downtown Cleveland, and I quickly lost interest. Not that it didn't sound exciting in its own right, but he started talking numbers and cost estimation and financial statements and cash-flow statements and profit projections and my eyes glazed over. I had never been one to think that business and accounting was an exciting career to consider, mostly because I hated numbers. I tried to remind myself that many people found the business world to be fast-paced and exciting, but I just couldn't make myself get incredibly interested in what he had to say about his job. Did that make me an asshole? Probably. But I tried and failed to show much genuine interest in what Andrew did for a living.

When we got to the restaurant, valet service parked Andrew's car, and we entered, Andrew making a big show of opening the door for me. I did my best to look impressed by his manners. We were seated without incident, though the host of the restaurant did a double take when he saw me. It was almost a look of recognition, but it quickly disappeared as the host seemed to convince himself that he was just being ridiculous in thinking that I was who I am. Once we were seated, Andrew ordered a beer, and I asked simply for water as I was trying to get over my hangover still. It wasn't bad, but it was lingering.

Immediately, I picked up my menu, giving it a glance before realizing that the Indian food offered was pretty standard. Andrew leaned in, using his finger bowl to wash his hands. I disregarded the finger bowls as I planned to eat with my cutlery. Andrew noticed that I didn't wash my hands and gave me a five-minute lecture about how all Indians eat with their hands and what the purpose of the bowl was. He also told me that traditionally, we would be sitting on the floor on comfortable mats to eat if we were eating like *real Indians*. I had asked him if he had ever traveled to India and he confessed that he had not, but he hoped to go one day.

It was difficult, but I kept myself from informing him that in Northern and Western India if you ate with your hands, they might tell you that you "ate like a Bengali," which was not a compliment, and that *not all Indians* ate with their hands. In fact, a lot of Indians regarded guests in their homes and at their table as higher than God. If cutlery was asked for, and it was available, it would be provided—no questions or comments. Additionally, it was quite common for restaurants, hotels, and upper-middle class homes in India to have tables and chairs for those who were dining.

When he gave me a lecture about how samosas were his favorite Indian pastries and how they had originated there, I had to hold my tongue again. Then he talked at length about how most Indian foods were highly seasoned but rarely had enough spiciness for him, I was tempted to "accidentally" kick his shin under the table. God, he was arrogant. And he knew the effect his looks and charisma had on other diners at other tables. I wanted to throw my water in his face. But I also found him very attractive and desirable, so there was an epic battle between good and evil going on inside my head. He seemed to put off some type of pheromone that made me want to drag him across the table and have angry sex with him right there. However, he was *just* arrogant enough that I wanted to throw my water in his face more than I wanted to fuck him.

After we had ordered—Andrew opting for Chicken Tikka (*Northern India*) and I opted for Bhindi Masala, also from Northern India—Andrew asked if I ever managed to travel much. Feigning ignorance, I told him that I didn't get to travel much and wished I could travel more. The second part was true, so I didn't feel too bad about the first part being a lie. Then I was treated to a lecture about how travel was the best education. He asked where I went to college. I told him I hadn't. He asked what I did for a living. I told him that right now I was between jobs. At first, I wanted to be embarrassed at my answers to his questions but realized that maybe sounding like a roustabout would make him less interested in dating me.

Unfortunately, it didn't.

Sounding like I was uneducated, not worldly at all, and unable to find gainful employment just made me a prime target for his arrogant belief that he was better than me in almost every way and needed to educate me. If it made the date easier, I was willing to have him believe that I was just some country bumpkin. However, when he told me that he really wanted to travel more because racism was almost solely an American problem—I wanted to hit him. For someone, who racism was obviously a very prominent issue, I thought it was so ignorant to not be aware of racism and ethnic cleansing and classism in other countries. Even people who looked similar to others in a country might commit acts of war and genocide over preconceived superiority.

I kept my mouth shut.

"So, what do you think you'll do, once you go back to work?" Andrew asked as he struggled to pull some Chicken Tikka off of its skewer with some Naan and shove it into his mouth. "Surely you have something in mind?"

I shrugged, using my spoon to scoop up some of my food.

"I don't know," I replied honestly. "I'm not so sure what I want to do next. If at all."

"Well, we all have to have money to survive, right?" He smiled at me, his thumb covered in sauce. "You can't just sit at home and live off of your savings forever."

I replied with a shrug again.

"You're not very forthcoming." He chuckled.

Another spoonful of Bhindi Masala was shoved in my mouth.

"Would you like some of my food?" I smiled simply. "It's really good."

"Thank you." He smiled and reached over with a piece of Naan to scoop some up, performing the action poorly.

I sipped my water, watching as he stuffed the entire bite in his mouth. I waited. His eyes grew wide, and he brought a hand to his mouth as the *spiciness* of the Bhindi Masala made itself known.

"Good, right?" I sat back in my seat and smiled sweetly.

"It's—it's very good." He coughed and reached for his water.

That simple act of douchebaggery on my part made me feel like a complete, well, douchebag. I decided to remind myself that I didn't want to be on this date anyway and I had only done it to be nice to Oma. It wouldn't hurt me to be nice and just suck it up for a few hours.

"So," I asked, picking up my spoon, "where do you hail from?"

"I live in Point Worth..."

"Did you grow up there?" I asked, shoving more food into my mouth. "I was born and reared there."

"Well, no." He coughed again and looked down, paying an inordinate amount of attention to his plate. "I grew up in upstate New York."

"Any more north than Utica and you may as well call yourself a hillbilly." I teased, bringing food to my mouth.

His eyes lit up with a smile.

"Around Adirondack State Park." He said vaguely. "I moved to Athens here in Ohio to go to the university...then I found my way to Point Worth."

"That's strange, right?" I was egging him on but trying not to. "I mean, Point Worth of all places. Who wants to move here if they haven't already lived here before?"

He took a page from my book and shrugged.

"Of course, it is cheaper to live in Point Worth and work in Cleveland or Toledo." I continued. "You can get a much nicer place in Point Worth for not even half the money you'd spend in Cleveland, right?"

He nodded.

I got the distinct impression that this line of questioning was something that he wanted to avoid at all costs. That made me want to ask more questions, simply because it would make him squirm. But I managed, somehow, to keep myself from following my instinct to behave like a complete asshole. I continued to eat my food as Andrew took a few moments to collect himself.

"So...Esther Jean says that you don't date much?" He asked, pulling another piece of Naan off of his plate. "I find that hard to believe."

"I've been too busy," I replied with the truth, realized how it sounded, and corrected myself. "You know, trying to figure out what I'm going to do with my life and all."

"Well, I figured it was a conscious choice on your part." That hungry, lascivious look he had shown at the center was back.

He was practically eye-fucking me.

I literally had to press my lips together to keep from saying something.

"Do you date a lot?" I asked simply, quickly shoving food into my mouth.

"I suppose so." He nodded with a grin. "I mean, I do okay."

Rolling my eyes was not beneath me, but I didn't do it.

"Well, that's good," I stated simply.

"What are you looking for?" He grinned evilly at me.

I stared at him, collecting myself so that I wouldn't say something mean to him. Something like "*you are incredibly sexy, but I'd rather punch you than fuck you, to be honest.*"

"Something long-term," I stated evenly. "A decent guy. Who is kind. Moral. Funny. Educated and well-traveled."

He smiled arrogantly.

"Nothing casual." I finished. "Ever."

"Well, serious long-term relationships can be good."

"They're the only kind I like." I nodded.

"I can see that you're interested in me." He smirked arrogantly down his nose at me. "And you want to start something serious..."

"Actually," I stopped him, "I find you insufferable, Andrew. You don't know the difference between dining etiquette in South and East India from North and West India but act like you do. You like generalizations. You aren't aware that tables and chairs are quite common in many areas of India. Or that a lot of the food in India can be quite spicy. Or that racism and ethnic genocide and cleansing occurs worldwide. Especially in the most *ethnic* countries in the world. Or that having a college degree doesn't make you an expert on hardly anything. You are absolutely insufferable. And eye-fucking me every chance you get is not the best way to ingratiate yourself to me. I don't know if you assumed that I'm just some wild and crazy sex maniac who is staying with Oma because he's down on his luck...or what...but I would love to hit you."

"Or fuck me." He leaned in, completely unfazed.

Maybe both. I found myself thinking.

"God, I despise you," I stated simply and sat back.

"That can lead to some fun." He waggled his eyebrows.

"Does this work?" I gestured vaguely at him. "Do guys see this confidence and arrogance and assume things about your virility and stamina? Or is this just who you are? Because, hard pass, Andrew."

"We don't have to get along to date." He was not letting up.

"We have to get along to keep me from slashing your tires and getting an Uber home." I snapped.

"An Uber back to Point Worth would be incredibly expensive."

"I'd *use all my savings* if I had to," I replied flippantly.

"Nah." He shook his head, bringing more food to his mouth. "I think you actually enjoy hating me. Most guys do."

"What does that even mean?" I rolled my eyes.

My mouth was getting ahead of me, but I just couldn't tolerate any more of this evening with the world's rudest financial manager. The evening hadn't started out bad, but it was quickly digressing into me wanting to flip the table like an entitled housewife from a certain T.V. channel. Of course, drawing extra attention to myself was always a bad idea. Calling an Uber was definitely not the worst idea that I had ever had.

If riding a half-hour back to Point Worth meant that I'd have to be alone with Andrew, I was willing to spend more money.

"A lot of guys don't really care to date me, but they don't mind *dating* me." He smirked.

"You're disgusting." I spat.

"You're intoxicating." He actually sniffed the air.

"Are all of your synapses firing properly or what?" I snarled lowly, trying to keep things discreet. "And did you just *sniff* at me?"

"You smell like cinnamon and citrus and something...*spicy*." He seemed almost drunk on whatever it was he was feeling. "You smell absolutely delicious, Rob."

"And you smell like Backpage." I snapped.

"*I want you.*" He leaned in with a snarl, his eyes ferocious, his teeth showing.

He looked deranged. I frowned deeply and sat back, putting as much distance between us as possible. Just as suddenly as he had seemed to become possessed by his overactive hormones, Andrew shook his head, and a look came over his face as though he couldn't remember what was going on. He looked around slowly, taking in the restaurant, the other diners, the tabletop, me. Then he looked chastened, and his eyes were on his plate again. My frown deepened even more as I just stared at him with disdain, but also concern. Concern for my safety and concern for his mental health.

Was everyone in this freaking state crazy as shit?

"I'm sorry." He shook his head.

"What is wrong with you?" I snarled lowly again.

"It's...it's a bad time of the month for me." He said.

"Like, you're on your period or something?" I snorted hatefully.

He chuckled nervously.

"Maybe we should go?" He said. "I should get you home."

"That's the nicest thing you've said all night." I tossed my napkin next to my plate as I stared blankly at him.

Andrew motioned for our waiter, and I had my credit card out and was shoving it in his hand as soon as he approached our table. Objections were made by Andrew, but I told the waiter to just hurry and bring back the receipt for me to sign as I glared at Andrew. I didn't bother trying to make conversation with my dinner companion as we waited, choosing to just glare at him the entire time instead. Once the waiter returned with my card, I signed the check quickly and rose from the table, thanked the waiter, and made for the exit.

I was out of the door before Andrew could even get out of his seat, but he was next to me at the valet station soon enough. When the valet came with the car, Andrew tipped him, and we both got into the car in silence. I folded my arms over my chest and stared blankly through the windshield as Andrew drove us away from Toledo. The sun was below the horizon as we left the city behind, on our way to Point Worth. I just wanted to be out of the car, back at Oma's house, telling her to never set me up with anyone ever again.

Regardless, I also had a niggling feeling that maybe I was still being unfair to Andrew—and I had no idea why I would feel such a way. The man had been nothing but a bore, arrogant, and sexually aggressive all night long. Maybe not all at once, but he had hit all of the checks on a list that would be titled "Stay Far Away from This Guy." Twilight started to settle in as we drove the mostly deserted highway back towards home. Andrew seemed to get tenser by the moment as we rode in silence, trying to ignore each other. His hands were clenching the steering wheel as he drove and I was getting more and more worried about my own safety as the seconds ticked by.

A few miles outside of Point Worth, where there was nothing on either side of the road except trees and fields, Andrew jerkily pulled the car to the side of the road. I clenched my teeth together as he put the car into park, wondering if I should just open my door and take off on foot. Whatever Andrew had in mind, pulling the car to the side of the road, I knew I was not in the mood for it. Whether it was to talk, argue, or apologize, I was done with this date and with Andrew himself.

"You really should reconsider your feelings about me." He turned to leer at me, his voice throaty and hoarse.

"You should really drive this car to Oma's house." I didn't keep my eyes on him, I was afraid of what I'd say or do if I did.

"I can really be quite nice." He reached over, his hand reaching for my knee. "If you let me."

I shoved his hand away violently, reaching for my seatbelt.

"Don't fucking touch me," I growled at him angrily.

"You know you want me." His hand was reaching for me again.

Swatting his hand away, I turned my hand to glare at him as I violently unbuckled my seatbelt. Andrew's face was distorted in some kind of sexually depraved stalker fashion, looking as if he would launch himself at me at any moment. For once in the evening, I was beginning to truly feel unsafe. This man was nowhere near as sweet and kind as Oma had wanted to believe. My mind flashed back to earlier in the day when Oma had shown concern about me actually going out with Andrew once the day had arrived.

I looked around quickly—only fields to the right and woods to the left. There were no other cars in sight, and it was entirely possible that Andrew had chosen to pull over at this place in the road for that exact reason. Why the Hell did this lunatic think that I wanted anything to do with him? Especially after such a disastrous dinner date? His mood flip-flopped back and forth so much—from arrogant, to tacit, to pervy, to quiet, to sexually aggressive. He was absolutely insane. Dark was falling quickly. I had to make a decision about how I was going to handle this. If I was going to walk the last few miles to Oma's, I needed to take off.

"You are an absolute asshole." I snarled at Andrew as his hand shot out at my leg again.

I attempted to swat his hand away again, but it was like trying to swat away a wrecking ball. Andrew was stronger than he had let on and his hand grabbed ahold of my knee as he leered at me. My hand reached for the door handle as I kept swatting at his hand and he leaned closer and closer, smiling wickedly, his eyes looking more and more crazed. Andrew ripped his seatbelt off and started to climb out of his seat towards me. With no other option, I let go of the door handle, reeled back, and punched out as hard as I could.

My hand connected with his eye and his head snapped back, bouncing off of the glass of his door window. I grabbed the door handle and pushed the door open violently, kicking at it with my foot. Leaping out of my seat, I exited Andrew's car, putting my feet upon the ground and feeling a lot safer all of a sudden. I turned on my heels and looked at a deranged Andrew collecting himself angrily in his seat.

"Fucking pig!" I bellowed at him and slammed my door.

The glass in the window spiderwebbed at the force of the slam.

Quickly, I began walking in the direction of Point Worth. I heard Andrew's door open, but I ignored it.

"Get back here, you fucking cocktease!" I jumped at the sound of Andrew's voice.

It sounded deeper, feral, crazed. Instead of heeding my instincts and continuing to walk in the direction of Point Worth, I turned around to scream back. I wanted to tell him one last time that he was a "fucking pig" and he should have his ass kicked for the way he had behaved. However, when I turned around, I didn't see Andrew the "fucking pig." Andrew didn't look like a pig at all. His face looked more wolfish...*very wolfish.*

Chapter 12

"**_Get...back...over...here!_**" Andrew took jerky steps towards me, his face twisting, his jaw seeming to stretch out.

"*What the fuck...?*" I whispered to myself, completely terrified.

Andrew moved jerkily towards me, his whole body jerking and twisting as he tried to close the distance between us as I stumbled backward to get further away. Absolutely terrified at what was happening before my very eyes, I jumped as Andrew leaned back and...*howled* at the sky. I looked over my shoulder. The full moon was beginning to show in the almost dark sky. Something deep inside of me told me an absurd, but obviously absolute truth, and I turned my head back to look at...*Andrew*?

The "person" before me dropped to his hands and knees in front of the car on the side of the road and howled viscerally as its body jerked and twisted. The face of this thing elongated, its hair began to grow longer, the seams of its clothes began to split, its body grew larger in front of my eyes. Hands and feet gave away to paws as shoes and clothes fell away. Andrew no longer looked like Andrew, but instead, he looked like a giant wolf. I was sputtering and mumbling to myself, still backing away as this thing that had been Andrew, but was now a wolf, started panting, shaking off the pain and agony of its transition from human to...*other*.

I stumbled slightly in my panic to back away. The Andrew...*thing*...suddenly realized I was still there and its eyes shot to me. Its eyes didn't look human. They looked feral and animalistic. And *hungry*. My eyes darted back and forth. I had so many options—but there was no way any of them were good enough. There was no way I could outrun a...wolf. There was no way I could dash into the woods and be safe. Running straight down the highway would only leave me an open target. Same problem with the field. I felt a scream bubbling up in my throat, but I knew screaming wouldn't help either.

Backing away still, I kept my eyes on this creature that used to be Andrew as it slowly shook off the remnants of its daze. I didn't know if a person could reason with a wolf—but I knew that I hadn't been able to reason with Andrew in human form. Werewolf Andrew had to be a lot harder to deal with. **_Werewolf?!?_** Did that thought actually go through my head?! I looked around quickly again, trying to decide what to do. Could I somehow fake this thing out and get back into the car and drive off? Could I fight it? What was I supposed to do in a situation like this?

AROOOOOOOOOOOOOOOO!

Andrew-wolf howled at the moon again, then its eyes were back on me.

And it lunged.

Then I was splattered with blood and...other things.

Tires squealed as I sputtered and wiped at my face.

A pickup squealed to a stop next to me.

The passenger door opened.

"***Get in the truck, Rob!***" I looked up, my face covered in Andrew juice.

Lucas was in the driver's seat of the truck, motioning hurriedly for me to get inside of his pickup. To say I was stunned was the least that could be said. I stood there and sputtered for a moment as Lucas waved me towards him. I didn't know what the fuck was going on. *What the fuck was going on in Point Worth???*

"***Get in the fucking truck now, Rob! Being hit by a truck isn't going to keep a werewolf away for long!***" Lucas bellowed.

I shook my head clear of thoughts, raced to the truck and leaped inside. Lucas shoved his foot to the gas as I closed my door and we sped away. Lucas kept glancing into his rearview mirror as we drove down the highway on our way into Point Worth. I grabbed the collar of my shirt and pulled it up in an attempt to wipe the blood and guts off of my face. I was shivering and muttering gibberish to myself as I tried to keep myself from upchucking Indian food all over the cab of the truck.

Lucas only let off of the gas slightly when we crossed the city line into Point Worth. He aimed his truck towards Lake Erie, and I sat there muttering and shivering, wondering what I had just witnessed. Had I really just seen a...*werewolf?* Is that what Andrew was? Is that why he had acted the way that he had? Werewolves weren't real! Were they? Had I taken my Paxil that morning? Was this an effect of taking medication and getting drunk the night before? Was I losing my mind??

"Sorry for screaming at you like that," Lucas stated calmly as he drove towards the lake. "But I couldn't risk him coming back before you got into the truck. He would've just been more pissed off. Werewolves don't get distracted from a meal for very long."

I turned my head slowly to Lucas, my eyes wide and my mouth in a disbelieving gape.

"*What. The. Actual. Fuck?!*" I squealed, which did not exactly make me proud. "*What the...who...why...**I'm covered in blood!***"

"Werewolves don't carry diseases." Lucas seemed to think this was soothing. "Besides Lycanthropy, of course. But you won't catch that unless he bit you or scratched you deeply. He didn't did he?"

"What?!" I squealed again.

"Did he bite or scratch you?"

"Well...uh...I mean...what? No." I stammered.

"Good." Lucas sighed. "Mrs. Wagner would absolutely destroy me if I let that happen to you. I mean, not that it would be my fault exactly, but she still wouldn't be in a forgiving mood."

I sputtered and stammered for several moments, unable to form a single coherent thought as I sat there, blood drying on my face. Lucas just watched me out of the corner of his eye as he chewed at his lip. We drove further, and it quickly became clear to me that we were going towards Lucas' house on the lake, away from Oma's house. I didn't even know if I wanted to be at Lucas' house since I had just seen another person I recently met turn into a wolf alongside the highway.

"Okay." I started to get my wits back. "Okay. Okay. Right. Okay. Um, just what the fuck, Lucas? What the actual fuck just happened?"

"Andrew." He jerked his head backward, indicating the road behind us. "Werewolf. Tonight's the first night of the full moon. Mrs. Wagner wasn't thinking when she set you two up. Well, she wasn't certain he was...well, that he was a werewolf when she started this whole thing."

I just stared at him with a disbelieving, shocked stare.

"She shouldn't have set you up with him at all, regardless," Lucas muttered.

"Okay." I nodded with an unhinged laugh. "Everyone here is fucking insane. Or I am. I've completely gone 'round the bend here."

Lucas squealed to a stop in front of his house. Then he threw the truck into park and turned the key in the ignition. He opened his door and leaped down as I sat there, looking around for answers that weren't going to present themselves in a way that didn't sound completely insane.

"You better get out and follow me quickly," Lucas said through the open door. "It's best to not be outside during the full moon around here."

Because I couldn't decide what to stay, I jumped out of the truck and followed Lucas up to his house, looking over my shoulder every few feet. Lucas unlocked his house and pushed the door open, ushering me inside quickly. I stepped over the threshold of his house and suddenly felt ten times safer than I had outside. Lucas promptly shut the door behind us and latched the door. I stood there and looked down at my hands, noticing that they were sprinkled and splattered with viscous blood.

Lucas stepped around me, coming to stand in front of me, his eyes meeting mine as I stood there looking at my hands. Finally, I looked up at him and lowered my hands to my sides. He was looking at me with concern—no longer looking confident and brave—now that we were inside. The Lucas I knew was staring out at me, shy and unsure.

"You...plowed into Andrew," I stated simply, almost calmly.

"Yes." He nodded. "Well, a werewolf, actually. It wasn't really Andrew. And he'll be fine."

I held my hands up, palms out.

"I'm wearing his blood."

"It takes more than a hit-and-run to kill a werewolf." Lucas chewed at his lip. "He'll be really sore tomorrow maybe, but he'll be alive."

"Yeah." I shrugged. "Sure. That's comforting."

I laughed crazily and then my whole body twitched in a shiver.

"Are you going to vomit?"

I just stared at him.

"Do you feel sick?"

"Uhhhhhh..." I looked around as though someone would pop up and tell me how to answer these questions.

"I know this is kind of...weird."

"If there was a more blasé way to describe what just happened, I don't know what it would be, Lucas." I snapped. "I just watched my date turn into a goddamn werewolf and get run over by a pickup!"

"I didn't run him over." Lucas looked down, chastened. "Just kind of...sent him reeling, really. He's fine. I promise."

"Honestly, I don't know if that's comforting or terrifying!"

"Well, comforting, I hope." He shrugged. "I mean, at least that way there can be a date number two, right?"

I sputtered.

"Are you completely insane?!? Why would I go on a second date with someone who just changed into a wolf in front of me???"

"He's just a werewolf." He frowned at me. "It's not like he's a serial killer or anything."

"I'd gladly take a serial killer right now!" I screeched at him. "Even if he wanted to use my skin to make a pashmina!"

"What's a pashmina?"

"It's like a shawl made out of Kashmiri wool," I said, then shook my head. "Wait! That's what has got you confused right now? My date just turned into a goddamn wolf!"

"Werewolf."

I growled at Lucas.

"Yes. Let's argue semantics when I'm covered in my date's blood and guts, Lucas!"

"You should really clean up," Lucas suggested gently. "Maybe it'll make all of this a little easier to—"

"I really don't think a hot shower is going to make me readily accept that my date was a goddamn werewolf! I am totally freaking out here, Lucas! I went on a date with. **a. goddamn. werewolf.** And werewolves are real! I'm losing my fucking mind! I mean, am I going to wake up in a mental hospital?! What the actual fuck is going on?!?"

Suddenly, my face was in Lucas' hands, and he was pushing his lips against mine. My whole body seemed to deflate as Lucas wrapped his arms around me and kissed me deeply. When he finally pulled back, I had somehow calmed down significantly.

"You have blood on your chin," I stated simply.

"It'll wash off." He looked deeply into my eyes, his arms still around me.

"You're gay."

"Yes."

"I thought you were straight."

"I didn't say I was straight."

"You didn't say I was wrong."

He shrugged.

"Let go of me. Please." I stated lowly.

Lucas slid his arms from around me, making sure I wasn't going to collapse as he let go of me. I stepped back slowly, putting a foot between us. I was so turned on, and I had no idea when or how that had happened. I had just gone on a date with the most arrogant and boorish man I'd ever met in my life. Then I watched him turn into a werewolf on the side of the road. Then I got splattered with his blood when Lucas ran him over with his truck. Lucas—the guy I'd just gotten drunk with the night before. The guy I thought was straight and was going to be my new best friend. Everything was spiraling out of control. If I weren't already insane, this night would get me there.

"I'm sorry." Lucas blushed but didn't look away. "I shouldn't have just kissed you like that without asking. It's just...well...it's hard not to kiss you."

"It was a nice kiss." I nodded.

He smiled.

I shoved him.

Lucas winced as he took a step back to correct his balance.

"What the fuck is wrong with you?!" I bellowed.

He looked down.

"What the fuck is wrong with *everyone* here?" I growled. "Ever since I got here, weird shit has been going on—and now my fucking date is a werewolf. I mean, I keep saying that—but how can you not keep saying 'werewolf' when you see someone turn into one???"

"Look, I'm sorry about the kiss, Rob." Lucas held his hands out defensively. "But, it's just, the danger, excitement, fear, you're so good looking and I just..."

Something took me over, and I pulled him to me and pressed my mouth over his, my arms wrapping around him as I kissed him passionately. His hands went to my head and his fingers laced through my hair as we fed at each other's mouths. Before I knew what was going on, he had pushed me against the wall next to the door, and his body was pressed along the length of mine. I was breathing heavy against his mouth as our tongues fought each other and our lips pressed against each other's. Then I came back to myself and pushed him away again.

"Jesus!" I growled.

"Why did you stop?" Lucas was panting.

"Because this is all so fucking fucked up!" I wanted him so badly. This wasn't like me. I didn't do things like this.

You never got splattered by werewolf blood before either. I thought to myself.

Then I rushed Lucas and was shoving my mouth over his again as we stumbled into the back of the couch, a tornado of arms and legs as our bodies did their best to become one. I pushed Lucas against the back of the sofa, my mouth feeding at his as his hands ran over my stomach, my chest, and around my body to settle on my ass. He grabbed my ass roughly and pulled me into him, almost sending us toppling over the sofa as my hands grabbed his coat and pushed it off of him and onto the couch behind us.

My fingers found the hem of his shirt and yanked it up roughly. I pulled back from him just long enough to yank the shirt off over his head and then my mouth was back on his. Lucas pushed my coat off of me, letting it fall to the floor at our feet as we continued to kiss and desperately explore each other's bodies with our hands. My mouth moved from his and traveled to his jaw, his neck, to the front of his throat, slowly trailing my way downwards. My mouth was on his chest, one pec, then the other.

Lucas' fingers trailed through my hair as he gasped and panted and I trailed my way down his chest. I slowly started to lower myself as I kissed a trail down his chest to his stomach. Lucas was moaning desperately as my lips and tongue explored his flesh and his fingers urged me to go lower. My fingers were trailing along the waist of his jeans as I sucked at his flesh, tasting as much of him as I could as I made my way lower.

You just saw a goddamn werewolf!

I stood quickly and pushed away from Lucas, growling loudly in frustration as I put distance between us and turned away.

"Wha..." Lucas was panting behind me. "What are you doing?"

"What is going on?" I panted. "This isn't like me. I don't...this isn't...I don't do this with guys I don't know. I feel totally crazy right now."

Lucas was trying to get himself under control behind me, his breath still coming out raggedly.

"It's the full moon." He stated hoarsely. "It makes everyone crazy."

"This isn't my first full moon, Lucas." I spat over my shoulder, but I couldn't put any real anger into it.

"You haven't been home for a full moon in a very long time." He said this like it explained everything. "Not since you became an adult."

"Makes perfect sense," I stated simply, though it didn't.

"Don't you want to..."

"Yes." I turned to him, feral and aroused. "But no."

I took a step backward, putting more distance between us.

"I want to." Lucas was biting at his lower lip.

Staring at him, I saw him completely bare-chested for the first time. Saw the definition of his chest, his perfectly sculpted abs, his honey-tan skin, the specks of blood that my clothes had transferred to him. The moistness of his lips. The dark waves of his hair. The gilded jade of his eyes. The veins at his waist that trailed beneath his jeans. I swallowed hard and steadied myself, forcing my eyes up to his.

"We need to slow down," I said, holding my hands out as though making a barrier between us. "Take a breath."

"Okay." He nodded shakily, trying to control his breath. "Right."

He was chewing at his lip. I wanted to chew his lip for him. I averted my eyes so that I might stop thinking those thoughts. I counted to ten, took deep breaths, tried to ignore my arousal. Lucas got his breathing under control as the two of us stood there, less than six feet apart, doing our best to not attack each other with our mouths, lips, tongues, hands, and fingers.

"You can't tell Mrs. Wagner about tonight," Lucas stated steadily.

"Do you think I'm going to tell people about this?" I looked at him like he was crazy. "I mean, she wouldn't believe me. She'd fucking commit me."

Lucas looked around anxiously.

"What?"

"Well," Lucas chewed at his lip, but out of nervousness instead, "she'd *believe you*, but she'd have my hide."

I licked my lips, not to be sexy.

"Are you going to tell me what that means?" I asked.

"I probably shouldn't."

"I really think you should," I growled.

"She'll think that I wasn't doing my job." He said simply. "And that will piss her off. And the last thing I need is someone like Mrs. Wagner mad at me. So...please don't tell her."

"Someone like Mrs. Wagner?" I squinted at him.

"Ya' know...*a witch.*" He leaned forward to whisper nervously. "No one needs one as an enemy."

I just stared at him.

"Did you...not...know that?" He cringed.

"How long have you been clinically insane?"

"You just saw a werewolf." Lucas frowned at me. "Why is your grandmother being a witch so crazy?"

"Because!" I threw my hands up. "Because...because she's my grandmother. I think I'd know if she were a fucking witch, Lucas! Not that I know what to actually look for...but...what the fuck is even going on?!?"

"It's not really my place to say." He looked away.

"What are you?" I laughed crazily. "A leprechaun??!"

Lucas frowned at me.

"I'm...I just help out sometimes." He said simply. "Ya' know, when there's...like, a werewolf attacking her grandson...or something."

"Makes perfect sense." I nodded with an exaggerated smile. "I mean, how crazy of me to think that all of this is absolutely insane. Andrew's a werewolf, my grandmother is a witch, and you're just lending a hand where it's needed. All perfectly reasonable and sane."

"You've been living in L.A. for ten years." Lucas snorted. "I'm sure you've seen crazier things, Rob."

Glaring at him was all I could manage.

"Are you mad?" Lucas was chewing at his lip again.

"I don't know what I am."

Lucas looked at my crotch.

"You look...*aroused.*"

I rolled my eyes, but then they wandered to his crotch.

"That's the pot calling the kettle black." I sighed.

"Well...I want you." He said simply. "I've wanted you since I laid eyes on you at Mrs. Wagner's house the day I delivered her manure and tiller. Well, that's a lie. I've wanted you since high school."

"I hardly knew you in high school." It was a dumb thing to say.

"I didn't care." He said quickly. "I still wanted you."

"Why?"

He just stared at me.

"That's what I thought." I started to turn away.

"Because," He said forcefully making me turn back, then he cleared his throat, "because you were the most talented guy I'd ever seen. Because you treated everyone nicely. Because you were kind. And because..."

All I could do was wait.

"Because you didn't talk to me like I was just a football player."

I kept my eyes on his for several moments.

"Oma said she tried setting you up before," I said lowly. "Who...exactly...did she try setting you up with?"

"Just some guy from the center." He shrugged. "I hadn't wanted her to because, well..."

"You're in the closet."

"Kind of."

"And you got mad because she was trying to ease you out?" I asked. "Is that why she said you got upset?"

"Sort of."

"What was it exactly?" I grumbled.

He looked up, blushing.

"Because when she said she had someone she wanted to set me up with, I had heard you were gay in the magazines, and when she said she was setting me up with someone, well, I thought maybe you were coming to visit, and...but it wasn't you. And it really disappointed me. I wasn't upset. I was disappointed."

"You know that sounds completely psychotic, right?"

"A little."

"You barely know me."

"Well, I know you now." He said with a smile.

"We got drunk and had dinner one night and acted like a couple of silly teenagers." I frowned. "You don't know the first thing about me, Lucas. I'm an extremely famous actor and rock star...that sounds douchey, but I'm just making a point...and highly trained in publicity. Do you think you'll ever learn anything *real* about me unless I want you to?"

"Are you really looking to settle down?" He cocked an eyebrow. "Are you looking for a kind, funny, loyal guy who wants to travel with you and devote himself to you? Live the rest of his life with you?"

"Well, yes, but..."

"What other prerequisites can there be?"

"For one, he can't have just run over my actual date!"

"Hit. Not run over."

"Semantics again!"

He rolled his eyes but looked chastened. Even that made me want to pull him into me and do vile, disrespectful things to him with my hands, mouth, and other parts.

"Don't you want me?" He blushed. "I think that maybe you want me as much as I want you, but you're holding back."

"Of course I am, you asshole!" I sounded like Oma. "When a guy I was on a date with turns into a werewolf and gets hit by a car, and I get splattered with his blood, it's a good time to take a step back and say 'maybe I need to rethink some life choices here,' Lucas! Not fuck the first guy who comes along!"

"So...you do want me?"

"You are so goddamn annoying!" I growled.

We both just looked at each other. He was staring impassively, I was glaring at him, trying to control my most carnal self. Lucas' honey-tan skin, his defined chest and abs, his strong arms, those gilded jade eyes...everything about him was drawing me in, telling me to ignore the little voice in my head. I had needed a guy like Lucas—sex—for so long. My body wanted me to give in and give myself over to my most basic needs.

"*Oh, fuck it,*" I grumbled hoarsely.

I rushed Lucas again and pulled him into me. This time he was waiting to move into my body as well. Our bodies crushed against each other as our mouths found each other again. Lucas hands went immediately to the front of my shirt and start undoing buttons. I moaned against his mouth as he pulled my shirt off of me and explored the bare flesh of my chest and stomach with his fingers, desperately, eagerly.

My hand slid between us and slipped inside the front of his jeans and Lucas groaned against my mouth, his eyes opening in shock and yearning as I stroked him. I took his bottom lip between my teeth gently, my eyes on his, then I was kissing him again, our tongues battling as I continued the movements of my hand. Lucas' body reacted to my stroking and my mouth on his as we did our best to make our bodies one right there in the middle of his living room.

Then we were on the floor, and Lucas was on top of me, kissing at my neck as his hands undid my pants. His mouth moved to my chin, the front of my throat, then sucked at the flesh on either side of my neck. Then he was pulling me out of my pants, and his mouth was on my chest. He moved lower, his tongue and lips tasting the flesh of my chest, my stomach, and then I felt him take me into his mouth. I screamed out in pleasure as his mouth sucked at me and his head bobbed up and down as my fingers wound their way through the dark silk on his head.

Lucas was then under me, and I was repeating his actions, doing my best to bring him to the brink with my mouth, lips, tongue, and fingers. Both pairs of our pants got kicked off somehow, and we were both naked and writhing on the floor, going after each other's bodies like wild animals. Lucas seemed utterly out of control, lost entirely to some unfulfilled desire as we practically consumed each other's bodies right there on the wood floor of his living room.

Then I was inside of Lucas. Then he was inside of me. For what seemed like hours we explored every inch of each other, back and forth, slowly building, then pulling back, building some more. When I thought that neither of us could take the pleasure of each other's bodies much longer, we'd pull back just enough to prolong this encounter. Finally, after what seemed like hours, but still not long enough, we both climaxed, screaming out in euphoria. When we finally collapsed on the floor, we were both panting like wild animals, sweat sealing our bodies together.

We lay on the floor, wrapped up in a tangle of arms and legs, panting, trying to get our breath back as our hearts thundered in our chests. My body was telling me that this had been the most explosive sexual encounter of my life. No one understood my body and how it worked like Lucas did. He had known every part of my body that was the most sensitive, the most erogenous, the most delicate...everything that drove me crazy in the best of ways.

When we finally calmed down, our breathing controlled and our hearts no longer galloping like horses within our chests, Lucas laid his head next to mine, staring at me. He leaned forward and kissed the side of my face. Then he moved to my lips and kissed me gently, his damp hair tickling my forehead as I kissed him back, my hand rising to caress the side of his face. He looked me in the eyes, his gilded jade eyes looking so soft and kind, and I wanted to do it all over again.

And that was confusing as Hell.

I didn't do these things.

I didn't have sex with guys I barely knew.

I had just seen a werewolf.

Everything in my life had been turned upside down in the matter of an evening, and now I was laying with a virtual stranger on his living room floor after having just had the best sex of my life. Not that there was a lot to compare it to—but it still came out on top. I sighed contentedly, pushing every other thought to the back of my head as Lucas placed a gentle kiss on my chest, then laid his head down upon it.

My date had been a werewolf.

I still had some of his blood on me.

Oma was a witch.

And I had just had sex with Lucas.

Did I love him?

Processing any of that information was too much for one person in such a short amount of time. How can one go from leading a seemingly normal life—even though being famous is never normal—and suddenly find out that werewolves are real? That their grandmother is a witch? That some guy they thought was going to be their straight best friend was actually a gay guy who had been pining for them for at least ten years? Lucas was suddenly asleep against my chest, his arms wrapped around me. And the sun was rising outside. I closed my eyes and decided to sleep. Everything could wait for a few hours.

Jacob Michaels Is Not Crazy

A Point Worth LGBTQ
Paranormal Romance
Book 2

Chapter 1

I had come home and hadn't felt so bad about myself for once during my life as a teenager. Face no longer riddled with acne, hair no longer greasy after eight hours in my sophomore classes, pits, groin, and happy trail had a dusting of hair, and my voice no longer squeaked when I talked. My body was filling out so that I wasn't gangly and lanky. My alto voice had settled into a range somewhere between a tenor and a bass, though I could still hit relatively high notes in the choir. Girls were starting to take notice, though that just fed my ego since I genuinely wasn't interested. Settling into my looks had a profound effect on my life in general, regardless.

When I auditioned for plays, I got the lead. When I tried out in choir, I got the solos. My guitar playing was getting better. When I talked to other people in my classes or in the hallways, or just…anywhere…they wouldn't treat me like I was invisible. I was becoming very visible. It was overwhelming but in good ways. Though, in other ways, it was disconcerting. Popular kids wanted to be my friend, and unpopular kids wanted to be my friend. Other people hated me while others emulated me. I just wanted to be Robbie Wagner—but also sing and act in the school choir and plays. Everyone else had other expectations of me. I was starting to look decent, so, of course, that meant I had to behave a certain way.

It was all exciting and thrilling…and exhausting.

When I got home from school, I dropped my backpack by the door and kicked my shoes off. Oma had immediately yelled at me to not "leave my shit right out in the goddamn open where any asshole could trip over it." I loved my Oma. She was colorful and fun and, regardless of her language, kind. She was also incredibly embarrassing. The few real friends I had loved coming over to hang out simply because of the floor show. Their parents didn't like the new words that they came home with, but that didn't deter Oma.

Rolling my eyes, I had scooped up my bag and shoes and headed up the stairs towards my bedroom. In the upstairs hallway, I still felt the pull to walk to the end of the hall and go sit in the room that had belonged to my parents. Somehow, I ignored the instinct, just like I always did. I wasn't ready for that. Not yet. Inside my bedroom, I set my backpack next to my little desk I used for doing homework and then put my shoes in my closet. I didn't need Oma getting onto me for leaving things unorganized and untidy.

Freshly laundered clothes were folded and laid out on my bed, so I took a few minutes to put those away. Oma went to the trouble of washing my clothes, the least I could do was put them away. I even ignored the movement in my peripheral vision as I put clothes in dresser drawers and hung shirts in the closet. The shadows were there from time to time, in the corners, peeking out of the closets and cubbyholes, dashing into cupboards and the pantry, slipping under pieces of furniture. It was just what life was like living in Oma's house.

Oma didn't like to be questioned about it, and if I gathered the courage to ask, I was told: "maybe in a few years." I wasn't sure what that meant, but I trusted my Oma. I believed in her. I knew that she was old and wise and would take care of me, especially once my parents were gone, so I revered her word. Her word was law, and her law was love. Why question such a thing?

So, I picked up after myself, did chores, did my homework, tried to be a good grandson, and I ignored the things that I never could quite lay eyes upon that scurried about the house. It was none of my business. At least not for a few more years. I could live with that. Even at night, when I could swear that something was crawling into the bed and curling up by my feet, I closed my eyes tightly, reminded myself that I could never be in danger. Oma wouldn't have allowed that. She would protect me. So...I just shut my eyes tightly and went to sleep. After a while, I barely even noticed when something laid down against my feet as I was drifting off to sleep. It was almost as comforting as knowing that I had Oma, even though I didn't have my parents anymore.

Oma's house was where I felt safe.

When I awoke, the room was bright with mid-morning sunlight. My eyes scrunched up as I yawned deeply and started to move my arms. I couldn't move my right arm, it was numb, and it felt like the world was standing upon it. I started to panic as my eyes shot open but then I saw the reason for the heaviness and numbness in my arm. Lucas was still pressed against my side, his arms wrapped around me, his head on my chest, and my right arm was still stuck underneath him. Both of us were as naked as the day we were born, which made me feel like I should be embarrassed and cover myself. But then flashes of all of the things we had done to each other hours previously came back to me, and I realized that being naked was the last thing that should embarrass me.

Heat rose to my cheeks as I thought of all of the things I'd allowed Lucas to do to my body and all of the things I'd done to him. Not that sex was shameful...but I barely knew Lucas. I had behaved like a sex-crazed, lovesick idiot with no regard for my health and well-being. I'd simply let my most basic needs overtake me and had fallen into the moment. I never did that. Even as a rock star and actor, my image, personality, behavior, everything was controlled down to each and every step that I took. I never deviated from how I wanted to present myself to the world. Because the way I presented myself to the world was indeed who I was deep down. Jacob Michaels, er, Robert Wagner, well, Rob Wagner, if I had my say about things, was a good guy.

Okay. Maybe I was looking through the wrong lens at things. Having sex with someone doesn't make a person bad, per se. People aren't sluts and whores and players just because they enjoy sex. But...it just wasn't *me*. I'd never just fallen into bed with someone whom I had only known for a week. Especially one with whom I'd never actually had a date. I laid there on the floor, my shoulder blades starting to ache against the wood floors of Lucas' living room. However, I didn't want to move because moving meant that Lucas would wake up and then we would talk. I wasn't too sure that I was ready for talking, especially after everything that had transpired the night before.

Andrew had been a complete and unforgivable douchebag. He had been insufferable over dinner and had practically assaulted me in his car on the way home afterward. After punching Andrew to get him to stop trying to touch my...*naughty bits*...I had gotten out of the car and slammed the car door so violently that I had broken the window. When Andrew had followed me...

Werewolf.

How was that even possible? How had I watched a human man turn into a fucking werewolf? I couldn't even wrap my mind around the possibility that werewolves were actually a thing, even though I had seen it with my own eyes. What is visible doesn't need evidence, but I still doubted that I wasn't just completely mental and had imagined the whole thing. But Lucas had plowed into Andrew with his truck, brought me back to his house, and we had had sex. A lot of sex. And here I was, laying on the floor of his living room, completely nude and wrapped up in his arms and legs. Surely that was further proof that I hadn't imagined the night before. If I could discount my memory, I couldn't ignore the fact that Lucas and I were, in fact, laying on his living floor completely nude.

"Good morning." I jerked slightly at the sound of Lucas' voice.

I looked down at my former sexual partner to see his eyes lazily opening and his mouth turning up into a content smile.

"Good morning," I answered simply.

"Did you sleep well?" He asked.

Lucas seemed so happy. So content. Like the previous night hadn't affected him in the slightest. Like werewolves and attempted murder—well, okay, he hadn't been trying to *kill* Andrew, just fend him off—and then sex with a virtual stranger was just a typical Saturday for him. Maybe it was? I mean, how much did I know about Lucas? I only knew what he had told me—and you can never be sure about what goes on inside a person's head unless they are willing to tell the truth. And how does one validate the truth if one isn't a witness to the things they're told?

"I guess so." I nodded.

Lucas leaned up, his lips moving towards mine. Without a trace of enthusiasm, I pursed my lips and greeted his. But I didn't close my eyes or lean into the kiss. I simply let it happen.

"Are you hungry?" Lucas asked, his lips finding my jaw, then my chest.

I allowed Lucas to plant kisses on my skin a few times before interrupting him.

"Can you stop?" I asked gently.

Lucas tilted his head to look up at me.

"What's wrong?"

"Really?" I gave a nervous laugh. "I mean, come on, Lucas..."

He chewed at his lip.

"Okay." He shrugged against me and finally raised his body enough so that I could slide my arm out from underneath him. Pins and needles ran along it. "I know what's wrong. But...can't we just enjoy this moment a little longer, Rob?"

I just stared at him.

"I don't know what this moment is." I shook my head and slid away from him, finally rising to a seat position. "I don't know what anything is right now, Lucas."

Lucas sat up beside me, a frown forming.

"We made love."

It was my turn to frown.

"What?"

"Is that what that was?" I asked. "I thought it was just two idiots throwing caution to the wind and doing something reckless."

"Do you regret it?"

I chewed at my lip. Did I?

"No," I answered honestly, I thought. "But I also feel like I should. I mean...look at us for God's sake."

I gestured at our naked bodies as we sat beside each other there on the floor. If two guys sitting completely naked on the floor—two guys who barely knew each other—wasn't something to cause concern, then I didn't know what was. Was this just a sexual encounter to get over the trauma of what had happened in an evening? Was it sex, comfort...*love*?

"Did you enjoy it?" Lucas looked away shyly.

Flashes of the things we had done sent a shiver down my spine. The smell of Lucas' skin was stuck in my nose, I could taste him at the back of my throat. Sure, it was pleasant and enticing...but it also concerned the hell out of me. It made me want to do more things that were against my nature. Right then. Right there.

"Yes," I replied evenly. "I enjoyed it."

"Do you want some breakfast?"

"I want to go home." I shrugged. "I need to get away from here. For now."

"Home...where home?"

I thought about that.

"I just want to go back to Oma's." I rose to my feet and shuffled over to the pile of clothes our sexual encounter had formed. "I need to...I don't know...clear my head or something."

I bent down and sorted through the clothes until I found my underwear and pants and pulled them on quickly, though I tried to not look as self-conscious as I felt at that moment. Lucas rose to his feet and joined me at the pile of clothes, and he pulled on his underwear as well. My eyes rose to take him in, and my mind screamed out that he looked nearly as amazing in his underwear as he did nude. I wanted to pull him into me, feel his bare skin against my bare skin once more, press my mouth to his. Devour him.

Shivering, a shaking off of thoughts, I reached down and snatched up my shirt and pulled it on over my head. Lucas mimicked me as I went through the motions. In silence, occasionally exchanging awkward glances, we dressed, covering up the evidence of the previous night. Of course, feelings, memories, and thoughts can't be covered up with something like a shirt, so the awkwardness continued as Lucas found his keys and we left his house. The sun was climbing into the sky, even though it was chilly, and the brightness of the sun made me feel a lot safer after the night I'd had.

I climbed into the passenger seat of Lucas' truck as he jumped into the driver's seat, his eyes darting over to me. Doing my best to ignore the questioning look, I just fastened my seatbelt and tried to ignore the scent of sex and regret coming off of my clothes. My tongue and teeth felt furry, and I knew that my hair had to look absolutely tragic. I just wanted to get back to Oma's house, where all of my fresh, clean clothes were, get a shower, get redressed...and then...I didn't know.

"Are you sure you want to leave?" Lucas asked softly. "Right now?"

I turned my head to look at him, to consider what it truly was that I felt and wanted. Lucas' eyes did not meet mine; instead they were fixed on a point somewhere past the windshield.

"What did you mean when you said Oma is a witch?" I asked.

Lucas turned to me.

"You're more concerned about that than your date being a werewolf?" His eyebrow raised precipitously.

I motioned toward the sky. "Sun's out. I figure that one can wait for a few hours. And a lot of things have me concerned right now, Lucas."

"I meant she's a witch." He shrugged. "But I would appreciate it if you wouldn't tell her I told you that."

There were a lot of things I could say to that.

"I must be going out of my fucking mind right now." I sighed and turned my head back to look straight ahead again.

"You're not crazy, Rob."

"I'm not exactly in a good headspace."

"I promise that you're not crazy." He reiterated. "I know this is all a lot to take in all of the sudden...even for someone like you."

"I think I'm in shock."

"That would be understandable."

"Andrew is a werewolf," I said it as though we weren't fully aware of the fact yet. "You hit him with your truck. Oma is a witch. And we just fucked like a couple of horny teenagers."

"Fucked?" Lucas frowned.

"What is wrong with me?" I shook my head. "I mean...what is really wrong with me? I came back to Point Worth to...rest and eat and be with my grandmother. And...I managed to fuck that all up within the course of fewer than two weeks. I mean, that's gotta be a record, right?"

"How did you fuck it all up, Rob?" Lucas turned, kicking his knee up onto the bench seat between us. "How is anything fucked up—and even if it was—how is that your fault?"

"I don't have an answer for that." I shrugged, my hands falling limply into my lap. "I just...I feel what I feel, okay?"

Lucas stared at me as I sat there, wallowing in self-pity.

"Did you really *fuck* me, Rob?" Lucas asked lowly. "Is that what you thought we were doing when we...*did what we did*? Because that wasn't how I felt about it at all. It was the best sex of my life, sure, but it just felt right to me. It didn't feel like *fucking*, Rob. It felt like...*home*."

I turned my face to him again.

"Do you want to do it again?" I asked.

Lucas nodded.

So, we got back out of his truck, went back into Lucas' house, and repeated the previous night's activities. Except we didn't repeat them on the living room floor. We used the actual bed.

Chapter 2

Oma was in the kitchen, talking to herself again when I walked in through the front door hours later. It was mid-afternoon, and I hadn't so much as gotten a text or call from her on my cell phone in the entire time that I had been gone since the previous afternoon. I closed the door gently behind myself, barely making a "clicking" sound as it shut. Standing in the entryway, I was barely breathing as I listened to the sounds coming from the kitchen. I could hear Lucas' truck slowly pulling away from the house. And Oma was talking to…herself?

Lucas and I had had sex again. Okay. We had had sex again twice.

I don't know why I had wanted to have sex with him again. Twice. But it felt right, so I did it. And it felt so very right both times. Then we had dressed again, got in his truck, and he drove me home in silence. He had tried talking to me about what it meant for us now that we had done all of the things we had done, but I was in no mood to dissect this new development. Lucas was a nice guy. I thought so, anyway. He was certainly fun to hang out with. And I…liked him, I thought. But there was no way that I was going to delve any deeper into it than that. So, that's what I told him. I just wanted things to be as they were for now. I needed to go home and just be alone to think. To not be inundated with anyone else's questions and concerns.

Quietly, I slid my shoes off next to the door and stepped away from them, sneaking across the entryway, past the stairs, through the living room, and towards the kitchen entryway. What was Oma talking about? Was she actually talking to someone else? What exactly was going on? And, could I even ask her about it without bringing up what Lucas had said about her? I had made a promise as Lucas and I had laid in his bed after having sex twice more. I had told him that I wouldn't say anything to Oma about him saying that she was a witch. So…I would do my best to keep that promise. But that didn't mean that I couldn't do other things to show her that I was onto her and whatever it was going on inside of her house.

"He better be home safe and in one piece soon, ya' little shit." I heard Oma hissing. *"Every second I wait is one more check against you. I'll have your ass if there's one hair out of place on his fuckin' head, ya' hear me?"*

I frowned to myself as I stood just outside of the entryway, trying to figure out who Oma was talking to—if anyone at all. Was the old bag as crazy as I felt?

"I swear he's fine." I heard a familiar voice. *"I'm not sure where he is, but I know that I didn't hurt him."*

It was Andrew's voice.

My eyes closed to slits as I listened.

"*You better fuckin' hope so.*" Oma snapped. "*How in the whole steamy pile of hell did you think it was okay to take my fuckin' grandson out on the full moon in your condition?*"

"*I usually have myself under control, Mrs. Wagner.*" Andrew peeped. "*I don't know what came over me.*"

"*I'm pretty sure you know what the hell came over you, ya' fuckin' moron,*" Oma growled. "*Of all the fuckin' idiot shit I've seen in my near seven decades. You oughta be ashamed of yourself.*"

I did nothing to muffle my footsteps as I stepped into the entryway, finding Andrew seated at Oma's kitchen table, his back to me. Oma was standing by the sink. When she saw me step into view, her eyes grew wide.

"What...*exactly*...came over him, Oma?" I asked, cocking my head to the side, smirking as Andrew jerked in his seat and spun to look at me. "A case of the handsy, *furry* douchebags?"

Andrew's face was one big bruise. He had a cut along his lip, and I was confident that, if it weren't for the fresh clothes he had on, I'd see several bruises and abrasions smattered all over him. Getting hit by a truck will do that to a...*werewolf*...I supposed.

"Rob." Andrew swallowed hard.

Before I knew what I was doing, I had crossed the space between myself and Andrew and punched him in the face. He fell out of the chair onto the linoleum floor and started scooting backward and away from me. Oma threw her hands up in the air.

"Oh, just fuckin' great." Oma huffed. "Those kitchen chairs are older than any of us! Don't you assholes break nothin'!"

"Really?!?" Andrew looked over at her as he backed into the wall, fear pouring off of him in waves.

"I care more about that kitchen set than you!" She put her hands on her hips and waggled her head. "It belonged to *my* grandmother."

I turned to Oma as Andrew cowered against the wall. She twisted up her mouth in a half-frown as she examined me.

"Well...you *look* fine." She said.

I stared at her for a very long time.

"Get him out of this house," I stated firmly.

Oma gave me a look as though her first instinct was to tell me that she'd be damned if I told her what to do in her house and whom to do it with, but she finally rolled her eyes and looked over at Andrew.

"Ya' heard him!" She shouted at Andrew. "Scat! Get the hell out of here. I'll talk to you at the center, ya' little shit. This isn't over!"

Andrew scurried to his feet and dashed out of the back door, somehow managing to close it gently behind himself as he got far away from us. He must have parked near the back of the house because I hadn't seen his car when Lucas had pulled up to the house. But I heard a car start up shortly after he ran out of the house, so I knew that he had to have his car nearby. Oma and I stared at each other as we stood in the kitchen, her with her hands on her hips and me with my hands clenched in fists at my sides.

"You. Crazy. Bitch." I finally spoke once the sounds of Andrew's car were in the distance.

"What did I do?" She threw her hands up.

I glared at her.

"Okay." She rolled her eyes as her hands went back to her hips. "So, he's a werewolf. I didn't exactly know that now did I?"

"So...we're just throwing that word around like it's not crazy as shit, huh?"

"Which word?"

"Don't play dense with me, you crazy old woman."

"Where was you?"

"Where was *you*?" I snapped back.

"Oooooh, sassy today, are we?" Oma leaned against the sink edge. "Go on one bad date, and suddenly you're full of piss and vinegar and out to blame me for all of it?"

"Are you insane?!?" I practically shrieked. "You set me up with a goddamn werewolf. In the history of all dates set up by meddling family members, this takes the goddamn cake, Oma! And...*werewolf! A fucking werewolf! Andrew is a goddamn werewolf, and fucking werewolves are real! And you knew they were real!*"

"Well, of course, they're real." She rolled her eyes. "Don't get your pressures up. It's not that big of a deal in the grand scheme of things. There's all kinds of things some of us know nothing about. No reason to give yourself a goddamn stroke, though. You're perfectly fine, ain'tcha?"

"I can think of a fucking mile-long list of people who would disagree with everything you just said."

She shrugged.

"Lucas is gay." I spat.

"Well, yes." She shrugged again. "I suppose he is."

"You didn't think that was information you should have shared with me?" I bellowed. "I made a goddamn fool of myself acting like he was just this cool dude I was going to be friends with...and..."

"Really?" She smirked. "You almost got ate by a werewolf last night like you was wearing a red cape on your way to grandma's house and you're worried about making a fool of yourself in front of Lucas?"

"Fuck you, old woman!" I pointed a finger at her.

"Don't you jab your goddamn finger at me." She actually jumped back, putting her back against the sink.

I lowered my hand but didn't back down. "After what happened to me last night, I should be jabbing every fucking finger at you."

"Oh, calm down." She rolled her eyes. "You're fine. Well, fine-ish. Andrew's gone, he's learnt his lesson, and life goes on. Tra-la-la. He won't be bothering anyone for the rest of the full moon, so just relax, damnit."

I glared at her.

"What's in this fucking house?" I asked firmly.

"What do you mean?"

"Don't play dumb with me, Oma." I shook my head angrily. "You know exactly what I'm talking about. I had a dream last night and..."

"Where exactly did you have that dream?" She waggled her head at me.

"*On Lucas' goddamn living room floor after we fucked!*" I spat the words out like they were bullets.

Oma's eyes grew wide as she laced her arms over her chest and stared at me from across the kitchen.

"Well...that's...that's something, isn't it?"

"What does that even mean?"

"Well, Lucas...he's not exactly promiscuous, is he?"

"How the hell would I know?"

"Because I'm telling you, ya' shithead." She snorted. "For a while, I suspected the little shit was a damn virgin or something. Especially after he got all pissed off when I tried to set him up down at the center. Then a week after you come to town, he's gettin' some strange on his living room floor from ya'. I mean, I knew he talked about you a lot whenever we watched your movies or saw you on the T.V., but who knew he was wanting to play 'Hide the Sausage' with you?"

"Is this real right now?" I shook my head and looked up towards the heavens. "This all has to be a fucking coma dream or something. I must have fallen and hit my head, and I'm in a hospital ward somewhere."

"Stop being so damn dramatic." She waved me off.

"Dramatic?" I snorted. "Try apoplectic, lady."

"I don't even know that word." She snorted. "There you go, being all fancy again."

"It's in the goddamn dictionary, Oma." I snapped. "Look it up. Suffice it to say, you should be glad you're not Andrew right now because I am far from happy and I'm about a day's hike, a canoe ride down the river, and a helicopter ride over the mountains from calm."

"Was he good at it?" Oma leaned slightly forward.

"Are you for real right now?"

"Just curious." She stated defensively. "Not like I got a lot of people to talk about these things with."

"I'm sure some of the 'boys' at the center would love to carry on with you." I rolled my eyes. "But, yes. He was very good at it. All three times."

"Three?!" She practically squealed. "When was the other two times?"

"Before he brought me home today!" I shouted. "I fucked him twice more trying to forget about goddamn werewolves and..."

I trailed off, stopping myself from saying what it was that I really wanted to say. Consciously, I gathered myself up and walked over to the kitchen table, picking up the chair Andrew had knocked over when I had punched him, then plopped down into it. I put my head in my hands and rubbed my bleary eyes, then ran my hands through my hair as Oma sauntered over and sat across from at the table. She folded her arms over her chest and watched me as I had my internal debate over what my next course of action should be.

"Well, I guess a good fuckin' did ya' good." She said.

"Don't start with me, Oma."

"Well, when's the last time you had a little strange, Robbie?" She shrugged. "Maybe that's part of what you needed? You said you came here to find some love...and I guess you found it."

"I don't love Lucas."

"Hm." She appraised me. "We'll see. Funny what a little tickle will do to a fella after all."

"I'm nearly twenty-seven years old, Oma." I sighed. "I think I'd know if I was in love, right?"

"You think he loves you?" She asked.

I looked up at Oma. Before I knew what I was doing, I slammed my fist down on the table. She didn't so much as jump. I guess a finger jab is unsettling but a fist slamming into a table isn't.

"Don't," I growled at her. "Don't act like this is settled, Oma. You lied to me, and..."

"I didn't lie about shit." She spat. "I didn't know that the little shit was a werewolf, so that's not my fault."

Rapidly, my conversation with Oma the previous day before Andrew had come to pick me up rushed through my head.

"But you suspected it." I snapped back. "You were worried about me getting home after dark because you knew it was the first night of the full moon. Don't try to lie."

"Fine." She relented. "Maybe I suspected that he got a little hairy 'round the full moon. But it wasn't like I could just ask him. The were-community is notoriously tight-lipped about their status and for good reason and..."

"The...were...*community*?"

I knew the disbelief and shock were painted all over my face.

"Well, yeah." She replied. "Andrew ain't special or nothin'. Surely you figured that out for yourself already."

I frowned at her. I didn't know if I was shocked, scared, dumbfounded, or resigned to the fact that things were even crazier in Point Worth than I had initially understood. Growing up in the small town there on Lake Erie, I knew that the place wasn't exactly...*normal*...but I thought it was just because it was full of country people. Obviously, other things were going on in the tiny little town that I had absolutely no clue about. Or...had I just chose to ignore those things when they drew my attention?

"Oma...I don't even know what to say right now."

"Guess you're gonna dash off in the middle of the night again, huh?" She sat back in her chair, a disappointed look on her face.

"Is the...can't believe I'm saying this...is the *were-community* confined to Point Worth?"

"Of course not." She snorted. "They're all over the damn place."

"Then where the hell am I gonna go, Oma?" I shook my head. "Where can I go that I wouldn't have to worry about crazy stuff happening?"

Both of us sat at the kitchen table with that hanging in the air between us. If I was truly only upset about the fact that Andrew was a werewolf—and werewolves could be found everywhere, even if I hadn't been aware of that fact—Point Worth was as good a place to be as any. I chewed at my lip and looked over at Oma, wondering if I could bring myself to ask the question that was on the tip of my tongue. Lucas had plenty to say about Andrew *and* Oma. Of course, Andrew had been the biggest problem in my mind because his...*issue*...had been a severe threat to my personal safety within the last twenty-four hours. Oma's...*issue*...wasn't really of a concern to me. Was it?

"Oma..."

Her arms still crossed over her chest, she just stared dully at me.

Well, dully wasn't correct. Oma never had dull looks—there was always fire behind her eyes, a gleam in her eye. A little danger mixed with humor.

"What?" She urged me on.

Could I really ask my grandmother if she was a...it was so ridiculous I couldn't even think it while looking at her. We were sitting at the kitchen table in the house I had grown up in—where I was visiting her and getting away from everything. A home where up until Andrew turned into a werewolf, I was considering living in until I sorted myself out. Now I wasn't so sure. There were answers to questions I hadn't even asked looming in my mind, and questions without answers I couldn't push out of my mind. If the question fell out of my mouth, would there be any coming back from that?

What would Oma say anyway? Who would own up to being a *witch*??

Maybe someone who speaks openly about werewolves and the were-community, Rob? Ya' think that might be a person who owns up to being a witch? Sound reasonable to you, dumbass?

"Nothing." I pushed away from the table.

"Where are you off to?" She frowned, her brow an expanse of furrows.

"I need to clean the...I need to clean up." I sighed.

Oma grinned widely.

"Piss off, old woman," I grumbled at her.

Stalking back out of the kitchen, through the living room, and up the stairs, I realized that I hadn't really come up with a battle plan for what was next in my little Point Worth saga. Obviously, I'd have to address with Oma whether or not she was a...*witch*...or did I? Was that any of my concern? Whatever she was that she hadn't told me about was none of my damn business. Right? It wasn't my place to demand to know everything about my grandmother, especially since I hadn't exactly been around in the last decade. Hell, I hadn't even been a good enough grandson to check in as regularly as I should have, so storming back down to the kitchen and asking very personal questions was out of the question.

But what did it mean that Oma was a *witch*? Was she turning into a crunchy, groovy, earthy old chick who grew herbs and produced handmade jewelry and worshipped nature? Did she brew special teas and tonics for herself and neighbors that she claimed would cure all that ails ya? Or...*was she a witch*? Like, did she cast spells and dance naked under the moon and convene with all sorts of...*things*? I frowned to myself as I reached the top of the steps, thinking of things curling up beside my feet in the middle of the night. Something was going on in Oma's house— something that had been going on for years, and her being a witch would certainly explain a lot of it.

This is all ridiculous.

I marched down the hall, entered the room I was using and closed the door a little more roughly than necessary. Lucas was probably just being dramatic and using poetic license when describing Oma. I had known the woman twenty-six years—my entire damn life. If Oma were a witch, one would think that I'd be the first to know aside from herself. Witches—real witches—weren't a real thing anyway. Magic wasn't real.

Neither are werewolves.

My breath was stuck in my throat as I yanked my shirt off and started to unbutton my pants. How had I been in California a little more than a week prior, skinny to an unhealthy degree, working myself into the ground, and living on caffeine and nicotine, playing at being Jacob Michaels—an incredibly famous actor and singer? And now I was in Point

Worth, being Robert Wagner—just a boy born in upper Ohio—living in his Oma's house, learning that werewolves and the supernatural and...*witches?*...were a real thing? How had my life escalated to such a summit in ten years and come crashing down within fewer than two weeks?

Jacob Michaels was incredibly famous, incredibly rich, incredibly connected...and ignorant. He knew nothing of these things going on behind the scenes of everyday life. He just wanted to do his work and get paid and hide behind the façade of, well, being Jacob Michaels. Robert Wagner was who Jacob Michaels really and truly was—and he just wanted to move back home and leave the fast-paced and crazy lifestyle behind. Robert Wagner didn't have the first clue about all of these things going on, either. But...maybe he should have? Shouldn't I know things like, oh, yeah, my Oma is a witch and a guy I go on a date with might turn into a werewolf at the full moon?

Then there was everything that had happened with Lucas. Actually, the one thing that happened with Lucas, *three times*. How had I become this guy in the space of fewer than two weeks? I had fallen into bed (and other places) with a guy I barely knew and for whom I didn't have feelings. Well, not romantic feelings. Actually, I didn't know how I felt about Lucas. I stood there, shirt flapping open and my pants rolled down to my thighs, staring off at nothing. How did I feel about Lucas?

Lucas was cute.

He was kind.

He was shy and adorably so.

He had steady employment.

Lucas knew who he was.

He had saved my life.

Fuck he was sexy.

But did I think that I could love him?

Abso-fucking-lutely not.

Lucas and I were cheese and chalk. We had nothing in common. He was some boy born in the country—so was I—but that's where it ended. He was country through and through. He liked working at his grandfather's hardware store and performing duties as a substitute teacher. And he liked living out on the lake in seclusion. And, for fuck's sake, being a vegetarian.

But, my God, wasn't he sexy?

Wasn't my body drawn to his?

Could I look at his lips without wanting to press mine against his?

Could I look at his body without wanting to feel my tongue drag along the length of it?

Didn't I, even as I stood in the bedroom at Oma's house, want to feel his hands grab ahold of me. Anywhere. He could grab me anywhere.

I shivered as I ripped my shirt off in frustration. Lucas was not going to become a *thing*. He was just a distraction in my journey to turning back into Robert Wanger—er, Rob. I just wanted to be Rob, and romantic or sexual interludes were out of the question. That was not why I had come back to Point Worth. Sure, as Oma had pointed out, I had come to Point Worth hoping to get a little love and friendship back into my life. However, not *that kind of love*. I didn't need a man. I had me. Regardless of what Oma thought, that was more than enough. I didn't want some guy dictating my future. One man—Jacob Michaels—had already done that for a decade. And I was done.

I just want to be Robert Wagner.

Welling up with tears, I rolled my pants down and stepped out of them. I started to cry because I didn't know how to be Robert Wagner. Because I had no idea who Robert Wagner was. I hadn't been him for at least ten years. And, even when I was Robert Wagner, I had no clue who he was. I was a man with two names and no idea who I was supposed to be. Tears were leaking down my cheeks as I stripped off my underwear and carried all of my dirty clothes to the hamper.

Less than thirty minutes later, I was drying off from my bath and sliding into fresh pajamas. Then I was sliding under the crisp, clean sheets of the bed. Sleep. Sleep always helps.

Chapter 3

Oma had knocked on the bedroom door at lunchtime. Then again at dinner time. I didn't get out of bed or even answer verbally. Pulling the covers more tightly around myself, I chose to ignore her. Tiredness had surrounded me, made my skin crawl and my bones ache and my eyes heavy and bleary. Knowing that I had acted out of character with Lucas—at least, what I thought was out of character—and finding out all of the other things I had found out about my life and Point Worth, made it impossible to exist for the time being. Sleep was the only thing that I could manage.

Finally, sometime around midnight, I felt the house go still. Darkness, though I couldn't really know, seemed to envelop the entire house. Quiet descended upon Oma's house, and everything was dead for the night. I rolled over onto my back and stared up at the ceiling. Reaching over, I took my cell phone from the bedside table, surprised it was still working since I hadn't charged it since the day before. The alerts on the screen told me that I had missed calls from my assistant, manager, and agent—but just one from each. I also had ten texts from Lucas, two from Andrew, and even one from Oma.

Upon listening to the voicemails left, I quickly ascertained that my team back in California had a new project they wanted me to consider. I deleted the messages and shot off a text to my assistant, Jessica, that I wanted to be left alone until I reached out to them. The texts from Lucas were what one would expect from someone they just had hours of sex with throughout a night and morning. Proclamations of missing me, still smelling me at his house, all kinds of vomit-inducingly nice things. Andrew's texts were profuse apologies, which were almost laughable. And Oma's was a quick text asking if I was going to eat dinner at least. I didn't respond to any texts.

When I laid my phone back on the bedside table, after a few seconds, it lit up gently, signaling a text or call, casting the ceiling in an eerie blue. I ignored it. My eyes were getting heavy again. And then I felt the foot of the bed being weighed down by something crawling up onto the bed with me. As I felt whatever it was curl up by my feet, I couldn't think of anything else to do.

"Don't get under the covers," I said as I drifted off. "And we will get along fine."

I heard something breathe out gently, contentedly. I took that as acquiescence. And then I drifted off to sleep.

When morning came, I woke up with the sun, rising as though summoned by that heavenly star itself. My eyes popped open, and I immediately looked down at the foot of the bed. I was alone. No critter was there, waiting for me to wish it "good morning" or scratch it behind the ears. Which was a good thing, because, unless it had been a cat or dog, that wouldn't have been in my wheelhouse. Even strange cats and dogs gave me concern since there was no way to know if they were friendly enough to pet. It's not until you've been bitten that you know a being's true personality.

I slid out of bed and went about getting bathed and dressed once again. Not that I wanted to put much effort in, especially since I was in Point Worth and not Hollywood, but I knew it would make me feel better. I noticed that my hamper was empty of dirty clothes, but I paid it no mind. Things were weird in Oma's house, and I was starting to just go with it. What I didn't know wouldn't hurt me. And what didn't kill me in the middle of the night could sleep at my feet without me knowing what it was. That was fair enough.

As I bathed, primped, and dressed, I plugged my phone into the charger on the bedside table and cued up some music. *Scissor Sisters* began to blare, and I smiled to myself as I waited. When the loud knocking began at my door, followed by the bellowing of Oma, I grinned wickedly to myself.

"*Go away, old woman!*" I bellowed back.

The knocking went on for a few moments longer as I busied myself about my bath and the rest of my routine. Once I was clean and primped and dressed in fresh underwear, jeans, and a sweater, I finally shut off the music. The pounding on my door and the bellowing from my grandmother had ended quite a bit before that, but I hadn't lowered the volume of my music. I had hoped that it had startled her awake and it had done exactly what I'd expected. Finally, I turned the music off on my phone, leaving the room in deathly silence. I couldn't hear Oma at all.

Before leaving the bedroom I was using, I made sure to tidy up, make the bed, and leave everything as it should be. Mostly because Oma had made a comment about being more thoughtful about the messes I made and not making messes in the first place. That was probably her way of telling me a secret without actually telling me directly. I wanted to test that theory. See if the scurrying I'd heard during the nights would stop. Just call it a hunch. When I got down to the kitchen, Oma was in front of the stove and had a scowl on her face, which she aimed in my direction when I waltzed into the room, a sweet smile on my face.

"You're a dick." She hissed.

"Good morning, crazy." I chirped as I went to the fridge and swung it wide.

I surveyed the contents of the fridge and grabbed the carton of orange juice before heading over to the cabinet to grab a glass. Pouring the glass of juice for myself, Oma watched me for a few moments as she continued to cook at the stove.

"Pour me a glass, would you?" She asked simply.

I looked over at her, maintaining eye contact, as I finished pouring the remainder of what was in the carton into my glass. Then I chunked the carton in the trash.

"Fresh out," I said simply. "I'll get some more when I go into town later."

She squinted at me.

I lifted the glass to my lips and took a long, refreshing drink, then smacked my lips as I stared at her.

"What the hell has crawled up your ass?" She snapped, poking at the bacon in the pan before her. "Going out of your way to be ugly when you were already born that way?"

"Too much." I shook my head. "Can't finish all that."

I tipped the glass slowly, letting it dribble into the sink. Oma glared at me as the O.J. waterfalled from my glass and down the drain.

"Okay, you little shit..."

"What's in your house, Oma?" I stopped her.

"What the fuck are you talking about now?" She snapped. "Have you been taking your...Paxil? Paxil. That's what it is, right?"

"Don't you turn this shit on me." I glared at her. "There is something in this house—*besides you and me*—and you're hiding it from me."

"You been taking them pills?"

"You been taking pills?" I snapped back.

She rolled her eyes and poked at the bacon.

"Something crawled into bed with me last night." I set my glass in the sink. "Just like every other damn night I've been here and wasn't too tired to notice. So...what is it? You have a cat? A dog? A raccoon or opossum or something?"

"Who the hell keeps an opossum as a house pet?"

"Crazy old country women from Ohio who think that the guy they set their grandson up on a date with turning into a wolf at the full moon isn't that big of a deal??!?"

Her eyes were rolling around again.

"You just aren't going to let that go, are you?"

"You have some douchebag try to grab your junk, turn into a wolf, and then get plowed into by a truck and see how long you hold onto that nut, lady."

"Who the hell hit him with a truck?"

"Not that that should be your first question, but Lucas did."

She thought about this for a moment.

"Well, I guess he had it coming." She shrugged.

"Oh," I laughed in disbelief, "you are crazy as a shit house rat, aren't you?"

"Someone's getting' the *Point Worth* back in their personality." She quipped. "Keep talkin' all folksy and maybe people will start to think you're actually from around here, no matter how much you've tried to act like you're better than all of us."

The heat poured off of me as I braced my hand on the sink edge. A shattering sound rang through the air as the glass in the sink practically exploded. Oma jumped back from the stove, putting distanced between the sink and herself. Glass ricocheted off of my knuckles and felt like pinpricks, but I didn't so much as flinch at the sound or the feeling. Internally, I couldn't help but wonder why the glass had shattered. However, I was not going to be distracted by Oma's nonsense or trickery.

"*What the hell do you think you're doing?*"

"What is in this goddamn house, Oma?!"

"There ain't nothin' in this house except my crazy damned grandson breaking my shit!" She growled back. "Your goddamn hand is bleeding."

I glanced down. My hand merely looked a little scratched up.

"Don't deflect."

"You need to take your pills!"

"I am not crazy, Oma!"

"You just tore your damn hand up, Robbie." She grumbled. "And you're worried about raccoons and opossums?"

"My hand is far from 'tore up,' Oma." I held it up for her viewing. Just a few small scratches. "What's been crawling into bed with me?"

"I have no idea, ya' asshole." She turned away from me to poke at the bacon in the pan some more. "But you need to take them pills."

"Fine."

Without another word, I ripped a few paper towels off of the holder next to the sink and blotted at my hand as I walked towards the doorway.

"Now where the hell do you think you're going?" Oma hollered after me. "You ain't even had breakfast!"

"I'll eat at the café."

So, I went and got my coat, wallet, phone, keys, and left.

Chapter 4

Lucas entered the Sunny Side Up Café, a smile on his face, and a spring in his step. I was sat in the same booth we had occupied on our previous visit, a cup of coffee half-drunk already. When I had left Oma's, I had shot off a text to him, asking if he wanted to meet for breakfast. Of course, he had responded immediately to the affirmative, which unnerved me. Lucas' immediate desire to see me again made me wonder if Oma wasn't on to something when she asked if he had feelings for me. One wouldn't think that one night of having drinks and one night of debauchery would enamor one to another so quickly. But Lucas had the look as he made his way over to my booth in the mostly empty café. Weekdays obviously weren't very busy after the breakfast rush, either.

When Lucas slid into the booth across from me, that smile growing broader and more genuine, I brought my coffee mug to my lips and took a long drink. The waitress, Jill, popped up and took Lucas' order for coffee as well and we both ordered our meals. I opted for another veggie omelet and fruit cup, which made Lucas smile, so he ordered the same. However, I desperately felt the need to explain to him that his vegetarian lifestyle was not rubbing off on me. I just desired to eat something at least halfway healthy instead of something like the heart-clogging fare Oma offered at home.

"Hey, you." Lucas grinned at me as he started to unbutton his coat in the seat across from me. "I was worried when you didn't return my texts last night."

"I slept from the time I got home until the sun came up this morning," I said simply.

There was no need to provide details that were unimportant in the grand scheme of things. The grand scheme being whatever it was going on between Lucas and myself.

"Did I wear you out that much?" He grinned wickedly, yet somehow still shyly as he slid his coat off. "Maybe you need to do more cardio?"

"Maybe."

"I'm glad you asked me to come have breakfast." He smiled widely. "I didn't really have anything to do this morning."

"Not working at the hardware store? High school doesn't need your skills either?"

He chuckled. "I usually have Mondays and Tuesdays off—if I have days off. They're the least busy days at grandpa's store...though you'd think some teachers would've called in today, right?"

"Look," I didn't want to banter, "Lucas, I wanted to talk to you about this weekend and...I don't know what to say really...I just know that we need to talk about it."

"I had a good time." His smile practically split his face.

Staring into his eyes, the color of gilded jade, from across the table, I didn't know if I had the heart to have this conversation with Lucas. I didn't know if I had the heart to talk to anyone about anything. Except maybe Oma and Andrew since it was easy to talk when I'm angry. Lucas hadn't really done anything to draw my ire. Sure, he hadn't told me he was gay—but that hadn't really been my business, and I hadn't asked anyway. Of course, he hadn't told me he knew that werewolves were real and Oma was allegedly a witch. Then again, if he had told me before I had seen it with my own eyes, would I have believed him? No. I wouldn't have. I would have called him crazy and avoided him in the future.

"Um, yeah, I mean, I had fun, too." I nodded, trying to gather my thoughts.

Lucas started to reach across the table for my hand that held my coffee mug, realized where we were, then slid his hand back into his lap. But his smile didn't falter. Which scared me more than anything—even more than his thought to grab my hand to hold.

"Are you busy tonight?" He asked. "We could go into Toledo and see a movie. Maybe have dinner first? There's a really good vege—"

"I'm not dating you." I interrupted him.

Lucas stopped abruptly, and I got to witness the heartbreakingly slow transition of smiling to frowning on his face.

"I—jeez—I didn't want to, I don't know, hurt you or anything." I shook my head. "But I wanted to make it clear that what we...*did*...doesn't mean that suddenly we're...*boyfriends*."

"Boyfriends?" He frowned.

"Yeah." I nodded warily. "A couple. Partners. Whatever you want to call it. Obviously, I haven't dated in forever, and I don't even know what to call two guys who are in a relationship. So, that should tell you that I'm not a guy you want to partner up with anyway."

"I see."

"And I wanted to get it out there before it became imprudent to bring it up again," I said. "So, there it is."

"Well, thank you for being prudent."

His tone was just this side of snarky.

I rolled my eyes softly.

"I know," I said. "I shouldn't have slept with you if I didn't know how I felt about...*us*...but..."

"What's wrong with you?" Lucas sat back in his seat. "Seriously, Rob. What is your major issue? Because I haven't been able to figure that out."

"I'm sorry?" I blinked at him.

"You have some serious boundaries and barriers." He said, frowning at me. "I mean, you have some issues with relationships of all kinds."

I couldn't stop myself.

"The weirdo vegetarian who couldn't even look me in the eyes or hold a conversation the first handful of times we saw each other in person is telling me that I have issues?" I snorted. "The guy who has lusted after a stranger since high school thinks I have issues? Really, Lucas?"

"Ouch."

Clearing my throat, I sat back, realizing that I was being snarkier than the conversation required. Lucas wasn't my enemy. He didn't have to point out my faults, but he wasn't my enemy. I didn't have to come back at him with snarky remarks like I would Oma.

"I'm sorry."

"Forgiven." He nodded.

"Just like that?"

"Yes. That easy."

"I'm not that easy." I realized what I said and couldn't help but grin evilly. "Usually."

He smiled back.

"I didn't ask for your hand in marriage, Rob." He said. "I just asked if you wanted to continue *this* with dinner and a movie. See where it leads. That's all."

"I don't know who I am, Lucas."

And there it was. The truth fell out of my mouth without me even willing it or realizing that I had it cued up to fall out of my mouth. Lucas frowned more deeply as he watched me from across the tabletop. Unsure of how long we just stared at each other, Jill showed up with our plates and set them down in front of us before we spoke again. We both thanked her for our food, and she wandered off again. Lucas broke eye contact first as he unraveled his napkin wrapped silverware.

"What does that mean?" He asked simply.

Unwrapping my own silverware with trembling hands, I refused to let my eyes wander away from Lucas. I wouldn't look insecure or vulnerable. I had seen this man's penis after all.

A very nice penis.

Shut up, brain.

"Who the hell am I, Lucas?" I said, grabbing ahold of my fork. "Who was Rob Wagner before I went off and became Jacob Michaels? Who was Jacob Michaels? Who is Rob Wagner if he's not Jacob Michaels?"

Lucas stared at me, wide-eyed.

"I've spent a decade pretending I'm someone I'm not to the point that I have no idea who I really am." I looked around surreptitiously and leaned in. "I didn't even know werewolves were real and that my Oma...there are a lot of things I don't know about...*anything*...because I've been too busy being Jacob Michaels and denying I was Rob Wagner. Now, I'm back here, and my intention was just to be whoever it is that Rob Wagner is...and I don't even know who that is. And werewolves are real. Happy Monday."

Lucas chuckled and cut into his omelet.

"I need to ask you a question," I asked tentatively as I skewered a piece of honeydew melon from my fruit cup. "Is that okay?"

"Of course." Lucas popped the bite of omelet into his mouth.

His beautiful, sexy, delicious mouth.

Stop. Stop. Stop.

"Who are you?"

"I'm sorry?" He smiled crookedly.

Popping the piece of fruit into my mouth, I kept my eyes on his. Those gilded jade eyes that were just a little too beautiful. Lucas had beautiful eyes. Lips that were just too kissable. Skin that was just too perfectly tanned and smooth. He was so appealing in every way.

"I'm sorry," I said. "That came out wrong. *What* are you?"

Lucas set his fork on his plate and sat back in his seat.

"What do you mean?" He chewed at his lip.

"Andrew is a werewolf." I shrugged, trying to appear nonchalant as I chewed and skewered another piece of melon. "Oma is a witch, I guess. What are you, Lucas? Did I have sex with a leprechaun the other night?"

"And twice the next morning?"

His grin was too appealing.

It was my turn to frown.

"Please answer me."

"I'm just...me, Rob."

"Human?"

"Mrs. Wagner is human." He said. "So is Andrew. Being a witch doesn't take away your humanity, Rob. And werewolves only lose their humanity in wolf form."

I'd hit a sore spot, clearly.

"Are you human or is there a hyphen, Lucas." I was sorry for having phrased my question the way I had, but I needed answers. "Is there an additional descriptor for 'Lucas' besides 'human'?"

"Would you believe me if I said I was just a human?"

"Maybe."

"What if I told you that I was, indeed, a leprechaun?"

"Harder to believe."

"Because werewolves don't exist, right?" He teased.

Watching him for a few moments, I tried not to get distracted by his perfect...everything. I tried not to let my brain tell me how much I wanted to ask him if we could go back to his house.

"What are you?"

"You're not going to let this go, are you?"

"I don't think so. No."

"I'm human."

"And nothing else?"

He shrugged.

"What does that mean?" I was completely frustrated. "All you have to tell me is if you're something in addition to being human."

"I don't know." He was shrugging again.

"How can you not know?"

"Everyone around here has some crazy family history." He said, grabbing his fork and attacking his omelet once again. "Well, maybe not everyone, but quite a few people have this or that in their bloodline. How should I know if there's a leprechaun in the woodpile?"

"Poorly executed, Lucas."

He blushed as he shoved more omelet into his mouth.

"I've never grown hair at the full moon or had lasers shoot out of my fingers or granted wishes, or anything." He replied, chewing his food. "If that helps any."

"Then why didn't you just say that you're human and that's all?"

"Because I didn't want to lie inadvertently." He shrugged, shoving more omelet in his mouth.

He was eating faster by the second, which made me nervous. Was he trying to finish this meal so that he could leave and avoid my questions about his genetics?

"It's not lying if you think you're telling the truth, Lucas."

"Okay." He said. "I think I'm telling the truth. Eat your food."

"What's the rush?" I cut at my omelet with the side of my fork.

Lucas shoved the last bite of his omelet in his mouth, chewed it just a few times and swallowed it in a way that looked painful. He leaned in as I brought the bite of my omelet to my lips.

"The rush is to get your food finished because we need to leave." Lucas' voice was thick as he stared at me. "Because I need to have sex with you again. Maybe a couple times."

I swallowed the bite of omelet, nearly choking.

"Eat your food, Rob," Lucas said firmly. "Then we're going to my house."

My brain told my mouth to tell Lucas that he couldn't just order me around and command me to hurry up and eat and then have sex with him. That's not what came out of my mouth.

"Okay," I said to Lucas, my fork digging into the omelet again.

Chapter 5

Rising to my knees, Lucas' legs fell off of my shoulders, and he stared up at me, panting and smiling widely, sweat beads decorating his torso and other places. I took a few moments to catch my breath before placing my hands on either side of him and leaning down to push my mouth against his. Lucas' arms went around my back, and he pulled me into him, both of our sweaty bodies sealing the space between us. I was still inside of Lucas as he did his best to devour my mouth with his own as arms tried to push us even closer together, though that would have been utterly impossible.

"My God, Rob." Lucas breathed out heavily as my mouth moved to his jaw, then to his neck.

What the fuck is wrong with me???

I wanted to do this again. And again. And again. I wanted to feel my tongue trace along every inch of his skin. To taste every part of him that I could. I never wanted my body to be withdrawn from his.

"That was so...so..."

Mumbling into Lucas' neck, I kissed and nibbled at him with a smile, making him squirm and chuckle beneath me.

"What did you say?" He practically giggled as I chewed at his neck like a sex-crazed, eternally horny teenager.

"*Amazing,*" I mumbled against the flesh my mouth was sucking at as he squirmed beneath me.

"That doesn't even cover it." Lucas sighed happily as his fingers twined in my hair and gently pulled my mouth back up to his.

Lucas' hands went to my face as he pulled me in for a long, passionate kiss and his legs wrapped around my waist. *How were we managing to stay connected so easily?* I adjusted my hips to rectify that situation. Lucas sighed as my body left his and our mouths continued to mingle, reacquainting themselves. Finally, I pulled my mouth away from Lucas' as I felt myself finally going soft, though it was hard to tell with our pelvises pushed together, and I gazed down at Lucas, unable to remove the lazy smile from my face.

"I could run my fingers through your hair all day." He whispered playfully to me as he did just that. "You were blessed with good hair, Rob. And, uh, other things."

I felt myself slightly blush as a laugh escaped my throat.

"You're not so bad yourself."

Lucas answered that with a smile and a gentle thrusting of his hips.

"No!" I admonished him, though I made no move to remove myself from our current position. "Not again. I'm worn out."

Lucas' hands slid from my face, over my shoulders and collarbones, my chest, and came to rest on the sides of my stomach. I continued to gaze down at him, holding myself above him.

"We need to get a little more weight on you." He tickled my ribs, finally forcing me to roll off of him in a burst of laughter. "Get your stamina up."

"You're a shit. I've had more sex in three days than I've had in the last five years." I spat playfully. "I think that counts for something."

"Maybe you need to make up for lost time?"

Lucas turned on his side, and his mouth was on mine again, and then he was rolling on top of me and pressing his body into mine. I reached up and held his face in my hands as we kissed and he tried to seduce me into going past my limits. It would have absolutely worked, but I knew that I needed to eat and I needed coffee. I hadn't eaten nearly enough in the day considering I had given up on finishing my breakfast at the café, letting my libido win over. And I hadn't even finished a full cup of coffee, either.

"Okay, okay." I slowly pulled his face away from mine, getting a whimper and slight resistance from him in the process. "I need food. And I need coffee. And you need to make it for me."

"You aren't afraid I'll burn it?" He kissed the tip of my nose.

It was a loving, romantic gesture. Too familiar. Too perfect. It felt too good. I ignored that nagging feeling in my gut and just smiled at him.

"The coffee? No. The food? Maybe."

Lucas chuckled and gave me another quick kiss before rolling off of me and then out of bed. Noon sunlight was streaming through the sheer curtains of his bedroom, and dust motes hung lazily in the air. It was still cold outside, but his bedroom was warm and toasty. I wanted food and coffee, but seeing Lucas stand at the side of the bed, pulling his jeans on without even bothering to pull his underwear on first, I wanted to drag him back into bed. Wrap him in my arms and curl up with him. Doze off. Sleep the sleep of death until we could sleep no more.

"What are you looking at?" He waggled his eyebrows at me.

"Go!" I shook the thoughts from my head. "Food! Coffee! Burnt as little as possible!"

He laughed and left the room, pulling a t-shirt on over his head as he stepped through his bedroom door. I rolled onto my back and stretched jerkily, smiling to myself and my bad choices and behavior. With the new activities in my life, I was going to have to start showering more. In my pre-Point Worth life, showering once a day usually did it on a typical day. Unless I was working on location or in the studio and makeup or the sweat of a long shoot had to be washed off at the end of the day. With Lucas in my life and all of the sex, it was nearly the same concept.

Finally, I rolled out of bed and found my underwear and jeans and slipped them on. Then I pulled on my sweater and slipped my feet into my socks. I wasn't planning to leave—was I?—but I didn't want to get cold walking on the hardwood floors in Lucas' house. It was well-insulated and heated, but I was still a ways from having an adequate amount of body fat, so I got cold a lot more easily than a normal person. I gave my hair a once-over in the mirror over Lucas' dresser, making sure I didn't look too "sexed up" and tiptoed from the room as well.

I could hear Lucas working away at setting the coffee pot to brew in the kitchen and searching the fridge for whatever it was he was going to make for me. How I felt at that moment made me almost stop in my tracks and reassess how I let myself tumble into this position again. I was playing house with Lucas. I hadn't even bothered to tell Oma where I was, how long I would be gone, hadn't even checked in with her. Lucas and I had met for breakfast, exchanged a few words in a tense discussion...then we were back in bed together like teenagers who had just discovered their bodies.

Everything felt *so right*, though. I felt compelled to tiptoe up behind Lucas and wrap my arms around him and nibble at his neck. Wanting to feel him jump in pleasant surprise and chuckle sexily as my mouth worked at his flesh. I wanted to make him feel even more enamored with me and my body. Wanted him to know that I loved his body. The desire to make him realize our bodies were made for each other's made my gut flutter.

That is batshit crazy.

You've known him for DAYS.

You've worked with some of the hottest, sexiest, most desirable men on the planet and never felt this way.

Maybe you thought they'd be good to see naked or have sex with, sure.

But you didn't daydream about them.

God, Lucas sets my skin on fire.

Stop it, brain!

Goddamnit!

"What do vegetarians make for breakfast at home?" I asked the most neutral question that came to mind.

Lucas looked up from the stove as I tiptoed into the kitchen and slid onto one of the barstools across from him at the counter. The guy made cooking look absolutely luscious.

"Well, I don't have any meat, but I thought I'd make eggs and hash browns?" He gave a slight shrug, his eyes on mine for a moment, then my arms, then back to my eyes. "I want to do bad things with you."

"You know this is ridiculous, right?"

"Yes." The word was a satisfied exhalation.

"Okay."

"Don't ruin it."

"I won't."

"Good." He nodded, then his smile reappeared. "I'm going to make you eggs and hash browns. And you're going to love it. And you'll have a big cup of coffee. After thirty minutes, it's back into the water, Rob."

"Is that what we're going to call it?" I couldn't help but laugh.

"It's the nicest thing I could think of to call it."

"It wasn't a bad effort."

"Scale of one to ten." He gave me an upward nod. "What do you think?"

"Of...*the water?*"

He made a humming noise in response.

"I don't want to answer that."

"Why not?" He chuckled nervously.

"Not because it's bad." I rolled my eyes playfully. "I don't want to talk about how much I like having—*the water*—with you. I'm not in love with you, Lucas."

"Yet."

"Maybe."

"How many more times before you are?"

"What if I never am?" I asked gently, bashfully, shamefully. "What if that never happens?"

Good Lord, this was a bluntly honest conversation.

"I love you."

"No," I replied. "You don't."

"Pretty close if not." He shrugged as he threw some butter in the skillet. "Enamored at the very least. You're absolutely addictive. Delightful. Obsession-worthy."

"Any more adjectives you want to throw in there?"

"I'll think of some, I'm sure."

"I've never been in love, Lucas."

God's honest truth. Another one fell out of my mouth. And I hadn't been aware that it was going to happen. Again.

"What does that have to do with me?"

"Nothing." I chewed at my lip. "And everything. What if I'm not capable of falling in love? With anyone? Even someone like you."

"What is someone like me like, Rob?" He teased as he threw some chopped onion into the skillet and nudged it around, not even bothering to watch what he was doing.

"Intoxicating," I said, then frowned. "I don't like how honest you make me. I don't do...this."

"You don't tell the truth?"

"I don't tell it so quickly and easily." I replied. "Especially to some guy I barely know."

"How's it feel?" He asked. "Telling me the truth just because you want to? Does it feel like—"

"It feels like I'm not in control." I stopped him. "Like I'm thinking with my dick instead of my head."

"Maybe it's a different organ." He jabbed the spatula at my chest with a chuckle. "Maybe it's not your dick—though that is very nice."

"Make my hash browns." I swatted the spatula away with a laugh. "But I need to know something. I really, really need to know something very badly."

"Ask away."

"Will you hate me if this is all it ever is with us?" I shifted on the stool uncomfortably, feeling very exposed. "What if...it...never happens and it's just what we have now? Will you not want to even be my friend?"

Lucas frowned down at the skillet as he added shredded potatoes from a bag. He nudged things around for a few moments with the spatula as I sat there and stewed in my own juices, thoughts racing through my head. If I was scared to have him disappear from my life, didn't that mean *something*? Sure, it was ridiculous to think that losing someone I had known less than two weeks would devastate me. Ridiculous that someone I had known for such a small amount of time and really didn't know all that well played such an important role in my life. But I enjoyed my time with Lucas. Even before the sex. Lucas was...he was my only friend.

Is that why you don't want to fall in love?

Might lose him?

Shut. Up. Brain.

"We'll still be friends," Lucas responded lowly, his eyes staying on the skillet. "Even if you don't ever love me the way I want you to."

"How do you know?"

He shrugged bitterly. "I just do."

"Okay."

"So, can we please not talk about this anymore?" He looked up at me with an easy smile. "Because I want you to eat and fuck me some more."

"*Fuck you?*" I scrunched up my face.

"Did that not sound right?" He asked way too innocently. "I mean, we weren't *making love*, so *fucking* is the right term, right?"

I glared at him.

"You don't love me, Rob." He smiled sweetly. "You couldn't' possibly have made love to me. You fucked me."

He wasn't angry or even upset. He was taunting. It was so enticing. I wanted to have my way with him again. And again. And...well, lots of times.

"Maybe I'm not in love with you." I relented. "And maybe that's a 'not yet' situation. I'll give you that. But I'm not *fucking* you either. I do care about you. Okay?"

"Okay." He shrugged nonchalantly, flipping potatoes.

"I mean that."

"Okay."

"Say 'okay' one more time," I growled playfully. "I dare you."

"What are you going to do?" He sucked at his teeth. "Fuck me some more?"

"You're asking for it."

"If you play your cards right, I might beg for it." He grinned so evilly that my stomach didn't care about food suddenly.

"I hate you." I laughed.

"No." Lucas moved so that he could lean over the counter and kissed me on the lips quickly. "You definitely don't hate me. Do you want salsa for your hash browns?"

I reached up to run my fingers through his hair.

"Vegetarians have something against cheese on potatoes?"

"Absolutely not." He kissed me again.

Then he was rooting around in the fridge and I was admiring his backside as he was bent over, fulfilling another one of my wishes.

Chapter 6

Other than the living room, the house was dark when I parked outside of Oma's house that night. Lucas and I had had sex in so many ways so many times I couldn't even remember how many times that was. My head was swimming with the thoughts still swirling through my brain, and the smells and tastes still clouding my limbic system. The smile on my face was genuine and not a single bit innocent as I got out of the car. Locking the car with my key fob, I climbed the stairs to the front porch and unlocked the front door, letting myself inside as quietly as possible. It wasn't even ten o'clock yet, and Oma had the living room lights on, so it was unlikely that she was in bed. However, I didn't want a fight to start first thing. I was too happy, too satisfied, to want to bring my mood down before bed.

"And just where the hell have you been?" Oma was waggling her head at me from the easy chair in the living room as soon as the door was shut.

I sighed to myself and flipped the lock.

"I've texted you fifty times today if it was a million." She seethed but didn't rise to her feet.

The T.V. was on but was muted, and it cast an eerie blue tint through the room and on her face.

"At Lucas' fucking again." I shrugged.

Oma frowned at me.

"Shocker." I raised my eyebrows.

"Surprising, maybe. Not shocking."

I held my hands out in a "there ya' have it" type of way.

"You two playin' house now, are ya'?"

"Playing something." I shrugged.

"Mm."

"What does that mean?"

"It doesn't mean nothing you little shit." She waggled her head. "Just a response so you knew I heard ya'."

"Charming."

"Oh, fuck you, Mister High-and-Mighty."

"Goodnight, Oma." I turned toward the stairs.

"Get back in here right now, you little asshole." She boomed.

That voice was the "Oma voice" from my childhood. I knew better than to ignore it. Not out of fear, but out of respect. It was Oma's way of letting me know that the conversation wasn't over. That she was my elder. That she, whether I liked it or not, was my grandmother, I was in her home, and I had to give her respect. I walked back into the living room and stood before her, arms crossing over my chest.

"Now, you look here." She looked up me, trying to be angry, but her expression was too soft. "I don't care that you and Lucas are seeing each other—"

"How kind."

"—but, ya' little asshole, you could at least return a text, so I know you're not lying in a goddamn ditch somewhere."

"Or eaten by a wolf on the way home to grandma's house?" I waggled my head this time.

"Or that." She snapped.

"Got it," I said evenly. "I apologize. I will text you next time."

"Good."

We stared at each other as the T.V. cast its blue haze around the room, casting eerie, late-night shadows even with the lamps on.

"You wanna watch some T.V. with me?"

"What are you watching?"

Oma looked at me for a second, then seemed to realize what was being asked of her. She glanced at the T.V. nervously and reached for the remote. She wasn't quick enough. I spun to the T.V. and saw my face on the screen. It was one of the action movies I had made two years previously. Something about terrorists trying to blow up the Statue of Liberty. It was complete crap. I had made twenty-million-dollars. Before taxes. It was a fair wage. The movie made twenty-times that much domestically and even more internationally.

"I'm going to assume you just wanted to see my face." I snorted as I turned to look at her again. "Because that isn't one of mine that I would have picked. Unless you're trying to go to sleep."

"Oh, fuck you."

I laughed.

Oma laughed with me.

"It was just on cable." She relented. "And, well, I was flipping and there you were."

I shuffled over and sat down, perching on the ottoman her feet were on, looking at the T.V.

"God." I shook my head. "I have lost a lot of weight, huh?"

"Look like a damn twig."

I nodded.

"You know they made me work out every day with a trainer for three months before I made this shit?" I gestured at the T.V. "They put me on this high protein, low-fat diet. I've never eaten so much salmon, chicken, and eggs in my life. I couldn't drink alcohol or have sugar. And I worked out for three hours a day every day for the entire three months."

"Well, you can tell." I sensed her waving at the T.V. from behind me. "That shirtless scene was something to behold, Robbie. Looked like you were carved outta stone."

I laughed.

"I felt like shit the whole shoot." I sighed. "I was so unhappy."

"Well, I'd be unhappy too if I felt like my neck was eating my head."

The laughter poured from my throat.

"Who's that wrestler fella?" She asked over my laughter, a few chuckles escaping her throat. "That guy who is always telling people they can't see him?"

"I was not as built as John Cena." I gestured at the T.V.

"Your neck was bigger than his, that's all's I'm saying." She cracked. "Looked like you could drink peanut butter straight from the jar."

"Yeah." I cackled. "It was ridiculous. It's the buffest I've ever been."

"Then why did you feel like shit?"

"I was so unhappy." I sighed. "I was lonely and miserable and bored and stressed and...I guess everything not good, Oma."

"Well, ya' can't tell." Her voice was soft. "Guess that's a testament to your acting skills, huh?"

"I suppose." I stared at my ex-body doing my possibly ex-job on the small screen in front of us. "I wasn't acting. I was posing."

"What's that mean?"

"I was doing what was expected of me."

"Isn't that what actors do?"

"I've never won any acting awards because I can't act, Oma." I sighed. "I just know how to be anyone but myself. That's what I do when I'm making movies or T.V. shows. Or I'm playing 'rock star' on stage. I'm anyone but Robert Wagner."

"Robert the youngest."

"Do you think mom and dad would be proud?" I didn't dare look back at her.

"Oh, Robbie." She sighed.

"It doesn't matter." I swatted my hand in the air over my shoulder. "That's stupid."

"Your father—even though he was a dumbass—was smart enough to be proud of you. And your mother—even though she was a triflin' tramp—was proud of you, too. As long as they were around, anyway."

I laughed. "You always do that."

"Do what?"

"Talk crap about them."

"Doesn't it make it easier to not miss them?"

"No." I sighed. "It makes me wish I could argue with you about your opinion of them. But I can't. Because I don't know them. I have nothing I can use to argue. Other than my feelings. And I don't even know if those are real."

"Robbie." I felt her scoot forward in the chair and then her hand was petting my hair. "Them feelings is real. We can have dumbass, triflin', trampy parents and still love 'em. I'm mean as a Pitbull with his balls in a vice, and you still love me, right? And you ran off without a word ten years ago, and I still love you. Facts don't factor into feelings."

"I suppose." I sat there and let her pat my hair.

It was a kindness, a loving gesture, that we hadn't shared since before I was in junior high. Though it wasn't exactly comfortable, seeing that we hadn't shared affection like that in so long, it was still comforting.

"Maybe you don't know who are 'cause you didn't stick around long enough to find out?"

I just listened.

"Ya' ran off when you was still figuring all that out and, well, that part of your growing up got stopped right at sixteen." She said gently, her fingers running through my hair. "Can't really keep figuring out who you're going to grow up to be if you're running all over God's damn creation and pretending to be anything but yourself, can you?"

"I guess not."

"And, well," she sighed, obviously having some internal struggle, "even if you are a goddamn shithead, I'm proud of you. And that's just gonna have to be enough, isn't it?"

That settled on the air between us. I let it linger for a few moments as I felt her fingers sliding through my hair.

"What's Lucas, Oma?"

"What do you mean?"

"You know what I mean," I said at a whisper. "Andrew's a werewolf. You're...Oma. What's Lucas?"

Her fingers froze in my hair for just a split second then continued their path downwards before starting up near the crown of my head again.

"I don't know, Robbie."

"But...he's *something*, isn't he?"

"I would say so. Yes."

"Have you been trying to figure him out like you were trying to figure out Andrew before the other night?"

Oma's hand left my head. When it didn't return, I shifted on the ottoman so that I could turn and look at her. She looked troubled, but not concerned. Deep in a difficult thought was the only way to describe it.

"He knows things."

"What's that mean?"

"He saw you coming, Robbie."

"What does *that* mean?"

"I think he knew you was coming back to Point Worth."

"So...are you saying he's psychic or clairvoyant, or..."

She chewed at her lip.

"He knew I was destined to be the love of his life?" It came out teasing, but it made my throat clench. "He knew I'd return and the two of us would fall in love or something? Because I'm not so sure he was one-hundred-percent right about that."

"It had nothing to do with the two of you." She shook her head.

Frowning was the only way I could respond to that.

"He just...said some things that let me know he was expecting you back." She said, her voice measured. "Not that he knew when, of course. He just knew it would happen."

My teeth chewed at my lip for a moment as the thoughts formed in my head. The right questions moving to the forefront.

"When he saw me that first day we met?" I asked. "He wasn't shy, was he? He was concerned."

"Might have been."

"Concerned about what?"

"How the hell am I supposed to know?" She threw her hands up suddenly. "Talk to him about it. Y'all are so close now."

I sighed.

"And we were having such a nice moment."

I rose to my feet and started to walk away.

"Oh, don't be so damn sensitive." Oma huffed from behind me. "How the hell am I supposed to tell you things I don't know? Someone needs to slap you upside the head."

Turning to Oma, I said: "And someone needs to drop a house on your sister."

Oma's eyes turned to slits. I let that hang in the air.

"Goodnight, Oma."
And then I went upstairs to bed.

Chapter 7

The house was on fire.
That's what woke me up.
Flames.
Smoke.
Heat.
Oma and I needed to get out.

Except, when I sat up in bed, my chest heaving, my heart thumping, sweat beading on my forehead, everything was dark and quiet. I heard something scurry away. I glanced in the direction of the sound but saw only a shadow slip through the bathroom doorway. Clutching my hand to my chest, I smelled the air, listened for the crackling of a fire. Within the space of heartbeats, it became apparent that I had only had a bad dream. With mild trepidation, I pushed the covers off and slid my legs over the side of the bed.

My feet touched the icy floorboards, but I didn't even wince; instead, I focused all of my energy on other senses. What could I see and smell? The room was pitch black, and I could smell nothing—other than how Oma's house normally smelled. Wood and cinnamon and a faint undercurrent of the lavender cleaner she liked to use when performing the task. I pushed off of the bed gently and stood at my bedside, my head turning slowly, my nose and eyes laser-focused on their assigned tasks.

Nothing.

I was alone, and everything was quiet and still. There was no fire. I had merely been dreaming. Nothing more.

Just as I was going to sit back down and slide my legs back under the covers, staving off the frostbite that was threatening my toes, I saw the light. A sickly, eerie green light slithering under the door. Something between a glowstick and radiation beamed from under the door and cast the room in an eerie, putrid glow. My eyes grew wide as I stared at the crack under the door where the green light was coming from. As I watched, the light grew brighter by the second as my eyes grew wider at the sight. Within ten seconds, the room was filled with the color of the light, and I had to reach up to shield my eyes in an effort to keep from being blinded.

When I opened my eyes, the sun was rising in the sky and was filling the bedroom with light. I was comfy, cozy, snug as a bug in a rug in bed. I had only been dreaming. I sighed to myself as I pulled the covers more tightly around myself. Spring was looming in the background, but upper Ohio had decided that one more really severe cold snap was necessary before winter would give up the ghost. I shivered slightly, tempted to roll up like a burrito and attempt to go back to sleep. As I rolled to my side in the bed, my phone on the bedside table caught my eye.

Text Lucas and tell him to come over and crawl into bed with you. He'll make things warmer.

Shaking my head clear of the thought, I gathered up my nerve and got out of bed, wincing and hopping from foot to foot on the icy floorboards. After making the bed and generally straightening up my room, my cell phone stayed in my mind. I wanted to text Lucas. But that wasn't the right move at this point in our...*relationship?* I needed to establish boundaries in whatever it was we had going on. Coming off as overly eager or ready to try and fall in love, or hell, even have an actual relationship wasn't the best move. Well, maybe Lucas would have welcomed such a move, but I wasn't so sure that it was something that I could commit to at the moment.

But you want to, dumbass.

Okay. So, yeah. I wanted to—for once in my life—jump headfirst into something besides my career and not care what consequences might come my way. Especially with a romantic relationship. As I went into the bathroom and went about my morning routine of getting ready for the day, I couldn't help but consider my past relationships. I'd literally only dated two guys in my life—and I wouldn't have categorized either as all that serious. Nice, sure. Serious? No. One was at the beginning of my rise to stardom in the industry, so we all know why that didn't work out. The other one was a few years before I had come back to Point Worth looking for silence and, love, I guess. It just fizzled out.

Passion is essential in a relationship. I hadn't been passionate about either. The sex had been mediocre, maybe because I hadn't been that into the guys I'd been dating, but I hadn't been that interested in sex, truth be told. When I was a teenager, I was pretty sure that I was gay. I had even told Oma that I was gay. I found guys attractive—even wanted to express my appreciation for them physically from time to time. But when I went to Hollywood, and my career started, I found myself less and less interested in guys and sex.

Guys had always been more sexually attractive to me. I had never found a single woman attractive in a sexual way. Beautiful? Hell to the yes. Did I ever want to have sex with a woman? Fuck no. Nothing against women, but guys were my thing. Or, so I'd thought. When I got to Hollywood, started working hard, traveling, becoming *Jacob Michaels*, I suddenly wasn't so sure about anything. No. I wasn't questioning if maybe I was straight or bisexual or something...but perhaps asexual? Sometimes the very thought of having sex completely turned me off.

Some of the hottest guys in Hollywood—sexual orientation is always debatable when it comes to a lot of rich and famous people—had tried to get in my pants. It was always a struggle to not throw up a little in my mouth each time. The whole concept of someone wanting to date me or have sex with me because they saw me as this "gorgeous movie-slash-rock star" made the bile rise from my gut and settle at the back of my throat.

That was it, though, wasn't it? After a long time, I began to realize that I was definitely gay and not asexual. I just couldn't get sexually aroused by people who wanted to have sex with me because I was *Jacob Michaels*. I wanted someone to want to be with me and have lots of sex with me because I was *Rob Wagner*. Or *Robert Wagner* or, hell, even *Robbie Wagner*. I wanted someone to want me for me—not all the glitz and glam and things they believed because PR and the media had told them to believe them.

Lucas likes Rob Wagner. A lot.

Was that why I was so drawn to Lucas? He had been attracted to me when I was just Rob Wagner in high school? He didn't care that I had become a celebrity and famous the world over? He didn't care that I had played concerts and performed on the most revered and storied stages all over the world. He didn't care how much I got paid for a single movie. He didn't care if I had won any awards or knew so-and-so or what kind of car I drove or if I had a big, fancy house. The first question he had asked about my acting career was whether I had gotten to see the Northern Lights while shooting in Finland.

Just invite him over. Nothing has to happen. Nothing has to be assumed.

When I walked down the stairs, my room was in perfect order, and I was wearing long underwear, jeans, a t-shirt, sweater, wool socks, and hiking boots. A suitable outfit for a cold Ohio day. Oma would be pleased. In fact, when I walked into the kitchen, hugging my arms around myself, she was at the stove, dressed similarly to myself and making breakfast.

"It's twenty-damn-degrees in here, Oma," I grumbled as I went to the fridge for orange juice, then remembering I hadn't picked any up as promised the day before, frowned as I opened the door.

Orange juice. Oma never failed.

"I turned the damn furnace up ya' titbag." She grumbled back with a smile on her face. "I didn't have it cranked that high because I thought they was lying about this cold front coming in. It's damn near the end of March, and it feels like the beginning of January."

"You aren't lying." I agreed as I poured a glass of juice.

"Now they're saying we might get one last snow tonight before all is said and done." She shook her head. "Can you believe that shit?"

"Well...yes." I laughed as I put the orange juice back in the fridge and poured myself a cup of coffee. "And you shouldn't have a problem believing it either. You've lived here over a hundred years."

"Sit your ass down at the table before I kick it." She jabbed a gravy covered spoon at the table with a laugh.

Following her command with a chuckle, I sat down and sipped at my juice, then switched to my coffee. I needed something warm and comforting on such a cold day.

"You know how to start a fire?"

"Are you thinking of arson, or..."

"In a damn fireplace, ya' idiot." She rolled her eyes even though she was amused. "I was gonna put a fire in the fireplace after breakfast, but if you know how, I'll put you to use for once."

"I can probably figure it out." I shrugged. "It's been a minute since I've used a real fireplace."

"What's that mean?"

"Most the ones I've used were gas and turned on with a button or the turning of a knob."

She waggled her head.

"Now, I've made some biscuits, good ole sausage gravy, bacon..."

"Oh, good. Heart attacks all around."

"...and you're gonna eat all I give ya'." She snapped. "You're still too damn skinny, and I don't want you to look like this come Spring. I wanna be able to take you out in public without getting looks. At least, not for the wrong reasons. Also, if you're going to be tumbling in the sheets with Lucas all the time, you need the extra calories."

"Ew."

"Just tellin' it like it is." She shrugged. "Besides, the food will help warm ya' up. Nothing like a thousand calories at breakfast to raise your body temp."

"I suppose." I chewed at my lip.

Oma looked over at me with a frown.

"What?"

"Just come out with it, ya' asshole." She waved the spoon in the air. "I can tell you got something on your mind. So just say it or ask it or whatever you need to do."

I sighed and took a sip of my coffee. How was it that Oma could always tell from one thing I said or one look I gave that I had something weighing on my mind? I guess she wouldn't have been my grandmother if she couldn't read my behavior.

"It's nothing really," I replied. "I just woke up and thought about texting Lucas to invite him over for...I don't know. No reason. Just to invite him over."

"So?"

"That just seemed a little odd is all."

"Robbie," Oma chuckled, "once you've seen a man's balls, it's hard to call anything else awkward, right?"

"Oma."

"Well, hell. If you can see *that*, you can surely invite a man over for breakfast or coffee or just for a nice leisurely chat. Not much is more awkward than a ballsack, Robbie."

"From the owner of a ballsack, and also your grandson, I ask that you never utter the word 'ballsack' again in your life."

"All's I'm sayin'." She shrugged. "I mean, you two are...*friendly*...he's my friend, he can be invited over without it being weird. I don't want to see you two going after it, though. My heart couldn't take that."

"Oh, you volunteer at the LGBTQ center, but two guys smoochin' is too scandalous for ya'?" I teased.

"It's not because it's two guys, ya' dipshit. I'm just old and ain't gettin' none myself. I don't need to be reminded that those years are behind me now. Your Oma is dried up like a prune."

"Ew."

She waggled her head.

"You could always give Mr. Barkley a call." I grinned evilly.

"You could always turn that chair over and sit down on it." She growled.

I laughed.

"Maybe I'll invite him over, then." I shrugged as Oma grabbed a plate from the countertop beside her and started making a plate. "He could have lunch with us or something."

"Text him for God's sake." She rolled her eyes as she ladled gravy on top of biscuits. "If he ain't busy and gets over here soon enough he can have some biscuits and gravy."

"Is there sausage or anything in it?"

Oma looked up suddenly with a smile.

"What?"

"Considering his dietary needs, huh?"

"Oh, fuck you."

"That spells out caring."

"I can spell other things if you like," I grumbled.

Rolling my eyes, I reached into my pocket and found nothing. I had left my cell phone upstairs in my room on the bedside table. For a split second, it pained me to not be able to text Lucas and tell him to come have breakfast with us. That thought immediately coming to mind just pissed me off. I was starting to get pissed that my mind would immediately think such a thing so quickly and easily about someone whom I was just...well, I didn't know what to call the thing Lucas and I had going on, did I? Were we "seeing each other"? "Dating?" "Fucking?"

No. That last one was crude, and we definitely cared about each other as people, so "fucking" was reductive. Maybe "friends with benefits" or something? We were definitely becoming friends, if not already friends, and there were definitely benefits to that, so maybe that was the best term. Then again, I wasn't sure how I truly felt about Lucas. I knew that my body was drawn to his. In fact, every time he popped into my head, I felt aroused. Not physically of course, but I felt that fluttering in my lower abdomen that was a signal that my body was pleased by the thought.

Also, I was irritated with myself that I was being such a whiny little bitch about the whole thing. Maybe I didn't vocalize every thought I had, but I definitely had some inner turmoil over the entire situation. That was high school type behavior, and I just didn't want to admit that my brain possessed such abilities. Then I'd remember that werewolves were real and Oma was a witch and wonder why I was wasting valuable thoughts on something like whether or not Lucas and I had a real relationship forming.

Andrew. That was a problem.

Why hadn't I thought about Andrew and that whole situation more since it had happened? No, plainly said, why wasn't I spending more mental energy on dissecting the new knowledge that Andrew was a werewolf? That werewolves were real? Why hadn't I thought about going to see Andrew during the light of day to speak to him? I needed to tell him what I thought of him. I needed to ask questions. Ultimately, I needed to let him know that next time I would ask Lucas—or whoever was driving— to back up and hit him again. I needed to have a confrontation with the guy I had been on a date with who had tried to force himself on me and then, I guess, murder and eat me.

What do werewolves do when they attack someone?

Do they just attack the person?

Do they turn them into werewolves?
Do they eat their victims?
What...exactly...had been Andrew's intent in werewolf form?
Did he even know?

"Oh, for Christ's sake, just use my phone." Oma rolled her eyes as she slapped the plate of food down in front of me. "Text the boy and get him over here so you can stop frothing at the mouth."

"That's not what I was thinking about, Oma."

My grandmother picked up her phone and tapped on it for a second then set it back down in the same spot.

"There." She put her hands on her hips. "I texted him for God's sake."

"Okay." I shrugged and picked up my fork. "But that wasn't what I was thinking about, either way."

I looked down at my plate and saw that it was covered entirely in biscuits that had been split in half, drowning in creamy gravy and slices of bacon to the side. Looking at all of the heavy food made my stomach churn a little. Partly in a good way at the thought of Oma's delicious cooking, but also from thinking about how my gut would feel an hour after eating it.

"What the hell were you stuck in your head about then?" She asked as she walked over to the stove to make her own plate. "You sure have been thoughtful lately. Wish you'd been like that a decade ago when you packed up and ran off in the middle of the goddamn night."

"Oma..."

"Oh, just tell me what you was thinking then." She stopped me. Oma's phone dinged. I reached over and looked at the screen.

I'd love to come have breakfast. Be there shortly. That's what Lucas had responded. He hadn't even asked what we were serving.

"I think I need to talk to Andrew, right?" I responded as I set Oma's phone down. "Lucas is coming over."

"Good," Oma said. "And why the fuck do you think you need to talk to Andrew? He done messed up. That ain't got nothin' to do with you."

Oma filled her plate and came to sit down across from me, immediately grabbing up her fork and cutting off a piece of gravy-laden biscuit. She stuffed the bite in her mouth with a satisfied, nearly orgasmic expression.

"Because I have questions."

"What questions could you have?"

I thought about that.

"You're just curious 'cause you found out he's a damn werewolf." She shook her head before stuffing another bite in her mouth. "Let that go, Robbie. It ain't gonna lead nowhere but trouble. He tried to attack you, Lucas stopped him, he learnt his lesson, it's over."

Andrew had said some things over dinner that I had questions about that were starting to come back to me. It was like experiencing a trauma—which I guess nearly getting attacked by a werewolf *was* trauma—and my mind had shoved details out of my mind in the moment. Like temporary amnesia. Now I was starting to remember the details of our conversation over dinner at the Indian restaurant. Things like how he thought I smelled. He had said I was "intoxicating." Lucas had recently said the same thing.

What does Oma smell like?

I smelled the air, pretending that I was clearing my nose. Everything just smelled like food. I couldn't pick out a particular scent on the air that could be attributed to Oma's person.

"I just want to know why he acted the way he acted." I shrugged, trying to play it all off.

"Because he's a damn werewolf, that's why!" She jabbed her fork at me. "You mind my advice and just push that out of your mind, Robbie. Andrew is no good, and you don't need to put up with his shit."

"This from the woman who described him as a 'sweet boy' just last week." I rolled my eyes playfully. "I mean, he seemed pretty contrite the other morning."

"Nothing like a fist to the face to do that." She snorted.

We ate in silence for several minutes before I heard the front door open and close. Oma looked up expectantly as my stomach fluttered again. I took a big bite of biscuit as footsteps sounded in the main part of the house. My mouth being full when Lucas entered would keep him from trying to kiss me in greeting in front of Oma, and I wouldn't be expected to have anything intelligent to say upon his approach. Lucas entered the kitchen, looking just as delectable as he had the past few times we had...*hung out?*...and it made me wish that we had met at his house instead of him coming to Oma's.

"Well, good morning there, Lucas." Oma cocked an eyebrow at him and then shot a glance at me.

Stuff it, old lady. I thought to myself.

"Good morning, Mrs. Wagner," Lucas responded. "Thanks for inviting me over."

"You're welcome, Lucas." Oma started to stand.

"I can fix my own plate." He gestured for her to sit. "Good morning, Rob."

I smiled around the mouthful, gesturing at my bulging cheeks with a finger, before giving him a nod. He winked back at me. Oma grinned at that and went back to eating her food. As Lucas prepared himself a plate of biscuits and gravy, I ate my food slowly and thoughtfully, trying to keep my mouth full but not eat quickly or appear anxious. Oma kept glancing at me out of the corner of her eye as she ate her food.

"Guess Jackson didn't need you in the store today?" Oma asked. "How's that old bastard doing?"

I frowned at my grandmother.

"Grandpa's fine," Lucas responded from his spot at the stove. "Thanks for asking. He said to tell you to wait at least three days after tomorrow before you start digging or planting. You should be good to plant then, though."

"Tell him thank you so much for his damn expert advice." She waggled her head. "Always tellin' me how to run my damn garden like I ain't been doin' it since he was learning to play with his pud."

"Oma!" I gasped around the mouthful of food.

Lucas just chuckled.

"Well, he's an asshole." Oma waved me off with her fork before popping the last bite of her food in her mouth. "If he ain't tellin' me what to do one way he's tellin' me another. Hope he falls in the shower with them rickety ole legs of his."

Lucas guffawed as he slid the ladle back into the gravy skillet and headed over to the table. Oma raised from her seat, her plate suddenly empty.

"You boys finish your breakfast." She said suddenly. "I'm gonna go in here and get a fire going and get my feet toasted up."

Lucas sat down in the chair next to me at the table, giving me a wink as Oma rinsed her plate off and deposited it in the sink. A few seconds later, Lucas and I were alone at the table, and I didn't have the first clue what to say to him. Which was odd, all things considered. We'd had meals together. Done...other things together. Surely, I could figure out something normal to say?

"Did you sleep well?"

That wasn't it.

"Did I sleep well?" Lucas grinned goofily at me as he stuffed a bite of food into his mouth. "Is that what you wanted to say?"

"No."

"Did you want to ask me if I slept well without you in bed next to me?"

I couldn't help but blush slightly and grin as I looked down at my plate.

"I think that's what you wanted to ask me."

Crossing my arms, I placed them on the table in front of my plate, ignoring my food as I swallowed the last bite I had taken.

"What if I did?"

"Then the answer is that I slept okay, but I would have slept *better* if you had stayed over and slept with me." He shrugged. "But that's moot now."

"Who would be the big spoon if we slept together?" I leaned in conspiratorially. "You or me?"

"We could take turns."

"I want first watch."

"I'd let you have anything you wanted."

"*Anything?*" I leaned in closer.

Who was this person I was becoming? I was mooning over some guy at Oma's table, acting like a lovesick teenager who was experiencing their first sexual relationship.

Who really gives a shit?

"Yes." Lucas looked me in the eyes as he shoved another bite into his mouth. "Anything, Rob."

I considered this.

"Why?"

"Because something inside of me tells me that I want to do it."

"What if that thing inside of you told you to burn down an orphanage?" I was only partly teasing. "Would you follow that instinct, too?"

"Apples to oranges." He shook his head with a smile. "Wanting to do anything to make someone happy and burning orphans alive are not even on the same spectrum, Rob."

"Okay." I nodded. "What if I wanted you to burn down the orphanage?"

"Are you the type of person to ask that of me?"

"No."

"Then it's moot."

"But would you?" I egged him on playfully.

"Okay, okay." He relented. "Maybe I wouldn't do absolutely *anything* you wanted. But pretty close."

I smiled.

"You enjoy this banter, don't you?" He grumbled.

"I enjoy messing with you, yes."

"Eat your food." He gestured at my plate. "Mrs. Wagner will get mad if you don't eat everything on your plate."

"You and Oma get awfully concerned with what's going into my body," I replied. "For obvious different reasons."

"Do you want to go to dinner and a movie yet?"

I looked over at Lucas as he chewed his bite of food and popped a bite into my mouth as well.

"Or are you enjoying the chase too much to commit to the next step?" He asked. "Because I think the reason you haven't accepted an invitation to an actual date is that you enjoy the foreplay too much."

My first instinct was to laugh at this statement, primarily because of how it was phrased and the words Lucas had chosen to convey his thought. However, what he said actually gave me pause. Was I avoiding moving forward with Lucas because we'd no longer be in a "honeymoon" phase and the magic would be lost that is there in the early days of a relationship? Isn't the first part of any relationship the best? Where two people aren't quite in a relationship, but they're getting used to each other as people, exploring each other's bodies, experimenting sexually, enjoying the pleasures each body can provide...flirting with danger?

"No." I shook my head, suddenly no longer playful. "Of course not, Lucas."

"Then...are you going to go have dinner and see a movie with me?"

"Fine." I shrugged. "If it's that important to you."

"It is."

"Fine." I shoved another bite of food into my mouth.

"Fine." He smiled.

So, that was done. The deal was made. A gauntlet had been thrown down. And I had accepted the challenge.

"Do you think I should talk to Andrew?"

"About what?" He turned up his nose.

"The other night? How he's a werewolf and all? I don't know."

"Why would you need to talk to him about that? He's learned his lesson. You won't have to worry about him anymore."

"Well, he'll see Oma at the center whenever she goes, so he'll still be around," I explained. "I mean, maybe I should at least try to get on an even keel, ya' know? So that there's no animosity or tension there."

"Why would there be?" He asked. "Just steer clear of each other and problem solved, ya' know?"

Looking over at Lucas, the redness in his cheeks, I couldn't help but grin at the thought that suddenly popped into my brain.

"Are you jealous that I'll talk to a guy I went on an actual date with?"

"Of course not." Lucas shoved another bite in his mouth. "That's just ridiculous, Rob."

"Okay."

"It's not what was on my mind, okay?" Lucas grumbled, looking down at his plate as he ate.

I popped my last bite into my mouth and sat back in my chair and stared at him with a grin.

"You're jealous." I cooed.

"I am not jealous."

"Say it enough times you might believe it."

"Why would I be jealous?" He looked up at me. "I mean, do I need to be jealous of some vile hairball?"

I laughed as Lucas realized what he had said and how it showed his hand.

"I'm pretty sure you are, although you don't need to be."

"Why do you want to talk to him, then?" Lucas asked firmly. "Why do you need to talk to him?"

"He said that my *scent* was intoxicating." I shrugged. "Maybe not those exact words, but...and then you said the same thing the other day. I want to know what that means. At least, what it means to him. Does it mean something different to a werewolf than it does to just some guy who finds me sexually attractive?"

Lucas frowned at me.

"That's all."

"You're going to go talk to some guy you went on a date with to ask him about your...smell?"

"No." I rolled my eyes. "Just why he said it. Why he said it that way. Why did you say that?"

Lucas didn't answer me, but he continued to eat.

"Because I have some suspicions."

"Just let it go, Rob." Lucas glanced up at me, then back at his plate, his mouth full of food. "Don't get into this."

"You said that a lot of people in Point Worth have a monkey in their family tree at some branch or another." I continued, ignoring his plea. "So, maybe I have a monkey in my tree? I mean, you said Oma is a wit—"

Lucas looked up at me with pleading eyes, so I stopped myself.

"Is that it?"

He glanced at the kitchen doorway.

"Don't." He whispered lowly. "Please."

My head tilted to the side of its own volition as I looked at him.

"Mrs. Wagner will be upset with me, Rob." He said simply. "Please don't start this right now."

"I'm not—start—anything, Lucas." I chewed at my lip. "I just want to know what's going on."

"Later." He said firmly. "Please?"

Why was Lucas so bothered with talking about this stuff in general, but even more so when it was possible that Oma would find out about it? It was almost as if he was scared of her.

"Fine." I sat back. "But we will talk about this."

He nodded. "Thank you."

I was exhausted with everyone in Point Worth being so damn weird. But, when I looked at Lucas, I didn't really care. When it came to Lucas, I had my qualms about him—but all of them were my own hang-ups about dating and guys in general. That didn't keep me from wanting to do very naughty things with him every time I saw him. I didn't even care if he was *weird*, too. However, he would have to be pretty severely weird to curb my appetite for him. Of course, I didn't want him to know that.

Examining the situation, I knew that I would eventually have to know what, if anything, was weird about Lucas. I would have to face that—just like I had to face the fact that I went on a date with a werewolf and Oma was a witch—which was still hard to swallow. Because, if I did get my mind and my body into alignment, and that meant I wanted to make Lucas a permanent fixture in my life, it couldn't be built on lies or even half-truths.

"Should we just spend this lovely, sunny day enjoying each other's company?" I suggested.

Lucas chuckled. He pointed to the window over the kitchen sink that looked out over the backyard of Oma's property. I turned my head and saw the snowflakes immediately.

"Well, shit." I sighed. "I knew I was being facetious, but still."

Lucas popped the last bite of his food into his mouth and grinned at me.

"Wanna go help Mrs. Wagner build her fire?"

"Absolutely." I smiled at him.

First, though, we did the dishes from breakfast. Then we joined Oma in the living room. She already had a roaring fire going and had her feet kicked up on the coffee table, roasting her feet, which were covered in big, fluffy, mismatched socks, a broad smile on her face as she lounged on the sofa. She just smiled at us as we took the other end of the couch. Lucas and I kicked our shoes off and kicked our feet up on the coffee table, setting our feet to roast as well. At first, things were odd, particularly when Lucas laid his head against my shoulder and wrapped his arms around me. Finally, though, we all settled into easy conversation and reminiscing.

Maybe things didn't have to be weird all the time.

Chapter 8

"*Jesus,*" I whispered. "*When they call for snow they aren't fucking around are they?*"

I didn't know why I was whispering. Of course, it was night time, and we were outside and something about being in the dark underneath the moon in the stillness of the night made me feel that I had to be quiet. Reverent, even. Lucas and I had decided, once the snow stopped, that we would take a walk down to the lake. The snow had started right as we were finishing up breakfast and had continued on at a fairly steady rate until just after dark. Oma guesstimated that we had gotten a foot of snow, and when the six o'clock news had come on, with the three of us still huddled in front of the fireplace, she was confirmed to be almost on the nose with her guess.

All day long, the three of us had taken turns adding logs to the fire, stoking it, keeping it blazing warm, as we sat and shared stories and just talked. When lunch came, Lucas and I had gone in and made all of us lunch to take into the living room. At dinner time, Oma had gone in and heated up leftovers from the day before and brought it into the living room as well. All we had really needed was for it to be Christmas time so we could have a lighted tree and it would all have felt as cozy as possible. But, since it was late March, we had to settle for things such as they were.

Oma had regaled us with tales about growing up in Ohio—when the *winters were really awful.* Obviously, Lucas and I knew nothing of a really harsh winter. Lucas told us about going to NYU and studying in the city. After much prodding, I shared stories of acting gigs and performances and maybe a few insider pieces of gossip about certain celebrities. I didn't have much else to share, story-wise, that the two wouldn't have known already, so celebrity insider stories it was.

Once the snow stopped, shortly after dinnertime, Lucas asked if I wanted to take a walk down to the lake. Of course, I didn't want to walk down to the lake in the freezing cold in nearly knee-high snow. However, I really wanted to put my mouth on Lucas'—and I really didn't want to do that in front of Oma. Even though she would have thought nothing of it, I just didn't feel right doing it. No one wants to kiss the guy they're involved with while their nearly seventy-year-old grandmother looks on.

"When it rains it pours," Lucas responded in a normal tone.

Obviously, he wasn't intimidated by the haunting silence of the snowy night around us.

"You're using that wrong," I replied in a sing-song voice as we trudged through the snow.

Suddenly, Lucas' fingers were sliding between mine, and he was holding my hand in his as we made our way through the woods towards the lake. I looked down at our intertwined fingers, wondering if I should take issue with this or not. I decided that it was a perfectly acceptable thing for two guys in a situation like ours to do and just went with it. We trudged through the snow and the woods for a few moments, our hands keeping each other's warm for several long minutes before I couldn't take it any longer. I turned and pulled Lucas into me and lowered my head to shove my mouth over his.

Lucas' mouth responded to mine as he pushed the length of his body into mine and his hands went up to my face. His fingers were ice cold, but I didn't care. I just wanted to kiss him, and I would have taken that at any temperature I could have gotten it. The whole situation was so surreal for me. I never wanted to kiss and have someone be so close to me as much as I wanted that of Lucas. Running my fingers through the silky waves of his hair, I let myself melt into him as we kissed in the snow and the dark quiet of the woods and let myself just be in that moment, not worrying about what it all meant. If it had been warmer, and there wasn't snow on the ground, I know I would have pushed him to the ground and done other things. Instead, I found myself finally pulling away from him, a smile growing easily on my face.

"That wasn't half bad." Lucas smiled up at me.

He slid his arms inside of my coat and around my middle, his body pressing up against mine. It was if he was trying to crawl inside of me, to join the warmth of our two bodies. To become one being. Under the darkness of the inky, early Spring sky, within the cocoon of quiet that the snow-laden woods provided, we held each other and dreamed of a life that hadn't quite developed in our imaginations yet.

"Do we talk now?" I asked softly, obviously having to ruin the moment.

"About what?"

"Don't do that, Lucas."

He sighed and gently pulled away from me, his arms sliding from around my middle hesitantly.

"What do you want to know, Rob?" He looked at up at me with a placid expression.

"What are you?" I asked the first question that came to mind.

"I already answered that."

"Not fully you didn't."

"Why do you say that?"

"*You saw me coming*," I whispered. "That's what Oma told me."

"What does that mean?"

I just stared at him. He sighed again.

"Okay." He shrugged. "So, maybe I have premonitions. So what?"

"I don't know." I shrugged back. "That's not normal though, right?"

"I guess not."

"How long have you had premonitions?"

"Long as I can remember." He replied evenly. "But I didn't recognize what they were, or that I was even having them until I was in college. So I'm still adjusting to it myself."

"What does that make you?" I asked. "Clairvoyant? Psychic?"

"Why does it make me anything?" His brow furrowed. "You seem awfully concerned with the arbitrary characteristics of everyone around you."

"I wouldn't call that arbitrary but a very big part of who you are and what makes you who you are, Lucas."

"What are you?" He actually snapped.

My neck jerked back.

"Sorry." He looked down.

"I don't know who I am," I said evenly. "I couldn't even begin to tell you who I am, Lucas."

With that, I turned and continued the journey towards the lake. After a few moments, I heard the shuffle of other footsteps through the loose snow, and I knew Lucas was following. We didn't speak again on our journey through the snowy woods, but once we exited the other side, the shore less than ten yards away, Lucas came to stand beside me.

"Do you ever feel like Robert Wagner and Jacob Michaels are not all you are?" Lucas asked gently. "But you can't put your finger on it?"

My head turned of its own accord to look at him.

"Yes." I shrugged. "And no."

"Explain. Please."

"I'm Robert Wagner. Robert the youngest." I said. "My parents are gone. My Oma raised me. I grew up in a household with weird shadows and weird happenings. I ran away at sixteen to join the circus, essentially. When I don't know who I am—it's a developmental thing. A personality quirk. I don't know how I feel about relationships and love and sex and whether or not I know the people nearest and dearest to me as well as I thought. I don't know what I want to do with the rest of my life. I don't wonder if there's a hyphen at the end of 'human.' That's what I mean."

Lucas looked out towards the lake, thoughtfulness and concerned etched on his face. Maybe he was starting to get a hint at the mess of a guy he was trying to build a relationship with. Was he concerned that he was making a bad choice in trying to make our relationship into something more—or was he just concerned for me? I didn't know. And I wasn't sure that I wanted to know. Nothing would have upset me more at that moment than knowing that he had changed his mind about caring about me in that way. I didn't want my own hang-ups to make Lucas run away. I wasn't sure that I cared for Lucas in the same way that he said he cared for me—but I didn't want to lose him either. Which was crazy. I barely knew him, after all.

"Why can't you just accept that you know who I am, Rob?" He asked softly, his face still turned towards the lake. "I mean, why does it matter if I have some weird premonitions? I don't turn hairy at the full moon. I'm not going to try and attack you. I don't have any ulterior motives. I'm not some creature of the night. I just have some quirks. Just like everyone else."

"Because I haven't lived with this knowledge for as long as you have, Lucas," I replied. "I didn't know werewolves were real. I didn't know that Oma was a witch. I didn't know that one day I would say those words so casually and not mumble incoherently at the craziness of it all. I'm trying to adjust. And the only way I can do that is by asking questions. Trying to quantify and validate all of this new information."

"I suppose so." He sighed.

"Staying with me...I mean, doing *this*...is not going to be easy for me." I shivered at the feeling of being nearly knee deep in snow as we stood there. "Or for you. You seem to have knowledge about a world I've only just discovered. It's normal for you. It's not for me. It's going to be confusing and weird for a while. If that bothers you..."

"What is that?"

"I just meant that—"

"No." He interjected. "*That.*"

Looking over at Lucas I saw, even in the low light that the moon provided, that he was staring off west along the shore of the lake. With a frown, I followed his gaze, looking for whatever it was that he was seeing. Finally, my eyes landed upon a figure standing out all alone on the shore, on one of the higher overlooks over the lake. It was about twenty yards away from our position on the shore. All alone and cast in shadow, the figure seemed to be doing a weird jig of some kind or thrashing uncontrollably. My eyes grew wide as I watched the gangly figure doing its bizarre dance on the overlook, wondering who in the hell, besides Lucas and me, would be out by the lake on such a cold, snowy night.

"*What is he...*"

"*I don't know,*" Lucas whispered back.

We both watched with morbid fascination as the figure "danced" a few moments longer, then seemed to lose its footing. As if in slow motion, the figure tumbled off of the overlook and plunged towards the water as Lucas and I both yelled out. The figure hit the icy water with a resounding splash and then Lucas and I were running through the snow towards the overlook. Snow pulled at our feet, but we ran as fast as we could until we were standing on the overlook, looking down at the dark, glassy water—which was surely just shy a few degrees from freezing over.

My breath was caught in my throat as we gazed down at the water in horror, wondering who had fallen into the water and if they could swim. The water surface was still rippling, but there was no sign of the person who had literally danced off the side of the overlook. Lucas and I glanced at each other before looking back down at the water below us. We both gasped as a shockingly white arm breached the surface of the water, flailing, as though begging for help.

Without thinking twice, I stripped off my coat and pulled my shirt off over my head. Lucas grabbed at me, trying to stop me.

"Rob, don't be ridiculous!" He pleaded. "There's no way that you won't freeze to death before you can save them."

"Are you kidding?" I scoffed as I started to unbutton my pants. "I can't just let them drown in front of us."

Lucas sputtered for a retort as I stripped off my pants and kicked off my shoes, standing there in only my boxer briefs and socks. Without another thought, I leaped from the overlook towards the water below. When I hit the water, my whole body screamed out in pain and terror. The water was so cold it was suffocating. Every breath I had left my body, and my instinct was to kick towards the surface, to get out of the water any way that I could. Pins and needles stabbed every inch of my body. It took several moments before I could clear my mind of all instinct to merely survive and I began groping for whoever had fallen into the water.

Seconds ticked by as the iciness of the water stabbed and pricked at my body and made me feel like I'd never be warm or breath again. Finally, after several painful seconds, I felt my hand wrap around another smaller hand. I grasped it tightly and pulled it towards me. Then my other hand had ahold of a forearm, then a bicep, and I was pulling the person towards me. I couldn't see under the water, even though my eyes were open—I think—but I pulled the body into me and kicked towards the surface. This was a child, not a man or woman. The body I was holding against me was too small to be an adult.

When I breached the surface of the water, I gasped for air, my lungs burning as I did my best to keep mine and the other person's head above water. I glanced at the person I was holding and could only make out a mop of hair in the darkness. Lucas was screaming from twenty feet above, still up on the overlook. Glancing around in the water, looking for the nearest shore where I could drag the person out, I began to swim, pulling the person with me.

The other person wasn't moving, at least as far as I could tell, as I pulled us towards the shore. When I finally got into shallow enough water, I grabbed the person under the arms and drug them towards the shore through the shallow water. My body felt numb and so cold that even laying down in a lit fireplace wouldn't thaw me out. Shivering violently, I pulled the person up onto shore and laid them down on their back. I fell to my knees beside the person and looked down. My whole body froze, but differently, when I saw what I was staring at on the ground before me.

This person was me. The way I looked as a kid.

Then the person's eyes shot open. I jumped back, falling to my ass in the dirt and sand covered shore. The person jumped to his feet, laughed maniacally, and dashed towards the woods. I began babbling to myself as I watched the person disappear into the woods, wondering if I was going crazy, but also terrified that I wasn't. Then I heard Lucas shouting in the distance, getting closer. I looked up, my face twisted in horror, icy water dripping off of me, threatening to freeze at any moment against my skin.

Lucas was suddenly next to me, squatting down and pulled me up. He pulled me into his body, and I was babbling yet incredibly grateful for the warmth that his body provided against mine. As he began shoving me back into my clothes, haranguing me with questions, I got myself under control and managed to stop babbling.

"What the hell were you thinking, Rob!?!?" He admonished me. "You could have fucking died!"

"I duh-don't nuh-know." My teeth chattered as he pulled my shirt on over my head and began pulling my coat on around me. "I juh-just duh-did it."

"Where is he?"

"Huh-who?" I chattered.

"The guy you pulled out of the water!"

"He ruh-ran into t-the wuh-woods." I pointed a brittle finger towards the woods near the shore.

Lucas frowned and looked off towards the woods. Then he was putting my shoes on me as I did my best to balance and keep on my feet. I looked off towards the woods, wondering how crazy I could be. Was I going crazy bit by bit the longer I stayed in Point Worth? How was it possible that I had pulled my younger self out of the lake? The nearly frozen lake.

"How the hell did he just run away?" Lucas grumbled as he stood up and pulled me into him again, trying to share his body warmth.

"It was me," I said.

"What?"

"Th-the puh-person I pulled out of the lake." I shivered violently against Lucas. "It was me. As a kid."

I felt Lucas' body tense against mine.

"What are you talking about, Rob?" He pulled back just enough to look me in the eyes as he held me.

I shivered and shrugged. Then a maniacal cackle sounded from the edge of the woods. Lucas and I both turned our heads violently towards the woods. A pale face peeked out from the tree line, finding the light of the moon perfectly. I gasped at the sight of my younger face staring out at me, an evil grin on his face. Lucas jumped against me at the sight of the face. We held onto each other as the younger me laughed maniacally again, its face twisting up grotesquely, then disappeared into the woods once again.

"*What the fuck...*"

"I don't know," I whispered in fear.

"What is going on, Rob?" Lucas gasped. "Where is...it...going?"

I stared off toward the woods for the space of a few breaths, then my eyes grew wide in terror. It was heading in the direction of Oma's.

"Come on!" I shouted as I grabbed Lucas' hand and drug him towards the woods.

Chapter 9

Lucas was one step behind me as I slid across the threshold of the front door to Oma's house. We had seen the footprints in the snow leading up to the house. The two of us had left the house through the back door to walk down to the lake, so unless Oma had left the house through the front door, only one person could have made the prints. When I burst through the front door, I nearly slipped and fell. Water spotted the floorboards beneath me, which made my head whip back and forth, looking for Oma and signs of an intruder at the same time. Lucas looked down and saw the water on the floor as well and started shouting for Oma.

"*Mrs. Wagner!*" Lucas bellowed from behind me.

I moved from the foyer and into the living room, frantically looking for *younger me* while I searched for Oma.

"*Mrs. Wagner!*" Lucas bellowed again.

The fireplace was still lit and keeping the living room comfy-cozy, the lights were still on, and everything seemed as we had left it before we went on our walk. My heart was racing, and I was trying to catch my breath after trudging through the snow in the cold on our run back to the house.

"I'm in here!" Oma hollered from the kitchen.

Lucas and I glanced at each other, relieved to hear her. We both dashed into the kitchen like madmen.

"What are you two bellowing about?" She grumbled from her spot by the stove.

The tea kettle was on the stove, and she was waiting for her water to come to a boil.

"Is someone here?" I asked quickly.

"Besides you two assholes?" She put her hands on her hips as she frowned at me. "Why?"

"Did you hear someone come in the front door?" Lucas asked quickly. "Before us, I mean."

Oma frowned at us a moment longer, looking back and forth between the two of us before finally answering.

"Well, no." She shrugged. "But I've been in here making my tea. What the hell is going on with you two idiots? Robbie, why do you look like you had a bucket of water dumped on ya'?"

"Long story," I mumbled as I moved to the back door, checking to make sure it was locked.

Oma watched me for a moment, then turned to Lucas, searching for answers to what was wrong with the two of us.

"You two are acting like you're drunk," She snorted. "What's going on with you two?"

"Rob jumped in the lake to—"

"You jumped in the lake?!" Oma bellowed. "It's a degree shy of icing over ya' fucking idiot!"

"Someone fell in," I said, then gave a quick shiver, realizing I was probably going to catch pneumonia if I didn't warm up quick.

"Well, where the hell are they?" Oma was wide-eyed.

Lucas and I looked at each other.

"Well?" Oma demanded.

"We don't know." Lucas sighed.

"I pulled them out of the lake, and then they got up and ran into the woods." I shivered again. "We thought they might be headed this way."

Oma rolled her eyes.

"That has got to be the dumbest goddamn story I've ever heard." She waggled her head. "If ya' fell in the lake, ya' fell in the lake. You ain't gotta make up some cock-and-bull story about it."

"I'm not—"

"Lucas," Oma stopped me, "run upstairs and get this idiot some fresh clothes. Something warm. And get a damn blanket for him."

"Mrs. Wagner, I—"

"Do as I said." She waved him off. "He's gonna catch his death of cold."

Lucas frowned and turned as if to head off to do what Oma had instructed. Quickly, I leaned into Lucas and whispered in his ear:

"Look out for...that thing."

Lucas gave me a nod, then a quick kiss on the lips, ignoring that we were in Oma's presence, and headed off towards the living room. Oma banged around for a minute, then walked over and ushered me towards the living room. I let her nudge me into the living room in front of the fireplace, then at her instruction removed my shoes and socks. I stripped off my coat and handed it over.

"What the hell are you doing falling into the lake?" Oma shook her head as she draped my coat over her forearm. "Ain't got the sense God gave a goose."

"I didn't fall," I grumbled. "I jumped in to save this person who was on the overlook."

She rolled her eyes. "Who the fuck is going to be out there this time of night, on a night like this no less, except you two morons?"

"I swear to you, Oma," I stated firmly. "There was somebody out there on the overlook dancing around like a weirdo, then they fell in the lake, and I jumped in without thinking and..."

"And what?" She asked after a beat.

"Nothing." I shook my head. "Nothing, ya' mean old woman. I nearly died trying to save someone's life, and all you do is call me a moron."

"Well—who the hell else would do such a thing?" She replied firmly. "I don't give a shit if some idiot wants to fall in the lake acting a fool. They shoulda know'd better anyway."

There was no point in arguing with Oma. Either she didn't believe my story, or she didn't care if it was true or not. Obviously, it was more important that I didn't die than it was to save someone who fell in the lake. *Someone who looked like a young teen me.* I shivered at the thought, which made Oma frown more deeply.

"Lucas!" She bellowed toward the ceiling.

Footsteps sounded on the stairs, and Lucas hurried in to join us in the living room. He had a towel and a pile of clothes in his arms.

"I got clothes," Lucas announced before glancing at me as though trying to convey something.

"Well, you get him out of those clothes and into fresh ones while I go put these shoes out back." She instructed. "You've seen him naked so it shouldn't be too embarrassing for you to help him."

Lucas blushed at that, but Oma ignored it and headed towards the kitchen. Once she was out of sight, Lucas chunked the clothes on the couch, and his fingers went to my shirt. I held my arms up, and he slid my shirt off of me. I stopped him from reaching for my pants and unbuttoned and pulled them off myself. Then I stripped off my underwear. Lucas' eyes shone hungrily in the light cast from the fireplace. I gave him an admonishing look, which made him grin sheepishly. He handed me the towel as he gathered up my wet clothes and set them by the fire. I dried off quickly and pulled on the boxer briefs he had brought for me. Then I pulled on the sweatpants and sweater he had gathered. Lucas took the towel from me and reached up to dry my hair better as we stood in front of the fire.

"*There was no one up there, Rob.*" He whispered softly.

"*Any wet footprints?*" I asked lowly.

"*Nothing.*" He shook his head.

I sighed to myself as he finished drying my hair. Then he was pulling my face down to his, and his lips were pressing softly against mine. He kissed me gently for several moments before pulling back, his eyes staying closed as he pulled me into a hug.

"*I'm not crazy,*" I said though I wasn't sure if I was talking to Lucas or reminding myself.

"*I know you're not,*" Lucas replied. "*I saw it, too.*"

I swallowed hard, grateful that he believed me. It made me care for Lucas more than I wanted.

"*What is going on?*"

"*I don't know, babe.*" He whispered.

That word coming out of his mouth made me pull back, though not to get away from him, but just in an effort to look him in the eyes.

"Don't call me that."

"Why not?" He asked.

"Because it felt right."

He didn't respond, but his lips found mine again. I ran my fingers through his hair as my mouth responded to his.

"Okay, you love birds," Oma announced grandly as she sauntered into the living room. "Break it up long enough for me to get them clothes."

Lucas cleared his throat and smiled up at me, and I relented and gave him a grin back.

"Jeeeezus." Oma whistled. "Nearly getting' hypothermia sure can work you two up, can't it?"

"Oma."

"Fine." She waggled her head as she scooped up my clothes and snatched the towel from Lucas. "You two sit down and get warmed up. I'm going to throw this shit in the washing machine. These aren't them fancy clothes that need to go to the dry cleaner's are they?"

I just looked at her.

Oma rolled her eyes and headed off towards the kitchen.

"Lucas, you may as well stay the night," Oma said. "Barkley surely ain't gonna open the store tomorrow, and I'm sure school's gonna be called off. And there ain't no point in you drivin' home in this shit."

Lucas looked over at her.

"You can take the couch if you're too uncomfortable sleepin' in Rob's room with me being around." She teased.

"Go away Oma." I said blandly, my eyes not leaving Lucas'.

"This is my house."

"Go to another part of it, then."

Oma muttered something under her breath but did as I requested. Lucas' fingers went to my hair as he stared into my eyes. He raked my hair into place as I looked down into his eyes.

"I'm not crazy."

"Who are you trying to convince, Rob?" He asked softly.

"I'm not crazy," I repeated.

"You're not crazy." He nodded.

"How is...is that even possible?" I exhaled. "What we saw?"

Lucas shook his head, but his fingers stayed in my hair as his other hand went to my chest.

"I don't know...babe."

"Stop it."

My hips pushed into him of their own accord.

"*Babe.*" He whispered playfully.

"I'm warning you." I moved my mouth down to his, my lips brushing against his. "You don't want to keep doing that. Especially if you'll be shy about sharing a bed at Oma's house."

"I want to go to bed now." Lucas sighed against my mouth.

We stared into each other's eyes as I felt something familiar poking against my hip. Lucas moved his hips slightly against me with a wicked smile. I wanted to drag Lucas to bed like a caveman and do very disrespectful things with him, but a sudden thought kept me from it.

"I feel nervous about leaving Oma alone," I said.

"There's no one here."

"I believe you," I said, shivering again at the thought of the younger me I had dragged out of the lake.

Remembering the maniacal look on the younger me's face and the matching laughter made my blood run colder than the icy lake could have ever managed. Why had there been someone who looked like me dancing on the overlook who then decided to plunge into the icy water of Lake Erie? Most importantly, why the hell was there anybody who looked like me roaming around on the property around Oma's house?

Something was going on at Oma's house. Something was going on with me. Something was going on in Point Worth. There were a lot of things going on with a lot of people and places all around. Within the span of two weeks, I'd started acting like a hormonal teenager, I'd found out werewolves were a real thing, Lucas had claimed Oma was a witch, and I'd run into an early teens version of myself. To my credit, though I wasn't feeling completely stable, I was handling everything admirably. At least, in my opinion.

As Lucas pulled me into a hug, to hold me close against his body, I turned my head to look at the fire. I wanted to know how my life had gotten from point A to point B. Sure, my life had never been normal. Being raised by Oma, running away at sixteen-years-old to be a movie and rock star, none of that was exactly normal. But, how did it all devolve into finding out that there was some world hidden just out of view for my entire life? Lucas' mouth was on my neck, kissing and nibbling at me gently.

"Okay, you two lovebirds!" Oma announced as she stomped in from the kitchen with her mug of tea. "Either cut it the hell out or go up to bed. I ain't lookin' at you two actin' like two teenagers any longer."

I did my best to smile as Lucas pulled back with a chuckle.

"*Let's make sure everything is locked up first,*" I whispered to him. He nodded.

"Okay, Oma." I sighed. "We're going to lock up for you and head up to bed."

She scoffed.

"I ain't had to keep my doors locked until you showed up." She waggled her head as she flopped down on the couch and kicked her feet up. "You've been living out in California too damn long."

"Just humor me, then," I said.

She waggled her head but didn't argue as she brought her tea to her lips.

Lucas and I made sure all the doors and windows were locked, then we said "goodnight" to Oma before we headed upstairs. It was nearly midnight when the two of us actually went to sleep, naked and content in each other's arms. As I drifted off, I felt something curl up in bed with us—but it wasn't by my feet, it was next to my legs. Obviously, whatever it was didn't know Lucas well enough to sleep by his feet. But it was perfectly fine sleeping in the crook behind my knees as I laid on my side and held Lucas.

Chapter 10

Green light was peeking out from under the door again when I awoke in the middle of the night. Whatever had been sleeping in the crook of my legs had jumped off of the bed and scurried away towards the bathroom as I stirred. The light under the door cast the room in a sickly green glow as I slid my arms from around Lucas. He didn't stir as I rolled and let my legs dangle off of the bed. I stared at the light coming from under the door. Nothing happened. Suddenly, I was filled with a wave of anger fueled by curiosity and exhaustion.

I stood from the bed, still naked, and grabbed my underwear from the floor. Slipping them on, I pulled on my sweatpants and sweater next. Lucas continued to sleep as I crept from the bedside to the bedroom door. After a short moment to take a breath, I reached out and turned the knob. I pulled the door inwards, expecting to be blinded by the light. However, the hallway was just cast in the eerie glow of the light as the bedroom had been. I stepped out of the bedroom and looked down the hallway. Wherever the light was coming from was drifting down the hallway and going down the stairs.

When I glanced back into the bedroom, Lucas was still curled up in bed, sleeping peacefully, so I left the room, closing the door gently behind myself. I crept down the hallway carefully, so as to not wake Lucas or Oma, and followed the light as it traveled downstairs. Step by step, I kept just within the shadows the light cast and followed it. Then down the stairs. When I got to the base of the stairs, the light was in the kitchen, casting it in an eerie glow as well. So, I followed it there. When I got to the kitchen, my feet making tapping noises against the linoleum, the light was behind the cellar door, peeking out in a slant across the kitchen floor.

My hand went to the cellar door, and I turned that knob as well, deciding to follow this light wherever I had to in order to find out what the hell was going on. When I opened the cellar door, the light was moving down the rickety stairs, further into the cellar. I took a deep breath and started to descend the stairs. Step, by frightening step, I descended the old wooden steps into the cellar, not knowing what might be waiting for me. However, when I got to the base of the stairs, the room seemed to be filled with the eerie green light. I couldn't remember the last time I had been in the cellar of Oma's house, in fact, when I really thought about it, I wasn't sure that I had ever actually been in the cellar.

That was weird, considering the fact that I had grown up in Oma's house from a very young age. I held a hand to my eyes, to shield them from the bright green light. Finally, after several moments, the light seemed to dull, and I pulled my hand back so that I could see what was happening. Before me, in the center of the cellar, was what could only be described as a stone well, roughly as far across as I was tall. The green light was emanating from somewhere deep within, seemingly disappearing deeper and deeper into the well, getting duller and duller as it descended.

Cautiously, I tiptoed over to the well, knowing that this was probably the worst decision I could have made in the situation. However, I tiptoed over to the edge of the stone well and braced my hands against the side, which came up to my waist. Against my better judgment, I leaned forward to look down into the well, needing to know where the light was coming from. When I looked down into the deep recesses of the well, all I could see was the green light flooding everything below so that I could not tell how deep the well actually was. I stared down into that green light for a very long time. Then it began to move upwards again, getting closer and closer until I was being blinded once again. I stepped back from the well, bringing my hand up to shield my eyes again as the cellar filled with the bright light.

I awoke to the feeling of Lucas' lips against mine. When I opened my eyes, Lucas' face was next to mine, his eyes were closed as he pressed his lips against mine, and the room was warm with late morning light. The light was that type of snow-reflected white that let one know, without getting out of bed, that it had snowed the night before. Of course, it had snowed all day long, so I wasn't sure if the light would have been enough of a clue if I hadn't already seen the snow for myself with my own eyes.

The sudden change from being in the cellar in Oma's house to lying in bed next to Lucas, being kissed awake gave me a mental jolt. I did my best to smile and return the kiss, but my brain was asking "*what the actual fuck?*" very loudly. Lucas finally opened his eyes and smiled at me as he pulled away from the kiss. He looked so content and warm in bed with me that it made my stomach flutter again. And, yet again, I was left with the nagging feeling that things felt too good—too right. That I was being too nonchalant about all of the odd happenings in my life recently.

"Good morning, babe." He said softly.

"Good morning."

"It snowed more last night."

I gave an involuntary shiver with a laugh as he pulled me into his body.

"Another few inches, I think." He spoke against my mouth. "I got up to use the bathroom in the middle of the night, and it was really coming down. But there's nothing wrong with getting a few inches."

"More than a few." I winked.

He chuckled throatily.

"You were having some dreams, huh?"

"What do you mean?" I asked.

"You were kicking a little in your sleep."

"I'm sorry."

"It was cute." He somehow managed a shrug as he laid there. "Made me want to wake you up and give you a real reason to thrash around."

I chuckled.

"Does Mrs. Wagner have a pet?" He asked with a half-frown half-smile.

"What?"

"I thought there was a dog or cat in bed with us last night." He chuckled.

I am not crazy.

Later in the day, just after lunch, Lucas bid adieu to Oma and me—after way too many kisses at the front door. I watched him drive carefully through the snow, away from the house, as I stood on the front porch. It was still below freezing outside, but the sun glinting off the snow was nearly blinding. As soon as Lucas' truck was out of sight, I gladly went back into the warm house, rubbing my hands together to knock away the chill. Oma was in the kitchen, banging away, preparing for an elaborate, stick-to-your-ribs meal seeing as there wasn't much else could be done, considering the weather.

Doing my best to not march, I went straight to the kitchen. Now that Oma and I were alone, we were going to have a real conversation about her and her house. When I entered the kitchen, she was pulling some potatoes, carrots, and what looked like fennel out to prep for the meal. A whole chicken was sitting in the sink. An evening roast. I wouldn't let myself get distracted by the thought of good food.

"Okay, Oma." I crossed my arms, standing ten feet away from her. "Tell me what the hell is in this house."

"What are you babbling about again?"

"You have a pet or...something...in this house," I demanded. "What is it?"

"I ain't got no damn pets." She placed the vegetables on the counter and turned to me with her fists on her hips.

"Something has been crawling into bed with me at night." She started to interject, but I continued quickly in order to cut her off. "And it crawled into bed with Lucas and me last night, and he noticed it, too. So, I'm not fucking crazy. That excuse isn't going to fly."

"You need to take—"

"I haven't taken my pills in days." I actually stomped my foot. "If this were withdrawal, I'd be over it by now. And that doesn't explain Lucas noticing it either!"

"I don't have any pets, I tell ya'." She snapped back.

"Then. What. Is. It?"

Oma started to say something, stopped herself, and raised her head haughtily.

"I don't know what in the world you're talkin' about, Robbie." She sniffed. "If somethin's crawlin' into your bed at night, it ain't no damn pet of mine."

I glared at her.

"Fine," I said. "Game on, old woman."

I turned to leave the kitchen.

"What the hell does that mean?" She grumbled.

"If you aren't going to tell me—I'm not going to tell you," I replied over my shoulder. "Elphaba."

"Who?"

"Read a book." I snapped as I walked away.

Chapter 11

That night, after a tense and relatively quiet dinner of roast chicken and vegetables and homemade rolls, I helped Oma wash up after dinner. I read a book, curled up in front of the fire, while she watched some television show about baking. When it was a reasonable time to go to bed, I announced my intentions and went upstairs. I changed into my pajamas and sat on the edge of the bed, waiting for signs that Oma had done the same. What seemed to be days later, I heard her come upstairs and enter her bedroom. After several minutes, the house was quiet and as dark as a tomb. So, I crawled under the covers and laid down in bed. I closed my eyes, making sure that I didn't drift off as I waited.

The quiet of the house was eerie as I laid there in the dark, waiting for whatever it was that crawled into bed with me to arrive. My heart was thundering within my chest as I laid there, listening to that infinite silence in the dark, wondering if I was making a bad decision. What if Oma was keeping secrets for a really good reason? What if the thing crawling into bed with me at night had nothing to do with Oma? Carrying out the plan I had in mind might have ramifications I couldn't understand. However, just as I had worked myself into a near fit of anxiety, I felt the...*thing*...crawling up onto the bed. I braced myself, still pretending to be asleep as I felt it crawl along the bed, coming to rest behind my legs again.

Almost like a dog, it seemed to turn in place a few times before settling down, curling up behind my legs. If I knew that Oma had a cat or dog, this wouldn't be that big of a deal—it would almost be sweet. But Oma denied having any pets, I hadn't seen any pets, and my door was closed. How the hell would a pet have gotten into the room anyway? This thing in bed with me didn't belong there, and I had to know what was going on. I held my breath for the space of a few breaths, then I leaped into action. I tossed the covers off and over the creature by my legs.

Squirming and thrashing, the creature created a whirlwind of movement under the comforter, as I leaped on top of it, wrapping it up in the blanket like a hobo's kerchief. Whatever was inside the blanket was strong, but it was small, and even though I wasn't at my ideal weight, it was no match for me. I laid on top of it as it wore itself out.

"Gotcha ya' little shit," I whispered down at the bundle of covers.

It thrashed once more within the blanket as I twisted the covers up and pulled it off of the bed. The thing weighed no more than a medium sized dog, but as it thrashed again in my arms, I almost dropped it. Wrapping my arms tightly around the bundle, I went to the bedroom door and threw it open. I marched down the hall, thrashing bundle of blankets in my arms, to Oma's bedroom. I didn't even knock, I just kicked the door open and entered.

Oma sat up in bed and flipped the light on in a panic.

"What the fuck are you doing?" Oma gasped, sitting up quickly in bed.

"Don't have any pets, do ya'?" I sneered at her and marched over to the foot of her bed.

I threw the bundle down on the bed.

"What the hell is that?" She growled.

"Oh, you know what it is, lady." I snapped. "And we're about to see it together."

I grabbed an edge of the blanket bundle and whipped it open. Oma gasped as a tiny body tumbled out of the bundle and landed on top of her legs over the covers. My eyes grew wide as I looked down at the little humanoid creature. It looked almost like a House Elf out of *Harry Potter*, except it was wearing normal clothes. *Small clothes that maybe belonged to a German peasant,* but normal clothes. And its skin more of a human shade. For all intents and purposes, I was looking at a miniature human...but not.

"Goddamnit, Ernst!" Oma bellowed.

The creature popped to its feet, its head whipping back and forth rapidly between myself and Oma.

"*Ernst?*" I was incredulous.

The creature on the bed looked scandalized. And a little pissed.

"Why'd you keep going into his damn room!" Oma swatted at the creature, which it barely avoided. "I told you to stay out of there not two hours ago!"

"*I'm sawwy Mrs. Wagner.*" The creature spoke in a high-pitched voice. "*His room be the warmest, 'tis all.*"

"That's no reason to keep fucking around, is it?" She growled at the little humanoid. "I oughta..."

The creature ducked down, expecting another swat.

"Excuse me?!" I bellowed. "What the fuck is going on? What is that thing?"

The creature turned its head violently towards me with a snarl.

"Oh. I'm sorry." I growled down at the creature. "You don't mind curling up next to my ass to sleep without permission, but *you're* offended?"

What the hell was I even doing? I was talking to this...*thing*...like it was the most natural thing in the world. Oma swatted at, I guess, "Ernst" again, which he managed to mostly avoid, though her fingers slapped against him.

"*I didn't mean no harm, Mrs. Wagner,*" Ernst responded, prancing about the bed anxiously. "*It's cold 'tis all.*"

"That ain't no excuse, Ernst." Oma threw the covers off of herself. "If you'd just fucking listen to me then—"

"Both of you shut the hell up!" I screeched, my face turning red. "I want some damn answers about what is going on in this house and what that...*thing*...is and why it's been curling up to me nearly every night since I got here!"

Oma and Ernst both looked up at me, parts chastened and parts irritated.

"This is Ernst," Oma said simply.

Ernst waved a tiny hand impishly.

"I figured that part out, ya' crazy old bat!"

"Ya' don' have much fat on ya', sir." Ernst peeped. *"Ya' put off alotta heat. 'Tis warm in your bed."*

"Um, thanks?" I snorted down at the creature.

"You're welcome." He nodded, a stern look on his face. *"But if ya' wrap me up in a blanket one more time—"*

I swung my arm back as though to strike him.

Ernst flinched. Yeah. He was a real badass.

"Well, don't hit him for God's sake!" Oma screeched.

"What. Is. That. Thing?" I asked again.

"He's Ernst." Oma reiterated.

When the expression on my face let both Oma and Ernst know that this was not an adequate, nor acceptable response, Oma continued.

"He's a Kobold." Oma waved her hand in the air as though that explained everything about Ernst.

Ernst bowed an introduction.

I just stared at them.

They stared back.

"Oh, fuck me silly." I slapped a hand to my forehead. "That explains everything, doesn't it? Ernst is a Kobold. How stupid of me to worry about him crawling up my ass each night to sleep."

"I didn't crawl up his ass," Ernst spoke to Oma out of the corner of his mouth.

I frowned at him.

"A Kobold is a household spirit." Oma rolled her eyes. "They do chores and mostly keep to themselves."

"In the shadows?" I barked.

"Well, fine, yes." Oma shrugged.

"We also are expert pranksters." Ernst peeped proudly.

I glared down at him.

"He won't bother you none sleepin' in your bed," Oma added.

I was apoplectic.

"Stay out of my room, Ernest!" I jabbed a finger at him.

Green light flashed through the room, and Ernst was propelled off of the bed and through the doorway into Oma's bathroom. Oma gasped and then the room filled with silence. After a heartbeat, I heard scurrying in the bathroom, and Ernst was gone. I turned my head to look at Oma. She was looking at me in horror as my hand hung in the air, my finger pointed at the bed. What had just happened?

"What the fuck did you do that for?!?" Oma screeched.

"What did I do?" I asked her with wide eyes.

"You just blasted Ernst's ass into the bathroom is what you did, ya' idjit!"

"What?"

"Put your damn finger down, Robbie!" She commanded.

Slowly, I lowered my hand. Had that green light come from...me? The same color of green light that had awoken me two nights in a row? Or had I been dreaming? I wasn't so sure of anything.

"You don't treat the Kobolds like that, damnit!"

"Kobolds?" I leaned in angrily. "Ernst isn't the only critter in this damn house?"

"He's not a *critter*, and no, there's a few others."

"How many?" I demanded.

Oma chewed at her lip.

"How many, damnit?"

"Well, there's Ernst, Hans, Oskar, Felix, and Lena." She counted off on her fingers. "So, five, I guess."

"There are five of those things wandering around here?" I jabbed my finger at the bathroom.

"Put your damn finger down, Robbie!" Oma screeched again.

I put my finger down, but I glared at her.

"You're crazy." I admonished her. "And you've been trying to make me feel like I'm the crazy one."

"I'm not crazy!"

"You've got miniature people...*things*...*Kobolds*...living in your house, creeping around, curling up to sleep with me, doing laundry, making beds, scrubbing floors..."

"Oh." Oma blushed. "Figure that out did ya'?"

"I always wondered how some crazy old woman kept this house so damn sparkling clean. I guess Ernst gave me the answer!"

"I suppose..."

"Is that what they all look like?"

"Sometimes." She admitted hesitantly. "They can look like other things sometimes."

"Pranksters?" I barked at her. "Was it one of those things I pulled out of the lake last night?"

Oma chewed at her lip.

"Well?!"

"Well, I don't know!" She bellowed back, though the blush deepened in her cheeks. "I mean, it's possible."

"Possible—or probable?"

She was chewing at her damn lip again.

"Great, Oma." I lost all of my fight and deflated. "One of your little household Gremlins nearly caused me to die of hypothermia, and tra-la-la must be a Tuesday, right?"

"That's not—"

"You keep those things out of my goddamn room while I'm here," I demanded. "Which won't be much damn longer! I'm sick of this shit, old woman!"

I turned.

"Where the hell are you going?"

"Back to my room," I growled. "Tomorrow...I don't know. I'm sick of your lies and bullshit."

Spinning back around, I glared at her.

"How could you, Oma?" I demanded of her. "You let me stay here, thinking I'm crazy, that I was seeing things...who would do that to their grandson? That's fucking sick."

"Would you have believed me if I told you that werewolves and Kobolds and...other things...are real, Robbie?" She snapped. "Or would that have made me some crazy old lady?"

"Oh, you're crazy all right."

"You ain't seein' this from my side."

"You absolutely aren't seeing it from mine, Oma!" I stomped my foot again but kept my finger down. "I've never felt right. I've always felt something was off about everything. Especially when I was younger. And you just let me go on feeling like that without giving me a hint about all of these other things going on around me all the time. That's fucking sick!"

"What—"

"The only time I felt normal was when I was in Hollywood, doing my job. I mean, yeah, that has its own fucked up things, but I knew what those things were. Here—I don't have the first clue what is real and what isn't. And you don't tell me unless I throw it on your bed in the middle of the night."

"Okay." Oma rolled her eyes. "Just settle down now."

"Why would I do you that kindness?!"

"Because you're my goddamn grandson, and for better or for worse, I've always tried to do the best by you that I could, that's why, ya' little asshole!"

I glowered at my grandmother as she sat in her bed, the covers tossed back. She looked so small and, for once, elderly, as she sat there, her cheeks red with embarrassment.

"I have so many questions, and I don't even know which one to ask first, Oma." I sighed.

"Well, I don't know where to begin either." She exhaled tiredly.

I stared at her for a moment, unsure of how to proceed.

"I'm going back to bed," I said simply. "Keep...*Ernst*...and any of those others out of my room. Please."

"I don't think you'll have to worry after blasting his ass into the bathroom."

She kept her eye rolls and head waggles to herself. Points for Oma.

I nodded and left.

Chapter 12

The library in Point Worth is not very well stocked, so two days later, once most of the snow was melting away, and the roads were clear, and the temperature was actually above freezing, I found myself in Toledo. However, once I got to the Toledo Public Library, I was walking up the front walkway and realized that I had a library in my pocket. I was so used to not using my phone for much of anything—a rarity for a celebrity of my age, I know—that I had forgotten that I could Google just about anything. I had sat down on one of the freezing cold benches outside of the library and pulled out my phone. A few seconds later, I had the story about "Kobolds" and witches and werewolves and...well, many other things which were unrelated. Sometimes you find yourself in an internet black hole, and you don't realize you've done it.

I thought about the things that I had learned. Kobolds were Germanic spirits that came in three different varieties: those that lived in homes, those that lived in mines, and those that live on ships at sea. Across the board, they were known for pulling malicious pranks or tricks if they were pissed off. However, the household variety was no bigger than small children, wore plain, peasant-like clothing, did household chores for their "room and board" and was generally harmless—aside from the pranks, like getting an adult man to jump in a nearly frozen lake. They could appear in many forms, such as animals, dolls, fire, candles (*what the actual fuck*), and humanoid.

Before long, I had wandered onto a webpage that talked about how Kobolds appeared in various games, such as Dungeons & Dragons and online RPG's, and I gave up. There was no reason for me to know anything about games that people used for roleplaying. Even if I had a reason, I surely wouldn't understand it. Those games were for the smart kids, and I was the proud owner of a general equivalency diploma. Not that I was dumb—but I was anything but studious.

Werewolves, when I got on Google, brought up far too many results, and most of those were geared towards fandoms and other craziness. Most of them agreed on silver bullets, changing at the full moon, being bitten being the cause of "lycanthropy," increased strength, agility, and healing while in wolf form, the normal things one who had seen any movies would expect. Witches brought up similar results. A bunch of crazies claiming to control the powers of the universe or communing with nature spirits or peering into crystal balls and throwing bones and reading Tarot. Of course, I couldn't really scoff at a lot of it because werewolves had been something I thought was ridiculous to believe in until my date with Andrew. And witches were just crunchy, earthy, groovy people who danced naked under the moon and called themselves "Wiccans."

I was pretty sure that wasn't what Lucas had been referring to when he had called Oma a "witch."

Then I thought about what had happened with Ernst in Oma's bedroom. I had jabbed my finger at him, and he was suddenly flying through the air. Oma had been afraid of me when I raised a finger to her. Had I...done something to Ernst in my fit of rage?

Wait a second—that was fucking crazy. If I had used my finger to propel a Kobold (*Jesus, even just saying that in my head made me feel crazy*) across a room, that would mean I...

I was so tired. I was tired of being angry. I was tired of being surprised. I was tired of weird shit. I was tired of being Robert Wagner just as much as I was tired of being Jacob Michaels.

That's when the thought struck me.

You have so much money. Take off. Make a new life under a new name. Who could stop you?

But then I realized that I looked like Jacob Michaels, at least once I gained my weight back. There would be no hiding for long. Surely tabloids and other "journalists" and paparazzo were already looking for me. I hadn't been photographed in two weeks. I imagined that most of the magazines and online websites were frothing at the mouth to get a photo of me. In fact, it had probably been months since I'd actually been photographed out and about. When I had started to really show my weight loss, my publicist and agent and manager had all agreed that I needed to get myself hidden until I gained weight back. When it had become apparent that I wasn't going to easily put on weight, I just stayed hidden away.

When my calendar cleared up, I took off for Ohio. And then I found a brand new set of problems. I slumped on the bench and stuffed my phone back into my pocket. I cupped my hands to my mouth and blew into them, trying to warm them against the chill. Upper Ohio was starting to warm up and trying to move into Spring after the last snow, but it was still far from Spring-like. We were probably in for pretty chilly days up until at least my birthday, which wasn't much further off.

I was going to be twenty-seven years old. How does a person find themselves on the downward slope towards thirty and not know who they are, what is going on in their life, who their family is...why was I nearing thirty and utterly lost? Why did I have such trouble feeling okay about dating some guy—especially a guy like Lucas? Why didn't I know more about Oma and the house I grew up in? Why, why, why? I had so many questions and feelings and...I was just tired of all of it.

Coming to Ohio, even though I hadn't been in a good place in my life, had felt like an exhalation of grand proportions. When I had crossed over the state line, especially when I entered Point Worth, I had felt relief that I was home. That I was away from "Jacob Michaels" and that I could be Robert Wagner again. Now, I wasn't so sure of anything. I hadn't even gotten two weeks of rest before everything was totally fucked up and confusing and if I was being totally frank, frightening.

That was the thing, though, wasn't it? I was handling everything remarkably, all things considered. Seeing a werewolf transform before my very eyes, seeing said werewolf get plowed into by Lucas' truck, having sex with a virtual stranger—many times—seeing my younger self plunge into the lake, catching Ernst in my comforter, finding out Oma was a witch—it all should have sent me off the deep end. I should have been a babbling idiot. I wouldn't have been surprised if I had driven myself to the nearest mental health facility and asked to check in for the longest stay. But there I was, sitting in front of the Toledo Public Library, calmly considering all things. Nothing was in sync yet everything felt fine.

All things considered, I had to admit, I actually felt like I was at home. Even with all of the craziness going on, I felt like everything was going to be fine. When I had problems in Hollywood, I was at a loss for what to do. In Point Worth, Oma and I could have the worst fights, but I knew we would shout it out and then forgive each other and go back to things per usual. If something weird happened in Point Worth, I'd learn as much as I could, then go back to my normal routine. Point Worth, Ohio just made me feel comfortable like I was where I was supposed to be. Even when I saw a goddamn werewolf.

Never had I felt that way in California. I'd always felt out of place, never liked any of the people I met, for the most part, and I never knew if I was doing the right things or the wrong things. Everything I did was by the seat of my pants and at the urging and guidance of others. In Point Worth, I knew that I could work my way through anything. I felt...*powerful.*

But that didn't make sense. How can one feel powerful just because they are in a certain place at a certain time? A thought suddenly popped into my head, one that I couldn't push away.

I had slowly, over a decade, become a shell of a human. When I came back to Point Worth, I began to feel better. Being in Oma's home brought me back to my old self—whomever that was.

Maybe I didn't know who I was—but Point Worth, Oma's house, was helping me to discover that. Being home started to bring Robert Wagner back and was pushing away Jacob Michaels, the man I had been pretending to be. I never liked being Jacob Michaels. Ever. Sure, it was exciting to act and sing and put on shows and travel the world. A life spent under the spotlight and in front of bulb flashes was thrilling. But it wasn't me. Robert Wagner—who I really was—was meant to live behind the scenes. Anonymity and secrets were who I was. Even when I was Jacob Michaels, no one really knew me.

Like Oma, I was meant to have my secrets and keep them. I wasn't meant for the spotlight. Because, more than a world-famous celebrity, I was something else. I didn't quite know what that was, but I knew that coming back to Point Worth was going to teach me. Something in my gut told me that the reason I had started to become unwell, to lose weight, to lose part of myself, was that the person I was started in Point Worth. Like Oma, the essence of Robert Wagner was tied to Point Worth.

What did that mean?

Andrew exited his building, still looking worse for the wear. He was limping slightly, and his face was a little swollen. If it hadn't been for his skin coloring, I probably would have seen a multitude of bruises. However, even with his dark skin, I could tell that he was sporting a few, even at the distance of several yards. I was sat on the waist-high planter, my feet dangling as he began to walk towards me, his head down. I held my hands in my pockets to keep them warm as he walked along the sidewalk, his head down to try and avoid the chilly breeze slapping against his face. I didn't speak until he was within six feet of me. And when I did, he jumped.

"Hey," I said simply.

Andrew looked up, his eyes landed on me, and his whole body jolted.

"How're the wounds?" I asked as he glanced around nervously.

"Um..."

"You seem to be getting around okay," I said.

"Um, yeah, I guess, yeah." He struggled to find the right words.

"I have questions."

Swallowing hard, he looked at me, his eyes not quite staying on mine for any length of time.

"I'm sure you do."

"And I want to ask them in a safe place."

He looked down at his feet.

"I'm not dangerous now."

"Were you ever?" I scoffed. "Admittedly, a truck is a big weapon."

He shuffled his feet.

"I'm not going to attack you." Andrew looked up briefly, then glanced around. "The moon is waning."

"Okay."

Andrew looked thoroughly chastened. Of course, losing control of himself close to the full moon, getting hit by a truck, having to heal, having Oma chew him a new asshole, and getting punched in the face for all of his efforts was probably enough to do that to a person. A lot of activity in a few days time, when you think about it.

"There's a coffee shop." He gave an upward nod. "We can talk there. It's usually busy enough that you would feel safe."

"I feel safe now." I shrugged. "But okay."

I'll blast your ass with my finger. Apparently, I can do that. Did you know that? 'Cause I didn't until recently.

Hopping down from the planter, I allowed Andrew to lead me down the sidewalk in the direction he had been headed, though I made sure to keep plenty of space between us. I wanted plenty of room and options if he decided to get handsy again or—I didn't know if werewolves could randomly get furry. Wikipedia wasn't really helpful when it came to situations applicable to fantasy colliding with the real world. But, whatever happened, I wanted to be ready to make my escape. After punching him again, obviously.

The coffee shop was around the corner from his office building, and while there were plenty of empty tables and booths, there was still enough people about that we were safely still in public. If Andrew did anything, it would be witnessed by several people. Of course, that could also mean collateral damage if it came to that, but, and this was cold-hearted, but I didn't mind if others got hurt if it kept me safe.

"I'll buy you a coffee," Andrew said, but it was a suggestion.

"I'd rather you didn't."

"Please?"

"Fine." I looked at him and his wounded expression. "Just a black coffee, please."

Andrew nodded and headed to the counter while I selected a booth that was private but still in the line of sight of the baristas and a few other customers. It also had an excellent straight shot to the front door if I had to bolt. I watched Andrew as he ordered, paid for, and grabbed our coffees. He had asked for two black coffees, either to make things easy or to not show weakness by ordering something like a frappe or something frou-frou.

"Black coffee." He said simply as he put my cup in front of me and slid into the booth across from me.

"Thanks." I dragged the cup across the table towards myself.

Andrew and I stared at each other for a moment as I brought my coffee to my lips. It was barely warm. That wasn't Andrew's fault, so I just set the cup back on the table.

"I really am sorry." He began.

"I'm not here for an apology," I said, keeping my eyes on his. "I want to know why you said I smelled intoxicating."

Andrew looked down, embarrassed.

"That means something," I said. "And I think you know what I mean. You meant I smelled...*special*. Like you'd never smelled another person who smelled like me."

Andrew sipped at his coffee, his eyes stayed lowered.

He wasn't going to be forthcoming easily.

"I'm not scared of Oma."

Andrew looked up at me, shocked.

"So, if you are, you may as well get over that," I said. "I want to know why you said I smelled special, Andrew."

"You don't understand about Esther Jean. She's—"

"A witch."

Andrew's eyes grew wide.

"I'm not scared of her," I said. "Maybe I'm lucky. I'm her grandson, so I know she would never do me any real harm. At least not on purpose. But I notice that a lot of people around here are scared of her. I don't care. I want to know things she won't tell me."

"Esther Jean would—"

"I don't give a shit." I scoffed. "Someone is going to give me answers, Andrew. And it may as well be you since you're already on hers and my shit list."

He grimaced.

"I'm scared of Esther Jean," Andrew said. "Well, I wasn't really scared of her until I was sure of what she was. I don't want to be on her bad side any more than I already am."

I snorted.

"A werewolf scared of a lil' ole witch."

He looked down and sipped his coffee.

"Tell me why I smell special."

Andrew grimaced, obviously having an internal debate, a struggle with himself.

"You owe me." Maybe that was low.

I didn't care.

"I can't."

"Then don't tell me directly," I said. "Tell me without telling me."

Andrew's head rose with a quizzical expression affixed to his face.

"Everyone around here is an expert at speaking in riddles and telling half-truths and using subterfuge to cover up dirty little secrets. Surely, with your condition, you have similar experience. So...tell me without telling me. I'm becoming an expert at deciphering that shit lately."

Andrew's eyes darted around.

"*Goddamnit. Tell me.*" I leaned in to hiss.

"I wasn't really scared of Esther Jean until I figured out what she was." He blurted it out lowly. "And I wasn't scared of you. Until...I figured you out. And I'm scared of you the same way I'm scared of Esther Jean."

I stared at him.

"That's why you smell special." He lowered his eyes. "But I wasn't aware of the reason when I said it."

This would be the moment where I should tell you that I sat back in shock, as though slapped across the face with a sudden realization. That my whole world came crashing down, and I had a sudden existential crisis—that I suddenly realized my entire life was a lie. That I'd been swindled. Bamboozled. That I didn't know how I could go on living knowing what I now knew. That's not what happened. I just picked up my coffee and brought it to my mouth. What Andrew said only confirmed the theory I had swirling in my brain.

"You don't seem affected by that." Andrew's brow furrowed.

"It's been kind of hard to shock me for a few days now."

Andrew just watched me.

"Okay." I tipped my coffee cup at him in thanks. "See ya' 'round."

I started to rise from the booth.

"Wait." Andrew frowned at me, his brow furrowing so deeply I thought that his face might crack wide open. "That's it? 'Okay'? That's all you're going to say to something like that?"

"If I had something to say, I wouldn't say it to you."

Harsh? Maybe. The man had turned into a werewolf and tried to attack me—after assaulting me in his car. Fair's fair.

"Ouch."

"I don't trust you, Andrew," I said, settling back into my seat. "I don't trust pretty much anyone right now. And the fact that you actually tried to kill me doesn't help your case for leniency."

"I didn't mean to—"

"Werewolf." I nodded, got it.

Andrew glanced around nervously.

"How does that work, by the way?" I sipped my coffee. "You turn at the full moon, obviously, against your will. But how'd you become *that*, silver bullets, all of it? Tell me about your people."

Andrew glanced around again.

"Oma said there's a 'were-community' and they're all about everywhere, so I'm curious about that." I couldn't believe I was having such a discussion in such a mundane place as a coffee shop. "I mean, do you have a pack? Like real wolves? Give me Werewolf one-oh-one here."

"I mean...I guess...it's the least I could do." Andrew mumbled.

I snorted, amused.

"I was...*that*...from birth." Andrew began. "My mom and dad were, *that*, so, of course, I am, too. I'm a birthie, I guess."

"*Birthie?*"

"It's just kind of an unofficial term people in the community use."

"Ah. Being werewolves, you'd have thought they'd be more creative with their nomenclature, right?"

"Like the uniqueness of a name like Jacob Michaels?" He replied impishly before looking down.

I stared at Andrew. That had shocked me. But I refused to show it externally, even if my heart started beating rapidly and I was tempted to glance around to see if anyone had heard him say my stage name.

"So, you've known."

He shook his head.

"No." He said, still looking down. "I didn't recognize you until you decided to assault me at Esther Jean's."

"Fair is fair, right?" I snorted. "You try to grab my junk I punch you in the face."

"We're   even?"

"Not by a long shot." I glared at him.

"You've punched me twice."

"And you deserved it both times."

Surprisingly, Andrew just nodded and reached for his coffee tentatively.

"There are a lot of other werewolves around, then?" I asked.

Andrew sipped his coffee slowly as he thought of how to best answer that without sounding like a total weirdo. We were way past either of us sounding like weirdos, as far as I was concerned, so it was pointless to try to pretend to be otherwise. I was a grandson of a witch who had run off to Hollywood and had come back to find out the world as he knew it was a lie. Andrew was a werewolf. That's just weird no matter how you look at it.

"I mean, I guess." He said slowly. "I don't really know a lot of werewolves, per se, but there are a lot of *weres* all over the country. Probably the world, too."

"But you haven't gotten outside of the country much, have you?"

He shook his head.

"Hard to travel when you're not sure if you can safely be...*this*...somewhere else."

"You the only one in Point Worth?"

"No."

"Who else?"

He frowned at me like I was stupid. Fair enough.

"It'd be like 'outing' someone, right?"

He nodded.

"Okay." I sighed. "Fine. I just want to know that when the next full moon comes, you won't come looking to eat me or mess with me and mine."

Andrew's face twisted up in disgust.

"That's not how it works, Rob." He sounded put out. "I was just in the beginning of the full moon cycle and wasn't in full control of myself. That's why I did what I did. We don't turn into werewolves and then suddenly have thoughts of revenge or vengeance. Basic, primal instincts take over and, while you have some cognizance about being human the other days of the month, urges sometimes take over and make you do things you wouldn't normally do. I'm not plotting out some nefarious plan to come *get you* or Esther Jean or...*anyone*."

I nodded. "Fine."

"The were-community," Andrew chewed at his lip, "is secretive. And strict. I'd really appreciate it if you kept it to yourself about what happened. *Jacob*."

I laughed loudly.

"Do you think threatening to expose who I really am is really that big of a deal that you can use it negotiate with me?" I snorted. "I mean, sure, it would make me have to avoid going out in public, but must be a Tuesday, Andrew. You have nothing to negotiate with or threaten me with so don't embarrass yourself by pretending you do."

He turned red.

"Except," I sighed, "no one would believe me."

Andrew looked hopeful.

"And I wasn't planning to say anything to anyone who doesn't know anyway." I sighed. "I mean, what good would that do?"

As I slid from my booth a second time, Andrew didn't try to stop me. I grabbed my coffee and stood next to the table end and looked down at him.

"As long as I don't have to worry about you doing that shit again, we're square." Andrew gazed up at me. "And stay away from my grandmother. I still don't fully trust you. At all."

"She's going to think it's odd if I don't talk to her at the center."

"You're smart. Think of an excuse."

Andrew watched me for a moment and then nodded. Obviously, we had an understanding.

"Thanks for the coffee." I motioned with the cup and started to turn away.

"Rob." He stopped me.

I turned back to him, my face a mask.

"Esther Jean isn't the only thing you have to worry about." He said lowly. "I wasn't kidding about the were-community. They're very secretive and strict. It's best if they don't know what happened between us. It wouldn't be good for me."

I stared at him for a moment.

"I'm not looking to cause you trouble, Andrew," I said evenly. "I just had questions."

And then I walked away.

Outside, the day was warming up, but it was still far from what normal people would refer to as Spring. I walked down the street, dropping the disposable cup into one of the city trash cans as I walked by. I hadn't really drunk any of the coffee. I had just pretended as Andrew and I chatted. I still didn't trust him in the slightest. Andrew had believed I drank it, though, so maybe I really could act.

Chapter 13

Ernst was on my bed, folding pairs of my jeans from a pile of laundry when I entered my bedroom, wanting to just be alone and have peace and quiet. After my early afternoon in Toledo and finding out very little useful information from Andrew, I wanted to go home and just think. Ernst or any of the little Kobolds being on my bed would distract from that activity. When I entered the room, a freshly purchased cup of coffee from a coffee joint in Toledo in hand, Ernst started at my appearance. He began folding the jeans quickly, obviously about to make a quick run for it.

"Once you've been seen it's easier to be caught in the act again?" I couldn't help but chuckle as I went over to the bedside table to place my wallet and keys.

Ernst was frantically finishing the folding of my pants.

"*I dunno, sir.*" He squeaked.

I rolled my eyes at the title.

"Don't call me that," I said evenly. "My name is Rob. Or even Robbie. Don't call me 'sir,' okay?"

He didn't respond verbally, but he nodded frantically. I sat down gently on the bed beside him. He barely made a dent in the bed where he stood. I watched as Ernst folded pants, watching me out of the corner of his eye yet pretending that he didn't know I was there. He was shaky and nervous, and I couldn't blame him after what I had inadvertently done the previous night. The guilt was rising up as I watched him do his, *chores*, I supposed. I reached out to grab a piece of clothing to help, and Ernst jumped. He topped over, falling to his ass on the bed in a tangle of gangly limbs as a t-shirt fluttered down to cover him as he lay there.

Not that I wanted to, but I found myself laughing. It was quite a sight seeing something, er, someone like Ernst fall out in such a way. Ernst looked ridiculous and comical, flailing wildly under my t-shirt as though he expected something or, more specifically, someone (like me) to attack him at any moment. I felt guilty that he was obviously assuming I meant him harm, and for having harmed him the night before, but the whole thing was ridiculous. Reaching out, I gently pulled the t-shirt off of Ernst, disentangling him from the fabric. Ernst jumped to his feet and moved to the foot of the bed quickly, getting out of arm's reach.

"I wasn't going to hurt you." I held the t-shirt up. "I was just going to help you fold the laundry."

Ernst eyeballed me suspiciously. Instead of saying anything else, I began folding the shirt. Then I laid it down and grabbed another to fold. Ernst watched me for a moment, his body language indicating his desire to flee. After three more shirts, Ernst expression turned from fear to that of concern and annoyance. I continued folding laundry from the pile.

"No, no, no." He stomped over and swatted the shirt out of my hand. *"You're doin' it all wrong, sir. 'Tis a disgrace. Haven't ya' ever folded laundry for yourself before?"*

I smiled as he proceeded to show me the *proper* way to fold a shirt.

"I usually hang my clothes up in the closet at home." I laughed. "Except for my underwear and socks, that is."

"Well, I can tell." He shook his head as he started in refolding the pile I had made. *"These won't do at all, sir. There are certain ways things should be done and this innit it."*

"Please call me Rob or Robbie."

Ernst looked pensive as he folded a shirt.

"That's not the way things are done either." He barked.

"Well, then just don't call me 'sir,' please."

"You're the master of the house are you not?" He scoffed. *"It wouldn't be prudent to call ya' anything but 'sir' now would it, sir?"*

"This is my Oma's house." I frowned. "I'm just visiting. So, as a guest, you don't have to call me 'sir,' do you?"

Ernst continued folding as his brow furrowed.

"I'm sorry I hurt you last night, Ernst," I said, wondering how I could be so comfortable sitting there next to a mythological creature and act so calm about it. "It was entirely unintentional. I swear."

"T'weren't nothin'." He sniffed haughtily.

Obviously, this was a sore spot for his ego.

"Well, I'm sorry." I reiterated and moved on. "And thank you for doing my laundry while I've been here."

Ernst's brow furrowed even more deeply by our interaction. He looked troubled by our interaction. I stood, which made Ernst fold slowly at alert as he watched me out of the corner of his eye. I pulled my wallet out of my pocket, along with my cell phone and keys and put them on the bedside table. I kicked off my shoes and carried them over to the closet to stow them away in an orderly fashion. Then I took off my coat and hung it in the closet as well. Ernst quietly watched me the entire time.

"Oma said there are some of your, um, friends, or family around here with you?" I asked. "She said there are other, uh, Kobolds, here?"

Ernst averted his eyes and went back to his folding.

"Yes...yes."

He didn't call me by name, but he dropped the 'sir' shit. That was good enough for me. For now.

"Who are the others, then?" I asked as I went into the bathroom and turned the tap on the sink faucet for warm water. "Are they your family, or...?"

"No," Ernst replied hesitantly. *"They be my kinfolk, true. But we aren't all exactly brothers and sisters if ya' understand my meaning."*

I made a noise that I understood as I ran a washcloth under the water and began to wash my face. Ernst was in my peripheral vision, standing on the bed, folding clothes, as I washed my face at the sink.

"Well, there's Hans." Ernst began tentatively. *"You'd mostly find him tinkering around', fixin' things that get broke. Lena likes to do the dishes and work in the garden. Then Felix mos'ly sticks to the attic and the walls, patchin' up drafts and the like. Oskar likes to do sweepin' and moppin' and general scrubbin'. Hans, well, he mos'ly keeps to 'imself and*

just does whatever he feels needs to be done. You won' see him 'bout much due to the fact that he's a miserable piece o' work."

"And you like doing laundry," I added.

"Well, it keeps me busy, I spose," Ernst said noncommittally.

"Out of trouble?" I teased, glancing over as I washed the day's grime off of my mug.

"There's always time for that." Ernst chuckled mischievously. *"Though the chores tend to keep us busy."*

"Why did...whomever...make me jump in the lake the other night?" I asked, frowning as I finished cleaning off my face. "That wasn't exactly the nicest thing to do to someone who hadn't done anything to any of you up until that point."

Of course, I had blasted Ernst ass into the Oma's bathroom, but that was after I had jumped in the lake.

"T'wasn't us." Ernst snapped. *"None of us would do such a thing. We may get up to some'tings but we ain't done that."*

I hung the washcloth on the rack by the sink and turned off the water. Patting my face dry with the towel hung on the back of the door, then hanging it back up, I went and leaned against the doorjamb to look at Ernst. He ignored me as he finished folding up clothes.

"Someone who looked like me jumped in the lake the other night," I said. "If it wasn't one of you, who was it?"

"I wouldn't be knowin'." Ernst shrugged his tiny shoulders.

I decided to let it go.

"Been sleepin' at your feet since you was a wee'un, wouldn'ta done nothin' to put you in much danger," Ernst stated casually as he leaped down from the bed.

He used his wee arms to reach up blindly and grab stacks of clothes, then went to the dresser and began stuffing them into drawers. Ernst looked like a mountain climber, stepping on knobs to get to higher drawers and struggling to open drawers to shove clothes into, working blindly but well. I walked over and helped open drawers and put away clothes. Ernst barely came up to mid-thigh on me when he was finally standing on the floor beside me.

Kobolds were unique looking little people and absolutely precious in size. I wanted to snatch him up like a dog and snuggle him, but I figured that would garner more anger. Besides, that would be admitting that I was perfectly comfortable with these mythical creatures roaming about the house in the shadows, and I wasn't certain I was there yet. It was still incredibly odd that all of these odd and magical things happened at Oma's house daily—and in Point Worth in general—and I was just becoming aware of it. If I hadn't gone on a date with Andrew, I probably would have never known.

If you hadn't come home to Point Worth to rest up, you'd never have known.

"Sir?" Ernst looked up at me curiously, realized his mistake, and corrected himself. *"Guest of the house?"*

"Rob, Ernst." I smiled weakly. "Please."

"Won't be doin' no such thing." He sniffed. *"I'll call you 'master' if that's better, seein's you are the madam's grandson."*

"Fine." I cringed. "Call me 'sir' if you have to."

He smiled widely. *"What's troublin' you, sir?"*

"I don't know, Ernst," I answered honestly. "I just don't know why this place is so familiar and not familiar at all."

"*This place?*"

"Oma's house." I shrugged. "Point Worth. It's like I don't know this place at all anymore. Not that I ever did, I guess."

"*Awh, hogwash.*" He slapped both hands in the air in my direction. "*You just been gone a'bit s'all.*"

"I guess."

"*Wouldja like a cuppa tea?*" He suggested eagerly. "*I'll get Lena to make ya' one ya' like?*"

"I have coffee." I shook my head. "But thank you. And I don't need all of you doing things for me."

"*Kinda the thing, innit?*" He headed towards the door. "*We get to live 'ere, and you get your chores done. Fair trade.*"

He turned in the doorway to look at me.

"*Ya' need anythin' you just let me know.*" He jabbed a thumb into his chest. "*I know the ins and outs of this house better'in the rest of 'em.*"

I nodded, looking down at my feet.

"*What's botherin' ya' now?*" He threw his hands up in the air.

I looked up at Ernst.

"I don't know where I belong, Ernst," I said lowly.

Why was I being so honest with...well, a Kobold...of all people?

"*Well, I says if you don't know where ya' should be, ya' should just stick where ya' are.*" He gave a firm nod. "*No point in runnin' 'round like an idjit if you dunno what you're lookin' for, right?*"

I smiled.

"*'Sides...one place is as good as any. Longs ya' got good food, a good bed, and someone to care for ya'.*" He grinned proudly.

Obviously, Ernst, and probably the other Kobolds I hadn't met yet, took a lot of pride in the place that they called home.

"That's good advice, Ernst," I said. "Thank you. And you can sleep in the bed if you want, but try to crawl in before the lights go out. When I'm drifting off to sleep and feel you crawl into bed, it's a little jarring."

The tips of Ernst's ears, which I suddenly noticed were slightly pointed, like an elf, wiggled as he smiled up at me. It was precious, but I was smart enough to figure out that I probably shouldn't mention such.

"Thank you for my laundry, Ernst." I motioned vaguely at the dresser.

Ernst blushed and gave a slight bow of his head before he disappeared down the hallway. I shut my bedroom door and went to relax on the bed with my cup of hipster coffee. That was how I spent the rest of my afternoon, immersed in scrolling through my phone and sipping at my delicious store-bought coffee while the rest of the house silently existed around me. I didn't see Ernst or any of the others for the rest of the afternoon and Oma didn't come in to bother me either. It was a perfect afternoon.

Around five in the afternoon, Lucas texted, disturbing my immersive Pinterest experience—which I had just created an account—and told me that he was on his way over to Oma's. The message was accompanied by smiley faces with hearts for eyes and a smiling face blowing a kiss. It was kind of cute, but it also made my stomach sink. It was a little too familiar and presumptive. We hadn't made plans to get together. We hadn't even decided what it was we were really doing with each other. Was it too early in the relationship to be sending kissy faces and heart eyes?

When Lucas pulled up in the driveway, Oma was in the kitchen, banging around and fixing dinner—possibly with Lena assisting just out of sight?—and I was sitting on the porch in my heavier Spring coat. Lucas' truck slid to a stop in the slush at the end of the mostly cleared driveway, smiling at me through the windshield. I gave him a smile and waved as he put the truck into park and shut it off. Immediately, he was leaping out of the truck and practically skipping over to the porch. I stood from the chair and walked over to the steps to greet him. His arms immediately went around my middle as he ascended the steps to meet me, and he smothered my mouth with his.

Returning his kiss, I ran my fingers through his hair as his body melted into mine. My body wanted to react to his, but I held back, not wanting to make this meeting something that it wasn't. Lucas must have sensed my reticence because when he pulled back from the lingering kiss, he had a confused smile affixed to his face. I let my fingers play in his hair for a moment before I spoke.

"We need to talk."

His body deflated and he was frowning.

"This isn't going to work out for you." He stated blandly.

"That's not what I was going to say." I pressed my forehead to his.

Lucas closed his eyes gently as he held his forehead against mine. His whole body was somehow tense but also slumped against mine.

"I can feel you want to say something that is going to make me sad, though." He whispered.

"You wouldn't be much of a psychic otherwise." I teased.

He opened his eyes and pulled back with a slight smile.

"I'm not psychic."

I grinned.

"Just tell me." He said.

"Before you come inside," I grabbed his hands in mine and held them between us, "I just wanted to say that I want to be very clear about what this is and where it's going."

"Okay."

"One, I don't know what it is." I shrugged, keeping my eyes on his. "Two, I just want you to know that it needs to slow down."

"How is it going too fast?" He frowned pitifully.

"It's going too fast because I'm working out who I am, Lucas," I said. "How can I know what *this* is, what *we* are, if I don't know who Robert Wagner is? I need you to give me space to figure that out before we dive into this head first. Is that okay?"

Lucas seemed to examine me for a few moments, his eyes on mine as we stood there, holding our hands between our bodies. Was he trying to see if there were any premonitions in that head of his?

"That's okay." He nodded.

I let a smile overtake my face.

"Good." I leaned down to give him a quick kiss. "Because being boyfriends is okay. We don't have to rush that, right?"

He grinned widely.

"Is that what this is?" He whispered, stepping up onto the porch in front of me. *"We're exclusive, babe?"*

"Don't push it." I shook my head, amused.

"Well?"

I looked around.

"Who else am I trying to be with?" I relented.

"Ya' know," He laughed, "I'll take it."

"You're so easy."

"For you."

"Lord." I rolled my eyes. "Come in here and have dinner with us."

Lucas chuckled as I drug him through the front door, both of us tangled up in each other's arms. Once inside, Oma hollered that she was still working on dinner, so Lucas and I got a fire started and curled up on the couch together. And we just talked. Okay, maybe we kissed a bit, too, but we talked. Not about anything particularly important but we didn't fill every moment with groping and kissing and lusting after each other. We acted like two adults trying to discover each other and decide if there was more between us than just how our bodies reacted to each others.

Dinner with Oma was a raucous affair, with Oma regaling us with stories about how proud she was when I was a teenager and acting in all the plays and doing solos in the choir. Lucas admitted how he always had eyes on me when we were in high school together, watching me, wondering if we could have ever been friends. I didn't know any of those things about my Oma and my, I guess, now, boyfriend. I was an oblivious teenager, I guessed. Maybe I was a bit of a dick. Self-possessed and obsessed. My eyes had always been on the prize of leaving Point Worth.

And here I was sat, in Oma's kitchen, not wanting to be anywhere else but with the two people I was with currently. I didn't want to be in Hollywood. I didn't want to be on set, shooting another movie, on another stage, performing another song. I just wanted peace and quiet and love. Becoming an adult and gaining experience changes priorities, gives credence to the simple things that youth takes for granted. When you get right down to it, being with people you actually like, or even love, and having a full belly, and a warm house, and not a care in the world beats fame and fortune hands down.

After dinner, Lucas and I spent a few minutes on the porch, kissing and acting as though we were the only two people in the world. Then I made him leave before I begged him to stay the night again. We didn't have to have sex every day, sleep in each other's beds every night. Space and time are what makes relationships grow stronger if they are meant to do so, after all. Proximity breeds familiarity, but longing to be with someone when they're not near shows how deep that love is. So, I sent Lucas on his way. And I was already missing him as I watched his truck drive away in the dark.

"Oma," I announced as I entered the kitchen and leaned against the doorjamb.

A figure scurried away into the cabinet under the sink. Probably Lena. I looked over at the slightly open door and then back to Oma. She gave an innocent smile.

"I don't want to go back to Hollywood."

"Well," Oma blinked a few times, "that's something."

"I want to stay here," I said. "For now."

Oma just stared at me.

"If that's okay?"

"Of course, it is, Robbie." She was gobsmacked.

"Okay." I nodded. "And I need space. And I need truth. So, tell...*Lena*...and the other Kobolds around here to stop scurrying around here like crazy and just do things like they would if I wasn't here."

Oma chewed at her lip. "Well, don't bother them too much. They like their space, too, ya' know."

"I wasn't planning on bothering them," I replied. "I'm just tired of all of the shadowy creepy shit in my peripheral vision."

She nodded.

"Are you a witch?"

Oma was blinking again.

"And is that what I am?" I asked. "Whatever the male version of that is, anyway? Is that why—is that why I am the way I am?"

"What do you mean by that, Robbie?" She frowned.

"I became Jacob Michaels so easily," I said. "You should see me in an interview. I can charm the pants off a journalist or reporter, make a television host fall in love with me. Heads of studios and record labels—producers, directors, agents, managers—they adore me. I'm not that charming, but for some reason, people think I am. And I don't even have to try. I was an ugly kid, and then I hit puberty, the worst time in a kid's life, and now...please tell me the truth."

Oma sighed and set her dishtowel down on the counter, her arms coming to rest over her chest.

"You ain't no witch." She said. "You're just Robert the youngest. You ain't got no reason to think you're a witch, Robbie."

"But...I'm something," I said softly. "Right?"

"You coulda been." She said it as though it pained her. "But ya' ain't. So, just get that out of your head."

"Why am I not?"

"I said just stop it." She said firmly.

"Please, Oma?"

"Look here." She pointed a finger at me. "You are just Robert Wagner. And that ain't gonna change. Ya' hear me? You want to stay here? Well, we'd love to have you. For as long as you like. But you drop that shit right here and now."

"But—"

Oma stomped her foot. The walls shook. The house groaned. I should've been shocked. Instead, a tear slid down my cheek. I felt something inside of me, something in my chest that I couldn't explain and didn't have a name for at all. It felt like something was missing from me and I didn't know what it would be.

"And you stay out of that goddamn cellar." She frowned at me. "Ain't nothin' in there for you."

I nodded. Oma gave a sharp nod and went to pick up her dish towel.

"You know you're eventually going to tell me, right?" I reached up to wipe the tear off of my cheek. "You're just delaying the inevitable. The only thing I don't know is why, Oma."

"Robbie," She growled, "I'm sick of this shit. You're not here for none of that. And I won't hear it. Fine. You know about Ernst and the rest. That's good enough. You leave the rest of that be! I want you to tell me you understand what the fuck I'm sayin' to you."

"But why?"

"Why does it matter?" She waggled her head. "When have I ever led you astray, Robbie? Trust that I know what's best."

I wanted to spit out some retort about something awful Oma had done to me that had caused me grief in the past. But, when I thought about it, there was absolutely nothing. Oma was right. She had always done right by me.

"Fine."

"Good." She gave that sharp nod again. "Now, do you want to wash or dry?"

I laughed wetly, my eyes shiny with unshed tears.

"Dry." I shrugged. "I guess."

"Well, get over here and make yourself useful."

Chapter 14

Ernst jumped up in bed when I sat up with a jolt. We glanced at each other in the dark, his shiny black eyes looking like onyx in the darkness of night. I reached over and glanced at my cell phone. It was just after two o'clock in the morning. I had been dreaming about the eerie green light yet again, and then something had jolted me awake. It had been a sound, I was pretty sure, but I couldn't remember what it was for the life of me.

Something in the night had been loud enough to disturb me from my sleep and had also rattled Ernst. I knew he was rattled because of his stance but also because he hadn't scuttled off into the darkness to wherever it was that he scuttled off to when I had woken up in the past. Of course, now that I knew of his existence, we had talked to each other, it was unlikely that he would avoid me much anymore.

"Did you hear something, Ernst?" I asked, peering over to look at him, alert at the end of the bed.

"*Aye.*" He nodded.

"What was it?"

"*Dunno, sir.*" He whispered. "*Someone hollerin' out, I think.*"

"Oma...?"

He shrugged his tiny shoulders in the dark. Together, we stayed there in bed together, listening for the sound of whatever it had been that had shaken us from our slumber. I cautiously slid my legs over the side of the bed as Ernst listened and watched me, as though concerned for me.

"*Careful, sir.*" He whispered.

"I'm sure it's fine." I tried to smile. "I don't hear anything now."

Ernst gave the smallest of nods as I stood from the bed. I stood there at the bedside, listening for any noise, watching for any movement. Of course, in the dark, how would I know if anything was moving? Ernst was quiet as a church mouse and stood still as a statue as his pointy ears stayed at alert, listening for any sound throughout the house.

Oma wasn't screaming out for me, and the house seemed as quiet and still as it did on any other deep night at two in the morning. My grandmother was probably still tucked tightly into bed, sleeping soundly. Maybe Lena or another one of the Kobolds asleep at her feet or side. Why had I been dreaming about the green light again? I had promised Oma I would stay away from the cellar, that I wouldn't search out whatever it was drawing me there.

That was another thing I had thought about while we were doing dishes after dinner. How had she known about my dreams about the cellar? Or had I been dreaming when I had gone down to the cellar? Had I been sleepwalking and she had caught me doing it? I shivered there in the bedroom in the dark as I stood, listening for sounds. Ernst tiptoed over to the side of the bed and tapped me on the elbow with one of his small, bony fingers.

I nearly jumped out of my skin, then laughed nervously. Ernst gave me an apologetic smile.

"Did you hear something?" I looked down into those black eyes in the dark.

"*No, sir.*" He shook his head. "*I dunno what woke us, sir.*"

I nodded down at him.

"Maybe I said something in my sleep?" I suggested.

He shrugged, appearing to be less worried than before.

"Are you okay?"

He beamed up at me. Obviously, he was fine. And me asking about his well-being made him happy.

"*Yes, sir.*"

I smiled down at him.

But then I heard it again. Well, I would have said I heard whatever it was again because what I heard was familiar. I hadn't known what noise had shaken us from our sleep, but the sound that came to me didn't sound foreign but like something I had just heard recently. Or, maybe that wasn't right. It just seemed like I should know the sound. Ernst's ears pricked up and his hand went to mine. His tiny hand managed to wrap around two of my fingers frantically as his head turned towards the window.

"What was that?" I asked.

Ernst nodded towards the window. I looked down at him. His hand stayed wrapped around my fingers. The child-like gesture would have made me smile if it weren't for the fact that I was concerned. Something was going on that wasn't right, even if I didn't know what it was. I slowly slid my fingers out of Ernst's grasp as I stepped towards the window. Ernst made concerned noises as I moved away from the bed towards the drapes. Turning my head slightly, I gave him a reassuring smile.

When I approached the window, I reached out cautiously and grabbed ahold of the drape, pulling it to the side so that I could peer out. Ernst was making concerned noises from behind me as I leaned forward and looked out into the backyard. My eyes grew wide as I looked down and saw a tall, hooded figure in the middle of Oma's still unplanted garden, hands raised aloft, his or her back turned to me. Several, shorter figures in hoods stood around the figure in a circle, their arms raised towards the sky as well.

"*What the fuck?*" I whispered.

"*What is it, sir?*" Ernst whisper-hissed behind me.

"There are people down there," I said lowly. "They're...I don't know what they're doing."

I let go of the drape and stomped over to the bedside table, quickly flipping on the lamp. Ernst shut his eyes against the sudden light as I shoved my feet into my slippers.

"*What are ya' doing, sir?*" Ernst asked frantically when his eyes opened incrementally.

"I'm going down there and finding out what the fuck is going on is what I'm doing," I grumbled as I went over to the bathroom door and grabbed my robe. "I'm sick of this shit."

"*No, sir. No.*" Ernst leaped down from the bed and landed on the floor with a soft 'thump.' "*Ya' shouldn't go out there. Ya' should stay here. It's safe inside the house.*"

"Ernst." I pulled my hand back as he reached for it. "I'm going out there and finding out once and for all what is going on here. You just crawl back up onto the bed and go back to sleep. I'll be back once I talk to those assholes out there."

My mind raced back to the night I had had dinner and wine at Lucas' house the first time. I had come home, quite a bit drunk, and seen those figures in the garden before. At the time, I brushed it all off as being under the influence of alcohol. Now, I wasn't dreaming, drunk, or under the influence of anything else. This was real, and I was going to get to the bottom of it.

"*Sir.*" Ernst raced along beside me as I walked to the bedroom door. "*Don't. Please.*"

I sighed and squatted down so that my eyes were close to level with Ernst's.

"Look," I said, "just get back up into the bed, okay? Try to sleep. I won't be gone long. I'll be okay, Ernst. Don't worry. When I come back, we'll both go back to sleep and forget all about this."

Ernst chewed at his lip, his eyes darting around.

"I promise." I laid my hand on his shoulder.

My hand was enormous in comparison to his bony shoulder.

"*Okay, sir.*" He gave a decisive nod. "*But if ya're not back in ten minutes, I will wake up the madam.*"

"Fair enough." I tried to smile confidently. "But give me ten full minutes, okay?"

"*Yes, sir.*"

I gave him another pat on the shoulder and exited the bedroom. As I gently shut the door, I gave him a wink. Ernst still looked as though he had eaten something funny and it had settled in his stomach. Once the door was shut, I crept down the dark hallway and tiptoed down the stairs, doing my best to be as quiet as possible. I padded through the living room, through the kitchen, and to the back door. Taking a deep breath, I unlatched the door and grabbed the knob. What would happen if I went out into the garden and demanded these people tell me what the fuck they were doing? Were they some cult or coven performing some ritual?

When I threw the door wide, though, I found the backyard dark, quiet, and absolutely empty. The fenced in garden area was empty, and there was absolutely no sign of anyone having been inside the fence. Everything was deathly quiet and still. My throat felt like a multitude of lumps needed to be swallowed down. My eyes scanned the yard, looking for signs of movement or absolutely anything that was out of place. Everything was as it always was. Still, dark, quiet, peaceful.

I was at the point of convincing myself to close and latch the door once again when my eyes affixed on the woods just beyond the yard. Shimmering, white and ghost-like, I saw a figure. I squinted and looked towards the sight, immediately recognizing it as the teen-Rob I had pulled out of the lake nights before. I swallowed hard as my eyes adjusted and I took in the figure peeking playfully from around one of the trees at the edge of the woods.

As if beckoning to me, teen-Rob's arm came up and its hand waved me towards it.

Close the fucking door, Rob.

Close the door.

Close the door.

Latch it. Go back to bed. Forget you saw this.

I found myself going down the back steps and stepping into the yard below. The figure continued to beckon to me as I glided across the soggy backyard, water seeping into my slippers as I was propelled by some unknown forced towards the woods. I knew that if I wanted, I could force myself to go back to the house, lock the door, go upstairs, and crawl back into bed. But something inside of me told me that there was no way out but through.

When I got within a few yards of the tree that my teenage self had stood behind, the ghost-like teen-Rob ducked behind it with an audible chuckle. I stopped in my tracks, suddenly concerned that I was in danger. However, I allowed myself the space of a few breaths to collect myself and then began walking towards the woods again. One more foot. Then two. Then three. When I was nearly close enough to reach out and touch the tree, my eyes grew wide as ghost-like teen-Rob appeared from behind the tree. He smiled at me for a split second...and then he was flying at me.

Teenage ghost-Rob flew into me, and I was flung backward, falling wetly onto the soggy lawn behind me. My back hit the soggy ground, and my head thumped softly against the muddy earth. The breath was knocked out of me as I hit the ground so that I ended up lying there, trying to collect myself and my thoughts as I gazed up at the clear, starry, early-Spring sky above. My mind went blank, and my vision hazed over. For a split second, I wondered if I was about to feel myself lose consciousness, blackout, only to wake in the yard with the sun beating down on me, Oma standing over me cursing and raving.

Then I felt myself inhale sharply. A gasp escaped my mouth as my eyes welled with fat tears and I came back to myself.

I remembered everything.

Jacob Michaels Is Not Jacob Michaels

A Point Worth LGBTQ
Paranormal Romance
Book 3

Chapter 1

'*Everything Little Thing She Does Is Magic*' by The Police was playing on the little radio on the kitchen counter when I walked into the room. Bright summer sunlight was pouring through the windows in the house, making everything look white and golden and nearly celestial. All of the curtains and drapes had been pushed back on their rods to help welcome the first day of summer. The house was sparkling clean and smelled of Oma's favorite lavender cleaner. I staggered down the stairs, all wonky elbows and joints, my hair surely sticking up in spikes all over my head, rubbing my fists into my eyes. My bare feet padded down the stairs and then across the floor of the living room towards the kitchen. It was my last summer before I started Big Boy School. Talks had been given to me over and over again about what to expect, the friends I'd make, the teachers I would love, the things I would learn. All I cared about that summer morning was getting some of the food in the kitchen that was scenting the house from top to bottom: bacon and eggs and butter and maple-y goodness.

When I entered the kitchen, I immediately saw her standing there, back turned to me, poking around in a skillet on top of the stove. My eyes lit up as an evil grin came to my face, and I tiptoed across the linoleum floor in the kitchen, sneaking up on her. I grabbed ahold of her sides, my head barely coming up past her butt, making her scream out in feigned shock. She had heard me walking up behind her, but it didn't matter. She let my five-year-old self pretend that I had snuck up and startled the daylights out of her. She spun around, hand to chest, gasping as she looked down at me with wide eyes. Then her face broke into a smile, and she dropped to kneel before me. Her arms went around me immediately as she smothered my face with kisses.

"Good morning, Robbie!" My mother managed to get out between my squealing and squirming as she smothered me with her kisses. "Good morning my little ray of sunshine!"

"Mommy!" I squealed, pretending that I wanted to get away but I was really wanting my mother's kisses to keep going until I was exhausted and collapsed in her arms.

I wanted to feel my mom's arms around me, comforting and loving me, leading me to the table for my breakfast. The smothering kisses and squeezing arms lasted for what was a very long time, but not to a five-year-old. Finally, my mom pulled back, her hands going to my shoulders so that *she could get a good look at me. Immediately, one hand went to my head, to try and pat down the multitude of cow-licks in my hair. She smiled to herself as she gave up after a few seconds. My hair never wanted to do what she wanted it to do, and that was a battle she was slowly losing. Her hand went to my chin, pinching it between her fingers as she winked at me.*

"Did you leave your appetite in bed or is it here with you?"

I giggled. So silly.

"I'm so hungry, mommy!"

"What do you want for breakfast, baby?"

"What did you make?"

"What do you want?"

I giggled. This was our game.

"What did you make, mommy?"

She smiled widely.

"What do you want?"

"I want eggs and bacon and pancakes!" I crowed towards the ceiling, excited for a new day, full of endless possibilities and wonder.

The way a five-year-old lives each day...with possibility.

"Well," Mom kissed my forehead quickly, "you must have read my mind. That's exactly what I made."

Cheering, I headed over to the table, my mom patting me on the butt as I turned away from her. I sat down, yawning and rubbing my eyes again as my mom got a plate from the cabinet in Oma's kitchen and went over to the stove to serve my breakfast. That was probably the best thing about being so young—no real responsibility, all the wonders of the world, and your mom served you breakfast. As I sat there, listening to the spatula scrape against the cast iron skillet, I couldn't help but wonder where Oma and my father were. They always had breakfast with us in the morning. In fact, Oma was usually the first person down in the kitchen. She usually made our breakfast. Sometimes mom did...but not very often. Frowning to myself, I rubbed my eyes with my balled-up hands again, trying to chase the last of the sleep away.

Just as I was turning in my seat to peek at my mother over the chair back, I felt it. The rumbling in the floor. At first, it just felt like a train passing nearby, though there were absolutely no train tracks anywhere near Oma's house. My eyes grew wide as the rumbling turned into shaking and the whole house seemed to shake with the movement. A low roar began, then louder and louder until it sounded like a tornado was about to rip the house apart. I looked at my mother in terror as she turned to me, the half-filled plate in her hand, her own eyes wide with concern. No...with absolute terror.

"Mommy?" I squealed as loudly as I could over the sound.

"Stay there, Robbie!" My mom replied desperately, her hand unsteady as she reached out to set the plate on the kitchen counter as the house shook.

The plate clattered to the floor, shattering, food flying everywhere as I grabbed onto the chair, trying not to fall off of my seat. Next, it was the small radio falling off of the kitchen counter, its crash to the floor muted by the roaring and shaking. The roaring and shaking increased until I knew that I would fall from my seat to the hard ground below. My mother held onto the kitchen counter, trying to stay on her feet and also not step on the broken plate shards or chunks of greasy food. Suddenly, as though it had never even started, the roaring and the shaking stopped. We were left in

Oma's deathly quiet kitchen, me holding onto my chair, terrified, and my mother gripping the kitchen counter as though her life depended upon it. Slowly, she turned to look at me, her face ashen, concern etched all over it.

"Muh-mommy?" *I peeped.*

My mother's mouth moved but whatever came out was muffled, as though she were speaking underwater.

Then the roaring and shaking were back, and green light filled the room.

"Robbie!" *My mother screeched.*

Whispers.

Whispers everywhere.

My vision was blurry as I looked up at the moon peeking through the clouds and tree limbs overhead. The moon was like color trails in my vision, haloes of red and blue and green, especially green. Shutting my eyes tightly, I pulled my arms away from the muddy ground to slap my hands over my ears. The whispers continued, indecipherable, indiscernible, coming from everywhere but nowhere at all. Were they coming from inside of my head? Who was whispering? What were they saying? I grimaced and shook my head as I held my hands against my ears. Slowly, the whispering tapered off. My heart was in my throat, pounding like a jackhammer. I could hear it inside of my head, replacing the whispers as the memories ducked in and out of the vault in my head.

Pulling my hands away from my ears, I laid there, looking up at the clouds passing in front of the moon through the tree branches overhead.

Did you see that?

"What?" I gasped, trying to rise to a seated position, my body not wanting to cooperate.

Who was I talking to as I laid there? Who was out in the backyard with me? I listened carefully, trying to ignore the sound of my own heart in my head. Off in the distance, a wolf howled.

Did you see that?

Immediately, I pushed myself out of the muck I had fallen into, jumping to my feet. Mud and muck dripped off of me. It had seeped through my pajamas, matted the back of my head, covered the entire backside of me. Dashing across the still nearly frozen ground at the edge of the woods, I ran as fast as my thudding heart and my aching joints allowed, heading directly towards Oma's house. The whispers had stopped, my vision had cleared, Oma's house was crisp and sharp in my vision as I crossed the lawn at top speed. Halfway across the lawn, the house getting closer, I noticed the stillness of the night around me. My feet crunching against the ground, my heart in my throat; they were the only sounds I heard. The clouds moving across the sky and me dashing across the lawn were the only things moving in the dark.

Spinning around, I turned and looked off towards the woods as my mind strobed memories and my breath came in gasps.

My mom was making me breakfast.

The shaking of the house and the green light.

My father was tucking me into bed.

"Mom will be back, Robbie."

He had said that.

Waking up the next morning and being all alone.
Oma showing up.
Dad never coming back.

As I stood there, my hands rising to either side of my head, pressing against my skull as the memories rushed in and then receded, then repeated the process, I sensed movement at the edge of the woods. I looked up; hands still pressed to my head as it did its best to split wide open from the strobe light of memories flashing through my brain. Everything was going so fast—I remembered everything but, then I didn't, over and over again until I thought I would go mad as I gasped for air, trying to get my lungs working correctly. Just as I felt the memories start to settle back into place, find their home within my consciousness again, the silence of the backyard was shattered by another wolf howl. But this one was close. So very close.

At the edge of the woods, though my vision was still somewhat blurry, I saw dark shapes moving through the trees towards the yard. I let my hands fall from my head as the memories fluttered away like dandelion seeds in a stiff breeze. My body felt frozen in place, from fear or the cold, I wasn't sure, as three large shapes moved past the tree line into the backyard. Three wolves, larger than I had ever seen before, stalked out of the woods, their red eyes glowing and zeroing in on me. All three had thick black fur, red eyes that seemed to glow in the dark, and toothy snarls affixed on their muzzles. A low, rumbling growl emanated from them as they inched towards me, their massive paws sinking deep into the muck with each step.

My feet began to move of their own accord—my brain was not involved—moving me backward and closer to the house. I screamed out in shock at the sight of the wolves, which only made them growl louder as they continued their forward movements. I slapped a hand over my mouth as I continued shuffling backward, wondering if I should make a mad dash for the house or if that would only make them run after me. There was no way that I could outrun three grown wolves with half of the yard left to traverse. However, if I merely kept inching backward, they would surely catch up to me. They definitely would not continue stalking forward at the same pace once they figured out that I was terrified and unable to make my brain and feet communicate effectively.

Three wolves continued to traverse the backyard, inching towards me as I inched back towards the house. My heart was in my throat again, and my eyes darted from one set of glowing red eyes to another to another. All three wolves snarled, their fangs dripping viscous saliva as they got closer and closer and the house seemed to get farther and farther away. Staring into the eyes of the wolves was like staring into my future—a future full of ripping jaws, clenching teeth, sinew and flesh torn from bones, guttural screams filling the air. I swallowed hard as I started to take more substantial steps backward, my eyes zeroing in on the middle wolf—the one I had decided was probably the leader of this small pack. The middle wolf's eyes squinted in what seemed like feral anger as I took another substantial step backward. He growled gutturally as the two wolves on either side of him leaned back and howled ferally at the sky.

Something inside of me connected my brain to my body once again, and my mind began to command my body to turn and rush for the house, to do everything I could to outrun these three wolves.

What were wolves doing along the shore of Lake Erie so close to Oma's house anyway?

What does it matter, idiot?

These wolves are going to tear you limb from limb regardless of the reason.

Then it dawned on me.

I glanced at the sky, but the moon was waning.

Were these werewolves?

How could that be?

The moon wasn't full.

Looking into the eyes of the wolf I had decided was the leader convinced me further that I wasn't dealing with standard wolves. There was a human intelligence there. A hunger and longing and anger that a standard wolf could neither express nor convey with their eyes. For several moments, I stared into the leader's eyes as he squinted ferally back at me. The other two wolves started to inch forward again, coming closer to me as the leader held back. Obviously, the two on either side were going to dash in and attack, and the leader would bring up the rear in case I tried to get around them. I had no choice. I had to turn and run for the house. Even if I could feint and dodge around them, the only place I could run was the woods—and they would surely chase me down before I got close to the tree line.

"*Sir?*" My eyes widened at the voice that came from behind me.

"Ernst," I spoke through clenched teeth but did not turn my eyes away from the wolves, "go back in the house! Right now!"

The space of a single breath passed before Ernst had dashed forward, coming to stand before me, putting himself between me and wolves. Ernst was quick. There hadn't been time to stop him from making himself a target.

"*No!*" He held a tiny hand up, palm out, towards the wolves. "*Ya' will leave the master alone!*"

"ERNST!" I screamed at his insane display of bravado. "GET AWAY FROM TH—"

The three wolves all howled towards the sky again, then they were dashing towards him, teeth gnashing and red eyes glowing angrily. There was no other decision to make. Ernst vapor-locked at the sight of the wolves barreling down on him. I dashed forward and wrapped an arm around Ernst, enveloping him within my grasp as the wolves ran towards us at full speed. I held my other hand out at the wolves, as though this would stop them.

I want them to stop.

I don't want to die.

I don't want Ernst to be hurt.

"NO!" I screamed.

My vision flared as blistering fire erupted from my hand, flowing out in a violent wave towards the wolves. Ernst's burrowed his face in my chest as the leader of the wolves ducked, barely avoiding the blast of fire. His counterparts were not so lucky. The wolf on his right was hit fully by the wall of flames, and the one on the left ducked a little too late, the wall of fire sliding across the side of him, singing off hair and melting skin underneath. I was breathing heavily, my hand still held out in front of myself, holding Ernst against me as the wolf leader snarled and growled but came no closer. The wolf who had taken the full force of the fire was whimpering and thrashing on the ground, and the other one was limping and yipping, putting itself behind the leader.

"*Sir.*" Ernst peeped.

"Shhhh, Ernst." I silenced him, keeping my hand up.

Fire had just erupted from my hand.

I didn't know how.

I didn't care how.

Ernst and I were safe. For the moment. I didn't want to drop my hand. The wolves needed to think that I knew what I had done, how I had done it, and that I was willing to do it again. They needed to believe that what I had done was very simple for me to do over and over again. Wolves that wanted to attack me didn't need to know that I felt woozy but also energized. I felt...*alive*. The desire to burn all three wolves until they were nothing but ash in front of me filled me up, made my heart beat faster, but not from fear. I wanted to see them as scared of me as I had been of them.

I wanted pain.

Shaking my head clear of those thoughts, grimacing at the very idea of wanting to bring down pain and destruction, I glared at the lead wolf. He glared back, but he was slowly inching away as the other half-burnt wolf yipped and whimpered behind him. The wolf leader and I kept our eyes on each other as he backed up until he was alongside the fallen, crispy wolf before he finally bent down to break eye contact with me. He bit into the fallen wolf's neck fur and started to drag the unconscious wolf towards the woods. Slowly, still keeping my eyes on the one-and-a-half wolves still on their feet, I rose from the ground as well, keeping Ernst firmly against me, and my other hand outstretched towards the wolves. As they backed off towards the woods, the leader dragging the unconscious wolf and the other limping and whimpering, I inched back towards the house.

Nearly stumbling, the heel of my foot found the steps up to Oma's house, so I finally lowered my hand and turned. Racing up the steps, I slung the door open and delivered both Ernst and myself to the safety of the kitchen once again. Immediately, I slammed the door shut behind us and locked every lock on the door. I fell to my knees on the linoleum floor and released Ernst from my grasp, placing him to stand on the floor before me as I knelt there. Ernst stood there, staring at me with wide eyes as I laid my too large hands on his shoulders. My hands covered both of his shoulders and part of his neck. He was so small, and he had put himself between the wolves and me.

"What were you thinking, Ernst?" I shook my head, terrified of what could have happened. "You could have gotten yourself killed!"

"*Me?*" He scoffed, though he looked more worried than anything. "*Ya' almos' got yourself killed, sir!*"

I pulled one hand away from him to place it against my forehead, my eyes closing as I did my best to slow my heart.

"*Are ya' awright, sir?*"

Taking a shaky breath, I did my best to nod as I squeezed Ernst's shoulder gently with my other hand.

"I'm fine."

That's what I meant to say. Instead, I said it roughly twenty times, as though trying to convince myself that everything was just fine.

I'm fine. I'm fine. I'm fine. I'm fine.

"*Sir?*" Ernst squeaked. "*Ya' are covered in mud, sir.*"

"Yeah." I nodded, my eyes shut tightly. "I know."

"*Le's go get ya' cleaned up, sir.*"

"What was that, Ernst?" I shook my head as a shiver overtook my body. "Were those..."

"*Werewolves?*" He squeaked out. "*If I were ta put muh money on it...aye, sir.*"

"The moon isn't full." I shivered again.

The mud and muck that had caked on the back of me felt cold and gritty and crackly and did nothing to make me feel better kneeling there in Oma's kitchen. If I had been so inclined, I was sure that I could have peeled the mud off in one big frozen piece. I felt stiff and woozy...and *alive.*

"What did I do?" I asked, my eyes finally opened to peer into Ernst's exaggerated wide-eyed face. "What happened? How did I do...*that?*"

"*I wouldn't be knowin', sir.*" He shook his head ever so slightly.

"I know." I shook my head. "I'm sorry, Ernst. It's just—"

I placed a hand on his head. A jolt went through me, memories flashing through my head rapidly. A fleeting glimpse of a past long since forgotten.

I was young. Ernst and I were sitting on my bed, reading a book. Ernst and I washing dishes together. Ernst and I jumping out and startling another of the Kobolds—Lena maybe?

Gasping, I yanked my hand away from Ernst and stared at him, aghast. My hands went to the side of my head again as I rose to my feet and stumbled away from him backward, my eyes shutting tightly, as though that would block out the things in my head. I shook my head and gasped for breath as the memories fluttered through my head like a film reel flapping to an end, slapping against a projector.

Slap. Slap. Slap.

"Stop it!" I growled, slapping my hands against the side of my head.

Suddenly, it felt as though something went through me, from the top of my head down to my feet. I felt empty. Somewhere, in the back of my mind, I heard a giggle.

Did you see that?

"What?" I gasped.

Then the memories were gone. I opened my eyes as my hands cautiously slid from the sides of my head. Ernst was standing in front of me, wringing his hands and looking up at me; concern etched all over his face. Suddenly and inconceivably, I suddenly missed Lucas. The longing to see him felt like a cord pulling my stomach downwards. When was the last time I had seen him? I wanted desperately to hold him, to kiss him, to have him hold and kiss me.

"*What is it, sir?*" He whispered.

"Ernst." I swallowed again. "I have something I need to do. I need you to check to make sure Oma is okay. Check on the other...your kin."

"*I can do tha', sir.*"

I nodded. "Okay."

Stepping away from where I had backed up against the counter, I made my way around Ernst and across the kitchen.

"I'm going to...go clean up," I said neutrally. "I'll...I'll see you in the morning. Um, later today."

But Ernst was gone. He had disappeared into the shadows to, presumably, check on the other Kobolds and, hopefully, Oma. As I stood in the kitchen, still shivering, I wondered if maybe I shouldn't pop my head into Oma's room to make sure she was okay, to see that she was fine for myself. However, I somehow knew she was safe and fast asleep. If something had happened to Oma, I probably would have heard her cussing and carrying on. Instead of checking in on my grandmother, trusting that Ernst would do as he promised, I made my way through the house to the stairs. I needed to strip off my muddy clothes and clean myself off. Once inside of my room again, I grabbed my cell phone, and with shaky hands, shot off a text.

Twenty minutes later, I was clean and in fresh pajamas, quietly opening the front door of the house. Lucas was standing on the front porch, still in his pajamas but with a Carhartt coat thrown on over them, bleary-eyed, hair standing up in all directions. I could tell that he had tried to pat it down to look more presentable but had failed miserably. Even his mussed hair made my heart leap. I quickly ushered him inside, closing the door behind him swiftly but quietly before locking it again. Lucas stood in the foyer, looking at me quizzically as I locked the door.

"*Come over right now but be super careful?*" He cocked an eyebrow at me. "What's goin' on, babe?"

"I just..." I turned to stare at him.

"Are you okay, Rob?" He looked as concerned as I would have expected after having received such a desperate, cryptic text at one o'clock in the morning.

"No." I shivered again.

Then Lucas' arms were pulling me into him. I folded my arms in so that he was hugging all of me against his chest. As soon as my body connected with his, I felt that feeling again. It was that feeling of being alive and powerful—just like when I had burned the wolves. Something that I felt had been missing, something that had once made me feel like Robert Wagner, something I hadn't even known was missing, was back for the briefest of moments. Before I could stop myself, I had pried my arms out from between our bodies and placed my hands on either side of his head. My lips found his, and I kissed him desperately, as though I were a man lost in a desert and his lips were water. Lucas gasped in shock, yet appreciatively, as I fed at his mouth. His arms pulled me tightly into him as I kissed him passionately, needing to taste him.

"Rob." He gave a nervous laugh as I pulled away from his mouth.

"I missed you," I said.

"You missed me?"

"Desperately." I felt my eyes water, but no tears fell. "I feel like I haven't seen you in forever. I don't know why."

"Does it matter?" He whispered against my mouth.

"No."

"I missed you, too."

"I need to have sex with you," I said, feeling that surge of power zip through my body again. "Right now. Can you do that? Can you make me feel better right now?"

"Right here?" He smiled wickedly.

"In my room." I jerked my head towards the stairs. "Now."

"Okay."

Moments later, we were a flurry of arms and fingers, tongues and lips, stumbling into my room together. My hands were doing their best to push Lucas' coat off of him and rip his shirt off over his head as he did his best to both shut the door as gently as possible and push me towards the bed. We fell onto the bed as one, a little too roughly, though my body told me not to worry if we woke Oma. I needed to feel every part of Lucas, have him feel every part of me, to forget about what had just happened less than thirty minutes prior in the backyard. I didn't want to think about wolves with red glowing eyes and flames shooting out of my hand. Lucas and his body were all I cared about at that moment.

Lucas gasped in delight as I flipped him onto his back on the bed and planted a knee on either side of his hips and leaned down to smother his mouth with mine. I ground my pelvis into his, grabbed one of his wrists in each hand and held him down, taking control of him. When I pulled my mouth away, his mouth tried to find mine again, but I held back, smiling wickedly down at him as he did his best to keep kissing me.

"Please, Rob." He pleaded.

Giving him another, fleeting, yet passionate kiss, making him groan once again, I slid down his body, kissing a trail to lower places. Muffled groans and whimpers filled the air as I did my best to bring Lucas to the brink with my lips and tongue as he twisted my hair in his fists. When I released him, I shimmied up his body again, presenting myself to his lips. Lucas accepted me eagerly as I braced my hands against the wall over the headboard, groaning in desperation as he returned the favor. Before either of us could fall over the edge, Lucas released me and we were ripping our pajama pants the rest of the way off. From seemingly nowhere, Lucas produced a condom, smiling hungrily up at me as he tore the wrapper open and slid it onto me. Then I was yanking his legs onto my shoulders and positioning myself against him. Lucas wrapped his arms around my neck, his eyes pleading with me to do the thing we both needed so desperately.

When we were both spent, my body on top of his, our lips and tongues dancing once more, I felt like Rob again. There were no flashing memories or incorporeal whispers or surges of power through my body. All I could feel was myself still inside of Lucas, his arms around my neck, his lips on mine, and a kind of sleepiness I hadn't felt in days. I was barely able to extract my body from Lucas' so that he could turn on his side and I could wrap myself around him. As I drifted off, feeling as though I couldn't stay conscious even if I had wanted, Lucas whispered to me.

"I still love you, Rob."

Chapter 2

"You buried the lead, babe." Lucas was shaking his head as we stood at the edge of the woods behind Oma's house. "I mean, I never want to turn down making love with you, but you could have told me about the wolves before."

Chewing at my lip, I glanced into the woods before turning my eyes back to Lucas. The sun was barely up, so I didn't know why we were. Lucas was standing before me, in his pajamas and Carhartt again—the only clothes he had brought when he came over—watching me skeptically. Not that I could blame him for his skepticism, of course. Three wolves the size of...well, really big wolves...with glowing red eyes attacking me in Oma's backyard was hard to believe. The fact that I didn't feel like I could tell him about *"Teenage Ghost Rob"* and Ernst made the whole thing even more difficult. I certainly wasn't going to explain to him how fire had shot out of my hand and hurt one-and-a-half wolves, either. An abridged version of events was relayed—three enormous wolves tried to attack me, and I ran for the safety of the house.

"I was...my head wasn't right after that." I gave a half shrug and shook my head softly. "I was scared and confused, and I didn't know what to do, Lucas."

He reached out and pulled me into a quick hug. He pressed his lips to mine softly before pulling away again.

"And I didn't think you'd believe me." I sighed, looking towards the woods again. "I still kind of don't."

"Babe." He frowned at me, though he didn't put his heart into it. "Of course, I believe you. It's just...odd, I guess."

Nodding down at the ground, I couldn't help but snort in disbelief at his skepticism for my story. Lucas looked down at the paw print the size of a human hand in the drying mud at our feet.

"I mean, obviously there was at least one huge wolf." He stated sheepishly.

"You *don't* believe me, do you?" The frown was unstoppable.

"Rob," He sighed, "I'm not going to say it again—*I believe you*—I'm just processing the whole thing, babe. I mean, this is just crazy, even though there was clearly a wolf here. Three huge wolves wandered up into Mrs. Wagner's backyard and tried to make you a nummy little treat? I'm wondering if we need to tell Sheriff Dennard so he can notify...I don't know...wildlife management or something? Who deals with this kind of thing? If wolves are wandering out of the woods—which wolves being around here is crazy enough—but if they're wandering out trying to attack people so close to their homes, that's a real problem. I don't know what to do in a situation like this. That's all. Okay?"

"Okay." A feeling of relief washed over me. "Lucas, I feel like I haven't seen you in years. Even now, here in front of me, where I can look into your eyes, I feel like I haven't seen you in forever."

Lucas' brow furrowed as he stared back. He was chewing at his lip.

"That's weird, right?"

"I guess." He looked towards the woods.

"I'm so glad you're here."

"I'm glad you're here." He replied. "So much."

Swallowing hard, choking back the feeling of loss, like a rock in my gut, I turned to look into the woods with him. There was nothing there but trees and deeper woods peeking through the leafless trees. Spring was coming. Everything felt electric, as though life was excited to push through and make itself known, to announce its presence to the world. I could practically feel the ground and everything around me vibrating with unfulfilled potential. It felt like an energy I hadn't felt in a long time. It made me feel powerful. But also sad. Something I had no name for was missing. I just knew it.

"I—and don't make fun of me—but I think they were werewolves." I spat it out, knowing that if I hesitated, I would stop myself.

Lucas turned, aghast.

I shrugged.

"I mean, they...look, their eyes looked kind of like Andrew's...*that night*," I explained. "They were glowing red, and they looked, I don't know, intelligent. Not just like wolves looking for a *nummy little treat*, okay? They had this look in their eyes that they knew exactly what they were trying to do. They were organized and stealthy, and if...if I hadn't run so fast, I guess..."

Lucas wrapped an arm around me and pulled me into him, side to side, standing there, looking out into the woods. Why wasn't I explaining to him about Ernst and *Teenage Ghost Rob*?

"It's just all so strange," Lucas stated neutrally.

"Yeah." I agreed. "Why do I feel so..."

Lucas let go of me and turned to watch me as I stared out at the woods.

"What is it, babe?"

"Right now," My teeth were gnawing at my lip again, "I miss you."

Lucas just stared.

"Why is that?" I asked, turning to him, my eyes pleading for an answer. "You know how someone comes home from a long trip, and you pick them up at the airport, and it feels like days or even a week have to pass before it feels like they're not still gone? Like you can't believe that you finally have them back? That's how I feel right now. I'm settling into the feeling of having you *back* in my life."

The face I was presented with by Lucas was impassive. Not knowing quite what to make of his hesitation to respond to my, admittedly, odd statement, I reached down and took his hand. Lucas' fingers reflexively laced through mine, though his eyes didn't meet mine. They stayed focused on the woods beyond us. Lucas' eyes looked as though they were focused on something that only he could see, that he wasn't going to share with me. It should have bothered me; it should have made me grab him and shake him and demand that he tell me what was on his mind. Instead, all I could think about was how glad I was that he was there. Only a few days had passed since I wasn't even sure that I wanted a guy in my life and now I found myself wanting nothing more than to have Lucas by my side.

All I could think about, besides how good it felt to have Lucas' hand in mine, to have him standing there with me, was memories. After my encounter with my ghostly teenage self, I had remembered...*something*. I had remembered a lot of somethings. My subconscious was a niggling voice in the back of my innermost self, telling me that if I could remember them, pieces would fall into place. Something...*or somethings*...very important had been lost to me, and I needed to remember them. Closing my eyes, I found myself wishing that by touching Lucas' hand, I might remember something about him like I had when I touched Ernst.

Nothing.

"That's weird, right?" My voice was soft and didn't match my conviction. "The fact that I'm even explaining how I feel to you—that I feel *compelled* to share this with you...it's all just weird."

"Rob," he said, "you're just rattled from last night."

"The sex?" I chuckled.

He chuckled as well. "Not from the sex. I hope."

"No, not the sex." I agreed. "Lucas, I need to ask you something, and I really want you to be honest with me, okay?"

"Okay."

"Why do I feel like I just got you back?" The question begged to be asked. "Do you know why that is?"

He just stared at me.

"Lucas?"

"Rob..."

I waited.

"...I...look, I don't know what compelled you to ditch Point Worth and everyone here. But obviously, you did feel compelled to leave ten years ago. Right?"

My head bobbed up and down before I even thought to do it.

"Do you know why you left?"

"To chase fame and fortune."

He frowned.

"I mean," I chewed at my lip, "I didn't want to be here anymore."

"Did you want to be rich and famous?"

"I guess?"

"Babe, I don't think you're being totally honest. Like, at all." He shook his head. "But I don't think you know you're being dishonest either. Does that help?"

"Not in the slightest."

As if summoned, the backdoor of the house swung open, and Oma appeared in the doorway, still in her nightgown and robe, looking as though she had just woken up. Lucas glanced over at me nervously as I looked across the lawn to Oma standing in the doorway, staring out at us as though she'd never seen us before.

"Well, what the hell are you idiots doing out there at butt-early-thirty when it's this cold?" She hollered. "You're gonna freeze your balls off!"

Lucas' hand was in mine again, his fingers lacing through mine. I looked down at his hand as he squeezed mine.

A warning?

"We're just talking, Oma," I hollered back automatically, jovially even.

"Damn fine place to do it." She gave an exaggerated shiver as she pulled her robe tightly around herself. "What the hell are you even doing here this time of morning, Lucas? Not that you ain't welcome, of course."

"I—"

"I invited him over last night, Oma." I interjected.

"I can only imagine why." She shook her head. "Well, when y'all get done playin' grab ass out there, come in and I'll get us some breakfast started."

"We're going to go on a walk first, Oma!" I hollered back.

"Freeze your asses off if ya' want!" Came her reply. "Breakfast will be waiting!"

Then she disappeared into the house once again, the door swinging shut behind her. Lucas let out a sigh at my side that seemed to come from the very soles of his feet.

"A walk?"

"Yeah." I nodded, not looking at him.

"You don't want to go inside?"

"Not right now."

Lucas had no response for that, but, instead, held my hand as I pulled him towards the woods. Together, watching everything in the periphery as we walked, Lucas and I walked side by side through the woods towards Lake Erie. Silence was the music of our march, though it was not uncomfortable, as we made our way through the skeletal woods. Spring was coming, but in the meantime, the woods were stuck in that fitful sleep between death and life. Lucas' fingers squeezed mine as we walked hand-in-hand through the woods, stealing glances at each other, both of us wondering what was on the other's mind. Why did I suddenly feel the way I did about Lucas...and why was he so cautious in speaking about it?

The woods that created a barrier between Oma's house and Lake Erie were not incredibly dense, yet they were thick enough that we had to be careful on our journey. All of the trees were clear of snow and ice, yet there were still patches of snow scattered throughout the woods where the sun had not quite reached. Spring would fully announce its presence soon, and any trace of winter would be gone within days, but winter was still clinging to the woods with bony fingers, refusing to give up until forced. When we broke through the woods, the shore of the lake was before us; I felt relaxed and free. My body didn't feel electric; every hair on my body didn't feel like a live wire, I could breathe. I gave a wide smile as I looked out at Lake Erie's—surely freezing—crystal clear waters and breathed deeply, squeezing Lucas' hand in mine.

When I turned to look at him, he was smiling back, but I could also see the concern in his eyes.

"What is it?"

"I'm worried." He said. "For you."

"I'm not crazy, Lucas." I let go of his hand.

He quickly grabbed my hand again, his fingers lacing through mine again, frowning at my yanking my hand away from him.

"That is not what I meant. I'm worried for you because of the wolves." He explained. "Andrew was one thing—I mean shit happens, right?"

"To say the absolute least."

"But to have three wolves—werewolves or not—wander up and try to attack you in the middle of the night…I mean, if they were werewolves, what if…"

I waited, but Lucas simply trailed off and did not finish his thought.

"Maybe Andrew and some of his buddies came to exact their revenge?" I prodded him.

"I mean, maybe?"

"I don't know."

"Could you tell if one of them was Andrew?"

"They were wolves." I reminded him. "How would I know?"

"Not all werewolves look the same." He said. "Just like regular wolves."

"Well, I'm on a learning curve here." I snorted.

Lucas smiled sheepishly at me.

"Do you remember what Andrew looked like in wolf form?" He asked softly, as though he didn't want to keep asking about Andrew.

The reasons for that were obvious.

Andrew and I had been on a date.

Lucas and I were now dating.

Andrew was the other man.

The fact that I had nothing but contempt for Andrew didn't factor into Lucas' reasoning in the matter.

"I, um," I chewed at my lip as I thought, "I honestly can't say. It was all so quick and confusing. Not to mention terrifying. Maybe I was in shock during the whole thing, but I don't remember much except that he turned into a wolf and I didn't even know werewolves were real, Lucas. I just remember how angry and feral he looked. And his eyes. These wolves last night had the same kind of eyes. Not like some wild animal with a hunger for dinner, but something intelligent. These wolves knew what they were doing. They hadn't just happened upon Oma's yard and—"

"What were you doing out in the backyard so late anyway?"

"I thought I saw people out there, and—"

"Real smart, babe." He teased.

Shrugging, I gave him a half-smile.

"People or wolves, there was obvious danger in the backyard." His brow furrowed. "Why did you think there were people out there? Did you hear voices or something?"

"Hey." I glowered.

"Not in *that* way." He snickered. "Please stop implying that I'm calling you crazy for two seconds, Rob. I mean, did you hear people talking or calling out, or…something?"

"I guess?" I chewed at my lip. "We—I—woke up because of some noise or something and then I heard it again, and it was coming from outside. I looked out of my window and there was a person in…"

Lucas just watched me.

"I swear if you call me crazy…"

"I won't."

"Some person in like a hooded…*cloak? Or robe?*…was standing in the backyard. Kind of looking up towards my window." I cringed at letting such a statement come out of my mouth. "Kind of like, I don't know, ritual robes or something?"

Lucas was frowning deeply.

"Like a witch?"

I gestured with my hand, validating the suggestion.

"It wasn't, ya' know...?"

"It wasn't Oma." I shook my head. "Too tall. Way too tall."

"But you were looking down from the window, Rob." He shrugged. "And you had just woken up out of a dead sleep, right? Maybe..."

"Look," I shook my head softly, "I've been no big fan of my grandmother's lately. I'll give you that. But don't try to implicate her in this. It wasn't Oma."

"Okay."

"Oh, stop that."

"Stop what?"

"That was sharp."

"I was just saying 'okay.'" He squeezed my hand. "Promise."

"Okay." I relented. "But I just know it wasn't Oma, okay?"

"I believe you, Rob."

"She's crazy as hell, mean as shit, and she definitely hasn't done much for me to want to like her a lot lately, but she wouldn't lure me out into the backyard for any good reason, let alone so wolves—or werewolves—could attack me. If she wanted to hurt me, she'd do it herself."

Lucas squeezed my hand. "I'm not lying to you. I believe you that it wasn't Oma. I'm just trying to come up with—"

"What was that?" I whipped my head to the side.

"What?"

"Did you hear a scream?"

"Um, no."

Lucas was looking at me like I was crazy again. I ignored his facial expressions and listened quietly, still holding his hand. No sounds, other than the water and the breeze and the crackling of the trees filled the air around us. Had there been a scream—or was I crazy? Unexplainably, I felt a tug in my gut again, something pulling at me, telling me to pay attention. A sudden urge to check on Oma came over me, overwhelming my senses.

"*Oma.*" I gasped.

Lucas looked shocked as I let go of his hand and whipped around, my feet moving of their own accord as I dashed towards the woods again. I was already past the tree line, running like crazy when Lucas finally managed to holler after me. Seconds later, I heard him running to catch up. My heart was pounding in my chest again, and I was gasping as I ran faster than I ever knew possible, trying to get back to Oma's house as quickly as possible. By the time I reached the other side of the woods, I felt like I might pass out from the sudden exertion. My body still wasn't back to one-hundred percent yet, so running through the cold woods through damp and muck wasn't something it was prepared to do. Lucas had to be far behind me in the woods, unable to keep up with such a pace.

As soon as I broke through the tree line into the backyard, my eyes landed on Oma. She had fallen back onto the steps, facing the woods. One of the Kobolds—my guess was Lena—was by her side, trying to get her back up onto her feet. The fact that Oma looked like she had fallen wasn't my main concern. The fact that a lady, completely nude, was stumbling through the backyards towards my grandmother was what had my focus. The strange woman's back was to me, so I was treated to an eyeful of asscrack as I dashed across the backyard, trying to get myself between my grandmother and some weirdo.

Had I heard Oma scream for me from the other side of the woods?

"Hey!" I screamed as I got closer, though I had no idea where I found the breath to do so.

The woman kept stumbling towards Oma as she laid back against the steps, looking at the approaching woman in horror. The Kobold was pulling at Oma, looking both terrified and annoyed somehow. The strange, completely nude woman came into focus better as I approached and I could see that she only had hair on one half of her head. One side of her body looked nearly melted, covered in scar tissue. Grimacing, I ran even faster, wanting to make sure that the woman got nowhere near my grandmother. I watched as Lena pulled at Oma and Oma's face changed from a look of astonishment to anger. Her hand slowly raised, pointing at the woman approaching her.

"Oma!" I screamed again. "No!"

Apparently, Oma hadn't seen me burst out of the woods and come running across the backyard. My screams had obviously not reached her ears, either. When her eyes settled on me, her hand stopped in mid-air. I didn't want Oma to suddenly send fire flying towards the woman when I was approaching from behind. Knowing my luck, she would miss, or the woman would duck, and we'd have Flame-Broiled Rob. A second later, I had reached the woman. I grabbed her by the shoulders, stopping her from moving any closer to Oma. She stumbled awkwardly, her body turning to face me as I gasped for breath, my heart thundering within my chest.

How I kept myself from screaming, I wasn't sure. Half of the woman's face was melted away. One eye was missing, half of her long brown hair scorched away, her scalp, face, half of her torso and lower half all looked like melted plastic—with just a touch of blood and other fluids to make her look even more frightening. The woman's mouth opened and one eye looked out at me in desperation.

"*Help me.*" She managed to croak.

Then she was collapsing into my arms. With no other option, I reached out with my arms, catching her around the middle as she fell into me, completely still. Slowly, I lowered the woman to the ground, wondering what in the Hell had happened to her and why she had wandered up into Oma's yard of all places. Oma was finally standing from the steps as Lena stood meekly at her side. I looked over at them, and Lena shyly stepped behind Oma, partially hiding behind Oma's legs. Oma looked down at me in shock. If it hadn't been for the sound of Lucas approaching the tree line, I wouldn't have known what to do.

"Lena," I whisper-hissed, "hide."

In less time than it takes to blink, she had jumped down and disappeared into the slight shadows cast alongside the stairs. Then there was nothing. Oma looked down at where Lena had been, and then her eyes shot back over to me. I shrugged and slowly pulled my arms from around the woman as I laid her onto the wet lawn and Lucas came barging out of the woods as fast as he could. Oma took a second to calm herself before she walked over to stand over the naked woman on the ground and me.

Then Lucas was next to us, his hands on his knees, doubled-over as he clutched his side and gasped for breath.

"How did you get here so fast?" He gasped for air.

I wasn't exactly ignoring him, but I didn't have an answer, either.

"What the fu—"

"Robbie?" Oma was aghast. "Who is that?"

"I have no idea," I responded robotically as I looked at the naked woman I was kneeling beside.

"Why the hell is she buck-naked?" Oma asked. "What the hell happened to her? I came out here to look for y'all to tell you breakfast was ready and she comes stumblin' up with her hoo-ha hanging out, looking like something that crawled out of a swamp!"

"Oma." I shot a disapproving glance up at her.

"Well, her cooter is hangin' out, Robbie," Oma grumbled, but her heart wasn't in it. "I know you don't want to see that any more than I do, for God's sake. What the hell is wrong with her?"

Lucas was still panting, his hands on his knees as he stood next to the woman and me and I had to control the urge to snarl at Oma that it was apparent to anyone with eyes what was wrong with the woman. The compulsion got swallowed when I took a moment to consider the burns that went from the top of the woman's head down to her foot on one side. When I noticed that her one remaining eye—which was open and lifeless—looked like a mix between a human eye and something else, it struck me.

"She's dead," I said simply.

"What?" Oma gasped.

"She's—she's dead?" Lucas was starting to get his breath back.

Looking up at Oma, I felt my stomach sink.

"You better call the police."

"I'll do it." Lucas straightened up and dashed towards the back steps, shooting a look at me over his shoulder. "Sheriff Dennard. I'll call him."

"Oh, fuckin' great." Oma rolled her eyes as the screen door shut behind Lucas. "Just what we need."

"Could you try and show some compassion?" I snapped up at her as I felt the woman's wrist, praying that I was wrong.

"I'm showin' more compassion than whatever did that to her, ain't I?" Oma threw her hands up. "Why the hell did she wander up in my damn yard? Couldn't she have gone over to The Irish to cause trouble?"

The Kelly's were "The Irish" that Oma was referring to as she stood there, flinging her arms in the air like a crazy person. A rotating cast from the Kelly brood had lived a few hundred yards away from Oma for more than a few generations. All Irish, red hair, annoying to Oma, and constantly being described as "ugly assholes" by her. Regardless of her thoughts on the Kelly family, I felt it was wrong to wish this upon them.

"She's been burned bad." I swallowed hard, ignoring my grandmother merely to state the obvious.

"No shit."

"Oma."

"Well," Oma sighed, "bless her heart. I don't mean nothin'. But this is certainly not how I saw my day startin'."

"I'm sure this wasn't how she wanted to start her day either."

"No one wants to wake up dead, that's for sure." Oma shrugged. "How the hell do you think she got burnt up like that?"

"No idea."

Lying hadn't been on my agenda for the day, wasn't how I saw my day starting, yet that lie was just the beginning.

Chapter 3

Lucas, Oma, and I were seated around the kitchen table, all of us with a mug of coffee and half-finished plates of food. None of us had found that we had a massive appetite after the Sheriff's Department showed up, so we all had some eggs and toast left on our plates. Somehow, we had all found the ability to eat all of our bacon. Funny how that happens—even death couldn't keep a person from wanting to finish any bacon that has been cooked. We all sat there, sipping at coffee, merely exchanging glances instead of talking, while the coroner worked out in Oma's backyard and Sheriff Department employees milled about. Some were coming into the kitchen for coffee, which Oma happily kept making for them, while others were walking around the backyard and the woods. Apparently, in upper Ohio—especially within the city limits of Point Worth—a burned up naked woman wandering into someone's yard, collapsing, and dying was a strange event.

"So, none of y'all know who this is?" Sheriff Dennard, who I had met for the first time an hour prior, poked his head in through the backdoor. "Because she obviously doesn't have a purse or a wallet with her."

"I done told you we don't know who she is, Wesley!" Oma turned sharply in her chair to growl at him. "Stop pokin' your damn head in here and asking every five minutes."

Lucas and I glanced at each other.

"You got a dead naked lady in your backyard, Esther Jean Wagner." He grumbled back. "You ought not act so rude to me."

"Unless you're gonna charge me with murder or interfering with your investigation, get your damn head back outside." Oma wasn't bothered one bit. "You're letting all the damn stank out."

My nose turned up of its own accord as Lucas snorted into his coffee mug. Sheriff Dennard squinty-glanced at Lucas, then snarled at Oma before he pulled his head back and closed the door.

"Bastard." Oma spat as she turned around in her seat to reach for her coffee mug again.

"I heard that Esther Jean!" Sheriff Dennard hollered from outside.

"I hope to hell you did!" She shot back over her shoulder. "Didn't exactly whisper it did I?"

"Oma." I reached over and squeezed her hand.

"Well, I'm older than his damn parents." She looked at me. "He can go take a running leap off—"

"Just stop." I shook my head at her as Lucas snorted again.

Shooting a reproachful, though amused glance at my boyfriend, I was glad to see that he had the common sense to look at least a little bit chastened. Though Lucas realized laughing at a situation such as the one we found ourselves in was inappropriate, Oma seemed to be taking everything in stride. She was so unbothered by everything going on that I had to wonder if there had been other incidents in the past where she had to explain dead bodies on her lawn to the police. In slightly more than a quarter-century of living, I hadn't had a single run in the with the police. At least not in a way that I would have been questioned.

Police often provided security at film premieres, film festivals, at Hollywood events, or even private parties. However, I'd never had to sit in a kitchen and pretend that nothing was wrong while a dead body was dealt with a few yards away. Considering the fact that I was pretty sure that I knew how the woman had been burned on one half of her body made me uneasy. I found myself stuck between pretending I knew nothing and was completely innocent and confessing to Sheriff Dennard that I shot fire out of my hand while the woman was in wolf form and burned her all to Hell. Of course, the only thing a confession such as that would lead to was me in a "Me Time" jacket in a padded room where I would be watched through one-way glass. Additionally, I hadn't been honest with Lucas about the night before, nor had I mentioned anything to Oma about the incident.

All around, and in every way, I was what the kids referred to as "fucked."

Whether I liked it or not, whether or not my conscious was happy with the decision, I had no choice but to sit and be Robert Wagner, innocent and normal. Sheriff Dennard hadn't asked much about Lucas and me when he first arrived on the scene, and it was evident that he was well-acquainted with Oma. Of course, if memory served, Oma had fired a shotgun at the Kelly kids once for sneaking into her yard, so even if Sheriff Dennard hadn't been from Point Worth, he knew of her. Also, I remembered that Jackson Barkley, Lucas's grandfather, who owned the hardware store, had said that Sheriff Dennard had been the one to deal with the case of the old lady and the shotgun.

Regardless, due to his familiarity with Oma, and probably Lucas, Sheriff Dennard didn't ask us many questions. Being Oma's grandson probably made him a little suspicious of me, but at least I qualified as a "local." That got me excused from a lot of initial questions. The fact that I was trying to rein Oma's mouth in probably won me brownie points with the Sheriff, as well. Of course, once the woman's body was gone, I didn't doubt that Sheriff Dennard would have follow-up questions. If I could get through the day without being outed as "Jacob Michaels," I would go to bed shocked.

"Ya' think they'll take much longer?" Oma sighed.

"They'll take as long as it takes, Oma."

"I'm sure it won't be much longer," Lucas added.

"Well," Oma grumbled, "I was thinking about doing some planting today. Ground ain't gonna freeze back, the ground's nice and soft, it would have been a perfect day. Come afternoon, the sun's supposed to be high in the sky, and I thought—"

"Do you think they can figure out who she is?" I interjected, suddenly nervous as I saw two people—coroner employees, maybe?—lifting a gurney with a filled body bag. "She obviously didn't have ID on her, and it was kind of hard to make out a lot of her face."

"I'm sure they'll figure it out." Lucas patted my hand, reluctant to actually hold it with all of the police around. "Surely, someone will report someone missing, two-and-two will get put together, and they'll find out who she is. Then maybe they can figure out what happened to her."

"Great." I swallowed.

"Probably a meth-head." Oma clucked her tongue.

"What?" I frowned at her.

"Burned all over." She shrugged. "Been a lot of them places been blowin' up, catchin' on fire. Hell, watch the news any night of the week and, well, them idiots just don't know when God is tryin' to tell them somethin'."

"Oma." I shook my head.

"I ain't sayin' nothin' bad about her for fuck's sake." Oma rolled her eyes and waggled her head. "Just sayin' that this is probably something innocuous like that. I doubt anyone went and set her on fire is all's I'm sayin'. Poor thing probably just didn't have enough sense and done did the wrong thing, and—"

"Mrs. Wagner." Lucas shook his head at her when he saw my expression.

"I ain't meaning to upset ya' none, Robbie." Oma reached over to pat my hand. "I know ya' been away for a minute. The Midwest is littered with them meth-houses. It's a disease...well, maybe a cancer. It's been spreading."

"Let's just...let's not talk about it."

Oma shrugged. Lucas patted my hand again. I felt guiltier than I had before. If this woman got labeled as some junkie when that wasn't the case at all, I'd never have forgiven myself, even if she had tried to attack me while in wolf form. If that was what happened at all. Maybe I really was in a mental hospital somewhere half out of my mind, waiting for some drugs or therapy to do their job. All things considered, I didn't know if I was crazier for wanting to confess to the previous night's events or because I didn't doubt that those things happened.

"All right." Sheriff Dennard coming in through the backdoor once again, looking official and concerned snapped me out of my reverie. "They're going to take her away, Esther Jean. Your plans to get out in the garden won't be completely ruined."

"Stuff it, Dennard."

"Mrs. Wagner." Lucas couldn't help but grin.

Sheriff Dennard wasn't amused.

"Esther Jean..."

"Yes, Wesley?" She waggled her head.

That was fair. Sheriff Dennard hadn't shown proper respect to an older lady of the community by calling her "Mrs. Wagner" or "ma'am," so why the hell should Oma have to use his title?

"I'm the Sheriff of this county."

"I'm the owner of this house." Oma started to stand, but I reached out and put a hand on her shoulder, pushing her back into her seat. Of course, that didn't slow her mouth. "And I ain't got nothin' to do with Miss Naked as a Jay Bird out there, anyway."

"Oh, calm down." Sheriff Dennard waved her off. "I didn't say nothin' about this even being anyone's fault."

"Damn right you didn't." Oma nodded once. "And you better not, either."

"I don't think none of y'all hurt her." He grumbled. "I wouldn't be standing here being nice if I thought y'all were responsible for what happened to her."

Regardless of how it made me morally feel, Sheriff Dennard's statement made me feel physically relieved.

"But you know that there might be more questions later on." He reached into his breast pocket for a small notebook and a pen. "I know she just stumbled up into the yard looking like that and then...Robert?...you eased her to the ground and she just...well, she died."

He was reading from the notes he'd made in his little notebook when he had first arrived and asked what happened.

"Yessir." I nodded. "She wasn't alive long after she came into the yard."

Oma threw her hands up in a "are we done now?" fashion.

"And, Lucas?" Sheriff Dennard glanced up at him. "You came running up after?"

"Yessir."

"Esther Jean, you were cowering on the steps of the backdoor here?"

"Look here, Wesley—"

"The...woman...frightened Oma, I guess from sneaking up behind her like that, Sheriff Dennard," I interjected to avoid another round of fighting. "Lucas and I were coming back from a walk by the lake when I saw the woman stumbling up to Oma. I ran up to help Oma—obviously, the woman being naked and stumbling around wasn't exactly normal— and then when I pulled the woman away, saw her condition, and eased her to the ground when she collapsed, she just...*died.*"

"All right." He shrugged.

"Jesus." Oma huffed.

Sheriff Dennard shot her a look. "What were y'all doing walking down by the lake?"

Lucas and I glanced at each other.

"Walking?" Lucas frowned at Sheriff Dennard.

"It's a way to get exercise, Wesley." Oma snorted. "Maybe try it." My grandmother gave the Sheriff's waistline a long stare.

"Oma." I scolded her. "Be nice. You're like a toddler."

She shrugged at me.

Sheriff Dennard pointed his finger at me. "I like you, Robert." Then his finger went to Oma. "But you are walkin' on thin ice, Esther Jean."

"Callin' a cop tubbly in your own home ain't a crime." She laughed. "You gonna haul me in and tell 'em to book me for hurtin' your feelin's?"

Lucas snorted again.

Sheriff Dennard glared at him.

Great.

Two of us were now on The Shit List.

For what seemed like forever, Sheriff Dennard glared at Oma and Lucas, as though he were trying to figure out some misdemeanor—or even felony—with which he could charge them. Oma glared back, and Lucas averted his eyes. The whole time, all I could think about was that this was all so unnecessary. Even if I confessed to what I thought happened, it would do no good, and the woman would still be dead. Oma and Sheriff

Dennard having a pissing contest wasn't fixing anything, either. Finally, I cleared my throat to break their concentration on each other.

"Sheriff Dennard?" I asked. "Do you think you can figure out who she is? Was?"

He finally looked over at me. "Eventually we will, Robert."

"Good."

"Esther Jean." He snapped at her. "Don't you put a toe out of line."

She flipped him off.

"No wonder everyone hates you." He snarled, then looked at me. "Robert, take a walk with me."

Sheriff Dennard turned on his heels and headed towards the backdoor. I glanced at Oma and Lucas, both of them looking concerned, but I rose from my seat and followed Sheriff Dennard to the backdoor. He opened the door and eased down the steps—Oma wasn't wrong, he was a larger man, though that was no reason to be mean to him—and I followed after, a little more athletic in my descent. Together, we watched the rest of the Sheriff's office employees disperse, giving half-hearted waves and salutes at us as they vacated Oma's backyard. Finally, once we were alone—but not walking, obviously—Sheriff Dennard turned to me.

"Look," He said, "this lady that died in your grandma' yard had obviously been burned all to hell."

I swallowed hard, my eye twitching slightly as I looked at the Sheriff in his very scary uniform and scarier handcuffs and absolutely terrifying weapons belt. Was he about to arrest me?

"I wouldn't be surprised if this wasn't drug related." He continued, making the knot in my stomach loosen slightly. "These damn meth labs are blowing up all the damn time."

"Oma said something about that." I gave a neutral response.

"Well, she was right about something. Imagine that." He rolled his eyes. "Now, I ain't seen or heard nothin' around here about a meth lab. We don't have much of a problem in Point Worth. Yet. But it's always inevitable, isn't it? Those types of things tend to find their way into every small town eventually. Even idyllic ones like Point Worth."

Idyllic? I was going to keep my opinions to myself as to avoid getting pretty new bracelets put on me.

"But, regardless of the hate I have for your grandmother," He continued, "I'm glad she has you and Lucas around. When something like this happens, it just keeps on happening. If the wrong sort is movin' into Point Worth, we need to start watching out for each other. You make sure to watch for any strange people around your grandma's property, Robert."

"Of course." I nodded.

I wanted to tell the Sheriff that only a crazy person would attempt to cross Oma. She did shoot a shotgun at teenagers, after all. Of course, bringing that up to the Sheriff was probably a poor choice, so I just kept my answers short when needed and my mouth shut otherwise.

"You see anything else odd and you call me right away." He gave me a stern look, his fingers hooking into the belt below his pudge. "If we got the druggies movin' in, I want to get on top of it and get 'em out of here just as quick as they came. They can go be Toledo's or Cincinnati's problem. Or, add to their problem, I guess."

"Yessir."

"You grew up around here, didn't you?" He asked suddenly.

"Um, yeah." I nodded. "In this house. I lived here until I was sixteen."

"You took off a while back, didn't you?"

I nodded.

"Now you're back."

"Yessir."

"You find all the fame and fortune you needed?" He gave me a knowing look.

Sheriff Dennard wasn't nearly as ignorant as Oma had portrayed him to be or as simple as his "Good Ole Boy" persona painted him. Eyeing Sheriff Dennard for a moment, I didn't know how much I wanted to get into my *other life* with him.

"The illusion is fleeting."

He nodded. "Well, I'm sure you're glad to be back."

"Yessir."

"Would you, uh..." He was reaching into his pocket for his notepad again, then flipping to find a blank page.

"Yeah." I shook my head, trying to affect an affable personality. "Sure. Of course."

"My wife," He cleared his throat, "she loves your movies, see?"

"Of course." I shook my head as though this was the most common thing to happen to me recently. Of course, being recognized as Jacob Michaels was the most common thing that had happened to me recently. "What's your wife's name?"

"Sarah Jean." He smiled broadly as I wrote out a little note and signed "Jacob Michaels" on a blank page of his pad. "We went and saw one of your concerts down in Chicago...gosh, three years ago, I think it was."

I nodded, still smiling as I handed his notepad back to him. That was the thing about Midwesterners. Everything was "down there"—even if "down there" happened to be in a western direction.

"Yeah." I agreed, as though I remembered the show he was talking about in his previous statement. "It was a great show; great crowd, of course."

Of course, I didn't remember playing Chicago three years prior since I had played Chicago at least two dozen times throughout my music career. However, it was always best, in my experience, to just go along with the things people said about seeing a movie or show.

"Down there at Millennium Park." He continued to smile as he inspected the autograph I had provided. "Hate Chicago. Too busy, crowded, loud—but it was a good show, Robert. Or should I say 'Jacob'?"

He chuckled at his cleverness.

"Rob's fine," I repeated my mantra.

"You've lost some weight, haven't ya'?"

"Yeah," I said automatically. "But Oma's helping me put it back on."

"Well," He reached out to slap me on the shoulder, "that's what grandmas are for, right? Even hateful, old, mean ones like yours, I suppose."

"Yessir." I smiled jovially, though I was not amused.

"Would you mind if..." He was reaching for his phone.

"Sure." I was flustered but managed to keep smiling. "How else will Sarah Jean believe you, right?"

He laughed at that. Sheriff Dennard moved into my personal space, put his head next to mine, then snapped a selfie of the two of us smiling into the camera. Of course, I probably still had bedhead, my hair wasn't styled, I was without my trademark beard...maybe Sarah Jean wouldn't believe he had met Jacob Michaels, regardless of the picture and autograph.

"Well, I thank you, Rob." He slid his phone back into his pocket after inspecting the picture quickly. "Sarah Jean will be beside herself."

"I'm sure." I smiled. "I'm glad I could get you husband points."

He laughed at that and slapped me on the shoulder again.

"All right." He made a move to walk away. "But you don't forget to let me know if you see anything else weird, ya' hear?"

"Of course," I replied. "If any more naked people stumble into the yard, you'll be the first to know after us."

I gave him a jaunty salute, which made him laugh all the way across the backyard and around the side of Oma's house. As soon as he was out of view, I let the smile disappear from my face and slogged back up the stairs into Oma's kitchen. She was at the window over the sink with Lucas, having just watched the entire display between myself and Sheriff Dennard in the backyard.

"Surprised the tubbly bastard didn't ask for one of your old t-shirts." Oma snorted as soon as I was inside. "Of all the unprofessional things!"

Lucas was merely smiling at me.

"Do you think him or his wife will tell people I'm here?" I asked.

"I would be shocked to shit if they didn't," Oma grumbled. "Wesley ain't got a lick of propriety, and Sarah Jean finds out and tells everyone's business. She probably figures out whodunit before Wesley can even begin to investigate. Hell, she probably knows a crime's being committed as it's happenin'."

Lucas laughed again.

"She is...I guess...interested in other people's affairs." He agreed.

"She's fuckin' nosy is what she is." Oma slapped at his arm.

"Tomato, tomahto." He chuckled at her before turning to look at me. "Babe, I've got to get down to the hardware store. Grandpa understood me having to stay here while the Sheriff was around, but..."

I waved him off. "It's okay. I understand."

Lucas gave me a soft smile and sauntered over, ignoring the fact that Oma was still in the room. Before I could stop him, my face was in his hands, and he was kissing me gently on the lips. Oma gave a wolf-whistle—appropriate more than she knew—as she headed back to the table. Lucas pulled back from the kiss with a smile, his eyes staring into mine.

"Why don't you come by the house later?" He grinned evilly since his back was to Oma. "I'll make us dinner."

"Vegetarian?"

"Of course."

"You're lucky I like you."

"Like?" He teased.

"Go to work." I spun him gently and swatted his pajama pants covered ass. "I'll come to your house later."

Oma wolf-whistled again.

"Stuff it, old woman." I snarled.

Lucas cackled before giving me a wink. Then he was gone. And Oma and I were alone in the kitchen. I stood there as Oma started sipping her cup of coffee again. Once I was confident that enough time had passed for Lucas to have gotten into his truck and pulled away, I went and sat down across from Oma. She eyed me knowingly as I grabbed my coffee cup.

"That your work out there?" She asked, calmly sipping her now, probably cold, coffee.

"Perhaps," I replied calmly. "Unless you were out wandering around last night or early this morning."

"Ernst told me last night when I caught him creeping around my room." She answered the obvious question. "So...ya' heard some weird noise and thought you'd go investigate like some teenager with big tits in a horror movie? That seem as dumb now as it should?"

"Did he tell you about the wolves?" I ignored her.

"He mentioned 'em."

"It wasn't a full moon last night."

"No." She gave a single nod. "It wasn't."

"I'm guessing that maybe werewolves are forced to turn into wolves at the full moon, but can—or at least some can—turn when they want. That about sum that up?"

"Just about."

"After my little incident with Andrew, don't you think that would have been good information for me to have?" I frowned.

"Why?" She snorted. "Andrew ain't one of them. He ain't nearly powerful enough to be changin' his skin any ole damn time the mood strikes him."

"Regardless." I tried not to be dazed by this conversation I was having with my grandmother in her more than ordinary country kitchen. "It would be good to have told me, *hey, since you know there are werewolves now, maybe you should know that you don't just have to worry about the full moon.* Especially since Point Worth seems to be teeming with them, Oma."

"Every damn time I turn around, you're scolding me for something." She sighed.

"Rightfully so," I stated though I couldn't put any force behind the words. "This is twice I could have been clawed or chewed up by a werewolf—*wolves*—because you decided to keep secrets, Oma."

"Fine." She rolled her eyes. "Some werewolves can change any damn time they please. Happy?"

"I guess."

"But I didn't know we had any of them around here." She waggled her head. "Usually they have to belong to a pack and have a pretty damn powerful Pack Alpha to have that kind of power, and—"

"Pack?" I stopped her. "Pack Alpha?"

"Well, yes. Wolves have packs and alphas so why wouldn't werewolves?"

"Ya' know," I shrugged, "I'll give you that one. Where'd Lena disappear off to?"

Oma looked around, as though Lena's whereabouts hadn't even crossed her mind until I brought her up.

"Lena?" She hollered.

Without so much as a sound, a bright light, a puff of smoke, or anything, Lena was walking out from underneath the table next to Oma. Seeing little humanoid creatures—Kobolds—appear and disappear on a whim would never be something to which I wasn't sure I could become accustomed. However, I did my best not to jump at the sudden sight of her or do anything that might make her think that I was hostile. I didn't even have Ernst's full trust yet—though he had been willing to take a mauling for me the previous night.

"*Yes, ma'am?*" Lena asked, her eyes darting to me for a moment.

Her voice was like Ernst's, barely distinguishable from his squeaky-toy-like voice. Maybe it was a little more feminine, but it was pretty close to the same. Even Lena's physical appearance was strikingly similar to Ernst's. For a second, I wondered if Ernst wasn't just somewhere with a trunk full of disguises, waiting to make an appearance in various parts of the house. However, Ernst soon followed Lena out from under the table, though he exited on my side of the table. I did jump when he appeared, only because I hadn't expected him. Ernst flinched and went to step away.

"Sorry, Ernst." I reached down to touch his shoulder. "You just startled me."

He looked up at me then and smiled widely, grateful that I hadn't been preparing to do something violent. His little pointy ears wriggled slightly, and I suddenly realized that Lena's ears were a bit more rounded at the top. Her eyes were somewhat more almond-shaped. I'd have to pay attention to tell them apart physically, but it wasn't impossible.

"*It's awight, sir.*" He beamed.

I patted his shoulder again and smiled at him before turning my attention to Oma and Lena.

"There y'all are." Oma sighed. "Thought you'd have slithered out as soon as everyone was gone."

"*He's still here.*" Lena whisper-hissed at Oma, one of her tiny little fingers jabbing in my direction in what she probably thought was a discreet manner.

"Well, he's gonna be around for a while, so you may as well get used to coming out with him in the room," Oma spoke down to Lena. "He ain't gonna hurt you none."

"*I heard what you done to Ernst.*" Lena squinted at me.

"It was an accident," I said, referring to accidentally blasting Ernst into the bathroom with my *finger rays*. "I didn't even know I could do that."

"*Well, don' go jabbin' yer fingers at me!*" She squeaked.

Oma chuckled. I wanted to giggle but didn't think it would be appropriate. Instead, I gave her a grave look and nodded. Of course, given what had happened the night before, the fact that the Sheriff's department had been in the backyard all morning...levity would not have been entirely appropriate.

"I won't, Lena," I said. "I promise."

She harrumphed, which was extremely adorable. Ernst looked up at me and winked, sharing an aside about Lena's prickly nature. I winked back and smiled.

"Lena," I asked, "did you see where that woman came from this morning before I told you to hide?"

"*Nosir.*" She stated sharply.

"You don't know which direction she walked into the yard from?" I asked again. "You didn't see her wander out of the woods or from around the house or anything?"

"*Nosir.*" She reiterated haughtily. "*I ran ousside when I heard the missus scream bloody mur'er and that woman was stumblin' up towards the house all nekkid-like.*"

"Oh."

"I think she was already stumblin' around the yard when I walked down the steps, Robbie." Oma shrugged. "I mean, I wasn't exactly payin' attention when I stepped out of the house. I think when I got to the bottom of the steps, I looked up and here she comes, all naked and burnt up."

Sighing, I patted Ernst on the shoulder again and stood. He didn't jump at me rising to my feet, but Lena stepped closer to Oma, as though she needed a shield from my laser fingers.

"Last night, I was attacked by three werewolves in the backyard," I said, just to hear myself say it aloud. "And I blasted them with a fireball I conjured up out of my freaking hand. I burnt one of them pretty good. Then this person wanders up in the yard covered in burns."

Oma looked at me, her eyebrows raised.

"Don't think the Paxil would have helped in this situation."

Oma rolled her eyes.

"Let's face it." I shrugged. "I killed a woman."

Blasé is my middle name.

"We don't know that," Oma grunted.

"We don't not know that."

"She probably had her meth lab blow up."

"On the same morning I roasted wolf people?"

"Werewolves."

"Semantics. The coincidence is unsettling, Oma."

"Oh, just settle down." Oma raised and lowered her hands, urging me to sit.

I didn't obey. Crossing my arms over my chest, I looked down at her stubbornly, waiting for whatever it was she had to say.

"Look," Oma sighed, "maybe you tossed around a little fire to save yours and Ernst's asses. That's fair play in any book—even the law book. But we don't know who that naked lady is, let alone if she is a werewolf. And if it was her, well, she got what was comin' to her, didn't she? You attack someone on their property in the dead of night, planning to do them harm, they have a right to defend themselves."

"I suppose there's logic there, Oma." I nodded. "But that doesn't make me feel any better about being a murderer right now."

"We don't know that." Oma reiterated loudly with a waggle of her head. "And even if we did, it still don't make you a murderer. It makes you a person who was defending hisself. Period."

"Where would I find Andrew today?"

"Why?" She snapped.

"If you wanna know something about wolves..."

"Don't you dare."

"Who else can give me an idea if this woman was a werewolf?" I shrugged. "Maybe she's part of his pack?"

"Oh, this is just ridiculous." Oma shook her head. "Andrew ain't got a pack anyway."

"You got any better ideas, Oma?"

"Yeah." She slapped the table. "Sit your dumbass down and finish your coffee and pretend it never happened. In a week, they'll decide they don't know who that lady is, give her a pauper's funeral, an unmarked grave, and we'll never have to worry about it again. You done nothin' wrong."

"We can debate the morality of all of this later," I said. "But that woman's family has a right to know what happened. Especially so they can claim her body."

"You're going to talk to Andrew, find out which pack this lady belonged to—if she was even a werewolf—and then tell them you killed her? Are you crazy? They won't care that it was self-defense. And after you tell 'em, you better hope you can burn a whole bunch of wolves at one time, because they'll just attack you. No questions asked."

"What?"

"If Andrew takes you to meet her pack—or even just her Alpha— they ain't gonna take kindly to her killer amongst them, regardless of the circumstances." She said. "You'll be putting a target on your back. And mine!"

"That kind of changes things." I sunk into my seat.

"I thought it would."

"So...what do we do?" I looked up at her. "Besides act like it never happened, I mean."

Oma shook her head in exasperation.

"I mean, can't I at least go see Andrew and tell him we think some female werewolf wandered up naked and burnt and died on your lawn so he can tell the...pack...or whatever? So at least the police might find out who she was? I don't have to say I did it."

"Where's the other two wolves, Robbie?" Oma snapped.

"The..."

"The other two wolves that was with her last night?" She clarified. "If that's really who she was."

"Um..."

"Exactly." Oma gave an angry laugh.

"Them other two wolves already know where, who, what, when, where," Oma said. "Obviously, they'll know what happened to her and can tell her kinfolk themselves."

Ernst was against my leg, his arms wrapped around my calf. I laid a hand on his shoulder to give him comfort. Lena was still hiding behind Oma but was looking up at her, terrified.

"They may just leave it at that, Robbie." Oma sighed. "But we may have more visitors with paws before it's all said and done. I don't think you need to go lookin' for trouble when it's probably already headed our way."

"Are you serious?" I gasped.

"Well, werewolves like to keep themselves secret, sure." She chewed at her lip. "But those fuckers sure can hold a grudge. And they pass those grudges down through the generations. The chances of them forgetting about you barbecuing one of their pack members last night are pretty damn slim. Don't know that they'll start any trouble—but they sure won't back down from any if it's brought to their doorstep."

"Fuck."

"Mm." Oma nodded and picked up her coffee mug. "So, drink your damn coffee and act like you're Helen Keller. I hear you know a thing or two about acting."

She said the last part with a smirk. I wasn't in the mood to joke.

Chapter 4

Lucas' house smelled heavenly when I walked inside without even knocking at dinner time. If I hadn't known better, I would have expected that he was making us a Sunday roast for dinner. Rosemary, and potatoes, and meaty, juicy flavors permeated the air. My boyfriend smiled at me from the kitchen as I closed the front door behind myself and tossed my coat on one of the hooks by the door. *"Hey, babe!"* he shouted as he smiled widely and I wiped my feet on the rug just inside the door.

The house Lucas was building just felt like Lucas. Lots of wood, rustic, rough corners, simple yet elegant in a masculine way. Utilitarian but not in a sterile or nondescript way. It was merely the house of an outdoorsy guy who also was more concerned with function than style. When he wasn't cooking it smelled like all of the types of wood he had used to construct the house and...Lucas. I loved the smell of Lucas. He smelled like the wild yet clean, masculine yet fresh, exciting yet peaceful. Whenever I smelled him, it was like my brain had been fried and I couldn't make a rational decision. All of my neurons were firing wildly at all times, and I could only focus on him, not what was next or next after that. That was Lucas' house. It was a place where thinking was not required. Existing was all one had to do.

Within the walls of Lucas' house, I felt that I could slide up to the kitchen bar in front of him, sit down on one of the stools, watch him cook, and I had nothing else with which to concern myself. I could just be Rob Wagner, and nothing else mattered. Besides the fact that Lucas was so easy to like, that was my favorite thing about him. I didn't have to be anyone but me. In fact, without so much as saying it, Lucas demanded that I just be Rob. He didn't want Jacob Michaels or Robbie or Robert. He wanted Rob.

"It smells...good in here," I said as I walked into the kitchen area.

"You sound surprised." Lucas grinned at me as he wiped his hands on a hand towel he had tucked into the waistband of his jeans.

Jeans that fit him perfectly. Lucas wasn't wearing a shirt. It was all just too distracting. As I sat down on the barstool, trying to control myself, he reached across the counter, took my shirt in his hands and pulled me forward. I met his lips with mine, more than happy to kiss him. Having Lucas' lips against mine was something that always made me feel safe. Of course, that thought made me feel anything but safe.

"You taste better than the food will, I'm afraid." He whispered against my mouth as he pulled back just enough so that he could speak.

"I'm sure it'll be delicious," I replied throatily.

"I could be a world-renowned chef and still not be able to cook something that tastes as delicious as you."

"Are you trying to get an appetizer?" I teased, my lips brushing against his.

"Are you offering?"

"How important is it for you to keep an eye on the food without burning it?"

Lucas deflated with a grin. "Kind of important."

I pulled away and sat on the barstool.

"I guess you'll have to settle for dessert." I grinned evilly at him.

"I hope you can eat quick."

"Don't I always?" I asked.

"Okay, okay." He waved his hands between us. "Don't distract the chef!"

"You started it." I teased.

Lucas winked at me as he checked pots on the stovetop and glanced through the window of the oven. Next, he produced a bottle of wine from the fridge and poured us both half-glasses, setting one carefully in front of me as he took a sip of his own. Picking up the glass by the stem, I looked over at my boyfriend, wondering what it was about Lucas that made me want to throw caution to the wind. What made me want to turn all of the burners off, flip the oven off, then bend him over the counter and—

"You look distracted."

"Do I?" I sipped my wine.

"A little bit." Lucas bit his lower lip, trying to hide his smile. "Do I need to put my shirt on?"

"Do you ever?"

"You tell me."

"You could stay naked all of the time, and it wouldn't bother me," I replied. "At least...not in a bad way."

"Well," Lucas set his wine glass on the counter and reached for the button of his jeans, "I could always—"

"Do you think there's value in talking to Andrew about the werewolves from last night?"

Lucas' fingers froze as the button popped out of place and he looked at me sternly from across the kitchen counter. I chewed at my lip, chastened without having Lucas say a word, as I grabbed my wine glass and took another quick sip. Lucas' hands slid away from the waist of his jeans to rest at his sides as he considered me from the other side of the kitchen counter.

"Really?"

"Just a thought." I cringed. "You can keep stripping. I was paying attention, I swear."

"I am not taking another single article of clothing off until you explain yourself." Lucas laced his arms over his chest. "You are on warning, mister."

"So, you're saying if I came over there right now and—" I smiled wickedly.

"Don't you dare try to change the subject."

I sighed. "Fine."

"Why do you want to talk to Andrew?" The way he said the name told me that Lucas still wasn't over the fact that Andrew and I had gone on a date.

Sure, the date had been horrible, and Andrew had been an insufferable douchebag throughout—not to mention the fact that he had turned into a wolf at the end and had tried to make me a nummy little treat. Regardless of the circumstances, Andrew was a man who was interested in me. Or, had been at one time. The status of present-day levels of interest was unknown.

"He's a werewolf," I answered, trying to sound as disinterested as possible. "Only one I know. I figured he'd know something about whether or not that woman this morning was actually a werewolf, too. Or if he had heard anything through the grapevine about what happened last night. Ya' know?"

"Rob."

"What?"

"Don't talk to the wolf."

"*The Wolf* now is he?" I teased.

"He's trouble."

"And you aren't?" I waggled my eyebrows.

A break appeared in Lucas' stern façade, and I knew that I had the upper hand in the discussion. Just keep him on the ropes and don't mention talking to Andrew anymore, Rob.

"I'm not that kind of trouble."

"You're the best kind of trouble." I licked my lips. "I like your kind of trouble, babe."

"Stop that." Lucas averted his eyes, a smile coming to his lips.

"We should see how much trouble we can cause after we eat this delicious dinner, babe."

"Rob." It had been his attempt at being firm, but he didn't quite manage.

"I bet it won't taste as good as you, though," I added.

"Okay." He shook his hands crazily. "Stop it. You're distracting me from cooking dinner. I need to pay attention to what I'm doing, or we'll have to eat charcoal."

"You used noodles and not, like, slices of zucchini, right?" I teased.

"I'm not a monster."

"Good," I said. "Now, how about you give me a kiss, and we'll forget all about everything but dinner and each other?"

Lucas rolled his eyes but eventually leaned across the counter, presenting his lips to me once again. Leaning forward, I pressed my lips against his, trying to forget all about Andrew and everything on my mind about the naked burned up lady, werewolves, Kobolds, hooded people in the backyard—all of it. As I pulled back from Lucas, he was grinning, his eyes slowly opening to look at me. He gave me a wink, and I reached up to take his face in my hands so that I could kiss him once again, but deeper.

It was dark outside.

Lucas was slowly walking up the steps of the bleachers in the stands of the football stadium.

He smiled at me.

"What are you doing out here all alone?"

Something like talking under water.

More talking.

"Did you...want someone to keep you company?"

Then we were running through the woods. His hand was in mine, and we were scared. Both of us were gasping for breath and scared out of our minds. Then we were standing in the dark of the woods, looking around frantically.

"Did you see that?"

I pulled back from Lucas, my eyes wide. His lips were still pursed, and his eyes were still closed. So, I leaned forward and gave him another quick kiss on the lips, then immediately withdrew my hands from his face. I sat back on the barstool, affixing a smile to my face.

"You still taste better than anything." He opened his eyes to smile at me.

"Still do." I nodded.

"Always."

I gave a nervous chuckle. "Always."

Chapter 5

Carlos looked as glamorous outside of drag as he looked when he was dressed as Carlita. When I had gone to the center, under the guise of helping out the community, I was hoping to run into Andrew. After Oma had thrown a fit about going to see Andrew, and Lucas had made it clear that he would never be okay with the idea, going directly to Andrew was a decidedly bad idea. If I went to his office building—or God forbid, found out where he lived and went to his home—I'd have a grandmother and a boyfriend out for blood. Running into him at the LGBTQIA center was pretty innocent, though. It couldn't possibly be my fault if Andrew and I showed up at the center on the same day.

It wasn't the best plan I'd ever come up with, going to the LGBTQIA center in Toledo to find Andrew, but my head hadn't been right for half a day. When I had touched Lucas' face—my *boyfriend's* face—I had the same experience I had had with *Teenage Ghost Rob*. And Ernst. Were these memories? Alternate realities? Dreams? Hopes? Wishes? What were these odd memories flashing through my brain?

After dinner, Lucas and I had had sex. A lot. In fact, we had fallen asleep so late in the night that I was afraid Lucas would not get out of bed for work in the morning. Even if he did, I knew he'd be sore. We had done it every which way we could think of, though my mind had been somewhere else the entire time. Not that I hadn't enjoyed having sex with my boyfriend—he was pretty stellar at it—but I couldn't help but feel a cluster of nagging thoughts and questions in the back of my mind.

When morning came, Lucas and I were roused by his alarm, and I had decided that it would be a good day to find Andrew. Lucas would be at the school, teaching young, fertile minds, and then helping at the hardware store, so he wouldn't be able to check in on me. Oma didn't follow me around much, thus avoiding her wouldn't be an issue. Ernst and the other Kobolds didn't leave the house as far as I knew, so I had to take advantage of the situation. Andrew might show up at the center. And, if he did, I would be there waiting with a laundry list of questions.

However, the only person there when I arrived, shortly after breakfast, was the center director, who promptly put me to work stuffing envelopes again. Apparently, the LGBTQIA community had need of a lot of reading material. I wanted to feel snarky and put out by the whole thing, but as I stuffed envelopes, I found myself wishing that someone had been sending out brochures and information to me when I was a teen—hell, even as an adult. It would have made everything about being a gay teen, and then a gay man, so much easier. At the very least, I wouldn't have felt so lost and alone. The thought that maybe one of my envelopes might be opened by a confused and lost teen caused me to smile as I performed the task. I had been like that, all alone, for an hour, before Carlos walked in the door.

Carlos was wearing jeans and a sweater, a stylish jean jacket—all of it well fitted to his slim body—a scarf around his neck that practically had its own wind machine, huge sunglasses, a large tan purse...and Louboutins. Apparently, even out of drag, Louboutins were acceptable footwear to Carlos. It made me smile. Not that he was wearing the shoes I had bought for him, but that he enjoyed them so much. He did look good in them, so why not wear them any chance he got, I figured.

"Well, look at you!" He whipped his overly large sunglasses off and smiled over at me as the door shut behind him. "I didn't think I'd see you here again, Rob, honey!"

I smiled as Carlos sashayed over to the table in his fancy heels. Carlos whipped his scarf off with a flourish and deposited it onto the table along with his sunglasses and purse. As he slid into the folding chair across from me, I continued stuffing envelopes but turned my focus to him. The fact that Carlos had remembered my real name and hadn't called me "Jacob" made me smile internally. Most *civilians* weren't so conscious of what they called me and when they called me it. Leave it to a drag queen to know when to use an alias and when not to—wise and magical creatures, drag queens.

"I thought I'd come help out a little today," I replied.

"Well, aren't you a doll?" He replied as he grabbed some of the envelopes and inserts to help out. "I hadn't seen you or Esther Jean since you first came here, so I figured you weren't coming back. Of course, I should have known better. I'm sorry for thinking you thought you were too good for us, baby."

Carlos gave me a wink from an eye that seemed to perpetually twinkle, causing me to laugh.

"How are you, Carlos?"

"Oh, lawd, help me." He fanned his face with the envelope in his hand then went about stuffing materials into it. "I have been trying to get a space to do my drag show at because the last place—Pixxxies?—it shut down a week ago. Apparently, after fourteen health code violations, they just shut you down. Who knew?"

"Fourteen?" I coughed.

"Well," Carlos sighed, "it might have been more, honestly. They didn't have real bartenders so things weren't as clean as they should have been. You'd think with all of the damn customers and money I brought through that door twice a week, they'd have had money to get at least one good bartender. Sleazy ass Enrique—*he's the piece of shit who ran the place?*—well, he cared more about money than quality. He never paid me enough to even keep a one-legged hooker in fishnets, and that's why all my wigs look like they were harvested from JC Penney mannequins. Bastard. Didn't even get paid for my last show."

"Wow." I shook my head. "That's...well, that's fucked up."

"To say the least." Carlos nodded, his lips pursed. "I find that motherfucker the soles of these heels will get even redder."

I laughed loudly.

"How you doin', baby?" Carlos reached across the table to swat the back of my hand. "You're lookin' like you might have put on a pound or two. You're simply glowing, baby."

"Thank you." I smiled. "Oma has been making sure that I eat."

"Vieja loca can throw down in the kitchen, I'm sure," Carlos responded. "All old women can. Even the white ones. So...that doesn't explain the glow..."

I shrugged.

"Mm."

"What?" I chuckled.

"I think you might be gettin' a lil' sum sum lately, that's what I think." Carlos nodded as if affirming something to himself. "You have that, 'I'm getting laid regularly' look to you."

Whether or not I liked it, I felt myself blush.

"I knew it." Carlos was nodding again. "Baby, ain't nothin' wrong with gettin' the bottom knocked out every now and again. Or doin' the knockin'. Just play safe. You can't be volunteering at the center and not know how to take care of yourself. You need some condoms?"

Carlos was reaching for his bag.

"No." I reached out pushed his hand away from his purse with a laugh. "I've got condoms. Plenty."

"Mmhm." Carlos grinned comically. "I knew that's what was going on with you. Well, good for you, baby. He any good?"

"In bed?"

Carlos rolled his eyes. "Of course not. I'm not *that* tacky. I meant is he good to you?"

"Oh." I grinned. "Yeah. I think so. Yeah. He's really good to me."

"It may be none of my business," Carlos looked around and leaned in, "but it wouldn't happen to be another man who volunteers here and Esther Jean set you up with, would it?"

I turned my nose up.

"Good God, no."

Carlos shrugged.

"Well, then I'm out of guesses, and you'll have to tell me all about him." Carlos quipped. "What's he like, what's he do, how tall is he...how jealous will I be when I see him? All of that stuff."

"Um," I chewed at my lip, "I want to kind of keep it quiet for now. We haven't been seeing each other long, and even though it became a *thing* pretty quickly, it's still new, obviously."

"Obviously." He said as he reached for more envelopes.

"But now that you mention Andrew...do you think he'll be in sometime today?" I asked. "I did want to talk to him."

Carlos' right eyebrow rose to precarious heights as he gave an envelope seal a comical lick.

"Not like that." I shook my head. "I just wanted to ask him some questions about his family."

"Mm."

"I promise that's all it is." I laughed.

Carlos studied me from across the table for a moment.

"Well...okay," Carlos said finally. "But if I find out that you're fucking around and being a bad boy, you'll be another reason these soles are red."

"You just can't help mentioning those shoes, can you?" I teased.

"They are fabulous." Carlos leaned in with a squeal and patted my cheek. "Thank you again, baby. All these other bitches around here are jealous as shit."

"You're welcome." I nodded.

Carlos patted my cheek again and sat back in his seat.

"Well, Andrew comes in whenever he sees fit, honestly." Carlos looked around before surreptitiously reaching into his bag to pull out an e-cig. He gave it a healthy puff and blew the vapor out of the corner of his mouth. "Tell me if you see anyone sneaking up."

I laughed. "Okay."

"I haven't seen him since the last time I saw you, frankly." Another puff on the e-cig. "He used to come in whenever he could if he wasn't busy at his office, or if he was on lunch, or...just whenever he felt the need. But, like you, I guess he is feeling too good for us commoners."

I shook my head with a smile.

"I'm just kidding, baby." Carlos took another puff and folded one arm across his chest, resting the elbow holding the e-cig against it. "He's probably just been busy. You'll probably have to go down to his office to talk to him if it's super important. You stick around here waiting, you might have gray hairs before he shows up."

"I guess I might have to walk down there later." I sighed.

"We all got bullshit to deal with." Carlos teased.

For several minutes, Carlos puffed on his e-cig while I stuffed envelopes and kept an eye out for the center director or anyone else who might narc on him. Once all of the envelopes had been stuffed, I sat back and looked over at Carlos as he puffed away, not a care in the world.

"You seem to be taking losing your drag show pretty well," I said. "You don't look too stressed."

"Stress creates Crow's Feet." Carlos quipped as he blew out vapor. "I can't afford that shit."

"Well, you're handling it remarkably well."

"I didn't lose my drag show, anyway." Carlos took a final puff and stuffed the e-cig back into his bag. "That's in here."

He jabbed a manicured nail into his chest.

"I just lost the place to perform it." He reiterated. "Clubs are a dime a dozen. Just, a lot of them don't have the stage space for a *good* drag show. I'll make the rounds, though. Talk to owners, see what I can do. This ain't the first time I've had to hustle. And there are other bars in town. They care more about ensembles, though. I'll figure something out."

"Let me know." I winked. "I'll come see the first show. Promise."

Carlos put a hand to his chest. "I would be honored, baby."

Standing up from my seat, I pushed the folding chair back in under the table as I smiled down at Carlos.

"Tell the warden I had to leave, would you?"

"Absolutely." Carlos winked. "Don't be a stranger."

"I won't." I agreed. "See ya' next time, Carlos."

"Bye, baby."

Exiting onto the street in front of the center, it became apparent that the day was going to warm up—maybe even be tolerable by lunchtime. Since the wind wasn't too strong and it wasn't too cold, and Andrew's office building wasn't too far away from the center, I opted to walk over to see if I could locate him. I gave the lock button on my key fob a quick click and my car honked at me as I made my way down the sidewalk. Being in downtown Toledo reminded me of being back in Hollywood—of course, it wasn't nearly as cosmopolitan or busy or, well, big, but it was a taste of being in a place more significant than the postage stamp that was Point Worth.

When I had come back to Point Worth, I knew that I wanted to get away from living such a busy lifestyle, constantly around tons of people, running from paparazzi, listening to a constant dull roar of noise. However, after what had happened over the last several days, I wasn't so sure if Point Worth was going to be the ideal place to settle down in, either. Apparently, the supernatural community—the *were*-community—were all over the place, so I couldn't entirely escape whatever it was that went on in the shadows. However, I certainly couldn't hide in a small town like Point Worth. It was everywhere at all times because there wasn't enough space to contain it.

In my heart of hearts, as I made my way down the sidewalk, hands in my pocket, eyes down so that no one could get a straightforward look at my face, I knew that Point Worth was home. If something like the date with Andrew and then the attack from the werewolves, Kobolds—any of it—had happened in Hollywood or anywhere else, I would have lost my mind. I wouldn't have known what to do. Something about being home in Point Worth, where I was born and raised, living in Oma's house, it all made me feel stronger. Braver. Saner. Powerful. Maybe Point Worth and even Oma's house wasn't perfect, but it just felt natural to be there. Hollywood and anywhere else in the world felt wrong.

Andrew's office building was large enough that I knew I would have to ask around quite a bit to find him. Hopefully, I wouldn't get recognized by anyone in the process, either. As luck would have it, I didn't have to enter the building, ask a receptionist where to go, talk to another receptionist, talk to other employees, so on and so forth until I had spoken to a hundred different people. Andrew was outside of his building, sitting on one of the benches, eating a sandwich and drinking something in a to-go coffee cup. Probably coffee, if I were to place a bet.

The setting was so peaceful and calm, and Andrew looked so happy to be enjoying his lunch that I almost backed out of talking to him. He obviously had not been in Oma's backyard the night of the attack, and maybe he didn't really have any pertinent information that could help me. Interrupting his lunch and causing him stress definitely wouldn't make me feel good about myself. However, my mind flashed back to the night we had gone on our date, and he had tried to get handsy with me in his car before turning into a wolf and tried to gobble me up. Ruining Andrew's lunch didn't seem so awful after I remembered that.

"What's on the sandwich?" I asked as I sat down on the bench next to him, making sure to leave adequate room between us.

Andrew smiled and looked over.

The smile quickly disappeared when he saw me.

He didn't change from smiling to angry or annoyed; he just looked concerned. Of course, in dealing with me, he had been practically run over by Lucas' truck, punched in the face—by me—and cussed out numerous times by myself and Oma. His track record when I was around was not great.

"Rob." He exhaled.

I smiled and shrugged, though it wasn't as light-hearted as I would have liked. Andrew wasn't someone I could ever trust, so I couldn't put my heart into trying to be jovial with him. Something about a guy trying to eat you really makes you wary of him, ya' know?

"How've ya' been?" I asked simply.

"Um, okay." His brow furrowed. "I guess?"

I gave an upward nod.

"Any fleas or ticks we need to worry about?" It was a low blow, but he still had insults coming as far as I was concerned.

Andrew's dark cheeks flushed as he gently started wrapping up his sandwich again.

"Don't stop on account of me." I gestured vaguely at the sandwich. "I'm not here to cause you trouble. I probably won't be super nice—but what's new?"

"I told you that I'm sorry."

"Takes more than a sorry after what you did, I'm afraid." I sat back, pushing my hands into my pockets. "But, I'm not here for more apologies or your attempt at contrition. Eat your damn sandwich."

Andrew waited a moment, observing me carefully as I stared straight ahead at the street before us. A car would drive by slowly every few seconds. People were walking by on our side and the other side of the road, but no one paid attention to us, nor were they close enough to hear us talk—as long as we didn't raise our voices. Raising my voice wasn't the plan unless Andrew did something douchey again. Finally, as though he realized it was safe, Andrew took his sandwich back out and took a bite.

"I was attacked by three werewolves the other night."

Andrew nearly choked on his bite.

"I wanted to know if you knew anything about that," I said, not concerned with the choking sounds.

It took a few moments, but Andrew finally managed to stop choking, finished chewing the bite, then swallowed in what looked like a painful way. Of course, I wasn't sure if he just hadn't chewed thoroughly or if what I'd had to say had rattled him more than I thought.

"I don't know anything about that, Rob." He spat, reaching for his coffee to wash down the bite he had swallowed.

"Well, you're the only furry fellow I know around these parts, so I figured you'd know more than anyone else." I shrugged. "So...here I am."

"I'm telling you, I don't know anything about anyone attacking you," Andrew replied quickly, desperately. "I'm still upset with myself over what I did. I'm really, really sorry, Rob."

I waved him off.

"I want to know if you know of any other werewolves in town," I said evenly, still staring straight ahead. "And...I managed to hurt one of the werewolves. And she died."

Why was I telling him that part?

"She got burned really badly, and the next morning she wandered up into the yard, naked as the day she was born, and her skin looked all melted. I wanted to know why she would turn back human before she died."

Andrew was staring at me like I was crazy. That was fair.

Who was to say that I wasn't?

"I don't know any other werewolves. Or packs. I mean, I know of them and sometimes speak with them casually—shop talk—but I don't *know* them." Andrew said finally. "I'm kind of a loner. I have been for years. Since before college."

Andrew was chewing at his lip, his eyes flicking around, deep in thought as he sat on the bench, holding his sandwich but not taking any bites. I watched him for a moment, waiting to see if he'd add anything else of his own accord, but it became apparent that he was not going to speak up unless prodded. His fingers were digging into his sandwich, his nails and fingertips sinking into the bread and the fillings inside. Mustard was oozing out of the sandwich around one of his fingers, but he didn't seem to notice. It takes a lot of distraction to not realize that you're losing the condiments on your sandwich.

"Andrew?" He started at the sound of my voice, his head whipping around to look at me again. "Why did she turn back into a human before she died instead of just dying in wolf form?"

"That didn't happen." Andrew shook his head, chunking his sandwich into the trash can at the end of the bench. "That doesn't happen."

"It did. Saw it with my own eyes," I said. "She got burned during the fight, one of her comrades drug her off into the woods, then the next morning some woman wandered up into the yard naked, and half of her body burned all to hell. I'm not making that up."

"I believe you saw what you saw, Rob," Andrew said lowly. "But...if someone is hurt when they're..."

"A wolf?"

Andrew looked around, suddenly aware that we were in public having this conversation. I laughed.

"If anyone heard us, they'd just assume we were crazy or talking about a video game or mythology." I snorted. "I think we're completely safe here."

Andrew swallowed hard and nodded jerkily.

"If that happens, then they die, or they recover." He explained. "And it takes a lot to kill a werewolf. As you know..."

I nodded.

"If I were hurt right now and could change into wolf form, it would heal me." He looked me in the eyes. "It's one of the perks. We heal well. And fast."

For a moment, I stared back into Andrew's human eyes. I nearly shivered thinking of what they looked like in wolf form. Red eyes and feral thoughts and blood lust.

"What if you're hurt with...*magic*?"

He shrugged, unfazed by the question. Points for Andrew.

"About the same." He said. "I mean, magic is more likely to deliver a fatal blow—nature of the beast and how they are related—but we can recover from any wound if it doesn't kill us really quickly."

Thinking about this, I wondered if the werewolf had died as soon as I had burned her and it had nothing to do with the naked burned lady. Maybe the lead wolf—*alpha?*—had drug a dead wolf away and the naked lady was just a coincidence? Perhaps she was just someone who had been involved in a meth lab explosion? Then again—why was she naked?

"When you, uh, change back to human, you are naked, right?"

Andrew flushed again.

"Yes." He exhaled. "Why?"

"Calm down." I squinted at him. "I was just wondering whether or not someone would change back fully clothed or what. That's all."

He nodded, looking away.

If I had burned a werewolf badly while in wolf form, logically, that person would be naked and burned when they changed back to human form. If the woman who had wandered up into the yard had been involved in something like a meth lab explosion, surely, she would have been wearing clothes. Or at least the remnants of scorched and charred clothes. The woman who had wandered up in the yard was burnt all along one side—just like the wolf I had blasted—and she was stark naked. It made more sense that the two events were connected than them not being linked.

"I guess that's all I needed." I stood.

Andrew stood quickly.

"Rob—"

"You're forgiven, Andrew." I turned to him.

My face was bland. Impassive.

"If I forgive you, you can stop worrying about it, right?" I said. "So, you're forgiven. I understand now that it's the nature of the beast. I don't believe you did anything on purpose. I still think it's fucking shitty that you chose to go on a date with someone when you knew that the full moon was coming...and I'm even madder that person was me. But I forgive you. I just hope you've learned to keep to yourself on *those nights*."

Andrew nodded with a sigh.

"Good."

"Rob," He stopped me from turning away, "do you think I could get another chance? I mean, we could go out again. Try to start over?"

I didn't mean to, but I laughed loudly.

"You can't be serious." I chuckled. "I mean, I'm not completely stupid, Andrew. I may believe that what happened was an accident—but I'm not going to give you the opportunity to make the same mistake twice."

"I won't."

"I'm seeing someone."

"Oh."

"Yup."

"Are you seeing someone, or is that the nicest way you could think of to make me stop asking for a second date?"

"Both." I nodded. "Always a pleasure, Andrew."

With that, I turned on my heels and strolled away. To Andrew's credit, he didn't chase after me, holler any apologies or promises or do anything to keep me from going on about my business, which was good. I already had too many things on my mind to spend any more energy explaining how little I would like a second date with him. Andrew was cute. Very cute, actually. But he was a werewolf who had tried to eat me alive on the one date we had gone on. Even if I could *genuinely* forgive that, I couldn't overlook the fact that he had been an utterly insufferable douchebag during the date leading up to him turning into a wolf in front of my eyes. Maybe his behavior had been connected to his *condition* and the oncoming full moon, but it was too hard to overlook.

Regardless of the problems with even thinking about Andrew in such a way, I also knew that I was showing bias. Andrew was a werewolf. Oma was a witch. Lucas was...*something*. And I certainly wasn't just vanilla-flavored human. Ordinary humans don't shoot green shit and fire out of their hands, do they? Of course, I had no idea what I was. The worst part was—that wasn't my biggest problem. I also didn't remember some essential things from my past. Flashes of memories I'd had proved that to me.

Even more disturbing than not having the best memory was the discovery that I had memories in my head that weren't entirely accurate. In my mind, I had lived with Oma until I was sixteen years old because my parents had...well, I didn't know. That was a sudden revelation. Where were my parents? What had happened to them? Were they dead? Had they run off? It dawned on me that I didn't know where my parents were or if they were even alive to be somewhere. Something in my mind had just made me accept that they were no longer around and I had never thoroughly and honestly questioned that. Why was that?

Remembering life with Oma before I ran off to chase fame and fortune was difficult as well. I knew I had gone to school; I had found Oma's house odd when I lived there, I had not had too many friends, I had loved school plays and choir and playing guitar, and...everything was vague. I honestly couldn't put a finger on a single complete memory while I was awake. But when I slept and dreamed or had nightmares, or sometimes when I touched other people, full and complete memories came back to me. But they became hazy as time went on. I was already forgetting the memories I had seen in my mind's eye when I touched Ernst and Lucas.

I stopped in the middle of the sidewalk and pulled out my phone. Pulling up the notepad app, I made myself notes about the memories still in my head. Just in case I forgot them again.

Chapter 6

"What the hell are you doing now?" Oma grumbled when she entered the kitchen through the back door.

Glancing over my shoulder at her, I took in the dirty bib overalls, the rubber gardening shoes, the too big gloves, the big sun hat, and the spade in her hand as she stood there. She looked like any grandmother from anywhere across the country getting ready to plant her garden for spring. The fact that I knew she was anything but the innocent old lady planting her garden made the ensemble look ridiculous. Lena was standing at her side, arms crossed over her tiny chest, glaring at me, helped me remember that Oma was not the little old farmer lady she appeared to be.

"*I told ya', sir,*" Ernst whispered up from my side, where he had been standing for the last few minutes. "*This was a bad idea.*"

"It's okay, Ernst," I replied and turned away from the cellar door I had been attempting to open.

The door in the kitchen that led down to the cellar was tightly shut, though I couldn't see anything that kept it sealed so tightly closed. A good lock would have kept me out, but the door didn't even budge a fraction of a centimeter when I pulled on the knob. Most doors will give at least a little, rattle in the frame, when yanked on forcefully. The cellar door did nothing but stay tightly in place, keeping me from gaining access to the room below.

"Where's the key?" I turned to Oma, crossing my arms over my chest as I stared her down.

"Why?"

"So I can open the door." I glowered. "Obviously."

"Why would you want to do that?" She said. "I done told you to stay out of there. There ain't nothin' down there for you."

"Let me be the judge of that. Where's the key?"

"You ain't goin' down there."

"It's either the key...or an ax." I shrugged. "Maybe I can figure out that fire throwing trick again...but I'm not entirely sure how that works so who knows what I'll end up doing. Up to you."

Oma glowered at me.

Lena's eyes had grown wide, and her arms had dropped to her sides.

Ernst was shifting from foot to foot by my side.

"Ernst." Oma barked. "How could you let this happen?"

"Ernst isn't my keeper." I snapped. "And you leave him alone. He hasn't done anything wrong."

I placed a hand gently on the top of Ernst's head, luckily without memories flashing through my mind. Like the green lasers and the fire, the memories came whenever they felt it was appropriate.

"So, I see he's your little pet again." Oma rolled her eyes.

"I'm sorry?"

Oma looked startled for a minute then was back to glowering at Ernst and me.

"Nothin', ya' shithead!" She snapped. "There's no key to the damn cellar and ya' ain't goin' down there. End of discussion."

"Fine." I nodded.

Calmly, I motioned for Ernst to move away. He gave me a pleading look but shuffled a few feet away. I gave Oma one last look, then turned around, took a step back, then attempted to put my foot through the door. All I managed to do was send pain up through the heel of my foot that settled in my calf. I didn't let it stop me. I kicked again. And again. And again. The door was rattling, finally, but I knew after the fifth kick that this was not going to provide the results that I wanted.

I spun around to glare at Oma, my foot aching.

"I'm going to get an ax."

"Oh, for fuck's sake," Oma grumbled before I could make a move for the back door. "You want in there so fuckin' bad, fine."

The fact that Oma hadn't screamed at me for trying to kick in one of her doors was not lost on me. Maybe she knew that I could pay to replace anything I broke? Or perhaps she knew I'd never be able to kick it in and one of her household helpers would fix any damage?

Lena and Ernst were both looking uncomfortable as Oma stomped across the kitchen to the sink and opened her "catch-all" drawer. I waited, trying not to wince at the pain in my foot as she rustled around in the drawer. Oma muttered to herself like a crazy person—naturally—and Ernst and Lena shifted nervously from foot to foot as I waited for the key to be found. With all of her mumbling and cursing under her breath, I couldn't help but feel that maybe Oma was stalling for time until she could figure out a way to distract me.

Kicking at the door had been a dick move. I knew that. However, with everything that had happened since I got into Point Worth—Kobolds, werewolves, magic fingers (not the sexy-time kind), naked burned up women, Teenage Ghost Rob—*everything* was making me desperate to figure out what was going on. If I had to kick in a door, or, try to kick in a door, then I was going to do that. Having more and more unfamiliar memories flashing through my head when I touched someone, ghostly apparitions of my teenage self, or more attacks from local werewolves, were things I could do without for the rest of my life.

Maybe I'd find something in the cellar that would put all of the pieces together. Or maybe there would be nothing. Maybe I'd go down in the cellar and have a revelation that would eventually drive me over the edge for good. After several dreams of the cellar and the ghostly green light, I knew that the cellar wasn't a terrible place to look for answers. No matter what I found in the cellar, once I gained entrance, at least it would settle my mind. If I found something that explained what was going on, that would be ideal. If the cellar held nothing of import, then at least I'd know to focus my attention somewhere else. At least I'd be moving in the right direction and taking action, not just standing around with my thumb in my ass.

"You and this damn cellar." Oma huffed as she yanked the key out of the drawer. "I don't know why the hell you got to go down there."

I held my hand out. "Just give me the key, Oma."

Oma slapped the key into my hand as if slapping me the angriest high-five ever. Ignoring her anger, I looked down at the common key and turned to the door. Ernst tugged at my pant leg with one little fist.

"*Sir.*" He squeaked. "*Maybe we ought-not go down there?*"

"It'll be okay, Ernst." I looked at Oma over my shoulder. "Right, Oma? We're not going to find anything too crazy down there are we?"

I smirked at her.

"Not unless old Christmas decorations and mouse shit are scandalous to ya'." She snapped. "Or if cobwebs are too much for your heart."

"There ya' go, Ernst." I winked down at him. "There's nothing to worry about. Even Oma says so."

He glanced over at Oma and from the way he twitched, I could only imagine the face she was giving him. The fact that Ernst had taken a liking to me so quickly...or so quickly *again* would eventually be checked off of my To-Do List of things I needed to try and remember. However, the Kobolds in the house were not my biggest concern. They lived and moved in the shadows and kept the house clean. Maybe pulled a few harmless pranks. Otherwise, they were not the reason why I felt the way I did. Not having access to my full Rolodex of memories was the problem. Oma wasn't going to explain it to me directly—even if she fully understood it or knew about it—so I was taking things into my own hands. I was going down into the cellar no matter how anyone felt about it.

The lock didn't do much once I had crammed the key into it. From the feeling of resistance, my first thought was that Oma had given me the wrong key. Either that was intentional or, she hadn't opened the door in so long that she didn't remember which key opened it. However, after a little steady twisting and turning, the lock started to move. Oma grumbled behind me, obviously not pleased with anything that was going on. I ignored her and twisted the key gently until the lock was disengaged.

Instincts took over, and I didn't stand there, looking at the unlocked door, breathing in my victory at getting access to the cellar. Instead, I turned the knob and pulled the door outwards. A cold blast of air shot up the stairs, chilling me to the bone, but only darkness greeted my eyes. Ernst shivered and moved to stand behind my legs as I peered down the dark stairwell. Looking into the darkness, all I could think about was what I would do if all of my answers were in the room beneath us. What if I went downstairs and had the biggest revelation of my life? What if I left the cellar a changed man?

"Spooky." Oma snorted. "Ain't it?"

"You got a flashlight?" I looked over at her.

"Turn the damn light on, ya' idiot." She snapped. "It's right there on the wall at eye level. You ain't just dumb, you're also blind."

"Thanks," I stated blandly before turning to look for the switch she had referenced.

Locating the light switch was easy enough. It was just inside the door, mounted to one of the wooden studs to the right. I gave it a quick slap and lights—well, probably *one light*—came on below. The cellar was still dark, but there was enough light for me to see that the floor was dirt. The stairs were wooden but solid looking, and shadows loomed everywhere. The walls of the stairwell were unfinished, as was to be expected, and there was a fair amount of dust with a scattering of cobwebs along the stairwell. Ernst was quiet, but his fingers were trying to dig into the backs of my legs. I reached down and patted the top of his head, feeling a surge of something again, but no memories flashed through my head. I laid my hand on top of his head for a moment, but nothing else happened.

Oma was still frowning when I looked over at her with my hand atop of Ernst's head.

"What?" She spat.

"Just wondering if I'm going to find any bodies down here," I said. "I mean, you are the resident witch around here, right? Are there bones of children down there?"

Oma squinted angrily at me.

"Double, double, toil and trouble." I waggled my head. "Fire burn and cauldron bubble."

"What?" She snarled.

"Read a book, Oma." I rolled my eyes. "For God's sake, pick up a damn book. Fuck, watch a play or a movie that doesn't star me."

She flipped me off with a snarl.

"Charming."

Oma ignored me.

"You goin' down there or what, smartass?" She shoved her fists against her hips. "Or are you just proving a point?"

Instead of responding, I stepped down and began my descent into the cellar as Ernst tried to keep ahold of my pant legs. Gently, I pulled his hands away from my legs and smiled at him. Wordlessly, I let him know that he did not have to come with me, then patted him on the head again. I didn't know if pats on the head were appropriate for Kobolds, as though treating them like a family pet, but he didn't seem to mind. Ernst seemed to find the gentle touches reassuring, so I ignored my desire to examine it.

Slowly but surely, I took one step at a time, descending further into the cellar, my fingers trailing the walls along the stairwell as I moved. After a few moments, I heard Oma stomp to the cellar door and start following me down. Whether or not that was a good thing, I wasn't sure. If she came into the cellar with me, would she try to distract me in my examination of the room, or would she just stand there and watch. Seeing as there was no option but to let her go into the cellar—it was attached to her house after all—I walked down the last few steps. My feet touched the dirt floor, and I moved away from the steps to survey the room around me.

Stone walls, lots of cobwebs, the kitchen floor overhead, a stack of boxes in the corner, a bare bulb mounted to one of the studs overhead. It was dank and dark and musty but otherwise looked like a fairly organized cellar. Save the dust and cobwebs, it was reasonably clean as well. Oma stepped down onto the dirt floor as well and looked at me, waving her hands around dramatically. Her grand gesture of "what did I tell you" made me want to flip her off. I controlled my instincts and just looked around the cellar at the absolute lack of anything.

In one of my dreams, there had been a well that had been waist high with green light beaming up from wherever the bottom of it was. Reality was a different story—just a solid dirt floor from wall to wall with very few things of interest scattered around. Oma appeared impressively organized in her storage skills. Someone easily could have converted the basement into a den, a family room, or even an apartment. It wasn't huge—but it was bigger than most apartments you'd get in New York City on a budget. Probably got more natural light, too.

"Find what you was lookin' for?" She snorted.

"You're a real peach, Oma," I stated blandly as I turned, looking around at...*nothing.*

"I can go get you a shovel if you want to dig up the floor." She added. "Just in case you ain't yet satisfied."

"If there's nothing down here...why were you so against me coming down here?" I turned to her, lacing my arms over my chest.

"All this damn nonsense you've gotten into your head—I don't want you to keep feeding it!"

"I'm sorry?" I laughed bitterly. "I think the Ernst, Lena and...the others whose names I can't remember right now—"

"Hans, Felix, and Oskar."

"Yeah." I waved her off. "Them. They prove that not everything my brain comes up with is just nonsense. You lied to me about them. You said I was crazy. Well, lady, I think we proved that I was not crazy. So it's gonna take a shit more than an empty cellar for me to believe everything is peachy keen in Fuckville, Ohio."

"Fuckville?" She turned her nose up.

"I don't know!" I threw my hands up. "I'm not really on top of my game today, all right?"

"Obviously." She mimicked my hands-over-chest pose and stared impassively back at me.

"I've had dreams about this cellar." I jabbed my finger down at the floor in a childish display of stubbornness.

Should've stomped my foot as well.

"There is something about this cellar."

"Well," Oma clucked, "since I have no idea what you're talking about, I guess you're just going to have to find it. Dig your way to China for all I fuckin' care. But everything better be back the way I had it before you brought your arrogant ass down here!"

Oma waggled her head and turned towards the stairs. She laid her hand upon the handrail, and her foot landed on the first step.

"Where's the well, Oma?"

Anyone who didn't know my grandmother wouldn't have caught it, but I saw the slight pause she took, the uncertain look on her face before she turned to me with a scowl.

"Who has a well in their goddamn basement?"

"There was one here in a dream I had."

"Then it must be true." She rolled her eyes. "Just like the other night when I dreamed that Sam Elliott had come to make sweet love to me years back."

"Gross." I turned my nose up.

"He's a fine lookin' man." She whispered conspiratorially. "And that voice. Oh, my."

"Well the voice is one thing, but he's too old for me and—stop changing the goddamn subject, Oma."

"I ain't changin' the subject! You're the one getting all hot and bothered!" She reached up to lay a hand at the front of her neck. "I'm just makin' a point that dreams ain't real!"

"Oh, you're not real!" I snapped back.

"What?"

"I don't know!"

"Well," She rolled her eyes, "I'm glad to see your mental health is in a grand state. Why don't you go lay down? Obviously, you need some rest."

"Blow it out your ass, Oma." I snarled.

Oma rolled her eyes as I stormed across the cellar, rounded her, and stomped up the steps. I didn't even wait to see if she followed. Once I was out of the cellar, I made my way through the house and upstairs to my room. Making sure my door was shut and locked, I threw myself on the bed. Moments later, Ernst appeared from the corner behind the dresser and tiptoed towards the bed. My eyes landed on him, and he looked up at me with a disconcerted frown. Sighing, I patted the other side of the bed. Ernst crawled up and sat down in the Lotus position, his hands in his lap. Together, we both used the bed as our place to go over our concerns and worries.

Chapter 7

Are you scared?
No. I'm just lost.
I'd be scared.
I have no reason to be scared. I just don't know what to do. Things are changing. She's worried.
What do you think we should do?
I don't know. I don't know anything right now.
I wish I could help you.
We could...run away.
Together?
Would you run away with me?
Of course, I...did you see that?
What?
Rob! Run!
Why? What did you see?
Rob!
"Rob?"
Knocking.
Lucas' voice.
When I sat up in bed, shaking off the afternoon nap sleep, Ernst was standing on the bed like a meerkat at attention. The visual made me want to laugh, but I chose to rub my eyes instead, wondering when I had drifted off. The way Ernst had been standing, the feeling that we had both drifted off for a nap gradually hit me. Everything going on around us was sure to tucker a fellow out, so climbing into bed led to the inevitable.

"Are you in there, Rob?" Lucas' voice and another round of soft knocking sounded from the door.

"Yeah." I croaked, then cleared my throat. "Hold on."

Ernst looked over at me warily.

"Hide for now, Ernst." I winked at him. "It'll be okay."

Ernst nodded, then hopped off the bed and disappeared underneath. Whether he was hiding under the bed or had used the shadows underneath to just...*leave*...I wasn't sure. It didn't matter. I bounced to the side of the bed and slung my legs over. Since I knew that Lucas wouldn't be ignorant enough to bring Oma to my room with him, I quickly unlatched the door and swung it wide. Lucas was standing there, a crooked smile on his face. He had on his work jeans, a long sleeve flannel, his Carhartt, and it was evident that he had been working all day.

Before I could stop myself, I had twisted my fingers in the front of his shirt and pulled him into the room. I slammed the door and locked it behind him and had shoved Lucas towards the bed before he could utter a word. Lucas looked at me with wide eyes as I pulled him into me and smothered his mouth with mine. My fingers traveled down to his waist to tug his shirttail out of his jeans before they moved to the front to start undoing buttons. Lucas looked up at me with wonder as I pulled my mouth away from his to work on extricating him from his shirt.

"What's gotten into you, babe?" He chuckled appreciatively.

"I missed you so much." I exhaled.

"I missed you, too." He reached up and ran a thumb along my cheek as my fingers continued working.

"How much did you miss me?" I asked as I pulled his shirt open and pushed it over his shoulders and off of him.

Lucas reached up and took my face in his hands.

"I know where this behavior is leading," Lucas whispered through a toothy grin. "And...I don't want to keep you from wanting to do that, babe. But what's going on here?"

"I told you," I said as I leaned forward to kiss him again. "I missed you."

"A few days ago, you didn't even want to admit you wanted me around, Rob." He moaned happily as my mouth moved to his neck. "And now you miss me all the time? I'm not complaining, but...unh!"

My hand had snaked its way into the front of his pants as I kissed and bit at his neck. Lucas' hips pushed forward of their own accord as my hand began to move and I licked a trail from the side of his neck down to his collarbone. Lucas' fingers found my hair as my tongue traveled down to the middle of his chest and my knees slowly bent, taking me to lower places. As my tongue trailed over his stomach, and my knees connected with the floor, I looked up at Lucas, grinning evilly as he looked down at me, his eyes wide, his fingers tugging at my hair.

"I hope you never stop missing me." He breathed out as I ripped the front of his jeans open.

Later, as the sun was starting to set, the sky turning pink, I was laid alongside Lucas in the bed. We hadn't gotten as far as removing the rest of our clothes, though both of us were completely satisfied. My head was just below Lucas' chin, pressed against his chest, both of my arms wrapped around him as I held myself against him. Lucas' fingers were raking through my hair gently, a gesture that would be soothing in most situations, but only kept me on the edge of hunger and satiated. My face nuzzled his chest as he kissed the top of my head, his breath wispy in my hair.

"What do you know about amnesia, Lucas?" I asked softly.

"Huh?"

"You're a college boy." I chuckled throatily. "What do you know about amnesia? Or memories?"

"I didn't go to med school." He replied, kissing my head again. "English. Remember? They didn't really explain neurology or anything like that much."

"Oh." I kissed his bare chest, my eyes moving to look at the top of his jeans, still flapped open.

Lucas was tucked away inside of his boxers, but just seeing his pants unbuttoned and wide open made me warm and think thoughts that were not conducive to what I wanted to achieve.

"I feel like I have so much to make up for." I whispered against the tight flesh of his chest. "So much time to make up."

"Well, you were gone for a decade," He laughed lowly. "That's a lot of years you weren't spending with me when it's obvious you should have been."

"Obviously," I replied. I wasn't being sarcastic. "A few days ago, I was sure that getting into a relationship...with anyone...was a huge decision. Now I feel like I should have run back home years ago—back to you."

"That doesn't make sense, Rob." He was pulling my face up to look at me.

Lucas planted a kiss on my lips then stared into my eyes.

"When did we first meet?" I asked.

He shrugged lazily. "I mean, Point Worth has three school buildings. I'm sure we initially met in kindergarten or first grade. I don't know. We never really ran in the same circles, so it's hard to pinpoint."

"I can kind of remember you from freshman and sophomore years," I said. "But, it's hazy. Like I don't really remember you there. And I feel like I've missed you since then. But I also feel like if we went to the same schools for so many years, I should have a better memory of seeing you around."

Lucas stared at me for a long time, his fingers trailing through my hair gently, slowly, as he thought. I could practically hear the wheels clicking in his brain as he considered what I was saying.

"What's this about, Rob?"

"Do you remember me?"

"Of course I do."

"What do you remember?"

"You played guitar a lot. And sang. And you were in plays, and the choir and...you were the *special kid.* The one everyone else wanted to be, even if they wouldn't admit it. Half the kids hated you, and half of them loved you—but they all wanted to be you. You never gave anyone a reason to hate you...or love you for that matter."

He laughed.

"But you were extraordinary."

"That's pretty vague."

"How is that vague?"

"You told me that you've been enamored with me since high school." His fingers stopped moving. "That night we first...made love."

"Yes." He breathed the word.

"Which locker did I have in school?" I asked. "Where was it? Do you remember a time you looked up at lunch and saw me walking by your table? What was I wearing? Did you ever talk to me in class? Ask me for a spare pen or pencil? Did we accidentally bump into each other in the hallway and chuckle and say 'excuse me' or even 'Go fuck yourself'? Do you remember me raising my hand in class to answer a question? Who were my friends? Give me some details."

Lucas just stared at me.

"I can't."

"I didn't think you could." I nodded.

"So...what does that mean?"

"I don't know," I admitted. "But...I've been having flashes of memories and weird dreams."

"What about?"

"I don't know." I felt my vision get blurry. "I can't remember after I have the flashes of memories or the dreams. But I remember how they made me feel."

"They make you miss me?"

"A lot of them, yeah." I nodded.

"I'm not sure what that means, Rob." He said, then kissed my lips again. "But I know that I always felt like I was supposed to be with you. It's why I was so upset when Mrs. Wagner tried to set me up on a date, and it wasn't you. I wanted you so badly...but I also knew that I was *supposed* to be with you."

"That doesn't make sense either."

"Obviously." He chuckled.

Both of us laid there, curled up in each other's arms, Lucas' fingers trailing through my hair again as I nuzzled my head against his chest and I held myself against him with all my might. In the furthest reaches of my inner self, I knew that it wasn't quite normal to have someone you barely knew feel like home. However, that same part of me told me that it wasn't normal to reject something that felt like home, either. Everything about Lucas made me feel warm and safe and...*like Rob*. Everything I was felt tied to this person whom I had only known well for fewer days than I had fingers and toes. Lucas made me feel like I was really getting back to being Rob.

As I lay there, Lucas stroking my hair, wondering if Oma was going to come knocking on the door to ask if we were going to have dinner or at least text, I felt a nagging feeling in my gut. Surely, there was some way to figure out why I was having weird memories and dreams that didn't make sense. If I couldn't figure out why I was having them, maybe I could at least remember what the memories and dreams contained. As if testing a hypothesis, I reached up and laid my hand against Lucas' cheek, trying to make it look like a loving gesture and nothing more. Lucas smiled at me and looked into my eyes.

Nothing.

How I felt about Lucas remained, but I didn't get a flash of a memory or a weird jolt of feeling. We were simply in bed together, doing what couples in...what couples in love do. That thought was more telling than any memory or dream I could have and then remember. Since my experiment had half-failed and half-succeeded, I leaned up to give Lucas a soft kiss.

"I hope you never want to stop kissing me." Lucas sighed as I pulled away.

"Highly unlikely," I whispered. "Would you humor me if I wanted us to check something out?"

Lucas grinned evilly.

"Not that." I laughed.

"Well," He was still smiling, "then what?"

"I want to go to the football stadium."

"Really?" Lucas cringed. "It's like a three-and-a-half-hour drive to Athens, and I have to work at grandpa's store tomorrow, babe, and—"

"Not Peden, silly." I laughed.

"Well, Cincinnati is like four hours away, too."

"Not Paul Brown, either." I reached up and thumped him gently on the forehead. "The high school football stadium. I'm not crazy. I don't think."

"Okay." He shrugged. "But why?"

Another kiss.

"Maybe it will jog some memories that I can remember?"

"Even if it doesn't, can we make out under the bleachers?" He wiggled his eyebrows.

"Of course." I snorted. "But you have to let me look around first."

"Can't I get some head under the bleachers?"

"You're pushing it, Lucas."

He laughed loudly before giving me another kiss, this one a little more aggressive than the last. I tightened my arms around him as our lips pressed together, savoring our final few moments in bed together.

"Well," he finally pulled away with a sigh, "if we're going, let's go. I want to get back in time to get head in bed."

"You're a horny bastard," I shook my head. "And that rhymed."

"What?" He winked. "You don't want to?"

I just stared at him.

"Fine. Let's go to the stadium, and we can go back to your place."

"In case we get loud?" His eyebrows were wiggling again.

"Yes."

Lucas pushed me away and bounced to the edge of the bed, quickly coming to stand beside it before buttoning his pants hurriedly. I watched as he found his shirt on the floor at the end of the bed and pulled it on. I'd never witnessed a man button a shirt so quickly. Once Lucas was pushing his feet back into his boots, he glanced up at me on the bed.

"Get moving, babe." He urged me. "I want to get this over with so we can get back to having fun."

"Going to the football stadium with me won't be fun?"

"Going to my house with you will be more fun."

"Fair enough." I chuckled as I slid out of bed and did my pants up once again.

Lucas waited, semi-patiently, as I pulled on my shirt and shoved my feet into a pair of kicks, then raked my fingers through my hair. Luckily, my hair had been cut in a way that made it always look stylishly sloppy, so I didn't have to try too hard to get it back into place. There was no set place for my hair. It did whatever it wanted to, and that was how it was supposed to look. I reached up to scratch my chin, feeling the beginnings of whiskers that would need to be shaved away soon. When I had shaved off my beard, I thought I was saving myself the trouble of trimming my beard regularly. Having to shave daily if I wasn't going to have a beard was a task I had forgotten about after so long of not shaving.

Lucas grabbed my hand and pulled me in for another quick kiss, and then we exited the room together. I glanced over my shoulder to see if Ernst climbed out from underneath the bed. I'd hope he hadn't just stayed under the bed and witnessed everything Lucas and I had done.

Sexuality and sex were probably not as taboo with Kobolds, but I still didn't want Ernst—or anybody really—witnessing what I did in my bedroom.

Down in the living room, once we had made our way down the stairs, I could hear Oma banging around in the kitchen. Literally. She was making much more noise than was necessary, which let me know that she was still agitated about the incident in the cellar. Instinctively, I wanted to go into the kitchen and hash things out with her. Whether we fought it out or hugged it out didn't matter, just as long as we settled the tension. Taking the fight to Oma's doorstep would mean delaying going to the football stadium, though. Lucas cringed as he looked at me and Oma banged things around.

"Oma!" I shouted. "We're going out. I'll be back later!"

"*Do I look like I give a shit?*" She snarled back.

Lucas cringed harder. I couldn't help but chuckle.

"She's cussing at me. Things will be okay." I winked at him.

Lucas produced a nervous smile and let me lead him to the door.

"Don't worry." I shrugged as I reached for the knob and opened the door. "Things always work out one way or another around here."

Of course, when you least expect it, another assault comes. When I opened the door, that's precisely what happened.

Chapter 8

"JACOB!"
"JACOB!"
"JACOB!"
"Over here, Jacob!"

The screams and flashes were coming from every direction. Lucas vapor locked in the doorway as the cameras went off and paparazzi screamed at me. Immediately, a friendly smile came to my face, and I affected my best "Friendly, Accessible Jacob Michaels" look I'd used with the paparazzi a million times before. Since I hadn't stepped outside yet, I nudged Lucas away from the door and let the door swing shut. Then I locked the deadbolt and turned to my boyfriend as he stood in shock beside the now closed door.

Estimating from the crowd I saw outside of Oma's door there had to have been at least twenty people waiting to scream a question at me or snap a photo. Automatically, I went into assessment mode, going through my head what happened from the time I opened the door until I had closed it. Lucas and I had been holding hands. No big deal there, everyone knew I was gay. They didn't know I had a boyfriend, but that wasn't that big of a deal, either. Unlike my heterosexual counterparts, the consensus was that if a celebrity was gay, people actually liked them more when they were in relationships, so it was a good thing that Lucas and I had been holding hands. I had smiled and had "twinkly, friendly eyes" for at least half of the photos, showing that once I was surprised by the paps, I had taken it in stride. Then I had shut the door without saying a word, so any made up quote could easily be fought by my team. Things had gone better than they should have.

"Babe?" Lucas peeped.

"Yeah?" I turned to him, chewing at my lip.

"What...the actual fuck?"

"I guess Sarah Jean phoned a friend." I shrugged.

I shook my head, kicking Jacob Michaels out of my brain. In Point Worth, especially at Oma's house, I was Robert Wagner. Robert Wagner did not stand in the foyer assessing a situation with the paparazzi. That was a Jacob Michaels activity, and I wanted no part of it.

"What the fuck is goin' on out there?" Oma stomped out of the kitchen, wiping her hands with a kitchen towel.

"The reporters found Rob." Lucas groaned.

"Paparazzi." I corrected him. "Reporters don't behave like that."

"What?" Oma's expression changed from angry with me to concerned for me. "Who found you?"

"You have a porch full of photographers." I sighed. "I guess people finally found out that Jacob Michaels is in Point Worth visiting his grandmother."

"Well, shit." She slung the towel onto her shoulder and put her hands on her hips. "It was goddamn Sarah Jean Dennard. She's like a Christmas Goose with a bell up her ass. Makin' noise is all she does."

"That was my assumption." I nodded. "None of us are getting out of this house without them harassing us now."

Lucas looked ashen but was slowly coming back to himself.

"Want to be my date to my next premiere?" I teased.

He turned green.

I took that as an outright rejection of my invitation.

"Sonsofbitches," Oma grumbled as she stomped over to the closet stairs and nearly ripped the door off of its hinges. "I'll be damned if a bunch of papa-whatevers are gonna park themselves on my porch rent free!"

"What are you gonna do?" I snorted. "Go out there and charge 'em twenty fucks a gander?"

Oma turned her head to gawk at me.

"You think they'd pay that?" She asked.

"Of course not." I laughed. "How did you not know that they were there anyway? Didn't they knock or ring the bell or make enough noise to make you suspicious?"

"Someone's been knockin' every now and again for the last thirty minutes." Oma went back to rummaging around in the closet. "Thought it was them damn Kelly kids—ugly assholes—or Wesley Dennard's tubbly ass. I didn't have time for none of that."

Oma pulled her arms out of the closet, her shotgun in hand.

"Whoa, Mrs. Wanger!" Lucas put his hands up.

I threw my hands up in the air in exasperation. "What are you gonna do, Oma? Shoot 'em all like they're looking for potatoes in your garden?"

Then I had a thought.

"Maybe I should call my publicist? Or manager?"

"While you're doing that, I'm gonna see how many of these shitheads I can put in the hospital." Oma waggled her head. "Or the morgue. Depends on how well they get low."

"Oma." I stepped in front of her, putting my hand on the shotgun. "You can't shoot paparazzi. Well, you can't shoot anyone without good cause."

"I'm gonna tell 'em to get off my private property." She snapped, glancing at the door. "Then I'm gonna count to ten. If they ain't gone, that ain't my damn problem."

"That's not good enough." I couldn't help but laugh.

"Mrs. Wagner," Lucas added, "you could get into real trouble."

"From who?" She hooted. "Wesley Fatass Dennard? I know I won't miss him. Wish to hell he'd come try to do something about me defending my property."

"Get real, Oma." I rolled my eyes. "You aren't shooting the people on the porch, and you're certainly not shooting the sheriff."

"I got a golf club in the closet." She suggested. "I can always go out there swinging with that if you think it'll cause less trouble. Be fun to watch 'em all scatter either way."

"That is absolutely rid—"

Then I had another thought.

I looked over at Lucas, and he frowned at the expression on my face.

"Oma," I said, "do you think you going out there with a shotgun will make them all run for it?"

"Unless they're complete morons." She snorted. "I mean, who don't run when someone shoves a shotgun in their face?"

"Fair point."

"You can't let her go out there with a shotgun, Rob." Lucas laughed nervously.

"Oma," I continued quickly, "Lucas and I need to leave for a little bit. But we can't go anywhere with all of them out there waiting to follow us. If you get them running for it, Lucas and I can jump in Opa's truck and take off before they know it's us. Well, me. They don't care about Lucas. No offense."

Lucas chewed at his lip while he thought this over.

"I mean," Lucas spoke slowly, "as long as no one actually gets shot, that is okay with me. And it'll probably work."

"Of course it will!" Oma announced. "This ain't the first time I've sent folks runnin'. By the time they know what happened you two can be long gone."

Nothing like a common enemy to make Oma and I get along. If only for a brief period.

"Good." I nodded as I pulled Lucas towards the kitchen. "After we're gone and all of them have collected themselves and taken off, get all the bullets and give 'em to Lena or Ernst and tell them to hide them. Just in case Sheriff Dennard does show up. Then you can claim you don't even have bullets for the gun and he can't get too mad."

"Shells, ya' asshole." She frowned at me. "It's a shotgun. My Glock forty-five takes *bullets*."

"Whatever." I waved her off and pulled Lucas into the kitchen before yelling back to Oma. "Count to ten and make 'em scatter, Oma!"

"Like this is my first rodeo." I heard Oma mutter under her breath.

Lucas stood by the kitchen table as I pulled the "catch-all" drawer out and quickly grabbed the key to Opa's truck. Hopefully, the thing wasn't frozen up due to the winter. Of course, Oma had used the truck to make trips into town during nasty weather or to go to Barkley's, so I was pretty sure it would start up fairly quickly. Lucas and I headed to the backdoor and waited. When we heard the front door open, and Oma scream something unintelligible, then heard the sounds of people screaming, I pushed the backdoor open and pulled Lucas outside with me.

As we were running to the side of the house where Opa's old truck was, I heard the first shotgun blast. I cringed internally, hoping Oma hadn't aimed too well at anyone. Hopefully, she had fired the gun into the air off of the porch or just in the general direction of one of the photographers. Worrying about whether or not Oma had shot a trespassing paparazzo was not my business, however. Lucas pulled open the passenger door and jumped inside, slamming the door quickly behind himself. I rounded the truck and climbed into the driver's seat, mimicking his actions.

As if the Gods of Luck were pissed at us, the truck didn't do anything when I turned the key. I growled under my breath as I tried turning the key again. Another shotgun blast sounded in the distance.

"It's a manual, Rob," Lucas announced desperately, looking around. "You have to get it in neutral, push the clutch down and put your foot on the brake and—"

Lucas looked over to find me just staring at him.

"City boy." He took a second to tease, though the worry didn't leave his face.

Two seconds later, I was sliding over Lucas' lap as he scooted across the truck into the driver's seat. I plopped down into the passenger side of the bench seat, and another second later, the truck was roaring to life. Lucas gave me a nervous wink as he put the truck into gear and quickly got the truck turned around, aiming down the driveway. Then he gunned it. We sped down the driveway towards the front of the house as we bounced in our seats.

"Don't hit anyone," I begged him with clenched teeth.

"I'll do my best." He chuckled through a grimace.

As we passed the front of the house, I glanced over to see Oma standing at the base of the porch steps, the shotgun raised to the heavens as she fired one more time. The blast from the shotgun looked almost like an exploding firework in the dark as Lucas drove us away. Paparazzi were scattering everywhere, trying to figure out how to get to the plethora of cars parked in the driveway—which Lucas had to steer around to get us away from the scene of mayhem. Turning in my seat, I watched the paps running around crazily, trying to get into their cars as quickly as possible as Oma fired another shot off. I could practically see her cackling as she scared the paps. Lucas had us at the end of the driveway and turning onto the main road before I saw a single paparazzo make it into their car.

When we were clear of the driveway and free from the type of mayhem that only Oma could create, I turned around to face the windshield and sighed with relief. Lucas was shifting into another gear, the truck roaring and speeding up as we drove down the road away from Oma's property. Silently, I said a prayer, thanking...*whatever*...for Oma's skill at causing a scene worthy of any movie I'd ever been in before.

"Mrs. Wagner sure knows how to cause a ruckus." Lucas laughed, sounding a lot less tense now that we were driving away.

"Oma lives to make a ruckus." I laughed with him.

Lucas looked over at me and smiled. The compulsion to kiss him was too strong to ignore, so I leaned across the cab and kissed him on the lips quickly. He was smiling even wider when I pulled back and sat back in my seat again, just like a good little passenger.

Chapter 9

Ohio in April is always chilly, but the wind was whipping down through the football stadium and whistling up through the bleachers as we sat on the bottom row of the stands at the fifty-yard line. So, it felt chillier than usual. Lucas had his arms wrapped around me, his head on my shoulder as I stared down at the field.

We had successfully gotten away from Oma's house without getting hurt and made our way to the stadium. Oma had texted minutes later to say that all of the paparazzi had taken off and: *"I didn't hit a damn one. Ya' happy?"* That did make me happy because at least she wouldn't be doing jail time if she got into trouble. I shot off a quick reply to her instructing her to let me know if Sheriff Dennard or anyone else came out and gave her trouble, but otherwise, I'd be home in the morning at the latest. *"Yeah. Yeah."* was the reply.

Lucas and I had parked in the field behind the stadium so no one would see Opa's truck in the parking lot and investigate. Then we had snuck over to one of the chain link fences that surrounded the property and hopped over. Easiest breaking-and-entering job ever. As soon as we walked onto the field, I expected to feel something. To remember something. *Anything.* But nothing came to me. No sudden realization or memory or thought. We were just walking along the grassy field, hand-in-hand, as though it were any other place for us to take a moonlit stroll as a couple.

After walking the field, Lucas and I walked up into the stands, up and down rows waiting for anything to strike me. Lucas had no idea what I was waiting for, but I honestly didn't either. I was simply hoping that some memory would be jogged or I'd have a sudden revelation about why I couldn't remember things like a normal human being who had lived nearly twenty-seven years could. But the football stadium felt as empty as my head—as far as memories go. Lucas stuck with me as we walked the rows of bleachers, holding my hand when it was possible. When I finally walked down to the front row and fell onto the bleacher at the fifty-yard line, Lucas sat down next to me and laid his head on my shoulder. It was comforting, but it didn't fix my problem.

"Nothing?" Lucas finally asked, his breath hot against my neck.

"Not a single thing." I sighed. "Fuck."

"What did you expect?"

"Something besides nothing."

We sat there for a few moments before Lucas said anything else to me or moved at all.

"Won't it be good enough to keep going the way we're going, babe?" He whispered as the wind whistled under our seats, making it hard to hear him. "I mean...I'm happy. Are you happy?"

"May as well get a lobotomy, Lucas." I sighed. "I mean, if we're just happy because we can't remember what led to this moment, is it really happiness?"

"Fair enough."

"Can you remember anything?" I asked again. "Anything else? Anything you haven't told me?"

"I remember a lot of things I haven't told you." He chuckled against my neck. "But nothing about us. I clearly remember you being the talented, *special* kid in high school. That you were kind. And, of course, hot. I remember always wanting you."

I could practically feel him blush against my neck, which made me smile.

"When you delivered Oma's manure and tiller the other day?" I questioned him. "She said you were starstruck. What did you truly feel?"

Lucas didn't answer for several moments.

"Completion." He said. "I felt overwhelmed."

"Please explain that to me."

"I had felt like something had been missing for a very long time." He sat up to look me in the eyes. "Then, I saw you, and I didn't feel that way anymore. I guess I had been missing you, too."

"That doesn't make sense, Lucas." I pleaded with him. "I know exactly what you're talking about...now...but it just doesn't add up."

"Do you believe in fate or destiny?" He shrugged. "Maybe we were always destined to end up together, and something inside of us knew that, so when you left, we both started to feel that something wasn't right?"

"That's a stretch, babe." I shook my head. "I mean, fuck, that's a beautiful thought. But we didn't know each other. At least not really. We *knew of* each other. Maybe exchanged a few pleasantries—but nothing memorable. How would something inside of us know that we were meant for each other? And, not to piss on your parade, but I'm still myself here. I don't know what the future holds for us. I love what's going on here...but I can't say, without a doubt, that we were meant for each other."

"Ouch."

"You know what I mean."

"Yeah." He sighed. "I know what you mean. Who knows what the future holds? Who knows if we're not just in the honeymoon phase here, ya' know? Who knows if this isn't just lust masquerading as something else?"

I looked at him, but he wasn't looking at me. He was looking down at the field. Slowly, his head turned, and he locked eyes with me.

"But...I know, Rob." He gave me a firm nod. "Even before you came back and I saw you there in Mrs. Wagner's backyard, I knew. You were coming back, and we were going to..."

I waited, but he just stared at me.

"What, Lucas?"

"We were going to be together again." He finished, biting off his last word like it was sharp and had pricked his tongue. "That we would no longer be forced to be apart. I knew that. I know things. Remember?"

"What else do you know?"

"Is Ernst one of the little creatures that live in Mrs. Wagner's house?" He asked lowly. "Lena? You said their names before we left the house."

My eyes grew wide.

Lucas tapped the side of his head with one finger.

"I know things. Maybe I can't fill in all of the details, but I know things." He said before I could ask. "Eggs, bacon, and pancakes was your favorite breakfast when you were young. You never made any friends in Hollywood because you knew you wouldn't be staying. You never bought a house because you knew you wouldn't be staying. You never stayed in one place for long because you never felt at home. You didn't leave Hollywood because you were worn out and lost all the weight. You left because you knew that if you stayed, you'd keep on not caring how much you wasted away."

I took a deep breath, shocked at how deep Lucas' words cut.

"When you met me...again...behind Mrs. Wagner's house the other day, you thought I was a weirdo vegetarian loner who probably had bodies in his basement."

He chuckled at that.

"Were you reading my mind?"

"I just knew." He shrugged. "Later."

"That's almost exactly what I thought."

"What do you think now?" He asked gently.

Shaking my head, I stood up.

"That none of this makes sense," I grumbled. "All of this makes sense, and it doesn't make sense. It feels right, but it doesn't add up."

Stomping up the steps, I ascended six rows and then plopped down on the end of one of the bleachers, feeling defeated. Lucas turned to look up at me as I leaned forward and put my head in my hands, trying to figure out what was wrong with my brain. Lucas knew absolutely true things—stuff I'd never told anyone. He knew everything I felt when I had gone off and lived the Hollywood lifestyle. Truthfully, he could have guessed any of those things—they weren't uncommon for people who sought out fame and fortune in such a way—but I knew that he hadn't guessed. I knew that as well as I couldn't remember the things that I wanted to remember.

"Hey, babe." Lucas sighed.

I lifted my head to look down at him.

"I'm so tired, Lucas." I shook my head. "Jacob Michaels is tired. But Robert Wagner won't come back and switch places with him. At least, not permanently. And that's frustrating as fuck because I'm not Jacob Michaels. I've never been him. I didn't go to Hollywood to act in movies. I went to Hollywood to act like Jacob Michaels. But I'm not him. It was like I was running away and pretending to be someone else so that I wouldn't be Robert Wagner for a while. And I don't know why. I don't know if I just don't remember why...or if I never knew why."

Lucas' face dropped.

"What could have happened that made me not want to be Robert Wagner so desperately that I just pulled up stakes and snuck away in the dead of night?" I was pleading with him as though he were an oracle. "Because I don't remember. My brain tells me that I wanted to get away. Live my life. Find fame and fortune. But...I swear to you right now...that's not true. I know it's not true even though my brain says it is. I know, without the shadow of a doubt, that that was something I told myself to make the whole thing easier. Easier to do and easier to understand."

"Rob..."

"Do you know what I did when I first went to L.A.?" I asked. "I found an agent on my first day. She let me stay with her until I was eighteen-years-old. We had to lie about my age. I had auditions the next week. Within two years, I was starring in movies and had a record deal. Two years, Lucas. I was already a multi-millionaire by age twenty. By age twenty-one, I had been around the world at least three times, filming here, filming there, performing concerts everywhere, being a household name."

Lucas was staring at me.

"That doesn't make sense either," I said. "I could charm my way into any job I wanted. And when I did the job—acted or sang or performed in any way, I could make people believe that it was a good job. I wasn't even trying. It was like something took me over, Lucas. *Jacob Fucking Michaels* possessed me. I don't even know who he is—but he's not me."

"That's really...messed up, babe." Lucas shook his head with a smile. "It's like you believe that you are literally two separate people."

I chuckled bitterly.

"No." I shook my head. "Not like two different people...but he's this personality that lived inside of me, peeking out when he was needed so that another goal could be achieved. Do you know how I know that?"

"How?"

"I was in London," I said. "I was about to do my first show there—before things really took off with the music. I was standing in the wings of the stage, totally petrified. Like, literally petrified. I couldn't move. But then, my cue came and that all just sloughed off. I strutted out there and gave a performance that would have made any season artist envious. Here I am. I'm Jacob Michaels, and I will make you love me. Then the concert was over, and I was riding a high—so damn chuffed. And when I got back to the hotel...and I was alone again...Jacob Michaels disappeared. I cried myself to sleep that night—horrified at how phony I was, how scared I had been the whole time I was on stage. Jacob Michaels was a buffer to all of the people and the cheers and the flashes of lights and the...insanity of being a celebrity. But, when he wasn't needed, Jacob Michaels dipped. I was Robert Wagner again. And I was terrified. Because I had no idea what I was doing there. Well, not literally. I'm not crazy. I knew that I was there, performing a concert, that I was also an actor...but I had no idea why I would want to be there. That began my day-to-day existence, Lucas. Every day I wasn't at home, in Point Worth, I used Jacob Michaels as a mask for Robert Wagner. To shield me from how I truly felt, to make myself feel like everything I was doing was exactly what I wanted. But I didn't want it. None of it."

Lucas was wide-eyed.

"I would have been happy staying here and going to college—if I could get into one," I said, "or working at Barkley's or the café or the bank or...wherever. I didn't need to be famous or rich. So...why did I get up and leave in the middle of the night and do exactly that?"

The wind whistled under the bleachers again as Lucas and I stared at each other with six rows of bleachers between us. Cold April Ohio air ruffled my hair, and I pushed it back onto my head to keep it out of my eyes. Lucas looked pensive as he stared up at me, as though unable to decide what it was he could say or do to help. Or he couldn't determine the answer to the multitude of questions I had posed.

"I'm sorry." I sighed, but I didn't look away.

"Don't be sorry, babe." He said though he was barely audible over the wind. "It's not your fault."

"Do we know that?" I gave a bitter laugh.

"I guess not." He returned the laugh as he reached up to rub the back of his neck. "I know the things I know. And I'm sure that I'm right. But those are the only things I am sure of, babe. I wish I could help more, but that's all I have. All I can offer."

"I wish I had something...*anything*...to offer." I snorted.

"Hey." Lucas frowned as he stood and moved into the aisle of stairs that led further up into the stands. "Don't say things like that. You are extraordinary, Rob. Even if your memory is shit."

I laughed.

"You wouldn't happen to want company up there, would you?" He grinned wickedly.

I shivered.

"What?"

"Did you want someone to keep you company?" He reiterated.

"Were you waiting for me?"

Lucas was standing at the bottom of the bleachers, his letterman jacket on, making him look as sexy as he was. I was sitting in the bleachers, my boring coat pulled tightly around my torso to keep me warm. I had been waiting on Lucas. Just like I always did.

"Of course I was waiting on you," I replied, my voice not as deep as it now was. "I'm always waiting for you."

He smiled.

"I thought I was always waiting on you."

"Well," I shrugged comically, "one of us is always waiting. But...the wait is always worth it, right?"

"Abso-fucking-lutely," He replied. "Don't you get scared out here all alone? What if someone tried to get you?"

"You'd protect me."

"How can you be so sure?"

I shrugged. "I just know."

"I'd argue," He said, "but I'd be wrong. And I don't like being wrong."

"You nearly fumbled the last pass."

"I held on. For you."

"For me?" I chuckled.

"So we'd have a reason to celebrate."

"How do you think we should celebrate?"

"Maybe you can give me one of your amazing kisses?" He said, glancing around, as though he thought we might not be alone.

"You're the football star," I said as I lifted my legs to place my feet on the bleacher row below me. "Show me your skills. Come get it. Make a play."

Lucas grinned wickedly then slowly stalked up the stairs, his eyes never leaving mine. When he got to my row, he stepped over my leg, then brought his other leg over it as well, positioning himself between my legs.

He looked down at me as his hand came up to cup the side of my face as I looked up at him. I wanted him to kiss me so badly.

"You're...beautiful."

I couldn't help but laugh. "Is that a compliment for a guy?"

"I wasn't talking about your looks."

That made me swallow back any retort.

"Do you want me to kiss you again?"

"Yes." I exhaled.

"Do you love me?" He asked.

"Yes." I breathed the word. "I love you."

Lucas sighed.

"I love you, too."

Then he leaned down...

The concrete behind me felt like a hammer against my tailbone and was icy cold when I hit the ground. My legs were still up on the bleacher row I had been seated upon before the memory flashback. My vision blurred, hazy, streaks of color, as I flailed, trying to get my bearings.

"Rob!" Lucas gasped from somewhere lower in the stands.

Suddenly, he was beside me, his hands sliding under my arms, trying to lift me off of the icy concrete. I flailed again, unsure of what was going on, unsure, really, of where I was. My vision continued to blur in and out as I felt him pulling at me, trying to gently fight my flailing and get me off of the ground. Through the blurriness in my eyes, I saw Lucas, though one second he looked like he was wearing a letterman jacket and then the next he looked like he was in his Carhartt. I shut my eyes tightly, willing away whatever it was that was blurring my vision.

When I opened my eyes again, all I could see was Lucas trying to get ahold of me in an attempt to pull me off of the ground. The wind was whistling under the bleachers again, cutting into the exposed flesh of my face and hands as I finally stopped fighting against Lucas. Then he was pulling me up until I was seated upright on the bleachers again and he was kneeling to look into my eyes, worry etched all over his face. I stared back into his eyes, barely able to breathe as he reached up to turn my head as if examining me to see if I was bleeding from hitting my head or had otherwise hurt myself.

"Rob." He breathed out heavily. "Shit. You scared the hell out of me. Are you okay, babe?"

I just stared back, my eyes wide, trying to process what had just happened. Had it been a real memory? Could I remember it?

Lucas. Letterman jacket. Banter. He was standing in front of me between my legs. I told him that I loved him. He said he loved me. We kissed.

The memory hadn't fluttered away. Mentally, I imagined wrapping an iron fist around the memory. It had been alarming, but it was also one of the most precious I currently held within my brain. There was no way I was going to let it go. *I had told Lucas that I loved him.* That should have terrified me. Instead, it made me reach out suddenly and wrap my arms around him. Lucas made an "oof" sound and then laughed as I hugged him to me, pulling his body into mine with all of my strength.

"Jeez, babe," He said, "it was just a little fall. I know you're an actor, but you don't have to be so dramatic."

I pushed him back, my fingers digging into his upper arms as I looked him in the eyes.

"I love you," I gasped.

Lucas' eyes grew wide and then a smile slowly formed on his face.

"I love you," I repeated.

"Say it again," He said.

"I love you," I said, "I've loved you for a very long time."

Lucas gave me a funny look.

"I love you, too," He said, "but...what's going on?"

"I've loved you since high school," I said. "I've loved you since you stood in front of me after a football game and asked me if I loved you."

Lucas pulled back slightly as his brow furrowed.

"What?"

"I just remembered something." I was shaking my head, still confused about what had happened, but knowing it was real. "You were at the bottom of the stairs, in your football jacket, after you guys had won a game, and you asked me if I had been waiting on you...and then we told each other we loved each other, and we kissed, and—"

"I don't remember that, Rob." His eyes were welling up. "But I know you're telling the truth."

"Is that one of the things you just know?"

"No." He shook his head. "I can just see it in your face that you're telling the truth."

Lucas gasped with happy surprise as I yanked him forward again and smothered his mouth with mine. My lips savored his, and then I was kissing him all over his face, cupping his face in my hands.

"Why don't we remember that, though?" He gasped as I kissed him and his arms went around my neck. "Or, at least, why don't I? Why don't we remember more?"

"I don't know," I said, still kissing him all over his face. "I don't care right now. But now I don't feel like you're missing. I don't miss you like I did. Now I'm just so glad that I have you back."

"I don't care right now, either." He sighed as I moved to kiss his neck, still holding him tightly to me. "I'm just glad I have you, Rob. I'm so fucking glad to have you back."

I shivered once again as I tightened my arms around him and hugged his body to mine, my face burying itself into his chest. Lucas held me to him, sighing contently as we held each other there in the stadium. Finally, I understood why Lucas felt like home, why I had missed him so much. All of the details weren't there, but things were falling into place. After my encounter with *Teenage Ghost Rob*, and I started having flashes of memories and weird dreams, I felt like I missed Lucas all the time. My relationship with Lucas wasn't new—even if we couldn't remember being in one before. Things were coming back to me, though. I prayed that I could help Lucas remember the same things that I remembered, too.

"What's that?" Lucas whisper against my ear.

"What?"

"That." Lucas whisper-hissed. "Look."

Pulling away from Lucas, but not quite letting go of him, I turned slightly on the bleacher to look up at the top of the stands where he was staring. I didn't see anything.

"*Did you see that?*" Lucas jerked.

"What are you—"

Shadows moved at the top of the stairs as Lucas and I slowly rose to our feet, our eyes staying fixed in place. Our arms had fallen away from each other, but my hand grasped Lucas', and I laced my fingers through his as I moved to his side.

"You did see that, right?" Lucas whispered.

"I saw...something."

As if summoned by my words, the shadowy movement returned to the top of the stairs. The shadows fell away as two men stepped out of the darkness at the top of the stadium and into full view. Illuminated by the dim blue light of the quarter moon, it quickly became apparent why these men were not security guards coming to tell us to go smooch somewhere else. The most obvious clue was that they both had red eyes that practically glowed in the dark.

"*Shit.*" I gasped, walking back down the stairs.

Lucas followed my lead.

"Are they..."

"I don't think they're about to ask us to join in on a game of touch football." I quipped.

Lucas nodded, and we turned in unison towards the field. Both of us jumped at the sight of the two men standing on the field just beneath the stands. Lucas twitched at my side.

"Rob." He gasped.

Turning my head to look in his direction, I saw another two men with glowing red eyes walking through the bleachers towards us. A glance to my side confirmed that another two more guys with red eyes were in the stands, helping to close us in on the other side. There were eight guys: two behind, two in front, two on each side. Maybe we could have taken one or two, perhaps even three, of the guys in a fight. At least get away from them. But two against eight just wasn't fair. Lucas and I whipped around as the men closed in on each side.

We looked up at the men coming down the stairs towards us, but they had stopped several yards away and were merely staring down at us. Lucas' hand tightened in mine as we looked up at the guys while trying to watch the guys in our periphery. Having eight pairs of glowing red eyes watching us was unsettling. I felt another shiver run up my spine.

"You believed me when I said I remembered us, right?" I whispered out of the corner of my mouth. "You know that I was telling the truth?"

"Yes," Lucas mumbled back.

"Do you trust me?"

"With everything I am."

"Good."

"We have a score to settle with you." The guy on our right on the stairs above us said blandly, his teeth flashing white in the dark.

His teeth seemed longer than they should have. The fact that I caught that detail in the dark made me want to shiver again.

"Well, come back on Monday," I mumbled. "I'm booked solid until then."

He snorted, finding my quip pathetic and funny at the same time, I was sure. Lucas gripped my hand tightly.

"I'm afraid this has to be taken care of now." He replied blandly. "Otherwise we may never get the chance, and we don't like to leave things unsettled. Rob."

That did make me shiver.

I didn't know these men.

Then again, I hadn't known Lucas.

"I truly hate to let an audience down," I replied, "but today just isn't your day, sir."

Lucas' hand gripped mine back as I squeezed his.

"*Run.*" I hissed.

Yanking on Lucas' arm, I pulled him after me as I ran up three steps and then cut to the right, between two sets of bleachers. Lucas let go of my hand so he could run behind me comfortably. The sounds of the men coming down the stairs sounded. Sounds of men scrambling up and over bleachers, like metallic thunder, reached our ears but I stared straight ahead, pumping my arms and legs as I ran. The only thing I cared about was hearing Lucas' breath and feet behind me, assuring me that he was keeping up and hadn't fallen.

A howl sounded behind us, and I flinched but, it did not slow my pace.

"*Go, Rob!*" Lucas growled. "*Run!*"

We reached the end of the aisle, and I made a sharp right down towards the field. The men that had been on the field and the ones who had been in the stands with us had been too busy trying to get ahead of us that they hadn't expected us to head towards the place they had previously occupied. They were now behind us. Another howl sounded. Then another. My heart was in my throat as Lucas and I raced down the stairs towards the field.

When we reached the fence at the end of the stands and the drop five feet to the field beneath us, I immediately leaped and started to clamber up the fence. Lucas was on the fence seconds after me, climbing as if his life depended upon it. And it probably did. At the top of the fence, I swung my legs over and slung myself down towards the field below us. Lucas followed my lead, landing less gracefully than I had somehow. I only took a second to make sure he was okay, and then I was leading the way across the field in the direction of the perimeter fence we had scaled to get inside the stadium.

"Rob!" Lucas gasped.

"Keep running, Lucas!" I screamed back.

"They're coming!"

Looking over my shoulder, I could see why Lucas was even more distraught than was to be expected. We didn't just have eight men chasing us across the field. Five men and three wolves were now giving chase, and I couldn't tell if the men or the wolves looked more bloodthirsty. Obviously, my theory about some werewolves not needing a full moon, which Oma had confirmed, was correct.

Greetings, powerful pack with a Pack Alpha.

Not so pleased to meet you.

Lucas and I reached the taller chain-link fence that surrounded the football stadium, and I could hear feet pounding the dirt, both wolf and human. Without looking back, not wanting to lose any ground, I jumped onto the fence and started clambering to the top. I felt Lucas hit the fence and start climbing and then both of us were scrambling to reach the top. Lucas somehow reached the top of the fence first and slung his lower body over, bracing his stomach along the top bar as he reached down for my hand. Reaching out, I slapped my hand into his, and he started to pull me up.

"Rob!" He screamed.

Then I felt the tugging.

I looked down, and one of the wolves had caught up to us. The heel of my shoe was in his mouth, his teeth holding on for dear life, his mouth salivating and his eyes glowing red fury at me.

"*No!*" I screamed, thrusting my free hand down at him.

I don't want him to hurt Lucas or me.

Please don't let him hurt us.

Fire shot out of my palm and splattered against the wolf's face like liquid heat. The wolf howled in agony and let go as he fell towards the ground, the fire traveled over his muzzle and around his head, then quickly crept over his entire body. I dangled there in Lucas' grip, my right foot pushing into one of the holes in the chain link. My eyes grew wide as I watched the fire envelope the wolf, burn away its fur, then sputter out in a plume of acrid smoke. The wolf was on the ground, unmoving, its mouth gasping over and over again in terror and pain. I glanced towards the two remaining wolves and the five men. They had all frozen in place, staring at the scene unfolding before them.

"Come on, Rob!" Lucas growled and pulled me upward.

I lifted my "fire hand" to flip off the men and wolves, then pushed off of the chain link with my right foot, pushing myself up towards Lucas. Howl after howl sounded behind me, but I didn't look over my shoulder to see the rest of the men shift into wolves. Lucas and I dropped to the other side of the fence, confident that the men, in wolf form, would have to find a different way out of the stadium. Without hands and feet, it was unlikely that they could scale the fence.

Running beside each other, Lucas and I didn't say a word as we ran through the parking lot of the stadium and into the field where he had parked the truck. The two of us didn't make the same mistake twice with seating assignments, though we both climbed in through the passenger door since it was the closest to us as we approached. Lucas tore the door open and clambered across the bench seat and started the truck as I jumped in and slammed the door behind myself. The roaring of the tires reached my ears before my ass was fully planted in my seat.

Lucas peeled out of the field, sending tall grass and mud flying as he punched the gas. I grabbed onto the dash as we bounced and shimmied in our seats. Once we hit the blacktop, I settled into my seat, my chin falling to my chest as I gasped for breath. Lucas' hands were vices on the steering wheel as he looked around frantically to make sure we weren't being followed. I wanted to scream at him to keep his eyes on the road—not out of anger, but fear. However, I found myself turning in my seat, looking to make sure that there were no wolves running in the road behind us or any other vehicles that might be in pursuit.

"*What the actual fuck, Rob?*" Lucas was breathing heavy as well.

I was trying to control my breathing.

"You shot fire out of your hand!"

"I do that sometimes." I grimaced, finally realizing that Lucas had no idea about my magic laser-slash-fire fingers.

"Since when?"

"I don't know." My chest was heaving as I tried to get my breathing and heart rate under control. "They knew my fucking name, Lucas. How did they know my name?"

Lucas stared at me for several moments, then seemed to decide that the throwing fire with my hand situation could wait.

"Do you know them?"

Turning to him, I just frowned.

"Well, I didn't think so." He gave a nervous laugh, trying to bring levity to the situation. "But...what other explanation is there?"

"Maybe I don't know them like I didn't know you," I mumbled.

"What?"

"Maybe I've forgotten that I know them?"

"That's just..."

"Crazy?" I snorted, my breathing slowly returning to normal.

"Well...yeah."

"Must be Tuesday, Lucas," I said. "Rob Wagner is crazy as shit. Or, at least, everything in his life is."

"If they knew your name..."

"What?" I turned in my seat to look at him.

"What else do they know?" He chewed at his lip as he kept his eyes on the road. "Do they know where you live?"

I thought about that statement for a moment, the realization of what that meant slowly dawning on me.

"Oma." I gasped.

Lucas gunned the truck.

Chapter 10

When Lucas came to a gravel-flinging stop in Oma's driveway at the front of the house, I had my door open before he had put the truck into park. The lights were on in the living room, and everything looked peaceful. No paparazzi, no strange cars, no wolves circling the house hungrily, looking for a little girl in a red cloak. Everything looked as it always did. Lucas' door popped open as I slammed my door and started for the house. Lucas fell in beside me, his hand finding mine as we hurriedly walked towards the house and up the porch steps, looking over our shoulders every few steps.

"Do you think they followed us?" Lucas whispered.

"I hope not," I said. "But I really hope they didn't get here before we did."

"Mrs. Wagner is okay, Rob." He nodded his head furiously, as though trying to convince us both. "I just know it."

"That makes me feel strangely better."

Making our way up the steps, I let go of Lucas' hand once we were on the porch so that I could open the front door, allowing it to swing wide. Before I had even stepped over the threshold, I spotted Oma. She was kicked back on the sofa with her feet up on the coffee table, enjoying the fire. A mug of tea was in her hand, and the shotgun was sitting on the coffee table beside her feet. My breath came out in a relieved sigh, and Lucas smiled widely at me as we entered the house. It wasn't until I was inside the house, with Oma within eyeshot that I felt my heart rate finally begin to return to normal.

Lucas' hand once again found mine and I turned my head to look into his eyes, a smile immediately coming to my face. He looked back at me, and his hand squeezed mine again. I didn't know what we had achieved at the football stadium, as far as memories go, but I knew that what I'd felt since the night the three wolves tried to attack me in the backyard was real. I could see in Lucas' eyes that, no matter what else had happened at the stadium, he was glad we had gone. The way he gripped my hand let me know that he never wanted to let it go if he could avoid that. I reached out and brushed his sandy hair off of his forehead and away from his eyes before giving him a quick kiss.

"Oma," I turned away from a smiling Lucas, "we're home."

"Ya' think I didn't hear the damn door?" She announced over her shoulder. "I'm old, not fuckin' deaf."

Lucas laughed.

"Are you okay?" I asked, heading into the living room, pulling Lucas after me.

"Don't I look okay?" She frowned up at me as we rounded the sofa to stand before her. She raised her mug in salute. "Got my tea, got my fire, and I'm pretty sure I peppered some of those sonsofbitches as they was runnin' away."

"I saw you, Oma." I shook my head with a smile. "You were aiming for the sky."

"Well," She waggled her head, "I still think a few of 'em shit their pants. Did some damage either way. You boys ever not touchin' up on each other? Jesus."

She gestured at our clasped hands.

Lucas and I smiled at each other and let our hands slide away from each other's as Oma took another sip of her tea. When Lucas gave me a stern look and jerked his head in Oma's direction, I knew pleasantries had to end sometime. I turned to my grandmother and sighed deeply.

"We have another problem."

"What the fuck did you idiots do now?" She pulled her legs off of the coffee table to sit forward. "Where the hell did you two go anyway?"

"The football field," Lucas responded for us.

Oma's brow furrowed as she looked over at him.

"We...needed to see something," I added.

"Thought you'd take a stroll down memory lane?" She rolled her eyes.

Her statement was like a punch to my gut. But I didn't have the time to dissect a statement from my grandmother that could have been completely flippant. The way Lucas' hand grabbed mine again let me know that my instincts were not off. Oma had said something spot on, my gut was telling me something, and Lucas' grip was letting me know that he *knew* something.

"We ran into more werewolves." I ignored the previous statement. "Eight of them."

Oma whistled with wide eyes.

"Well, I'm impressed." She took a sip of her tea. "If I was bettin' on you two idiots against eight werewolves, well, I would have been expecting to lose that bet."

"Thanks." I snorted.

"Just sayin'." She shrugged. "That's four on one. You two can barely wipe your own asses without accidentally finger-bangin' yourselves on accident. Didn't think you was capable of handling yourselves so well."

"Oh. My. God." I looked upwards as Lucas laughed nervously.

"I just meant you done a good job."

"I only got one of them, Oma." I snapped. "We ran."

She jabbed a finger at me.

"That sounds more accurate." She nodded.

"Yeah, well," I stammered, "I don't really have a response for that right now. But they knew my name, Oma—not *Jacob Michaels*. They knew my real name. But I'd never seen any of them before in my life. Since I didn't know those guys and have never seen them before, I don't know how they knew my name, Oma."

"What they look like?"

"I mean," I glanced at Lucas, he shrugged, "just normal guys, I guess. All of them had eyes like the wolves the other night and then that dead woman the other morning. Red. Glowing. Kind of. One of them said we had a score to settle. I assume it's because of what I did to their pack member the other night."

"I hope you never get called as an eye witness for nothin'." Oma shook her head in disgust. "Didn't notice hair color, heights, sizes...*nothin'*?"

"Well, no." I sighed.

Lucas was no help. He just looked at me and shrugged nervously as Oma examined us both.

"Eight of 'em?" Oma set her mug on the coffee table and rubbed her chin. "All fellas?"

I thought about that.

"Yes." I nodded. "I'm pretty sure they were all male."

Oma waggled her head.

She opened her mouth as if to say something, but the sound of distant rumbling engines sounded outside, far away at first but growing closer. Oma sighed to herself as headlights flashed through the front room windows. She looked up at me and then stood from the couch.

"Stands to reason they'd know more than your name, I guess." She motioned for Lucas and me to step aside. "I guess we'll have to talk to 'em. See what the hell they want."

"What?" I gasped, refusing to move. "You're not going out there, Oma. And we know what the hell they want!"

Somehow Oma pushed between Lucas and me in order to get to the front door. Lucas reached down and snatched the shotgun off of the coffee table quickly as I tried to reason with Oma. The engines shut off outside and I could hear doors creaking open. The headlights died off, and the front room was left in the ambient glow of the lamps and fireplace.

"Ain't no shells in it, Lucas." She waved him off. "Won't do you no good."

"Where are the shells?" I asked desperately.

"Gave 'em to Lena to hide 'em, smartass." She waggled her head. "One of your brilliant ideas—like burning up werewolves and going out to the football stadium at night."

"You still can't go out there." I grabbed her arm. "Those men are not playing around, Oma."

"Get your damn hand off me." She snapped. "I can still whip your ass if I have to, Robbie."

My hand slowly slid from her arm as I frowned down at her.

"I'll go out here and talk to these fellas and send them on their way." She gestured vaguely. "I'll clean up your damn mess."

"How is this my mess?"

"Ya' killed one of theirs didn't ya'?"

"Maybe?"

"You was so certain the other day." She waggled her head. "I'll get rid of 'em."

"Oma." I pleaded. "Seriously. Let's call Sheriff Dennard."

She scoffed. "Yeah. Get his tubbly ass out of bed and get him over here in under an hour. You go on and do that while I talk to these assholes out on my damn lawn. Probably left tire tracks."

"Mrs. Wagner—" Lucas tried to help, but Oma had already reached for the knob of the door.

My grandmother flipped the porch light on and swung the door wide until the knob bounced against the wall behind it but not hard enough to leave a mark or indention. Lucas and I chased after her. We didn't want to go outside and face a group of men who were out for our blood, but we couldn't let my grandmother do it on her own either. Oma walked across the porch and stood at the top of the steps, her arms crossing over her chest and coming to rest there. Lucas and I ran up behind her, Lucas taking her right side and me taking her left.

Three late 80s model single cab pickup trucks had pulled up in Oma's yard, all in a row, side by side. All of the men had climbed out and lined up in front of the trucks in a wide arc, surrounding the front porch. I reached out to grab Oma's arm but she gave me a look, and I pulled my hand away as though I had been slapped. Lucas glanced at me, fear in his eyes as Oma crossed her arms over her chest and looked down at the men. There should have been seven men in the yard since I had wounded one of them when I climbed the fence to get out of the stadium. A quick count let me know that there was exactly eight men standing before us.

All of the men, now that I had time to look at them without the immediate danger of being hurt, looked strikingly similar. All of them had dark hair, though some of them had long hair, some short, some nearly buzzed to their scalp. Some were tall, some were average, but they all had a generic look to their faces—if it weren't for the red eyes. The porch light shining on them made it harder to tell if their eyes were actively glowing. They all wore jeans and denim shirts with familiar tan coats thrown over them to ward off the early Spring chill in the air.

"Well," Oma looked out at the men, "it's a little late to be comin' for a visit, boys. But if I'd known you was comin', I'd have baked a cake."

"Esther Jean." The guy at the center of the arc of men stepped forward.

"Put one foot on my steps and you'll be running with three paws come the full moon, Jason Morris," Oma replied blandly.

The name sounded familiar.

Jason Morris chuckled but didn't move any closer.

"Whatchu boys doin' on my damn property?" Oma asked, her hands movin' to her hips. "Pretty sure I told you if I saw you on my property I'd have to do somethin' about it."

"We don't have any quarrel with you, Esther Jean." Jason, the obvious leader, replied. "We're here for Rob."

"Well," Oma said, "that's unfortunate since he's on my damn property, ain't it?"

"Esther Jean—"

"You don't show me the respect you was raised with, and I'll take two of your damn paws, Jason Morris." Oma snapped.

"Oma," I grumbled.

Jason Morris seemed to flush, but he didn't snap back at Oma or make a move towards the porch. All of his cohorts seemed to snicker, though they did their best to hide it.

"Mrs. Wagner." He said finally. "We don't want to cause trouble."

"I don't need no damn puppies thinking they can piss wherever they want." Oma snapped. "You started your damn trouble when three y'all wandered up into my yard and tried to attack my grandson. He was just defending himself."

"He's been hurting weres," Jason replied evenly.

"Only when they attack him." Oma waggled her head. "Stop actin' like y'all ain't got no damn sense, and maybe you won't get hurt."

"Bullshit, Mrs. Wagner." Jason spat, suddenly very angry, though he was smart enough not to move a single inch forward. "He hurt Andrew and he hurt Katie."

Andrew said he only talked to other werewolves about shop. I suddenly realized that he had told more details than needed.

"Andrew got handsy with him and then tried to make him dinner." Oma shrugged. "And I'm assuming Katie was the naked girl who wandered up into our yard the other morning. She tried to attack him, too. Along with two more of y'all. If y'all came that night to get revenge for Andrew's boo-boo's—I'll be talking to his sorry ass about this, by the way—then you was misled. Andrew is perfectly fine. And, technically, Rob ain't had nothin' to do with Andrew gettin' banged up. This one here ran into him with a truck."

Oma hooked a thumb at Lucas.

Lucas was ashen as he swallowed a lump in his throat.

"Fine." Jason snarled. "He'll take the punishment for Andrew and Rob will take the punishment for Katie."

The rest of the pack snarled along with Jason. Seeing eight grown men snarling like wolves in human form, along with the sound of it, made my stomach drop.

"One you bastards gets even the slightest bit furry," Oma warned, "and we're gonna have another damn barbecue right now."

Oma raised a hand, and the snarling stopped. One of the guys actually yipped as though he had been kicked.

"We're owed justice!" Jason snapped.

More snarls sounded, but they were silenced quickly by a glare from Oma. She turned her head slowly, looking at all of the men in turn, her eyes finally returning to center, to focus on Jason.

"You got a dick in your ear, son," Oma said calmly, her hand going back to her hip. "Andrew got hit because he tried to attack Rob. Rob wasn't the one who hurt him. Then y'all came up on my property in the middle of the goddamn night to try to get revenge on the wrong person, and that person defended themselves. Seems to me you should be kickin' each other's asses for being so goddamn dumb. 'Course, y'all wasn't exactly the top of your class, so I don't expect you to be very damn smart now."

Jason just glowered at Oma.

"Tell me," Oma continued, "why was...Katie...still burned all to hell the next mornin'? She shoulda been fine once she had a few hours. But she came up in my yard lookin' like someone melted half her body like a candle."

"She was one of our young ones."

"Young?" My head whipped to Oma.

"He just means new," Oma spoke out of the corner of her mouth. "She wasn't no damn child."

"She wasn't an old woman who was ready for death, either!" Jason bellowed.

More snarls.

Lucas and I fidgeted as the men all glowered up at us, their eyes really glowing, even in the light provided by the porch, their teeth gnashing.

Oma started to cackle.

Slowly, the snarling and teeth gnashing tapered off and all of the men were looking at Oma again, unsure of themselves.

"If I didn't know better, I'd think you just threatened me, Jason." Oma actually bent down to slap her knee. "And that is just too damn precious for words. I done told you that if you boys showed up on my property again that I wouldn't be happy with you and now here you are testin' my patience. Your balls are bigger than your brains. Though I'm sure both are tiny."

Jason Morris looked around, fidgeting slightly as he looked at his comrades. The way that they were twitching, I wasn't so sure that they were loyal enough to have his back against Oma. Though, I wasn't sure exactly why that was. I had never seen anything besides Oma's shotgun and her tongue that did much damage.

"Now," Oma shook her head with a sigh, "the way I see it, you feel you're owed something over Andrew's little boo-boo's even though he ain't in with y'all—again, he will be hearing from me, so you let him know that— and you're owed something over Katie's death. Even though both was their own damn faults. Am I right?"

"That's about the size of it." Jason nodded, trying to look menacing, but failing spectacularly as he stared up at my elderly, small grandmother.

"Mm." Oma snorted. "Well, I know where you live. We'll be sure you get money to pay for Katie's funeral. Make sure she's buried proper- like and has a decent headstone. So her family—if any still claim her— ain't put out with anything more than grief. You'll need to make up a story to Sheriff Dennard, so he knows who he's got in the morgue."

"Oma..."

"Shut up." She snapped at me out of the corner of her mouth.

"What about Andrew?" Jason snarled.

His cohorts didn't do anything but look up at Oma.

"He ain't one of yours." Oma shrugged. "If he feels he's owed something for getting banged up by someone defending themselves, he knows where to find me. But I guarantee you he won't come looking for compensation. So, that settle your hash, Jason Morris?"

Jason stood at the base of the steps, looking up at Oma, the wheels creaking in his head. Finally, he nodded.

"I need to hear you say it out loud in front of your pack here, Jason." Oma grinned. "Let's hear ya' say, 'Yes, Mrs. Wagner. That will settle us up.' Can you be a good boy and do that for me?"

Jason glowered at her, but he still followed directions.

"That will settle us up, Mrs. Wagner."

"Good." Oma's hands fell from her hips.

"Now, Robbie, say you're sorry for giving Katie what she deserved." Oma turned her head to me with a shit-eating grin.

"You just hold on!" Jason jabbed a finger up at Oma, which was not all that threatening considering how docile he became just from her chewing him out. "What about Darrell? Your damn grandson set him on fire back at the stadium!"

Oma turned back to Jason with a roll of his eyes.

"Is Darrell dead?"

"No." Jason snapped, but his heart wasn't in it. "He'll be fine when he changes back. But he probably won't have much fur until he changes at least a dozen more times."

"Poor thing," Oma stated simply.

"What are you gonna do about that, old—Mrs. Wagner?"

"What part of 'don't attack people and you won't get burnt' don't you understand, you fuckin' moron?" Oma snapped. "I ain't doin' shit about someone gettin' hurt by someone defending themselves. I'm only havin' pity on Katie 'cause she's dead, and everyone deserves a proper funeral."

"That's not good enough!"

"You just said it was, ya' dumb shit." Oma was raising her hand again. The men before us all blanched. "Now y'all just hear your Pack Alpha go back on his word?"

Jason looked around nervously at his "men."

"That's not fair!" Jason squeaked. "You tricked me, Mrs. Wagner!"

"Like that's really damn difficult." Oma snorted. "I spoke plainly to you about the terms, and you forgot about Darrell until it was done. Besides, Darrell will be just fuckin' fine from the way it sounds. Send him my best."

"Your grandson can't just go around acting like he's so goddamn special, setting our people on fire, thinking he can just get away with it!"

"I was wrong." Oma shook her head in disgust. "You got a dick in both your damn ears, Jason Morris. This matter is settled."

"No the hell it is not." He growled and stepped forward.

My vision flashed hot and red, then suddenly Jason was jumping backward, and his men were scattering. I hadn't even suspected Oma would react in such a way, nor had I seen it happen, but Oma had blasted him back without a single thought about it. Once the red cleared from my vision, Jason was on his ass, and all of his pack members were scattered, hiding behind their trucks. I glanced over at Lucas, and he was looking at me with wide eyes, a grin slowly blooming on his face. I gave him a nervous smile, trying not to laugh at what Oma had just done to a group of men with more testosterone than neurons.

"My fuckin' tea is in here getting' cold, and you think I'm just goin' to have all the patience in the damn world, Jason?" Oma snapped down at him, her hands on her hips again.

The soles of Jason's boots were sending up plumes of smoke. Oma hadn't taken a "paw," but she had made her decision on the matter clear.

"If you had any damn sense you'd call this a wash and get the fuck off my property, Jason." Oma continued. "If you want to keep negotiating, I'm going to ask how you're going to make up for the fact that you came up on my property after I illicitly told you—"

"Explicitly," I interjected.

"You shut the fuck up." Oma jabbed a finger at me. "Unless you want the ole hot foot as well!"

I shrugged.

Jason was getting to his feet, his knees wobbly and his shoes still smoking as his pack members slowly came out from behind their trucks.

"I told you to stay off my property, and you didn't listen." Oma snarled down at Jason as he stood before her, shaky and smoking. "If I wanted to, I could demand my own damn compensation for your transgression. I could refuse to do a damn thing for Katie. Or I could take a paw or two. I'm bein' pretty goddamn generous here, Jason Morris. You better consider that before you say one more damn word to me."

Jason took a step backward towards his truck as his eyes stayed on Oma.

"Fine." He spat.

"Don't you take no sass with me, damnit!" Oma crossed her hands over her chest, making all of the men jump again. Lucas and I exchanged another grin. "Now get your asses back into those trucks and get those pieces of shit off my lawn. You're making the property value in the neighborhood go down by the minute."

Jason gave a sharp nod and started to turn.

"And if there's one damn rut in my fuckin' lawn, we won't be done here, ya' hear me?" Oma spat.

Jason and his pack members all rushed to their trucks like their asses were on fire, doors closing loudly as they all made their getaway. The speed with which they all pulled out, turned around, and made their way onto the driveway to get away from Oma's property was at a much slower pace, though. They didn't want to risk leaving any ruts. Oma watched as they all drove away down the long drive, her arms staying across her chest. When the last pair of taillights disappeared as the last truck turned onto the main road, she shook her head and turned around.

"Oma," I said, "that was...messed up."

"You're telling me." She huffed. "I'm gonna have to make a fresh cup of tea 'cause of those assholes."

Oma entered the house, wiping her feet on the rug as though she had ventured anywhere but the porch. Lucas and I glanced at each other, exchanging confused looks. I shrugged deeply as we followed her into the house. Oma was grabbing her mug off of the coffee table and was heading towards the kitchen as Lucas closed the door behind us. My grandmother looked wholly unbothered about everything that had just happened out on her front lawn. In fact, if I hadn't witnessed it myself, I would never have believed that a group of men had come to threaten us. I certainly wouldn't have believed that Oma took care of the whole thing on her own.

"Oma, can we—"

"You two just take your asses to bed." Oma turned and rolled her eyes at us. "I ain't got the energy or patience to deal with any more bullshit tonight."

"I have a lot of questions, Oma." I pleaded.

"Well, the answers will taste better with some biscuits and gravy."

I guess that was her way of saying: "*Save it for morning.*"

With that, she turned around again and went into the kitchen, slapping the light on in the process. I turned to Lucas and held my hands out in a way that showed how put out I was and how desperate I was for answers. Lucas grabbed those empty hands and pulled me into him. I tucked my face into his neck as he kissed my forehead. Together, we turned towards the stairs, not letting go of each other. As a unit, we ascended the stairs, with nothing better to do but go to bed. There was always one way we could make each other feel better about everything.

Chapter 11

Brushing my teeth with Ernst standing on the toilet seat lid, watching me with wide-eyes, was slightly odd, but he was not ready to come out and introduce himself to Lucas yet. He was watching the movements of me brushing my teeth with morbid fascination, as though someone jamming a brush into their mouth over and over was the oddest thing he'd ever seen. Either Oma never brushed her teeth or Ernst had never been allowed to watch the process. Once my teeth were thoroughly clean, and I had spat and rinsed, I reached for a washcloth so that I could knock the day's grime off of my face. Ernst finally spoke up as I was running the cloth under the hot water that came out of the faucet at a temperature just shy of boiling.

"*Sir,*" he said, "*is everything okay now?*"

"It's okay for now, Ernst." I nodded.

"*Good.*" Ernst nodded furiously. "*That's good, sir.*"

"Yeah," I replied as I brought the cloth to my face.

"*The missus is not goin' ta be happy with me for a long time, sir.*" He squeaked. "*She wouldn't speak ta me after we were in the cellar, sir.*"

Ernst's squeaky voice and high pitch made me wonder if Lucas could hear him out in the bedroom where he was waiting in bed. Even if he couldn't hear Ernst, I knew that he could probably hear me. I didn't like thinking that he might be in my bed, waiting for me, wondering why I was having a conversation with myself. After everything that had happened since we had started seeing each other, the last thing I needed to do was give any indication that the elevator didn't go to the top. The thought of Lucas not wanting to be with me anymore felt like a lump of cold clay in my stomach.

You shouldn't feel that way at all.

You've only been dating for...

"She'll get over it, Ernst." I smiled at him as I washed my face. "She just has to get over feeling like we were disobedient. Besides, you didn't do anything wrong. I did. If she keeps being mean to you, you let me know, and I'll talk to her, okay?"

"*I'll be doin' no such thing!*" He was scandalized. "*Sir, you cannot tell the missus what ta do!*"

"I wouldn't tell her what to do, Ernst." I chuckled. "I'd just reason with her so she'd know she should be nicer to you."

"*She is nice enough,*" Ernst said haughtily.

Apparently, this was a sore spot, and the conversation on the matter was over as far as he was concerned.

"Ernst." I frowned, then finished wiping my face clean before turning to him. "Why was there nothing in the cellar?"

"*What do ya' mean, sir?*"

Blinking at him, I wondered if Ernst would actually tell me anything or not. Maybe he would keep his mouth shut after how Oma had treated him. There was no point in not trying to get information, though, so I plodded on, hoping I wouldn't make Ernst upset with me.

"I feel like maybe there is supposed to be something down there."

"*What should be down there, sir?*"

I swallowed hard.

"A well."

Ernst did his best not to let it happen, but his eyes grew marginally wider as he stared at me.

"I feel that there should be a well down there, Ernst." I reiterated. "But it wasn't down there when we went into the cellar earlier. I don't know why."

"*Maybe you are confused?*" His squeak was higher than usual.

Gotcha.

"I don't think so, Ernst." I shook my head gently. "Do you know why it wasn't there when we went down into the cellar?"

Ernst was wringing his hands in front of himself, his eyes darting all over the room. For a minute, I thought he might slip into a shadow by the claw-foot tub or into the linen closet and disappear. Remove himself from a difficult and awkward situation. Instead, he stayed perched on the toilet lid, still only coming chest high to me, wringing his hands.

"I won't tell Oma whatever you say."

"*Well,*" he whispered, "*I dunno, sir.*"

"You don't know if there's supposed to be a well in the cellar or you don't know why it wasn't there?"

Ernst stared up at me, his hand wringing increasing in intensity and speed. I was worried that he'd snap off one of his small, delicate fingers from all of the twisting and pulling.

"Please, Ernst?" I asked as gently as possible, but the desperation was there in my voice.

Ernst eyed me a few moments longer, his hand wringing slowing down gradually before he let his hands fall to his sides. He gave a full-body sigh, looked away for a moment, seemed to decide something, then looked up at me. The look on his face was determination, a decision made.

"*Some things don' react ta anger well, sir.*" He said cryptically. "*Even things like...wells...can hide when they sense there is danger.*"

"What do you..."

"*When the missus gets angry, we tend to jump inta the shadows, ya' see?*" He whispered. "*But when the missus is happy, we like ta be 'round her. When she is sad, we like ta comfort her. Anger is never good. Nothin' likes to be 'round people who are angry, sir.*"

"I don't understand." I shook my head.

Ernst climbed down from the toilet with a sigh. The way he climbed down like a full-grown person trying to scale a wall was precious, but I knew better than to say so. Ernst headed for the linen closet, which was open and ready for him to slip inside and find his favorite mode of transportation through the house.

"Sir," Ernst turned to me at the doorway, "*maybe the next time you go down to tha cellar, you shouldn't be angry.*"

I just stared at Ernst as he gave me a single nod and slipped into the closet. Then he was gone. Sighing to myself, I laid the washcloth over the edge of the sink and inspected myself in the mirror, making sure I looked okay to join my boyfriend in bed. Finally, I flipped the bathroom light off and exited the room. Lucas was still on the bed in his boxers. Apparently, my offer to let him borrow some of my pajama bottoms and a t-shirt had been ignored. Of course, why put clothes on when they'll probably just be pulled right off? Spring was coming to Ohio, anyway. It wasn't as cold in my room as it had been every other night I had been in Point Worth. Seeing Lucas laying there waiting on me made it feel even warmer.

"Who were you talking to?"

"Ernst." I shrugged.

Lucas accepted this at face value with an upward nod. As I started to walk over to the bed, the bare floorboards cold on my feet, Lucas rose to his knees on the bed, a grin blooming on his face. Grinning back, I came to stand beside the bed as Lucas gently walked on his knees over to the side of the bed to stop right in front of me, his face directly in front of mine. I wasn't going to pass up the opportunity, I leaned forward and pressed my lips against his. Lucas reached up, and his fingers twined through my hair as he started to gently kiss me, then began to feed at my mouth.

"Do you think we were always this great at kissing each other?" Lucas asked. "You know...*before*?"

"I think so." I nodded gently, my eyes not leaving his.

"I wish I could remember." He said. "I don't ever want to forget a single kiss of yours."

"Try to forget this one."

Leaning forward, my lips found Lucas' again, and I fed at his mouth as my hands came up to his hips. Slowly, yet passionately, I kissed my boyfriend as my hands rubbed along his sides, moving to his stomach, feeling the soft flesh that covered firmer muscles. My hands moved lower, and I was cupping him in the palm of my hand. Lucas gasped against my mouth as I rubbed him slowly and firmly as I did my best to keep my mouth on his, to stifle his gasp with my lips and tongue. Lucas' fingers twisted in my hair roughly but stopped just short of pain as we kissed, and I rubbed him roughly.

Then he was yanking me onto the bed and pulling me on top of him. Kissing Lucas one more time, I slowly moved down his body, smiling wickedly up at him as I hooked my fingers in the waistband of his boxers. I moved downwards, pulling them over his hips, down his thighs, lower and lower until I yanked them off over his feet. Lucas was laid out before me, naked and so tempting as I sat there on my knees, wondering about the best way to attack him.

"Rob." He sighed.

My body moved of its own accord until I was on top of him, trapping the hardest part of him between us. I pushed down on him, putting pressure against him as I met his mouth with my own again. Lucas shivered beneath me, his hips giving an involuntary thrust. I moved my groin against his, making him pull away from my mouth to moan.

"I have so much money." I heard myself say. "We could just stay in bed forever, making each other feel this way all of the time. We would never have to worry about forgetting anything because nothing would leave this room. The two of us, all of our memories, we could trap it all in this room. We could just make love and live in a house of memories stacking up around us."

"Tempting." Lucas groaned as I moved my hips again. "So, tempting."

"You don't have to go to work ever again." I sighed against his mouth. "Just stay here. Be my everything all day every day. Never leave me. I could make every wish you had come true and then some, Lucas. All you have to do is stay with me all of the time."

Lucas pulled back and looked up at me, his brow furrowed.

"What?" I leaned forward to kiss the tip of his nose.

"I don't want Jacob Michaels in this bed with me." He said softly, his fingers now stroking my hair. "I want Rob Wagner. *My Rob.* No more no less. Give me Rob."

I just stared at him, unsure if I could do that.

"Besides," his fingers played along my cheek, then my jaw, "I'm perfectly capable of making my own wishes come true."

Suddenly, his hand was between us, and he was rubbing me. I gasped in shock and pleasure, suddenly aware of nothing but how much I loved Lucas. How much I loved having him touch me. I didn't want to possess him. Not like that. I wanted him to be with me because I was Rob Wagner. Period. Lucas and I were two separate individuals. We were just happier when we were together. Nothing, not even him going to work in the morning would change that. Nothing could change that.

Lucas rolled our bodies, coming to rest on top of me, his mouth still locked to mine and his hand still rubbing me as I moaned into his mouth. After what seemed like a lifetime, but still not long enough, he pulled back to grin wickedly at me. Then he was kissing his way down my chest, my stomach, and he was pulling my pants off of me. When he traveled back up my legs from pulling my pajama pants off, I felt his mouth on me, and I could barely keep myself from crying out in ecstasy.

Do you love me?

Yes. I love you.

Chapter 12

Being awoken abruptly was something I was just getting used to so it didn't startle me as much when I sat bolt upright in bed. Had I heard something again? Had Lucas snored or talked in his sleep or was he moving around due to a nightmare or dream? Did I need to go look out the window to find some hooded figure staring up at my window like a weirdo? I wouldn't go outside even if I saw that again. I refused.

Glancing over at Lucas, I could tell he was in a profound sleep. The fact that I could see him well because he was cast in an eerie green light was not lost on me. It dawned on me that I could see everything in the room very well due to the illumination that the light provided. Looking over at the door, I found the source of the light, just as I expected. The green light was pouring through the cracks around and under the door, reaching into the room like slender fingers, searching me out.

I twisted my hips to let my legs hang off of the bed and then pushed away from the bed, landing on my feet. I was naked, never having bothered to dress after Lucas and I brought each other to two of the most intense orgasms we'd ever had. I reached down to the floor and retrieved my pajama bottoms, sliding into them quickly as I kept my eyes on the green light sneaking into the room through the door cracks.

For a few moments, I stood there, my feet cold on the floorboards, staring at the door. Somehow, like Lucas, I knew what was going to happen. I knew that the light had returned at that moment because it was time. I was ready to follow it down to the cellar again. Padding across the room quietly, though I knew Lucas would not wake up, I made my way to the bedroom door. Just as before, when I pulled the door open, the light was moving down the upstairs hallway. I glanced back at Lucas. He was peacefully and deeply sleeping. I smiled over at him and exited the room, closing the door gently behind myself.

I'm coming back with our memories, Lucas.

I promise.

Nervously following the light down the hall, I tiptoed along, though I knew that Oma and the Kobolds would not awaken to come investigate either. The light moved down the hallway just a few yards ahead of me, then started down the stairway to the floor below. When I reached the top of the stairs, the light was moving into the living room below. Step by step, I followed along, making sure it never got so far ahead that I lost sight of it. The light moved along at a pace that matched mine, only moving towards the kitchen when my feet touched the foyer floor.

Through the living room, I continued to tiptoe, as though there was any reason to be quiet. As I walked through the living room and headed towards the kitchen, through the large kitchen entryway, I could see the cellar door was wide open. The light moved across the kitchen, towards the door, then started to slip down into the cellar, illuminating the usually dark stairwell. My feet hit the cold linoleum, and I jumped slightly at how cold it was, but I continued my forward movements towards the cellar door.

Once I reached the top of the stairs, the light was halfway down, partially illuminating the room below. Without thinking about my decision, I stepped down, my foot connecting with the top step. My other foot followed. Then I went down another step. And another. One after another, the green light moving slowly, beckoning me to follow it. I knew where we were going, so it didn't have to wait, but it was considerate of the incorporeal light source. Finally, my feet touched down on the dirt floor of the cellar, and I was staring at the stone wall before me.

I took a deep breath.

Turning to see what was there was...big.

It was significant in a way that I hadn't fully understood before.

I needed a moment to collect myself before I took the final step in this journey with the green light.

Breathing deeply, I collected myself and my thoughts, then finally turned towards the center of the room.

The well was there, and the light had collected inside of it, making it look like it was shooting a beacon into the sky, stopped only by the ceiling above. Though, if I had been outside of Oma's house and seen a green searchlight reaching into the sky, I would not have been surprised. I swallowed hard as I looked at the well, the glowing green light within, the way it beckoned me forth, to peer into its depths.

The dirt floor was rough beneath my feet, made the spaces between my toes feel gritty as I walked cautiously towards the well. Inside the well, the green light seemed to pulse or throb, though it did not sink into the lowest recesses of the well like it had before. It stayed near the top, illuminating the well and the cellar around it as I approached. When I was next to the well, I placed my hands on the stone side, taking in the dimensions of this illuminated entrance into the Earth beneath my feet.

At least as wide across as I was tall, the sides coming up to my waist, the well was impressive. I probably could have climbed up onto the side, spread my arms wide and fallen forward. Falling, falling, falling, never once hitting the sides as I descended into whatever was below. Something told me that if I did that, I would never hit bottom, though that had to be impossible. Reaching out, I pushed my hand towards the light in the well. Though obviously light, it felt like something between a liquid and gas between my fingers. There was resistance, but it did not moisten my hand.

What have you been keeping from me?
I dipped my hand into the well's light again.
Did you want company up there?
Do you love me?
Have you been waiting on me?
Did you see that?
ROBBIE!

I shuddered as the voices seemed to come from within my own head, though I knew that they emanated from the well. Without giving it another thought, I climbed up onto the edge of the wall around the well and stared down into the light. I could see nothing but bright green light shining up to me, preventing me from seeing anything below. If I leaped, the light would swallow me whole, wrap my body up.

Then what?

"You couldn't wait for breakfast, could you?"

I started and nearly fell into the well, as though being yanked out of a dream. Correcting my stance, I turned my head to look over my shoulder. Oma was standing at the bottom of the stairs. Her hands weren't on her hips, and her arms weren't crossed over her chest. She didn't look angry or furious or frustrated. She looked concerned. Maybe sad?

"Hi, Oma." My voice sounded trance-like.

"Robbie." She shook her head and moved forward cautiously.

I watched her move towards me, but she didn't come directly to me. She rounded the well as my eyes followed her and she became illuminated by the green light as it poured out from fathoms below. I stared at her as I stood there on the well wall edge, the light still beckoning to me.

"What are you doing?" She asked gently, so unlike herself.

I pointed down into the well.

"I'm going to take back what's mine."

Oma stared at me. She wasn't shocked at what I had said, but she looked even more concerned.

"Robbie." she said, her voice sounding like a plea. "Don't do that."

"Why not, Oma?" I sounded like a robot.

"Because what's down there you can never forget again, Robbie," She said. "If you do this, there will be no way to take it back."

"I need to remember, Oma."

"You *think* you need to remember," She replied. "But you're wrong. And there will be no fixing that. I won't be able to do anything about that, Robbie."

"I can't not be me anymore, Oma." I sounded a little more like myself. Briefly. "I can't be Jacob Michaels anymore. I don't want to be...*that*...anymore."

"You don't know that." A single tear slid down her cheek. "Because you don't know the alternative."

"I can find out." I looked down into the well, green light nearly blinding me.

"Robbie," She said urgently, "you look at me, son."

It was a struggle, but I pulled my eyes away from the light in the well to look over at her again. Oma's eyes were pleading with me, begging me to reconsider. To think about all of the options. To me, there was only one option. One course of action. I spread my arms slowly to my sides as I stared into Oma's eyes.

"Don't." She shook her head frantically. "Once you do, it's done, Robbie."

"This is the only way."

"What about Lucas?" She asked quickly. "What will happen with you and Lucas if you do this? Don't you care about him? He's up there. In bed. You can get down from there and go right back upstairs and crawl back into bed with him. I know he is probably missing you right now, Robbie."

Staring at her, I considered this as best I could as my arms dropped to my sides slowly.

"He loved me before, Oma." I nodded. "He'll love me after."

Oma's eyes grew wide, and her hand went to her throat.

"It's already started, Oma." I felt a tear slide down my cheek. "It will happen no matter what I choose. You can't keep protecting me from it."

Then I spread my arms out to my sides again.

"*Robbie!*" Oma shouted.

And then I was falling down an endless hole.

Jacob Michaels Is Not Here

A Point Worth LGBTQ
Paranormal Romance
Book 4

Chapter 1

High heels with red soles were rare in places like Point Worth, Ohio. I only knew one person in the entire town who owned a pair of Louboutin heels, and that was because I had gifted them to her. The dead body laid out in the street was wearing a pair of Louboutin heels, and I knew without looking that they were on the feet of the person for whom I had purchased them. Point Worth was on fire. Well, maybe not in a 'Sir Thomas Bloodworth was indecisive after a baker's house went ablaze' way, but fires were scattered throughout the town. It was the only light to illuminate Main Street as I stood there, my eyes lingering on the red soles of those shoes.

Barkley's Hardware's windows were smashed out, and flames were flickering inside, smoke rolling out thick, black, and lazily towards the sky. The Sunny Side Up Café was decimated, only one wall was standing, and it was greasy with soot as smoke curled up from the foundation. The corner convenience store looked like a giant bonfire. The bank was basically a mound of bricks with more fire and smoke rising into the sky from the rubble. Lifting a hand to shield my eyes, I took in the devastation around me.

Glinting glass shards caught the firelight and made the street and pavement sparkle around me. A dozen other bodies littered the walkways and the middle of the street, as though God had sprinkled finishing salt onto this little macabre scene of mayhem. Why weren't there sirens or cop cars or firetrucks or the distant wail of help coming soon? I walked down the street, averting my eyes as I passed the body wearing the red-soled heels. Looking down at Carlita again was something I hoped I'd never have to do again.

Where was Lucas?

Oma?

Were Ernst and Lena and all of the others okay?

Was Oma's house on fire? Razed?

What had happened to Point Worth?

"Hello?" I looked around, hoping I would find someone else alive.

Seeing dead bodies, for some reason, had neither unnerved nor scared me—even though I had recognized the first one I had laid eyes upon. Something about the scene in downtown Point Worth felt odd. Even if I were able to remove the burning and decimated buildings, the broken glass, and the dead bodies, I still would have felt that something was off about the whole thing. Something about the air, the dark barely permeated by the flickering of nearly silent, roaring fires—all of it just seemed...off.

Your home town on fire. That's definitely not a normal occurrence. At least not one to be calm about.

The scene would have felt odd, regardless of the circumstances.

However, looking down the street laid out before me, littered with broken bodies, collapsed buildings, some on fire...it was like watching it on a 24-hour news channel. Like I had tuned into CNN for breaking news.

"This just in! The tiny, forgettable town of Point Worth, Ohio, future potential locale for meth labs and esoteric cult compounds, is lit!"

Something about how I was viewing the street unnerved me as I hesitantly took a step forward, intentionally making a wide berth around Carlita's lifeless body. Shouldn't I feel compelled to kneel down next to her, hold her broken body in my arms, and mourn her? Sure, I didn't know her all that well, but I knew she was good people. Carlos was a great guy, and his drag persona, Carlita, was an angel. She didn't deserve to be laid out in the middle of the street, her dead body exposed to the elements. Would anyone come to get her? Claim her?

Putting one foot in front of the other, I pushed the thought out of my mind. Carlita was dead. There was nothing mourning could fix about that. Mourning would come later.

A lot of mourning would come later.

My feet automatically stopped when I stepped directly in front of Barkley's. The front entrance to the store was unusual for me to see since Oma and I had always parked at the back of the store whenever we came to Barkley's. My throat felt tight as I looked at the store before me, windows were blown out, fires were roaring from inside, the front door was hanging on by a single hinge. Had Lucas been at work when this happened? My whole body tensed at the thought of my boyfriend being anywhere nearby when this...mayhem...began.

What had started all of these fires?

Had there been an explosion?

Had this been caused by gangs?

Vandals?

Terrorism?

White nationalists and other extremist groups had absolutely no reason to want to live in Point Worth, let alone make it a target for terrorism. My mind began to replay things I'd heard in the news and read about online, trying to formulate a theory as to why Point Worth had been...attacked? Who or what would want to attack a tiny town in Ohio? What did my minuscule town have going for it that would make it a prime target for such an act? Even if a wanton act of terror was not the reason for the devastation, random violence and vandalism were rare in Point Worth, in general, to begin with. The town was too tiny to have any real gangs...wasn't it?

Why hadn't I seen anything in the news about the things going on in Point Worth?

Why did I have to discover what was happening on my own?

Why hadn't I known the town was on fire until I arrived on Main Street?

This was something that seemed like word would spread about quickly.

Then again…

Why didn't I know where Oma and Lucas were and if they were okay?

Why didn't I know if Oma's house was affected?

Why didn't I know…anything?

Putting one foot in front of the other, I entered Barkley's, not feeling the heat of the random roaring fires still burning inside. I walked through the vacant and desolate store, stepping over toppled and spilled paint cans, piles of tools, puddles of screws and nails, fallen ceiling tiles and exposed wires, wondering how a once thriving business could suddenly look like a scene from a dystopian novel. I walked down aisles, unsure what I was looking for or how I would find it. The shelves on either side of me littered with detritus and a few lucky products that had not been damaged. The raging fires cast eerie shadows throughout the store as I made my way to the rear of the store.

The check-out counter and register area had completely folded in on itself, a pile of useless technology and wood, charred and sending up wisps of smoke. I stood there, staring down at the piles of…nothing…wondering once again whether or not Lucas had been present when the store had been…attacked? More questions swirled through my head that I knew I would not get answers to that would satisfy my curiosity. The scene laid out before me inside of Barkley's Hardware let me know that nothing would diffuse my confusion about the things I was seeing. As I strolled through the store, it dawned on me that I could not feel the heat of the fire or smell the smoke. The soot and ash did not settle upon my skin and make me feel dirty. It was almost as though I was removed from the situation in which I found myself.

Exiting through the automatic sliding glass doors into the back area of the store that contained gardening items and lumber was easy. The doors had shattered outward, spraying glass all over the concrete beyond; I merely had to step through the frame of the door. Outside, in the dark of night once again, fires raging in the town around me, I found that the back part of the store was just as bad as the interior. Plants were strewn about, bags of mulch and soil and concrete mix had been blown open, spewing their contents like the world's dingiest New Year's Eve party had ended. Standing there just beyond the doorway, I surveyed the damage, still going over a list of questions in my head.

Groaning sounds, as though being broadcast through water, emanated from a few yards away on my right. Without a second thought—though I felt that I was not being led by my own thought processes—I turned robotically on my heels and headed towards noise. In the corner, sat on the floor, his back against a pile of half-disintegrated bags of mulch, was Mr. Barkley. His face was bloodied, half of his face indistinguishable from a flat of hamburger meat as he groaned and gasped, his chest heaving and falling with each panicked breath.

His shirt was in tatters under his overalls, and the legs of the garment were shredded and charred by the fire. Most of his hair had been burned away, and I wasn't sure that his eye on the wounded side of his face was completely intact. Mr. Barkley looked like he had been worked over by a meat grinder. A meat grinder that had also been on fire. When I approached him, his eyes darted up to mine, stricken with fear. Our eyes locked as he gasped a final time.

"He's coming."

Then Mr. Barkley's eyes closed, his chest heaved one last time, and he went still. Standing there, staring down at the body Mr. Barkley had once inhabited, I wondered why I was not panicking instead of planning to walk back through the store and out onto the street. But that was where I found myself suddenly, unaware of how I had arrived from the back of Barkley's Hardware. The town was still partially and eerily illuminated by sporadic fires throughout town, but Barkley's was no longer there. There wasn't a pile of burning rubble or debris strewn about like after a major catastrophe. The lot to my right, where Barkley's had been, was now just a slab of concrete on the street, as though waiting for someone to build a new store.

I turned away, something about that blank space made it difficult to keep looking at it. Instead of looking at where Barkley's used to be, I walked in an even measure down the street towards the Sunny Side Up Café. Why had Carlita been on Main Street in Point Worth? She lived in Toledo as far as I knew. What had brought her to town—especially on a night when something like this would happen? Of course, I had no idea what happened, so how was I to know if Carlita being in town was unusual? In fact, I didn't know Carlita's habits or anything about her life in general—other than she was a drag performer—so, it might not have been all that unusual for her to be in Point Worth at all.

My vision suddenly blurred, and I felt a sharp pain right between my eyes, and I stopped in my tracks, wincing at the feeling emanating from within my skull. Instinctively, I bent down and put my hands against my knees, bracing myself as the lightning bolt of pain shot through my head and made everything in front of my eyes dance like I was on a bad acid trip. Firelight continued to dance, making everything I saw look like it was coming from behind a veil of gasoline fumes. As if out of place frames had been inserted into a glitchy reel of film, a dark figure appeared farther down the street, snapping in and out of the movie playing before me.

Shaking my head to chase away the pain and to clear my vision, the figure blinked out of existence and the haziness altering my vision slowly evaporated. I kept my hands against my knee for a few moments longer as I took a deep breath, trying to steady myself. The sharp pain in my head eased until I felt nothing at all. I righted myself and carried on down the street, looking around slowly for the dark figure. Without question, I knew it was crazy, but I knew the dark figure that had appeared in the street. Even with the pain behind my eyes and the hazy vision...I knew it.

Outside of the café, I didn't bother climbing the steps to enter but instead stepped around them to the side of the café to peer through one of the large windows. Just as I had expected, I was sitting on one side of a booth, and Lucas was across from me. Only, it was Lucas and me as we had been during our high school years. A little thinner, a little lankier, a little more awkward, a lot younger. We were talking animatedly to each other across the tabletop, smiling widely as we kept company with each other there in the Sunny Side Up Café.

Only, that wasn't true.

The Sunny Side Up Café had not existed when we were in high school.

It had been The Red Rooster Tavern.

We never would have been allowed inside at night at that age.

It had been twenty-one and up after dark.

Neither teenage Rob nor teenage Lucas saw me standing there, staring at them through the window of the tavern. They continued their conversation, hands gesturing wildly and excitedly, smiles shared, stories told, obvious affection passing through looks and body language. I smiled tightly at the scene before my eyes. Lucas and I had never been to The Red Rooster Tavern at night, only during the day. But I liked watching the two of us there together anyway.

Once, Lucas had taken me out onto the lake in a rowboat Jackson Barkley, his grandfather had owned. It wasn't the only time we had found ourselves in the rowboat on the lake, but we had laid back together and watched the stars and talked about our dreams. We had imagined that each star was a dream we had cast out into the universe, begging for...something...to hear our desires. To grant us a wish. I remembered those dreams. Those wishes. None of my dreams or wishes involved becoming famous—in any way. There had been plenty of wild things I had wished and hoped for, but fame had not been one of those things. A single tear slid down my cheek, and I quickly brushed it away with the back of my hand.

"Do you like remembering?"

I didn't even start at the sound of the voice.

I had expected it. And I knew the voice.

"This isn't a real memory," *I replied evenly, my eyes staying on the two boys inside of the tavern.*

"No."

The hooded figure stepped up beside me, its face peering through the window as well. Glancing out of the corner of my eye, I could only see the figure's nose peeking out from within the depths of the hood. My eyes went back to Lucas and me inside of the tavern.

"Why is it here?" *I asked.* "This memory?"

"Why wouldn't it be?" *The figure replied.* "This is the memory of the time the two of you obtained fake identification and, even though Clancy knew you were not old enough, he overlooked it. Your first real date."

"That never happened."

"Are you so sure?"

"Yes."

"You remember everything?"

"Yes."

"Are you entirely sure?"

I nodded. And I knew I should have panicked, remembering everything I had forgotten, all of the memories that had returned to my brain; but I wasn't panicking. I just felt complete.

"Seems Point Worth is on fire."

"Seems to be."

"There were no firemen to call."

"I know."

"That's your fault."

"I know."

"You don't seem to care at all," *The hooded figure said.*

"I do," *I responded, still looking through the tavern window, though the scene inside was slowly growing dark, casting teenage Lucas and me in deeper shadow.* "I just don't know what other choice I had."

"Don't you?"

I had no answer to that.

"Fortune may be smiling upon this worthless little town." He added.

"It's not worthless."

The hooded figure chuckled, the sound like ice being rubbed along my spine as I watched the scene before me grow darker still.

"You have returned."

"Yes."

"Why?"

"It was time."

"Running away didn't suit you?"

"No."

"Are you ready, then?"

I turned to the hooded figure.

"Let me see your face," I said. *"Again."*

The figure continued to stare into the tavern.

"Please?"

"That is your choice, then?"

"Do I have another?"

Another chuckle; another spine tingle.

"Of course, you do." Said the voice. *"You can just wake up. Go on with your life as it was. Go back...to Hollywood."*

The way the figure said *"Hollywood"* made me shiver. I turned back to look through the window, only to find that the tavern was just a concrete lot...just like Barkley's now was.

"Where is everything going?"

"You are taking too long to make your decision."

"I already told you my choice."

"Did you mean it?"

Turning once more, I stared at the figure.

"Let me see your face."

The figure stood there, ignoring me for a moment, then slowly turned to face me, though the figure's face, aside from its nose, stayed in shadow. My eyes connected with the mass of shadow within the hood, but I could see nothing apart from that nose. Of course, I knew the face within that hood, so it was not absolutely necessary for me to see. However, before I could make my choice official, I had to see that face once more.

"I have been waiting for this day, Robert," The figure said. *"I knew it would come."*

I swallowed hard as the figure seemed to loom over me

"We've wasted so much time. That vexes me."

"You shouldn't have presented me with options, then," I replied.

A chuckle once again, though it held no humor.

"I had no choice then," I added, *"but now I do."*

"Are you so sure?" The figure asked. *"Or have the years and distance emboldened you?"*

"Where are we?" I ignored the question.

"In the place between." The figure answered. *"The place between places, the time between times. The past, the present, the future, the here, the now, the then. What was, what is, and what could be."*

The figure gestured with its pale hands as it spoke.

"But this place is disappearing. Maybe forever."

"I've made my choice," I said with finality.

Gesturing around, the figure drew my eyes around the street as fires slowly faded out, and another building snapped out of existence. The post office, I think.

"Have you?"

"Let me see your face."

The figure chuckled a final time as the gas station blinked out of existence.

"If I see your face, I will make my choice." I pleaded.

Another building blinked itself away, and the darkness crept in around us before another building disappeared, leaving nothing but a concrete slab in its place. The dark figure reached up, and pale, nearly skeletal fingers grasped the sides of the hood as I locked my eyes on the shadow within the hood. Slowly, the figure pulled back the hood, and as the face of the figure came into view, the darkness began to swallow us. Finally, before the last of my vision was swallowed by nothingness, I saw the face I had been longing to see once again.

"Thank you." I managed.

"You've made your choice." The figure responded.

"Will it hurt?"

"Oh, you will have your pain, Robert." It responded. "There will be plenty of pain. All you have to do is wait. But this...will just sting a little bit."

Then everything went black.

Oma was in the kitchen like she always was, preparing another breakfast, humming a tune to herself, cupboards suddenly slamming shut and shadows shifting as I gamboled into the room. Bacon and biscuits and sausage gravy perfumed the air—the signature scent of Oma's house in the morning. Too hungry to entertain propriety, I plopped down into one of the kitchen chairs, prepared to eat. I was hungry. I was always hungry.

"What have I told you about flingin' your ass into my kitchen chairs?" Oma turned around, the large kitchen spoon in her hand was coated with gravy.

It made my mouth water.

"I'm sorry, Oma." I blushed. "Your cooking just always smells so good."

"I guess I can take that as an apology."

She cackled and turned back to the stove. Oma had rules in her house and a strict sense of what was and wasn't proper behavior. While she was quick to correct breaking the rules or displaying improper behavior, she was just as ready to laugh and forgive. Oma wasn't one to ever genuinely hold a grudge against anyone. Besides the Kelly family. As far as I knew, she'd never actually punished me for anything. Of course, Oma had a way with her looks and her words that let one know you would never want to suffer one of her punishments. So...I was a pretty good kid.

"Now," Oma said, the metal spoon scratching against the cast iron skillet, "what have you been up to the last few days?"

Summer sun was streaming through the window, making everything look soft and lazy and warm.

"Nothing." I shrugged.

"Nothin'." She snorted. "Nothin' my wrinkled ass, Robbie."

"Oma..."

She waggled her head. "Rob."

"Thank you." My pubescent voice cracked.

"I'll never get used to calling you that." She turned to me, putting her fists against her hips. "You're not a 'Rob.' You're too damn sweet to go by 'Rob.' I'm just goin' to call you 'Robbie' and you can hate me if you want."

She gave me a wink and turned back to the stove. Since Oma's back was turned and she couldn't see it, I let myself smile.

"You've been stayin' away from the house from sun up to sun down the last few days." Oma teased over her shoulder. "To me, that spells out that you're sweet on some girl."

I shrugged, though Oma couldn't see it, as I sat at the table.

"You just gon' be quiet about it?" Oma chuckled to herself. "Ain't nothin' wrong with a fifteen-year-old boy catchin' sweet on a girl. All y'all go through it. Bunch of hormonal idiots just waiting for a chance to smooch...and do other things...with some willing girl."

My cheeks were red, and I was staring down at the table. Oma talking to me about the birds and the bees—such as it was—was bad enough. The fact that I didn't have a thing for any of the girls at school was another. Oma turned to me, her eyes locking onto mine.

"You're going to be a heartbreaker, Robbie," She sighed. "I mean, hell...just look atcha. Now that you're growing into yourself. You make sure you're bein' a gentleman until they tell you it's okay to act otherwise. Don't you let me hear a single word about you treatin' a girl wrong."

"You won't, Oma," I mumbled.

"Good."

She turned back to the stove.

"I don't have any crushes on any girls anyway." I found myself practically whispering.

"Well, that's okay, too." Oma nodded to herself. "Ain't nothin' wrong with bein' a late bloomer. Keep you out of trouble as long as we can."

Oma laughed. I didn't.

There's a time in every young person's life where they decide the person they want to be with their parents—or their parental figure. Do they want to show their most authentic self and risk that it won't be good enough...or do they try on a persona so that they don't have to find out if the person they truly are is good enough to be loved? My teenage self chose the former.

"There's a boy I like, though." I felt the truth slide from my mouth.

The "skritch-skritch" of the spoon in the skillet stopped, and Oma seemed to freeze at the stove. My teenage heart palpitated within my chest as I waited for whatever was to come to...come. Thick, heavy silence grew between us in the kitchen as bacon sizzled in the other skillet, creating a soundtrack comprised of delicious sounds and smells. Just when I thought that I might scream out just to break the tension, the "skritch-skritch" of the spoon in the skillet started up again. Oma let the spoon rest against the side of the skillet and turned to me again, her hands on her hips once more.

"You know they got one them 'LGBT' centers over in Toledo?"

I shook my head nervously.

"Well, they do." She nodded. *"I been thinkin' about goin' over there to volunteer while you was in school all week long. Help the boys and girls out. I guess that's just what I'll do."*

Then she turned back to the stove and started stirring the gravy again. I allowed myself to give a wary smile.

"Maybe you can go with me?" She suggested gently.

"Maybe..."

"Who's this boy?" Oma didn't let my hesitance overtake the conversation. *"Do I know him? I should. I know everybody around here. Better not be one them Kelly boys. Ugly, Irish assholes."*

"Are you ever going to be nice to them?" I teased. *"Besides, they're all a lot older than me, Oma."*

"I'll sit up in my coffin to spit at them if they show up at the funeral." Oma waggled her head as she cooked. *"Who's the boy, damnit?"*

"Luc-Lucas Barkley?" I stammered, suddenly very nervous.

Oma turned to me again, the spoon in her hand dripping gravy onto the floor. She didn't notice.

"That Jackson Barkley's grandson?" She asked quickly. *"The one who plays football?"*

I nodded jerkily.

Oma cackled and then noticed the gravy on the floor.

"Shit." She admonished herself before retrieving a paper towel to clean up the mess she had made.

Oma bent down to wipe up the gravy.

"Well," She grunted as she wiped, *"Lucas is a good kid. But Jackson Barkley will shit his britches knowin' that his grandson is..."*

She glanced up at me, stopping herself from saying whatever it was she was going to say. I stared at her.

"I wasn't gonna say nothin' too bad." She waved me off as she stood up and deposited the soiled paper towel in the trashcan. *"I don't even know if Jackson will give a shit, to be honest."*

"Oma..."

"Well, I'm sorry." She snapped, but she didn't have the heart to put the full force of her sass behind it. *"I was just gonna say he 'had a little sugar in his tank' is all."*

"It's not the most offensive thing you've ever said," I mumbled, and Oma shot a squinty-eyed look over her shoulder, silencing me.

The cellar door creaked open suddenly, and I looked over to see Ernst come out, looking around as though to make sure that there were no visitors. Once it was clear to him that it was just the three of us, his eyes locked onto me.

"Good morning, Ernst." I beamed.

"Good-mornin', Rob." He smiled back.

Ernst exited the cellar and shut the door gently behind himself as Oma gave him a *"good mornin'"* over her shoulder. Ernst returned the sentiment and sauntered over to the table to stand beside me, his head barely higher than my lap in my seated position.

"Didja sleep well, Rob?"

I didn't respond verbally. Instead, I smiled and scooted my seat back, making the legs scrape against the linoleum unpleasantly. Ernst didn't hesitate as he climbed up and sat on my knee. Oma cast a disapproving glance over her shoulder and shook her head as she began piling a plate high with the heavenly concoction she had whipped up for *breakfast. Doing her best to not slap the plate down on the table, Oma set the breakfast in front of Ernst and me before shaking her head once more. I picked up my fork while Ernst grabbed a strip of my bacon and began nibbling at it happily. It had taken a few years for him to sit at the table with me, under the watchful eye of Oma. He had become less fearful of showing impropriety when it became clear that Oma wouldn't say anything while I was around. Ernst was my friend. Oma let it slide.*

"You two are thicker than thieves, ain'tcha?" Oma stated blandly as she made her own plate.

Ernst nibbled nervously and looked up at me, and I just gave him a wink.

Lucas never liked meeting anywhere we might be seen by the other kids we went to school with each day. Being a naïve, mostly sheltered country kid myself, I assumed it was because I was a theater kid and he was a football player. It was a personal "head-slapping" moment for me when I realized the actual reason behind his secretive behavior. Of course, when Lucas and I had first started hanging out, I thought we were becoming just friends. I had known that I was gay...or, at least, I had a pretty good idea. Lucas hadn't indicated that he was gay when we started becoming friends, so it never crossed my mind that anything besides friendship was developing. Later, when we kissed for the first time, I had an Oprah "Ah-ha Moment." Obviously, he was gay—or gay-ish, which were the only LGBT terms I understood at the time—and wanted more than friendship. Knowing this, he wanted to keep the fact that we hung out a secret, even though I was not out of the closet to anyone except Oma at the time. I had just been too dense to understand what was unfolding before my very eyes. Lucas, of course, had been much quicker at figuring things out than I had been. He had always been smarter than me.

"We could go down to the bowling alley," I suggested as we walked along the shore of Lake Erie, beyond the woods bordering Oma's property. Lucas was skipping rocks sporadically, and I was collecting interesting pebbles in my pocket. We were fifteen and should have had more exciting things to do. "We could go see a movie or something. Ernst said he would show us some more tricks if you want."

Oma wasn't aware, but I had introduced Lucas to Ernst within days of becoming friends with him. I had known that he would be able to keep a secret. Just as I had suspected, and though Lucas had been gobsmacked by the appearance of a Kobold, he had kept his lips shut. He and Ernst had taken to each other after Lucas' initial shock wore off and they always talked at least a little bit every time Lucas showed up to hang out. Lucas stayed clear of the house, though. He hadn't wanted Oma to see him. We always met at the edge of the yard or down by the lake. But Ernst would always at least say "hello" to Lucas before the two of us left to do...whatever it was we decided to do.

Lucas' reply was slow to come, "I like just being out here."

"Okay." I shrugged and bent down to grab a rock so black and shiny that it looked like obsidian.

Shoving the rock in my pocket, I turned to watch Lucas skip another one across the eerily calm surface of the lake.

"The play was really good," Lucas stated as he slid his hands into his pockets and stared out at the lake.

"Thanks." I smiled widely. "Oma took me to Toledo afterward last night. We got burgers and milkshakes and saw a movie and...it was kind of cool, I guess."

Lucas smiled, still looking out at the lake.

"I mean, it was kind of stupid, too." I backtracked. "I kind of just wanted to hang out with the cast. Grandmas, right?"

I sighed as though the weight of the world was on my world-weary fifteen-year-old shoulders. Cool kids don't feel happy about spending time with their parents or grandparents.

"I think it's cool."

Surveying Lucas' face for hints of a lie as he looked out at the lake, I found none.

"It was cool," I confirmed.

"Mrs. Wagner seems really nice."

"You never come inside..."

"I know. You were an amazing Professor Harold Hill."

"When in Rome."

"Ohio?"

"Close enough."

"Don't let an Iowan hear you say that." Lucas laughed. "They'll be fit to be tied over in I-Oh-Way."

"We're both going to be in trouble with a capital 'T'." I teased.

Lucas smiled crookedly as he turned his gaze from the sun-sparkling water and looked at me. I did my best not to swallow down whatever it was that was making my belly feel the way it felt as he looked at me. His blonde hair seemed to practically glow in the spring sun. His eyes looked even more like jade than they usually did. Puberty was having its way with Lucas—in all the best ways. His jaw was becoming sharper, stronger. His baby fat was being shed, and days playing football was making him lean and muscular. But none of that accounted for what hid behind the jade of his eyes. Kindness can be exercised, but it can't be learned. Lucas was intimately familiar with the concept.

"You're really funny."

I shrugged.

"What does that mean?" Lucas mimicked my shrug with a small chuckle.

"I don't know." I had to keep myself from shrugging again.

Lucas stared at me for a moment before turning to walk along the shore of the lake again. I followed silently, my hands still in my pockets. Suggesting more activities we could do instead of nothing came to mind, but I let it go. Spending time with Lucas at the lake had actually become my favorite activity very quickly. I just didn't want him to get bored with it.

"Are you coming to the football game on Friday?"

"I guess," I said, "I mean, I always do, right? Everyone does."

We both chuckled.

"Do you usually watch the game...or do you ignore it like everyone else?"

"I watch."

He glanced out at the lake quickly then gave an upward nod.

"Do you...I mean, you cheer for me, right?"

I gave him a nudge with my shoulder as we walked.

"Obviously."

He smiled, his eyes down.

"Grandpa cheers really loudly, so if I can single anyone out in the crowd, it's usually him."

"I guess I'll have to cheer louder." I shrugged, regardless of my desires.

"You don't really like sports, do you?"

"Honestly?"

"Yeah."

"No," I said. "Not really."

"But you still go to the football games?"

"Something to do on a Friday night, right?"

"You could go to the 'bowling alley or the movies'," He teased.

Again, I was shrugging.

"Why do you keep coming?"

How to respond to the question evaded me as we walked along the shore, the perfectly still water and lack of breeze making the silence palpable. Initially, I started going to football games because that's just what high school kids did. They went to football games and socialized and flirted and hung out. Sometimes they actually even cheered for the team. Over time, I realized that football was no more exciting than any other sport I despised. I enjoyed socializing with my friends...mostly...but I was also incredibly bored at the games, too. In sophomore year, when Lucas started playing, though, things changed.

The blonde, good-looking guy—though I wasn't entirely sure how I felt about that at the time—that I vaguely knew from classes and the hallways, caught my eye. It made the games more tolerable. After the very first game, I made sure to say "hello" to him in the hallways anytime I saw him. I'd smile at him in classes if I didn't actually talk to him. A friendship slowly began to form. Lucas glanced at me as though he would add a follow-up question, so I knew that answering his first question was important; otherwise, he'd think of ten more.

"Well," I said, "I have to support you, don't I?"

"I guess."

"I guess?" I feigned a chuckle. "I don't have to come, do I?"

"No."

"Then show some gratitude, damnit." I genuinely laughed.

But the laugh was cut off when Lucas turned to me, took my face in his hands and pulled my face into his. My eyes opened wide in shock as his lips connected with mine. Lucas' eyes were closed firmly with concentration and determination. The kiss itself was too wet, too firm, too...perfect. After a moment, I let my eyes close as Lucas held his mouth to mine, though that was all the kiss really consisted of—two pairs of lips pressed together firmly and wetly. When Lucas finally pulled away, I let my eyes flutter open to find him staring fearfully at me. His hands didn't leave my face.

"You didn't pull away."

I shook my head.

"Oh, shit." He swallowed as his hands slid from my face, obviously concerned at my lack of verbal response. "I didn't...look, let's just...Rob, I didn't mean to—"

I ignored his sputtering and reached up to lay my hand against his cheek, letting my thumb jerkily brush over his cheek. His words, fortunately, ceased, which gave me the perfect opportunity to lean in and kiss him back. Lucas shut his eyes forcefully, eagerly, as I eased my face to his. The corner of my mouth turned up in amusement as I closed my eyes and gently pressed my lips to his. Lucas seemed to melt into me as I kissed him, my thumb learning to slide along his cheek more expertly as I did so. The kiss didn't last long—I didn't want to attempt more than a simple kiss. When I pulled away, Lucas' eyes stayed closed several moments longer than mine, as though he had lost himself in the moment, but when they finally opened, they looked greener than ever.

"You like me, too?"

I nodded.

"Was the kiss...okay?" He looked away but made no effort to pull his face away from my hand.

"The first one or the second one?"

"Either."

"They were both perfect."

Then Lucas was amateurishly pulling my face to his again right there on the shore of Lake Erie, pressing his lips against mine. It was perfect, too.

"Is that what you think?" I spun on my heels to growl at Oma.

"Of course, I do." She snapped back. *"I think you're not thinkin' with your head. You're usin' another organ."*

In case I was confused, she tapped a finger against her chest. At least she hadn't tapped her crotch. I rolled my eyes and turned back around, headed for the living room. Oma would never let me storm out on her, especially during an argument, but I was sixteen. What sixteen-year-old hasn't jumped on a huff and rode it away when the mood struck them? I hadn't even stepped from the kitchen into the living room when Oma snapped at me.

"Where the hell do you think you're goin'?"

"To my room!" I screamed over my shoulder.

"The day pigs fly!" She bellowed.

Chair legs scraping against linoleum sounded, and I picked up my pace slightly as I made my way to the stairs and started up them in a sturdy march. If I could only get up the stairs, down the hall, and to my room, maybe I could lock the door and avoid Oma. Of course, if I thought a locked door would keep Oma from continuing the argument, I was dumber than dirt.

"You swivel your ass and get back down here!" Oma shouted at me from the bottom of the stairs.

I turned on the landing to glower at her.

"No."

"Don't you sass me." She put her hands on her hips and glared up at me.

"It's my life!" I snapped. "And just like everything else, you're telling me how to do everything!"

"Robbie," Oma looked at me through squinty eyes, "this isn't about gettin' your driver's license or a curfew. This is about your damn life."

"Right." I nodded firmly down at her. "My life. Not yours. Not Lucas'. Just mine. I can do with it what I like."

Oma crossed her arms over her breast and cocked an eyebrow at me as she looked up at me standing on the landing.

"You're plannin' to do a damn fool thing, is what you're plannin'." Oma waggled her head. "You think you understand everything. Just like every other dumbass teenager. Well, you don't know shit, Robbie."

"What don't I know?" I demanded. "I know exactly what this means, and you're trying to convince me that I don't understand."

"You don't understand, damnit!" She replied sharply. "Your mother and father—"

"Where are mom and dad?" I looked around dramatically. "I think the only people who get to be involved in an argument are the ones here, don't you?"

"More fuckin' sass." She rolled her eyes.

"I've made my decision." I crossed my own arms over my chest.

"You're goin' to let yourself get kilt because—for what?" Oma demanded. "What's that gonna do for any-damn-one?"

*"What's the alternative, Oma? Tell me that. You knew—**you knew**—this day was coming, and you just stayed silent. The only time you've ever stayed silent—"*

"Don't you—"

"—and now I have exactly two choices, and you're telling me which one to make without even discussing it!" I bellowed. "This isn't about you. It's about me, Oma!"

"It's about everyone!"

"Why'd I have to be born?" I screamed down the stairs at her. "If I hadn't been born I wouldn't have to deal with any of this!"

Oma's eyes grew wide as a hand went to her chest.

"I wish I didn't know any of this shit!" I continued. "I wish I wasn't here! I wish I didn't know what I know! I wish I didn't have to look at you! I wish I didn't have to worry about Lucas! I wish Ernst was safe! I wish I had more time—"

"Shut up, Robbie!" Oma hissed, her foot rising to the first step of the stairs.

My mouth stayed open, but I didn't say another word. Oma's hand was on the newel post cap and the other on her chest. She glanced down at the floor fearfully, then up at me desperately.

"Don't make wishes, Robbie. Not even in your own head," She pleaded. "You know better."

"Sorry." I snapped, but my heart wasn't in it. "I'm still learning all the rules."

Then I stomped the rest of the way up the stairs. Once I'd made my way to my bedroom, I made sure to slam the door as hard as I could. The whole house shook.

"Stay down," Lucas whispered as we huddled behind the bleachers.

"Okay."

We had almost been seen. I managed to peek over my shoulder as I crouched there in the dirt under the bleachers in the football stadium. Jason and the other football players were walking through the bleachers, searching. I knew who they were searching for, but I wasn't sure why.

"Why are they looking for you?"

Lucas looked over at me, his eyes locking onto mine.

"They still want me to join them."

My eyes grew wide.

"But you're not—"

"It doesn't matter."

"Why would Jason-fucking-Morris think you'd want anything to do with them, Lucas?" I whispered. "They're assholes."

Lucas chewed at his lip.

"You're obviously so not."

He gave a nervous smile.

"You're not—you're not going to join them, are you?"

"I'd rather die."

"I don't want that either." I teased.

"They're going to make my life—our lives—really hard, Rob." Lucas sighed. "I'm so sorry I got you into this."

"We both cause trouble for each other." I gave him a crooked smile.

Lucas returned the look.

"Trouble won't stop us, though." He stared into my eyes. "Right?"

"If it does—it'll only be temporary."

I held out my pinkie.

It was a juvenile gesture.

Lucas stared down at my pinkie with a wicked smile. Then he pulled me into him and smothered my mouth with his. When he pulled back, he was still smiling.

"That's how I make promises."

"I like your method."

"LUCAS!"

Lucas was out of breath, and his fingers were laced through mine as we slid to a stop behind the tree. The moon was dark, and I could barely *see any stars through the skeletal canopy above us. Somehow, I felt like the moon was watching us, tracking our movements through the woods. Hopefully, it knew how to keep its mouth shut. I pushed Lucas against the tree as he tried to control his breathing and not pant loudly so as to not give away where we were. How was I breathing normally and the football player was out of breath after our jaunt through the cold, slumbering woods?*

"**ROBERT!**"

"Oh, shit." Lucas hissed, his eyes fearful.

"It'll be okay." I grabbed his face between my hands and made him look at me. "I promise you it'll be okay."

Lucas looked into my eyes, the fear slowly melting away.

"You can run." I pleaded with him. "Run to the lake. Then keep running along the shore until you get to the road. Keep running until you get home."

"I won't leave you."

"This is only going to end one way, Lucas," I whispered desperately. "I don't want you to see it."

"I can't let you do this alone."

"I won't hate you if you run."

"You will eventually."

"Do you think I'll love you forever if you stay?" I managed to tease though I was terrified as the sound of crisp, cold leaves being stomped sounded in the distance. "Is that why you're doing this?"

"I know you'll love me forever." He responded, then kissed me roughly.

It was a quick kiss, but perfect like every kiss that came before it. Lucas pulled back, his hands on the side of my face.

"Everything is temporary," Lucas stated firmly. "Everything."

"Everything." I nodded. "Are you sorry?"

"I'll never be sorry."

"Me either."

"Can we make it back to the house?" Lucas swallowed hard. "Before...will I just slow you down?"

"I want you with me." I grabbed his face in my hands. "I want you to be the last thing I see."

Lucas' eyes started to leak.

"I'm going to miss you."

"I'll miss you more."

"What if—what if it's not temporary?"

"Hey!" I whisper-hissed, holding his face firmly in my hands so he had to look at me. "Every-fucking-thing is temporary. Except us. Except us, Lucas. I promise you that."

Lucas stared into my eyes, two trails of tears winding down his face.

"I believe you."

I nodded.

"Are you ready?" I asked.

Lucas took a shaky breath, doing his best to stop the tears from escaping his eyes. Finally, he steadied himself, resolve settling on his face. He nodded.

"I can do this."

"I will do this."

"You'll come back."

A voice in the back of my head wasn't so sure.

"I will come back."

"Promise?"

"Yes." I nodded once. "I promise."

"I love you." Lucas whimpered. "Just in case I haven't told you enough. In case I never get to again."

"I love you, too."

I kissed Lucas again, then laced my fingers through his, and we raced away from the tree towards the house.

Did you see that?

Chapter 2

The ground connected with my chin and my head snapped back roughly right before my sternum slammed into the dirt. An "oof" sound escaped my throat as I crumpled to the ground, dust and dirt floating upward in a cloud around me. My nose and mouth received a fair share of the cloud, and I sputtered for a moment as my eyes opened and adjusted to the darkness around me. Without the green light, the only illumination in the cellar was the little bit of moonlight that managed to peek through the awning windows high up on the walls.

At first, I just wanted to lay there and pity myself over the stinging sensation in my chin. The memories now in my head—they weren't slowly flowing back into my consciousness; they were just there—made my skull ache right behind my eyes. Immediately, I knew that I should be going mad, writhing around, cackling like a loon, but I wasn't compelled to do it. If the phrase "it is what it is" had a perfect situation to be used, that would have been it. I had gotten my memories back. What did that mean?

What now?

"You happy with yourself?" Oma sighed.

I looked up from my spot on the cellar floor to see her still standing where she had been before I had jumped into the well. Of course, and I was pretty sure this was true, the time that had lapsed between me falling into the well and then hitting the floor had been less than a second. At least for Oma. It had been longer for me.

I pushed off of the ground with my hands with a wince and a groan, rising to my knees to stare up at her. She laced her arms over her chest and stared down at me in what looked like anger in the dark, but I could feel the fear emanating off of her.

"Are you?" I returned.

She just stood there in the dark, staring down at me. Blue moonlight was slashed along one side of her face.

"I've never been less happy, Robbie."

"Rob."

Oma continued to stare.

"At least now you won't have to pretend to be mad at me for...*running away*," I stated blandly.

My grandmother deflated only marginally.

"He's coming," I said, simply.

"Well, no shit, Sherlock."

"When?"

"How the fuck should I know?" She snapped. "But it'll be sooner rather than later if you don't keep your mouth shut about it. Don't you dare tell no one."

"Who the hell am I going to tell?" I snarled up at her.

"You know who the hell you would tell." She jabbed a finger at me.

"He needs to know." I found myself pleading. "He deserves to have his memories back, too, Oma."

"He deserves to stay alive, ya' fuckin' idiot," Oma replied, though her words held no malice. "You want to endanger yourself, me, Ernst and the others, well...*well, it's too late to fix that now, isn't it?* But don't be a complete idiot and start building a bigger target, Robbie. You're smarter than that. There's more than one danger to Lucas, Robbie."

"I want him to remember, Oma."

"Of course, you do." She sighed. "You promised. Didn't you?"

The last four words came with a sneer.

"I told him I'd come back."

"You came back, Robbie." She sighed, her arms falling to her sides again. "That's all you promised."

Oma walked past me, her hip brushing against my shoulder though she easily could have rounded me in the large cellar without bringing herself so close. I rolled my eyes as her hip nudged against me. I started to rise to my feet with a groan as Oma headed towards the steps that led up to the kitchen. When I was finally on my feet, I turned to find Oma standing on the third step, staring over at me.

"What?"

"You never listen to me." She shook her head, her eyes gently closing, as though she were in pain. "Listen this one goddamn time. Keep your damn mouth shut."

I just looked at her.

"You can't stop what's comin', Robbie." She sighed. "But we might be able to keep Lucas out of it. Everything you remember? Keep it to yourself. Don't say a damn word. Not even to me. Don't even think about it if you can help it. The longer you can keep from talkin' about it...the longer you can keep from thinkin' about it...the longer we have."

"Then what?"

"Then we'll do what we have to do." She gave a firm nod, her hand going to the banister as she turned to continue her ascent.

Suddenly, a thought came to me.

"What about mom and dad? We could—"

Oma spun on her heels, a furious look on her face.

"You gonna make another fuckin' wish, Robbie?" She hissed at me. "Is that what you're going to do? How'd that work out for you last time?"

I leveled her with my eyes.

"It bought us ten years, didn't it?"

"Yeah." She snorted. "How'd that work out for you?"

"We're both still here."

"Barely." She snarled.

I had no retort for that.

"That's the last of it, Robbie." She made a vague gesture at the floor. "We're all we got now. There's no more wishes or prayers or hopes or..."

I stared up at her.

"Go back to bed, Robbie." She sighed. "Crawl back into bed with Lucas. Be in love. But don't let one word cross your damn lips, ya' hear me?"

For what seemed like hours but was probably less than five seconds, we stared into each other's eyes from across the dark expanse of the cellar. Finally, I gave a firm nod.

"Okay."

Oma nodded back, then started to stomp up the stairs, mumbling under her breath and shaking her head. Waiting until I heard her footsteps crossing the kitchen and going into the living room, then start up the main stairs in the house, I went over to the cellar stairs. As I stepped up onto the first step, I braced my hand on the banister and turned to look where the well had been. Where it would never be again. Nearly four hundred years of history ended with me. Of all the things I had to atone for, that one made my chest ache the most. If I had known then...

Shaking my head to clear it of thoughts—which was nearly impossible—I padded lightly up the stairs into the kitchen. Ernst was creeping out from the shadows under the kitchen table as I closed the door behind myself. I didn't lock it. There was no point anymore. Ernst looked up at me, his eyes somehow sad and full at the same time as he wrung his hands together at his waist. There was nothing I could think of to say to him that would make things better.

"How's your memory?"

"*'Tis back, Rob.*" He blinked.

"Don't tell Oma. At least...for tonight." I warned him.

"*I won'.*" He shook his head vigorously, fearfully.

"Do you think...I mean...the others...?"

He shook his head again. "*Dey weren' down there wif us.*"

I agreed with Ernst's assessment. Only the two of us had been in the cellar ten years prior. Lucas, the other Kobolds—they were in the house but further away. Oma hadn't been in the house. Things would be different for us all in one way or another.

"I'm sorry, Ernst," I said, simply. "I'm really, very sorry."

"*'Twas worf it.*" He held his head high. "*I don' blame ya'. Ya' did the only thin' ya' could-o.*"

Ernst speech was even more muddled than usual. The gleam in the corners of his eyes that caught the moonlight let me know why.

"Not the only thing."

"*Ya' made the righ' choice. I said it den, and I say it now.*"

"We shall see, won't we?"

Ernst inclined his head further. "*I will be righ' here with ya', Rob.*"

For a moment, I stared into Ernst's eyes, wondering how he had been treated during the ten years of my absence. How the other Kobolds had treated him, how Oma had punished him with silence or sneers...all for being my friend and agreeing with me. For an entire decade, he hadn't had the memory to realize why he was being treated poorly. Ernst had been my best friend growing up...and I supposed he still was.

"I've missed you," I said. "I didn't realize it until now. Because of the whole..."

I wiggled my fingers over my head.

"*I've missed ya', too.*" He beamed.

"See you in the morning?" I asked with a smile, then had a thought. "Later today?"

He smiled back with a nod.

"Goodnight, old friend."

"*Goodnight, best friend.*" He replied.

I placed my hand over my heart and nodded at him, then continued my tiptoeing through the kitchen and into the living room. As I ascended the stairs, my hand brushed over the newel post, and I stopped to run my fingers along it, wondering when Oma had finally replaced it. How long had I been gone before she decided that a blackened, partial newel post was unsightly? Taking a deep breath, I continued on my way up the stairs, wondering what Lucas would be like when I got back to my room. Oma had seemed totally sure that Lucas would know nothing, as long as I did nothing to remind him. As long as I did nothing to jog his memories, they would stay lost. I wasn't so sure. Someone like Lucas—*someone who knew things*—was a little trickier than others. But I would face whatever he said or did once I was back in the room and sliding into bed with him.

In the upstairs hallway, outside of Oma's room, I stopped to stare at her door, wondering how different life would be when the sun rose once again. Would Oma and I be able to pretend that things had been before I had gone down into the cellar? I knew in my heart of hearts that Oma was right—that it was the safest thing to do. To keep pretending. It wasn't a foolproof plan, but it was all we had.

"I made the right choice," I said softly to the door.

"*No, you didn't!*" Oma's voice grumbled from inside.

I rolled my eyes.

"*Asshole,*" I whispered and turned to walk to my room.

"*I heard that!*" Her voice came again.

Cringing, I faltered, but then began walking towards my room again. My room was still dark when I pushed the door open slowly, doing my best to make sure I didn't make any more noise than was necessary. My eyes stayed down as I entered the room and shut the door gently behind myself. A soft "click" sounded as the door closed, and I winced, hoping that it had not bothered Lucas' slumber. When I turned back to the bed, I could see Lucas' form under the covers, illuminated by a beam of moonlight that managed to peek through the drapes. Padding over to the foot of the bed, I looked down at my sleeping boyfriend, bundled up warmly within the bedclothes. He had a smile on his face, and he looked so peaceful there in my bed. Just like he had ten years prior. When we had both made a choice together, knowing what was to come.

> "*Open the door, Lucas!*"
> "*Go, Rob!*"
> "*Lucas—*"
> "*We'll huff and we'll puff!*"
> "*Run, Rob! Go! Hurry!*"
> *Laughter. Evil laughter.*

"I'm sorry," I whispered.

Lucas wiggled in his sleep, his dreamy smile broadening. I swallowed hard and rounded the bed to climb into bed on my side. As I slid under the covers, Lucas pushed backward in his sleep, shoving his body into mine, soft, whimpering sounds of longing coming from him. As I pulled the blankets over my body and wrapped my arms around him,

Lucas rolled over in bed, his head coming to rest on the pillow next to mine. Instinctively, I leaned forward to press my lips against his. Lucas' eyes fluttered sleepily as I pulled away, and then his eyes were locked on mine. He smiled widely.

"I was having the best dream."

"Were you?" My voice was thick.

"Yeah." He smiled sleepily, then looked confused. "But I can't remember a bit of it now. I know it was about you, though."

"Is that one of those things you just know?"

"I just assume all of my good dreams are about you."

I kissed him softly again.

"All of my good dreams are about you, too."

"Can I..."

Lucas trailed off, but gently wrapped his arms around me and buried his head against my chest, shifting his body to adjust for his height. He held me snuggly to him as he breathed warmly against me. I felt him sigh deeply, contentedly against me as he held me and started to go still once again.

"Lucas?"

"Mmmm...?"

"Do you..."

I stopped myself, knowing that no matter how I felt, or what my heart was telling me, Oma was right. Thinking with my head was the only option.

"I love you," I said, simply. "You know that, right?"

"*Mmmm. I lurve ya', too.*" He mumbled against my chest and pulled me even more tightly against him.

"I'm glad I came back."

"I'm glad you came back, too." He said, a little more clearly. "I knew you would. *That* is one of those things I just knew."

You saw me coming, Lucas. I thought it meant something different...but you've been waiting for a decade.

As Lucas started to drift off, his hold of me not lessening, I couldn't bring myself to tell him why he just knew things. I couldn't force myself to lay a hand on his forehead and help him remember. I couldn't rationalize waking him from his peaceful, unbothered sleep to tell him anything. Lucas loved me. Even if he didn't remember loving me before. Even if he didn't know why he felt his love for me so profoundly. I had to be okay with that. For his sake.

Chapter 3

Lucas smelled like bacon, but not because he had eaten any—he had just been in the kitchen while Oma had made breakfast. He had planned to leave the house as soon as he got bathed and then head straight to work, but Oma had insisted that he eat something first. While he had been in the kitchen with Oma while she cooked breakfast, I had gotten bathed and dressed. By the time I had made my way into the kitchen, Lucas was wiping his mouth with his napkin and getting up from the table. When I entered the kitchen, Oma shot me a furtive glance and went back to eating her breakfast. Lucas attempted to pick up his plate to take it to the sink, but Oma waved at him as if to say: "I'll take care of that." He shot her a smile and a wink and turned to me.

"You clean up nicely." He chuckled before grabbing me and pulling me into him. "Very nicely."

"You're not so bad yourself," I replied, giving him a quick smooch as Oma decided her food was very interesting. "You off to work?"

"Yeah." Lucas sighed happily as he stared into my eyes. "Grandpa is needy. Are we having dinner?"

"Your house?" I suggested. "Seven?"

Lucas gave me a wink and a lingering kiss before finally forcing himself to let go of me. He thanked Oma for a delicious breakfast and headed for the door. He turned in the kitchen doorway, as though he forgot something.

"I love you." He smiled at me.

"I love you, too," I replied.

My boyfriend beamed at me, looking as though leaving was a struggle, but somehow managed to force himself to exit the kitchen and head for the front door. I turned to Oma, and we locked eyes as we listened for Lucas to actually leave. We listened to his footsteps through the living room, the foyer...then the front door opened and closed and we were left with silence. Oma looked up at me as I stood on the opposite side of the table, her face impassive as I looked down at her. Since there was nothing else that could be done, I slid into the seat that Lucas had vacated, pushing his plate aside. It had nearly been licked clean.

"You didn't say anything to him," Oma said.

It wasn't a question.

"What's for breakfast?"

"You made the right choice." She said.

"What's for breakfast?"

"So now you ain't gonna talk to me?"

"I'm talking to you," I said. "I'm inquiring about breakfast."

"Look here—"

"You told me not to talk about it," I said, then mimicked her. "*Not even to you. Don't even think about it if you can help it.* So...what's for breakfast?"

"Biscuits, gravy, bacon...or you can have biscuits and jelly like Lucas did if you want." She snapped.

"I wish I had a nice bagel with cream cheese." I sat back and stared at her. "I wish there was a decent coffee shop within ten miles of this town. I wish that—"

"Oh, shut the hell up," Oma growled.

"Why?" I shrugged. "No one's listening anymore anyway."

"We don't know that."

"So...what now?" I asked. "We go on like this until whatever happens...happens? Wait until shit goes down?"

I wasn't dumb enough to reference *him* directly.

"I mean, I've had a decade of practice," I suggested. "I can act like everything is a-oh-fucking-kay for as long as it takes, I guess. But that's not really a plan for the long-term, is it?"

"Ya' got a better one?" Oma seemed to deflate as she set her fork alongside her plate and looked at me from across the table.

Oma was never one to look defeated or at a loss—she always had a plan or scheme of some kind or at least a smart retort for anything anyone said. Looking across the table at my grandmother with absolutely no guidance from her made me feel more nervous than I had felt in a very long time. Of course, I hadn't exactly taken her advice to stay away from the well in the cellar, so how could I expect her to guide me along for whatever came after? Suddenly, I very much felt like the asshole I had been for many years.

Visiting the cellar and the well the first time—a decade prior— had been my choice, even though Oma had warned me against it. Going back to the cellar and jumping into the well in the middle of the night had been my choice, too, even though she had warned me against it. Oma didn't have a plan for what would happen if I came back to Point Worth and reversed what I had done in the first place because she never thought it would happen. She had stuck with the route of going along with the whole "Rob was a teenage runaway who became a big Hollywood star" scenario for the rest of her life if she could have. She had known that not all magic was powerful enough to shield us forever, but she had hoped. She certainly hadn't counted on wishes having an expiration date, either.

"I'm sorry," I said.

Oma glared at me for a moment, then her expression softened.

"Well, if that solved the world's problems, I'd make a call to Washington, D.C., wouldn't I?" She snorted.

I smiled wanly.

"I thought your advice was you being bossy and trying to control me," I said. "If I had known then what I know now—"

"I told you what you know now."

"I know." I sighed. "I should have listened. But...where would we be now if I listened to you ten years ago, Oma? Would we even be here? Alive, I mean? We'd all be dead because we would have fought."

"Well...that, I don't know." She relented. "Things might have gone poorly either way, I suppose. But all this done is delay the inevitable, Robbie. We was gonna end up here one way or another, wasn't we?"

"I suppose." I nodded. "But I'm not a sixteen-year-old kid anymore, either. I'm not scared and weak and impulsive."

Oma cocked an eyebrow at me.

"Well...not as impulsive."

She nodded. "We can only speak about this broadly, mind ya', I don't want to say nothin' out loud about what was..."

She glanced at the floor.

"...or say a certain name. But we do need a plan, Robbie."

"The pack will have to be dealt with obviously."

Slowly, Oma started nodding.

"You should have dealt with that the other night." I rolled my eyes. "You had the chance. I wish I remembered then so I could have said something at the time."

"You wanna hide that many bodies and vehicles?" She was amused at my callousness. "And what would your boyfriend have done if he saw me murder a bunch of puppies in front of 'im? Huh? Never mind that—what would *you* have done? You didn't have your mind about you then like you do now."

"Point taken." I agreed. "But they're going to expand their membership. You know that. I know that. They may not remember...things...but they obviously remember enough to know what they are, why they are, and that they were tasked with creating a gang, right?"

"I'd say so."

"So...they'll keep searching out members." I shrugged. "They have ten now?"

"Dozen, I think."

"Have they gotten the attention of anyone besides us?"

"The were-community is always keepin' tabs." Oma rolled her eyes. "But don't expect The Council to do jack shit until it's too late. Like me, they ain't too fond of takin' on a pack that big at one time. Too many chances to fuck it up."

"Well, picking them off one by one is going to prove difficult, Oma." I chuckled angrily. "That's a dozen different chances to get caught, isn't it?"

"Perhaps." She leaned in. "But it's what we gotta do. People ain't as powerful if they don't have their armies, Robbie. Cut the legs off your enemy."

"I don't know how I feel about this, Oma." I shook my head, feeling sick. "I didn't like it ten years ago, and I don't like it now."

"You got somethin' else to suggest?" She held her hands out. "Wanna invite 'em over for tea and *reason with 'em*? You done seen how Jason acted just 'cause you went and rightfully defended yourself."

I sat there and thought about that. Jason and his "puppies"—as Oma liked to call them—were a pack of werewolves. They had been after Lucas to join them before because they sensed his abilities—though I would certainly never talk about those abilities out loud. They had managed to break into Oma's house and nearly get to him the night...well, everyone in the house had lost something. Some lost more than others. Jason and his pack had forgotten that they were after Lucas—or why they were after him at all. The magic that had been summoned the first time I jumped into the well ten years prior had reached every inch of the house. Those closest to the well got the brunt of it. Others...well, that was tricky.

Magic is fickle and unpredictable. I knew that Jason and his pack remembered enough about what their main goal was since they had only been six that night ten years prior.

"Do you think maybe Jason remembers everything but is playing dumb because he's scared to really take us on before he has a bigger pack?" I suggested. "Maybe he wants to double or triple the size of his pack before he comes knocking on our door again?"

Oma waved me off. "He's dumb as dog shit. He'd try to take us on now if he remembered everything. 'Try' being the operative word."

I nodded.

"Do you think...everyone will slowly start remembering now that I...did what I did?"

Oma thought on this.

"I don't think so." She shook her head slowly. "The first time was a...*release*...this time, well, it's all gone now. The river's run dry—if you catch my drift, Robbie."

"Got it." I thought about the fact that the well in the cellar was gone for good—the source of all my family's magic. No future generation would have to endure what we had—if I ever lived long enough to have kids—if I even wanted them some day. I didn't let myself think too long or too hard about it for fear of what that might summon. *Who* that might summon. "You think that pack's like a Hydra?"

"What the fuck's that mean?" Oma twisted up her nose.

"Cut off the head...will two grow back?"

Oma stared at me, surprised I would think of such a solution.

"Well," She finally began to speak slowly, carefully, "in my opinion, Robbie, you can never be too damn careful. Why take a chance that a plan won't work and you'll just have to follow through with your original plan anyway? Havin' said that...it might work. If Jason ain't around, flappin' his yap and playin' Billy Bad Ass, the rest of 'em may scatter to the winds. Maybe."

"I'd like to see if that will work." I was more asking permission than making a statement. "I don't want to hurt anyone...but if I have to, Jason would be my first choice. Or Andrew."

Oma frowned at me and waved a hand at me.

"Andrew ain't done nothin' but be a goddamn idiot." Oma chastised me. "He may be a damn fool and hornier than a toad, but he ain't got nothin' to do with any of this mess here."

"Fair enough." I shrugged. "He's still a dick. He told Jason about Lucas and me hitting him with a truck, though. He knew what would happen—even if he didn't know about our history with Jason."

"Being a *dick* ain't no crime. Otherwise, the two of us would done been locked up by now. Agreed?"

I waggled my head for once.

"Don't you bring no trouble to him!" Oma growled. "Just let that sleeping dog lie. Andrew ain't no part of none of this. He just ignorantly got involved."

"Correction." I held a finger up. "You got him involved."

Oma started to launch in on me.

"But I won't bother him unless he bothers me. Let's not argue, okay?" I stopped her. "We have enough to worry about, right?"

"Fair enough, Robbie." She gave a firm nod.

"We bought that tiller for nothing, I guess." I sighed and sat back. "No point in planting a garden anymore, is there?"

"Well...no. I suppose not." Oma mimicked my actions, saddened by the sudden realization. "Won't be long before the woods start to reclaim the land anyway."

My eyes grew wide.

"How long?"

Oma rolled her eyes and waved me off.

"We'll both be long dead before then." She chuckled bitterly. "Even if we manage to die of natural causes. But that mag—it's all gone. All we got is what's inside us. Everything we done is gonna eventually give up the ghost, I suppose."

She glanced around nervously.

"The others will be the first to go." She leaned in to whisper. "Without...*that*...they'll slowly fade, too."

I looked up at the ceiling, willing my eyes to not water as I thought of Ernst—my only real friend throughout my mid- to late childhood.

"But...they'll probably last as long as us, I'd say." She sighed. "Everything here will eventually fade, though, Robbie. It's just a matter of when."

"There's no way to fix that?"

"Unless you wanna go back in time, ya' asshole." She snapped at me, but her heart wasn't in it.

I just stared at her.

"Look...Oma...I can't say I'm sorry enough. As you pointed out, it won't fix a damn thing anyway. But you tell me one person in our family who had to make that choice at sixteen-years-old and I'll apologize until I lose my voice, okay?"

"Not since the old days." Oma shook her head.

"I knew that." I snipped at her. "It was a rhetorical question. Hell, it wasn't even a question. I wish you'd find it in yourself to remember that while I may have fucked things up—this was forced on me—*when I was a child.* I made the same choice any child would have made. I chose to not see everyone I know die before I bit the bullet myself. It wasn't fair, but it is what it is."

"Perhaps."

"If mom and dad had just—"

"You shut your mouth right now, Robbie," Oma warned me, then glanced around nervously. "Don't say one more word 'bout them. I'm warning you."

"Fine." I reached up to squeeze the bridge of my nose. "I guess that's settled, too. But I'll never forgive them. I want you to know that. There's nothing they could do. Ever."

"Well," Oma looked at me, her eyes sad, "I don't think no one would blame ya'. Most of all me. We both got bent over and greased up, didn't we?"

Nodding, I glanced over my shoulder towards the living room.

"Book still in the same place?" I asked, having a thought.

Oma assessed me for a moment.

"It's still there."

"What'll happen if I open it?" I asked, shifting in my seat. "To refresh me?"

"I don't know." Oma shrugged. "I ain't opened it since you left. I certainly ain't opened it since last night."

"You think it's empty, too?"

"Hope not." She replied evenly. "You didn't exactly finish your education before you ran off, didja?"

"I didn't run off." I snapped at her. "Well...Robert Wagner didn't run off. *A version of Robert Wagner* ran off."

Oma stared at me for the longest time, her eyes not leaving mine as she took me in—her actual grandson sitting before her instead of some version of him. I wasn't Robert Wagner pretending to be Jacob Michaels. Or vice versa. I was Robert Wagner, back home, ready to finish what he had avoided. My memories restored—of everything before—made me a complete person again.

"You pretending for Lucas?"

"How do you mean?" I squinted angrily.

"Ten years is a long time." Oma rested her forearms on the table. "You seen a lot of the world. Met a lot of people. He still as appealing as you're actin'? Or does that situation look different with more time and wisdom under your belt? Maybe things have changed?"

Slowly, I pushed back from the table, the legs of the chair squealing against the linoleum. I stood from my seat and gave Oma a firm look.

"No one is that good of an actor, Oma."

"I hope you're right. Because if you ain't bein' honest, it's best to sever that cord now, Robbie. That would solve another problem. Make you less likely to make the same dumbass mistakes later."

"Lucas isn't a mistake."

"Makin' choices based on your heart instead of your head is." She snapped.

Shaking my head angrily, I turned away, shoving the chair back under the table roughly. I stomped over to the kitchen door before I finally turned back to Oma. She was still sitting there, watching me.

"My choice wasn't based on the love of one person, you old hag," I growled at her. "I didn't just make my choice for me. Or my love for Lucas. I made it for this place and everything that involves. Even you. Though, now I truly know I made the wrong choice."

Oma smiled.

"Fuck you." I snapped.

Oma was cackling to herself as I stomped through the living room to the bookcase. I fell to my knees in front of it, angry, but my eyes threatening to leak. I did my best to ignore my feelings as I reached down and pulled away the panel at the bottom of the bookcase, revealing a small slot underneath. When I shoved my hand into the hole, my fingertips touched the smooth leather of an ancient book. I closed my eyes, giving myself a moment before I pulled it out. Lowering myself to my ass, I pulled my legs in "lotus style" and laid the book in my lap. The book, thick as an encyclopedia written by a writer with mental diarrhea, bound in darkish brown leather, the cover mottled in dark spots, looked up at me. It took a moment, a long sigh to steel my nerves before I tried to open the book. The cover didn't budge.

Shaking my head and smiling to myself at my ignorance—a memory that had been lost naturally, unlike the others, coming back to me. It took a few seconds, but I found the corner of the book that had the sharp sewing needle sticking out less than a fourth of an inch, and pushed the tip of my index finger firmly against it. I winced as the needle pierced my skin. When I pulled my finger away and turned it over to inspect, a single drop of blood, barely more significant than the head of a sewing needle, sparkled up at me. Without another thought, I pressed my fingertip against the book cover. The book vibrated ever so slightly in my lap. When I pulled at the cover again, it opened with ease.

The book was blank.

I wasn't all that surprised, but I was utterly disappointed. Maybe a little bit worried as well if I was being completely honest with myself. Now that I had my memories back, knew the things that I knew, and what was to come, it would have been nice to have the book. I could have picked up my magical education and learned a lot more before the shit really hit the fan. But the blank parchment-like paper in the book just stared back at me, offering nothing. Sighing, I closed the book gently. When I tried to open it again, it stayed shut.

Why did it still want blood if the pages were empty?

"Oma!" I hollered from my spot on the floor. "Book's being an asshole!"

"*Well,*" she hollered back, "*what did you expect?*"

Then I heard the water running and the sounds of our morning meal being cleaned up. Signing to myself, I gently returned the book to its place under the bookcase, though I wasn't sure there was any point in hiding it away now that it was blank. Something inside of me told me that the book still needed to be kept from prying eyes, though, so I returned it to its spot. When I slid the panel back into place, pounding against it with the side of my fist to make sure it was secure, I stared off at nothing.

What could be done now?

Spring was announcing its arrival outside, gusts of wind whistling against the house as Oma clanged around in the kitchen, and I rose from the living room floor. Doing my best to not think about things I wasn't supposed to think about or *people* I wasn't supposed to think about, I tried to go through the details of the night before. In the cellar.

Going through what I'd seen, vision by vision, a few people came to mind. One of them I could never go talk to—unless, *maybe*, someone's life depended on it. The other...I wasn't so sure. Instead of standing in the living room, wracking my brain for an answer that wouldn't come easily, I walked over to the kitchen and stood in the doorway, leaning against the doorjamb. Oma was standing at the kitchen counter, her hip against it, resting while Lena stood on the step stool, elbows-deep in dishwater. Another Kobold was sweeping the floor with a dainty broom.

"Hi, Oskar," I said automatically.

Oskar started and looked up, the "swish-swish" of the broom going silent as he turned to look at me. His ears were slightly more elongated than the other Kobolds, drooping at their tips. Small fleshy bags of skin hung under his eyes, and his skin was somewhat mottled, as though he had liver spots. He was the oldest of the Kobolds—and I had forgotten him for a decade. He looked older than he had ever before. His little brown cloth bib-style overalls hung limply from his shoulders, and the Kobold-sized t-shirt underneath looked baggy as well. His tiny slippers, always clean, clung lightly to his feet, the heels popping away from his foot with each small step he took. It was sad and precious at the same time. If

I had to bet which Kobold would be most affected in the future by what I'd done…

"*Master Robert.*" Oskar's eyes were slow to light up as a smile crept up his face. "*It's so good to see you.*"

"Good to see you again, Oskar." I smiled back.

"*This house always needs tidying up.*" Oskar shook his head, the broom restarting its dance across the floor once more. "*Seems there's always something that needs tending to around here.*"

Oskar spoke more eloquently than the other Kobolds, but he had more years to practice, I supposed. Returning his smile for a moment as he worked, I didn't bother to respond verbally to him. He had basically been chastising Oma and me for having so much space for the Kobolds to clean and essentially being slobs. It wasn't true—but that's what some Kobolds did. They accused their human counterparts of living like animals simply because a crumb was found on the floor. It was their way, and there was no reason to argue with it.

"Oma." I turned my head to her. "Do you know anybody else…*like us*…around here?"

"Wouldn't you know if I did?" She waggled her head. "I'd-a done told ya', wouldn't I have?"

"Maybe."

"Well, I don't." She snipped.

"Then I'm going out," I said simply and started to turn.

"And do what?"

"I'm gonna go hunting." I shrugged.

"*Jason?*" Oma hissed, her eyes wide.

"Don't be ridiculous." I rolled my eyes. "It's daylight anyway."

Vaguely, I gestured at the kitchen window. Oma glanced at the window as though she had forgotten this fact. Lena continued to wash the dishes, her head down and eyes averted, obviously ignoring the two humans in the room in an effort to not be noticed. Though, I wasn't sure why she thought being noticed would get her involved in the minor argument. Oskar started humming a slow, yet happy tune as he continued to sweep. When it became clear that Oma was going to stare out the window and get lost in her thoughts, I made my exit. The longer I waited the chances of becoming distracted increased.

Chapter 4

It wasn't even lunchtime, yet the manager of Lounge in Toledo had allowed me to come inside to see their new act. "Lounge" was a funny name for an LGBTQ+ bar, in my opinion. Although I was utterly unsure why, I suspected it was because it was such a straightforward, if not lazy, name for any kind of dinner club. Lounge. I mean, yeah, I guess that's kind of what it was...but that's it? Not *The Rainbow Lounge* or *The Executive Lounge* or *Unicorn Lounge* or *Meet Your Next Hookup Lounge*—just...*Lounge*. Of course, I was going to keep my opinions to myself and not tell the manager my thoughts. One, she had been kind enough to let me come in during off-hours, and two, she had recognized me as "Jacob Michaels." If I acted like a brat, it was possible she would tell some media or news outlet, and I'd be national news.

I was still waiting for more paparazzi to descend on Point Worth now that it was clear where I had run off to, thanks to Sheriff Dennard's wife.

Certainly, my luck would run out eventually. There'd already been one incident before Jason and his pack had attacked Lucas and me at the high school football field. The paps don't give up that easily.

Regardless of everything else, I was at Lounge to see if maybe my feeling about something was correct, now that I had all of my memories at my disposal. When I had my visions after jumping-slash-falling into the well, I had seen dead people on the streets and in buildings of Point Worth. Obviously, this was a vision of what was to come—or could occur. Point Worth was not on fire, had not been on fire, and two of the people I had seen in the vision were very much alive, I knew for a fact. So...why had I seen those two people in particular?

It was odd to me that in my vision I saw the dead body and saw the death of a person I was not all that close with in life. Why would seeing them dead or dying be important? How would their deaths affect me? If the hooded figure really wanted to rattle me, wouldn't it be more effective to show me Oma's or Lucas' dead bodies or deaths? Even Ernst or one of the other Kobolds would have hit closer to home than the other two people. Maybe I was barking up the wrong tree or pulling at the wrong thread...but it seemed very suspicious to me. Oma and Lucas had been shown in other visions...so why not the first one?

Mr. Jackson Barkley, Lucas' grandfather, and owner of Barkley's hardware died in front of my eyes in the vision. Right after he had told me, "he's coming." Who Mr. Barkley was referring to was not the mystery. Why Mr. Barkley was the one to deliver the message was the confounding part. Not that I didn't care whether Mr. Barkley lived or died—especially since it would destroy Lucas—but I had no personal emotional attachment to the man. Not like I did with Lucas, Oma, or Ernst.

The other person who was dead in my vision was currently prancing across the stage at Lounge, though the red high heels were nowhere in sight. Of course, you can't *always* wear the same shoes— especially when you're in the entertainment business. You have to switch things up, give people the ole razzle-dazzle with different fashion looks. Otherwise, you'll come off as a cheap hack who doesn't care about optics and presentation. Carlita, even though she was only regionally known, was not the kind to ignore her wardrobe.

Carlita was strutting across the stage, singing the opening number to *Chicago*—except the song had been retitled "*All That Jizz.*" So...it was tacky. But you don't go to a drag show to get Shakespeare or a family-friendly rendition of your favorite songs. It was evident from watching Carlita command the stage as I sat at a table at the back of the room that she was a natural performer. Multiple times I blushed and laughed out loud at the lyrics she had come up with for her rendition of the song. Carlita obviously couldn't see who was laughing since the spotlight was in her face for the performance, but I could tell that my laughter made her work harder. It was apparent that my laughter let her know that her routine was going to kill...once she actually performed it for a real audience.

As the last words roared from her mouth and the music came to a dazzling end, I stood at my table and clapped loudly, whistling to give it a little extra "oomph." Carlita smiled grandly and held a hand to her eyes, trying to block out the spotlight so that she could see who was watching. Instead, the manager of Lounge approached the stage, wringing her hands as she walked up to the area at the front of the room. Carlita stopped trying to find me in the room, and instead, looked down at the manger, crossing her arms over her chest aggressively.

"It was wonderful, Carlita," The manager said, simply. "But, do you think that...maybe...*maybe*...it's a little too...*colorful?*"

Carlita assessed the manager for a moment before speaking.

"Well, darling," She held her head up regally, "if you see a school bus pull up out front, warn me before the show. Otherwise, I think the boys and girls can handle it, don't you?"

"I suppose so, but—"

Carlita waved her off and marched to the side of the stage and down the steps into the room of tables and booths. Once the spotlight was out of her eyes, and the manager was left with nothing to do but worry about the bawdiness of the song, Carlita's eyes landed on me. Looking slightly taken aback, but pleasantly so, Carlita stared across the room at me.

"I'm starting to think that you're stalking me, Rob." She smiled wickedly. "The right way to woo a lady is with flowers and chocolates, and I see neither."

Holding my hands out apologetically with a smile, I replied: "Will dinner sometime suffice, my love?"

"Oh, you!" She threw her hands up dramatically. "How could I ever be mad at you?"

"I assume it would be difficult." I winked.

"What's going on, sugar?" Carlita asked in a quieter voice as she sashayed across the room towards me, her hands outstretched. "Since you're here, I can assume you know that I found a new home for my show?"

I took her hands in mine and kissed the backs of them with a flourish.

"The song was amazing."

"Why, thank you."

"You'll bring down the house whenever you do your first show." I nodded. "When is it? Maybe I can come see it?"

"I would be offended if you didn't." Carlita tapped me on the cheek playfully with the palm of her hand. "It's Friday night, baby. Bring vieja loca and your...gentleman friend?"

"Lucas."

"Lucas." She parroted. "Sounds delicious. Boys with country-ass names are always scrumptious. A weakness of mine. Living in booty-ass Ohio means that I'm always weak."

I laughed loudly.

"Of course, that doesn't explain why you're here now." Carlita slid her arm through mine and pulled me towards the stage, walking slowly. "Sneaking a peek before the show is completely ready will give you the wrong idea. You didn't get to see all of the lights, my dress—the confetti at the end! It will be fabulous, baby."

"If it's even better than tonight, you may as well pack up and move to Hollywood." I cooed.

"Oh, you." She giggled. "But, seriously, what in the fuck brought you down here in the middle of the day?"

Laughing again, I turned to her, letting her arm slide from mine. "Carlita...can I ask you a question that might seem odd?"

Her eyes lit up with a devilish glow.

"Those are my favorite sort of questions."

"Have you ever met the man in the black hooded cloak?"

I asked the question firmly, evenly, making sure that my eyes locked with Carlita's as I spoke. There was no point in pretending my question was a joke or that I might be testing her. Carlita had some answers. I was sure of it. For several tense, breathless seconds, though she didn't bother to look shocked, Carlita stared at me. Finally, she sighed, an exhalation that seemed to come from the tips of her toes.

She crossed her arms over her chest again as she stared back at me, one eyebrow raised precipitously. "You know what? I suspected that you'd eventually put two-and-two together, being Esther Jean Wagner's grandson after all. But I had no idea that people with the gift could be like...*you*."

"Meaning?"

"More alluring than he."

"I don't know if that's a compliment." I frowned.

"It's not." Carlita shrugged, though neither the gesture nor the words held malice. "The deadliest, wickedest creatures are usually the most enticing. Wouldn't you agree?"

I couldn't argue, so I shrugged.

"What business do you have with him?"

"Old," I said, nodding slowly, my eyes locked on hers. "Very old business."

She cackled loudly, her arms dropping to her sides.

"Old business is all he has." Carlita continued to cackle as though I had said the most ridiculous thing she had ever heard. "He has so much business that he hasn't had time to make new enemies, has he?"

"How old is your business with him?"

Carlita waved a hand, and the air shimmered around us, like fumes rising from a gas puddle on hot cement in the middle of summer. Everything around us froze. The manager, who had been walking towards the back of the room stopped in place. The ceiling fans five feet above our heads stopped in mid-whirl, and everything was deathly silent. Carlita looked around slowly, her eyes twinkling, taking in her work before turning her attention back to me. The act was impressive—something I never could have done, no matter how much I had wanted or tried. But Carlita and I were like apples to oranges. There was no reason to be jealous of her power.

"I'm betting...*Oracle?*"

She presented me with a delighted smile.

"What else?" She held her hands up dramatically.

"The theatrics would have given it away if it hadn't been for a little memory problem I've had for...well, a while."

Carlita just grinned, her hands going to her hips, marveling at her magics working around us. It was impressive, I had to give her that. The little magic I had was impressive by most standards, but what Carlita had whipped up on a whim was downright outstanding. Of course, I had a lot of questions, and Carlita had essentially stopped time, so I was going to take advantage of the situation.

"How long has Oma known?"

She shrugged. "We knew each other before she came to Point Worth."

I nodded.

"Is it rude to ask a lady how old she is?"

"Carlita would never reveal her age!" She gasped playfully. "But Carlos might tell you that your grandmother was not the first—or even second or third—Wagner he's dealt with."

Her eyes were practically twinkling.

"Got it," I said. "Can you tell me if there is any point in trying to avoid what seems inevitable? What will happen if I...if I face him?"

Carlita leaned in conspiratorially. "You know he's not a 'he,' right? Well, it's not a 'she,' either, I suppose. They're all things at all times, appearing as they are expected to look—what a person expects them to look like at any given time. It is interesting that they appear to you as the man in the long black coat, though, right?"

"It's a hooded cloak."

"Style, baby." Carlita tapped my cheek again. "But the meaning is the same."

"I guess." I nodded. "So...what will happen?"

Carlita sighed and gave a small laugh. "Baby, I'm an Oracle, not a psychic. Right now, I'm just a busted ass drag queen trying to get these shitheads to recognize my obvious talent."

I smiled.

"If you want the future...maybe talk to Lucas." Carlita went stone-faced.

My smile disappeared.

"My boyfriend is not a psychic," I stated firmly.

"Your boyfriend knows things." She twiddled her fingers in the air vaguely. "What is to come. That's closer to being a psychic than I will ever be. Of course...he's having a bit of a *memory problem* himself, isn't he?"

"Yes."

"Pity."

"Oma says if he gets his memories back, he's in as much danger as we are," I said. "Do you think that's true?"

"That's a better question." Carlita popped her tongue approvingly. "Well, of course, he is, sugar. Even if he *doesn't* get his memories back. And you know why."

I was chewing at my lip.

"No one can hear us, sugar." Carlita shook her head, then waved vaguely around us. "I took care of that."

"Are you sure?"

"He hasn't found me for several centuries—and I've said his name plenty of times here." She shrugged. "I would say I am nearly one-hundred-percent sure that we are safe."

"Good."

"Lucas having his memories back only puts one person in danger, Rob." Carlita continued. "And it ain't himself."

I frowned. "Who?"

"You, baby." Carlita looked at me like I was stupid. "You mean so much to him as it is. And he, of course, is everything to you. If he gets all of his memories back, well, baby, he's going to be as protective of you as you are of him. When it comes time, you'll both be trying to push the other one out of the line of fire. The firemen will abandon the fire."

Staring intensely into Carlita's eyes, I wondered why she had repeated an expression that the man in the black hooded cloak had used.

"You only have one job, Rob." She shrugged. "Lucas will distract you from that. That is why Esther Jean Wagner doesn't want you to...*do anything*...to change what Lucas does or doesn't remember. That's why she's kept him close ever since you left. To make sure he stays ignorant to everything that went on, is going on, will happen. Lucas could be collateral damage...or cause it. And she doesn't trust you to keep that from happening."

"Bitch."

Carlita snorted, amused.

"Sorry."

She waved me off. "Esther Jean cares about you, Rob." Carlita shook her head at me. "If she didn't, she wouldn't give a damn what you did or didn't do. Maybe you should do as she says?"

"Maybe."

"Besides...how could you give Lucas his memories back without tipping off your friend in the cloak, after all?" Carlita asked slowly. "I mean...he has ears everywhere magic can reach, right?"

Carlita's eyes twinkled as she leaned in. I watched her for a moment, then she blinked at me and pulled back just as something dawned on me.

"Where doesn't magic reach?" I grinned.

"You're smart." She was tapping my cheek again. "Maybe he'll have trouble with you after all."

"Carlita..."

"Before I answer you, can I tell you something?"

I held out my hands, a gesture of consent.

"When someone is in danger, it is natural for the people they love to try and protect them," she said. "It's just human nature, baby. A parent jumps in front of a car to save their child who wandered into the street. A lover jumps in front of a bullet to save their beloved. It's just what people do. Humans, by instinct, protect the people they love—without thought or consideration."

"Not always."

"Usually." She shrugged. "When the time comes, Lucas will do everything he can to save you. Whether you give him his memories back or not."

"So...there's no right course of action is what you're telling me?" I shook my head in frustration, though I couldn't help but give a bitter smile.

How was I to choose what to do if either thing could possibly have catastrophic results? Carlita stood there, perfect makeup, beautiful, skintight dress, gorgeous waves of black hair piled expertly on her head, her eyes alert and sparkling, the air still shimmering—quite literally with magic—around us. My main concern should have been the fact that I was stuck in a magic bubble with an Oracle who was surely centuries old, yet hiding away as a drag queen in Toledo, Ohio. All I could think about, though, was the fact that I didn't know what to do about my boyfriend and his magically-induced amnesia.

"That's not what I'm telling you." Carlita corrected me, looking down to pick at one of her beautifully manicured nails. "What I'm telling you is that Lucas is his own person. We all have free will to do whatever it is that we choose to do when we're faced with what is right and what is wrong. We all choose a side when the time comes. Whether we know why we chose what we chose or not. Do you want Lucas to make an educated decision—or just blindly follow you?"

Ah. *That* I understood.

"I got you."

"I knew you would." Carlita winked.

"Whose side are you on, Carlita?" I asked.

"Isn't it obvious?"

"No."

"That is a truly ignorant question." She giggled. "I think you know exactly which side I am on. You've seen it."

Carlita. In the street. Dead. Fashionably dead in Louboutin heels, actually.

"I thought you weren't psychic?" I raised an eyebrow.

She smiled. "I don't have to be psychic to see that you look like you're prepared to miss me, Rob."

Swallowing hard, that hit me in the gut like a hammer. Was I really that transparent?

"I have to thank you, baby." She sighed wistfully. "I have never had someone willing to mourn for me. It makes the whole thing a little bit easier to swallow, ya' know?"

"It wasn't real." I shook my head. "What I saw. It's something that could happen, not what is going to happen."

"Regardless," she shrugged, "thank you. No matter what happens, at least I won't be forgotten."

"Never."

She produced a genuine, toothy smile.

"Do you know people used to think spells, curses, and jinxes could be broken by swimming across moving water?" Carlita said, waving a hand. Things slowly started to creak back to life around us, and the shimmering began to fade. "That's just bullshit, obviously."

"What are you trying to say?" I asked quickly, knowing our time was coming to a close.

"People thought running water protected them from evil."

"So?" I asked desperately as things around us picked up speed.

"Maybe they weren't wrong." Carlita shrugged. "Running water has a way of clearing away a lot of evidence—probably why so many dead bodies get dumped in rivers and oceans."

"So...?"

"Even your friend in the cloak can't sense things that happen in moving water." Carlita winked. "Traces of magic just get swept away."

Then everything came to life at full speed around us. The manager of Lounge walked past us, still wringing her hands and looking concerned about what was to come with Carlita's routine. The fans started circulating air again, the shimmering was gone, and life was as it had been before Carlita had done her magic. My eyes stayed on Carlita's for several moments as I considered her words. Carlita stared back, looking like a regular drag queen and not an Oracle—not that there had been much to differentiate the two. Other than the shimmering and whole time stopping stuff suddenly, anyway.

"I have so much to do before Friday, honey!" Carlita announced dramatically. "Nine o'clock. In case you and Lucas want to come to see it. I'll make sure you have the best table in the house."

Smiling, I nodded.

"I'd like that."

Carlita grinned and gave my shoulder a squeeze before stepping around me and heading back toward the stage stairs again. As if she had a sudden thought, she turned to me once more, the spotlight hitting her, though I knew it wasn't just because the technician had seen her approach the stage. An Oracle creates his or her own lighting. They're very dramatic—Oracles.

"It could be a romantic evening, ya' know." She suggested. "Dinner, a show...maybe a walk along the Maumee? Whatever you decide, of course. I'm sure you'll plan a wonderful date for you and Lucas."

Chewing at my lip, understanding the implication, I nodded at her.

Carlita winked once more and then she was strutting up on the stage to give her song another run through. Oracles and drag queens are always interested in getting every little detail perfect. That's why people trust them.

Chapter 5

Lucas was in just his jeans, no shoes, no shirt, but that didn't keep me from considering giving him service right there in the kitchen. There was something about Lucas in just his jeans, barefoot and shirtless, whipping up a meal, that made me desire him even more. The fact that he hadn't burned a single meal since he got over his initial shyness—something he never would have experienced if he hadn't lost his memories—made it even sexier. Outside, the rain was dancing upon the windows and roof, providing a symphony for dinnertime. Lucas hummed to himself and practically pranced through the kitchen as he worked, lightning flashes showing periodically through the kitchen windows as thunder rumbled in the distance.

Jacob Michaels, professional actor, was doing his best to pretend to be Robert Wagner—*Robert the Youngest*—blissfully unaware of his past, the urgency of the present, and the uncertainty of the future. It was early in the evening, but I felt that I was doing a pretty good job of acting like I still didn't remember anything from before. Lucas certainly hadn't indicated that he didn't believe that I wasn't the same Rob I had been the day before. Of course, it hadn't been a full day since I had wandered down into the cellar at Oma's house, so everything was still fresh. Pretending I was still confused about the past was not that difficult.

When I had left Lounge and Carlita, I had shot a text off to Oma, letting her know that I didn't plan to return home for the rest of the evening. "*Be careful*" was the only response I got. What Oma had meant by those words was apparent to me, though I did not reply with an affirmative. Then again, I didn't tell her to go fuck herself either, so things were still up in the air as far as Lucas and his memories went.

Watching Lucas, happy as a lark, dancing around the kitchen, preparing a vegetarian dinner of epic proportions—his exact words—made me wonder if things weren't fine. Lucas was happy. Other than the fact that strange things had been happening, Jason and his pack had caused a little trouble, and he couldn't remember why things were the way that they were, he didn't have a care in the world. Did I really want to take that happiness away from him if I didn't have to do it? Would he rather be happy and oblivious...or know everything and risk the chance of being miserable? Then again, he hadn't been miserable before he lost his memory. Things had just been...*scary*?

"You know," Lucas shot a devilish look at me as he worked at the stove top, "people can make all the vegetarian and vegan jokes they want, but you can do amazing things with potatoes. Cruelty-free things. Buttery, creamy, cruelty-free things."

"Not vegans."

"There's vegan butter and cheese and cream."

"Look," I grinned, "I totally respect vegetarians and vegans. I mean...it takes dedication and commitment to a lifestyle that most people aren't strong enough to live. Okay? Let's get that clear."

Lucas just grinned widely at me.

"But bacon is fucking delicious." I continued. "Not some bacon made out of rice paper or plant proteins—real. pork. bacon."

"You don't even really eat that much meat." Lucas rolled his eyes, though he wasn't unamused.

"Don't sell yourself short." I teased.

He ignored me, though his grin widened. "Unless Mrs. Wagner sticks it on your plate or it just happens to come with your meal, I've noticed that eating meat is not the first thing on your mind. So—"

"Don't even start."

"—why not try being a vegetarian?" He ignored my statement as he leaned over the bar to put his face close to mine. "The rewards are amazing."

"Are you talking about the health benefits or the meat alternatives?" I wiggled my eyebrows at him.

"Both." He planted a quick kiss on my lips.

"One more."

Lucas gave me another kiss, though his lips lingered against mine longer than they had with the first kiss. I reached up to run my fingers through his hair as I stared into his eyes. His blissfully unaware and happy eyes. I sighed as I took my turn to lean forward and kiss him, sighing as I pulled away.

"I love your kisses," I said. "More than bacon."

"I'll be happy to give you as many kisses you want to make up for the lack of bacon." Lucas sighed happily. "If you give it up."

"You'll give me kisses anytime I want anyway." I tugged at his hair playfully. "I can't resist you, and you can't resist me."

"Don't." He bit his lower lip with a groan. "I didn't do all of this work just to let the food burn while we're in the other room."

"We don't have to go to the other room." I teased but let my hand fall from his hair. "You can work on the food while I work on you."

Lucas kissed my lips quickly once more then pulled away, putting space between us with a chuckle.

"Rob," He shook his head, "you are a bad influence. I like it."

"I try."

"Also, I think you're putting on weight." He winked. "In a good way."

I looked down at my body, though I wasn't sure where my eyes would find the pounds I had gained.

"Couple weeks with Oma will do that to a guy," I said. "Well, that's what being back in Point Worth will do to a guy."

Lucas smiled as he poked around in a pot on the stove.

"Maybe I can fill out so my hip bones don't hurt you so much." I winked at him. "And so Oma will stop shoveling so much food on my plate at meal times."

"You probably weigh less now than you did in high school." Lucas laughed. "Though...that's all kind of hazy."

I did my best to ignore his statement.

Lucas wasn't that easy.

"Maybe one day we'll remember it?" He suggested, glancing up at me from the stove. "I mean, we can't forget forever, right?"

"I guess not."

"You might want to start thinking about what you're going to do about Jacob Michaels." Lucas, mercifully, changed the subject.

"What do you mean?" I frowned.

"Well," He said, opening the oven to look inside, then shutting it once more, "I know you haven't been back all that long, but you haven't said anything about what you're going to do about your alter-ego, babe. Is Jacob Michaels still with us?"

Explaining to Lucas that Jacob Michaels, the identity and name I had assumed when I left Point Worth for Hollywood, was a thing of the past was going to be difficult. When I was sixteen, and I had jumped into the well for the first time, I had been granted a wish—even if the magic involved had taken me way too literally. Jacob Michaels was born out of a need to escape my previous life—to give myself a new identity and help me forget the things I had asked to forget. It had hidden me from...people it needed to hide me from. With my memories returned and the well gone...Jacob Michaels served no purpose anymore. Why pretend he did?

"Jacob Michaels is not here anymore, Lucas." I slowly shook my head.

"That's a funny way to say you're done being a movie star." He gave me a crooked smile.

"I'm not him anymore."

"Okay."

"I don't want to ever be Jacob Michaels again."

"Okay." He said once more.

"Say 'okay' one more time." I grinned wickedly at him.

Lucas stared at me for several moments, his face impassive as my wicked, teasing grin slowly and nervously melted away.

"I'm glad that I'll have you around here, Rob." He said simply. "It's nice to know you won't be running off to some faraway land to film a movie or record an album or put on a concert or..."

Lucas trailed off, his eyes drifting to look out the window.

"What?" I asked. "You don't want to be my boyfriend if I'm not going to be a famous actor and musician anymore?"

The smile that came to Lucas' face was tight, and the lightning flash from outside illuminated his face for a moment. Suddenly, I wasn't sure if I wanted to know what my boyfriend was thinking about me.

"I was so sure that you'd want to keep being Jacob Michaels." He said. "At least part-time."

"Is that one of those things you just knew?"

He shrugged.

"Are you disappointed?" I asked. "I mean...if I'm just Robert Wagner, I can stay in Point Worth and just live a simple life. With you. And Oma. And...the others."

"The creatures in Mrs. Wagner's house?" He asked but didn't turn his face back to look directly at me.

"Yes." I nodded slowly, watching him carefully. "Ernst, Lena, Oskar...all of them. I can just live my life."

Lucas' head slowly went up and down, agreeing with me as he continued to look out of the window as rain spattered against it and lightning flashed again. Northern Ohio. The snow had barely been able to melt for Spring. The ground was nearly still frozen and saturated. So, of course, a torrential downpour was in order. If Lucas' property wasn't one big marshland in the morning, I was going to be stunned.

Finally, Lucas turned back to look at me.

"It just seemed so important to you to be someone besides Rob Wagner." Lucas shrugged. "Almost as if..."

Waiting for Lucas to finish his thought proved fruitless.

"Nevermind." A smile brightened his face suddenly as he shook off his thoughts just as the oven timer went off. "You, my handsome, sexy boyfriend, are about to taste the best meatless Shepherd's Pie you've ever tasted before."

"It'll be the first, so the bar is low." I snorted.

Lucas gave me a stern look.

"Sorry." I was chastened. "I'm sure it's delicious. Yum!"

With a laugh, Lucas opened the oven and reached in to pull out the large casserole dish, lifting it up to the counter before using his foot and a swivel of his hips to shut the oven once more. Looking down at the perfectly browned potato topping of the dish made me realize that maybe it wouldn't be so bad after all, though I couldn't imagine not using some beef or lamb in the dish. Mushrooms were tasty and all, but I was a meat eater. Maybe being around Lucas so much would change my thoughts on that aspect of my lifestyle. Lucas did have a point when he said that my first thought of food was never meat.

"Will you miss it?" Lucas asked suddenly as he leaned down to sniff the dish he'd just retrieved from the oven.

"Meat?"

"Not being Jacob Michaels." He clarified. "Traveling, acting, putting on concerts. All the screaming, adoring fans?"

"None of it." I shook my head slowly as he pulled back from the casserole to look across the counter at me. "Not as long as I have you."

"You don't need to try to get my pants off of me, ya' know?"

My smile was immediate.

"I wasn't buttering you up," I said.

"Sure, sure." He waved me off as he stepped away to fetch some plates and silverware for us. "I'm sure giving all of that up for me will be no big deal, of course, but I thought you might miss it?"

"Can we talk about something else?" I grumbled, crossing my arms and laying them on the counter in front of myself.

Lucas set a plate gently in front of me and handed me a spoon and a fork with a shrug of his shoulders.

"If you want."

"Good." I was feeling grumpy all of a sudden.

Being grumpy in Lucas' presence made me feel poorly about myself immediately. Lucas hadn't done anything to intentionally upset me—he just wanted to have a conversation that any couple in our situation would have over dinner. Turning into a sourpuss over something as simple as whether or not I'd continue my career in Hollywood was ridiculous. It was a fair question to be asked by my boyfriend, after all. So...why was I being a grump over something that didn't really matter?

"I'm sorry." I sighed. "I just—"

Lucas stopped me. "It's okay, babe." He shoved a large serving spoon into the casserole and dug out a healthy portion which he deposited on my plate expertly. "I get it. I really do. There's...a lot going on, right? I mean, you left Hollywood, you're here to relax and get better, put on weight. Weird things have been happening, your life has been in danger multiple times—"

"Tra la la." I twirled a finger in the air comically.

"—and you just need a moment to take a breath." He smiled at my comment and finger twirl as he began serving himself up some of the Shepherd's Pie. "I won't bother you about it."

"Thank you. But I am sorry I'm a grumpy bastard about it, Lucas. Everything has just been a bit much lately."

He winked at me as he shoved his fork into his food and brought a bite to his mouth before he had even hopped up on his barstool. Lucas moaned happily as he savored the bite, obviously overdoing it to make his meatless meal seem even more delectable to my heathen, meat-eating self. Shaking my head with a laugh, I shoved my fork into the concoction and brought a bite to my mouth as well. It was good. Really good.

"It's really good." The thought left my mouth as soon as I had swallowed the bite.

There was no point in lying to Lucas and saying I didn't like it. Even when I felt like being petty; lying just to lie is a waste of breath.

"I told you." He grinned widely before sliding onto his barstool as he shoved his fork back into his food. "Mushrooms are a great meat substitute for a lot of dishes. And no one gets hurt."

"Unless you cut your finger while making dinner, I suppose." I quipped. "When did you become a vegetarian?"

Asking Lucas this question was pertinent. He hadn't been a vegetarian when I had left Point Worth ten years prior. Of course, I couldn't tell him that I remembered that.

"I don't really remember you being a vegetarian...way back when." I added for good measure. "Though my memory is a little fuzzy, too, I guess."

Lucas shrugged at this.

"I mean, I guess it was about the time I went to college?" His brow furrowed. "Does it sound weird that I don't remember?"

I looked over the bar at him, my fork halfway to my mouth.

"Weirdest thing I've heard all week, obviously." I snorted.

Lucas laughed.

"Fair enough." More lightning flashed as we each brought more food to our mouths. "I don't remember making a conscious decision to not eat meat. I just stopped one day and never started again."

"Sounds like you."

"How so?"

"Organically deciding something." I shrugged. "I mean, meat just became something you didn't eat, you didn't question it, you just went with it. You're good at just going with things."

"Is that your way of saying you like when I let life lead me?"

"I like it when you let me lead you." I let my fork rest on my plate.

"Where do you want to lead me?" He grinned before popping another bite in his mouth.

I looked down at my food, contemplating this question.

"I've never really paid much attention, but is your shower big enough for two?" I asked.

"Big enough for four." He replied, still eating nonchalantly. "In case you want to get really wild."

"Just you is more than enough."

Lucas bit his lower lip sexily as he set his fork down.

"Do you want to play 'drop the soap'?" He asked, wiggling his eyebrows. "Because I only use body wash."

"I don't care what you bend over to pick up."

"Why, you charmer you." Lucas drawled.

Before I knew what was happening, Lucas had reached down and popped the button on his jeans. The zipper came down lightning quick, and Lucas had his jeans pushed down to his ankles. He was stepping out of them before I realized that we had been dealing with a commando situation throughout meal prep and what little of the dinner we had eaten. I popped my tongue against the roof of my mouth with a wicked grin.

"You've just been waiting to do that, haven't you?"

"I've eaten enough." Lucas kicked his jeans out of the way and stood on the other side of the counter, his stance playful, though his eyes conveyed a different feeling. "We can always eat more later."

"Then let's work up an appetite so—"

Lightning flashed again, and every light went out, casting the house in complete and utter darkness. Lucas somehow kept himself from jumping, but I didn't manage to keep myself from gasping at the sudden extinguishing of all of the lights. Once more, lightning flashed, letting me know that Lucas was still standing around the counter from me, still naked, but then it was dark once more. I wasn't sure if I was upset that the lights were out because it was creepy or because it kept me from enjoying the sight of my boyfriend completely nude and ready to do bad things with me.

"Well, shit." Lucas sighed.

"Do you have a generator?"

"No." Lucas groaned pitifully. "Even if I did, I wouldn't go outside to start it up. I mean...it's really coming down."

I stared through the darkness in Lucas' general direction, my eyes starting to adjust to the darkness enough to see his shape on the other side of the counter.

"Hm." I moaned. "Your hot water heater electric or gas?"

"Gas." He said, and I saw his shadowed shoulders move. "Why?"

"We can still take that shower," I replied playfully. "I don't need any lights to take advantage of you, ya' know."

Lucas moved to walk around the counter, though I heard him more than saw him. His bare feet padded against the floorboards as I turned on my barstool so that I would be facing him as he came around to my side of the counter. Within seconds, I felt his hands reach out and land upon my chest, feeling his way towards me. Once his hands found me, he moved forward more confidently, his hips pushing between my legs until he was nearly pressed against me. My lips found his in the dark as my arms snaked around him so my hands could lay against the warm flesh of his back.

Sighing happily, Lucas returned my kiss and moved until he was pressed fully against me. I could feel his groin firm against me as his tongue rolled into my mouth, and his fingers twined through my hair aggressively. My fingers dug into the flesh of his back as I drank him in, suddenly overwhelmed with an urge to throw him down and do a number of things to his body right there in the kitchen. Lucas pulled back before I could continue this train of thought, as though he could look deeply into my eyes as he stood there.

"Why is that when I kiss you, all I can think about is all of the things I'd let you do to me?" He whispered from mere inches away.

It wasn't nearly enough room for all of his body to not be touching me now.

"Do you want to tell me those things?" I asked in the same tone.

Lucas leaned back slightly, groaning with frustration.

"I want to be able to look at you as I *show* you those things."

Whether or not it was instinct or an impulse that had lived inside of me since my teenage years, and I had merely forgotten during my ten years of memory loss, I put one hand between us, open wide, palm facing upwards. How I did it, I would never be able to explain since it seemed like such a fundamental part of who I was, but a flame slowly grew within my palm. Red and yellow, warm colors that put off no heat but lit the space between us. Lucas' eyes sparkled in the light of the flame in my palm, though he did not look even the least bit surprised at my magic. I stared into his eyes as I held the flame in my hand without being burned.

"Is that better?" I asked softly.

"Every little thing you do is magic." He said.

"What?"

My mind flashed back to a memory.

"From one minute to the next, I never know what you'll do, Rob." He sighed happily. "You surprise me at every turn."

I just stared into his eyes as fiery shadows decorated his face.

"How do you do that?" He glanced at my hand then back to my eyes.

"I don't know."

I wasn't lying. I really didn't know. If he had asked if I had my memories back, my answer would have had to be different. But he hadn't asked that. He didn't ask if I had suddenly remembered that I could do magic at will and not just when attacked by werewolves. Of course, Lucas didn't have his memories, so he didn't remember all of the times I had done it before. That led to another problem. If Lucas didn't remember all of the magics I had performed in the past, why wasn't he surprised?

"When you saw me coming," I began, "did you see this? Is that why this doesn't surprise you?"

Lucas shrugged.

"That's not an answer."

He grinned wickedly.

"This isn't me being playful," I said softly. "Tell me. Oma said you *saw me coming*. What did you see?"

Lucas examined me for several moments, his eyes lingering on mine as my other hand stayed against his back, keeping him from escaping. Not that I expected Luas to make a break for it just to avoid a question, but I didn't want him to think that I was going to let him off easy. For several moments, Lucas stared into my eyes over the flickering flame in my hand, his eyes showing the internal debate he was having with himself. Something Lucas had seen had bothered him, and he either didn't understand it, didn't want to tell me, or wasn't sure he should tell me. Regardless, I was going to do my best to make sure that he shared it with me.

"I saw fire."

"Fire?" I glanced down at my hand.

"No." Lucas gave an almost imperceptible shake of his head. "Point Worth was on fire."

I swallowed hard. Lower parts of Lucas were still pushing against me. Nothing would deter the man when he was ready for me to use his body in any way that I wished.

"And that made you realize I was coming back?"

Slowly, Lucas began to nod, his eyes not leaving mine.

"Didn't that scare you?" I asked gently. "Seeing our town on fire and knowing that it meant I was returning?"

He shook his head in the same way he had nodded.

"Why?"

"Because you're a fireman."

The soft gasp, more like a rough inhale, escaped my mouth before I could even stop to think it. Lucas just stared at me. The gravity of what he had said didn't register with him, though I desperately wanted to know why he had chosen those words.

"I'm a fireman?" I mumbled.

He nodded. "You don't start fires. With few, small exceptions." He glanced down at my hand with a soft smile. "But..."

Waiting for Lucas to finish his thought, I grew nervous, but lower parts of Lucas seemed to push against me harder.

"...you're always there to release the floods."

"Where did you hear that?" I gasped, the fire flickering in my palm.

He shrugged. "It feels like something I heard in a dream. It feels like something I've heard before, but I don't remember where. Do you remember where I might have heard it before?"

Sometimes a person finds themselves being forced to choose between lying to a person they love to protect them and telling them the truth and risking that it will put them in danger. Putting Lucas in danger was something I couldn't bring myself to do in that moment. My choice was clear.

"No."

He shrugged once more. "Then I don't know how to explain it."

"Are you being petulant because you think I'm lying or you really don't know?" I asked the obvious question.

"Do you think I'm capable of being petulant with you, Rob?"

"No."

"There you have it." He leaned forward and kissed my lips gently.

The top of the flame in my hand was licking against his chin, but it did not burn him. How Lucas knew that he could get so close to the flame and come away unscathed was another mystery. Of course, did he know that the flame wouldn't hurt him—or did he trust me so much that he knew I wouldn't let it hurt him? I didn't know which scenario scared me more. Eventually, I knew that I would end up hurting Lucas. I didn't know it like Lucas knew things, but I knew my history. People around me got hurt.

"Is there anything else you know that I need to know?" I asked as he pulled away, his chin sliding over the flame once more.

"I'm here until the end." He said firmly, yet his voice was a whisper. "Whatever comes...I'm here until the end."

"Do you know the ending of our story?" I asked though I wasn't sure I wanted to know it if he did.

"Yes."

"Tell me?"

"No."

"Why not?"

Lucas reached up and smoothed my hair back on my head, his eyes only looking kinder and warmer as he stared into mine.

"Because," he said softly, "I know you. You'll do something to affect it. And that will only fuck things up worse."

"Why do you think I'd want to change the ending? Is it bad?"

Lucas smiled.

"I think you'll try to avoid it." He explained. "And...I can't explain it...but I think avoiding things is what has led us to where we are now, babe. I wish I had my memories so I could make more sense. But I think something in our past—something we did when we were teenagers—put us where we are today."

"I like where we are today."

"I'd like us more if we were in the shower together." Lucas tried his hardest to distract me and change the subject.

It worked.

Chapter 6

Lucas did his best to stifle a laugh as I slipped behind him once more, my hands clenched on his shoulders, nearly making us both slip in the shower. My hands on his shoulders were the only things keeping me from ass-planting on the slippery floor of the large shower. The water was at a temperature between boiling and pure steam, and with the electricity out due to the storm, I couldn't see anything in the bathroom. The two small windows on the other side of the bathroom only provided illumination when lightning flashed, which was happening in intervals that grew further apart as time went on. Rain was still coming down steadily, though it wasn't quite the doomsday style storm it had started out at as early in the evening. Regardless, the bathroom, without electric lights, was just one big black box providing the stage for our sex-shenanigans.

"This is impossible." I grumbled though I couldn't put any 'oomph' into the words.

I was too turned on.

"You've never had trouble before," Lucas mumbled playfully over his shoulder.

At least, I think he was speaking over his shoulder. It wasn't like I could see him if he cast a glance back in my direction. The thought of him looking over his shoulder into my eyes as I did my best to join our bodies in the shower turned me on even more than I already was. My desire to make things work in the slippery, steamy shower was becoming an ache in my groin. I felt like I was going to explode before things would actually get underway. Suddenly, I found myself wishing that I was as buff and in shape as I had been when I had filmed my last action movie. If I had that heft and agility, I would have just scooped Lucas up and pounded away at him without any difficulty. I would impress him with my skills and addict him to my body. Not that he wasn't nearly jones-ing for me normally.

"I got this, don't worry," I mumbled back as I stepped gingerly up behind him again.

"Please." He sighed. "Come on, babe. I really fucking need this right now."

"How much do you need it?" I teased as I guided myself towards him, doing my best to hit my target in the dark. "Tell me how much—"

When I placed my hand against the shower wall to stabilize myself, my palm slipped against the tile, and I slid forward, my face smashing into the back of Lucas' head. Instead of screaming out in pain, Lucas began laughing uproariously as I stepped back and grabbed my nose with a groan. I could hear Lucas turn gently around in the shower in front of me. I still had my nose in my fist, rubbing it as Lucas' hand grabbed ahold of another part of me and began to stroke.

"Do you need me to take charge, babe?" He cooed.

I groaned as his fist pumped slowly up and down the length of me, and his lips found mine in the dark. Reaching out, I tried bracing a hand against the shower door and the other on the wall of the shower again, only to find myself slipping once more. Lucas laughed against my mouth as he caught me, wrapping his arms around my middle to hold me upright.

"I think you might be more comfortable with fire than water, babe." He whispered seductively into my ear as the showerhead forcefully sprayed water against his back.

"This is ridiculous." I couldn't help but laugh. "Why did I think this was such a good idea?"

Lucas moved his hand down to my length again as his other arm stayed around me, eliciting another moan from me.

"Because doing this together seems like a good idea anywhere." He cooed once more as his arm slid from around my middle.

Lucas continued to slowly work me in his fist as he reached behind himself to turn the spray of the showerhead off. It was almost as if Lucas could see in the dark and know where everything was, the deft way he handled every situation in the shower. Of course, it *was* his shower, so he probably knew every inch of it by heart.

"You probably say that to all the guys you've had in this shower." I teased; my voice gruff as he continued to use his hand on me. "Make all of the guys feel good about themselves so you can have your way with them."

"You're the only guy I've ever had in this shower." He squeezed me tightly, just this side of painful, before the stroking resume. "But I don't have to convince you to let me have my way with you, either."

"Never," I grunted.

"Let's dry off and move this to the bed, babe." He stated gently, his fist slowly sliding away from me.

Feeling his hand loosen and then slide away from me made me want to scream out in frustration but, instead, a low growl escaped my throat as Lucas shoved the door of the shower open and nudged me towards the opening. Obviously, I was not to be trusted to exit the shower after him. He wanted to stay behind in case I slipped and needed to be caught. I rolled my eyes, knowing that he would not catch the expression in the dark bathroom, and stepped out onto the mat in front of the shower. Once my other leg had followed, and I was on solid ground, Lucas followed. I didn't venture far from the shower for fear that I would bump into something, or trip, or commit any number of blunders, thus giving Lucas something else to tease me over. Instead, I moved just far enough aside to allow him to exit the shower and close the door after himself. We both were outside of the shower, dripping water onto the mat and floor as I yanked the condom off of myself and let it fall to the ground. We would need a fresh one before we continued.

Before I could make a move towards the door—or, at least, in the direction I thought the door was—Lucas pulled me into him and pushed his lips against mine again. We had barely completed the kiss before his mouth was on my neck, then my chest, then trailing lower to my stomach. I moaned as Lucas worked his way down my stomach, planting kisses over and over again against my wet flesh, his lips sucking at my skin as he lowered to his knees. He was taking me into his mouth as his knees hit the bathroom floor. He moaned hungrily as his mouth began to move on me, and my fingers clutched at his hair. My other arm wanted to shoot out to brace myself against the wall or the shower door, but I was afraid that I would slip again, pulling my body away from his mouth and ending my ecstasy. Instead, my other hand grasped at his hair as well, using him for support as he sucked at me.

Everything ended too quickly because soon Lucas was back on his feet, his mouth searching out mine. As we kissed again, I wondered if his lips tasted like what he had just had in his mouth. My fingers stayed tangled in his soaking wet hair as we fed at each other's mouths and lower parts of us fought and strained against each other. Suddenly, Lucas was pulling at me, his mouth staying on mine as he directed us towards the bathroom door. We tumbled out of the bathroom, somehow keeping our lips pressed to each other's as we collapsed in a heap on the bed. Lucas pushed me back onto his bed, obviously unconcerned with the fact that we were both still wet.

Using my elbows, I pulled myself entirely onto the bed and turned my body so that I was laying along its length. In the dark room, I saw Lucas' figure walk around to the foot of the bed in the dark, and then he crawled up between my legs. Within moments, his mouth was back on me, and my fingers were in his hair, urging him to keep doing the thing that he did expertly. Lucas' moaning on me and his head bobbing hungrily only aroused me more as my fingers pulled at his hair. Groans escaped my throat as he did his best to bring me to the brink with nothing more than his lips and tongue.

Just when I thought I might be moving towards the point of no return, Lucas pulled his mouth away from me. Obviously, he sensed me starting to buck my hips towards him as he bobbed his head and knew that only meant one thing. He didn't want things to end so quickly. Lucas kissed the tip of me, and I knew that if the lights were on, I'd see him grinning devilishly up at me. It was a good thing the electricity was out. That would have sent me over the edge and made a real mess of things.

As I ran my fingers over every inch of Lucas in the dark, he crawled up my body and reached over to the bedside table. Working like he had night vision, Lucas found the condoms and lube quickly. The tearing of a wrapper sounded, and I immediately felt him sliding a tube of latex over the length of me, his hands moving swiftly, desperately. Then a sound of thick liquid squirting and his hand moving over me again. Lucas chucked the lube to the side, aiming wildly in the dark and I felt his slick, lube slathered hand slap against my chest as he raised himself up to position himself over me.

Doing this thing, Lucas letting me enter his body in such a way, wasn't new to either of us, but it still took work. My mind drifted to thoughts of how people think that slipping a penis into someone else is an easy, painless task—something movies would like you to believe. I'd done enough sex scenes—with men and women—to know that Hollywood wanted everyone to believe that sex is never messy, uncomfortable, gross, or clumsy. But it is never that simple. The work it takes is frustratingly pleasurable, but it is never effortless. Lucas shimmied and wiggled and pushed, his hand holding me still and against the target as he eased down on me bit by bit, moans escaping his throat as he took me inside of him.

My hands found his hips and my nails nearly dug into his flesh as I bit my lip, trying to keep myself from screaming out at the feeling he was providing.

Once I was fully inside of him, Lucas put his other hand on my chest as well, now slick with the residual lube his other hand had smeared on me, and he began moving. Lucas was slapping against my belly each time he bounced on me, so I hungrily reached out and took him in my fist. Groaning loudly, Lucas' movements became more frantic as I pumped him with my fist, and he moved up and down the length of me. Even though Lucas' intention at moving from one activity to another was to stop things from ending too quickly, it became clear very quickly that things were going to end soon for both of us.

"Oh, God!" Lucas groaned. "Not yet, not yet."

I didn't know if he was talking about himself or me.

Regardless, I pumped him harder, making him moan even louder.

"Fuck, Rob!" He groaned suddenly, and I felt him release on my stomach and chest as his movements on top of me got faster and more harried.

Lucas' bucking on top of me, his release, the tightening of him around me, his groans and moans—all of it sent me over the edge. I found myself gripping his hips and holding on tightly as my own hips started to rise and fall, meeting his movements as I released as well. Lucas' hands were like claws on my shoulders, his nails digging into my flesh—I didn't care—as we both finished our climb up to the top of ecstasy and plummeted down to satisfaction. I looked up at Lucas as wave after wave of pleasure flowed through my body.

His eyes seemed to glow green in the dark.

Then that glowing was gone. Had he shut his eyes? Had I imagined it? I didn't care. I just rode those waves of pleasure as our orgasms seemed to go on forever. When they finally started to subside, Lucas' hands slid away from my shoulders, and he collapsed on top of me, his chest falling into mine. He didn't pull himself off of me, but instead, let me stay inside of him as he gasped for breath on top of me. I wrapped my arms around him and held him to me tightly as I attempted to catch my breath as well. Several minutes passed with Lucas' face nuzzled against my neck, his gasps of breath hot against my skin, though I didn't care. Finally, we both caught our breath, and Lucas shifted just enough to remove my body from his with a content sigh.

"*I love you, Rob.*" He moved to whisper against my mouth.

"*I love you, too, Lucas,*" I whispered back.

Our feeding at each other's mouths was languid and lazy. But we fed.

Chapter 7

The electricity was still out, and the bedsheets were still damp from our wet, naked bodies when I woke up hours later. We'd probably both have a rash in the morning. It was the middle of the night and the absolute silence, other than Lucas' breathing, let me know that the rain had abated. Moonlight was pouring through the bedroom window as I laid there in the bed, Lucas turned on his side, facing away from me. I frowned to myself over this. Lucas always slept with his head on my chest, and his arm draped over my torso. Or I held him and put my head on his chest. We both liked to cuddle. However, he was curled up in the blankets like they were a makeshift womb, as far away as the bed would allow.

Sniffing the air, I noticed the scent immediately.

Sulfur.

It wasn't coming from inside of Lucas' room, and if I had to guess, it wasn't coming from anywhere inside of the house. Like walking past a bakery, it was a fleeting aroma that beckoned to me, sought me out, begging me to come see what was being offered. The thought frightened me. Regardless, I found myself sitting up in bed, my hips swiveling as I rose, my legs sliding over the side of the bed. My feet hit the cold floorboards—Spring was still trying to get its legs in upper Ohio—and I began to grope for something to yank onto my naked body. Underwear, jeans, anything really, just so that I wouldn't venture far with *everything* exposed to the cold and elements.

Finally, my fingers found my jeans and I fumbled in the dark to pull them on, wondering if the noise would awaken Lucas. When I glanced over in the dark, I could see his sleeping form in the bed, still wrapped up in his cocoon of slumber, not stirring a bit. I zipped up and buttoned my jeans and decided that I had no idea where my shoes were, so I would just have to go barefoot. Tiptoeing from the bedroom, glancing over my shoulder to make sure Lucas didn't stir, I made my way into the main part of the house.

The smell of sulfur was stronger in the living room, but it was still faint enough, like the ghost of a scent, that I knew it was not coming from inside of the house. The thought occurred to me that most people would wake their sleeping partner if the smell of sulfur started to permeate the house. However, I knew just enough to know that the smell of sulfur was a calling card, not any type of real danger. Experience and my restored memories let me know that Lucas would be fine if he just stayed in bed and dreamed...whatever it was that he was probably dreaming about.

Making my way to the front door, somehow not tripping over anything in the process, I quietly exited the house. If the floorboards in the house had been cold on my bare feet, the porch was like ice. Deftly, I shut the front door behind me, being as quiet as possible still, then made my way to the edge of the porch. I wrapped my arms around my bare chest, as though this would protect me from the cold, and gazed out towards the lake. The moon, no longer hindered by the storms from earlier in the evening, shone large and bright, making the water look gleaming white where it wasn't cast in black.

Just as I expected, the figure stood at the lake's shore, mere feet from the water's edge. The lakeshore was several yards away from the house, but close enough that I could see the black hooded cloak easily. Sighing to myself, no longer afraid—well, not entirely—and supremely annoyed, I started down the steps towards the yard. The ground was like a bog under my feet, water and mud squishing up between my toes as I walked along. The hem on the legs of my jeans felt wet against my ankles, letting me know how much the storms from earlier had let loose.

As I walked, the figure by the lake just stood there, turned away from me, staring out at the gleaming white and black waters of Lake Erie. As I approached, the figure didn't move at all, even though I could sense he knew that I was there. With another sigh, I stopped beside him. I glanced over at him for the briefest of moments, then looked out at the lake as well.

"*This isn't real,*" I said.

Or...didn't really say.

Do we actually say things aloud when we talk in our dreams?

"*It is not.*" He replied.

"*Why have you come for me in a dream instead of marching down Main Street in town setting things on fire?*" I asked what I felt was a logical question, all things considered. "*I mean...we can just get this all over with. See where the pieces fall.*"

"*All of your wishes came true. Or so it seems.*"

"*Wishes don't last forever. Apparently.*" I sighed.

I just knew he was grinning inside of that dark hood.

"*Perhaps.*" Came the voice once more. "*Sooner or later, things fall apart, don't they? Of course, you could always make things easier on me. Help move things along.*"

My eyes darted over to the hooded figure nervously before I glanced out at the lake once more.

"*I really don't think I want to do that.*"

The figure chuckled, entirely amused.

"*I had assumed as much.*" He replied. "*That is why I have come to you, such as I have.*"

I nodded, and though the figure wasn't looking at me, this was a dream, so I knew that he would see the gesture. Together, the figure and I stood on the shore of Lake Erie, just a few yards away from the front porch of Lucas' house, and stared out at nothing. It occurred to me that there was no sound to anything. Unless one of us spoke, I heard nothing. I could feel the cold, but I didn't hear the water lapping at the shore, early Spring birds in their roosts, furry little creatures searching out the night for food. Nothing.

"*I don't know what to say,*" I said.

"*There is nothing to say.*" He replied. "*Eventually, I will find a way to you. Finding you is easy, releasing myself so that I can is a bit of a conundrum. You made serviceable wishes.*"

"*I suppose.*"

"Though you could have done much better." He chuckled. *"I'm quite disappointed that you did not do a better job of things."*

I shrugged. *"I was young. If I made wishes now, they would be much different. Of course, it was all kind of forced upon me. Give me a break."*

Smiling, I glanced over at the figure.

He chuckled.

"It will be delightful to face you in battle once more."

"That's a little dramatic," I said evenly. *"But okay."*

"You won't be as lucky the next time."

I stared at the figure a moment longer, then sighed and turned my attention to the lake once more.

"That has always been my assumption," I mumbled. *"How many times can a guy get lucky?"*

"You are not scared?"

"Terrified."

"But you know this is inevitable?"

I nodded.

"You can release me and be done with it, then."

"I can't do that."

"Of course, you can. It is what you do. It is what you were born to do."

"No. It's not." I stated firmly. *"It is what my father was born to do. I just got shafted, didn't I?"*

He was chuckling again. *"I suppose that is accurate."*

"I won't release you. Ever. You will have to find your way to me. In the meantime, I will be preparing for you. My memories aren't so foggy anymore."

The figure stood there, staring out at the lake.

"So...when you find your way to me, you'll have to work up a sweat to claim your prize. I'm stubborn like that."

"That is why I am so eager for us to meet once more." The figure said, finally turning to me. Icy blue eyes glowed out at me. I wanted to shiver, but I wouldn't give him the satisfaction. *"I think you will be the most satisfying opponent I have seen in...a very long time. Breaking you will be thrilling."*

I laughed lowly.

"I'd like to see you break me," I replied firmly, staring back into those icy eyes. *"You might win, but you will never break me."*

Those eyes stared back at me for what felt like an eternity.

"You could have run away. Like your father. Saved your wishes for another day."

"That would have meant I was broken, wouldn't it?"

*"You **are** a stubborn creature."* He chuckled.

"You have no idea."

The hooded figure turned slowly away, glancing out to the lake once more and I mimicked his movements.

"Dawn will be arriving soon." He said simply. *"I cannot be here for that."*

"Then leave."

"I will soon. But you must know, if you won't release me, I will do my best to convince you otherwise. I may not be able to reverse what you've done, but my wolves do not need their memories to take orders. They are

always eager to please." His voice dripped with sadistic humor as he spoke.

"*I hope you like dead wolves.*"

The figure cackled loudly, his head falling backward. He continued falling back until he was falling in on himself, bending over backward until he was nearly a circle, then he blipped out of existence. Looking into the space he had just occupied, I sighed to myself and looked out at the lake once more. Dawn would be arriving soon. The sun would peek over the horizon and make the water warm and golden instead of cold black and white. Lucas' lawn would start to dry and not be so swampy. And life would go on. For the time being.

There had barely been enough time to stare at the lake and think about the arriving morning when I startled awake in bed once more. My eyes shot open, but I did not sit up or jerk—I just simply woke up suddenly. Lucas had his head on my chest, and his arms wrapped tightly around me. He was breathing deeply, contentedly. And the only thing I smelled in the air was Lucas' soap. But I could swear I heard a cackle on the wind outside.

Chapter 8

Oskar was finishing up sweeping the kitchen floor when I walked in the backdoor later in the morning. Oma was sitting at the kitchen table, drinking her coffee and eating her breakfast while playing on her phone. No other Kobolds were in sight. Oma looked up from her phone, rolled her eyes at me, and then went back to whatever it was she was doing. Oskar gave me a warm smile before disappearing into the broom closet, shutting the door behind himself. He could put the broom away and make use of the shadows. No point in coming back out again.

I made my way over to the coffee maker and grabbed a mug from the cupboard so that I could pour some of the delicious dark brain juice for myself. It was going to be needed. Looking into the pans on the stove, I saw sausages, eggs, hash browns, and fried tomatoes. So, I made a plate for myself as well. When I slid into the chair across from Oma, she set her phone down and picked up her fork, her eyes settling on me. Instead of immediately launching in on her, I picked up my fork and cut off a chunk of sausage, bringing it to my mouth quickly. No matter what Lucas said, I could eat meat sometimes as my first choice.

When I had left Lucas' house, he was leaving as well, on his way to do sub duties at the high school. He had warned me that he was going to help Mr. Barkley out at the hardware store after, so he wouldn't be able to come by the house until much later in the evening. That was fine by me—in fact, I was hoping that he might not be able to stop by the house after work at all, that he would be too tired. There were other things I really wanted to attend to first.

"I saw him last night," I said to Oma. "In a dream."

Oma's eyes grew wide, but it didn't stop her from shoving another forkful of hash browns into her mouth. I popped another piece of sausage into my mouth and chewed thoughtfully, taking my time, figuring out what I wanted to say and how I wanted to say it.

"He's not coming anytime soon." I continued. "He can't. I mean, for now. Eventually...anyway, we're good for now. Talking or thinking about him is not going to be that big of a problem. It won't make any difference."

"You sure about that?" She snorted. "Your track record ain't great."

"Seeing as I am only oh-and-one, I wouldn't call that much of a record, right?" I quipped, scraping up hash browns onto my fork. "So...why don't you stuff it, old woman?"

"Sassy," Oma said. "It's a wonder it took me so long to figure out you was gay."

"You didn't figure it out," I said nonchalantly. "I told you."

"I guess you wasn't lyin' about your memories bein' back." She grumbled. "Why the hell are we talkin' about this anyway? What difference does it make? What's gonna happen is gonna happen, so—"

"He threatened me with the pack," I interjected, still shoveling food into my face. "If I don't do something to help him come back from...wherever...he's going to use the pack. He can't give them their memories back—about why things are the way they are—but they're always willing to be violent if commanded."

"Christ in a goddamn gravy boat, Robbie!" Oma dropped her fork alongside her plate and threw her hands up. "Ya' buried the damn lead."

"Well, I figured you'd ask how I knew that, so I lead with that. You're always asking questions."

"You don't ask enough!"

I rolled my eyes.

"So, that's it, is it?" Oma grumbled, picking up her fork once more. "We gotta worry about the goddamn wolves before we can even take a damn breath? Is that it?"

"Essentially." I shrugged. "It shouldn't be a problem, though."

"How the hell do you figure that?"

"I'm going after Jason tonight if I can," I explained. "Lucas works late and probably won't feel up to coming over—"

"Hm."

"—keep your comments to yourself." I snapped, though I was somewhat amused. "So, I figure it's a good night to go cut the head off a Hydra."

"You and all your damn uppity references."

"It's Greek mythology, Oma." I sighed, shoving eggs into my mouth. "It's not uppity."

"Whatever you say." She replied snootily. "You want to slow down on them eggs before you choke yourself?"

"I'm hungry."

"I see that." Oma snorted. "Probably lost a lot of calories last night, I'd imagine."

"Ew."

Even being disgusted by my grandmother wasn't enough to keep me from continuing to shove food into my gob. Within a few more scoops of my fork, my plate was empty. I felt ravenous.

"Guess your appetite's improvin'." Oma reached out and snatched up my plate while I was still chewing and swallowing the huge wad of food in my mouth. "I'll get you another plate."

"I don't—"

"Shut up." She cut me off. "Obviously, everything is gettin' back to what passes for normal around here. Just let sleepin' dogs lie, damnit."

"No pun intended, I'm sure."

"Look here, ya' smartass," Oma growled at me as she stomped towards the stove and I finally swallowed the mouthful of mostly masticated food. "Why are you gonna go stir the pot when the burner ain't even on yet? You start the attackin' first, and he's gonna bring down any trouble on our heads he can conjure up. Is that what you want?"

"That's a...messy metaphor." I rolled my eyes. "Besides, all he has right now is that pack. If we can deal with them, that'll take the pot off the fire completely. At least for a while. Don't you want some peace and quiet for a while, Oma?"

"Sure, I do." She shrugged as she filled the plate and stomped back over to slap it down onto the table in front of me. "But if you go rilin' up the pack, we ain't gonna have no damn peace."

"So," I was shoving my fork into my food immediately, "you're suggesting we just sit around and let Jason and his pack expand and see what happens? That's not very 'Esther Jean Wagner' of you."

I scoffed as my mouth got stuffed full of more of Oma's delicious cooking. As I ate, all I could think of was how food hadn't tasted as good since I was a child. Having my memories back reminded me how much I had missed having homestyle cooking. How all the fancy foods in the world, all the expensive plates of...whatever...all over the world never compares to food made with love and attention by a grandma. Even something as simple and humble as eggs, bacon, and hash browns beat nearly anything else in the world if it was made by your grandmother.

"How do you know that doing that won't help him be released, Robbie?" Oma asked gently, sipping her coffee as I stuffed my face. "How do you know that sliding back into your old self so effortlessly isn't exactly what he needs you to do? Maybe that's why he threatened you? How do you know if he even has the power to summon the pack right now, anyway? If he's trapped, how's he gonna sic the dogs on ya'? Did that ever cross your mind, ya' idiot?"

Looking up at my grandmother, my cheeks like a chipmunk's, I had to admit that those thoughts had never occurred to me. Luckily, since I couldn't have with the mouth full of food, my eyes did my talking for me.

"That's what I thought." She frowned. "You wanna load up for bear and go on the hunt, and you ain't even thought it through completely. You just want to go off half-cocked."

I swallowed the lump of food painfully. "Says the lady who shot at paparazzi—not to mention the Irish—with her shotgun?"

"One of them was *your* idea."

I shrugged and went back to my food.

"Worked out, though, didn't it?" I quipped.

Oma was waggling her head again as she brought the coffee mug to her lips. Luckily, she stopped her head movements before trying to take a sip of the scalding hot beverage.

Sitting there, I finished my second plate of food at a slower, but still record pace, contemplating Oma's viewpoint on everything. My mind was reeling somewhat from the events that had unfolded in the previous (not quite) two days. Something inside of me, a nagging thought, was telling me that I should be stark-raving mad, cackling, flailing, completely broken, by what had happened. Memories that had been stolen from me, events that had been warped in my mind, magics that had been used— just so I could survive—were suddenly un-warped and returned. Within the time it took to snap one's fingers, everything had been unraveled. My life had been returned to what it had been before I had jumped into the well in Oma's cellar a decade prior. Should I be falling back into line with my previous life so easily?

When I had been a young boy, my life had been pretty simple. Eat, sleep, go to school, take a bath, play with Ernst, watch T.V. Then repeat everything the next day to some degree or variation. I hadn't had my mom and dad around since I was very young, but I had had Oma. I always felt loved, cared for, and protected. It was an odd way to grow up, or so I thought at the time, not having a mom and dad, but it was good.

As I got older, I realized that a lot of people had different looking families, so I settled into my belief that my life with Oma was no stranger than anyone else's home life.

Instinctively, I knew not to mention the Kobolds to anyone who did not live in our home, though I would later break that rule with Lucas. I knew that anything unusual—erm, magical—that happened at Oma's had to be kept a secret. Though I knew this without being told, Oma told me once to keep certain things to myself, and I only had to be told once.

When my teenage years came, and I found that Oma and the Kobolds were not the only magical beings in the house, things got more complicated. At first, the magic was slow to reveal itself. I'd think of wanting a glass of water when I'd awake in the middle of the night…and a glass of water would be on my bedside table. I'd wish that my room wasn't so dark as I tried to drift off to sleep and suddenly it would seem as though there was a nightlight somewhere in the room when I knew there was none. I'd wish for the hours to go by quicker in school…and before I knew it, the last bell was ringing. Strange, inexplicable things began happening to me, and before long, Oma had to give me "The Talk."

Not the normal talk teenagers get from their guardians—a much different one. I had known that the strange happenings in Oma's house, the Kobolds, the displays of magic—all of it was unusual. But I had accepted it. When Oma had pointed out that magic was something passed down to me, it wasn't hard to accept initially. At first, it was just a fun thing that I could do. Hold out my hand, and the salt shaker would slide across the table towards me. Think really hard about the lights shutting off and they would. Simple, harmless, amazing things. But, then again, Oma had only given me half of "The Talk." She hadn't explained that a man in a long, black cloak with a hood would enter our lives. Oma hadn't said that it was something I should expect. Especially with my parents gone.

That's when everything went to shit.

Unfortunately, it was after I had drug Lucas into it.

"You know," I sighed and sipped my coffee as I stared across the table at my grandmother, "if I understood things as I understand them now, this would be a non-issue, Oma. One, I never would have given Lucas a second glance. I certainly wouldn't have allowed him into this…mess. And I would have just faced…*him*."

Oma stared impassively at me.

"But even magic can't fix that." I shook my head. "Oh, that it could. Or…maybe if I had been better prepared. Shoulda, coulda, woulda, right?"

Oma smiled sadly at me.

"We're here, this is the problem, and we have to fix it." I shrugged. "And I think going after Jason is the best course of action."

"You sure you're not doin' this for other reasons than ensurin' our safety for a little bit longer?" Oma asked gently.

"What do you mean?"

"Revenge for him tryin' to turn your boyfriend into one of his puppies back when?" Oma gave me a look that let me know she wasn't falling for my attempt at deflection. "Two enemies with a long history will find any ole excuse to come at each other, ya' know."

"It's not that."

"Ya' sure?" She asked. "'Cause, if someone went after my boyfriend like Jason did yours, well, I'd have lit their ass on fire at the very least. So...you sure ya' ain't just jonesin' to get some revenge?"

In response, I just stared at Oma blandly.

"Well?"

"Look...I may have been confused about what Lucas is—what's hidden in his family tree—for the last few weeks, years, whatever. But I remember what Lucas is now. I can understand why he was such a desirable target for Jason. I mean, who wouldn't want to add Lucas to their pack?"

Oma smirked.

I ignored the expression.

"So, I understand why Jason tried to recruit him and don't hold that against him, okay? He would have been a desirable addition to the pack. I get that."

"That's mighty reasonable of ya', Robbie." Oma smiled widely. "Gee, that's kind of you to see things from Jason's point-a view."

I rolled my eyes.

"You're pissed off." Oma jabbed a finger at me, which made me want to jump, now that I fully understood what a finger jab could do. "You can pretend that all these memories floodin' back into your thick skull ain't got your hackles up, but we both know better."

"It's not—"

"If you want to go mark your territory in blood, well, you just feel free." Oma snapped. "Don't bring none of that to my doorstep, ya' hear? I won't get you out of no trouble you started without cause."

"Yes, you will."

"Of course, I will." She snapped again. "I ain't lettin' the damn wolves have their way. But I'll take you over my knee the second I have to clean a damn bit of your mess up."

Rolling my eyes, I slugged back the rest of my coffee. It wasn't quite cool enough to do, but I managed to not choke as I swallowed it down and set my coffee mug on the table. Oma stared at me, her arms folding across her chest as she examined me, trying to figure out which way I would fall on the issue.

"Tell me what we do if the pack grows, Oma," I said. "If you can tell me you have a plan for what to do in a worst-case scenario, I won't do anything to anger Jason."

"If that pack starts gettin' too big for its britches, I'll take care of it my damn self." Oma nodded firmly. "And it won't just be Jason whose ass is smokin', either."

"They're already mad at me for all their wolves I've hurt," I added. "Even if they don't remember everything in our past. And they want to punish Lucas for Andrew getting hit by his truck, and—"

"We done settled that." Oma waved me off. "We'll send them a nice big bundle of cash—your cash, not mine—and that should keep 'em out of our hair at least for a while."

"Can't wait to call my accountant for that."

"And in the meantime, while they're over there plottin' their little schemes and watchin' for a reason to be mad—while *he* is out of commission—we'll get you up to snuff. That's the only way you win a war—plannin', preparin', and plottin'."

"Those are all kind of the same thing."

Oma sighed.

"Do you really think there's any way that this will end well, Oma?" I asked. "For me, I mean?"

"Not if you go off half-cocked, no." She snapped once more.

"Fine." I rose from the table, the legs of my chair squealing on the linoleum. "I won't go after Jason and his pack unless they come after me first."

Oma looked up at me, her eyes squinting at me, disbelieving.

"The Toledo LGBTQIA Center oracle sends her regards," I stated evenly.

Oma's looked like the cat who caught the canary.

"Drag queen." Oma shrugged. "What else would you expect?"

"What is he when he's Carlos?"

"Robbie, Carlos likes to be Carlita," She said. "Carlos is an oracle, and Carlita is an oracle. The rest is makeup, wigs, and shoes. Ya' live long enough, you need a few hobbies."

"Drag is a hobby?"

"Well, not really." Oma shrugged. "But it ain't been but half a century or so that Carlos has been able to be Carlita. So, he's takin' advantage of it. I think that's probably his favorite thing about livin' this long. He finally gets to be himself when he's her."

"Must be nice."

"You bein' snippy with me?"

"No." I shook my head. "I'm glad that Carlos—or whatever his real name is—lived long enough to be able to be Carlita, too. I'm happy for him."

Oma nodded slowly.

"I'm glad I got her the shoes."

"I know she appreciates it." Oma gave a firm nod. "Oracles have a hard time makin' a livin' as it is nowadays."

"Not many people believe in them anymore." I snorted ruefully. "Hard to get a job when your main skill is advice and prophecy, huh?"

"You could say that." Oma smiled. "But she sure can sing and dance, that Carlita."

"That she can." I agreed. "I'm going to call some people."

"Who?"

"Nosy." I waggled my head. "One, my accountant. Need a wad of cash for Jason's pack, don't we? Two, my agent, manager, and assistant. Letting people know their services are no longer needed is best done face to face, but I'm not going back to Los Angeles. Three, I guess my lawyer. Gotta figure out what to do about...everything."

"Point Worth is your home now?"

"That was an inevitability, Oma." I sighed.

"Don't you think you should go out there to California if you want to fire people?" Oma suggested. "Gettin' told you ain't got no job anymore is even worse when the person tellin' you don't bother to look you in the face."

"Fine." I shrugged. "I'll call my accountant and lawyer. I'll save the rest for when I can 'go out there to California' and do it in person."

Before anything else could be said, I left the kitchen. I'd already let Oma have her way enough.

Chapter 9

Jason was more than a little surprised to see me when he swung his front door wide. Of course, when you come to your own front door in nothing but basketball shorts at dusk and find your archnemesis standing there, it's reasonable to be surprised. Outstretched in my hand, I held a thick envelope from the bank, my eyes staring into Jason's as he fumbled with what to say to me. I could sense, without having to look around, that Jason was all alone. His pack wasn't there to back him up if he decided that he wanted to fight for whatever reason his mind pulled out of his ass.

Oma had asked me not to take the money over to Jason and his pack alone once my accountant had arranged for it to be wired to the First Bank & Trust in Point Worth. She was suspicious of my motives. Coincidentally, the teller, and then the manager, at the bank, had been suspicious of me and my twenty-thousand-dollar cash transfer. When it became apparent who I was—Jacob Michaels, not Robert Wagner—they were less suspicious. Throwing in that Esther Jean Wagner was my grandmother had sealed the deal. Apparently, they were used to dealing with crazy from her, so my twenty-thousand bucks were no big deal in the grand scheme of things.

Being suspicious of me taking the money to Jason alone was not entirely wrong of Oma if I was being honest. Having Jason by himself to talk to any way I wanted, about anything I wanted, was a big motivator for me. Knowing that I might say or do something that Oma might not approve of meant that I needed to keep her away from the meeting. Besides, if things did get hairy—every pun intended—I figured it was best to keep Oma out of it. Oma had power, but she didn't have discretion. Thinking of Point Worth being on fire in my dreams flashed through my mind before I decided she should not be involved in any way.

Jason sized me up, angry heat in his eyes as he stood in his doorway, one hand still clenched against the door itself. His whole body seemed to be quivering with pure, unadulterated animosity as he stared out at me. Of course, surprising him at home as the sun was going down, when he didn't have his pack to back him up, and he was not fully dressed for a fight probably didn't help. None of that concerned me since Jason's feelings about being surprised at his home by me and my envelope of money were the least of my problems. However, I had to do my best to not look concerned for my own safety. While I knew that I could probably take Jason in a fair fight, Jason and his pack were not known for fair fights.

"Funeral money," I stated evenly as I held the envelope out to Jason.

Jason was muscular but lean, not pasty nor tan, his eyes human, not glowing red. Stylish short hair, the shorts hung just so on his hips.

Big hands, strong arms. Tall. He looked like the type of guy any Hollywood casting agent would choose as "Werewolf Number Twelve" in some movie where a teenager has to choose between an immortal and a werewolf. I'd met plenty of those guys that I felt comfortable making that mental generalization.

"What?" He glowered at me once he shook off his surprise.

"For your friend who attacked me and I had to defend myself against," I explained slowly like he was an idiot—because he was. "This is the money Oma promised you for her funeral."

"Her name was Katie." He squinted as he snarled back at me.

He hadn't reached out to take the envelope from me, so I held it at chest height between us.

"Katie," I replied simply.

"You killed her."

I stuck my bottom lip out and batted my eyes.

"And it hurts my soul so much that she got hurt while trying to attack my friend and me in my grandmother's backyard unprovoked." I faked a sob. "Whatever will I do to feel better about this?"

Jason actually growled at me. Not the way a human growls when mimicking a wolf, but the way a wolf growls. Period.

"I really wish you would." I snorted, still holding the envelope out. "I only need one reason to light your ass up, too, Jason. I've been waiting a long time to do just that. And I'm a big boy now."

"Fuck you." Jason leaned forward slightly to growl again. "Don't talk to me like you know me."

Jason growling at me reminded me that he didn't remember the things that I remembered. Of course, it was obvious that losing his memories hadn't made him lose his feelings about me. I shook the envelope playfully.

"Twenty-thousand bucks, Jason," I said, ignoring him. "That will do plenty for Katie's family."

"That's how much a life is worth to you?" He snapped before stepping across the threshold and onto the front porch.

I'm no idiot. I took an equal sized step backward.

"No." I shrugged. "Her life is worth nothing to me. Neither is yours. But a promise is a promise, so here's money to bury her."

Jason was growling again, his shoulders raising up as heat poured off of him, and his eyes started to glow red. I lowered the envelope arm calmly and raised my other, the flame already visible and ready

"I'm not kidding," I said evenly. "Your life means nothing to me. I'll burn you and this whole piece of shit house down."

His house wasn't a "piece of shit." It was small but fairly nice. Looked well-kept and clean. But I find it best not to pay compliments to people whose lives you are threatening. Takes the sting out of it, really.

Jason's eyes caught the flicker of the light, and he backed up marginally, his shoulders no longer looking like hackles. His eyes got stuck somewhere between their usual shade of brown and the red color of werewolves. I didn't lower the hand with the flame, but I pulled it closer to myself and held the envelope out to him once more.

"Do you want the money or not?" I asked. "Because if you don't take it now, I won't offer it again. No matter what my grandmother promised to you."

"You'd defy Esther Jean Wagner?" Jason was amused.

"A lot has changed. I'm a new man, Jason." I grinned widely. "Actually, I'm my old self again."

He considered me for a moment, his eyes boring into mine as I held the envelope out towards him, not breaking his stare. Suddenly, he reached up and snatched the envelope away from me. Lowering my arm slowly, so as to not look as shocked as I was by the sudden movement, I kept my eyes on Jason. I didn't want him to get any sudden ideas that he could take me in a fair fight. I hadn't gone to Jason's house with the money, hoping he would attack me so I could set him on fire. That wasn't my plan at all.

"That all you wanted?" He snarled at me, his eyes now back to brown.

"That's about the size of it." Jason just glared at me. "Now you have your money for your puppy, and you can leave us alone, right?"

Jason didn't respond, but his eyes continued to bore into me— eyes he wisely controlled and kept their usual brown color. For a few moments, I stared back, but then I realized it was like staring into a painting. There were a pair of eyes to stare into, but there was really nothing behind them. Jason didn't have a thought in his head other than he hated me—even if he had no idea why. Of course, he didn't have a real reason to hate me. Only orders. Instead of continuing our stalemate, I turned to leave.

"I remember you, ya' know?" He spat when my back was turned.

I smiled wickedly to myself, feeling justified in the things I'd said to Oma about Jason and his pack.

"Prancing around school." He snarled. "Always thinking you were so much better than everyone else with your stupid fucking plays. Choir. Your fucking guitar you carried around like you were the next coming of Springsteen. Everyone thought you were such hot shit, but you're no better than any of the rest of us, ya' know."

Damnit.

Jason didn't *really* remember me.

My hope had been that he remembered *everything* and would give me a reason to provoke him into a fight so that I could hurt him.

"Better than you." I turned my head to answer him over my shoulder.

Before I knew what was happening, Jason had rounded me and came to stand face-to-face with me, his eyes glaring into mine. I could feel the heat coming off of his bare chest as his eyes bore into mine. Somehow, I wasn't afraid. I didn't feel like Jason wanted to harm me. He just wanted me to know that I wasn't better than him.

"Lucas wasn't like you, ya' know." Jason spat in frustration. "He was going to be one of us until you got in the fucking way."

So...maybe he remembers a little bit.

"Is that what you think?" I had to look up to stare into his eyes with his body so close to mine. "Because he was on the football team with the rest of you Neanderthals you figured he'd be chomping at the bit to join the pack? He'd beg you to bite him, initiate him, and demote him to being a total loser?"

God, he was tall.

He smelled like pine and musk.

Wild dog smell.

"You think that I stole Lucas from you and your litter of puppies?" I scoffed.

"No."

"Good. 'Cause, not to burst your bubble or anything, Jason," I laughed lowly, "but I didn't have to steal Lucas away from you guys. He never would have wanted to be one of you. Even if I wasn't around. But I didn't steal him."

"You're a liar." He stated through clenched teeth.

"You can feel however you want to feel." I shrugged, my right hand starting to feel warm, ready to produce fire in the blink of an eye. "But that doesn't make it so."

Quicker than a human can blink, Jason moved towards me. Sensing the movement, I threw my hand up, the palm of my right hand coming to rest right over his heart. There was barely room between us for my hand to fit there, but Jason stopped when he felt my hand land against his bare chest. Once again, we were staring into each other's eyes as I felt my hand getting warmer against my enemy's hairless, bare chest. Jason wasn't snarling. He didn't even appear angry; he just looked curious. My face was a blank slate as I stared back at him. Moments ticked by as we froze in this position.

Jason's head tilted back slightly as he sniffed the air.

"You smell like cinnamon and citrus." He sighed. "Spicy."

"So I've been told," I stated evenly. "Back up."

"You smell delicious."

"Been told that, too."

"I want to taste you."

Immediately, I wanted to ask if Jason meant that in a threatening way...or some other way. With his face so close to mine, my hand on his chest, and the lack of space between us, the pushing against my lower stomach let me know the answer. I didn't dare look down.

"Back up," I whispered.

"Will you burn me if I don't?" He smiled wickedly.

"Ah." I sucked at my teeth. "Lucas isn't the only fella you'd like to see in the doggy-style position."

That made Jason's grin broaden so that every last one of his teeth was bared to me. He seemed to have more than any human I'd ever met, and he hadn't even tried to shift.

"In totally different ways. *Jacob.*"

I stared into Jason's eyes. He wasn't as stupid as I thought. Or, at least, he wasn't blind.

"I'm so glad you came back." He sighed hungrily.

"Yeah?" I said lowly. "The feeling varies for me from day to day, honestly."

"Maybe you need me to help you remember what's so great about being back in Point Worth?" Jason's eyes lit up—but not in a wolf-red way. "Because if you're not sure you like it here, Lucas isn't doing his job."

"Back. The. Fuck. Up."

"Burn me."

"I will."

"No, you won't."

"You wanted to kill me the other night," I glowered, "and now you want to fuck me? How many brain cells does being a werewolf kill, Jason?"

"I didn't want to kill you." Jason sighed. I could still feel lower parts of him pushing into me. "Just punish you."

His grin got even more wicked.

"You're disgusting."

"You have no idea."

"I've got a pretty healthy imagination." I snapped. "And, luckily, a pretty strong stomach. Get the hell away from me. Last warning, Jason. I told Oma I wouldn't attack you unless you gave me a reason and—"

"You're even more enticing than you were in high school." Jason's voice was guttural. "God, I hated you then, and I hate you now. It makes me so fucking hard how much I hate you. I'm betting that you hate me the same."

"Oddly, I'm flaccid."

Jason laughed throatily, undeterred.

"You are an odd duck." I shoved my hand against his chest harder. "You're like the kid who throws rocks at the girl he likes in second grade."

"Something is like a rock." Jason bit his bottom lip, and his pelvis moved against me.

"Back up, or I will make you back up." I snarled, suddenly very angry.

All I could think about was the fact that Lucas was my boyfriend. I loved Lucas. I didn't give a damn about Jason. Actually, I cared a lot about Jason—but none of those feelings were good. Or sexual. They all involved pain, and not in a 'pull my hair and spank my ass' kind of way.

"You gonna burn me, witch?" Jason taunted. "I think you want to do something besides burn me, Rob."

Unless I was willing to burn Jason, make the first real aggressive move towards a fight, there wasn't a way to respond.

"Two people who hate each other usually have the most fun in bed, ya' know." He said. "*And I hate you sooooo very much.*"

Staring into Jason's ravenous eyes, eyes that told me all of the awful and depraved things he had planned if I even gave a hint that I'd allow it, made me go very still. It chilled me to my core. Jason needed to burn until there was nothing left but the ashes of his bones. The nagging voice in the back of my head that reminded me I had promised Oma I would not attack Jason without a good reason kept me from doing it. Technically, Jason had not attacked—he was just an unrelenting, disgusting pervert. I found myself wishing he had hit me or changed into a wolf instead of telling me all of his depraved thoughts. Then I could have set him on fire and felt perfectly reasonable about it. However, since that wasn't an option, I used my magic for something else.

A loud "*popping*" sound came from within Jason's house.

Then the roar of water gushing sounded from the open doorway.

"*What the—*" Jason shifted his stance to look over my shoulder through his front doorway.

"I think you have a leak." I smiled up at him.

Jason growled in my face before he was dashing around me towards his house. I turned to watch him race into his house towards the kitchen area at the back of the main room where the kitchen and dining area were. Water was gushing from the broken faucet in his sink, hitting the ceiling and falling to the ground, creating a giant puddle.

"Shut off valve should be under the sink," I stated just loudly enough to be heard.

"*Fuck you, witch!*" Jason bellowed as he dropped to his knees and started ripping open the cabinets.

Smiling to myself, I turned quickly and headed to my car. Oma had said before that I was no witch. That I could have been, but I wasn't. Well, sometimes you can change the past. Especially when magic is involved.

Chapter 10

When two people finally find each other—maybe it is different for closeted gay teens—but when they find each other, everything happens at the speed of light inside a bubble. Whenever they are together, they are each other's world. They are the only two people that they can be themselves with all day long. Things happen at an accelerated pace. What might take years to learn about each other happens in the blink of an eye for two gay teens. It is a microcosm of first love that only LGBTQ people can fully understand. Two boys may seem to fall in love too quickly to some, but to others, it is understandable that they fell so deeply so quickly. Their relationship was accelerated due to conditions beyond their control.

Because two gay teens in a rural town in Upper Ohio find it difficult to announce to their community that they are, in fact, a couple, their world goes askew. Two people, afraid to say something as simple as "I have a boyfriend" are often reluctant to speak up about anything that is dangerous. One of the teenagers might not talk about being pressured to try drugs or alcohol. The other might not tell his parents that he is engaging in risky behaviors, such as unprotected sex, drunk driving, or illegal activities. Both teens may not tell their parents or guardian that a gang is trying to recruit one of them as a member.

Not that any of these things happened to Lucas and me, but we often found ourselves in situations where a parent or guardian knowing what was going on would have kept us out of trouble. Even though I had told Oma about liking Lucas Barkley, Lucas made me promise not to tell her anything else about us. He wasn't ready to face his own parents, his grandparents—and neither of us was prepared for any of our friends to know about us. Two gay teens trying to figure out their sexuality and their love for each other shouldn't have to worry about acceptance. But that was forced upon Lucas as well.

Lucas and I were laying down on our stomachs in the rowboat on Lake Erie. The sun had been setting when we started rowing back to shore, but now the moon was out, shining down on our backs. One Saturday afternoon, after Lucas had come to my house after football practice in the early fall, and we had hopped into the boat and paddled far from shore. Being away from shore, out on the middle of the lake, away from everyone else, we could talk about anything, kiss, just be ourselves. We didn't have to worry that anyone would see us and make Lucas more uncomfortable than he already was at figuring out his sexuality at that age.

The afternoon had been spent holding hands in the boat, talking about our deepest wishes, dreams, and desires. Talking about school. Laughing about our idiot friends and the stupid things they said and did during class. Music, movies, what we were going to do once Point Worth was a distant memory—because we were obviously not going to live in the town our entire lives. We had kissed. A lot. It had been a perfect afternoon. But as the sun began to set and I lounged in the boat as Lucas rowed the boat towards shore once more, things fell apart. Jason and his friends were walking along shore, just far enough away that they didn't see us before we saw them.

Lucas had pulled me down in the boat, and we huddled there on our stomachs, waiting for them to walk far enough away that we could get to shore and run for it before they saw us. As we laid there, the sun setting incrementally with each passing minute, I had turned my head to look into the eyes of the boy who meant everything to me. What I saw in those eyes wasn't fear of being called "fag" or "queer" by guys who had only recently become his teammates on the football team. It was something else.

"Why are they always looking for you?" I had whispered.

"I don't know."

"What will they do if they find out we've been hanging out? Why do we always have to hide?" I asked. "I mean, guys hang out. We can tell them we're friends."

"They don't care that I'm hanging out with you, Rob," Lucas whispered.

"Then...why are we always hiding?" I asked gently. "Are they mean to you or something? Do you think they'll be mean to me?"

"They wouldn't even care if they caught us kissing." Lucas croaked. "They don't give a shit about that stuff."

I stared at him for several moments.

"I don't stay in the closet to protect me."

There was nothing to say to that either.

"I stay in the closet for you." He added. "To protect you."

"You staying in the closet protects me?" I was confused. "I thought you didn't say anything because your family and friends would...I don't know...like disown you or call you names...or worse?"

"I don't want anyone to know how much you mean to me."

That touched my heart but confused me more.

"Are you ashamed of me?" I asked, the bottom of the boat hurting my sternum as we laid there.

"No." Lucas insisted immediately. "I would never be ashamed of you, Rob. I just...I don't want you to get hurt."

This statement I found to be even more confusing than any of the others. For the entirety of my relationship with Lucas—once it had become romantic—I had assumed Lucas kept me a secret due to shame or fear of what his friends and family would do. But he was afraid for my safety?

"Why would I get hurt?"

"You'll call me crazy."

I did look at him like he was insane then.

"I would never call you crazy."

Lucas swallowed hard, his eyes burning with fear.

"They want me to...they want me to be like them."

"Like...well, I mean, you're already a football player, Lucas." I whispered back.

"They want me to be part of their pack."

"They're a gang or something?"

"No." Lucas looked green. "They're werewolves."

Then I was submerged, gulping in water, and flailing for my life.

Jerking up to a sitting position, frothy bubbles covered my eyes, and my hands reached out to grip the slick sides of the cast iron tub as I sputtered and tried to fill my lungs with air. I was still coughing when I reached up to wipe my eyes clear of the lavender bubble bath Oma always kept in the bathrooms. I had sloshed water over the side of the tub and created a fairly impressive puddle that would need to be sopped up before one of the Kobolds saw it. If Oskar or Lena saw the mess I had made, they wouldn't curse me out, but I would be getting the stink eye for an entire week at the least.

Sputtering, I dunked back under the water again to get the rest of the bubbles out of my hair and off of my face before I sat upright again. I pulled my knees up to my chest in the still warm water and looked out at the bathroom with stinging eyes. I had fallen asleep. *Smart move, Rob.* After leaving Jason's house, giving him the money for Katie's funeral expenses, and somehow managing to avoid his sexual advances, I had wanted a bath. I wanted to wash the smell and thought of Jason off of me. Oma's lavender bubble bath seemed like the perfect way to do that.

I shivered, though I wasn't cold, as I looked out at nothing from my spot within the deep tub. The old claw-foot tub was so deep that the water came up to mid-chest on me as I sat there holding my knees against my torso. It felt like having someone give birth to me, half in and out of the womb. If I sunk back under the water, would I feel safe, warm, and insulated from the dank, dark ugliness of my world?

For a decade, I had spent so much time being Jacob Michaels— A-list movie star and international rock star—and forgetting who I really was that even getting my memories back hadn't really reformed me as Rob Wagner. Memories are not trustworthy all of the time. Perception and our own wants and desires help mold them, and as time passes, those wants and desires shape them even more. I had remembered that Jason and his pack had actually wanted to recruit Lucas to be part of their pack before I had jumped into the well when I was sixteen-years-old. But my mind had pushed out the peripheral information, the things I hadn't realized were important to the story at the time I made the memories. Things like Lucas telling me that Jason didn't care if he caught us kissing. That didn't matter to him.

Obviously, that part of the memory would have been helpful to have before I had gone to Jason's house to deliver the wad of cash.

Remembering that Lucas had wanted to protect me from what might happen if the pack thought I was in the way was important, too. Lucas wanted to protect me from bad things, just as I wanted to protect him from bad things. We were both fighting similar battles but on different fronts. If we weren't careful, a battalion of soldiers was going to separate us while we were distracted. But Lucas had no idea what battles we were fighting. He didn't have his memories back like I did.

Water flew as I reached up to slap myself on the side of my head in rapid-fire succession, my teeth gritting together as I willed myself to not get emotional. I was so confused and disoriented and...I felt like a giant ass. Everything that had happened—before Jacob Michaels and after Jacob Michaels—was entirely my fault. But then again...there had only been one other choice at the time. Sure, if I had thought out my wishes a little better, worded them better, maybe there would have been more, or better, choices. Since you can't always change the past—even with magic—I had to admit that I had royally fucked things up.

Just as I was set to slap myself in the head again, a modified type of self-flagellation, Ernst peeked his head out of the linen closet. I sniffled roughly, making sure that my emotions were in check before I looked over at him. I was going to make a joke about "knocking first," but Ernst seeing me naked was nothing new. The joke would have fallen flat, especially with a Kobold.

"Hey, Ernst," I said blandly.

"*Are ya' okay, Rob?*"

"I'm fine." I gave him my best 'Jacob Michaels' smile. "I just fell asleep for a minute and tried to drown myself."

I capped that off with a laugh that I hope sounded genuine.

Ernst smiled pitifully at me.

"Are you okay?"

"*I'm fine.*" His little ears wiggled as his eyes lit up. "*The mistress is in-a rather righ' state, though.*"

"Isn't she always?" I snorted.

"*She, uh,*" Ernst looked around, "*she's dow' in the cellar diggin' at the dirt, Rob. Cursin' and-a diggin'.*"

Without meaning too, I burst out with laughter. I had to put a hand over my mouth in an effort to stop myself. Thinking about Oma flipping her lid, the realization of the well actually being gone, and digging at the dirt like a crazy old hag made me want to laugh until I died. Before I knew it, tears were coming to my eyes from trying to keep myself from laughing. Ernst smiled oddly at me as his ears wiggled. Finally, I was able to calm myself down and push the visual of Oma digging at the cellar floor out of my head.

"Well, Oma's gone 'round the bend." I shrugged. "We all knew it would happen sooner or later, Ernst."

"*I 'spose.*" Ernst replied. "*She wen' dow' there right after he showed up.*"

Ernst hooked a thumb over his shoulder in the direction of my bedroom.

"He...?"

My eyes widened as I stood quickly from the tub, water splashing everywhere as I reached for my towel. Ernst leaped out of my way as I dried myself hastily and rather poorly, then wrapped the towel around my waist. I dashed for my bedroom, prepared to face whoever had the nerve to come to Oma's house and enter my bedroom without my permission. When I tore open the bathroom door and stomped into the bedroom, my right hand already feeling warm, my eyes immediately began looking for my target.

"Hey, babe."

I jumped as Lucas' voice came from my bed. He was laid out on my bed comfortably, only in his boxers, reading a book. I looked over at Ernst, an irritated look on my face. Ernst shrugged and ushered me away.

As he was closing the bathroom door behind me, I saw him grab a towel and start mopping at the water on the floor.

"When did you get here?" I asked stupidly.

"Ten minutes ago?" Lucas shrugged, not looking up from his book. "Mrs. Wagner said you were up here taking a bath, so I thought I'd wait. She had a shovel in her hand, and it's after dark, so I figured it probably was best to just wait up here instead of getting in her way."

He laughed lowly at the thought of Oma and her shovel. I couldn't give him an explanation without telling him more than he needed to know.

"So...you just stripped down and crawled into my bed like you own the place, huh?" I chuckled as I tucked the towel into itself so that I wouldn't have to hold it in place.

Lucas frowned and looked up, his eyes finally landing on me. They lit up immediately, seeing me standing there, still damp and essentially naked, straight from the bathtub.

"Well," Lucas smiled widely, "if I had known this was how you'd greet me, I would have gotten here a lot sooner."

"You smooth talker." I teased.

Lucas pulled the flyleaf out and used it to mark his place in the book before setting it on the bedside table. Then he patted the bed suggestively, his eyes hungry as he stared across the room at me.

"That's your side now, is it?"

"Well," Lucas shrugged slightly, his eyes burning with desire, "you always sleep over there, so it just seemed logical to me. Just like at my house. You sleep on the right, I sleep on the left."

"Did you always sleep on the left, or did that become a thing once I came along?"

"I slept in the middle before you came along." He said simply. "But I prefer the left."

I nodded. "The right side is better than the middle for me, too."

"Did you sleep a lot in the middle while you were off being Jacob Michaels?" He asked.

"When I slept."

"How do you sleep now?"

"Better."

Again, he was smiling and patting the bed.

"You're not too worn out from work?" I grinned at him as I pulled the towel from around my waist, leaving myself bare before him so that I could dry my hair better. "I mean, teaching kids and working in the hardware store is bound to tucker a guy out."

Lucas' eyes danced all over my body as I stood there, running the towel roughly through my hair. I was pretty sure that he licked his lips at least once. When my hair was no longer dripping, I ran the towel over my body and tossed it in the direction of the hamper in the corner. Then I stood there, staring at Lucas, naked and completely comfortable.

"You should have done at least one nude scene in one of your movies." His Adam's Apple bobbed as he stared at me. "Even skinny as hell, you're sexy."

"Maybe I did do a nude scene." I shrugged. "You don't know."

"It never made it into a movie." He replied. "I've seen all of them."

"I'm sorry." I teased.

"I'm not."

"Even though there were no nude scenes?"

"No." He shook his head, his eyes coming to rest on mine. "I'm glad I'm the only person who gets to see you like this. I love seeing you like this."

"How was your day, dear?" I crossed my arms over my chest and smiled lasciviously at him.

"Who cares?" He gestured for me to come closer.

"Don't make me feel cheap." I turned my nose up playfully. "How was your day?"

"Doing work and waiting for the hours to pass so I could see you again," Lucas said. "I was worried I would work too long and miss the chance, so that was stressful. But I'm here now. Come to bed."

"Nothing exciting or funny?"

"Nothing more exciting than this."

"Funny?"

"Nothing funnier than you making me work this hard when you know you don't want that." Lucas smiled. "So, why don't you get in bed? Now."

"I love it when you're demanding." I cooed as I sauntered towards the bed as sexily as I could manage.

Lucas used his elbows to pull himself up further on the bed until he was sitting up, his back against the headboard. When I reached the end of the bed, I climbed on, one knee, then the other, kneeling at the foot of the bed and looking up at my boyfriend as he stared hungrily back. Slowly, I walked towards him on my knees and came to straddle his legs. Lucas reached out with his hands to grab my hips and pulled me towards him faster, obviously unable to wait for me to perform the action on my own. I gasped as his fingers dug into my hips, then laughed as my body was smooshed against his.

"I've been waiting all day for this." Lucas looked up at me as I knelt over his lap, then he leaned forward to kiss my bare chest.

I sighed. "Sounds like a reasonable way to spend your day to me."

"*Mmmm*," Lucas responded as he nibbled and sucked at my flesh, and I reached up to run my fingers through his hair. "*Di-oo-iss-ee-all-ay-oo?*"

I laughed loudly at Lucas' attempt to talk while devouring the flesh of my chest as his hands ran down to cup my ass firmly.

"Did I miss you, too?" I asked, leaning down to whisper in his ear.

"Mm."

"Yes," I said. "I missed you all day."

"Do you still love me?" He pulled away from my chest long enough to ask, his eyes looking up at me suddenly.

"What kind of question is that?" I ran my fingers through his hair as I gazed down at him. "You know the answer to that."

"Remind me." His hands slid up to my lower back.

"Of course, I still love you, Lucas." I shook my head in disbelief. "I've always loved you. I'll always love you."

"I love you, too." He replied quickly.

Leaning down, I let my lips find his as my fingers continued to rake through his hair gently. Suddenly, it occurred to me that I had gotten hard very quickly and was pressing into Lucas' stomach. He obviously didn't mind in the slightest as he returned my kiss.

"I've always loved you, Rob." Lucas sighed as I pulled away from his mouth. "And I'll always love you, too."

"How can you be so sure if you don't have all of your memories?" I was only half-teasing.

"You're sure." He shrugged. "Why can't I be?"

I had no answer for that—at least no answer that wouldn't give away more information than I was prepared to provide.

"My memories wouldn't change my mind about it anyway," He said, then, for good measure, added: "That's one of those things I just know, Rob."

Staring down into Lucas' eyes, I suddenly realized there were some things I just knew, too. Like when Lucas was telling the truth. Though, it wasn't difficult to figure out, since he almost always did. Hearing him say the things he said made me realize a fundamental truth about our relationship, what was going on around us, and what was to come. I made a decision.

"We still haven't gone on an official date," I said softly.

He smiled up at me.

"You won't feel like a real man until I've bought you dinner and movie tickets?" He teased.

"I can pay my own way." I flicked his nose gently. "But a real date would be nice."

"Okay." He grinned happily. "Where do you want to eat and what movie do you want to see? I'm assuming one you're not in?"

I laughed gently.

"Actually, a friend of mine has a show at a dinner club in Toledo on Friday. Lounge? Heard of it?"

Lucas indicated that he had. "You make new friends quickly."

"She's an old friend of the family," I replied with a wink.

"Then she's an old friend of mine."

"Maybe we could go see her perform?" I suggested. "Then...a moonlit stroll along the Maumee? Maybe walk the birding trail out by Cullen Park?"

"All alone with you in the dark under the moon?" He grinned.

I nodded.

"Sounds more romantic than dinner and a movie."

"A lot more romantic."

"Then it's a date, babe." He kissed me.

Chapter 11

There is a peninsula out by Cullen Park on the north side of Toledo. It's more like a skeletal finger of land that juts out from the Cullen Park and Docks area, pointing into the Maumee Mooring Basin towards Grassy Island. It isn't big enough or stable enough to allow vehicles to drive onto it, but it has an excellent birding trail—which is essentially just a trail for walkers or joggers. I suppose it is good for spotting birds during the warmer months, but as far as I was aware, most people used it as a simple walking trail to get in a bit of exercise. Of course, I didn't know of anyone who would venture out onto the trail late at night, other than Lucas and me. Of course, everything about our lives was strange, so taking a moonlit walk along an unlit path on an unnamed road on an unnamed finger of land was not that unusual.

As I had suspected it would happen, Carlita put on a show worth every bit of the cover charge at Lounge. Of course, Carlita had given mine and Lucas' names to the manager (Rob Wagner, not Jacob Michaels, thank goodness), so we didn't have to pay the cover. It would have been worth it if we had, though. For nearly thirty minutes, Carlita treated the audience to one of the funniest comedic monologues I'd ever heard. She interacted with the audience (luckily, sparing Lucas and me, although we were sat up front and center), made quips, told jokes, and had everyone roaring with laughter from her off-color jokes.

Of course, then we were treated to a few songs, the least of which was not *All That Jizz*. Carlita exited stage left to a thunderous standing ovation, which I am pretty sure that Lucas and I initiated when we leaped from our seats. After the show, I expected Carlita to come out into the crowd to mingle or say "hello" to people, but she never did. I was a little disappointed that I did not get to introduce her to Lucas, though it was probably for the best. Lucas *knew things*, so he probably would have known that she was no ordinary drag queen immediately upon meeting her. In fact, he probably knew it just from watching the show, but he kept that observation to himself. Obviously, he knew a lot of things in my life were not quite what they seemed, so I'm sure he took all of his observations in stride. Besides, it wasn't like his life was "normal."

As we slowly strolled along the pathway along the skeletal finger of land, I held Lucas' hand in mine, our fingers interlocked, as I used my other hand to try and pull my coat even more tightly around myself. The cold didn't seem to bother Lucas as much, but he had lived in Ohio and New York his entire life. A decade in Los Angeles and other warmer climates had left me unaccustomed to the fact that even Springtime in Upper Ohio was still essentially winter. Luckily, Lucas' hand was warm, and the wind wasn't blowing too hard. However, when I thought of what I had planned, even Lucas' warm hand made me feel chilled.

Carlita's show was great, and she had set me up to have a reason to bring Lucas out to the Maumee so that he would not be suspicious of my intentions. Not that Lucas would have been completely put off by what I had planned, but I didn't want him to think about it too much. I wanted to present him with his options and then just go with the one he chose. I did not want another decade to go by where we were left in limbo. We needed to either "piss or get off the pot" as Oma would say. The only way to get Lucas to quickly make a decision would be to present it to him at the Maumee. If I asked him in bed at night, and he chose, the next morning, his answer might be different. He might change his mind. I didn't want him to waffle.

Maybe that was selfish of me.

At least impatient.

But, like Lucas, there were some things I just knew.

I knew that a storm was brewing.

We didn't have time to fret over relatively simple decisions.

"You'd think they'd put at least a few lights out here, right?" Lucas asked, cutting the stillness of the dark night around us. "I mean, if we had a new moon tonight, I might not even be able to see you."

He chuckled

"Hey," I nudged him with my shoulder, "it's romantic."

"And a little creepy." He added. "There's a reason there are no other people out here on moonlit strolls, babe."

"How do you know that?" I asked ominously. "There could be someone right behind us, and you'd never know."

"Stop it." He chuckled nervously.

"There could be lots of people just hiding beyond the trees, waiting for us to drop our guard, babe," I added. "Maybe if we look closely, we can see their eyes shining in the moonlight, watching us walk along like a perfect little snacky-snack."

"Are you thinking of people or zombies?" Lucas nudged me this time. "And stop trying to scare me."

"I didn't know you were so easily unnerved." I leaned into him, pulling my hand away from his to wrap my arms around his middle.

It made walking along the path a little awkward, but neither of us really cared all that much.

"I don't even watch horror movies." Lucas sighed "That movie you did, *Eyes in the Darkness*? I nearly shit my pants in the movie theater."

I laughed loudly.

"Mrs. Wagner loved it."

"I can imagine," I replied cheerfully. "Well, as far as I'm concerned, you'll never have to watch another one of my movies ever. Especially a scary one."

"Was it scary to do that movie?" He asked.

"Let's not talk about that."

"Why not?" Lucas asked. "My memories are jumbled about the past, and I have no idea what you've really done for the last decade. Humor me."

"It wasn't scary," I stated simply. "The movie looks all dark and spooky, but most of the time I was on a soundstage that was fully lit. Post-production does all that creepy shadowy lighting stuff you see in the theater. All of the reactionary stuff I was in front of a green screen. I didn't even know what the things I was reacting to looked like."

Lucas turned his head to look at me in the dark as we walked.

"Not the exciting answer you expected?" I teased.

"Not exactly."

"That's how most of my movies have gone. Soundstages, sets, green screens, editing geniuses throwing it all together." I shrugged. "I mean, I've had scenes where the people I had dialogue with weren't even there. It's all just clipped together afterward. Movie magic."

"That seems...boring."

Laughing, I nodded in response.

"Yeah." I relented. "Making movies isn't nearly as exciting as people think. At least not when you do those big budget movies with lots of special effects and stunts. I'm sorry I pulled back the curtain, Dorothy."

Lucas chuckled at me, pulling me more tightly into his body.

"It's okay," He said, "I guess I was just hoping that you were as scared making it as I was watching it."

"Sorry. I almost always had stage fright when I did concerts, though, if that helps. Paralyzing, crippling fear where I wasn't sure I could even take one step towards the stage without tossing my cookies. Or pissing down my own leg. Facing thousands of live people on a stage is much worse than being on a set giving reactions based on what was shouted to me by the director."

"Directors shout what to do?" Lucas laughed. "How the hell does that work? I mean, wouldn't that end up in the audio or whatever?"

"The audio is stripped," I explained. "Then they add in ambient and environmental noise, sound effects, maybe music. ADR saves it."

"ADR?"

"Looping, dubbing, whatever." I shrugged against him as I snuggled deeper into his side. "I spent a lot of time in a sound booth, making breathing noises, stuff like that. Just so they could add it to the audio so that no one would know that the scene was originally silent."

"That seems like a lot of work."

"Time-consuming but not all that difficult," I replied. "There are a lot of things you could do at work that are worse than breathing into a microphone."

Lucas laughed loudly.

"I wish I could have been there with you." Lucas sighed as he held me close, leading us along the trail. "If we knew then what we know now, we would've stayed together, and I could have seen it all with you. I hate that we lost a whole decade of being together, babe."

"Me too."

"Don't sound so sure of yourself." Lucas chuckled and kissed the top of my head.

"I'm sorry." I looked up at him. "I didn't mean to sound unenthusiastic at the prospect."

"Good."

Lucas continued pulling me along beside him, our arms finally loosening and our bodies moving apart so that we could hold hands, fingers intertwined, and walk along the trail easily. We continued to walk in silence, no more questions about the less than magical process of making movies. Every now and then, Lucas would pull my hand up and plant a kiss on it before smiling at me as we walked along. The gesture, though it would have made me uncomfortable when I had first returned to Point Worth, now felt wonderful. Having Lucas show me affection in any way—especially now that I remembered everything from my teenage years—made me love him even more.

The depth of my love for Lucas threatened to unnerve me deep down since Lucas and I had only been "going out" for a little over a year before I left for Hollywood. Then we were separated for a decade before we even so much as laid eyes on each other again. How did a love that barely had time to bloom pick up almost exactly where it left off—especially since we hadn't remembered anything when I returned to Point Worth? Was that a sign of fate or destiny? That we were meant to be together? Or was it just proof of our love for each other that we never forgot how right we felt together?

"Are you sure you want to do this?" Lucas panted from above me, both of us naked, the rough ground in the woods our bed.
"We may never have another chance," I replied.
"That's not a good enough reason."
"It is for me." I had said. "If I never get a chance to do this with the only person I've ever loved..."
Lucas smothered my mouth with a kiss.

Before I had left Point Worth for Hollywood, before I had jumped into the well the first time, Lucas and I had made sure to consummate our relationship. Maybe that was what made the memory of our love for each other so strong that it just couldn't be broken. Even by magic. I wanted to be scared, realizing that mine and Lucas' love affair might be destiny, but I wasn't. My only concern involved what was to come—which I had no idea what was to come. Butterflies danced a rave in my stomach as I considered that Lucas might end up hurt. I could never live with myself. Especially if it happened before he had a chance to remember the same things I did.

We got to the end of the peninsula, and I stopped, looking out at the dark lake and the darker Grassy Island in the distance. Lucas was pulling at my hand, urging me to round the trail so that we could walk back towards Cullen Park along the other side of the peninsula. Instead, I let his hand slide from mine as I stared out at the cold water, the moonlight catching the crests of the small waves as they lapped towards shore. My mind was made up. I just needed Lucas to go along with it.

"What are you doing, babe?" Lucas asked as he stepped back over to stand beside me. "See something?"

I turned to Lucas.

"No." I shook my head. "If I asked you to do something with me, would you do it? Even if it's a little crazy?"

Lucas grinned evilly in the moonlight, half of his face blue, the other nearly black.

"Not that." I smiled. "At least, not right now."

"Damn." He sighed. "Then what?"

"Come on." I reached down and twined my fingers through his and stepped towards the water.

Lucas started to follow me automatically before he realized that I was headed towards the water.

"Wait." Lucas jerked at my hand gently. "Rob. That water is freezing. Do you—do you want to go in the water?"

"Yes."

"Why?"

"I can't tell you until we're in the water," I said.

"Why?"

"Say 'why' one more time." I teased.

Lucas produced a gentle smile.

"Explain, please." He said.

"I will." I nodded slowly. "If you walk out into the water with me. Just up to our knees. We don't have to get too wet."

"Why can't we talk here?"

"We need to be in moving water."

"Sure." He nodded humorously. "Makes perfect sense."

"Do you trust me?" I asked. "Because I need you to trust that I'm not doing this to just fuck with you."

"Of course, I trust you." He replied quickly. "Can I...at least take my shoes and socks off?"

I chuckled. "Yeah. Let's do that."

Lucas kicked his shoes off slowly, as though convincing himself that he really wanted to follow through with the thing I was asking him to do. I followed suit, kicking off my shoes, using the toes of one foot to pry off one shoe, then repeating the action. I stripped my socks off and tossed them down on top of my shoes, then held a hand out for Lucas to hold for support as he pulled his socks off. When we were both barefoot, I pulled Lucas toward the water once more, and he didn't hesitate this time.

The water was freezing. Lucas hadn't been wrong. It bit at my toes and ankles as I stepped into the Maumee. Lucas hissed beside me as the water touched his bare flesh, but I kept my hand on his, pulling him deeper into the slowly moving water. Walking through the water wasn't quite excruciatingly painful, but it was far from pleasant. However, I knew that having water moving past our legs was the only way I could tell Lucas what I needed to tell him. It would be the only way I could do what I needed to do if Lucas agreed. Carlita had said so—and I was prone to trusting Oracles. Especially if they also had a drag queen persona.

Finally, once we were standing knee deep in the water, the pants of our legs soaked and our feet freezing as we stood on the smooth pebbles under our feet, I turned to Lucas. He mimicked my action as my hand slid out of his. Reaching out, I put a hand behind his head and pulled him down to me, placing my lips gently against his. Lucas seemed unsure of what was going on, but his lips met mine. And when I finally pulled away, the confusion was replaced with happiness as his eyes fluttered open to look at me.

"I love you," I said.

"I love you, too."

"No." I shook my head. "I've loved you for nearly twelve years, Lucas. I've loved you since we were...I guess, *boyfriends*...before I left for Hollywood. You kind of know that part. But I've loved you since we decided the only way to be safe was for me to disappear."

"Wha—"

"Since before we decided that I should use magic to make us safe. I've loved you that long, Lucas."

Lucas just stared at me, his face etched with worry.

"I've loved you since we made love in the woods behind Oma's house when we were sixteen—the night before I left for Hollywood." I felt my throat clenching up. "I've loved you since Jason and his pack were trying to recruit you. I've loved you since I told you about the Kobolds in Oma's house when we were sixteen, and you weren't even unnerved. I've loved everything about you since we first met."

"Rob..."

"Do you want to remember how long you've loved me?" I asked gently.

"When?"

"A few nights ago."

"How?"

"I won't tell you." I shook my head slowly. "Unless you want to have your memories back. If you don't want your memories back, then we will act like this never happened. We will go back up there—"

I pointed towards shore.

"—put on our socks and shoes, finish our romantic walk, then go home and make love all night." I continued. "But I want you to make the decision for yourself which thing you want to do. Because I don't want to force you one way or the other. Having your memories back can put us both in more danger. Not having your memories could put us in danger. And, who knows, maybe having your memories back will make you go whack-a-do. I don't have the answers to any questions that might be flooding through your mind. But I have your memories. If you want them."

"Where?"

I tapped a finger against my head.

"Those are your memories." He whispered.

"I brought yours with me," I said. "Just like I promised I'd do. Ten years ago. When we promised that everything was temporary and I would come back. I will never break a promise to you."

Lucas stared at me for the space of several breaths, then his arms rose, and he took my hands in his. He looked down at his hands holding mine, both of us chilled to the bone, though we couldn't concentrate on the cold. I waited as patiently as I could as Lucas looked at our hands in the near darkness, only the moon shining down on us, then he finally looked up.

"Why didn't you tell me you got our memories back?"

"I didn't know how much danger it would put you in," I said apologetically. "I didn't know if telling you would make things better or worse. But now I know that either way we may be fucked. And I knew it was your choice to decide if you want to know everything you're supposed to and be fucked, or be ignorant and fucked."

The corner of Lucas' mouth turned up.

"Are all the memories happy?" He asked, reticently.

"The ones about us are."

That was the best answer I had.

No one has only good memories.

"Will they make me feel differently about you?" He was chewing at his lip.

That made my heart soar—but I would not be distracted from the task at hand. Lucas had to make a decision.

"I don't think so," I said. "But...you can remember everything. Know me as a complete person. Then you can decide if you still feel the same about me. I'm willing to take the risk that you won't love me anymore if having your memories back is what you really want. I don't want to take away your autonomy, Lucas. I want us both to be whole people. To know each other fully. I don't want this relationship to go forward with anything but the full, unadulterated, ugly truth."

"Then, I want my memories."

"You sure?" I squeezed his hands. "I won't be mad if you don't."

"Rob," He sighed, "I want to love you and everything about you. You telling me that you don't want to take my choice away from me lets me know that this will not change how I feel about you."

I nodded and slowly slid my hands away from his.

"Will this hurt?" He asked softly, barely audible over the sounds of the gentle waves of the lake lapping towards shore.

"Just stings a bit." I smiled.

Lucas smiled back.

"Look at me," I said.

Lucas squared his shoulders and planted his feet, his eyes locking onto mine as I stared back up into his. I'd never performed magic like this before, but I somehow just knew what to do. Lucas' jaw seemed to clench as I raised my hand to lay it against the side of his head. His eyes bore into mine as I smiled up at him, hoping that he felt at ease, not scared. I didn't want Lucas to be afraid of what was to come, because I knew that it would be okay. At least, I was pretty sure that Lucas would not be sorry for the choice he made.

"Ready?" I asked gently.

His nodded as I held my hand against his head, caressing his hair under my fingers. I nodded back and took a deep breath. Below us, I could feel the water insulating us from the world, ready to sweep away anything that we might do, to hide our acts from anyone who might use it against us. Setting a werewolf on fire doesn't draw a lot of attention. Reversing a magical act would set off beacons all over the place. And there was one particular person I wanted to make sure wouldn't notice it.

With a small force of will, I concentrated on wanting Lucas' memories, where they were trapped in my brain, to be returned to him. I wanted every decision he made moving forward to be informed, not based on something he *just knew*. Just knowing things is okay, if that's how you're wired, but memories and experience help to make informed decisions. Lucas could love me all he wanted, but it couldn't be the only thing he based his decisions on.

The jolt of magic that shot from my head, down my neck, around my shoulder, and up my arm, into Lucas' skull was quick and powerful. But it was completely invisible, imperceptible—unless you were one of us. I winced at the pinching sensation that traveled like a bolt of lightning, only to find Lucas' eyes rolling back in his head. Quickly, I moved my hands to his shoulders to steady Lucas so that he would not crash into the river, thoroughly soaking and chilling himself. Lucas swayed on his feet as his eyes flicked to the back of his head, the whites of his eyes appearing to shimmy in his head as I kept him on his feet. Suddenly, he was looking at me again.

"Lucas?" I whispered.

For a split second, Lucas looked confused, as though he had no idea who he was or where he was. Then he gasped, and tears started to well in his eyes.

"Rob."

"It's me," I replied, simply.

"Oh, my God." He croaked. "I missed you so much."

I felt my eyes begin to well with tears as I reached out to pull his body into mine. But then we were both falling into the river, water gushing up around us in waves.

Chapter 12

Icy cold water gushed into my mouth and up my nose as my back slammed into the rocky river bottom. Lucas was torn away from my arms when he went flailing as well. Immediately, I began trying to spin in the water, searching him out, but I couldn't push away from the river bed. In fact, it felt like I was being shoved harder into the river floor. As my arms flailed, they found purchase on the thing holding me down. Someone's foot was on my chest, pushing into my sternum, holding me against the rocks that were digging into my shoulder blades through the layers of my coat and shirt.

Water continued to gush up my nose, but I wisely shut my mouth tightly as the boot the person was wearing attempted to crush my sternum as it held me under the water. My heartbeat was thundering in my ears as I thrashed and flailed but still could not get myself out of the water. A headache started to form as my oxygen began to be depleted. I hadn't had time to think to take a big breath before I was pushed under the water. I knew I would pass out quickly if I didn't figure out how to get out of the water and take a breath, fill my lungs with life-giving air.

With my last surge of brainpower, I wrapped my hands around the ankle of the person standing on my chest and thought: *fire*. Even underwater, the magic sparked in my hands and red and golden fire poured forth, enveloping the ankle and foot of my attacker. The person leaped away, and I pushed away from the riverbed with the last bit of strength I had.

Breaching the surface of the water was quick—we had been standing in less than two feet of water—and I gasped loudly, water flying in all directions as I flailed. I continued to suck in air as I whipped my head around, sending droplets of water flying off of my head and body in a million directions. Screaming and the light cast by the fire caught my attention, and I whipped my head around, anger rising up within me. A man who I had never seen before was dancing around in the water, fire dancing up his leg as he did his best to extinguish it. But neither the slapping of his hands against his leg or the water itself would put it out. Water doesn't extinguish fire if it's started with magic.

I rose to my feet in the water as the man's eyes locked on mine, pleading with me to make the fire stop. Instead of feeling pity for the man's agonizing shrieks and the fear and pain quite obviously displayed on his face, I felt rage. Willing more fire to the palm of my hand, I stared into the man's eyes as they grew wide at the sight of me holding fire in my palm. Then I shoved my hand in his direction and fire shot out in a pillar of destruction towards him. The man howled like an animal as the fire washed over his body, enveloping him in red and golden flames. The shrieking seemed to go on forever, but it wasn't long enough for me as I watched him burn, then fall to the water. The fire suddenly went out. Not because of the water, but because it had finished its job.

*"**Rob**!"*

I whipped my head around at the sound of Lucas' scream from behind me, searching out my boyfriend, wanting to make sure that he was okay.

When my eyes landed upon him, I saw that he had his own attacker. Lucas didn't have some guy trying to drown him in the shallow water of the river close to shore. In fact, I wasn't so certain that the person attacking him was actually a man. Or even human. Though the body of the thing attacking him looked human, it didn't have human hands or head, but instead, large furry paws that ended in sharp claws, and he had the head of a wolf. Lucas was facing towards me, being pulled back towards the werewolf's gaping jaws.

*"**Lucas**!"* I screamed, trying to dash through the water to help him.

The water pulled at my legs as Lucas' eyes filled with terror at what was happening to him. Before I could make my way through the water, my eyes locked on the werewolf's—and something seemed to gleam out at me, as though this thing knew precisely what it was doing. Our eyes stayed locked for a moment as I ran towards Lucas and his attacker and the werewolf froze, its teeth inches from Lucas' shoulder. A second later, the werewolf bit down, its teeth sinking into Lucas' shoulder.

Lucas screeched in pain as the bite was delivered and I gasped in shock and fear as I watched blood begin to soak the shoulder of his coat. The werewolf latched onto him quickly, and just as promptly ripped its jaws out of his flesh, then shoved him away. The werewolf watched as Lucas fell into the water, a tornado of legs and arms, trying to catch himself. There was barely time for the werewolf to look into my eyes again before my fire found him as well. I screamed with rage as I sent another pillar of fire crashing into my second victim of the night.

This time, I did not watch my victim burn. Immediately, I began racing towards Lucas, ignoring the tug of the water at my legs as I slid in next to him, and he flailed in the water. I wrapped my arms around him and pulled him up to catch a breath, both of us kneeling in the water as the werewolf burned and danced a few yards away. Lucas looked into my eyes and we shared a scared look before both pairs of our eyes were drawn towards the werewolf I had just lit up like a bonfire. For several seconds, we watched him burn, his flailing and dancing slowing down until he finally was standing like a burning mannequin before us. Then, slowly, he tipped forward, crashing face first into the water. He hit bottom and slowly rose to float on the surface of the water.

Lucas' face turned back to me as I held him. "He bit me."

"Get your coat off," I demanded, ripping at the buttons along the front. "Get it off right now."

"What the fuck, Rob?" Lucas gasped, helping me to undo the buttons of his coat. *"Why...what...how...is that Jason?"*

Desperately, I glanced up at Lucas, remembering that he now had all of his memories back.

"I don't think so." I shook my head jerkily. "The other guy I've never seen before, either."

"Are they his pack, though?" Lucas asked as we pushed his coat off of his body, and it landed in the water behind him. "Did he send them to attack us or something? Does Jason have his memory back, too?"

"No, he doesn't," I answered. "But he still doesn't care for us much."

I began pulling Lucas' shirt out of his pants, untucking it and yanking it over his head. Needing to see Lucas' bare chest really didn't matter. I had seen the rips in his coat, the torn material of his shirt, the oblong circle of blood that had soaked the shirt around his wound. He had been bitten. There was no mistaking that fact...but I just needed it confirmed.

Lucas looked down at his shoulder once I had his shirt pulled off of him and we both groaned. The bite from the werewolf was unmistakable. Teeth had definitely penetrated his flesh. Both of our faces turned up to look at each other as my hand went to his shoulder. It wasn't bleeding much, but something inside of me wanted to apply pressure. Doing anything useful when I knew there was nothing that could be done.

Lucas had been bitten by a werewolf.

We both knew what that meant.

Jason had gotten his way. One way or another.

"Rob." Lucas swallowed hard, his eyes pleading with me.

"It'll be okay." I shook my head, refusing to believe what was right before my eyes. "It'll be okay, Lucas. I swear. We'll talk to Oma. We'll talk to anybody we have to. We're not going to let this—"

"*What are you two doing?*"

Then we were both bathed in light.

Jacob Michaels Is Trouble

A Point Worth LGBTQ
Paranormal Romance
Book 5

Chapter 1

Putting myself in front of Lucas to protect him, I threw an arm over my eyes to shield them from the blinding light. Lucas didn't exactly cower behind me, but his body seemed to shrink in on itself as I shielded him. Of course, having just been bitten by a werewolf, and having what seemed to be a spotlight shining in our eyes, it was understandable that he wasn't at his best. Certainly, I wasn't going to think less of him for needing a moment to collect himself before we faced something else. One more person present for me to also use as a shield for myself would have been nice, though.

The water was freezing, though I couldn't spare worry on the iciness of the Maumee when my main concern was that we were bathed in light. We were in the icy water with two burnt-to-a-crisp dead bodies floating nearby. If there was ever a visual representation of "cluster fuck," our situation would have nailed it. I felt Lucas' hand on my side, gripping onto me for reassurance and strength as we stood there bathed in that harsh light. Unfortunately for Lucas, all I knew I was good for was being a shield. What to say or do completely eluded me.

"Fire fingers" was my next thought.

"What's going on?" I heard a voice shout from the shore again.

A very familiar voice.

"Who's there?" My voice was shaky as my arm dropped marginally so that I could glance into the beam of light. "Who are you?"

Abruptly, the beam of light lessened in strength and I could finally see that a mere high-powered flashlight of some kind was what had produced the spotlight. After a few moments of staring out beyond the less bright beam of light, I could see the shape of the shadowy figure that held it on us. Lucas' fingers clenched at my side again as I slowly lowered my arm. The outline of the person on the shore came into focus as I lowered my arm to my side, but stayed at alert in case more fire was needed.

I was in the mood for more fire.

My mind was crazed with the thought.

"What in the..."

"Rob." Lucas whispered into my ear. "Is that..."

My eyes turned to slits as the figure behind the flashlight became discernible. Jason, werewolf pack leader extraordinaire, stood on the shore of the Maumee, shining the flashlight in our direction, illuminating us as we stood prone in the icy water. One of us was bleeding and shirtless, one of us probably looked deranged with anger and power, and surely, he had spotted the two bodies floating nearby. Two choices came to mind. Lucas' fingers clenching my side, warning me, kept me from being impulsive. I didn't immediately raise my hand and aim it at Jason, though the compulsion was at the forefront of my mind.

"Jason." The word carried heat as it left my lips, but it was a struggle not to shiver as I stood there in the icy water with Lucas.

"Who are those people?" Jason's eyes were wide, nearly horrified as he took in the scene before him.

Unsurprisingly, a thought seemed to come to Jason as he stood on the shore, holding us within the beam of his flashlight. That confused and horrified look slowly started to change, the corners of his mouth slowly turning upward until he looked like the Grinch. When his eyes landed on mine, practically staring into my soul as Lucas stood behind me, I knew we were fucked. Jason had found us in the most compromising of positions, and only one thing would get us out of it. I started to raise my hand.

"*Rob.*" Lucas whisper-hissed, his fingers clutching at my wrist. "*Don't.*"

"Seems you boys have been up to no good." Jason grinned evilly, his eyes practically twinkling in the dark. "No good at all."

Glancing angrily down at the fingers clenched around my wrist, it was all I could do to keep myself from screaming obscenities at Jason or yanking my arm free to send a column of fire in his direction. Lucas' fingers squeezed my wrist firmly, yet lovingly, trying to keep me from doing something that might make our situation even worse. Of course, when I thought about it, burning Jason to a crisp would solve the third problem. Problem number one and number two were slowly starting to float towards shore. Keeping my eyes on Jason instead of the dead bodies floating toward him was an insane exercise of self-control. Visions of fire and a desire to create more destruction continued to assault my mind, speed my pulse, hurry my breathing. Lucas' fingers around my wrist were the only things keeping me from going completely around the bend while we stood in the beam of light.

"Why are you here?" I demanded.

Jason gave an amused snort, the beam of light jiggling.

"Is that really what you want to ask me?" Came his reply. "Don't you think you ought to get out of the *freezing-fucking-river* before you lose a toe first?"

Considering this for a moment, my first thought was to tell Jason how to apply suction to a particular part of my anatomy—only metaphorically, of course—yet I knew he was right, no matter how much I hated to admit it. Lucas was ashen-faced when I glanced over my shoulder at him. The pain, loss of blood, and cold were doing nothing for the love of my life. In fact, my pride was going to turn into the cause for one of us losing a toe to frostbite. Lucas' teeth were chattering when I glanced over my shoulder at him, so I had nothing else to do but swallow down my rage and take a shaky step towards the shore.

Lucas' hand slid down my wrist so that his fingers could slide between mine, holding onto me like a life raft as we headed towards shore. Jason lowered the flashlight to point at the water so that it wasn't in our eyes any longer, and we quickly made our way out of the water. Both of the dead, original recipe men were beached by the gentle waves caused by the early Spring breeze, but we avoided them, averting our eyes from my handiwork. Or, my craftiness, I guess.

Jason grinned evilly and started to speak, but I silenced him with a glare, though the grin didn't disappear. Doing my best to ignore the smug asshole standing next to us on the shore, I knelt next to Lucas and grabbed his socks. His hands went to my shoulders to steady himself as I struggled to get his socks on over his cold, wet feet. Once Lucas' feet were covered up, I quickly pulled my socks and shoes on, glaring over at Jason as I worked. Then I was back on my feet and pulling Lucas into me, though holding my boyfriend against my wet, cold body was doing nothing to help bring his body temperature back up.

"You two are morons," Jason stated, the flashlight dangling from at side, casting the ground next to him in a halo of yellow. "You're both freezing. Wet. He's bleeding all over you. Neither of you has made a move to get out of here and go back to your car. And your two murder victims are right. fucking. there."

"Rob was defending us." Lucas' teeth chattered as I held him to me.

That statement gave me pause. Lucas was right, that I had been defending us and not just wantonly setting men...*werewolves* on fire...just for the hell of it. However...*Rob. Rob did it.* He didn't include himself in the reason for the men's deaths. Shaking my head to chase that thought away, I turned my attention to Lucas' bite, which was still seeping blood. The seeping had slowed considerably, probably from how cold his body was, but it had not completely abated. I pressed a hand against Lucas' chest where the teeth of the werewolf had entered, then attempted to press against the ones on his back with my other hand.

How to treat a bite wound from a werewolf was not exactly part of my repertoire, but I knew that putting pressure on a bleeding wound was usually the best thing to do. Lucas grunted and winced slightly as I pushed against both sides of the wound, hoping that the bleeding would stop on its own. Causing Lucas further pain was not optimal, but of course, he had no idea how to treat a werewolf bite either, so he wasn't offering alternatives. The fact that an actual, live werewolf was standing next to us flooded my mind.

"What do we do?" I half growled, half pleaded with Jason, though my eyes stayed on my hands covering Lucas' wounds.

"There's nothing you can do." Jason was rolling his eyes—I knew it without looking at him. "He got bit. He's gonna turn, dumbass."

"I'm talking about the blood, you fucking—"

"Rob." Lucas stopped me. "What are we going to do? We need to get to the hospital. Or something"

"Jeeez-zus." Jason groaned. "The bleeding will stop on its own. Our saliva helps our bites heal quicker—unless we decide to bite enough that even our saliva can't help it. It makes it easier for us to turn others without worrying about accidentally bleeding them out. By morning you might not even be able to tell you were ever bitten."

"Until the next full moon," I mumbled angrily under my breath as I pulled my hands away from Lucas' chest and back and twined the fingers of my right hand through his.

"Let's just get out of here." Lucas ignored Jason's comments, though they had to soothe his worry a little.

"And go where, assbags?" Jason snorted, strolling grandly over to the shore to shine the flashlight on the beached and burnt bodies. "Are you just going to leave the evidence lying around like a couple of amateurs?"

Lucas' teeth chattered as he gripped my hand tightly, his eyes piercing into mine. I squeezed his hand, trying to reassure him before I turned to Jason. He was pushing at one of the bodies with the toe of his right shoe, making a disgusted face and noises that matched.

"What do you suggest, Jason?" Lucas' fingers squeezed mine. "Apparently you feel you have more expertise about what to do with dead bodies, so—"

"You're going to have to weight 'em down and get 'em further out into the river. Or take 'em out onto the lake. Or you're going to have to drag 'em out and hide 'em somewhere else." He shrugged. Finally, he crouched down and grabbed a handful of hair from one of the bodies and lifted it with a sickening wet sound so that he could examine the dead guy's face. "Not one of mine."

"Wouldn't you know if one of your pack members had come to try and kill me and turn Lucas?" I snapped. "Or are you not able to keep your puppies in line?"

Jason laughed, curiously not in an angry way.

"My boys have gotten a little unruly lately."

"Why are you even here?" I demanded, sliding my hand out of Lucas' in case I needed it as I took a step towards Jason. "How did you know we would be out here?"

"I didn't." Jason stood up, affecting a bored expression as he turned his head to look at me. "I didn't know anything until I followed you to that club to watch the drag show. Then I followed you here. So, I didn't *know* anything until I followed you out here. Obviously, you exceeded my expectations. I thought I'd catch you two lovebirds out here giving each other Handy J's by the romantic light of the moon, but—"

"You're disgusting." Lucas chattered behind me.

"—you came out here to kill two guys and...then, I guess give each other Handy J's or something."

"You sure you're not mixed with pig instead of wolf?" I asked blandly.

Jason chuckled evilly, his eyes looking hooded in the moonlight as he stared Lucas and me down. I could practically hear my boyfriend's teeth chattering behind me as I kept my eyes on Jason, wondering what his plan was now that he had found us. Why had he followed us out onto the peninsula anyway? Now that he had and he found out what had happened when we found ourselves out there alone and two werewolves from a different pack had attacked us, what would he do with that information? How much had he seen? Did he see Lucas and I standing in the water, Lucas getting his memories back? What was he going to do with any of the information he might have?

I felt my arm start to raise.

The water.

I had made Lucas stand in the running water when I had given him back his memories for a reason.

Was it safe to do much magic on the shore?

Slowly, my arm sank back to my side. My palm itched and burned with unused magic. The genie had been let out of the lamp and did not want to go back inside for long. Lucas must have sensed my desire to harm Jason—not that it would have taken a genius, especially now that he had his memories back—because he stepped up behind me and twined his fingers through mine once again. Lucas gave me a nervous yet loving smile as I glanced over my shoulder. Jason just stared impassively at us as the flashlight beam shone at his feet.

"What is it with you guys?" I barked at Jason. "Do any of you have   fucking   manners?"

That made Jason smile.

"I don't even know why we're still standing here looking at you, let alone talking to you." I continued. "Obviously, I need to get Lucas home and—"

"And leave two dead bodies beached on the bank of the Maumee that could easily be tied back to the two of you?" Jason's eyebrows raised precipitously. "Is that your plan?"

"How could they be tied to us?" Lucas asked suddenly. "We don't even know who they are."

Jason glanced at the dead bodies.

"Bet it'll take a couple days to identify them." He shrugged, looking back over at us. "But I imagine they're carrying identification of some kind. So, it probably won't take a few seconds for the police to figure it out. And you were just going to leave them here for the police to do just that. You two really are stupid."

"Why do you care?" I snapped.

"Because," Jason replied evenly, "you killed two shifters on my pack lands. So, that shit's going to come down on me first and foremost. And they won't care if I know who *really* killed them, will they?"

"They?" Lucas asked, stepping up to stand by my side, his fingers still laced through mine. "Who's *they*?"

"The Council," I answered at the same time Jason did, which made him smile evilly at me.

"They'll have my ass and then come for yours." Jason shrugged. "Because I'm not going to lie for you. Not if this is how you want things to play out, anyway."

Lucas' fingers tightened, squeezing my hand.

"Why are you here?" I asked again.

The grin that flowered on Jason's face begged to be slapped right off of it. With a two-by-four.

"Problems follow you wherever you go, Jacob Michaels." He said.

"Rob. Wagner." I spoke through clenched teeth.

"Rob. Jacob. Tits McGuinness—whatever you want to call yourself." He snorted. "Everywhere you go, trouble follows. It was here when you were in high school...and now it's back. I have no fucking idea what is going on, but I know something is wrong. And it has something to do with you."

"You couldn't have said something when I was at your house the other night?" I spat.

"You were at his house?" Lucas peeped.

"I hadn't quite put two-and-two together then." Jason glanced at Lucas; then his eyes were back on me. "But it finally dawned on me. You were trouble before. Every time I ran into you, it was a fucking shitshow.

Then you disappeared suddenly and things…things changed…now they're changing back. I want to know what the fuck is going on, *Rob Wagner*, and what it means for my fucking pack. Are my guys in danger?"

"If they keep fucking with me, yeah." I sneered.

Jason started to step forward, so I raised my hand. He stopped moving but didn't look happy about it. Lucas' fingers clenched my other hand as Jason and I glowered at each other, both of us ready to tear the other limb from limb. So…Jason didn't have all of his memories, but he was, surprisingly, smart enough to take notice of things changing around him. Apparently, magic could mask problems but not completely solve them. Not when you had a werewolf with more curiosity than brains.

"What have you been up to, Rob?" Jason demanded, ignoring my threat. "I thought maybe you just came to my house the other night—"

"Why were you at his house?" Lucas asked again.

I held a finger up to him, pleading with my boyfriend with my eyes.

"—because maybe…well, whatever." Jason looked away for a second, conveying everything he was thinking without saying another word. "But then it came to me. You know—when you made my sink explode? Jacob Michaels is trouble."

"For the last time," I growled. "My name is Rob Wagner."

"A rose by any other name." Jason spat back.

Lucas was tugging at my arm. I turned to look at him, all pale and troubled, his fingers clenching at mine.

"What?" I asked as gently as possible.

"Why were you at his house?"

Jason snorted derisively, which made me shoot him a glare.

"To give him money for Katie's funeral." I turned back to Lucas quickly. "You know, that woman who wandered up in the yard naked and burned up? Then he tried to put the moves on me, and I made his sink explode."

It took Lucas a second, but a grin slowly bloomed on his face.

Oh, yeah.

My boyfriend knows things.

Probably, like, if someone is lying.

And he knew I wasn't.

"Whatever." Jason snarled. "You're a fucking disaster zone. And there's two bodies right here that prove it."

Lucas and I smiled at each other a moment longer, and then I turned back to Jason, my glower in full force.

"What do you suggest, doggy?" I waggled my head at him, refusing to let go of Lucas' hand. "I have bigger problems than two dead bodies. Lucas got bit, and that means—"

"I know what the fuck it means." Jason interrupted angrily. "I think out of the three people standing here, I have the best understanding of what being bit means, asshole. But he's not going to turn at the next full moon, so why don't you stop shitting in your shoes and focus on the real problem. Dead. Bodies. Two of 'em."

"I thought the problem was that I'm trouble?"

"That'll be the next issue we'll address." He glared at me. "Trust me."

My body jerked towards Jason automatically out of anger, but Lucas pulled me back.

"What do you mean?" Lucas asked quickly. "Why won't I turn at the full moon?"

"It takes a couple of lunar cycles to kick in," Jason answered Lucas, though his eyes stayed on me. "Making magic is hard work, isn't it?"

I just glowered back.

"How many?" Lucas asked quickly.

Jason stared at me a moment longer, then rolled his eyes and turned his attention to Lucas.

"Two or three." He sighed. "Three is the most I've ever seen."

"Well, what determines how long it will—"

"Ladies!" Jason boomed. "This isn't a coffee klatch. I'm not here to answer your stupid ass questions about your bite. It ain't from one of mine, so I really don't give a shit if you turn or not."

"What does that mean?" I brought Jason's attention back to me.

"Your boyfriend there turns?" Jason grinned evilly and jabbed a finger at Lucas. "His pack is going to come looking for him. And I have no idea what pack these guys belong to—so...good luck with that."

"Fuck." I stomped my foot.

Lucas stammered. "How will they know? I mean, those guys are dead now. Rob killed them. So, who is going to tell them?"

My eyed twitched at Lucas' proclamation once more. Again, he had laid sole blame for what had happened on me. How he would hold up in a court of law if someone did find out about the two dead bodies ran through my mind. Was my boyfriend the "plea deal" type or the "ride-or-die-bitch" type?

What all didn't I know about Lucas?

"He'd make a horrible pack member," I added. "He's a vegetarian."

Jason grinned.

"I don't think that matters right now, Rob." Lucas snapped, though he couldn't put any anger behind it.

"Yeah," Jason smirked. "We'll see when the cravings come."

Lucas made a retching noise. By the time I had turned to him, he was doubled over in the opposite direction, the contents of his stomach spilling out onto the inky ground below. I kept my eyes on Jason, but slowly rubbed Lucas' back as he vomited what looked like a week's worth of meals onto the shore of the Maumee. Jason rolled his eyes at us, then turned his back and crouched down next to one of the bodies beside his feet. Since he wasn't watching us, I felt better taking my eyes off of him.

Rubbing on Lucas' back as he puked made my stomach turn, especially when the smell wafted up to my nostrils, but I steeled myself and played the stoic boyfriend who was immune to being grossed out. It seemed to go on forever, but finally, Lucas' stomach stopped expelling its contents, and he slowly straightened up. He practically fell into me, his arms wrapped around my middle as I held him against me. Whether I liked it about myself or not, I was embarrassed that Jason saw my boyfriend being scared. I didn't want him to think that Lucas was weak. Also, I couldn't help but think about how I wished Lucas had rinsed his mouth first.

"Fuck, Rob." Lucas whimpered into my ear.

"It'll be okay, babe." I rubbed his back gently as he held me. "It'll be okay. We'll talk to Oma. We'll figure something out. Maybe there's—"

"Well," Jason interrupted again, "you guys lucked out. There's not a single thing in either of these guys' pockets. Unless their wallets fell out while they were still in the water, I guess. But the odds of that happening to both of them would be pretty low, so I'm guessing they don't have I.D. with them."

"Could you give us a second?" I barked.

"Sure." Jason stood and gave an exaggerated smile and nod of his head. "Let's take our time dealing with the evidence of your crime here."

"Rob was defending us." Lucas managed to mumble loudly into my neck.

God, I hoped his mouth wasn't covered in puke.

"It was self-defense." I clarified.

"If they'd been shot, sure." Jason shrugged, bending down again to one of the bodies. "These guys look like they've been tortured. Unless you want to show the cops your little laser hands there, give 'em a display, I don't think they're going to believe this was self-defense, Rob."

Whether I liked it or not, Jason was right. The scene did not scream "self-defense," and there was no way that the police would believe in magic. Or that the bite on Lucas was from a werewolf—if it was still there when we talked to them. Also, if I started shooting fire out of my hands, the cops would probably just shoot me and ask questions later.

"Fine." I relented. "Now what?"

Jason was yanking something out of one of the bodies' hands.

"Well," Jason sighed, "this is part of your boyfriend's shirt."

He held a scrap of cloth towards us. Lucas pulled away from my neck and let go of me slowly. We both just stared at the scrap of fabric in Jason's hand; both of us aware that it was indeed part of Lucas' shirt.

"I'm betting there's other forensic evidence here," Jason added, then smiled. "I sound like I should be on one of those procedural cop shows or something, huh?"

"Why are you here, Jason?" I demanded.

"Right now, I'm helping you decide how to cover up murder." Jason spat. "At least, that's the way the cops will see it. After that, we can get back to our little talk about what the fuck is going on with you and the bullshit that hovers over you like a nuclear cloud."

Swallowing hard, I refused to respond.

"So," Jason tossed the cloth, which Lucas caught, examined for a moment, then shoved into his pocket, "I'm going to take your two friends here and dump them. The pack lands are full of wooded areas. These guys don't have I.D.; I don't know who they are, no one but us three knows what happened here—I don't think anyone is going to find out about this anytime soon. In fact, no one may ever come looking for these guys. They don't exactly look like they were the deacons of their churches, so maybe no one will even miss them."

"How kind." I frowned.

"Kinder than what you did." Jason retorted. "Why don't you take your boyfriend home and kiss his boo-boos for him? We'll talk later."

"Listen here, you piece of—" Jason smiled wickedly as I started to move towards him again.

"Rob." Lucas jerked at my hand firmly. "Let's just go. Please. You guys can fight later."

Turning to Lucas, I saw the desperation in his eyes, his desire to get off of the peninsula and into the car in front of the heater to warm up, and forget about our night. At least, the best he could after having been bitten by a werewolf. I wanted to tell Lucas that Jason would probably just screw us over if we left him with the dead bodies, but then I remembered that Lucas knew things. If he felt safe leaving Jason and the bodies alone, he must have known how things would turn out. The fact that it didn't worry him made me feel less nervous about leaving.

"Fine." I replied gently to Lucas, then over my shoulder: "We'll fight later."

"Bet your ass." Jason snickered.

My hand was raised in a one-finger salute over my shoulder as I let Lucas lead me away from the shore of the Maumee. Jason's flashlight beam bobbled in the distance as Lucas and I walked away quickly, putting distance between us and the biggest clusterfuck imaginable. Getting Lucas into the car and turning on the heat for him was all I cared about at that moment. That, and getting back home so we could get clean and put on dry clothes.

Chapter 2

Lucas had his hand on top of mine as it laid on his chest and the hot water cascaded over us. Steam filled the shower and was spilling over the top of the shower wall into the bathroom. Green, gilded-jade eyes were locked on mine as the flesh of my palm stayed against the raw bite wounds on his chest. Already, I could tell that they were healing. The puncture wounds from each individual tooth were not as deep as they had been. They weren't as red and angry looking as when we had first entered Lucas' house. Lucas didn't seem to notice nearly as much as I did, but I was also concerned that he might be in shock from everything that had happened throughout our evening.

The attack had come so suddenly, out of nowhere, he hadn't even had the chance to process the sudden return of his memories. A werewolf was chomping down on his shoulder before he could even think about what all of those memories meant. Before he could even mentally sort through all of the events of his past that had been stripped from his consciousness. Then he was watching two guys get burnt to a crisp. Then he was bleeding and freezing and bathed in a flashlight beam. Everything had gone to shit, and there was no way that my boyfriend had been able to take it all in without going a little cuckoo in the process.

Right?

"Rob." Lucas leaned forward to lay his forehead against mine. "Thank you for saving me."

"Did I?" I asked, chewing at my lip.

Lucas looked up at me, his eyes boring into mine for a moment, then he gently kissed me on the lips.

"You stopped him before he could do worse." He sighed against my mouth.

"I didn't save you, Lucas." I shook my head jerkily. "All he wanted to do was bite you. He did that."

"He might have—"

"If he had wanted to kill you, he would have." I stopped him. "He was looking to turn you. I didn't save you."

Lucas stared at me as he kept my hand held against his chest and water poured over us, creating sheets of liquid warmth over our bodies. Against my desires, I was aroused, and I could feel that Lucas was feeling the same way. Standing there in the shower with my hand against his relatively fresh wound made me feel anything but aroused inside, though. Sex was the furthest thing from my mind. All I could think about was that wound that one day would mean so much more to both of us.

"I wasn't fast enough." My head was still shaking remorsefully. "You shouldn't have been bitten."

"Shhh." Lucas pressed his lips against mine once more. "Rob. You can't protect me from everything. And I can't protect you from everything either."

"Then what?" I asked after another gentle kiss. "This is my fault. If I had just left you alone..."

"Do you really wish you had *left me alone*?"

"No," I said. "I just don't want you hurt. And you've been hurt. I'm trouble, Lucas. Jason wasn't wrong."

"You must be upset if you're agreeing with him."

The attempt at humor was half-hearted at best.

"I remember everything, Rob." Lucas' forehead was against mine again. "You can't convince me that everything is your fault anymore. If this had happened last night...maybe...but not now. And if you hadn't given me back my memories, you would have lied to me."

"I know, but—"

"You promised you'd come back." Lucas gave me a sharp look. "And you brought my memories with you. You did exactly what you said you would do, babe. No more. No less. You did nothing wrong."

"It feels like everything I do is wrong." I sighed, the sound of the water nearly drowning out my words. "Coming back to Ohio was bad, Lucas. We both know it. If I had known when I got into my car to drive here what I know now, then..."

Lucas just stared into my eyes, his hand still over mine as it rested against his chest. I sighed and slumped forward, my forehead falling against his again as I considered what a mess I had made of everything over the last several weeks. Hell, the last decade. Everything that I had done in the last ten years was going to come back to bite everyone in the proverbial—and maybe literal—ass. All I had done was cause confusion and chaos—delayed the inevitable. There was no way that I would be able to keep Lucas from getting hurt in the process. The bite on his chest was proof enough. I slid my hand out from under his and let it drop to my side.

"Why did you take me out into the Maumee to talk to me, Rob?" He asked softly, just audible above the water. "Was it to shield the magic?"

"Sh," I stated quickly, though it lacked energy. "Yes."

"Does it have to be a natural body of water?" He asked.

Frowning to myself, I moved my head so that I could look my boyfriend in the eyes again. The corner of Lucas' mouth was turned upward, and he glanced at the showerhead.

"I...I don't know," I said cautiously. "I didn't even know that running water did that until...someone...told me."

"But now I have my memories back," Lucas said. "That's all that matters."

"I guess." I shrugged, staring into those curious green eyes.

"Do you want me to show you something amazing?" Lucas grinned.

I wanted to frown—getting frisky seemed inappropriate, all things from our night considered—but a smile crept to my face instead. Anything amazing that Lucas wanted to show me, I wanted to see it. Of course, I had seen everything on Lucas—and it was all amazing—but he seemed to be implying that he had something amazing hidden away for a special occasion. What better time to pull a trick out of the bag than when I needed cheering up?

"What?" I asked, my voice huskier than usual. "What is it?"

"Give me your hand."

My smile widened, and I lifted my hand once more. Lucas laid his palm against the back of my hand and pulled the palm of my hand against the bite wounds on his chest once more.

"Before they have time to heal," Lucas said.

"Okay..."

"This might feel weird." Lucas turned his eyes to mine.

"Huh?"

"Do you trust me?"

"Of course." I frowned. "I trust you with everything I have, Lucas."

A smile bloomed on his face a mere fraction of a second before it felt like someone was tugging my skin on my arm. Instinctively, I started to jerk back, but Lucas kept my hand held to his chest. My eyes grew wide as I stared into his. He wasn't pulling at my hand or my arm, and nothing was trying to pull the skin off of me. Something was being sapped from me.

My magic.

I didn't know how I knew that was what was happening. Something inside of me, something ancient and primal told me instinctively.

Lucas stared into my eyes, trying to wordlessly comfort me as dull green light leeched out around the seal our hands created on his chest. Bit by bit, the light seemed to glow brighter and brighter, filling the shower, then the bathroom, growing brighter until all I could see was that green light. I couldn't even see Lucas inches in front of me, but I could feel his hand holding mine tightly to his chest.

Lucas was drawing magic out of me and into his wound.

A gasp escaped my mouth, but I couldn't see Lucas. I was blinded by the green light that was so bright that I finally had to shut my eyes or risk going blind. Wincing, I didn't fight Lucas holding my hand against his chest as my magic leeched out of me and into the wound. I didn't know if him drawing magic from me was just a matter of "borrowing" or "taking." Would the thing he was doing steal my magic from me, or was he just...*using it*?

What the fuck?

Lucas knows how to use magic?

Why didn't I remember this?

I had my memories, too.

When it no longer felt like my skin was being tugged at, I let my eyes open to slits. The green light was slowly fading, and Lucas' form was coming back into view, the falling water starting to become visible as well. Slowly, I let my eyes open at a pace with the light fading away, creeping back to hide away beneath our hands against Lucas' chest. My eyes went to my boyfriend's—and for the briefest of moments, they were not green. They were brown. Lucas stared back as the light slid back under our hands, then he slid his hand off of the top of mine.

He blinked.

His eyes were green once more.

They hadn't changed to brown and back to green for real. It was a vision. Like my boyfriend, sometimes I just knew things.

I just stared at Lucas, my hand still held against his chest, neither of us saying a word. Finally, I let my hand slide from his wet skin as the water continued to cascade down around us.

"Your eyes," I said.

"They weren't always green," Lucas said.

I nodded as though that was the most rational thing I had ever heard in my entire life and turned my attention to his chest. There was absolutely no evidence that he had been bitten. His skin was intact. Perfect. Just as it had been before. I didn't bother staring since I knew I wasn't seeing an illusion, nor was I confused or crazy.

"You know magic."

"I know how to *use* magic," Lucas spoke in a small voice. "I have none of my own."

"Did you...*take*...some from me?"

"No." He shook his head softly. "Just borrowed it. I promise."

Nodding again, I glanced at his chest for the briefest of moments.

"Did you just heal the wounds, or..."

"I was never going to turn into a werewolf, Rob."

My eyes shot back to his.

"But we don't want Jason to know that." He gave a cautious smile. "If those guys weren't his pack...then we need to know who they were, right? If they think I'm going to turn...maybe they'll show up. Right? If they really were his pack, and he's lying to us, we need him to believe that they did what they set out to do."

My head nodded of its own accord again.

"Would you have turned into a werewolf if you hadn't just done that?" I asked gently.

"No."

"Why not?"

He shrugged. "I'm immune."

"I can't nod again," I said it aloud. "This is weird. Even for me, babe. Why don't I have this memory? Why don't I know this about you?"

"I never told you." Lucas turned his eyes from mine. "I've never told anyone. Except...grandpa."

"Right." I shrugged.

The water was slowly getting cooler. We were using up all of the water in the hot water tank.

"Don't be upset."

"I'm not upset." I shook my head. "I'm...confused. Why wouldn't you tell me, Lucas?"

With a sigh, he reached behind himself and shut off the now cold water, then he turned back to me, and his hand went to my chest.

"You're not the only one here who's trouble, Rob." He sounded defeated. "And I didn't tell you because I didn't want to make more trouble for you. Not back then. There was already...so much. And I would have told you as soon as you came back, but..."

"You weren't yourself."

"I wasn't myself." He agreed.

"You seemed to think you were going to be a werewolf earlier." I frowned. "I mean, you upchucked all over the place."

Lucas cringed. "Not because I thought *that*...I just couldn't imagine having cravings for meat. Especially human meat or something."

Together, we stood in the shower, which was no longer running, and stared at each other, slowly getting cold without the hot water to keep us warm. It was probably less than a minute that we stood there, staring at each other, with Lucas' hand against my chest, but it felt much longer.

When I could no longer take the silence and curiosity, my lips parted once more.

"Is tonight the night we unpack everything?" I asked gently. "Or...do we want to make love for only the second time as two people who have loved each other for a very long time—and actually remember it?"

Lucas' expression softened further.

"I remember that night." He choked out. "You were so brave."

"So were you."

"I really thought I'd never see you again, Rob." He gave a pained sigh. "Will you hate me forever if I tell you that I let you go into that basement, truly believing that you were lying about coming back to me?"

I shook my head slowly.

"*There is no way he is going to come back for me,*" Lucas whispered. "That was the last thought I remember having. I thought you lied to me to make me not be sad to see you go. It didn't make me hate you. It just made me sad anyway. And, maybe, a little proud. You were my boyfriend, and you were going to take that risk..."

"I was proud to be your boyfriend," I replied. "I *am* proud to be your boyfriend."

"I missed you so fucking much, Rob."

"Oma kept an eye on you." I smiled gently. "But I missed you so fucking much, too."

He smiled. "She did, didn't she? I think...I mean, I'm not sure...but I think I wanted to be around her because something inside of me told me that being around her meant that I would know as soon as you got back. Or at least, pretty quickly after."

"I guess that was something you just knew." I teased. "And you were right."

"I don't think I ever really forgot you." He said. "At least, my body didn't. Maybe my mind was scrubbed, but something way too deep to be scrubbed away didn't forget you. It never would have forgotten you."

"Hey," I said, "if you're trying to get into my pants, I don't even have them on, babe."

Lucas laughed and glanced down.

"We should probably get out of the shower." His eyebrow raised. "It's kind of cold in here."

I glanced down at my junk.

"Hey!" I leaned forward quickly, wrapping my arms around him.

Lucas did his best to pretend to get away, but my lips found every inch of his face as I kissed him over and over and he laughed uproariously there in the cocoon created by my arms around him. Maybe we had some unpacking to do. Eventually. But Lucas had his memories back. And he wasn't actually going to turn into a furry, fearsome creature at the next full moon. Unpacking could wait until after we had taken time to become familiar with each other's bodies again. Now that we both remembered them fully.

The room was cold.

Bitterly cold.

And I had no memory of the room.

But that didn't keep me from opening my eyes to find that I was lying on the bed in the middle of the room.

It wasn't apparent at first, due to my confusion at waking up in a strange room, chilled to my bones, but I wasn't even in Lucas' house. In fact, I wasn't sure whose house I was in, actually. The room did not look familiar—but it looked somewhat familiar at the same time. Maybe because it looked like a child's bedroom—the dark shape of an overflowing bookcase in the corner. A desk for homework along one wall. A toy chest that was overflowing. Cartoon sheets of some kind that I had kicked off in my sleep.

With my child-sized feet.

I gazed down at my body only to find that I was not staring at my body but that of a child—or a very young teen. Maybe a tween? This revelation should have sent a shock of terror up my spine, but I was getting used to the odd things in my life. Instead of screaming out in shock or panicking in any way, I sat up cautiously and swiveled my hips to let my legs dangle off of the side of the bed. Giving a quick glance around the room, looking for any sign of danger, I lowered myself to the floor.

Icy cold floorboards slapped against my feet, and I winced, though I made no noise. It was dark, I had no idea where I was, and there was no way for me to know if there was anyone else in the house. Would someone come to investigate if they heard me? And if someone did come to investigate, would they be dangerous? Harm me in some way? I let my feet adjust to the cold of the floorboards as I scanned the room slowly with my eyes.

Just a typical tween's room.

Nothing unusual.

Other than the darkness.

Nothing looks normal in the dark.

As I stood there, my feet adjusting to the cold and my eyes adjusting to the darkness, my ears began to pick up the voices.

Beyond the door positioned at the opposite side of the room, someone was talking. Low and rumbly, the voices sounded muffled and hollow. My feet began to move without me willing it, and I found myself being drawn towards the bedroom door. The cold was pervasive, making my feet—well, the feet I now had—feel like blocks of ice. It pushed through the cotton of the pajamas I was wearing. It slid over and around my body, doing its best to compel me back into bed. To forget the voices and the door.

Suddenly, I found myself in front of the door, my hands reaching out to brace myself against it as my ear moved towards the cold, smooth wood. My ear connected with the icy surface, trying to hear the voices better. To try and figure out what it was they were saying.

The voices became louder with my ear pressed against the door, but I still couldn't make out what it was they were saying. After a few moments, listening to what sounded like two voices quarreling or, maybe, debating, I crouched down next to the doorknob. I leveled my eye to the keyhole and looked through into the room beyond.

What I saw...was I really seeing this?

In the room beyond, seemingly lit by fire or candlelight was a pile of raw bones, gleaming white and splattered with blood. Sat upon what could only be described as the "throne" of bones was a hooded figure.

I knew that figure.

As if he knew I was watching, the hooded figure's head turned towards the door.

Red eyes peered out of the hood and into the keyhole.

Then I was falling backward.

"Wake up, babe." Lucas' voice sounded muffled. "You're having a dream, Rob."

Red filled my vision as my eyes flew open, and I jerked awake in bed. A second later, the ceiling of Lucas' bedroom came into view, illuminated by early morning sunlight streaming in through the windows. Jerkily, I looked around, checking the room for the hooded figure and those red eyes and the throne of bones. All I found was Lucas, in bed next to me, propped up on his elbow, smiling down at me like I was a dullard.

"Good morning, crazy." He smiled wickedly.

"What the..."

"Bad dream?" He suggested.

Again, I found myself glancing around the room, making sure that I was really in Lucas' bed, and the sun had washed away the darkness of the dream. Lingering in the back of my mind, I could practically see the room like an aura superimposed over the view of Lucas' bedroom in his house. My first instinct was to tell Lucas about the dream, to explain how it made me feel. Something in the back of my mind told me that doing so would sound crazy. At the very least, it would not be received well. So, I kept my mouth shut, closed my eyes tightly and shook my head gently, clearing my vision, and chasing away the thought of the dream.

"You okay, babe?" Lucas had a furrowed brow when I opened my eyes.

"Yeah." I gave a shaky sigh, then smiled. "Weird dreams because of a weird night, I guess."

Lucas grinned. "It wasn't all weird. Some of it was good."

"There were some pretty good parts." I agreed, propping myself up on my elbow so that my lips could reach his. "Did you sleep well?"

"I always sleep well with you beside me, Rob."

The expression on his face let me know how stupid he thought the question had been.

"Same here." I agreed once more.

Lucas' eyes lingered on me, hungrily taking me in as I laid there beside him.

"Don't you have work?"

"Yes." He grumbled. "I wish I didn't. But grandpa will be fit to be tied if I am not on time. Last week I was a few minutes late—because I had to run a mower down to Fremont. He about tore me a new asshole when I showed up at the store."

A laugh escaped my throat, and Lucas silenced it with a kiss before he slung his legs over the side of the bed and slid away from me. He walked around and stood at my bedside, looking down at me, completely nude, creating a problematic situation for both of us. Grinning up at him, I attempted to act innocent.

"You better go," I said, reaching up to push my hair back on my head.

Lucas reached down, his fingers finding their way into my hair. His fingertips massaged my scalp, and I couldn't help but notice the proximity of my face to a particular part of him.

"Is there something you needed before you left?" I bit my bottom lip playfully as I gazed up at him.

Lucas groaned with frustration and his hand fell away from my head.

"I don't have time." He moaned.

"You underestimate my skills and overestimate your staying power." I teased.

"Rude." He leaned down to kiss me again with a laugh.

His lips lingered on mine for a moment, then he pulled away with another groan and stepped away before he could be dissuaded. I watched his bare backside as he went to his dresser and began finding his clothes for the day. The sun was barely over the horizon, and golden light was shining through the window, illuminating one of the many parts of him I loved. Lucas had a nice ass, there was no denying it. Every time I saw it—clothed or not—I wanted to grab ahold of it, give him a squeeze. Use those handfuls of him to pull his body roughly into mine.

I had to shake my head to chase away the tempting thought.

"It was weird that Jason was out on the peninsula last night." Lucas state blandly as he pulled a pair of underwear out of the top drawer.

"It would be weird if it was a coincidence." I nodded to myself. "It is fucking gross since we know he followed us out there. I thought that after I gave him that money that he'd—"

"Why did you go to his house, Rob?" Lucas sighed, turning to me finally.

Lucas bent and pulled his underwear on, but his eyes were on me.

"To give him the money for Katie's funeral." I frowned. "Okay. And maybe to threaten him a little. Once I got my memory back and knew what I was capable of, I figured that maybe he needed a warning. Oma wouldn't let me outright kill him so—"

I stopped when I saw the look of horror on Lucas' face as he stood there before me in his underwear.

"What?"

"He...he's a threat, right?" The realization that I had said too much dawned on me. Lucas had his memories back and knowing that fact made me feel comfortable speaking more openly than I should have been. "He serves—well, his pack serves...you know."

Lucas' expression softened, but he didn't look any less horrified at the casual way I discussed contemplating murder.

"He doesn't know that," Lucas said. "You said he doesn't have his memories back, so—"

"For now." I shrugged as I sat up in bed, letting my legs dangle off the side. "It's only a matter of time. I figured that we didn't want him to keep growing the pack in the meantime, right?"

Lucas frowned.

"Look." I sighed. "I know you're kind of against harming other living creatures and all, but—"

"This is more than *Lucas is a vegetarian*, babe." Lucas gave an incredulous laugh. "You were seriously considering fixing a problem with...murder. Doesn't that seem...batshit crazy to you?"

"Is there any way I can answer that without admitting I'm crazy?"

Lucas shook his head.

"It was just a thought," I explained. "You, me, and Oma know where this story is headed. I was just trying to think of some things that might turn things in our favor before it's too late to try. That's all."

"Murder is not one of those things, Rob."

"Not even, like, a little?" I grinned impishly.

"Not even a little." Lucas couldn't help but crack a smile.

I rolled my eyes.

"I probably wouldn't have done it anyway." I was chastened. "I mean, it was merely a thought. Okay. Maybe I had a plan formulating in my brain, but I hadn't gotten to the charts and graphs stage of the plan."

"Don't go past the 'thinking it' stage, babe." He replied before turning to his closet. "So...you didn't go to...just see him?"

Lucas ducked into his closet, and I let a frown overtake my face as I considered what it was that he was getting at with his question. It took longer than I was proud to admit before I figured out what Lucas had meant. The frown on my face was replaced with a wide grin.

Lucas was jealous.

"Are you jealous?" I asked.

"Of course not." Lucas' voice was muffled.

"I don't know," I said, sitting back, bracing my hands against the mattress. "You were upset about Andrew—who is harmless, by the way. Probably not even a douchebag like we thought. I mean, it was the full moon, so...anyway, now you're being all cagey about me going to Jason's house to give him money for a funeral."

"Do you know what cagey means?" Lucas stepped out of the closet, a pair of work jeans in hand. "Because I think you got lucky."

"It means guarded." I waggled my head. "You're being guarded in asking me about Jason. You don't want me to know you're jealous. Worried at best."

"I am not jealous or worried."

I just stared at him.

"Fine." He spat, though there was no heat in the word. "I'm worried."

I continued to stare.

"Jealous." He hissed. "Are you happy?"

"Immensely," I stated blandly.

"The guy is good looking, okay?"

"So are you."

"And you're good looking."

"Thank you." I smiled. "So are you."

"Maybe I'm worried that your hormones will get the better of you and you'll...fumble."

I laughed. "Like slip and fall on his dick? Or slip and slide mine into him? I don't think people can *fumble* when it comes to cheating, babe. You either do it, or you don't. And I didn't. I won't. And it takes more than a guy who is generically attractive for me to have sex, ya' know."

"He's not generically attractive." Lucas sighed. "He's hot."

"Are *you* planning to cheat on *me* with Jason?" I quipped.

Lucas couldn't help but smile then.

"Stop it." He said. "I'm trying to be serious. I don't like you being alone with these guys. Even if I didn't worry about your hormones—"

"Kind of you."

"—I still worry about them."

"They can't make me do anything I don't want to." I shrugged. "So, if you're not worried about me, you shouldn't be worried at all, Lucas."

With a frustrated sigh, Lucas began pulling his jeans on a little more roughly than was necessary.

"It's funny, isn't it?"

"What's that?" Lucas huffed.

"We both have been through some really traumatic shit over the last decade, and you just got your memory back last night, then a werewolf bit you and Jason is hiding two dead bodies," I explained. "And we're here in your bedroom after a night of lovemaking arguing about you being jealous of two guys I have no interest in. We haven't even talked about your memories. How you feel. All of that. Do you think we're fucked in the head?"

"Obviously." He was buttoning and zipping his jeans.

"Seriously." I stood and walked over to him, still nude, and took his face in my hands, making him look at me. "Isn't it weird that we're just like 'tra-la-la just another day in Point Worth?' This is some really heavy shit, Lucas. Magic, werewolves, dead bodies, recovered memories, Kobolds, witches, fire-laser shit coming out of my hands...*the person we won't talk about out loud*...a handful of months ago, I was finishing up filming a movie in Morocco and now...this. What the fuck is life, ya' know?"

Lucas smiled warmly, and his eyes lowered.

"I'm sorry, babe." He sighed before looking up at me once more. "I know this isn't the best time for my jealousy. I'm really sorry, okay?"

"Don't be sorry," I said before leaning in to give him a quick kiss. "Just promise that we're a team, Lucas. Because...that's all I care about. I want to know that no matter how this all ends, my hand will be in yours."

Lucas stared into my eyes and reached up to take one of my hands in his as my other stayed against his face, cupping his cheek.

"Our story isn't about jealousy and cheating." He nodded. "I know that."

"It's more of an erotic novel." I winked.

"With a bunch of weird paranormal romance shit thrown in, right? Like Laurell K. Hamilton." Lucas laughed.

"Hopefully more *Anita Blake* than *Merry Gentry*." I rolled my eyes. "But only if she had sex with just Jean Claude. Or Richard."

Lucas cackled.

"Hopefully we won't be executing any vampires." He added.

"It's still kinda early." I shrugged. "We've got werewolves, so...who knows, right?"

He just smiled.

"This hand in mine 'til the end?" I asked, squeezing his fingers with mine.

"This hand in yours 'til the end, babe." He leaned forward and kissed me gently.

When we finally separated so that Lucas could find a shirt to wear to work, all I could think was: *whatever that end may be.*

Chapter 3

There were three people sitting at Oma's kitchen table when I walked into the house through the backdoor, and only one of them was Oma. While I had no real way to explain it, I had known that Jason would be waiting at Oma's house for me. SO, seeing him sitting there was not that unnerving at all. The fact that he was sitting peacefully with Oma in her own home was unusual, however. Of course, the two of them acting civilly towards each other could be explained away by the third person at the table.

Nelda Hammersmith.

My manager.

That was definitely a plot twist that I had not seen coming—my manager flying in from Los Angeles to make a surprise visit. Honestly, I hadn't known that people in the entertainment business even knew that Ohio existed, let alone how to get there. Well, maybe that wasn't fair. A lot of people in entertainment know where Ohio is on the map and how to book a flight there. But for people like Nelda Hammersmith—high-power, high-profile talent managers—asking them to go to Ohio was like asking them to go to Narnia. It was a magical land which existed only in storybooks about Middle America where everyone wore bib overalls and work boots.

Not that that was entirely inaccurate.

At least, not as far as Point Worth was concerned.

"Good morning," I stated neutrally as I stood in the open doorway and stared into the eyes of each person at the table in turn.

"Jacob." Nelda gave a relieved exhale.

I smiled tightly at her.

Oma's face was blank and unreadable.

Jason was smirking.

Obviously.

"Hi." I nodded before turning to shut the door. "What are you doing here, Nelda?"

Oma presented a raised eyebrow surreptitiously as Nelda rose from her seat dramatically, her actual, honest to goodness, fur capelet nearly twirling all the way around her neck like a Hoola-Hoop. I thanked my lucky stars that Lucas had not come home with me to see the menagerie of dead animals around my manager's neck.

Nelda Hammersmith was Old Hollywood, though she had actually been born in the early fifties and was no older than Oma. However, the way she presented herself, from her dress to her demeanor, to the flourishes she gave her speech and body language, you'd have thought she attended the premiere of the first talkie and sat on Jack Warner's lap for the entire showing. The fact that she had the fur capelet and a *fucking turquoise headwrap* on did nothing to dispel the myth that she was a one-hundred-and-twenty-year-old woman in the body of someone nearly half that age.

"What is on your head, Nelda?" I asked evenly.

One hand gently went to the side of her head, laying lovingly against the material of the wrap. Diamond teardrop earrings hung from her ears.

Alzheimer's or Delusional. Those were the only excuses.

"It's vintage, Jacob." The blood-red gash on her face parted, and the vibrant blue lids of her eyes danced as she answered. "Do you like it?"

"It's...a look." I tried to be polite, then turned my attention to Jason. "What are you doing here?"

"Just getting to know your Hollywood manager here." The smirk deepened. "Hearing all about your time out there in California while we waited on you this morning, *Jacob.*"

He pronounced "Hollywood" as "Hall-ee-wood" and "California" as "Cal-ee-for-nee-ya."

It took all I had to not roll my eyes. And then punch him in his.

"Jacob—" Nelda began.

"Robbie," Oma spoke, startling Nelda. "Mrs. Hammertoe here—"

"Hammersmith, dear." Nelda corrected her with a sniff. "Hammersmith."

"Mrs. Hammersnatch." Oma nodded. Nelda sniffed again. "Seems to think that you need to be back out in California instead of out here with us country bumpkins."

I sighed. Nelda Hammersmith didn't have the wherewithal to look offended at the butchering of her name or the insinuation that she thought everyone in Ohio was a rube. Of course, if I knew Nelda, she had probably declined any offer of drink or food from Oma, attempted to smoke in her house, and refused to let Oma take her fur capelet for her. Nelda Hammersmith was not known for knowing how to blend in, conform to social norms other than the ones she had made up in her head, or generally, just be polite. If she didn't know everyone in Hollywood and hadn't gotten me project after project to work on, I wouldn't have put up with her over the years. Harmless, yes. Asshole, definitely.

"Nelda." I reached out, offering my arm. "Why don't we go to the living room to have a talk? In private?"

That red gash on her face split again, her shockingly white, bleach-enhanced teeth beaming out at me.

"Oh." Jason leaned back in his chair, making Oma give him a quick glare. "We're all friends here. Whatever y'all have to say we sho' don't mind, do we, Mrs. Wagner?"

Oma's lips curled up in distaste as she stared at him and shook her head in response.

"Jacob—" Nelda said.

"We'll go in the living room, Nelda," I said as she laid her hand on my arm.

Classy.

Leading Nelda to the kitchen doorway, I pointed out the living room to her, gesturing towards the sofa, indicating where she should have a seat. The look on her face let me know she wished she had brought a drop cloth for the occasion. Maybe she thought the critter around her neck was going to catch fleas from the davenport.

You really are reverting to your old self, Rob.

"I'll be in to talk in just a second, Nelda," I assured her, patting her hand as it laid on my arm. "Then we'll get squared away. Do you want me to bring you a drink or something to eat?"

Nelda gave a last glance back at the kitchen as her hand slid from my arm.

"No." She said dismissively. "I wouldn't think so."

Oma started to rise from her seat. I shot her a look and eased Nelda through the kitchen door with reassurances that I would be along "in just a minute" to have a little chat with her. Oma lowered herself to her seat begrudgingly as I watched to make sure that Nelda found her way to the sofa and hesitantly found an acceptably clean spot to perch upon. Once it was clear that she was settled for the time being, I spun around to face my grandmother and my nemesis du jour.

"What are you doing here, assface?" I whisper-hissed at Jason as I stomped over to the kitchen table.

"*Assface?*" He snorted. "Are you twelve?"

"Shut up, assface," Oma answered for me. "What *are* you doing here? He ain't told me shit since he showed up here."

"That dinosaur was here." Jason shrugged and gestured vaguely at the living room. "Not like I could talk much with her around now, could I?"

"She's Oma's age." I crossed my arms over my chest. "Are you implying my grandmother is ancient?"

"Assface." Oma gave a firm nod in his direction.

Jason rolled his eyes. "We have unfinished business from last night, Rob. So, don't act surprised to see me."

"I thought you was with Lucas last night?" Oma's attention was suddenly on me.

"I was." I waved her off. "We ran into assface here while we were out."

"Oh." Oma nodded, then frowned. "Where the hell did you run into assface? It's not like any establishments around here let him inside."

"Can we all stop calling me assface?" Jason seethed.

"Dicklick?" I offered.

Jason sighed.

"Do you prefer 'dicklick,' assface?" Oma leaned in. "I can call ya' 'dicklick' if ya' like."

He just ignored her. Oma and I could be like cats and dogs, but we knew how to gang up on someone we mutually hated.

"What unfinished business y'all got anyway?" Oma sat back in her seat, crossing her arms over her chest to match my body language. "Ya' gave him Katie's funeral money, didn't ya'?"

"Yes," I answered. "It's complicated."

"Mm." Oma hummed.

"You want a fancy new nickname, too, old woman?" I grumbled.

"Bet," Oma warned me.

"Where the fuck are you learning these things?" I threw my hands up. "Who's fucking grandmother talks like this?"

"The T.V." She jabbed a finger in the direction of the living room, which actually made Jason smile. "I got a life outside of putting up with your uppity ass, ya' know."

"T.V. is a life?" I asked.

"It's one of my hobbies." She was picking at a fingernail.

"Right." I shook my head, then turned my attention back to Jason. "Look, assface—"

"I'm not leaving until I talk to you." He said firmly, then glanced towards the living room. "As well."

"Fine." I snapped. "Oma, keep assface in line while I go get rid of Nelda."

"But—" She started to stand.

"Please." I snapped once more before whipping around like I was trying to twirl a capelet myself.

Nelda was still sitting in the living room, looking around the room as though she had never seen what looked like the inside of an *L.L. Bean* catalog. Frowning to myself, I walked over, pulling her attention from the interior design around her, and sat down a reasonable distance from her on the couch. My manager, though I hadn't seen her in over a month, looked and smelled the same. Flowery, gaudy, and clueless to the things that happen in the real world outside of Hollywood and the entertainment machine.

"Did you fly out here alone, Nelda?" I asked, genuinely concerned for her well-being. "That's a long flight for...you."

"Of course not, Jacob." A laugh that sounded like tinkling bells emanated from that red gash on her face. "Randy came with me. He's waiting in the car."

A delicate hand waved towards the front door.

Randy was Nelda Hammersmith's personal assistant. He was also her much younger husband. He had tried to get in my pants once. It's a long story.

"You made Randy wait in the car?" I frowned, though I was glad Randy had not been invited into the house.

"He's fine." She gave a dismissive wave again. "He has his games on his phone and the radio, I suppose. Now, dear—"

"I'm not coming back to Los Angeles right now, Nelda." I shook my head. "I have...family stuff...I have to deal with and making movies or new music right now is just—"

"We just got an offer, Jacob." She indicated that she did not want to hear my excuses. "That movie you made...what's it called...the one with the terrorists who are trying to blow up...the White House...or...something?"

"The Statue of Liberty." I shrugged. "What about that piece of shit?"

"Well," Nelda reached into a pocket to withdraw an actual cigarette case, "they want to make a piece of shit sequel."

She opened the case, which made my mouth water, but I reached out and took the case from her, snapping it shut gently.

"No smoking in the house," I said evenly as I held onto the case.

"Of course, of course." She said as though this was perfectly reasonable, though her facial expression said otherwise. "Anyway, they want to pay you double what they did for the first one. Piece of shit, eh?"

"You can add a sunroom to a shack, but it's still a shack, Nelda." I shook my head. "I don't want to go on a special diet, work out six days a week for four months of my life, then go to Toronto, pretend it's New York City or D.C., and fight imaginary terrorists just because the price was right. The first movie was shit, this one will be shit, too."

"They don't make these movies for the Rotten Tomatoes scores, Jacob." She laughed as though everything I had said was ridiculous. "They make these movies so everyone gets rich. Including yours truly. So, do us all a favor and get your ass on the next plane to Los Angeles and get ready to swallow your pride."

"Nelda." I sighed, trying to control myself. "You came all the way to Bum Fuck Ohio for no good reason. I'm not coming back to Los Angeles. So, go out there, get in the car, and let Randy drive you back to the airport."

"Jacob—"

"Just call me Rob, Nelda." I sighed, my body deflating. "Jacob Michaels is long gone at this point."

"You can't mean that!" She brought a hand to her chest. "If you walk away now, who knows if you will ever work again, Jacob?"

"Who cares?" I shrugged. "It's not like I have to have the money. I mean, not to be a snob, but it's not like I need any more money at this point."

"You're not even thirty yet, Jacob—"

"Rob."

"—why would you even think about quitting now?" She squealed, the gash of red on her face flapping wildly. "You have decades of work ahead of you! Millions! You could be richer than a Middle Eastern Crown Prince!"

I rolled my eyes. "That's not offensive. Look, Nelda, I'm done. There are a million generically good-looking guys with good features and palatable acting skills waiting in line behind me. Sign a new Jacob. You're acting like you're watching Jack Nicholson walk away when I'm more like a Kellan Lutz."

"Well, you were never *that* buff." She replied earnestly.

"Fair enough." I had no other way to respond to that.

"But none of that matters, Jacob."

"Rob."

She waved me off.

"No one cares that you have no talent, and there is nothing truly remarkable about your looks." She said. "You just have...*that thing*...that producers and directors are looking for in a star, dear."

Ouch.

Well, actually, it would have been an "ouch" if I hadn't already gotten used to the way actors got treated in the business.

"That *thing*..." I stopped.

What I had wanted to say, I kept to myself. Because "that thing" that Nelda was referring to, was *magic*. Only she didn't know that. Casting directors didn't know it. Producers and directors didn't know it. The moviegoing public didn't know it.

"I can't, Nelda," I said. "I'm done."

Nelda huffed, the red slash across her face turning into what looked like the mouth on a Tragedy Mask. She snatched her cigarette case from me and stood angrily. Damnit. It was fun holding the cigarettes. I was actually hoping she'd forget that I had them and leave them with me. Then I could have one. Just one...

"You are a pain in my ass." She snapped down at me. "I will ask them for more money if you want to play hardball."

"Ask them for the Taj Mahal, Nelda." I shrugged as I peered up at her passively. "But it won't make me change my mind if they say 'yes' to anything you demand. Besides, if you push back, they'll just get Vin Diesel to replace me in the sequel."

But Nelda was already in motion, stomping angrily towards the front door. Her claw reached out and turned the knob, ripping the front door inward—which was quite a feat for someone of Nelda's age and stature.

"We'll see about that!" She snarled triumphantly. "The next time you hear from me, I'll have an offer you can't refuse!"

Then she was gone, and the door was slamming angrily, a gust of Ohio Spring air blowing into the living room to ruffle my hair. Sighing to myself, I listened for the sound of a car door opening and closing, the sound of an engine roaring to life, and then the tell-tale sound of tires crunching on the driveway. I stood from the couch and went over to the door to lock the deadbolt. I certainly didn't want Nelda coming back inside unannounced, uninvited, and unwanted.

Back in the kitchen, Oma and Jason were still sitting at the table, glaring at each other, though they both had mugs of coffee in hand. The thought of each of them having a solid object to launch at or hit each other with made me nervous, but I went to the cabinet to get my own mug. If things started getting thrown, I wanted scalding liquid and heavy porcelain as a weapon, too. Once I had pulled a mug down from the cabinet and filled it with piping hot coffee, I strolled over to the table as though all was right as rain, and sat down in the chair across from Oma, putting Jason to my right. Since I'm righthanded, I figured that would make it easier to throw the mug at him or send a ball of fire splashing into his face.

"Talk, assface." Oma barked before I had the chance.

Jason squinted angrily at her, but he was soon turning his attention to me.

"You owe me." He stated simply.

"I owe you shit."

"I hid two bodies for you."

"What?" Oma gasped.

"You hid the bodies of two of your kind who tried to kill Lucas and me." I brought my coffee mug to my lips and blew at it before taking a sip. "I mean, what are you going to do? Lead the cops to the bodies and tell them that you were an accessory to murder? That you hid dead bodies for the person who killed the two men out of self-defense? Good luck with that, assface."

"Why do we have dead bodies?" Oma snapped, turning her glare to me. "Again?"

"Two werewolves attacked Lucas and me last night." I sipped my coffee again. "One of 'em bit Lucas. Both of 'em got dead in the process."

"Lucas got bit?" Oma's eyes grew wide.

Jason was smirking again.

"Yes." I nodded, though I wasn't looking at either one of them directly. "And assface over here said he'd hide the bodies. So, he hid the bodies. Now he expects me to be grateful."

"I could have just called the cops."

"Or I could have roasted your ass, too." I snapped at him. "Then the cops would've had three deaths to investigate. What's your point?"

Jason actually snarled.

"Keep it in your pants, puppy," Oma warned him. "Why the fuck are your people attacking Lucas and Robbie? Answer me that. I thought we already settled this shit about your quarrel with them?"

"They weren't my pack." Jason snapped.

"I didn't recognize the guys," I added for good measure.

Oma looked back and forth between Jason and me several times before she responded to what we were saying.

"Who the fuck was they?" She bellowed. "You're telling me we got another pack of shifters in this damn town now?"

"Seems to be." Jason shrugged, though the anger was still etched all over his face. "They weren't my guys, so..."

I sipped my coffee.

"You're taking this well." Oma snarled at me from across the table.

"I don't think we should discuss theories with assface present." I jabbed a thumb at him.

"Stop calling me assface!"

"Oh, shush." Oma waved him off. "What do you mean, Robbie? What theories? You talkin' about maybe we had the wrong werewolves in mind when we was...talkin' 'bout what we was talkin' 'bout the other day?"

I nodded.

"What are you two talking about?"

"Shut up," Oma ordered, then her attention was back on me. "Well, fuckin' hell, Robbie. Why didn't you come home immediately and tell me?"

"Lucas and I were busy tending to his bites."

"Amongst other things." Oma snorted. "I think playing *Pass the Pickle* ain't nearly as important as letting me know we got another damn shifter problem on our hands, damnit."

I shrugged.

"It is what it is, Oma." I sipped my coffee. "Unless you have a way to turn back time, then—"

"What are you two talking about, goddamnit?!" Jason growled.

"Shut. Up. Assface." Oma snapped.

Before I could blink, Jason had slid both hands under the table and pushed upward. As if in slow motion, the table began to flip end over end in the air between the three of us. Oma pushed back in her chair, the legs squealing against the linoleum as I dropped my mug, slid from my chair to my knees, and held my hand out towards Jason's solar plexus. With a force of will, I sent a column of green light crashing into his gut. A loud "ooph" sound emanated from Jason as he took the full force of the blow and he and his chair slid backward until he hit the kitchen counter.

Oma raised her hand to the table in the air, and it suddenly stopped spinning end over end. She glanced at Jason, flicked her hand to right the table, and it landed back on all four legs on the linoleum. The legs of the table squealed loudly on the floor as she sent it towards Jason, effectively pinning him against the cabinet. Jason was grunting in pain again as the edge of the table bit into his sternum, trapping him against the kitchen cabinet. With anger, but also fear in his eyes, he looked up at Oma and me on the other side of the kitchen.

"Ya' couldn't take one of us, assface!" Oma admonished him. "Why the fuck would you mess with both of us at the same time?"

Jason growled angrily, his eyes starting to glow red.

"I see any fur, assface, and I'm burning it off," I warned him, raising my hand once more.

An actual whimper escaped Jason's throat, and he went still, though his hands still gripped the edge of the table. Oma let out a frustrated sigh and turned to me, a concerned expression on her face.

"You just sit there and think about what you done now." She spoke over her shoulder to Jason before speaking to me. "Well, you done screwed the damn pooch again, Robbie, ain'tcha?"

"How is every damn thing my fault, Oma?" I crossed my arms over my chest, trying to look her in the eyes while keeping Jason in my peripheral vision. "Everything that goes wrong, you just conveniently blame on me. You seem to forget that none of this would be happening if you had just been honest with me when I was a kid. Maybe I would have made better choices. Or...better wishes, actually."

"Maybe you'd be pullin' at your pud wondering what the hell to do, too!" She retorted. "You ain't exactly reliable when it comes to makin' decisions, are ya'?"

"Oh my god." I groaned and looked at the ceiling. "I didn't make two werewolves—shifters, whatever—attack Lucas and me when we were out walking along the peninsula, did I? That's not my fault."

"It's your fault you didn't come tell me that—" She froze.

"What?"

"Why was y'all out at the Maumee last night?"

"We were talking."

"About what?" She was squinting at me angrily, and her arms were folded over her chest once more. "What the fuck did y'all need to go out to the Maumee to talk about?"

"We were at Lounge watching Carlita perform and—"

"*Carlita.*" Oma hissed.

I rolled my eyes.

"That bitch." Oma actually shook her fist.

All I could do was grin evilly.

"So," Oma snapped at me, "I guess you did what I think you did out there in the Maumee."

"Depends on what you mean." I feigned innocence with a shrug and glanced over at Jason, trying to warn Oma with my eyes. "I mean, all kinds of sordid things could have happened out there, Oma."

"Oh, fuck him." Oma dismissed the thought of Jason listening in on our discussion. "Does Lucas have his memories back now, too?"

"Oma," I warned her again, my eyes darting to Jason.

"Assface won't remember none of this." She snarled. "I'll make sure of it."

"Stop calling me that," Jason grunted, trying to push the table out of his chest.

"Stay still, assface," Oma growled at him this time.

"He does," I said when Oma turned back to me.

"Who?" She hooted.

"Lucas." I gave her a deadpan look. "Memories."

"Fuckin' great." She threw her hands up wildly. "Just fuckin' great, Robbie. I told you not to do that, and you did it. Do you ever just listen to what the hell I tell you?"

"I guess I'm just a rebel."

"You're a goddamn idiot is what you are."

I shrugged.

"You're the band on the Titanic, Robbie." Oma admonished me. "The boat is sinkin,' and you reach for your violin. No, actually, you're shooting holes in the deck is what you're doin'."

"Nice analogy."

"And now you act like you don't even care that you're helping things along." Her eyes were wide with disbelief. "What the hell has gotten into you, Robbie? You're reckless and careless at times, but this is just downright batshit crazy."

"He had a right to his memories, Oma."

"It. Don't. Matter." She snarled.

"We're going to have to agree to disagree on this one, lady."

Oma shook her head, her eyes piercing into me as she considered everything that we'd said to each other. The things I had done the night before—actually, all of the things I'd done since I was a teenager. She was not happy with me. I wasn't entirely happy with myself either, but that was beside the point. When I was old enough to find out about magic, my family history, what was expected of me, I had been cornered. All I was doing was my best—both to survive and also not go down without a fight.

"So...now what?" Oma asked sharply. "What's the big plan, Robbie? We're just gonna wait around until you know who shows up with some strange pack of shifters we don't even know about? This one over here ain't even a threat, and we're havin' to deal with his bullshit right now. This is one big clusterfuck."

"It's not my fault," I said. "No matter how you slice it, Oma. I'm making things up as I go, sure...but what else can I do?"

Oma sighed and looked down, her whole body seeming to deflate before me as she considered that statement.

"Robbie, no matter what you do...son...he's gonna come. And you can't stop it. You won't be able to stop him. It's just a matter of when."

"Then why does it fucking matter that Lucas and I were in the Maumee last night?" I snorted.

Oma shook her head.

"Wait. Are you two talking about the man in the black hood?" Jason grunted.

Oma's head shot up and her eyes locked on mine. Together, we slowly turned to look at Jason. He had stopped trying to push the table out of his chest to free himself, having realized that Oma's magic had effectively and permanently trapped him against the kitchen cabinets.

"What the hell do you know about the man in the black hood, assface?" Oma asked him.

"He came to me." Jason swallowed hard, fear filling his eyes. "Once."

Oma shot a look at me, which I returned.

"He offered me—the pack—power," Jason said. "I said, 'no.' He...he scared me."

Oma and I didn't laugh at Jason.

His fear was well-founded.

"He scares everyone," I said gently.

"He said his name was Bl—"

"*Don't say that name!*" Oma hissed quickly. "*Never say that name.*"

Again, Oma and I were exchanging glances.

"I didn't believe him," Jason said. "I mean, I'd heard stories about...that...but I didn't know it was more than just a scary bedtime story. Something parents tell their kids to make them stay in bed at night. Are you two not shitting me right now? He—he's coming?"

For several moments, Oma and I continued to stare at each other, wondering what options we had, trying to speak nonverbally. Finally, I sighed, and Oma flicked her hand, the table sliding slowly away from Jason. Gently, so as to not startle one of us into doing something else to harm him, Jason rose from his chair and stood before us.

"Let's have a talk, assface," I said.

Chapter 4

Oma went about pushing the chairs in around the table after I had centered it back in the kitchen. Jason watched us cautiously from his position backed up against the kitchen sink. Apparently, he thought he could escape down the drain if the two of us decided to throw a bit of magic his way again. As far as I was concerned, he had been lucky that neither of had decided to just burn the whole house down out of frustration. Neither Oma nor I had dependable temperaments, so a ball of fire being slung around the kitchen for nothing more than a table being flipped was not out of the question.

"Acted like you was auditioning for *The Real Housewives of Toledo*, flippin' my table like that," Oma grumbled as she lowered herself back into her chair. "You're damn lucky you ain't hurt nothin'. This table and these chairs are worth more than twenty of you. And your pack."

Jason's Adam's Apple bobbed as he just stared at her.

"Come sit down." I sighed as I lowered myself into the chair across from Oma. "We probably won't hurt you."

"To Hell." Oma snorted. "He flips one more thing, and I'm gonna flip my chicken."

Jason blinked at Oma, confused, then looked over at me. I shrugged.

"Old people are folksy," I said. "Or so I've been told."

"Sit the hell down already!" Oma boomed, nearly coming out of her seat with frustration. "If one of us has to tell you again—"

Jason scuttled over—which was quite a feat for someone of his build and ego—and sat down in the chair to my right again.

Stupid, stupid werewolf.

"Anyone need more coffee?" Oma barked, her eyes on Jason, then me.

"I could use a cup," I said. "Jason?"

He shook his head jerkily.

Oma got up from her seat, the legs squealing against the floor again, and she set about the task of getting two fresh mugs of coffee for her and me. The three mugs that had been toppled in our little scuffle had somehow found their way into the sink. The coffee that had been inside of them had been cleaned up as well. Either the Kobolds were quicker than even I knew—and even better at making themselves invisible—or Oma had used a few tricks of her own. Either way, fresh coffee had to be poured for the two of us.

"So," I started as Oma busied herself at the coffee pot, "how do you know about the man in the black hood? And don't say his name. Unless you want to see him again. Real soon."

Jason swallowed hard again.

"I don't *know* him," Jason stated finally. "I just, well, he came to me once. In a dream."

"That's how he usually travels," I stated blandly.

"He likes flair." Oma deadpanned from across the room.

Jason glanced at her before his eyes landed on me again.

"He...he just came to me in a dream." Jason shook his head, his eyes closing tightly as though trying to drum up an old, painful memory. "Once. I never saw him again after that. But...once was enough."

Oma had finished pouring fresh mugs of coffee for her and me and was standing next to the counter, both mugs in hand, staring across the kitchen at the man we had just tag-teamed in the world's quickest fight. Examining Jason, I could tell that he wasn't lying—and he hadn't been lying just so we would let him loose from being trapped by the table. Something in his eyes let me know that he had seen the man in the black hood and it had stayed with him ever since. Even without his past memories—what had happened the night the man in the black hood had disappeared—hadn't erased the memory of the man. Something like that just stays with a person.

I found myself wondering what my options were in discussing everything with Jason so openly. As things stood, he was still an enemy to Oma, Lucas, and me. He may have hidden the bodies of the two werewolves who had attacked Lucas and me the night before, but he had done so with the intent that we would owe him for that service. Altruism had not been his intention when he had offered to help us out of our mess. Additionally, there was still the matter of things Jason had said to me when I had been at his house alone. Obviously, there was some...sexual tension...at least on his part, between the two of us. I hadn't been candid with Lucas and Oma about what had happened at Jason's house.

Furthermore, even if there was some other pack of wolves that the black-hooded man had been referring to—it wasn't Jason's pack he controlled after all—that presented another question. Why had Jason and his pack been at Oma's house the night the black-hooded man had attacked a decade previously—the night I managed to pull a metaphorical rabbit out of my metaphorical ass? That couldn't have just been coincidental. Had Jason and his pack decided that they were tired of Lucas refusing their offers to let him join their pack? Would things have been different if they had known that Lucas could never turn into a werewolf?

Was that even true?

Was I choosing to believe a lie Lucas made up?

Or maybe it was a lie he thought was the truth?

Would we really know the truth until we had lived through a few more moon cycles?

Question upon question began piling up in my brain, and none of them seemed close to having an answer. Being unable to talk too openly about the man in the black hood made things even more difficult. The fact that Oma and I had to be careful who we told anything to compounded that fact. Everything had changed since I had come back to Point Worth, yet everything was the same as it had been before I left Point Worth. A decade had not been long enough to truly change anything about the danger we found ourselves in by merely existing.

More disturbingly, I felt angry. All of the time. As I sat there looking at Jason and Oma in turn, all I could feel was frustration and anger at my present situation. Had I always been so angry, or just since I found out my life was not like other kids back when I was a teenager? Even though I had my memories back, none of them told me that I had felt perpetually angry before. Now, as an adult, and having returned to Point Worth, everything upset me. Of course, I conveyed that anger through removed indifference...but it was there. Just bubbling under the uppermost layer of who I was.

I was beginning to be afraid of myself.

What the hell can happen to someone who loses themselves so quickly and deeply?

"Robbie?" Oma's voice was gentle, obviously concerned with my mental removal from the situation. "Ya' still with us?"

Shaking my head to chase away the ghosts of everything in my head, I turned my full attention back to the two people physically present with me.

"What did he say to you?" I asked Jason since Oma's question had been made rhetorical by me responding at all. "When he came to you just the once, Jason? What did he want?"

Jason appeared to be going over his options in his head, obviously reluctant to share any information with the two people who just attacked him with magic as though it were no big deal. Logic won out over attitude and Jason gave a sign, finally indicating that he was going to answer.

"Look," He stated defensively, "it really was just once. I'm not jerking you around here, okay? He came to me in a dream. Offered me and the pack power if we would help to build him an army. But I refused."

"An army for what?" I asked.

"You know what for." Oma snorted.

Jason glanced at Oma quickly before answering. "To help him destroy a couple of witches. I'm now assuming that is you two."

Oma bowed her head with a grin.

"What's he got against you two?"

"Long story," I stated evenly. "Why did you refuse?"

"I'm not crazy, Rob." Jason spat, though there was no heat to his words. "I know real trouble when I run into it. I knew the guy in the black hood was not someone I wanted to attach myself to. I knew he was trouble just as much as I know you're trouble."

"Of a different sort." I shrugged.

"Trouble is trouble." Jason shook his head though a small grin reached his lips. "Doesn't matter how you dug the hole if you end up stuck in it, does it?"

"You and Oma should trade folksy sayings sometime." I rolled my eyes, but before Jason or Oma could respond, I continued. "So, if you refused him—to create this army of puppies—why are you still taking on members? Why did you go after Lucas so much when we were younger?"

"We're a pack." Jason looked at me like I was an idiot. "It's like a family, we just reproduce differently."

"Gross," I responded blandly, to which Oma chuckled. "Why Lucas?"

Jason was chewing at his lip. A tell-tale sign that he either didn't want to say what he was thinking or he had no idea how to answer the question.

"He was one of us," Jason responded suddenly. "On the football team. We knew he'd make a good pack member."

"That's a lie," Oma replied.

"No shit, Shirley," I answered her, though my eyes never left Jason's.

"I'm not lying."

"You already know we're witches, assface," Oma responded. "Do you think we're goin' to buy some cock-and-bull story that you just felt like you had to have Lucas in your pack because he played football with ya'?"

Oma's statement gave me pause as I sat there, helping her to stare down Jason and intimidate him into talking.

Witches.

She had said I wasn't a witch before...

"Fucking fuck." Jason groaned as he reached up to run his fingers through his hair, which he had obviously not bothered to stop by his house to wash after disposing of the two bodies. "Look, Lucas...we were just supposed to make him part of our pack, okay? That's all."

Oma looked over at me, a frown adorning her face.

I stared back at her, thoughts of *witches* on my mind.

Pushing away my questions—for the moment—I squinted at Jason.

"What do you mean you were supposed to make him part of your pack, Jason?" I demanded. "Who told you that was something you were supposed to do?"

Jason's head fell back in defeat and he stared up at the ceiling, as though saying a silent prayer.

"When I told the...guy...that I didn't want his offer of power, he got mad, okay?" Jason explained, almost pleading for understanding. "I guess not many people turn him down and when they do, I guess it pisses him off."

"Yeah." I nodded slowly. "He's been pissed at my family for a while now."

Oma agreed with a firm nod.

"Yeah." Jason shrugged. "He told me that he was going to destroy my pack, make me watch...then he was going to kill me. I mean, this was a...a...dream, right? But I knew he meant it. I knew that the next time I would see him it was because he had come to kill me and my guys, right?"

"He doesn't make idle threats, no," I replied.

"Before I could tell him I was sorry and that we would accept the power—or ask what could be done to appease him—he offered a solution, Rob. He told me if I did him a favor, he would leave us alone forever."

"What favor?" I asked, leaning in.

"He gave me a name." Jason nearly shivered.

"Lucas Barkley?" I seethed.

Jason nodded.

Glancing over at Oma was all I could do to keep myself from instinctively punching Jason is his, well, punchable face. Oma looked as though she had picked up on the fact that I was feeling murderous, her eyes warning me to keep myself under control. When it came to magic, Jason didn't stand a chance against me, most likely. In a fistfight, he'd probably kick my ass. So, it wasn't fair to punch him in the face and then defend myself with magic. Even if he had been begging to be punched in the face for over a decade.

"Get out," Oma answered the two of us when my eyes stayed on hers. "And don't come back ya' miserable little shit."

"What?" Jason squeaked.

"Get the hell out of my house, assface." Oma turned her head to growl at him.

In the corner of my vision, Jason made a movement as though he might protest being told to leave Oma's house. Another sharp look from her made him rethink his decision, and he was quickly removing himself from his chair. Oma's eyes followed him as he got up, pushed his chair back in cautiously, and moved toward the backdoor. My eyes stayed on Oma, keeping tabs on her as well as following Jason's movements by following her eye movements. Then I heard the backdoor squeak slightly, and a fresh Spring breeze met the back of my neck.

"We'll talk soon, Rob." Jason had the nerve to speak. "You still owe me."

"We'll see about that," I answered simply, my eyes still on Oma.

Jason's footsteps sounded, the door closed, and Oma and I were left staring at each other once more. Thoughts swirled through my head, and I couldn't separate one emotion from the next, so I simply sat there, staring at Oma with her staring back for a moment before I lifted my coffee mug to my lips. My hand shook slightly, and I had to pause for a moment to collect myself before I took a drink so as to not spill the steaming liquid down my front.

Oma sighed to herself and brought her own mug to her lips.

Once upon a time, I had been a sixteen-year-old kid with two very different and tough choices. Neither of which had been acceptable to me. So, I had made a new choice for myself. A choice that no one in my family before me knew was even an option. And my memories had been stolen from me. Sure, that had kind of been the deal when I had made the choice I had made, but with those memories back, I had even more questions than I had before I had jumped into the well in the cellar the first time.

"Oma." I managed to speak without my voice cracking. "I had a dream last night while I was at Lucas'."

"Yeah? So?"

Thinking of what I had seen in my dream, I felt my ability to speak being siphoned from me like water from a well. The scene of the darkened child's bedroom, being inside of a body I was unfamiliar with, feeling the ice-cold floorboards beneath my feet, the throne of bones, the hooded figure, the red eyes...it was all too much for me to verbalize. The fact that something inside of me told me that it wasn't so much a dream as a memory made it even more challenging to consider speaking of it. Worst of all—it wasn't one of my memories. It was someone else's.

"I—I need the book to not be blank," I said. "I need to see what is inside of it again."

Oma pushed her chair back and stood up gruffly, her coffee mug held in her fist like a shield.

"Well, good luck with that." She snorted as she made her way to the counter. "That thing's been as stubborn as you for the last ten years."

Oma dragged the sugar jar across the counter and began searching through the utensil drawer for a spoon. Apparently, Oma needed more than just caffeine to get through the day this once.

"Did it just...go blank when I...left?"

"Well," She looked thoughtful as one, then two spoons of sugar got dumped into her mug, "I'd say 'yes,' but I ain't certain. It was blank the first time I looked at it after you run off to Hollywood, though."

"That's weird, right?" I asked, my stomach suddenly feeling like lead. "I mean...*why?*"

Oma chuckled to herself as she stirred her coffee and shoved the sugar jar back to its place on the counter next to the flour and brown sugar. With the amount of cooking and baking Oma did, I never did understand why she poured the ingredients into decorative jars from their original sacks.

"'Bout par for the course, I'd say." She turned around with her sweetened mug of coffee gripped in her hand as she propped herself up against the counter. "You decided to take things into your own hands, ran off to Hollywood—things have been weird for a long time, Robbie. Hell, if something wasn't weird around here at least once a day I'd probably cream my britches."

"*You're the weirdest thing around here,*" I mumbled to myself.

"What's that?" She glowered.

"Nothing."

"Mm." She eyed me warily.

Sitting there in Oma's kitchen, thinking of the previous night's events, I found myself pouring through my old memories that still seemed to be adjusting to being back in my brain. Things that Oma had said when I was a teenager. Things Lucas and I had done when we were younger. Things I had seen, things I'd been taught, things I had known on a deeper level than I seemed to know them at present. There was a nagging pull at the back of my skull, something telling me that I should remember something that I couldn't. Not because the memory wasn't in my mind but because I was human and humans are forgetful. At best, humans don't have the extraordinary brainpower to connect the dots that link memories together.

With no better obvious course of action, I slammed back a swig of my coffee, wincing at the slightly too warm liquid, and stood from the table. Oma watched me from her place by the counter as I walked over and emptied my mug down the drain and rinsed out my cup before setting it in the sink. I laid my hands against the counter edge and stared out of the window that provided a view of the backyard. The white picket fence that surrounded the garden looked so pitiful with no garden to protect. Frowning to myself, I thought about all of the years Oma had tended to the garden dutifully, and how I was sad that she seemed to have no intention of ever doing it again.

"What are you thinkin' about?" She asked. "All the money you're losin' by not takin' your dumbass back out to Hollywood?"

"I don't need the money," I said, then corrected myself. "I don't want the money."

A sharp whistle emanated from Oma's lips.

"Ain't you fancy as shit?" She waggled her head slightly. "Guess your retirement plan is good if you decide to give up work before thirty?"

"I don't have a retirement plan." I looked at her out of the corner of my eye. "Just a shit ton of money."

Her face twisted with disapproval.

"Wouldn't have said it if you hadn't pushed." I shrugged, looking out the window at the barren garden once more. "Like you always do."

"Well, what are you gonna do when you run out of money, smartass?" She asked though she wasn't trying to be rude.

She was just being Oma.

"Unless I lived to be a thousand, I should be okay." I retorted. "But the way things are going, I'll be lucky to make it to twenty-eight."

"You'll be lucky to make it to twenty-seven, ya' brat." She replied nonchalantly. "If you keep sassin' me you won't make it another two weeks."

"Oh. Yeah." I said, vaguely remembering that my birthday was not far off.

"Mm," Oma repeated her go-to humming noise. "What kind of cake you want for your birthday anyhow?"

Turning with an incredulous look, I pushed my hip against the counter and crossed my arms over my chest as I stared my grandmother down.

"Really, Oma?" I snorted. "Do you want to get me a cake and throw a party? Play Pin the Tail on the Donkey?"

"There'll be more than one jackass gettin' something stuck in its ass if you keep being a shithead." She replied. "Thought it might be nice since we ain't seen each other on your birthday for ten years. Have a cake. Blow out some candles."

"Make a wish?" I teased.

"Oh, fuck you." She dumped her coffee mug in the sink.

"Think it'd work?" I continued. "Close my eyes tight, wish with all of my might and blow out a whole bunch of candles, and everything will be hunky-dory once more?"

"That ain't what I was getting' at, and you know it."

I shrugged.

"Why are you such a damn jackass lately?" Her hands went to her hips. "Can't say two damn words to you without getting' a load of sass."

"That's rich, Oma." My mouth turned into a wide grin. "Unless you want to go get the tiara out of the box in the attic and dust it off, I think you can hold onto the title."

When I felt the hand on my leg, I nearly came out of my skin. Jerking sharply, I looked down to find Ernst next to me, his head coming up to my hip, his eyes wide with shock. Oma jerked in surprise at my movements, saw Ernst, and let out a string of muffled curses. When Ernst realized that I had only jumped from surprise and not anger, his shocked expression turned into a happy one, and his hand went back to lay against my leg. I reached down and patted his head with a smile while Oma cursed a few moments longer.

"Hey, Ernst," I said, ignoring Oma's prattling on.

"*Mornin', Rob.*" He squeaked back.

"Where's everyone else?" I asked.

He shrugged. "*Ev'ryone's been keepin' to themselves. S'pose they've all 'ad enough excitement for a while.*"

I laughed gently.

"Makes sense." I shrugged. "Sometimes, I wish my family knew how to keep to themselves and give me some peace."

Ernst's ears wiggled happily.

"At least you know where your kin are, though." My mind wandered, bringing up thoughts of my mother and father.

"*S'pose,*" Ernst said simply.

As if lightning had shot out of the sky and struck me in the forehead, a memory came back to me. Not an old memory, but a recent one. An important one. Ernst frowned up at me as my eyes grew wide with excitement. Quickly, I gave Ernst another pat on the head and stepped away from him and Oma, turning towards the main part of the house.

"Well, where the shit is you goin'?" Oma asked.

"I need to go see a man about a wolf."

"What?" Oma coughed.

I was already taking the stairs two at a time before the word finished coming out of Oma's mouth.

Chapter 5

Andrew's office was nicer than I had imagined it would be. When I had only been back in Point Worth for a little over a week, Oma had introduced us while we were volunteering at the Toledo LGBTQ+ center. Probably because we were both gay and for no other discernible reason, such as she thought we'd actually get along. Regardless of our compatibility, Andrew and I went to dinner, he acted like a douchebag, and then he turned into a werewolf on the drive back to Oma's house—after trying to grab my junk and generally act like a turd. Just like any other normal first date, really.

Due to the epic failure that was our first date—Andrew essentially trying to murder me when he was in wolf form—I had decided immediately that Andrew was not to be trusted. Of course, a short amount of time and regaining my memories had given me some perspective. It's funny how that happens, really. Someone pisses you off, and you try to push them out of your mind, relegate them to the "distant memory" file, and then when you forget that there was information in that file when it becomes possibly useful later. Andrew's and my date, and our few discussions afterward pointed towards information that I likely needed.

"Well," Andrew reached up to rub his head which had recently been shaved again, giving it a nice, clean sheen, "now that you kind of demanded that I see you, Rob...what's up?"

I sat back in the chair, crossing my legs gently as I stared across the desk at Andrew.

"Did you recognize me the first time we met?" I asked though that was not why I had come to Andrew's place of employment.

"Uh," Andrew seemed perplexed, "yes."

Slowly, my head started to nod. "It kind of dawned on me that you were poking around for information about my job and financial situation during the date because you wanted me to admit who I was. Of course, I didn't realize it until much later. Thought you were just a massive douche at the time."

Andrew frowned.

"Is that why you came all the way from Point Worth?" He asked evenly. "To ask if I knew you were Jacob Michaels and insult me further?"

I waved him off.

"Not especially." I shook my head. "I realized that people often say things without actually saying them. Or they say something that kind of relates to what they *want* to say, hoping that the other person will pick up on it and do the talking for them."

Andrew just stared at me.

I figured there was a button for security under his fancy desk and soon his manicured hands would be groping for it.

"You don't have a pack," I said, leaning forward.

"No."

"That's weird, right?"

"How would you know if that's weird?" His brow furrowed so deeply I worried his face might crack and bleed. "You're not exactly an expert. Are you?"

"No." I shook my head. "It just seems that all shifters—werewolves—belong to a pack or 'family' of some kind, right?"

"I guess."

"You don't," I said. "Why?"

"There's only one pack around here that I know of and I don't want to be a part of it."

"Jason's pack?" The corner of my mouth turned up.

"Uh, yeah."

"You don't have a problem giving them information, though." My eyebrow raised against my will as I stared Andrew down from across the desk. "I mean, Oma is pissed at you. Like, super pissed. She already threatened to...uh, *flip her chicken*...on Jason. Her words. Not mine. Obviously. You will probably be the next person she goes batshit crazy on."

"What did she do to Jason?" Andrew's eyes were like saucers.

I waved him off.

"After I blasted him into the kitchen counter, she just pinned him there with the table." I rolled my eyes. "Nothing all that drastic. He walked out of the house on his own two legs. Nary a scratch."

Andrew gave me a horrified look yet said nothing as I smiled evilly at him.

"She was all upset because he disrespected her multiple times, nearly broke her kitchen table, yada yada yada." I gave a vaguely bored flip of my hand. "She might be madder at you for running to Jason and crying about Lucas plowing into you with his truck. Like you aren't perfectly fine."

Andrew's horrified expression changed to one of "fight or flight." Maybe I was lying a little to him in order to put him on edge, but the fact was that Oma had been pissed off about Andrew talking to Jason after the whole incident with Lucas' truck. Of course, she had probably forgotten all about being upset with Andrew due to other things that had occurred since. Oma had a good memory when it came to getting even with people who had pissed her off, so maybe I wasn't entirely off base.

"But," I said, holding a hand up as Andrew started to rise from his seat, "if you were maybe able to help me out a little, maybe she'd be less pissed off when the time came for her to talk to you."

If she remembered.

Big "if."

Andrew didn't have to know that Oma had probably already forgotten about being mad at him.

"What do you want, Rob?" Andrew sighed, his exhausted eyes closing slowly. "Jacob. Whoever you are."

"Where is your pack? Family? Whatever you call them." I asked. "Back in New York?"

"That's where they are based, yes," Andrew replied, his eyes sliding open cautiously to appraise me from the other side of the desk.

I smiled.

"Things have happened in the last week. A few days ago," I shook a finger at him, "I would've missed what you just did there, Andy."

"What?"

"Where are they now?" I asked. "I don't care *where they are based out of* regularly, I want to know where they are *now.*"

Andrew rolled his eyes and sighed, sinking back into his seat.

"I don't know."

"Sure ya' do." I grinned goofily as I laid my hand on his desk, palm down, and pushed out a little magic.

When I raised my hand, the scorch marks were very noticeable.

"Jacob...*Rob.*" Andrew pushed his chair back slowly. "Don't."

"I wonder if I set this office on fire with magic if anyone would believe you?" I asked thoughtfully. "Or would they think you'd gone 'round the bend and haul you outta here in a 'Me Time' jacket?"

Andrew stared at me, nearly emotionless, as we sat across the desk from each other in his fancy-schmancy office in the tall, fancy building. I'd had many a meeting with self-important people in fancy-schmancy offices in tall, fancy buildings. Typically, I used my charm and charisma to deal with their bullshit—especially since my memory had been a problem during those meetings—but that would not work with Andrew. Magic was the answer.

"You seemed like such a nice guy." Andrew finally sighed, his head slowly shaking as he stared into my eyes.

I frowned.

"But you're kind of a douche, too, ya' know." He said.

"I don't think the guy who verbally and physically assaulted me on a date has a right to tell me about my manners."

"What's happened to you?" he asked, his head cocking to the side marginally. "I mean...I'm getting a vibe from you now that wasn't there before. That trick there is new, too."

He pointed at the scorch marks.

"It's funny what happens when someone remembers how exhausted they are, Andrew," I replied evenly. "I've been tired of my circumstances for a very fucking long time. And I'm looking to correct them. Immediately. Where is your fucking pack?"

With each word spoken, I leaned in closer and closer, pushing myself into the desk and further into Andrew's space.

"What's that even mean?"

"Don't worry about it." I clenched my teeth tightly. "I got—well, we—got attacked by two werewolves the other night. I want to know whose pack they're a part of because Jason doesn't claim them."

"That's convenient." He snorted.

"Why would he lie?"

"Why wouldn't he?"

"Don't you think I'd recognize local boys, Andrew?" I quipped. "Even if he were lying, I'd know if the guys looked familiar. These guys were bigger than any of Jason's—even in human form—and they weren't from around Point Worth. So...where is your fucking pack? They in town for a visit?"

Andrew chewed at his lip.

"What do you want me to burn first?" I asked, sitting back nonchalantly. "I can start with anything that I think looks super important."

I reached to grab a stack of papers off of Andrew's desk. When he reached out suddenly to grab my wrist to stop me, I didn't jerk away or react with violence. I just looked up at him, waiting to see what he would do.

"Don't." He pleaded. "Please. This is my fucking job. I can't lose it because you're a fucking psychopath."

"Pot meet kettle."

"I'm not a psychopath." He sat back, his long fingers sliding from around my wrist. "I'm a werewolf."

"Tomato, tomato." I shrugged.

"You mean tomato, *tomahto*."

"No." I chuckled. "I really don't. They're too interchangeable for that."

Andrew squinted angrily at me.

"Look," I sighed, leaning in even more, my ass barely hanging onto the edge of the seat, "I don't give a shit what you and your furry brethren do when it doesn't involve me. I don't care if you're bathing in other people's blood under the light of the full moon and getting your rocks off to it, either. What you guys do has absolutely no effect on me whatsoever, puppy. But...*we were attacked*. Lucas got bitten by one of these assholes. I want to know who they are and why they are here if they are not part of Jason's pack. That simple."

Andrew stared at me impassively.

"Or I burn this fucking building to the ground with us in it." I sat back with a sigh, my ass squeaking against the leather of the cushion.

Rolling his eyes, Andrew sighed. "They're Jason's people, Rob. He's finding new members outside of Point Worth, obviously. I know for a fact that my people are not anywhere near here, though I would rather you burn me alive than tell you where they are."

"He's recruiting elsewhere?" My head fell back in frustration. "I should have thought of that. Could-a saved me from having to look at you."

"I'm surprised you and Esther Jean hadn't thought of it," Andrew said.

"Fair enough." I relented as I rose from my seat. "Of course, you could have saved both of us a lot of trouble if you had just said that when I first asked. So...you're still a major douche."

Andrew glared up at me as I stood before his desk.

"Have a nice day, Andy." I gave him a half-wave as I went to turn towards the door.

"I guess," Andrew's voice stopped me, "the question you aren't asking that you should be asking is why they're attacking you and Lucas, right? I mean...shifters usually only care about business that involves shifters. Neither one of you is a shifter, are you?"

Turning to look at Andrew, one of his eyebrows was raised, questioning.

"That's yet to be seen," I said. "I know I'm not. Lucas did get bit, though."

Andrew smiled.

"Your boyfriend is not going to be a shifter."

My brow furrowed deeply as Andrew snickered to himself, very confident in what he had just said.

"What do you mean by that?" I asked, pretending I didn't know what he said was the truth. "He got bit by one of those ass—"

"Everyone in Point Worth knows about those people." Andrew shook his head, amused. "There's no point in pretending that he has to worry about something like a bite, Rob."

"*Those people*?"

"The Barkley's." He replied. "But...if shifters are acting out of the ordinary...that is a concern, isn't it?"

I swallowed hard. Apparently, not everyone knew about the Barkley's—whatever that meant. A million questions spilled into my head, but I didn't have the first clue as to whether or not I wanted to ask them of Andrew. Nor did I know how to ask those questions. Anything I asked or said would only give him more information about my family and Lucas'. Something in the way Andrew was looking at me and smiling let me know that he knew more than he ever let on. In fact, I was beginning to think that he wasn't actually afraid of me burning down his building at all.

"Go fuck yourself, Andrew," I said simply.

"Close the door on your way out, Rob." He winked.

Chapter 6

The horizon was that lazy red color that's trying to decide how long it will be before it turns purple. Higher in the sky, the deep, nearly black, blue color was encroaching on the blood-like color pouring towards the ground. Somewhere between the two colors, a pale-yellow moon was climbing higher into the sky, watching the war between the two colors. Day and night fighting each other as the moon stayed out of the way and did what it was created to do. The sky could fight with itself as long as it kept out of the moon's way, for it had to bring forth destiny.

Nearly a quarter of a million miles beneath the moon, a scream of agony cut through the woods as the man fell to all fours. Writhing and gnashing, the man screamed out as his bones shifted, and his skin crawled. Popping joints and stretching sinew, like being stabbed repeatedly with hot pokers, the man knew that the pain alone would be enough to kill him. The moon shone down, indifferent to the man's suffering as he went through the transition—the first to ever experience a pain so unique...so exquisite. A pain that demanded to be felt, for reward was on the other side of that wall of agony.

Throwing himself back to his elongating knees, the man looked up at the moon, his eyes wide and yellow, lengthening and glistening as his mouth opened wide. Teeth, impossibly long, glistened with drool that fell to the ground in fat, viscous globs. His yellow eyes connected with the yellow light of the moon, and his soul learned a truth that had never been whispered to another soul. He was now part of the night—a part of the frightening uncertainty of darkness that forced the first people to walk on two legs to hide in caves when the God in the sky went to sleep each night.

As the first patch of fur split the skin on his back, the knobs of his spine spilling forth from that crevice, he understood everything. His eyes were drawn to the edge of the clearing, where a man in a black hooded cloak watched, his red eyes glowing out from the shadows of that hood.

Magic.

It was connected to everything.

His wish had been heard.

Carlita slowly slid her hand out of mine, her fingers trailing across the top of the table between us in the corner booth. My eyes opened, and I looked over at her, wondering what there was to say.

"He's been around for a very long time, baby," Carlita said as her fingers found her coffee cup.

It was evident that she was trying to keep her hand steady, but she couldn't quite manage it as her shaky hand nearly upended her cup before her fingers latched onto it. My own hand was cold and clammy and just a little shaky as I slid it back across my side of the table and into my lap. She brought the disposable to-go cup to her lips and took a sip from the minuscule hole in the plastic lid, but her eyes did not lose their hold on mine.

What she had just shown me didn't answer many questions, it merely added more to the growing "List of Things Rob Doesn't Know." So, my friend in the black hooded cloak was around when the first man became a werewolf. What did that mean? Had he created the first werewolf? Or was he merely an observer to something that the magic of the world had brought forth of its own accord? Why would someone wish to become a creature like a werewolf and where would such a primitive person get such an idea when no such thing had existed before? Someone doesn't just wake up one day and have such a thought, nor make such a wish.

Why are the shifters acting weird in Point Worth?

That had been my question for Carlita when I had found her at the LGBTQ+ center in downtown Toledo. Instead of answering, she had led me to the coffee shop—the same one I had been to with Andrew before—and ordered us both a coffee. Then we had slid into the corner booth, mostly out of everyone else's sight since it was the middle of the day, and business was slow. Her hand had reached for mine, and I had placed mine in hers willingly. My mind had been treated to a memory that wasn't my own.

But whose memory was it?

Memories were a tricky thing. What is a memory comprised of? Are they flickers of electricity being fired by synapses in the brain? Then again, does the brain contain memories...or is it memories? No matter the answer, I knew one thing for certain, the memory had to be Carlita's. How else would she have it to share with me? My hand was finally steady when I reached for my own disposable cup and lifted it to my lips. As the warm, black liquid flooded my mouth, I found myself wondering if anything would ever make sense again.

When I had first gone off to Hollywood, all of my pertinent memories about magic and the history of my family taken from me for safe-keeping, things were rough. But they made sense. I didn't wander through each day blindly, wondering what this thing or that thing meant. I didn't develop one question after another about every event in my life. One foot in front of the other was how I lived my life because everything was linear and logical. Now...I felt like, with my memories returned...I understood nothing.

I was worse off than I had been before.

"Why don't you people ever just give simple answers?" I sighed as I set the coffee cup back on the table.

"I'm an oracle, baby." Carlita smiled as her cup was set back on the table. "Not *Dear Abby*. Knowing my role in all of this doesn't mean I can just tell you any-damn-thing that pops into your handsome little head."

"Thank you," I said quickly before launching in on her again. "Carlita—"

"Yes, baby?"

"Why did someone become a werewolf?" I reiterated. "Why do they exist?"

"You saw why they exist, Rob." She replied.

I had to keep myself from rolling my eyes.

"When the first," She looked around and leaned in, "*magic*, was used, someone had to be around to keep that shit under control, right? I mean, you can't have people just running around batshit crazy doing whatever the hell they want without someone there to make sure they didn't go too far."

I wasn't sure she was answering the question I had asked.

"So," I said, "they came about because some guy wished to be a wolf?"

"No." She looked at me like I was stupid. "And yes. They came to be because some guy wished to be a wolf without realizing that magic is everywhere. It sees everything and hears everything. Be careful about what you wish...because you might just get it."

"Why was...*he*...there?" I asked quietly, nervously reaching for my cup.

"Baby," The look didn't leave Carlita's face, "he's been around for a lot longer than you know."

"Like you." I sighed.

"Like me."

"Is that your memory?"

She smiled at me, took another sip of her coffee.

For several moments we stared across the table at each other, enjoying sips from our own coffee cups in amiable, comfortable silence. I tried making a timeline in my head but found it too complicated. With everything that had happened throughout my childhood, all of the unexplained, weird things, then my teenage years, discovering my sexuality, meeting Lucas, then...*the well*...it was driving me mad. Having been gone for ten years with the effects of what I'd done, then coming back and having all of those memories back...my mind just couldn't handle it all.

The things in my past never got talked about, even with Oma. Everything was vague and referred to as though something we'd best just forget for fear of making things worse for ourselves. We were always on eggshells, doing our best to not draw attention to ourselves. At first, I thought it was just Oma's way. When I was a little kid, that made sense to me. You just followed the lead of the person who was your guardian, whoever that may be. As I got older, I realized that we were trying to be discreet. In my mid-teens, I found out whose attention we were trying to avoid.

I just wanted to say things to say them.

I needed to process everything I knew.

But my head wouldn't allow it.

Was that a side effect of being a kid and suffering through tremendously tricky events? Post-Traumatic Stress Disorder or something? Is that why things seemed to be somewhat blocked in my brain, keeping me from processing them? Was it a side effect of having my memories wiped clean when I jumped in the well the first time? Doing my best to think back to my life before I had jumped in the well at sixteen-years-old, I knew that I didn't have PTSD or anything really psychologically wrong with me. My brain had just been programmed to push these things away, out of sight, out of mind. So much so that when I tried to think about them, my brain threw up a type of veil to keep me from thinking too hard.

"When I was a kid," I said in a whisper, speaking to no one and everyone, "my mom just disappeared one day. My dad was at work. Mom was making breakfast, and *The Police* were playing on the radio."

Carlita looked over at me, her face a blank slate.

Like my brain had been wiped clean of memories right after I jumped into the well the first time.

Tabula Rasa.

"I remember the house shaking." I shook my head in frustration, trying to conjure up thoughts and memories that hadn't been in my head for years and only came to me in dreams. *Nightmares.* "Lights and loud...*fucking loud*...sounds. Like a freight train and an earthquake all in one. Things were falling to the floor."

Carlita was still staring blankly at me, and I was staring back as I spoke, as though in a trance placed by my own thought processes. I didn't know why I was speaking so openly with Carlita, but I assumed oracles tended to have that effect on people. A drag queen oracle, even more so.

"Everything stopped, and everything was really still."

Carlita waited.

"What happened after that, baby?" Carlita asked gently, her hand reaching for her coffee cup once more.

"I don't know." I shook my head jerkily. "I don't remember seeing anything. But...I don't remember anything after that until my dad was putting me to bed that night. He was tucking me in and reassuring me that mom would be back."

No follow-up questions from Carlita.

"But she never came back." My eyes locked on Carlita's. "And Dad was gone in the morning. That's when Oma showed up. To take care of me."

"Who called Esther Jean?" Carlita asked lowly.

"I guess Dad?" I shrugged shakily. "I mean...I guess he knew someone had to watch me at that age if he was just going to up and take off as well, right? Grandparents are usually the first choice in those situations, right?"

"I suppose."

Chewing at my lip, I stared at Carlita.

"I don't remember Oma before she showed up. We were living in that house before Oma came to take care of me." I said dryly. "I've never not lived in that house before or after Hollywood."

Carlita stared.

"That's not Oma's house. Is it?"

More staring.

"A lot of my life is a lie," I said with finality.

Carlita gave me a tight, concerned smile. With a shaky sigh, I slid from the booth seat and came to stand beside the table, looking down at the drag queen oracle known as "Carlita."

"Thank you." I shrugged.

"For what, baby?"

"Listening," I responded. "I guess."

She stared at me for a breath. "What will you do now?"

Again, I shrugged.

"About which problem?"

Then I left.

Chapter 7

Nelda Hammersmith was using an honest to goodness telescopic cigarette holder as she stood before me outside of the Sunny-Side Up Café. My phone had been vibrating sporadically in my pocket since the sun had begun its march towards the horizon, but I knew the list of suspects was small. Honestly, I wasn't sure if I wanted to speak with anyone on that list anytime soon, so I just continued to ignore the vibrations emanating from my pocket as I took in my manager's outfit right there on the main thoroughfare of Point Worth, Ohio.

Full evening dress, another fur capelet, a headwrap, alabaster skin with a red gash for a mouth, bright blue eye shadow, high heels, actual opera gloves, and sunglasses so dark I doubted she could see anything. My manager was a walking, talking caricature of what people thought Hollywood talent managers and agents looked like. Well, at least the female ones. It was probably all tailored suits, greasy, slicked-back hair, and chomping cigars for the male managers. Then again, I had no idea what gender stereotypes everyone had in their heads, so I could have been dead wrong. Also, I had no idea if people would have pegged Nelda Hammersmith as having anything to do with Hollywood at all.

Maybe people just think she's batshit crazy?

My phone buzzed again, and I ignored it once more.

"Now I see why you never return my texts or calls, Jacob, dear." Nelda cooed as she unclasped her tiny satin clutch purse for a lighter. "You've been positively ignoring your phone since we got here."

Since we got here was two minutes prior. Nelda had been standing outside of the Sunny-Side Up Café when I had been driving down Main street towards home. When I had seen Nelda standing there, draped in her Old Hollywood cosplay regalia, I had to stop. Not just because I was afraid she would be accosted by backwoods Ohioans with asinine questions about her provenance—not to mention her mental state—but because a thought struck me upon seeing her there. So, I had pulled into the parking lot of the café and approached my manager as she stood in the middle of Point Worth, looking as though she was waiting for the bus from the rest home.

After speaking with Carlita in the coffee shop in Toledo and having the revelation that I had, my mind was racing. When I drove home to Point Worth, to the house, I would be faced with Oma. Knowing what had transpired at the coffee shop, remembering the things that I remembered, I wasn't sure that was something I was prepared to do. In fact, I wasn't sure if seeing Oma was something I was incredibly keen on.

What I had said to Carlita had been true—as far as my memory served. My mother had disappeared one day after something...*violent*...had happened at the house. Then I remembered nothing until my dad was putting me to bed. When I awoke, Oma was there, prepared to watch over me since my father was gone as well. Both of my parents disappeared in less than a day after something shook the house and made a light show of epic proportions. What had happened at the house that would cause such an event—and make both of my parents run for the hills?

Had they even run away—or had they been chased off? Worse...had something terrible happened to them, and I had spent the entirety of my life thinking they were negligent and irresponsible parents? That's what Oma had led me to believe for two decades, anyway. Oma had told me that my mom was a trifling ho-bag, and my dad was dumb enough to fall in love with her. It all led me to believe that my parents had just been horrible at the job and had decided that they were meant for different things besides raising a child. But I had enough of my early memories to know that my mother had not been negligent. In fact, she had been very attentive. She had been warm and loving, to both my father and me. There was no way she had just run off in the middle of the day. Even if she had, my father wouldn't have followed suit, knowing that I had already lost one parent to a whim. Would he have?

If everything I had remembered, everything I now believed to be true was real, what did that mean for me and Point Worth? Where did that leave Oma and me? What about Lucas? The Kobolds? Any of it? Why did anything in Point Worth, Ohio even matter to me anymore? Couldn't I just disappear like my parents had? Make a clean break? I had all of my memories. My magic. I could just go back to being Jacob Michaels, make movies, live in California, and pretend that none of this had ever happened. Oma had insinuated that it was possible I should just go back to Hollywood.

That was curious, though.

Maybe even more curious than other thoughts swirling through my brain like a gathering storm.

No one who was looking to cause me harm would tell me to take myself out of imminent danger's way.

Right?

"Let me help you." I sighed to myself as Nelda's shaky hand extracted a silver-plated lighter from the small clutch.

Nelda smiled vaguely as I pulled the lighter from between her fingers and clicked it open. One cupped hand created a windscreen around the end of her cigarette as the other operated the lighter. I spun the wheel of the lighter...and nothing. Instead of trying again, I simply pushed a little magic into the lighter, making it produce a small flame on which Nelda could light her cigarette. I waited as she puffed a few times, then exhaled a plume of smoke, before I pulled the magic back, extinguishing the flame. Clicking the lighter shut, I held it out to her, which she readily accepted and dropped back into her clutch before clicking the purse shut once more.

"What's waiting for me, Nelda?" I asked. "Is it just action movies and bullshit like that? I mean...if I came back?"

"Bullshit like that makes us millions of dollars, Jacob." She clicked her tongue at me, disapprovingly. "I think—and don't quote me— but I think if this sequel does as well as the last one, maybe we can get you in one of those awful Marvel movies."

"Don't say that too loudly," I mumbled, though not unamused.

"Marvel   movies?"

"No." I frowned. "Don't call them awful. You're in middle-America for God's sake, Nelda. Superhero movies are up there with Hot Dish and Jesus on Sundays."

"What," She gave a distasteful look, "is a *Hot Dish?*"

"A casserole." I waved her off.

My stomach grumbled at the thought of greasy meat, cheese, and tater tots. Obviously, I needed to eat. If I was getting hungry thinking about Tater Tot Casserole, then I was starving.

"I don't want to go back to Hollywood," I shook my head slowly, "but I *really* don't want to stay here. But, I guess, even Hollywood is better for me than staying here and being...me."

"That's perfect." Her brow raised, and surely her eyes lit up, though the sunglasses kept me from confirming the fact. "They're going to film the sequel in Turkey of all places."

"Seriously?" I cringed.

"Mm." She nodded and delicately spat a piece of tobacco from the tip of her tongue. "We're going to have to put some weight on you, of course. Get you back into the shape you were before. If the producers see you like this—"

"If I did it once, I can do it again." I waved her off. "Where's Randy?"

"He's waiting in the car." She gestured vaguely at the Town Car parked a few spots down from mine. "I told him to wait while I checked to see if they could seat us. I figured that since we had to stay here tonight before our flight out tomorrow, we may as well have a decent meal."

Glancing at the Town Car, Randy beeped the horn at me sharply and waved from the driver's seat. He looked as out of place and clueless as Nelda Hammersmith did, though he seemed to be dressed more appropriately for Buttcrack Nowhere. I waved back with a confused smile before turning my attention back to my manager.

"Nelda." I sighed. "This is Point Worth, Ohio. It's a diner. It's a walk-in place. They have never even thought of the idea of reservations. You seat yourself when you go inside."

Nelda frowned, confused at the concept as she glanced at the squat, though charming building behind us.

"Quaint." She stated magnanimously.

"It is that." I agreed, not wanting to defend the café since it would distract from my point. Trying to explain that the rest of the world didn't work like Hollywood elite believed was not on the agenda, either. "Look, what's the latest I can come back? I have some...things...I need to do before I hop a flight."

"No later than a week, Jacob." She was shaking her head admonishingly. "You should just fly back in the morning with Randy and me, though. I can book you a flight right now."

Nelda reached for her clutch again, probably to pull out her iPhone or some other device she had no clue how to use well enough to buy airplane tickets on the spot. Holding my hand out to slow her down, I drew her attention back to the matter at hand.

"I'll be back before a week is up." I nodded slowly, my hand on hers as she clutched her tiny bag. "I promise. And I'll get my own ticket."

"Well," She turned her nose up, "if you insist. Personally, I would make my assistant do it if I were you. What else do you pay him for?"

"Her," I said blandly. "Jessica is a woman."

Nelda shrugged and brought her cigarette holder to her lips once more.

"It's not even a unisex name." I shook my head. "Nevermind. Look, I'll see you in a week, Nelda. Okay?"

One shoulder rose and fell as Nelda blew out a plume of bluish smoke, right into my face.

God, I missed cigarettes.

"See you in a week, Nelda," I state hurriedly as I turned and headed back towards my car, pulling my phone out of my pocket in the process.

"Hopefully sooner!" She stated grandly in response.

As I was sliding into the driver's seat of my car, Nelda was waving for Randy to get out of the car and join her. Randy was exiting the car as Nelda plucked the cigarette from the telescopic holder and dropped it daintily to the ground before crushing it with the toe of her shoe. As Randy approached, he held an arm out to her, and together, they made a grand entrance into the Sunny-Side Up Café. I shook my head as I watched them disappear inside, wondering what they would think of Midwestern café food. Hopefully, they both would end up puking after eating more grease than they'd both collectively ever had in their lives. At the very least, a nasty case of The Trots was in their futures.

Once I was certain that they were safely inside and making asses of themselves in the café, I unlocked my phone and brought up my notifications. Several from Oma—which I had no intention of returning quickly—one from Jessica, probably to warn me about Nelda's impending arrival, and two from Lucas.

You are still coming over for dinner, right?

The question was followed by the grinning devil emoji.

But I didn't know if that little devil would still be smiling after I told Lucas what my future plans were going to be. Then again, I wasn't so confident that I knew how to tell Lucas that I was giving up on my previous idea of staying in Point Worth. My head fell back against the headrest as I groaned, thinking of everything that had happened in the last few weeks. If I had been smart—which was something no one had ever accused me of—I would have left to go back to Hollywood as soon as I had gotten my memories back. Staying and giving Lucas his memories back had been the worst decision I had ever made. Really thinking about it, I felt that it might have also been the cruelest as well.

My phone got tossed into the passenger seat, and I pulled out of the Sunny-Side Up Café parking lot. Meeting Nelda Hammersmith outside of the café had helped me make a decision about my future—and how I really felt about staying in Point Worth. Lucas, on the other hand, was a major fly in the ointment. It was one thing to give Oma "deuces" and jump on a plane. I'd done it before without so much as a single word, so it wasn't beneath me. Telling Lucas I couldn't stay any longer and keep my sanity was another issue. Not just because it would be cruel to him...but because I genuinely did love Lucas.

That was one thing my memories didn't contradict.

Chapter 8

Upon entering Lucas' house, one thing was made clear to me once again. My boyfriend knew how to be alluring to the point that all other thoughts were pushed from my brain, and I was left in a hormonal puddle of stupid. Lucas was in the kitchen, peeking into the oven, clad only in boxers. When I came through the front door, his eyes came up to meet mine, and he smiled widely, the sheer joy at seeing me plastered all over his face. How could I possibly say or do anything to hurt him in any way? It would be like kicking a dog...well, no...my boyfriend wasn't a pet. But he always looked as happy to see me as a beloved family pet would. How do you say or do anything cruel to someone who loves you as deeply as you love them? Aren't those the people you are supposed to go out of your way to be as loving and kind to as possible?

"Hey, babe." He greeted me. "How does pork chops, roasted potatoes and carrots, roasted Brussels sprouts, and warm, buttery biscuits for dinner sound?"

"Amazing," I responded automatically. "What are *we* having?"

Lucas laughed.

"Everything except the pork chops." He bit his lower lip, making lower parts of me stir. "But I did pick up a cake from the Super Walmart on the way home from Toledo this afternoon. Double Double Fudge."

"Ooooh." I wiggled my hips suggestively as I sauntered toward the kitchen. "You treat me so fine with your big city store-bought cake."

My boyfriend tried not to look amused.

He failed.

"Bite me, city boy." Lucas teased as I hopped up onto the barstool on the other side of the counter from him. "I wanted to get home in time to get cleaned up so your *second dessert* would be fresh."

"When you put it that way." I pursed my lips as he leaned over the counter to give me a kiss.

"I thought you'd see it my way." He spoke against my lips before pulling away. "Second dessert is always more important to you than first dessert."

"I don't even give a shit about dinner if you want to skip right to second dessert." I teased, though my stomach grumbled at me, admonishing me for saying one of the dumbest things I'd ever said in my life.

"I heard that." Lucas jabbed a finger at my stomach. "Tummy Robbie is not going to let you just lie and not call you out, babe."

"Tummy Robbie?" I scoffed. "I have a flat stomach, thank you very much."

"I wasn't implying otherwise." Lucas admonished me. "But, for the record, I wouldn't care if you had a gut, ya' shallow turd."

I laughed loudly as Lucas winked at me as he slipped on an oven mitt. Lucas turned his attention to the oven, which he opened smoothly to pull out a sheet pan full of roasted vegetables as if doing a magic trick which involved a rabbit and a top hat. As my boyfriend found hot pads to place on the counter and placed the sheet tray of vegetables atop it, I unfurled my napkin and laid it in my lap. Lucas ducked again and another sheet tray with the buttery biscuits he had promised upon it. My mouth watered as I thought of stuffing one biscuit after another in my mouth, savory the warm, liquified butter dribbling down my chin and throat as I chewed hungrily.

"Is that look for me or the food?" Lucas asked, pulling me away from my thoughts.

"Huh?" I looked up.

"You're drooling, babe."

"Oh, shut up." I rolled my eyes as I chuckled and reached up to wipe my mouth to make sure he had been joking.

"I'm glad that what I have to offer appeals to you." Lucas was biting his lip again, making lower parts of me tingle once more. "There's nothing like seeing my man enjoy my goods."

"If you keep biting your lip, I'm going to start thinking one of two things," I said as I reached for my fork, trying to control my urges.

"Which two things?" He was smiling wickedly as he leaned against the counter.

"Either you are trying to seduce me—which is unnecessary—or you are secretly Anastasia Steele." I raised my eyebrows questioningly as Lucas started shoveling roasted carrots, potatoes, and Brussels sprouts onto my plate with a large spatula. "Seducing me is okay, though."

"Who is Anastasia Steele?" Lucas asked as he piled my plate with vegetables. "Did we go to high school with her?"

"Really?" I frowned as I pierced a potato with my fork.

Lucas looked over at me briefly, his shoulders rising and falling as he transitioned to making his own plate.

"What kind of English teacher are you?"

"Substitute." Lucas corrected me. "Literature usually. Is Anastasia Steele some famous book character?"

Lucas looked at me imploringly as he filled his plate and it dawned on me that there was no reason why Lucas would know who Anastasia Steele was. Of course, there was no reason that I should have that knowledge stored away in my brain, either.

"*Fifty Shades of Grey.*" I cringed before shoving the potato in my mouth.

A sharp, genuinely amused laugh escaped Lucas' throat as he pulled up a barstool to sit down across from me. Once he had his own fork poised over his plate, he looked over at me with a sly grin.

"How dirty is the book?" He asked, then skewered a vegetable. "I've never read it. Obviously."

"I shouldn't have." I sighed.

My boyfriend chewed and urged me on.

"Not that dirty." I shrugged. "I mean, other than people thinking BDSM is taboo and everything, it's not that bad."

"They tie each other up?"

"Um, I think he tied her up," I replied, focusing on my food as we discussed one of the worst—but most fun—books in American literature. "I don't think the BDSM went the other way."

"Doesn't seem fair."

"True."

"Does he spank her?" Lucas asked. "Mr. Grey, I presume."

"Well, duh." I chuckled as I skewered a carrot. "I mean, it's BDSM. You have to have a little spanking, right?"

"Agreed." Lucas chewed. "Blindfolds?"

"I think, yeah."

"Whips and chains?" Lucas asked. "Handcuffs?"

"Probably." I shrugged as I chewed and skewered another vegetable and reached for a biscuit. "I can't remember specifically, but that sounds right."

"Toys?"

I made an "mm" sound as I bit into the biscuit. Warm, melted butter greeted my lips and tongue, and my eyes closed in ecstasy as my stomach growled appreciatively again.

"What would Mr. Grey—"

"Christian," I mumbled around the mouthful of half-masticated biscuit.

"—Christian make Anastasia do while she was all tied up?" Lucas asked. "I mean, after he spanked her, of course."

"Sex stuff." I shrugged.

"Babe," Lucas said.

"Yeah?" I looked up and stuffed more of the heavenly biscuit into my mouth. "What?"

Lucas stared at me blandly.

"What?" I laughed nervously, barely understandable due to the mouthful of buttery biscuit in my mouth.

Lucas merely shook his head, an amused grin creeping onto his face as he stood from his barstool and slowly rounded the counter. Once Lucas was around the corner of the counter, and my view was unobstructed, I realized that Lucas Junior had joined our party. I swallowed the half-chewed biscuit in my mouth, nearly choking at the sight of my boyfriend's boxers straining out towards me as he approached. Lucas stopped short of actually pushing against me, but he was close enough that one slight movement and part of my body would be touching one of my favorite parts of his.

"Oh," I said simply, clearing my throat.

"You should have known better."

"Talking about literature really does it for you, huh?"

"Literature?" He laughed.

I shrugged as a grin formed on my face. I was having a tough time keeping my eyes on Lucas'. Keeping my eyes from trailing down to lower parts of him was more than difficult.

"Isn't any book technically literature?"

"Debatable."

"Webster's definition?" I teased.

"Maybe." He grinned.

"Yay me," I stated simply.

"Do you want to be Christian or Anastasia?" Lucas asked suddenly, making my eyes take on a saucer-like quality.

"Like...I mean...you want to do *that*?"

"Why not?" He was biting his lip again.

"I've never done those kinds of things before," I said though I was already turning on the barstool to face him, intrigued. "I've barely done anything before, really. What if I do it wrong?"

"What do you think will go wrong?" Lucas moved closer, positioning himself between my knees.

We were definitely touching, and Lucas was getting closer.

"What if—what if I spank you too hard?"

"So, you want to be Christian?" Lucas' mouth was so close to mine. "I can be Anastasia. I'd love to be your Anastasia."

I grunted as Lucas' groin ground against me.

"Okay." I moaned. "But let's use a different name. I'm one-hundred-percent gay here. And you're definitely not an *Anastasia*."

Lucas chuckled against my mouth before kissing me. His arms weren't wrapped around me, but he was still grinding against me. I moaned into Lucas' mouth, realizing that I was hard as a rock and had no idea when that happened.

"What do I call you?" Lucas asked, barely pulling away from my mouth in his effort to speak.

"Huh?" I moaned, trying to seal my lips over his once again.

"Do I call you 'sir'?" He teased. "Or is 'master' more appropriate?"

I groaned.

"Baby steps, Lucas." I chuckled, though I was more aroused than I'd ever been in my life. "I don't know if I would know how to handle that right now."

"I've got other things you can handle."

Without even willing it, my hands shot out and grabbed ahold of Lucas' ass through his thin boxers and pulled him into me roughly. Lucas gasped as his groin connected with my stomach, a particular appendage of his sliding up and getting squeezed between our two bodies. Hungrily, I looked up at him as Lucas looked down at me, first in surprise, then with excitement.

"Don't get smart with me." My voice was gravelly as I squeezed his ass with both hands and held him tightly against me.

"Okay." He exhaled with a slight shiver.

"If you get smart with me, you'll have to be punished."

Lucas gave a slight smile.

"Then maybe I should."

"Maybe." I agreed.

"Do you need more motivation?" He asked lowly as he moved his hips slightly, sliding himself between us.

The movement made me throb and him gasp. Before Lucas could do anything else, I hopped off of the barstool and moved my hands to his wrists, pulling both of his arms behind his back roughly. The length of our bodies were still pressed together as I stared at him. I tried to look intimidating, though Lucas was just slightly taller, as I squeezed my hands around his wrists and held his arms behind his back. Lucas groaned and tried shifting his hips again to rub himself against me once more. With a wicked grin, I moved back just enough to deny him that pleasure.

"Babe." Lucas moaned.

"You have to earn that."

"How?"

"Go to the bedroom," I commanded in a growl, my mouth against Lucas' suddenly.

Lucas gasped again as my hands tightened around his wrists.

"Now," I said firmly.

"Okay." Lucas eagerly nodded.

Jerkily, I let go of Lucas' hands, having to keep myself from grabbing him and having my way with him right there on the kitchen floor. The front of Lucas' boxers was still announcing his excitement and willingness as we stared at each other hungrily for a moment. Lucas looked as if he could attack me as much as I probably looked like I was debating the idea myself. Before I could command Lucas to do as I said again, he hesitantly and jerkily stepped away from me, towards the bedroom. My eyes burned into his as he made his way toward the bedroom, walking backwards so that his eyes didn't have to leave mine. When I saw him approaching the bedroom door, his eyes dropped to my crotch, and a slight grin appeared on his face. That was the rest of the motivation I needed to complete this experiment of Lucas'.

"Get in there," I commanded firmly again.

Lucas jumped, though the grin didn't leave his face and he darted into the bedroom as I began stomping across the room towards the doorway. When I stormed into the bedroom, Lucas was standing at the edge of the bed, his boxers no longer on. He was standing at full attention, the tip of him glistening. I did my best to not lick my lips as I sauntered over to him, prepared to provide my boyfriend with the release for a fantasy I hadn't known he had held onto since...whenever.

"Did I tell you to take off your boxers?" I asked as I stepped into my boyfriend's space and put my face in front of his. "Why would you do that if I didn't tell you to?"

"I guess you'll have to teach me to listen better." He grinned slightly.

Reaching up, I ran my fingers through his hair as he sighed and looked into my eyes desperately. When my hand got to the back of his head, I tangled my fingers in his hair and pulled just roughly enough to be on this side of pleasure. Lucas' mouth opened, but nothing escaped as my eyes burned into his. As my eyes lingered on his, I felt resolve fading away. My desire to do anything that might be painful melted away like ice on a hot summer sidewalk. Lucas' eyes were pleading with me to do the thing I wasn't sure I could without feeling poorly for it.

"Please, Rob." Lucas exhaled, obviously aware that I was having second thoughts. "But only if you want to."

His exposed cock was pushing against me, surely leaving a wet spot somewhere on the tail of my shirt. I leaned in and kissed him roughly, my lips forcing his lips open so that my tongue could slide into his mouth. Lucas moaned against my mouth as our tongues fought and his body moved desperately against mine. Groaning, I pulled at his hair, yanking his mouth away from mine.

"You'll tell me if you don't like it," I grunted.

Lucas nodded.

"Please." He nodded jerkily. "Please, Rob."

"I want this," I confirmed.

"I really want this." He parroted.

"I don't want to hurt you," I whispered huskily. "At least, not more than you want me to."

"You won't." He gasped again, making my pants feel even tighter.

"Because you'll tell me if it goes too far." It wasn't quite a command but not quite a question.

Maybe a firm request.

"Yes." He was nodding desperately again. "I'll tell you."

Grabbing Lucas' upper arms, I pulled him into me a final time and kissed him deeply, no tongue, no tricks, just a loving, deep kiss. When I gently pushed him away from my lips, I looked deeply into his eyes.

"Then I need you to turn around and put your hands on the bed, Lucas." I was biting my lips this time.

"Yes." Lucas sighed dreamily. "Yes, sir."

Lucas' head was on my chest as we laid naked on the bed together, both of us worn out yet satisfied. My boyfriend's ass was a slightly brighter shade of pink than a slight sunburn would provide, but the dreamy smile on his face let me know that he didn't mind in the slightest. Every now and again, Lucas would turn his face so he could tenderly kiss my chest, as though thanking me over and over again for what we had just done. My mind reeled at the thought of everything we had done that I had never thought of doing before. I wasn't so sure that either of us would ever do those things again, even with each other, but the evidence that we both had enjoyed the experience immensely was evident.

Only once had Lucas told me that it was all too much during our session in his bedroom. But it wasn't because he couldn't physically take the pleasure bordering on pain. It was because he was so turned on that he needed me to stop so that he could turn around and drop to his knees in front of me. He needed to do things to me to show how much he was enjoying what we were doing. And I was happy to let him. My fingers had twisted, curled, and tugged at his hair as he used his mouth on me in a way that only he knew how to do. After that, my mouth was on him as I held his hands behind him against his ass. Then he was on the bed on all fours again, but for an entirely different reason than punishment.

It was all too much and not enough for both of us. Lucas and I were not known for ending our sessions too quickly, but this once I think we both would have been unhappy to go all night. Our experiment had aroused us both too much for that to be a possibility. Our excitement made it impossible for us to not thrust and suck and stroke and spank towards one goal as quickly as possible. Things ended much more rapidly than usual, but I was pretty sure that neither one of us was going to complain.

"Can it be like this forever?" Lucas whispered against my chest before kissing it gently again. "You and me. *This*? I want this to be our life, Rob. I don't want to never not have life be like this."

"It can be like this as much as you like, Lucas." I sighed happily.

"Promise?" He asked with a sigh.

Responding to Lucas was not the easiest task once my mental processes started to catch up with me. When I had come to Lucas' house for dinner as we had planned, I had also been keenly aware that I needed to tell him that I wanted to go back to Hollywood. I needed to leave Point Worth, Ohio—put everything behind me and go back to the life that I thought I hated. After being in Point Worth and everything that had happened in such a short amount of time, Hollywood was looking better than it ever had. It looked better than it had after I jumped into the well in the basement, my memories got stolen, and my wish had been granted. Now that I knew I had the charisma and personality—enhanced by my innate magical abilities—to be a movie star, I knew that I could escape all of the craziness of my hometown once more.

The Kobolds were one thing. Discovering the things creeping around Oma's house was jarring before I had retrieved my memories from the well, but I could have dealt with it. Finding out that there were werewolves...I probably could have dealt with that as well. I mean...there are tons of things out in the world that a lot of us know nothing about. Only five percent of the ocean has been explored, so there could easily be things living in the deep that would turn a person's hair white as they shit their pants.

Having the encounters with Jason, seeing strange visions, pulling my teenage self out of Lake Erie...I probably could have learned to deal with those things. Oma being a witch, the same. Once I jumped into the well and recovered mine and Lucas' memories and really understood about the man in the black hooded cloak, things got unbearable. Now I knew that unknown werewolves were roaming Point Worth, looking to cause trouble. Lucas had some odd powers. Jason and Andrew would never stop being a bother. Oma would never stop keeping secrets. And sticking around Point Worth would lead to its decimation made my path clear.

Leave.

Get on a plane.

Never look back.

The man in the black hooded cloak will have no reason to return if you are not here, Rob.

He won't have the ability.

In the furthest, deepest corners of my mind, I knew that my plan was full of holes and there were a million problems that Lucas and I should probably deal with before we made any major decisions. Together, we had a lot to discuss, questions to ask, things to tell each other, but I just didn't care. I had come to Point Worth because I was tired and done with Hollywood. What would be so wrong about going back to Hollywood for the same reason? Point Worth and everyone and everything in it was going to have the same effect eventually. In fact, Point Worth would probably lead to mine or several other people's deaths.

Get out while the getting's good, Rob.

"Lucas," I whispered into his hair as he kissed my chest again.

"Mm."

"Do you want to live in California?" I asked gently.

Lucas' lips froze against my chest. As if time was moving at a snail's pace, his head slowly turned, and I was greeted with his confused, and possibly horrified gaze.

"What?"

I chuckled nervously.

"Would you want to live in California?" I asked again, refusing to lose my resolve. "With me. I want to leave Point Worth. Soon."

"Rob." He started to pull away.

Tightening my arms around his body, I kept Lucas' body against mine as we stared into each other's eyes. Lucas' started to look slightly aghast at what I had been suggesting, but he stopped trying to pull away from me.

"How soon?"

"Tomorrow if we could."

"Oh my god." Lucas' lips parted in shock. "You told me you wanted to stay here. Find a guy to live your life with. Who loved you. Travel. Live to be old and happy, and live a quiet life. What changed, Rob? I mean...did you not mean all of that when you said it?"

"Lucas." I shifted in the bed, bringing myself to a seated position against the headboard. Lucas slid from my arms but did not pull away as he came to kneel in front of me. For once, his nudity presented to me in such a way was not a distraction. "I meant every word when I said it. But you know everything that's happened since then. Can you honestly say that you want to stay here now? After everything that's happened? Now that we know everything that we know? Again? We have our memories back, babe."

Lucas stared warily at me.

"Don't tell me you don't remember everything that led up to me going into the cellar when we were sixteen and why. And don't tell me thinking about not knowing me when I came back out doesn't break your heart now that you have those memories. We loved each other, then and we love each other now. Those ten years away from each other were the worst ten years of my life. I want to leave this town—again—and never look back. Fuck Oma. Fuck the house. Fuck Jason and Andrew and werewolves and Kobolds and Oracles—"

"Oracles?"

"Fuck magic." I finished. "I want to leave. But I don't want to leave without you. I don't want to do *that* again."

"Rob—"

"I don't know what is up with you and *knowing how to use magic* and all of that." I shook my head. "I don't care why werewolf bites don't affect you, okay? I don't care if I know your family history or any of that. Because...if we leave here...together...it won't matter. We'll just be Rob and Lucas—well, I'll be Jacob Michaels again—but we'll be together. Living a normal life. Well, kind of normal. Don't you want that, babe? Don't you want to forget about all of the weird things that happen here and having to deal with them just so we can be together? We can ditch all of that shit and just have the being together part. Isn't that what you want, Lucas?"

"Rob—"

"Please." I pleaded, a single tear dropping from my eye. "Please, please, please Lucas. Don't tell me, 'no.' Okay? I can't hear 'no.' When I decided this, there was something inside of me telling me it was okay because I knew you would go with me if I asked."

Lucas looked as though he was going to cry as well.

"Of all things I know—the one I know the strongest is that I'm meant for you and you're meant for me." I shook my head, refusing to think of any alternative. "And I know that will work even better in California. I promise."

"I have a job here, Rob," Lucas said gently. "Two jobs. I'm a substitute English teacher, and I sling hardware for grandpa. What would I do in Los Angeles, Rob?"

"Nothing," I answered quickly. "Or anything you wanted. I have money. I'll work, babe. I'll do whatever it does to make you happy or nothing at all. Whatever you want. Anything you wish is my command, Lucas. I swear."

Lucas stared into my eyes.

"Wishes got us into this, babe." He answered softly.

"Don't." I slowly shook my head, both eyes leaking now. "Please don't blame me for all of this."

"I'm not."

"I know it's all my fault. Okay?" I was on the verge of sobbing. "All I can think of is...*shit*...how we got here. I can't even have a coherent thought about most of it because it's all too much. I couldn't explain it if I wanted to. And I know it's my fault. I get that. I thought I was doing the right thing, babe."

"The road to Hell is paved with good intentions, Rob." Lucas sighed.

I swallowed hard, willing myself to accept that Lucas had made up his mind about me. He had made a decision. The blame for everything was squarely on me in his mind...and California was the last thing he would choose. I sniffled, hoping that I could save some of my dignity.

"But I don't blame you." He looked up at me. "I know it's not your fault. What happened."

Hope filled my mind and my heart as I looked at my boyfriend cautiously, wondering if he was being honest.

"This whole town is full of secrets, Rob." He whispered. "Everything here is...*fucked*. No kid should have had to make the decision you were forced to make. You found an alternative. I don't blame you—because that's not your fault at all."

My eyes were freely leaking now.

"You did what had to be done when other people just ran away, babe." He shook his head in disgust. "And it worked. Maybe not great, but it worked. How can I blame you for that?"

I gave a wet laugh.

"And you came back." He smiled gently. "Just like you said you would. You brought me back, too. If you want to make a new wish for the future, I will be by your side for that one, too."

"Are you saying..."

"I'll go to California." He gave a firm nod, though he looked nervous.

A heavy, relieved exhale poured from my throat as I pulled Lucas forward so that I could hold him against me. He chuckled as our bodies pushed against each other's once again.

"I don't know what the hell I'm going to do in Los Angeles." He grumbled. "I mean...the people. The lights, cars...it's pretty...uh...busy, right?"

"I'll buy you a house in Hidden Hills or Calabasas with a big yard and a swimming pool and hills and trees around us so you can still feel like you're not in the big city. I'll buy you any fucking house you want, babe. A mansion if you want it." I laughed as I started kissing his face, which made him chuckle. "If you don't want to drive, I will, or we'll get

Ubers or hire a driver. We can have groceries and dinners delivered. We can do whatever needs to be done so that you're comfortable there, okay? Anything."

"Promise?"

"Anything."

"Just make sure that I can look out the backdoor without seeing a stream of cars driving by on a highway and I won't complain about a single thing, Rob." He smiled at me.

I laughed. "I can do that."

"What if you—uh, what's it called?" He frowned. "You have to shoot on location or something? Like in some other country for months on end?"

I looked at him like he was crazy. "You'll come with me, babe. I mean, unless you want to find some job and stay home while I'm off on location, you'll come with me. But that's totally up to you, too. Anything you want, remember?"

He smiled.

"I mean, I guess I could be your personal assistant and just travel with you." He said. "You'll have to fire the one you have."

"I could use two." I teased. "Besides, you'll be assisting me with things that Jessica doesn't have the qualifications for."

Lucas laughed and gasped as I grabbed a particular part of him as I held him against me, overjoyed that he had agreed to my request. I kissed Lucas repeatedly, kisses he happily returned as we smiled and held each other, confident in our decision. We probably would have ignored our cold dinner in the kitchen, forgone showers, and laid in bed together, kissing and snuggling until we fell asleep, completely exhausted. In fact, we probably would have been more than happy to kiss and snuggle until dawn came. The loud boom that echoed through the house, right before all of the lights fizzled out, kept us from doing that, though.

Chapter 9

Lucas and I were frozen in time, startled into a near-catatonic state as the darkness overtook the house, and the booming sound echoed off of the walls. As quickly as it sounded, the booming sound disappeared, and the echo of its existence stopped bouncing off of the walls. Lucas and I turned our heads to look at each other, our eyes not used to the darkness that was suddenly thrust upon us. The two of us knelt there together, listening, barely seeing, waiting for something to pop up out of the darkness, to clue us in on what had caused the sound and the lights to go out. There was nothing but the darkness and the silence, other than the sound of our own breathing, however. Slowly, I indicated to Lucas to get out of bed and put his pants on.

Quietly, and in unison, the two of us let go of each other and shifted to the edge of the bed, making as little noise as possible. My brain started to concoct reasons for the noise and the sudden extinguishing of all of the lights in the house. Maybe a transformer blew outside. There was no rain or storm of any kind to have caused problems, but it was totally possible that an equipment malfunction happened randomly. A flipped breaker was also possible, especially since Lucas had built the house himself—I had no idea if he did the electrical work himself—so that was added to the list.

It was also possible that a storm was starting to roll in that we had not noticed due to all of our fun and dramatic talking in the bedroom. A sudden rainstorm, accompanied by lightning and thunder, was not an oddity in upper Ohio in early Spring. More times than I had fingers to count, crazy, violent storms had popped up out of nowhere during Spring in our neck of the woods. It was not totally out of the question that we had Mother Nature to worry about more than anything else. The only problem was the twisting and turning in my gut, letting me know that whatever happened was not natural.

As though I could simply sense it, I knew something was very wrong, even though I had no evidence to support that feeling. With everything that had happened in my lifetime, though, I did not feel in that moment that I had to be rational. All things considered, I had every right to be as irrational and come up with as many crazy theories as I wanted. The first thing that came to mind was:

Magic.

Whether what had happened was a genuinely intentional act committed by a magical practitioner or some other type of act accompanied by magic was beyond me. I knew of no one—besides Oma and myself—who could cast magic in Point Worth, though my knowledge was limited. It wasn't like I went to the monthly conventions to network or simply to make new friends in the community. I wasn't even sure that those in the world who could do magic wanted others to know about it. Oma and I were pretty damned secretive about it, after all. As far as I knew, it was a pretty rare ability, so I was guessing that any convention I could have gone to would have been pretty lame and not worth the cost of admission. Of course, that thought only led to two other possibilities.

Black-hooded cloak.

Werewolves.

Lucas slid off of his side of the bed as I slid off of the other side, and together, we found our pants in the dark. Sliding into my jeans, I could see Lucas sliding into his boxers in my peripheral vision, though the darkness distorted things a bit. For all I knew, he was trying on a pair of yoga leggings. The thought, regardless of the seriousness of the situation, made me smile slightly, though I was still ill at ease.

"What was it?" Lucas whispered before looking around the bedroom floor in vain for something to put on over his boxers.

"I don't know," I whispered over my shoulder as I started to creep towards the bedroom door.

"Don't go anywhere." He hissed desperately. *"We'll go together."*

I paused and turned my head slightly to watch Lucas as he scrabbled around for a second, finally locating what he was looking for by the large window that looked out at Lake Erie. He stood from his stooped over position, triumphantly holding a pair of what looked like basketball shorts. Time and darkness seemed to press in on us as I waited quietly for him to slip them on. Lucas tied the drawstring in the shorts, giving me a proud look from across the room, the whites of his eyes and his teeth the only clearly visible features in the darkness of the bedroom. I shook my head nervously with a smile at him as he beamed back from his place next to the window.

"Now we can—"

The window shattered, shards of glass slicing through the air towards me as Lucas' eyes grew wide in horror. I crouched quickly with a scream, my hand flying up out of instinct, as I focused my magic outward. A halo of barely visible blue light appeared, and every piece of glass that hit it turned to sand. The other shards of glass flew past me, not connecting with my vulnerable, exposed flesh. Before I could pull my magic back in or stand from my crouched position, two arms, several times more massive than a normal man's—and much hairier—came through the window and encircled Lucas' waist.

He barely had time to look at me in disbelief.

"Rob." He gasped.

Then my boyfriend was yanked out of the window and into the night.

Roaring with rage and fear, I darted to the window, launched myself through it, and landed on the soft grass below. Werewolves are fast. By the time I had landed, corrected my footing, and raised my hand in preparation to send some fire towards the werewolf, he was nowhere in sight. Neither was Lucas. A scream to the left made me whip around, hand at the ready, searching desperately for some sign of my boyfriend. My stomach sunk when my eyes landed on the werewolf, Lucas over his shoulder like a sack of potatoes with flailing human appendages. I screamed angrily as the werewolf jumped into the back of a pickup truck at the side of the house.

Taking off at a full run, I thought about sending fireball after fireball towards the pickup and the werewolf who had Lucas wrapped up in his arms. However, I knew that there was no guarantee that Lucas would come away from the assault unharmed, so I lowered my arms to my side, pumping them as I ran as fast as I could towards the truck. The taillights lit up red, casting the surrounding yard in an ominous shade and it took off, werewolf and Lucas in the back. Screaming with rage, I ran faster, doing my best to catch up to them, to give myself a clear shot at Lucas' captor. But a human is no match for a pickup truck. Dust and gravel flew out at me as the truck sped off and I was forced to slide to a stop, barely staying on my feet, so that I could watch the truck drive off into the night.

Two red, rapidly shrinking eyes taunted me as they flew off into the night.

My whole body shook as I looked up to the heavens and screamed with rage.

Chapter 10

Jason barely had a chance to get out of the way as his door flew inwards. As soon as he had unlocked the door and began to swing it open to see who was banging away on it, I had violently kicked it in. He screamed out in shock as he jumped back and the door slammed into the wall behind it, the doorknob busting through and sticking into the drywall there. Jason stood there, merely in pajama pants, breathing heavily as he stared at his door now affixed to the wall. Heat and anger poured off of me as I stood framed in the doorway, glaring at him. I started to raise my hand, to do something to harm him. Not because I thought he had anything to do with Lucas being taken, but because he was *one of them*. He was a werewolf—just like the person who had ripped Lucas out of his own home and stolen away into the night as I pathetically tried to save him.

After the truck disappeared into the darkness, those two red eyes practically laughing at me, I screamed into the night sky. Fire shot from my hands into the sky, flying in an arc over the front lawn and landing far out from the shore into Lake Erie. There it sizzled and steamed and sent up more proof of my rage and fear. Why hadn't I gone back to Hollywood sooner? Told Lucas that I didn't want to stay in Ohio? He would have gone with me sooner—before it was too late. I had shaken those thoughts away. *Too late.* Lucas had just been taken, not harmed.

Hewasfinehewasfinehewasfine.

Please, God. Let him be fine.

He better be fine.

I will burn this entire state down if he is not fine.

He didn't do anything to deserve this.

Slowly, I lowered my hand at that thought. Jason was a total douchebag, but he hadn't done anything to be turned into a piece of bacon, either. *Yet.* His eyes shifted from the door and the wall to me, a look of anger trying to chase away the fear in his eyes. Glaring through the doorway at him, I stepped over the threshold into the house.

"They got my fucking boyfriend," I growled.

"What?" Confusion shadowed his face. "Who? Who got Lucas?"

"Your fucking people." I snarled. "Werewolves."

"My pack?" He was actually shocked.

"I have no fucking clue." I snapped. "You all look alike when you're furry, you piece of shit."

"No, we—" He stopped himself. "That's not the point. A werewolf took your—Lucas?"

"Yes."

"When? Where?"

"From his house, asshole," I growled again, stomping closer. "We had just got done...*stuff*...and some furry shit-hook came through the window and grabbed him like a sack of potatoes."

"Did he hurt him?" His eyes grew wide as he observed my menacing form stalking towards him.

"He jumped into the back of a pickup truck with Lucas, and it sped away," I replied sharply. "I wasn't able to stop them. But that means there was at least two of them working together."

"Why would anyone want Lucas?"

"Why would anyone want to bite him, you dumb bitch?" I snapped.

"Fuck you."

"Why have you always been after Lucas since we were kids?" I demanded. "You *always* wanted him in your pack. Because, it's kinda fucking suspect now, Jason." I stalked closer. "In the last day, two werewolves have attacked us and bit him. Now, one came through his fucking window to kidnap him. What the fuck is going on?"

"I told you and your crazy ass grandmother this morning why I tried to recruit Lucas when we were kids." Jason snapped back, though he was slowly inching away from me, obviously not as dumb as he looked. "The man in the black hooded cloak told me to."

"Yeah?" I hissed. "Partial bullshit, Jason. You might have done it to appease him, to keep him from doing you and your pack harm, but I think you also know why he wanted you to do it. And I swear to God you're going to tell me."

I raised a hand, red fire already encircling it, lapping and flickering, though not harming my flesh.

"Be careful!" Jason practically squealed as he backed into the island in his kitchen.

"Tell me, goddamnit!" I bellowed.

"Because Lucas was a distraction!" Jason spat, though his eyes were still wide with fear. "Because he was in the way, all right?"

"What does that mean?" I glowered at him, my hand and the fire staying in position, threatening him.

"Dude." Jason was shaking his head violently. "Just stop. I've already told you enough, okay? Put your fucking hand down and let's talk like normal people—without fangs, claws, or fire."

"I'm beyond being civil, Jason." I inched closer as menacingly as possible. "You're going to tell me what the fuck you are talking about—what you actually mean, and not some half-truth bullshit—or I'm going to burn this whole fucking house down. And you'll be the kindling."

"Fuck." Jason hissed to himself, aware that his choices were severely limited.

He realized he had to decide if he wanted to tell me what he knew and risk putting himself in danger...or not tell me and certainly get barbecued alive.

"Fine!" He growled back at me. "Put your hand down."

"After you tell me, asshole."

"Lucas made you more powerful." Jason spat, firelight dancing in his eyes, I was so close. "He gave you something to fight for. To live for. *He. Got. In. The. Way.*"

"Whose way?" I demanded.

"Who do you think?" Jason shouted back.

"Him."

Jason gave a single sharp nod.

"He wasn't concerned about Lucas' powers? How Lucas just knew things? Why he's immune to werewolf bites?" I asked. "Do you think maybe that's why *he* was so damn fixated on Lucas?"

Jason stared at me for a moment, the anger and fear melting from his face, leaving him bewildered by me. After a few breathless moments, a grin slowly started to form on Jason's face.

"You really are a clueless son of a bitch, aren't you?" Jason snorted sharply. "I always thought you were pretty fucking dumb, but—wow."

"I'm still holding fire, fuckface."

"He doesn't care about Lucas' powers. Or mine. Or anyone else's." Jason was on the verge of laughing. "There's nothing for him to be curious about, you idiot."

"What does that mean?" I asked, pushing the fire closer to Jason. He didn't even react.

"He's the reason we have our powers, you fucking nitwit." Jason chuckled. "He's the reason this whole fucking town is the way it is. Why everything is upside down. I mean...God, you're simple. I know it's hard to believe that werewolves and witches and magic are all not real. But you know that they are. Didn't you ever wonder why there are so many in the little fucking town of Point Worth, Rob? Did that ever cross your mind?"

"I've been kinda busy not having my memories for a decade." I snapped.

"What?" Jason frowned.

"So," I realized I had said too much, "that's where this comes from?"

Indicating the fire in my hand, Jason's eyes were drawn to it. He grinned so widely that his teeth reflected the flame, painting them in reds and yellows.

"No, you dipshit." He turned his eyes back to mine. "You're the one person in this town whose powers have nothing to do with him. That's why he wants Lucas out of the way. To make it easier to get to you when the time comes. When *your* time comes. Your power is not his. And it makes you so...*enticing.*"

Jason sniffed the air as his eyes closed slowly, his tongue darting out to lick his lips.

I swallowed hard.

"What?"

"You're only here for one reason, Rob." Jason was shaking his head as he smiled, his eyes opening once more. "Your parents had no clue when they came here what drew them here...but...you're going to release him. Finally. You're going to open up the ground, and it's going to swallow this whole fucking town, and out of that, he'll be born again. When you sent him away, you just helped him out. He's growing stronger by the day, man. And when he finally comes...it's going to leave this place in ruins. You've seen it. I know you have. Because I've seen it, too."

"You look happy about that." It was the only thing I could think of to say.

"Happy?" Jason snarled suddenly. "Of course I'm happy!"

I inched back marginally at the fire-illuminated crazy expression on Jason's face.

"Who the fuck wants to live like this?" He swept an arm vaguely through the air. "In this shithole town with limited opportunities, turning hairy off and on, walking the thinnest tight-rope in the world, hoping that you don't anger *him*. Pray he doesn't decide you and your family aren't living up to the bargain?"

"Bargain?" I felt sick.

"Ask your boyfriend." He snorted.

"I'm asking you." I darted forward, shoving my flame covered hand into his face, nearly singing off some of his five o'clock shadow. "I'm asking you because I know where the fuck you are, Jason."

"The Barkley's have been here as long as my family has." Jason didn't even look scared anymore. "Do you think Lucas is the only one who is...*special?* His family knows *him* as well as mine and everyone else's family in this town does, Rob. We all get powers...he uses us as he sees fit. Every damn person in this town is some flavor of strange. Some more so than others."

Jason looked down when he said that part, obviously considering his own special "power."

"Only problem is," Jason looked up, squinting angrily, "Lucas doesn't like playing the game."

"You get powers you don't want, and he uses all of you?" I was confused as I backed up marginally, pulling my hand away from him. "That's it? Why do any of you play the game?"

I scoffed at him.

"I mean," I continued, "if you don't want to be a werewolf and the Barkley's don't want...whatever it is they have...why go along with it? What's he going to do? Especially now that he's gone?"

"He's not gone," Jason whispered. "He's resting. You didn't stop him. You just slowed him down. Sure. We all hoped what you did got rid of him for good. So we could all go on living as close to normal as possible. But...he's been reminding us periodically that he'll be back. And any of us who think we're safe now will find out otherwise."

"What's in it for you?" I repeated like Jason was deaf. "Even if you know he'll come back, he's going to destroy this town and everything in it. Why play along?"

"Have you seen any homeless people here, Rob?" Jason asked gently. "Seen anyone go hungry? What's the dropout rate at the high school? Who doesn't have a job? Who can't pay their bills? We've only had social problems in this town in the last ten years. Since you did what you did."

"I see." I swallowed.

"Maybe we're all going to be fucked when he pops up again," Jason said. "But we're all going to die eventually anyway. At least here we know we'll be taken care of until then."

"Yeah." I nodded, my hand dropping to my side as the fire went out, leaving us in shadowy darkness. "Because living under a bridge is so much worse than a fate worse than death, right? And you call me stupid."

Jason just glowered.

"Everyone in this fucking town is a few red Solo cups short of a frat party, man." I laughed bitterly. "I knew it when I was a kid...and these last few weeks have confirmed it. Especially now that I have—"

I stopped myself.

Jason grinned evilly.

"What are you smiling at, fucker?" I snapped.

"Nothing." He snickered.

"Fucking tell me," I replied. "Or do I need to threaten to burn you alive in this house again?"

"Your memory." He snickered again. "It's back."

"What?"

How does he know anything about that?

"You wished to not know anything about any of this." Jason was gesturing vaguely once more. "You thought so hard about how you wished you and Lucas didn't know about any of the stuff that happened when you were kids. To escape from what was coming. You wished your little friends in your house were safe, too. You thought, when you came out of that well, that you had stopped *him*. That everyone was safe."

I stared at him, my gut sinking towards my feet.

"All you did was make everyone on your side dumber than ever for the next ten years." Jason was full-on laughing. "And the rest of us just went along with it, let you believe it while *he* started planning his return. He's inevitable, Rob. All you did was give him more time to plan. You fucked up. And you didn't even realize it until Lucas was snatched and I told you. You've already lost and are just now realizing it, man."

"Fuck you," I grumbled angrily.

"And so few of you there were, right?" He was so amused that I wanted to punch my fist through his face and out the back of his head. "You, Lucas...and some *creatures* who live in that house. You better hope you can handle *him* on your own, Rob. Because those creatures are nothing...and Lucas will be dead by the time the sun comes up."

A snarl started to build in my throat as I glared at Jason, the fear and worry for Lucas twisting my guts. But then a thought dawned on me, something I should have thought of long before that moment. Something that I'd been told but didn't quite want to believe. Shaking my head at how stupid I was, I couldn't help but smile bitterly.

"Of course, these guys are your pack." I sighed, angry at myself. "The guys who attacked Lucas and me and bit him...the guys who took him just now. All of these wolves are your pack. You've been expanding for ten years."

"Largest pack in the whole northwest." He leaned forward and winked evilly. "Though, that's not really saying much since no one comes close to our size."

I nodded slowly.

"You really are simple, aren't you?" Jason sighed with a smile. "All you have is your magic and a blank book. You don't even have Lucas anymore. Well, soon, no one will have Lucas."

The book.

How does he...

Oh.

Oh, yeah.

"The book won't be blank for long." I shrugged. "And Lucas won't be dead soon. I may be slow...but I'm steady, assface. I can win this race."

Jason threw his head back and laughed with incredulity.

"But first," I stopped him with my sharp tone, "I'm going to do what I told Oma I was going to do."

"What's that?" Jason rolled his eyes.

"I'm gonna cut the head off the Hydra." I smiled sweetly at him. "I don't care what happens."

Jason gave me a confused look. When I smiled at him and drug a finger across my neck, his confused look turned to a mixture of anger and fear. Rage welled up in me as I started to lift my hands towards Jason. His head fell back again, but instead of a laugh, it was a howl that came from his throat. In less time than it takes to blink, Jason's flesh seemed to explode from his body, his werewolf form bursting forth. The howl still coming from the wolf's throat echoed off of the walls as his head tilted back down, much higher than it had been before, to stare at me with red eyes.

I wasn't afraid.

Werewolf Jason leapt forward, and I stepped aside, making a slashing motion with my hand as he flew by. With a resounding crash, the werewolf that was Jason fell to the ground. Well, his body crashed to the ground. His head came tumbling after a split second later.

You don't need silver to kill a werewolf.

Almost everything needs a head to live.

The puddle of blood began blooming around the beheaded werewolf as it laid there, motionless and useless.

So, I went to Jason's kitchen to find some Tupperware.

Chapter 11

The front door of Oma's house creaked only slightly as I pushed it open, cautious, attempting to be sly as I made my way into the house in the middle of the night. Darkness, like that in Lucas' and Jason's house, pervaded, but my eyes were adjusted to trying to see in the dark now. Cradled in the crook of my arm was the Tupperware I had taken from one of the cabinets in Jason's kitchen, being careful so as to not drop it. Once I was inside, I gently shut the door behind myself, making sure that a mere *click* sound was made by the lock engaging. I knew that Oma would not hear the noises of the door opening and closing—I'd snuck in and out enough as a teenager and as an adult to know that. But I didn't want to wake Ernst or any of the Kobolds, either. Especially Ernst, actually. He'd be inquisitive, and I couldn't have that.

I didn't bother kicking my shoes off, though my footsteps would have been lighter if I had. Sticking around Oma's house was not in my plans, however, and kicking my shoes off just to put them back on in a few moments would only slow me down. Lucas needed me as quickly as possible, so I had to work fast. If I happened to wake Oma or the Kobolds up, that was something that I would just have to deal with when the time came. Until then, I was going to do things the only way that I knew how—like a bull in a china cabinet.

When I got to the bookcase, I knelt down, gently setting the Tupperware onto the ground beside me. The house was as quiet as a grave as I reached down and gently pried the false board away from the bottom of the case. My hands slid into the darkness of that cubbyhole, and my fingertips connected with the old leather of the book. I slid it out of its hiding place and set it onto the floor before me. I didn't bother pricking my finger and trying to open the book the way that I'd always been taught.

The magic I'd done when I was sixteen fucked everything up.

It needed more than just a touch of my magic.

The book wasn't going to do anything for anyone until it was satisfied with a significant bit of magic.

With more blood than I could give.

"Thirsty?" I whispered in a bland tone as I picked up the large, full Tupperware container and slowly peeled back the lid.

The viscous liquid inside—Jason's blood—looked black in the dark of Oma's house. I shut my eyes for a moment, saying a silent prayer—to who, I wasn't sure—and tipped the container forward. Blood flowed over the edge and onto the book. Blood I had let seep into the Tupperware from Jason's open neck. At first, all I could think about was how I was going to make Oma's living room look like a murder scene—like Jason's. But when the blood connected with the book, it seemed to disappear into the leather of the old book, as though it was being drunk into the book itself. I smiled to myself as I continued pouring the container onto the book until the very last drop dripped off of the plastic lip of the Tupperware.

Pressing the lid back onto the Tupperware, sealing it tightly, I set it to the side for the time being. The book was heavier than I ever remembered it being as I lifted it from the floor. It was almost as if it had a belly full of blood it was digesting, giving it more heft—though I wasn't sure that was a bad analogy for what was actually going on. When I brought my fingers to the leather cover to open the book, it gave no resistance. Looking down at the book, I smiled at the sight of the dark shapes and words on the pages that I couldn't quite read due to being in the dark, but could still see were now there.

The book was no longer hiding its secrets.

All it needed was more magic.

Rising from my knees to stand once more, I closed the book and bent down to grab the plastic storage container from the floor. Creeping again, I made my way to the kitchen and set the book on the counter. I methodically cleaned out the bloody container in Oma's sink, once again being as quiet as possible, then shoved it into the dishwasher. Either it would be cleaned so thoroughly that no one would know what it had been used for, or by the time someone figured it out, I'd be long gone. Neither situation particularly bothered me in the slightest.

No Kobolds were in sight, and I hadn't heard a single sound in the process of retrieving the book and washing out the Tupperware in the kitchen. So, when I started to tiptoe back through the living room towards the front door, I was startled out of my skin when the light came on suddenly. I jumped back, nearly dropping the book, when I saw Oma standing by the front door, her arms crossed under her breast, looking at me like I was crazy. Hiding the book or pretending that I hadn't been creeping around didn't even cross my mind. I simply adjusted my facial expression to a more normal one.

Not that it mattered.

"Where you been?" She asked.

Simple question.

"Where have you been?" I countered.

"In bed, of course."

Looking her over, it was evident that Oma had not been in bed. She had on her button-down shirt and jeans, her makeup had not been washed off, her hair was still perfectly coifed. The only article of clothing that indicated she had been ready for bed was the hard-sole slippers on her feet.

"Okay." I shrugged.

She just stared at me.

"Out of my way, old woman." I gestured vaguely.

Oma's eyes grew wide. "You gonna just come home and be bossy and sassy with me? What reason you got to do that?"

"Move."

"You little—"

"Move, or I'll move you," I stated blandly. "I've got better things to attend to, lady."

She scoffed. "Like you could. Where the hell you been?"

"Cutting the head off of a werewolf who had it coming," I answered. "By the way, there's crime scene evidence in the dishwasher.

You might wanna let it run through a cycle before you use anything out of there. Not trying to be a jerk, but I'd put money on it that Jason had Hep-C or something. Ginga-vita-cockus at the least."

I started towards the door again. Oma didn't back down.

Oma should have been shocked at my statement about Jason, but she didn't even try to pretend that she was.

"You got the book." She looked the tome tucked under my arm.

"I got the book." I nodded. "It's my family's book, so I'm taking it."

Oma squinted at me, searching my face for more information than I was providing verbally. Outwardly, I was trying to project a calm façade, but my mind was racing with one thought.

Save Lucas.

However, I knew that I couldn't get too rushed when dealing with Oma, especially when I had just killed Jason and was taking the book away from the house. She obviously hadn't even gone to bed but instead had been staying up, waiting for me to come home. That, in itself, was an indication that the theories swirling around in my head were accurate and not just batshit crazy ideas my paranoia had cooked up.

Why had Oma been dressed and awake when I came home? Had she been doing something in the middle of the night that required her to be fully dressed and prepared? As long as I'd known Oma, anything past midnight was asking too much of the woman. But there she was, blocking me from the front door, fully clothed, looking as spry as I'd ever seen her. I couldn't help but wonder if she knew that I would be coming home in the middle of the night.

And how would she know that?

"Move."

"I'm not moving."

"Oma," I stared deeply into her eyes from across the expanse of the living room, "there are at least two other werewolves I need to fuck up tonight. My plate is full. So, unless you want to be on the list—"

"Where's Lucas?" She interrupted. "Wasn't you supposed to be at his house tonight?"

Fighting back the urge to let a groan of frustration and agony escape my throat, I just stared at Oma. There was nothing to say that I felt comfortable saying to her.

"Shouldn't you be with him?"

"I should." I nodded. "So, let me go be with him."

Oma didn't move, and her arms seemed to tense up in their folded position under her breast. Instead of fighting further with Oma, I shrugged and turned on my heels, pointing myself in the direction of the kitchen. As I started to stomp away towards the back door, I heard Oma grumble and then heard her footsteps padding against the floorboards to catch up with me. My feet moved faster across the kitchen linoleum as I made my way to the backdoor—the only other exit unless I wanted to go through a window.

"You stop right there!" Oma huffed as my hand connected with the doorknob to the backdoor.

"Goodnight, Oma," I said simply as I pulled the door open.

The door had moved inward mere inches before it jerked back into place, pulled my hand with it, making my arm feel as though it would be ripped out of its socket. Instead of screaming out at the jerking motion applied to my arm, I swallowed it down and turned towards Oma, rage boiling up within me. Oma was standing in the kitchen doorway, glaring at me as I rounded on her. A stand-off was what she had in mind, I imagined, but I had no time for her questions or diversionary tactics. Lucas needed me.

Jason had something critically important when I had been in his house, speaking with him before he lost his head.

You're the only one in this town whose powers have nothing to do with him.

I couldn't trust Oma any more than I could have trusted Jason.

He hadn't told me why because Jason hadn't explicitly told me that Oma was not to be trusted. However, I had already figured that out for myself. All I had to do was remember my parents, the house, and their disappearance to know why I couldn't trust Oma.

"Where does Jason's pack meet?" I asked Oma, rage tinting my voice as I stared at her from across the kitchen. "They have Lucas, and I'm going to get him back."

"You're not getting him back, Robbie." Oma shook her head. "What's done is done."

"I thought Lucas was a friend of yours, Oma?" I asked, not surprised in the least at her remark. "I'd have thought you'd want me to go save him. Hell, I'd have thought you'd want to come along and help out."

"It's too late to help anyone, Robbie." She shook her head, her face pinched up. "I think you know that."

"Fuck the big city," I stated blandly. "Things move quickly in Point Worth, huh?"

Oma rolled her eyes.

"Let it go." She replied. "Put that damn book back, go upstairs, get cleaned up, and go to bed."

"Where's Ernst and the rest?" I asked, realizing that Oma and I arguing should have brought at least one of them out to investigate.

"Gone."

"Gone where?" I seethed.

She shrugged. "All the magic's gone. It's all gettin' sucked up. I think you probably already knew that."

She gestured at the book.

"Everything in this town that's got any bit o' magic is disappearin'." She continued. "Including Ernst *and the rest.* Pretty soon, it'll be you and me, too, Robbie. Soon as he manages to come back."

"I thought we had longer." I felt my eyes watering as I thought of Ernst and the rest of the Kobolds. "The well...I mean, yeah, I used all of that up myself, but I thought we'd have longer before things started getting fucked up beyond recognition."

"You guessed wrong, I s'pose."

"This is crazy." I shook my head as I reached behind myself for the doorknob. Oma's eyes shot to the door, watching it closely. "Everything is fucking crazy. None of this makes sense, and everything is spiraling out of control. I don't even know up from down. I have to go, Oma. I'm going to find Lucas—even if you won't tell me where Jason and his pack meet—and then the two of us are hopping on a plane out of this fucking state. And we're never looking back."

"You ain't goin' nowhere, Robbie." She shook her head, looking guilty. "You know damn well I can't let you leave."

"I know," I said. "But I'm going to. Are you going to tell me where Jason's pack meets when they're measuring their dicks or what?"

Oma didn't answer, but her head slowly shook side to side.

"Fine." My fingers connected with the doorknob. "But don't try to stop me, either. I'll burn this house down without thinking twice about it, Oma."

"You won't." Her eyes grew wide.

"Don't be the second person tonight who tests me, old woman." My hand twisted the doorknob. "It didn't work out so well for the last person."

"You threatenin' me?"

"That's what it's come to tonight, Oma." I pulled the door open, cool Spring air greeting my backside. "You have no idea what I'll do to save Lucas, so if you're not going to help me—not even tell me where he is—it's in your best interest to not get in my way. If the Kobolds are gone..."

I took a second to collect myself.

"And you're the only thing left in this house I'll burn it to the fucking ground if you force me," I said. "I don't even care if I'm in it, too. Understand?"

"You won't burn down our family home." She gasped. "What the hell you got left if you ain't got that?"

Unable to help myself, a barking laugh escaped my throat.

"Our family home?" I cackled. "What are you even talking about?"

"This house." She stomped her foot against the linoleum. "This is where our family made roots in this damn town. And you think I'd believe that you'd just burn it down without a second thought?"

"You're worried about this house?" I shook my head in disgust. "I'm worried about Lucas' life."

"What are you hopin' to achieve by goin' after him, Robbie?" Oma snarled. "You gonna just saunter into a werewolf pack's meet-up and take Lucas back? Is that your idjit plan? Is that how you think it'll work out for you? You think you're capable of takin' on that many werewolves at one time?"

Slowly, a smile formed on my face.

Oma was showing one card in her hand at a time.

"I thought we'd agreed before that Jason's pack was still relatively small, Oma?" I cocked my head to the side as I inched my way backward. "But you seem to think there's more now? Why is that?"

A cloud passed over her face, as though she realized she had said too much or the wrong thing. Instead of trying to backtrack or explain herself, she just glowered at me.

"It don't matter." She snapped. "What's done is done."

"Where's the pack?" I asked again.

"Most likely out at that damn football field." She shrugged. "Waiting on Jason to show up, even though—I guess—he ain't gonna."

"Okay." I inched further backward.

"You don't need to worry about that, though." She commanded. "Just get back in this house and forget about all of that, now."

"You telling me to let Lucas go let's me know that I shouldn't listen to a word you say, lady."

"Get back in this house." She stomped her foot, the walls of the house rumbling. But I'd seen that trick before. I didn't even jump. "We need to just stay home and figure out what to do to save ourselves. If you go and try to save Lucas, you'll ruin everything, Robbie."

"No."

"Wouldn't you rather be safe in your family home rather than out there gettin' yourself killed?" She asked.

I smiled.

"This may be my family home," I replied, "but there's no family left in it."

Then I ducked out of the backdoor and ran for it before she had a clear shot. I didn't have all of the time in the world to argue with Oma about family homes, family, keeping myself safe, not saving Lucas...none of that was an option. Lucas was the only thing in the entire town of Point Worth that made it tolerable. Not saving him was never an option.

None of this makes sense.

Chapter 12

Locating Lucas so that I could start formulating a plan wasn't nearly as difficult as I had anticipated, because when I got to the football field at the old high school, he was simply tied to the field goal post. Not the designated home team end, but the visitor end. *Kinda like rubbing salt in the wound*, I thought to myself as I peered down from the shadows at the top of the stadium. I did my best to keep myself out of view of any werewolves who were certainly watching and waiting for me. Even though none of them had probably figured out that Jason was no longer amongst the living, they would be angry to see me there, trying to save my boyfriend. If they found out about Jason before I managed to get to Lucas, things would be even worse for both of us, especially if we got caught trying to escape.

Looking down at Lucas, I could kind of tell that he had been stood up in front of the goal post, his arms pulled back and secured with rope around the post and affixed to his wrists.

Did you see that?

I shook my head, clearing away the thoughts.

What about that?

My hands went to the side of my head as I fought to concentrate on what was happening with Lucas. I needed to get down on the field and untie him, rescue him from the pack of werewolves. If I waited too long and one of them went to find out where Jason was, saw that he was dead, things would turn into a total shit show. They probably wouldn't hesitate to simply kill Lucas and move onto whatever their next planned activity was. Maybe they'd go on a rampage and start indiscriminately killing everyone in town. Just go door to door and kill anyone who answered.

Were werewolves like vampires? Could they enter homes without an invitation?

Were vampires even real?

Searching my memories, I wasn't so sure I had that knowledge stored away from some encounter with one in my past.

Then again, it didn't really matter what was real and what wasn't because my boyfriend was currently tied up and awaiting slaughter.

When I looked down at Lucas, I could tell, even from that distance that his head was slumped forward. As though he was passed out or knocked out. Or worse. Would I get down to rescue him, only to find that he was actually...not alive...and it had all been a trap to lure me out into the open? My eyes searched the stands of the stadium, and not a single person was in sight. There were no people slowly stalking the stands, waiting for signs of my arrival. There was nobody on the field. No one in the stands on the other side of the field as far as I could tell. That made me feel slightly better but was also concerning. If no one was at the stadium, watching over their captive, did that mean there was no reason to watch over him? Did it mean...

I stepped out of the shadows and slowly began my descent to the field. My eyes darted back and forth, searching the stands as I made my way down to Lucas. No one was stepping out of the shadows or popping up out of nowhere to cut me off or jump me. The only audible sounds were those of my feet on the aluminum steps that led downwards. A rhythmic "clunk" sounded with each step, but nothing else moved in the stadium.

By the time that I reached the bottom level of the seating on the home side, there was still no movement on the field or in either side of the stands. It was merely dark, quiet, and motionless. I waited a moment, making sure that I was not being overly confident, then walked to the stairs that led from the stands down to the sidelines for the home team. As I descended those stairs, my footsteps were the only sounds once more. I kept my eyes peeled but continued my trek to the goal post where Lucas was. No matter what Oma had said, there was nothing that was going to stop me from saving him.

No matter what condition I found him in when I got there.

As I got closer to Lucas, I could tell that he had been roughed up a little—there was a bruise on the side of his face—but I could see his chest slowly rising and falling as he hung loosely against the goal post. Whatever the wolves—the pack—had done to him, he was alive. He was fine. My heart soared, and my feet began moving quickly, bringing me closer and closer to Lucas at a pace that made a smile form on my face.

When I finally reached Lucas, I couldn't help but grab his face in my hands and kiss him gently. The movement against his face woke him, and his eyes slowly fluttered open. Duct tape had been slapped over his mouth, but I could see the smile in his eyes. The shifting of the makeshift gag let me know that the smile was not just in his eyes. His body began to quiver with excitement as I reached up and starting to work at a corner of the tape.

"Fast or slow?" I winced as I spoke. "Blink once for fast."

One blink.

I ripped the tape off without a second thought. Lucas, to his credit, merely cringed, holding back the scream that had probably begged to be released from his throat. Again, I leaned forward and kissed his mouth, now that I had access to his lips, hoping it would take some of the sting out from me ripping off the tape.

"Babe," Lucas sputtered when I pulled away. "They all left, but I know they're coming back. Get me the fuck out of here."

"They didn't hurt you, did they?" I asked as I moved around him and started to work on the ropes at the back of the goal post.

"Not badly enough." He stated simply. "How did you find me?"

"Well," I said quietly as I worked on the knots. "It's not like the football field is some random place, right?"

I laughed nervously.

"Where's Jason?" He asked. "He wasn't with these guys, but I know that they're his pack. They were talking about it earlier. They said Jason would deal with you eventually. I wasn't sure what that meant, but I knew it wasn't good."

"Jason's been dealt with."

"Did he try to hurt you?" Lucas gasped as the first knot came undone.

I just laughed.

"I guess that's an answer," Lucas stated lowly. "I probably don't want to know the rest, do I?"

The last knot came undone, and Lucas fell away from the goal post, barely catching himself with his feet as he stumbled. I walked around the post and pulled him in for a hug, then kissed him roughly on his mouth. When I pulled back, I looked into his eyes as I smiled.

"You're a vegetarian," I stated simply. "You don't like to hear about animals getting hurt. So, I won't tell you what happened to Jason."

Lucas cringed, but then a new look overtook his face.

A look that said: *"Well, he probably had it coming."*

"Where's Mrs. Wagner?" Lucas asked as I grabbed his hand and pulled him towards the stands.

"Home."

"Why didn't you bring her?" Lucas gasped as I drug him toward the stands. "Wouldn't it be useful to have her if the pack shows back up, Rob? I mean, your grandmother—"

I spun to face him, stopping us both in our tracks.

"She's not my grandmother," I stated sharply. "Esther Jean Wagner is not and never has been my grandmother."

Lucas stared at me for a moment, then a smile overtook his face.

"Rob..."

I tried to turn to lead us towards the stands again, but Lucas jerked my hand, pulling me around to look at him again.

"You're being crazy." Lucas shook his head. "I have my memories, remember? Mrs. Wagner has been with you since you were a little kid, Rob. She's your grandmother. You started staying with her when your parents...um, left...remember, babe? What are you even—"

"I lived in that house with my parents before they ran off, Lucas," I said sharply. "That isn't Oma's house. It was my parents' house. Then they disappeared, and Oma showed up. I have no memory of her before she just showed up one day."

"What?"

"That's odd, right?" I asked, cocking my head to the side. "I mean, she's supposed to be my dad's mom, but I never met her before he disappeared. No family reunion where she showed up with potato salad. No Christmas visit where she brought a gift. No phone calls to catch up. She didn't exist in my life before my parents were gone, Lucas. She is not my grandmother."

Pulling on Lucas' hand, I managed to get Lucas to take a few steps towards the stands while in his stupor before he was pulling on my hand again. With a groan, I turned to face him again.

"That's insane, Rob." He admonished me. "I mean...maybe you don't have memories of her before then. You were young, right? Maybe you just don't remember? Or maybe she wasn't in your life before then—I mean, you said that she didn't like your mom much and didn't get along with your dad, so—"

"That's what she's told me my entire life." I hissed. "But I have no proof of that—just what she told me. How am I supposed to keep believing someone without proof? Especially with everything that's going on now?

Lucas—everyone in this fucking town is in cahoots with the man in the black hooded cloak. Even...the Barkley's."

Lucas stared at me with wide eyes.

"And I think you know what I'm talking about but don't want to admit to it," I said. "You know where your particular type of powers come from. I've seen what happened to you when you were a kid in your bedroom late at night. You met *him* before you and I became friends...and more. Maybe you've forgotten. Maybe you've repressed it. I don't know what's going on anymore, Lucas. The longer I stay in this fucking shithole town, the stranger things get. The less anything makes sense."

Lucas shivered.

"We don't have to talk about it if you don't want to." I said. "Especially here, right now. But we both know that things are getting worse by the minute in this town. We both know that *he* is coming back sooner rather than later. This is how things felt before he showed up the first time, right? So...let's just go. Let's get in my car, go to the airport, and get the fuck out of this fucking state."

"Tonight?"

"You still want to leave me with me, right?" I asked.

"Of course."

"Then let's go." I urged him on. "We can't risk staying here any longer, Lucas. If we do...something really bad is going to happen. I can feel it. If we leave...maybe things won't get better, but *he* won't have any reason to return. I won't be here. And if he still wants me, he'll have to come to California. Because we won't be here."

"But, babe—"

"Let's get into the car, Lucas." I pleaded. "We'll drive straight through to Hopkins. We'll buy two tickets for the first plane going to L.A. and then we're gone. We'll never look back."

"I don't have clothes..."

"Babe." I smiled at him. "I'll buy you anything you need or want when we get to L.A. Fuck your house. Fuck my family's house. Fuck our things. Fuck our *families*. Fuck this town. Right now is our one chance to get out of this town and stop what's coming. If we don't leave now...we're never going to leave. And you know it."

Lucas looked sick but nodded.

"Yeah." He said, the nodding becoming more confident. "Let's get the hell out of here, Rob. You're right. You're right. I just...okay."

Grabbing his face in my hands, I looked him in his eyes.

"It'll be okay," I said. "I promise. If you're worried about your grandpa, you can call him from the plane. Or once we land. He'll understand."

"I don't think he will." Lucas shook his head. "But that doesn't matter, does it? We have to leave."

"Exactly," I said. "So...you are all in, right?"

Lucas nodded.

"Yes." He said affirmatively. "Let's go, Rob. Let's just get the hell out of Ohio and never look back. It'll be okay as long as I'm with you. I know that."

"Just one of those things you know?" I smiled warmly before kissing him gently.

"Yeah." He smiled as I pulled away. "I know it'll be okay if we get out of this town, babe."

Instead of saying anything else, I grabbed Lucas' hand once more and pulled him towards the stands. We raced up the stairs to the stands and then up the stairs that led to the top of the stands towards the parking lot where I had left my car. Whether or not Lucas' family would be upset that he stole away in the middle of the night with me didn't matter to me in the slightest. We were leaving—together—and we weren't looking back ever again. That's all that mattered to me. That both of us would be safe.

Of course, when we reached the parking lot, and our eyes landed on the dozen men surrounding my car, I couldn't help but laugh.

Of course, I should have expected that.

Chapter 13

Lucas gripped my hand tightly, his body freezing up as we slid to a stop several yards away from my car and the pack that surrounded it. He gave me a concerned look as I laughed loudly at the sight of the large men—all of them cookie-cutter versions of what werewolves in human form should look like according to movies made for horny teenagers. It wasn't so much that the pack was waiting by my car that I found amusing—though it was funny that I hadn't seen it coming—the fact that Jason was with them was the most entertaining part. And he still had his head.

Jason stood there, evilly smiling ear to ear as Lucas and I kept back, our hands clasped together for support and courage.

"So..." Jason began, "you cut off my head and just leave. Didn't even shut the door."

Lucas looked over at me.

"Rude." Jason shook his head.

I half expected it to partially detach like a character from *Harry Potter*, lolling around like a balloon on a stick for a moment before he shoved it back into place. Surely it wasn't completely healed and reattached so quickly after having been lopped off. It looked pretty secure as he grinned and chastised me, however, so I decided that the next time I took his head off, I wouldn't leave it behind. *Get a bowling bag*, I thought to myself. Then you can carry it around like Melanie Griffith in *Crazy in Alabama*.

The thought made me chuckle, which caused Lucas to look at me with concern once more.

"Head in a bowling bag," I mumbled to myself with a chuckle.

"Rob." Lucas squeezed my hand.

"Sorry." I glanced at him before turning my attention to the pack and its leader that had my car surrounded. "Get away from my car, assface."

"Don't think we can do that, Rob," Jason said, reaching up to scratch his head.

Or reposition it, I wasn't sure.

"We're not allowed to let you leave." Jason shrugged. "We have to keep you here until *he* comes."

"Well, we have other things going on," I replied, clasping Lucas' hand tighter as I took a step forward. "So, please, give him our regards, but we don't have time to wait around."

Under our feet, the ground vibrated for a split second. Lucas gasped and moved closer to me. Jason just grinned over at us like the dipshit that he was. His entire pack started growling and yipping, their heads turning towards the sky. My heart started beating faster in my chest, but I did my best to appear outwardly calm as I stared down my rival.

Who should be deader than a doornail.

"Your head's good." I shrugged.

"That's what they say," Jason smirked.

"Fuck you," Lucas responded for me.

Jason gave a barking laugh, which his pack echoed.

"I cut his head off earlier this evening," I mumbled to Lucas out of the corner of my mouth as we stared at the pack.

"Really?" Lucas' eyes were like saucers.

"Didn't take, I guess." I shrugged.

"Apparently not," Lucas mumbled.

We waited for the bark-like laughs to grow silent and for Jason to turn his attention back to us before either of us said anything. There was no point in trying to talk over a pack of puppies that were all riled up. The ground shook faintly once more.

"Okay," I announced once the barking had stopped. "Get the fuck away from my car. Maybe cutting your head off didn't do the trick, but I know fire will do the job."

I held my hand out, a flame blooming immediately from my palm. The red and yellow flame illuminated Lucas' and my face with dancing lights, hopefully making me look way more intimidating than I probably did to such a large group of werewolves. Jason smiled at me a moment longer, then sniffed the air, his head tilting skyward. Frowning to myself and casting a glance at Lucas, I didn't know what to make of the behavior. The ground rumbled roughly underfoot, and my heart began beating faster. Jason stopped sniffing the air and turned his attentions back to Lucas and me.

"He's coming." He said.

"I know," I replied. "Move your asses or get used to 'em being crispy."

For the space of a few breaths, Jason and I stared at each other across those few yards that separated us. Then, he suddenly stepped aside. His pack didn't even look confused by his actions but instead started to move away from my car. Lucas' hand gripped mine tighter as we watched Jason and his pack give us a clear path to the car. When they moved, I fully expected the windows to be smashed in, the tires to be flat, wires and parts lying everywhere on the ground. However, my car looked fine, and they all continued to move until they were far enough away from the car for me to feel safe enough to start walking towards it.

I'm not an idiot. I knew that Jason and his pack giving in so easily was a bad sign. However, I had no further plan for how to make an escape from Point Worth, so my car was my only option. Lucas and I needed to be in my car and headed in the direction of Cleveland as soon as possible. With the way things were progressively getting crazier and crazier in Point Worth, every second we spent lingering in the fucked up little town brought us closer to a situation we couldn't resolve. I squeezed Lucas' hand and pulled him towards the car.

Easing our way into it, the two of us walked towards the car, keeping all of the pack members in our line of sight as we walked. They had given us access to the car too easily. Either they knew something we didn't know, they figured we'd never get in the car and out of town quickly enough, or they were planning to pounce on us as soon as we got close to the car. However, Jason and his pack continued to stand clear as we made our way over to my car. Usually, Lucas would get in on one side, and I'd get in on the other, but I knew that separating was the worst plan.

As we approached the car, my hand still held out with the flame flickering in my palm, I indicated to Lucas to get the keys out of my pocket. Lucas' hand went into my pocket, which drew some snickers from pack members and made Jason smirk, but I ignored them. He fished the keys out and let go of my hand to unlock the driver's side door. The pack continued to just watch us as Lucas opened the door and I jumped in, sliding over to the passenger's seat. Lucas followed quickly and slid into the driver's seat, slamming the door behind himself.

We glanced at each other nervously as I mentally extinguished the flame in my hand. As Lucas started the car, I watched the pack members through the windows, my head jerking around to look at each of them, to make sure that nothing odd was going on. They were all still watching, which was why I had chosen to ride passenger in the car. If Lucas was driving, I was available to shoot balls of fire at anyone or anything that got too close to the car. The car started when Lucas twisted the key in the ignition, and I wasn't sure if the rumbling feeling beneath us was the car or the ground beneath us. My stomach was in knots as the idea of the car blowing up entered my mind, though I knew there was no one in the pack smart enough to make and plant a bomb that would go off when the car was started.

"Go," I stated when Lucas glanced over at me.

"They're all around us," Lucas muttered.

"They'll move or get run over."

Lucas looked at me for a moment, then gave a firm nod. He threw the car into gear and started to pull forward. For a second, it looked as though Jason and two of the pack members standing beside him would refuse to move aside for the car, but at the last second, they dashed to the side, letting the car pass. I stared out of the passenger seat window at Jason as we eased by. He merely smirked down at me as I squinted in anger up at him.

"Go." I said again. "Faster. Get us out of here."

Lucas gunned the car, gravel and dirt kicking up behind us at the pack. I smiled to myself as I watched pack members jumping out of the way, silently cussing and stomping angrily as debris pelted them. As the football stadium and the pack grew smaller in the rear window, I turned around in my seat to find Lucas smiling proudly. I couldn't help but smile at his expression. He was happy to have caused a little pain and anger. I definitely couldn't blame him. The ground was still rumbling. Or maybe it was the car?

"How much gas do we have?" I asked.

"Enough to get to Cleveland," Lucas replied.

"Good."

"Are we just going to leave your car here?" He asked. "I mean...won't you need it in L.A.?"

"I have another." I shrugged.

"Babe." He glanced over at me with a grin.

"I know." I chuckled. "But I never want to come back here. Ever. I don't care if leaving a car behind is douchey."

Lucas chuckled, but his facial expression betrayed him.

"They let us go too easily." He said. "Why even bother meeting us at the car if they were just going to let us go?"

"They were killing time," I said.

"Huh?"

"Don't you feel it?"

"Feel what?"

"The ground," I said. "It's shaking."

"Yeah." Lucas looked sick again. "I felt it."

"He's coming," I said. "We just have to get out of this town before that happens. If we get out of here quickly enough, we won't have to worry."

"What do you mean?" He asked. "Just because we're gone doesn't mean he's not a problem."

"He won't come back if I'm not here," I said. "Just trust me. Okay?"

Lucas gave a sharp but understanding nod.

"Gun it, babe," I said, reaching over to squeeze his shoulder. "Drive like the police don't exist, okay?"

"What if we get pulled over?"

"I'd like to see a Point Worth officer try," I said.

I held my hand out again, producing another small flame.

Lucas looked at me with concern.

I gave him a wink.

"Don't worry," I said. "If you drive fast enough, it's not something we'll have to think about, babe."

Lucas stared at me for several moments as the car carried us onto the highway, and he pressed the accelerator down. Finally, he gave me a smile and a nod, then turned his attention back to the road. I sighed to myself, extinguishing the flame, as I stared out at the road before us. I wanted to grab Lucas' hand, to feel his hand in mine as we watched Point Worth fly by and felt the ground rumbling underneath us. However, I didn't want to distract him on his mission to get us outside of the city limit in record time. So, I stared out the window on my side of the car and counted the stars.

All we had to do was get out of town.

It was that simple.

A few minutes later, when I watched the "Welcome to Point Worth" sign pass by the car, I let go of a breath I hadn't known I was holding. Lucas kept the accelerator down for several miles before easing off and letting the car drop to a reasonable speed. Finally, he looked over, a smile coming to his face much more easily than it had mere minutes before. He reached over, grabbed my hand, and laced his fingers through mine. I accepted his hand in mine. Quickly, I leaned over and gave him a kiss, noticing that the ground was not rumbling under the car any longer.

If we were lucky, we'd be in Cleveland before the sun came up.

CARNAVAL

Oma stopped the car right outside the gates of the carnival, her foot slamming on the brake pedal, which caused Opa's truck to skid to a shuddering stop. I hadn't been wearing a seatbelt, so my sternum used the dashboard to stop my forward momentum. Dust and gravel from the country road kicked up around the sides of the pickup. Unfortunately, my window had been down, and I had been talking, so I was also treated to a mouthful of dust and dirt. Coughing and hacking, I bent forward, trying to clear my eyes and throat of crud. Oma threw the truck into park, though she didn't bother killing the engine, and leaned over to slap me roughly on the back. Oma slapped, and I coughed, and finally, I was able to breathe again, though I had to slide the sleeve of my shirt over my hand to wipe at my eyes. It's hard to wipe your eyes clear of dirt and tears when your grandmother is pounding on your back. That's just one way to really hurt yourself, though I somehow managed to avoid any serious injury.

"Jesus Ladling Up Gravy, Robbie!" Oma grumbled, finally pulling away from me, her hand no longer assaulting my back. "I told you to roll that damn window up and put your damn seatbelt on."

I gagged and coughed again.

"Goddamn teenagers think they know better than everyone." She shook her head.

"If you hadn't slammed on the brakes—"

"Don't you sass me." Oma barked. "I drive just fine, thank you."

"*You drive like a crazy person,*" I mumbled.

"What was that?" She snapped.

"Nothing," I grumbled and pulled myself up to sit properly in my seat once more, trying to breathe the crisp October air that poured through my window. "I like the taste of dashboard and dirt."

Oma waggled her head as she hiked her knee up on the bench seat and turned to look at the gates just beyond my side of the pickup. Following her lead, but still wiping gently at my eyes, I turned to look towards the tall wrought-iron gates outside of the carnival grounds. There was a lump made of pure dread in my throat that had been present since I had first heard about the carnival coming to Point Worth without warning. I mean, carnivals are kind of scary to begin with when you consider the death-defying rides, the creepy clowns and circus-style tents, the carnies, all of the thrill-seekers pushing against and past you—not to mention all of the delicious food that would come right back up after a ride on some gravity-defying roller coaster. I swallowed hard, hoping the lump would sink somewhere lower where it could more easily be ignored.

The Owens farmlands, which abutted Lake Erie, had been vacant for a decade, ever since a fire had claimed all of the buildings and a lot of the land. Most of the locals liked to say that if Lake Erie hadn't been there to stop the fire, it would have burned straight across and into the central part of town, devouring everything in its path. That in and of itself was pretty creepy, to think that the town of Point Worth, as tiny as it was, could have been devoured whole by a raging fire. The fact that kids in school were always talking about the ghosts and spirits that lurked the acreage made it even creepier. It was ridiculous to think that actual spirits or ghosts had nothing better to do than to haunt some desiccated old farmland. Fourteen-year-old high school freshmen, such as myself, rarely used logic when considering their fears. As far as I was concerned, the place was haunted.

Adding to the mystery and creepiness aspect was the fact that the vacated farmlands had basically just been open, unattended fields in the decade since the great fire. However, a week before word of the carnival coming had spread through town like a wildfire itself, a large wrought-iron fence, complete with a locked gate at the south end of the property, seemed to have been placed overnight, encircling the entirety of the land. A day later, tarps, or some type of heavy cloth, had been hung on the other side of the fencing, blocking the view for any prying eyes that happened by the old Owens farmlands. A day after that, multi-colored tents and rides could be seen peeking above the tops of the fences, which were considerably taller than one would expect.

Alternating Fleur-de-Lis and savage-looking spikes topped each pole in the fencing, giving it an elegant, yet unsettling appearance. A day after the tops of tents and rides began appearing, people who happened by could swear they smelled popcorn and cotton candy and any manner of deep-fried treats. They could see multi-colored lights that were at all times ominous and alluring. The carnival put off an enticing aura of light at night, making every Point Worthian both excited and anxious to attend. However, no one was ever seen going into or coming out of the carnival at any time of day, so we all found ourselves speculating on how the carnival had even arrived, let alone been assembled. The police didn't seem too keen to investigate the matter since no one was technically being harmed by the appearance of a carnival.

Who had erected the tents and rides, though?
Who had built the fence?
Why were there coverings on the other side of the fence?
Who was making the popcorn and delicious smelling foods?

Then, nearly a week after the carnival arrived, posters were found plastered on the front windows and walls of every shop on Main Street.

Oma and I had not been present when Point Worthians wandered onto Main Street, both horrified and transfixed by the sudden appearance of the posters overnight. The posters were also confusing since they listed no location for the carnival—though it wasn't really needed—no hours of operation, no information about ticket costs or where they could be purchased, or who was actually behind the carnival. Or...*CARNAVAL?* Later, it was relayed to Oma by Mr. Barkley, and to myself by one of my friends in English class, that no one had to stare at the posters for long. As everyone lined up along the main thoroughfare of town, gazing at the posters with their backs to the street, a bell started ringing.

Startled citizens of Point Worth jumped and spun, turning to find a man, no shorter than seven-feet tall, meandering down the middle of the street. He held a large handbell in one hand, raising and lowering it in time with each slow step. His face was gaunt and expressionless, his cloudy eyes staring straight ahead, seemingly unaware of the townspeople around him. He wore a suit that could only be described as something you'd expect a ghoul driving a hearse to wear. Or maybe something you'd see on Lurch from *The Addams Family*.

Meandering and raising and lowering that bell in time with his steps, paying no attention to the curious and uneasy townspeople around him, he didn't speak until he was halfway down the street. He just walked, rang his bell, and let people stare at him all they wanted, seemingly not noticing. Then, suddenly, continuing to look straight ahead, his expression unchanging, he spoke. A booming, gravelly voice escaped his mouth.

We are The Council. CARNAVAL welcomes all high school-age children. Free of charge. This Saturday. Dusk 'til dawn. Enter through the south—and only—gates at dusk. No adults will be admitted.

He said it only once, and he said no more. He didn't have to repeat himself. He spoke clearly, and no one had tried to interrupt him. He continued meandering down the street, that arm rising and falling, the bell ringing with each step. Then he turned the corner without looking back. Everyone said he "just disappeared," but they also admitted that no one ran after him to see where he went. So, he probably didn't disappear, but instead just kept walking. Everyone said that the sound of the bell was gone as suddenly as the man, leaving Main Street deathly still and quiet as everyone just stared, open-mouthed and shocked, at the end of the street where he had disappeared. I hadn't even been present for the man's stroll down Main Street, but it gave me the shivers to think of it.

As I sat in Opa's pickup truck with Oma, looking at the south gates of CARNAVAL, I felt a shiver go up my spine and the flesh at the back of my neck crawl. My very soul felt chilled as I looked at the gate that was open just wide enough for a teenager to slip through. What was beyond those gates? Who was waiting on the other side? Were some of my friends inside, already enjoying free carnival food and rides?

That's impossible. None of the lights are on. I can't smell food being cooked. I don't hear the "whoosh" of carnival rides or the cries of carnival barkers trying to ply teenagers to play their games. I don't see balloons or…anything. This can't possibly be right.

"Well," Oma sighed, "what do you think? Still feel like testing your mettle?"

I swallowed again.

"Robbie," She said softly. "It's okay if you don't want to go inside and see what's goin' on. I bet half your friends don't even come out here. Hell, I bet most of their parents ain't as dumb as me to bring 'em out here. I reckon there ain't nothin' in there but a bunch of carnies tryin' to spook some local kids, and give 'em a thrill, but I'd understand if you don't want to find out."

"I haven't seen any other cars," I said stupidly.

"It ain't quite dusk, yet," She answered. "Maybe we're here early?"

"Maybe."

"Do you want me to come in with you?"

"They said adults weren't allowed."

"To Hell." Oma snorted. "I'd like to see 'em stop me."

She thrust her arm across the cab of the truck so that I could see her hand, even with my back to her. A small flame flickered to life in the palm of her hand, casting the cab of the truck in a reddish hue. I couldn't help but smile.

"Oma." I chided her. "Don't. Someone might show up and see."

I hadn't known about Oma's powers for long at that point in my life, but I had known about them long enough to figure out that no one else should find out about them. Not that anyone would have believed me if I had told them.

"I think I'd see a car pulling up out in the middle of ass-end nowhere, don't you?" She chuckled, though the flame went out, and she retracted her arm.

"Maybe they did all this to add to the mystery?" I suggested, wrapping my arms around myself. "Ya' know? To make it creepy and stuff?"

"Well, it is the season for it."

"Yeah."

"I won't think nothin' of it if you don't wanna go inside."

"But...I mean...come on, Oma." I shrugged, my arms still around myself. "What if I'm the only guy at school who doesn't show? I'll look like a pussy."

She chuckled.

"You see any of them other boys around here?"

"No."

"So?"

"I'm going inside," I stated firmly, though I didn't move a muscle.

Oma sighed, and I heard her sit back in her seat. Then I felt the truck being put into gear. Quickly, I reached out and grabbed the door handle. The truck went back into park, jerking slightly as I popped the door open and leapt down from my seat, my feet slamming into the dirt of the road. I turned, my hand still on the door, to look at Oma in the cab of the pickup. My grandmother sat there, her hands on the wheel of Opa's truck, smiling over at me, obviously proud that I had taken the first leap towards the carnival.

"I'm gonna park down the road," She said. "If you decide you just don't wanna be here, you come runnin', ya' hear me?"

I nodded, that stubborn lump threatening my throat once more.

"All right," She said, then in an attempt to squelch my fears, added: "I bet you get in there and it's abandoned, Robbie. You'll look around, see nothin' but a bunch of carnival crap, then you can come to the truck, and we can leave. Then all them other boys who didn't show up will be the pussies come Monday."

Laughing, I gently shut the truck door, pushing it shut with both hands.

"Don't go home," I said suddenly, looking in through the open window at Oma. "I mean...ya' know...just go down the road. I'll, uh, need you to take me home even if the carnival is...uh, real."

Oma gave me a wink and gently put the truck back into gear once again. I barely stepped back from the truck far enough for her to drive away without running over my feet with the back-right wheel of the truck. I hadn't wanted to let go of the door, or even get out of the truck because that would mean that I genuinely was left at the carnival alone. Being left alone at the carnival meant I would either have to run after Oma or go beyond the gates into the carnival. Waiting outside of the gates for several minutes before running after Oma was an option, too, but somehow, waiting outside the gates alone made me more nervous than just going inside. Waiting outside the gates would mean that anyone arriving would see me standing there, terrified to go inside by myself.

If I was the only guy in school who didn't show up to the carnival, that was one thing. Any excuse would have worked to tamper suspicions that I had merely been afraid. I could have said Oma wouldn't let me go. Or I was sick. Anything, really. But if one of the other guys from school showed up and saw me standing there all alone, nearly pissing my pants, I wouldn't have any excuse for that. So, I had to make a choice. I could run after Oma and hop back in the truck when she stopped—I could still see the truck kicking up dirt on the road in the distance—or I could go through the gate. With a steeling of my nerves and a deep breath, I turned to the gates.

The sun was setting, and dusk was upon me. No lights were on beyond the gates, and I heard no sounds coming from rides or barkers, but I decided to not think about all of that. My feet carried me swiftly to the gates, as though I hadn't been nearly wetting my pants moments before, and I slipped through the opening and into the carnival. As though attached to someone else's brain, my eyes shut on their own, afraid to see what might be lurking beyond the wrought-iron fence and tarps that surrounded the land. As I stood there, just a few feet beyond the gate opening, I heard and felt nothing. No smell of food being made, no sounds of rides, no voices asking me who I was or why I had been dumb enough to show up. No sounds of my friends from school running around gleefully without adult supervision.

Slowly, I let my eyes slide open.

It was a carnival.

But it was an abandoned carnival.

Booths for games where you threw darts at balloons or balls at old-fashioned milk bottles stood well-kept but abandoned. Food stands that proclaimed there was popcorn, and cotton candy, and corn dogs, and kettle corn, and funnel cakes were in the distance. There was a Ferris wheel and a carousel—all of the other types of rides one would expect to see at a carnival. In the very center of the land, at least a hundred yards away from me, I spotted the big tent. It was a canvas tent in alternating greens and reds and tans—like you'd see at a regular circus, not yet lit up, nor with the flaps open to allow entrance.

Frowning to myself, I found myself looking around, wondering what I had been afraid of when I came to the carnival. Even though it seemed to be abandoned, it was relatively harmless. No creepy clowns jumping out and surprising anyone. No carnies barking at me to come try my hand at luck. No freaky contortionists or men on stilts looming over me menacingly. It was just an empty fairground that seemed well taken care of, yet unmanned. I shrugged and shoved my hands into my pockets.

Even if I were the only guy in my school to show up, no one would know. None of my friends were on the carnival grounds waiting for me. When I went to school Monday and told everyone that I showed up and no one was there, no one would believe me. The whole thing had been a waste.

Well. Maybe not.

Taking a tentative step forward, I headed deeper into the carnival. At least if I could provide more detail about my visit to the carnival, maybe the kids at school would believe me. Walking along, my hands in my pockets, I felt somewhat anxious at seemingly being the only person in the carnival, the sky getting darker as the sun went down. However, I hadn't forced myself out of Opa's truck to chicken out so quickly. The least I could do was walk around the grounds, see what all they had, compile a full mental list of details to share with my friends on Monday—and then I could run up the road to Oma like my ass was on fire.

As I walked along, I noticed that everything seemed so new. The paint looked fresh. The rides—especially the carousel—looked like they had just been finished at the factory and shipped out to Point Worth, Ohio. The lands that the carnival had been constructed on had been moved down and raked. Everything was shiny and perfect, but unused. As the sun sank below the horizon, and the stars started to twinkle dimly above, my nerves began to jangle, and I began to wonder if I had made the right choice. Even if I was all alone—I was still going to be out in the middle of nowhere, in the dark, in a creepy carnival. I shivered at the thought.

For how long, I wasn't sure, but I walked in a circular path around the carnival. Memorizing the rides that they had, the types of food you could buy, and the games you could play. Committing every little detail to memory would be my only weapon on Monday when everyone claimed to have been at the carnival. I would know they were all lying, and I would be able to prove it. Probably. The sky was getting darker as I walked, casting long, shadowy figures on the grounds around me.

Just when I thought my nerves would get the better of me, a loud electrical clicking, nearly a "boom," sounded throughout the carnival. Startled, I jumped at the sight of thousands of lights coming on and rides and attractions coming to life around me. The Ferris wheel, the bulbs decorating the steel beams and spokes, started to turn brightly. The game booths were flooded with multicolored, cheerful lights. The carousel slowly began to turn, picking up speed until it was spinning at a slow, even pace, the horses bobbing up and down on their poles. The sound of popcorn beginning to pop over by the food stands made me jump, and then whip around to see what was going on.

Swallowing the ever-present lump in my throat, I meekly began walking towards the wooden stand, which was painted in red and gold stripes with a large marquis overhead that proclaimed popcorn was, in fact, the product it sold. As I approached, I could see movement—but more shadows than actual shapes—behind the counter of the popcorn stand. My first thought was to run away.

How did I not see this person when I entered?

Where were they hiding?

Instead, I steeled my resolve and approached the popcorn stand from across the expanse of the carnival grounds, my steps measured and confident. Actually, I probably looked like a cat ready to jump straight into the air at any sudden movement, but I felt confident. I approached the counter of the popcorn stand, just as the last of the popping sounds faded away, and looked around, trying to spot the shadowy movement I had seen from across the carnival. No one was there. Sighing to myself, I placed my hands on the counter, smiling at the tricks I was letting my mind play on me.

As if appearing out of thin air, a man rose from behind the raised counter of the popcorn stand. Jumping back, I wasn't sure what had startled me the most about him. Was it the fact that he just rose up from behind the counter, as though this were a normal thing to do—jump out and scare kids? Was it the fact that he was holding a super-sized bucket of perfectly piled buttery popcorn out to me, a grotesque, toothy grin plastered across his face? Or was it because he looked like Marcel Marceau dressed up as Bip the Clown?

"Holy shit." I gasped, clutching my chest with both hands, a laugh erupting from my throat. "You scared me."

The Marcel Marceau lookalike slowly cocked his head to the side, his smile unchanging as he held the popcorn out to me.

"How much does it cost?" I asked, unsure if I wanted to be speaking to this creepy guy.

Please don't try to touch me, sir.

The clown just stared and held the popcorn but raised his other hand skyward to the sign above. My head slowly tilted back so that I could see the sign but not lose sight of the man.

FREE.

"Oh." I looked at the creepy French clown again. "I...I, uh, didn't see that."

The clown just smiled.

Of course, I considered the fact that taking a massive bucket of popcorn from some creepy guy in clown mime gear was a bad idea. However, the popcorn looked to be absolutely glistening with butter, freshly popped, and it smelled delicious. I hadn't eaten anything before Oma drove me to the carnival so that I would have room for all of the treats that were offered. Instead of showing caution, I stepped back up to the counter, and slowly grabbed the bucket at the sides, keeping my hands from touching the clown's. As soon as I had the bucket in my grasp, he yanked his hand away, and both of his hands went up to his face, framing it like a dramatic and grotesque picture of glee as he affixed a new smile to his face and looked out at nothing.

"That's...odd, sir."

He didn't move.

"Um," I tentatively scooped up a handful of the popcorn and shoveled it into my mouth, so buttery and warm, "wuff da big deel? Where if errybuddy?"

For several moments, I shoved handfuls of warm, buttery popcorn into my gob as I stared at the clown, waiting for any type of answer. Finally, he moved in slow motion, his hands still framing his face, his grotesque, toothy smile still shining, until he was looking directly at me with his wide-open eyes. Suddenly, his hands shot out, making me jump and nearly drop my bucket of popcorn. Instead of reaching for me, I realized he was gesturing to something behind me. Slowly, choking down my mouthful of half-masticated popcorn, I turned to see what he was trying to make me understand.

He had been gesturing at the striped circus tent at the center of the carnival, which was now well lit by large yellow bulbs running up the sides and across the top to the tent pole at the center. I could now see the tiny flags attached to the strings of lights flapping in the light October breeze. The tent flaps were now open. I turned back to the creepy French clown, to ask him why it was suddenly open and what was going on, but he was gone. Instinctively, I thought to step up to the counter and lean over until I could see on the other side since he had probably just squatted down out of view. However, my courage—or lack thereof—didn't allow it. Instead, I slowly shuffled backward and away, grabbing another handful of popcorn to shove in my mouth.

Across the carnival grounds, I strolled again, getting closer and closer to the circus tent. The flaps were open, but I could only see darkness inside, as though there was no illumination within. That alone made me rethink the idea of checking out what was going on at the supposed main event of the carnival. Curiosity had always been one of my flaws, so I shoveled popcorn into my mouth, barely chewing before swallowing the delicious treat, as I walked closer and closer. When I was still several yards away from the entrance of the tent, I realized that it was not dark within the tent. There was a second set of flaps made of heavy black material blocking the entrance.

I knew this because they suddenly opened, yellowish-orange light, like that produced by fire, shone brightly from within as the flaps came open only long enough for a man to emerge. Entirely unlike the Bip the Clown at the popcorn stand, this man was dressed like you'd expect a circus ringmaster to be dressed. Red topcoat and tails with fancy gold embroidery on the sleeves, white gloves with buttons at the back of his wrists, black riding pants that traveled down his legs to meet black leather booths, a yellow vest with a white blouse underneath, and a riding crop in hand—he looked every bit the ringmaster. He even had a black top hat upon his head, his eyes rimmed with black kohl, and his cheeks rouged with bright red powder. I wanted to laugh with glee when I saw him.

The ringmaster marched a few yards away from the black flaps of the tent, a jovial smile on his face and a swagger in his step. Suddenly, he stopped, and the black flaps opened like bat wings once more. A half dozen people in leotards and intricately painted faces emerged, running out and encircling the ringmaster, dancing around him in a way I could only describe as Cirque du Soleil-ish. The ringmaster held his hands aloft theatrically and spun as the acrobatic performers danced and leapt and undulated around him in ways that seemed humanly impossible. My hand continued to shove popcorn in my face as I watched with wide eyes, transfixed.

After several moments, the tent flaps opened again and two performers who were dressed like Pierrot the clown, but with brighter colors, exited. They joined the acrobatic performers, dancing and stumbling around the ringmaster comically as he continued to twirl and cheer them on in a booming voice in a language I did not know. The almost empty bucket of popcorn got transferred to one hand and lowered to my side as I wiped my other hand on my jeans and watched the show before me with fascination.

No one is going to fuckin' believe this.

The acrobats twirled and danced and kicked high kicks, sometimes boosting each other dramatically to leap over the ringmaster or each other. They lifted each other in the air and did somersaults, flips, backflips, and dives. The clowns danced drunkenly, stumbling and bumping into each other but somehow avoiding the acrobats easily. The ringmaster continued cheering them on in what I was beginning to deduce was French, smiling euphorically at the multi-colored performers around him. Just when everything reached a fever pitch, and the performers were moving at what seemed an inhuman speed, they all fell to their knees in front of the ringmaster, facing me. They spread their arms dramatically, and the ringmaster turned to me grandly. He raised his arms in like fashion, the riding crop pointing in the air from one hand as he jabbed the other arm out at me, as though beckoning me forward.

All movement and sound from them stopped, and I was left dumbstruck.

"*Welcome! To CARNAVAL!*" The ringmaster announced grandly.

The performers all cheered and began clapping frantically for several seconds, making me laugh. Just as suddenly, they all leapt up and ran for the tent, disappearing one by one through the black batwing flaps, leaving me alone with greasy hands, an empty popcorn bucket, and the ringmaster. His riding crop was tucked under his arm, and he was walking toward me.

"Welcome! Welcome!" He cheered, his French accent apparent, bowing his head grandly as he approached.

"That was a big show for one person." I chuckled nervously.

"No show is too big for any person, my boy!" He proclaimed, bowing grandly when he was a yard away. "No show is too good for you!"

Somehow his top hat did not fall off.

"You don't know me," I said with a laugh. "Maybe I'm not worth all of the effort."

The ringmaster stood back up, looking aghast.

"Robbie!" He held a hand to his chest. "We are honored to put on a show for you! And all of your friends who have arrived while you were touring the grounds!"

"My friends?"

"Yes!"

"Wait." I shook my head. "How do you know my name?"

"The Council knows all, Robbie!" He stepped over to me and slid an arm through mine, effectively making me drop the empty bucket.

Littering didn't seem to bother him, but I figured that since this was his carnival, I couldn't really chastise him for it.

"Here at CARNAVAL, we welcome all boys and girls who are still filled with wonder and fear and excitement and joy! Our shows are for them and them alone. At CARNAVAL, we have the most delicious treats, the greatest death-defying rides, the most fun games, and the grandest shows for your eyes! CARNAVAL is not just entertainment—*IT IS ART!*"

The man's enthusiasm was infectious, though odd, as he pulled me towards the tent at a brisk, yet nonchalant stroll.

"What do you mean...*my friends*?" I asked, wondering if I should enter the tent with the man. "I didn't see anybody else come in."

"You must have missed them." He stated jovially, his voice like that of a French Santa Claus. "They arrived while you were enjoying the sights. We did expect more of your schoolmates to join you here, but we are happy to put on our show of wonders for one or all of you. Every child is deserving of a wondrous show at CARNAVAL!"

"But—"

"Inside! Inside!" The ringmaster proclaimed, ignoring my protests as he dragged me towards the tent flaps. "Inside, you will see your friends!"

"Look, mister, if you're going to try to touch me or something—"

"No one will touch you—they're more likely to bite!" The ringmaster found this incredibly funny, booming, theatrical laughter escaping his throat as we got closer to the tent flaps. "There is nothing to fear at CARNAVAL, Robbie!"

Again, how do you know my name?

"Hey!" I screamed at the top of my lungs as I dug my heels into the dirt. "Stop!"

The ringmaster let go of my arm abruptly, turning to me as though he was entirely confounded that a fourteen-year-old boy did not want to be dragged into a dark tent by a strange man who was dressed like a modern-day P.T. Barnum. Straightening up, pulling myself up to my full height, and pushing my chest out as confidently as possible, I stared the ringmaster in the eyes. I took a small step back, just far enough so that he could not reach out and grab my arm again without my consent, and glared at him.

"I want to know what's going on," I said as firmly and evenly as possible, though my age and hormones betrayed me.

"You are here to see CARNAVAL are you not?" He asked, his head tilting to the side.

The man continued his habit of speaking in dramatic capitals when he mentioned the name of the carnival, and it was becoming annoying.

"Well, I mean, I guess, yeah." I shrugged. "But...I mean...I don't know what's in that tent, sir. How do I know you're not going to hurt me or something?"

The ringmaster looked up contemplatively for a moment, considering my question, then, just as suddenly as he had appeared to perform his act with the dancers, his eyes lit up, and his head snapped back to look at me once more.

"A show of good faith!" He jabbed the riding crop in the air. "Yes?"

"I guess?"

The ringmaster stepped forward jauntily and held the riding crop out to me.

"If you would?" He asked.

Tentatively, I reached out and took his theatrical prop from him. It was cool to the touch, leathery, and appeared to be brand new. It had never been used for its purpose, for which I was grateful. I stared at the prop for a moment, then focused my attention back on the ringmaster as he jiggled his body, as though shaking off nerves. Then his eyes were back on mine, and he smiled brilliantly. He held one arm out towards me so that I could see up his sleeve, then the other arm shot out beside it. He stood like that for a moment, then started to bend his arms until his right hand was going up his left sleeve, and his left hand was going up his right sleeve. Once both hands had disappeared up the coat sleeves, he winked, then yanked his hands out at the same time.

He held a stick with a cloud of blue cotton candy in his right hand and one with pink cotton candy in his left. Smiling brilliantly, he bobbled the sticks the fluffs of cotton candy were attached to in the air before me, as though putting on a puppet show. I watched, my mouth watering as the clouds of sugar danced before my face. Nearly dropping the riding crop, I had to shake my head to clear away the thoughts of how much I wanted to shove all of that sugar into my face. Clearly, the man had just pulled cotton candy out of the sleeves of his coat, so I wasn't sure it was something I wanted to put in my mouth. Or he had used real magic to pull cotton candy out of thin air. That option didn't scare me as much. Oma could create fire in her hand, who was I to judge a man who produced cotton candy from his sleeve?

"So...I'm just supposed to get in your van?" I frowned, crossing my arms over my chest, the riding crop jabbing me in my ribs.

I did my best to not let out a yelp.

"It is perfectly safe to eat." He waved the sticks around in the air like a fire juggler, a toothy grin on his face. "Do you like blue or pink?"

"If I come in that tent with you, I'm getting both," I stated firmly, though not wisely.

"You may have both." He stopped 'juggling' the sticks and bowed forward slightly, holding them out to me. "We aim to please all of our guests at CARNAVAL!"

Tentatively, I reached out and grabbed the stick that held the blue cotton candy, then held the riding crop out to him. He took the prop from me, and I used the hand that was now free to take the stick of pink cotton candy from his other hand. The ringmaster seemed overjoyed at my having chosen to take the cotton candy because that obviously meant that I would come watch the show.

"What's your name?" I asked, chewing at my lip and eyeing the cotton candy before me.

"I am Richart." He bowed grandly once more.

"Why wouldn't it be?" I mumbled.

"Right this way, Robbie!" Richart gestured grandly towards the tent, ushering me forward as he reached for the tent flap. "Right this way! Fill your belly with clouds of sugar and let your eyes feast upon our sights! Be taken away by the *magic...of...CARNAVAL!*"

Richart ripped the tent flap back, and my senses were immediately overwhelmed by the sounds of lively carnival organ music, lights of every shade of the rainbow, and the smell of carnival food. *How had I not heard the music from outside of the tent? Maybe the black material on the other side of the circus tent blocked out the lights and shadows, but nothing could muffle that music.* My hands, still holding onto the cotton candy, went to my ears, trying to muffle the deafening sound, though my lips split into a grin as I peered into the tent. The clowns and acrobats from before were in the middle of the performance floor at the center of the huge tent. Dancing, tumbling, stumbling, leaping, cartwheeling, putting on a show. Overhead, trapeze artists were swinging to and fro, jumping and catching, performing death-defying stunts.

Urging me forward, Richart moved me into the tent as I stared up in wonder at the acrobats in the sky. My eyes didn't know what to focus on the most, so I allowed myself to be shoved forward as I held onto my cotton candy and stared. Once we had gotten past the sides of the bleachers—something I failed to notice at first—Richart leaned down to scream into my ear. I couldn't hear him, but when I turned my head to him, I could make out that he was telling me to choose a seat. Begrudgingly taking my seat eyes off of the show going on in the center of the tent, I turned to look at the bleachers lined up on either side of the tent opening.

The bleachers were ten rows high and climbed nearly halfway up the inside of the circus tent. Frowning, I noticed that they were practically empty. To my left, I noticed a group of about a dozen older boys from my school, and I immediately recognized them as football players. A couple of their snotty girlfriends were with them. Their asshole leader, Jason Morris, was sitting in the very center of the cluster of boys, all of them scarfing down food and watching the show, luckily not noticing my entrance. Jason Morris had a giant turkey leg he was gnawing at like a caveman, juices and grease covering his lips and chin. His friends had hot dogs, or cotton candy, or popcorn, or corn dogs, or giant buttery, salty pretzels.

I would have rather sat alone.

Looking to my right, I noticed that the bleachers on the other side of the tent opening had a sole occupant. A vaguely familiar-looking blonde-haired kid was sitting five rows up, clutching a bucket of popcorn in his lap as he stared up at the acrobats in the sky with wonder. Looking up at Richart, I nodded at him, and then at the boy in the bleachers. The grinning ringmaster gestured grandly with a bow towards the bleachers, and I stepped up onto the first row of seats. My first thought was to just sit down on the first row, or even the second or third. Maybe it would be weird to go sit with a kid I didn't really know. However, Jason Morris and all of his dumbass friends were clustered on the other bleachers, and I didn't want to look like a lonely geek with two sticks of cotton candy waving around. So, I climbed the bleachers and approached the blonde-haired kid.

The boy, I suddenly remembered, was named...*Lucas*? Yes. Lucas. He was in one of my classes, and I remembered maybe smiling at him when we passed in the halls. He didn't even notice me as I settled down on the bleacher next to him, leaving ample space so as to not make things too weird. As I settled into my seat, my eyes flitting between Lucas and the acrobats in the air, I wasn't sure if my seatmate would appreciate my presence. Just when I had convinced myself that I should move to a different row, Lucas saw me out of the corner of his eye. He started, looking shocked, then laughed, drowned out by the carnival music. I laughed with him, aware that my sudden appearance to someone transfixed by the performers had to have been startling.

Lucas tried to say something, but I had to do my best to indicate with two full hands that I couldn't hear him. He nodded, understanding, then nodded up at the ceiling and gave me a thumbs up. I nodded, agreeing that the performers in the air were amazing. Then I remembered that I had the cotton candy and held them out to him, jiggling them in front of his face. Lucas smiled widely at the gesture and reached out tentatively for the blue cotton candy. At the last second, he reached over and grabbed the pink one. I could have sworn that he blushed when he looked down and away from me after his choice. Looking down reminded him that he had a huge bucket of the buttery, delicious popcorn in his lap, so he picked it up and set it on the bleacher between us. Gesturing at the bucket with a smile, I understood his intention and returned his smile before shoving my hand into the buttery goodness. He followed my lead, and moments later, we were staring up at the performers again, shoveling greasy popcorn into our wide-open mouths.

Soon we were alternating between shoving fistfuls of popcorn into our mouths and slurping strands of cotton candy off of the sticks, barely sucking the flossed sugar into our mouths before it dissolved. In the air above us, the trapeze artists were flying and somersaulting through the air, being caught at the very last moment by their performance partners. Every nerve in my body was on edge, watching the acrobats perform their feats without so much as a wire or a net for safety. Popcorn and cotton candy were devoured maniacally as the trapeze act came to an end, and the performers climbed down from the platforms and disappeared. Another performer climbed the impossibly tall ladder to one of the platforms, and it was evident that we were about to be treated to a tightrope act.

The tent fell silent, even the music stopped as the clowns and dancers below stopped and stood, staring up at their cohort about to perform a feat of pure insanity. Lucas and I were holding our breath, our food now gone, as we stared up at the woman who was wearing what looked like a brightly colored ballerina clown costume. The deafening silence of the room, the only sound I could hear was my heart in my own ears, only added to the suspense of the moment. Everyone was staring upward, watching as the performer took her first step onto the tightrope.

Step by slow step, the performer made her way out onto the cable strung between the two towering platforms. She was laser-focused, staring straight ahead at the platform she was trying to reach before gravity won this game. Halfway across the expanse between the two platforms—which I had been calling "Life" and "Death" in my head, she wobbled precariously, nearly losing her footing. Lucas jumped in his seat, a hissing breath sounding from between his clenched teeth, and I felt his hand fall on my hand that was on the bench between us. I glanced over at him nervously, and he smiled sheepishly, quickly pulling his hand back to his lap.

You could have held my hand if you wanted.

Lucas gasped, and my attention was drawn back to the tightrope walker. She was still wobbling, one foot off of the cable as she tried to correct herself. Everyone in the crowd was either gasping or groaning in desperation, and though there were not that many of us, it seemed to fill the tent. We all were hoping that we were not about to witness the death of a performer. Luckily, as quickly as she lost her footing, the performer corrected her stance and began advancing across the cable again. In my mind, I knew that this was probably an act she put on every time she did the tightrope, just to give the audience a thrill, but it was still absolutely terrifying. When she reached the other side, Jason Morris and his pack of friends, Lucas, and I all cheered loudly. The clowns and dancers below the tightrope cheered as well, congratulating their friend on not plummeting to her death. The tightrope walker performed a grand bow from the platform that had saved her life and then began to descend the ladder.

The organ music began again, drowning out any chance that I could turn to Lucas and tell him it was okay to hold my hand. Not that I would have been brave enough to do so. Surely, telling another boy that he could hold my hand if he got scared, would label me as...something I wasn't ready to be labeled as. Instead of attempting to convey that message to Lucas with my eyes, I kept my attention on the show before us. The dancers and clowns on the floor struck up their routine again as they were joined by flame throwers and fire dancers in loincloths, their bare chests exposed, which made me tingle in places I didn't want to mention. Women balancing on balls, rolling around the circus ring, joined in. At a feverish pitch, more and more performers joined at the center of the ring and did their stunts and tricks.

Lucas and I laughed and cheered along with the other group of kids as the performers put on what surely had to be the greatest show ever performed. For what seemed like hours, but I knew that to be impossible, the performers did their jobs, keeping us entertained as we stared at them, smiling and wide-eyed. The organ music was jostling my insides into jelly and assaulting my ears. The performers' tricks and the lights were assaulting other senses, and I knew that it wouldn't be long before I was overwhelmed. However, the performers of CARNAVAL proved once again that they knew when they had hit a climax. Just when I thought I couldn't take the sights and sounds another single second, the music came to a clanging end, and all of the performers reached for the sky dramatically.

They were all smiling out at us, panting for breath, grinning grotesquely, their jobs well done.

All of us in the stands stood and cheered and stomped our feet, showing the performers our appreciation for a show one would never catch outside of something from Cirque du Soleil. The performers stood there and panted and smiled as we cheered until, finally, the ringmaster appeared from the side of the ring and hurried in to join them. He gave a grand bow as we all continued to cheer as if he had anything to do with what we had just watched. Finally, the performers all seemed to relax but stayed in position around the ringmaster as he began gesturing for everyone in the bleachers to take their seats once more. Even though there were few of us, it took a minute for everyone to stop cheering and return their butts to their seats. Once we were settled, and our cheers had tapered off, the ringmaster's booming, theatrical voice rang out.

"Once again, ladies and gentlemen, we welcome you to CARNAVAL!" He boomed, his toothy grin never leaving his face. "We hope you've enjoyed our dancers, our acrobats, our aerial feats!"

Ladies and gentlemen? I thought to myself. That was quite a greeting for a little more than a dozen teenage kids from the local high school.

"We know that you are all frothing at the mouth and gnashing your teeth to ride our death-defying, heart-pounding rides! To stuff your faces with hot dogs and popcorn and—"

Uh, yeah. The show's cool and all, but the whole point of a carnival is the food, games, and rides, sir.

"But we entreat you—stay in your seats!" Richart held his hands up, his ever-present riding crop jabbing skyward. "We have one final performance—the likes you've never seen! No carnival—no performing troupe—in the world has an act like this!"

Yeah, we'll see.

"Ladies and gentlemen—"

This shit again.

My eyes shot to Lucas. He looked electrified, absolutely twitching in his seat with excitement at what was to come. Suddenly, he glanced at me, a wide, toothy smile coming to his face. An easy smile came to my lips, and we shared a brief moment of wonder and excitement, then his attention went back to the center of the ring. I followed his lead, and my eyes went back to Richart. It was only then that I realized Richart had paused and was scanning the bleachers, making sure that he had everyone's attention. As soon as my eyes landed on him, I realized he was looking directly at me, waiting for me to pay attention. *How odd.* When he saw that he had my attention once more, he continued.

"Les Loups du CARNAVAL!"

Even though there were around a dozen of us in the bleachers, it seemed like the tent suddenly filled with murmurs. None of us were dumb enough not to realize we had just heard Richart give us the name of the next performance in French...but what high schooler in Point Worth, Ohio understands French? Richart was stepping backward, sinking into the crowd of performers who were still posed around and behind him. Glancing over at Lucas, he met my eyes, and I could tell he was just as confused as I was about what we'd just heard. I turned my head to look at Jason Morris and his pack of idiot friends. They were utterly transfixed, totally unconcerned with what Richart had said to us. It was almost as if they were all under the spell of CARNAVAL!

I shook my head. Even I had started screaming the name of the performance troupe in my mind. Lucas nudged me suddenly, drawing my attention. He was pointing at the center of the tent, a concerned look on his face. Turning my eyes back to the spectacle at the center ring of the tent, I could no longer see Richart. Not really. All of the performers were writhing around, like an undulating mass of arms and legs, only flashes of the red and gold of Richart's coat appearing between them sporadically. One second, I'd catch sight of his black top hat, and then the next, I could no longer see any part of him in the mass of undulating and twisting bodies.

Goosebumps prickled my forearms as I watched the performers at the center of the ring begin to writhe and twist, making inhuman shapes with their bodies in a mass of flesh and limbs. I felt, more than saw, Lucas scoot across the small space between us, knocking the empty popcorn bucket to the floor. His hip and thigh pressed against mine as we watched the performers move and writhe in the ring before us, Richart completely swallowed up by their movements. I glanced over at Jason and his friends once more and saw that they were leaning forward in their seats, practically an advertisement for teenage lust and hormones.

Admittedly, there was something sexual about the way the performers writhed around each other's bodies and pressed against each other, even if they all had clothes on. However, the impossible angles of limbs and torsos, the way that they seemed to melt into each other, slide around other bodies, all seemed more grotesque than sensual. All of the bodies working together seemed like a throbbing womb, about to give birth to a horror that no human eyes should ever have to see. Somehow, I knew in my gut that what was going on was not good. It was not something that a dozen teenagers should be watching. Underlying that, I felt...*danger.*

Without thinking twice about it, I reached down and grabbed Lucas' hand, gripping it firmly. He jumped at my sudden touch but did nothing to try and yank his hand free of mine. When I stood jerkily, he followed my lead. Then I was quickly leading him down the bleachers, each step bringing us closer to a run. The bodies in the ring continued to writhe and twist as a low growl began emanating from the mass of bodies. Stepping off of the bottom bleacher, my feet hit the ground, and I was pulling Lucas towards the tent's exit. Jason Morris and his pack of friends, I could see out of the corner of my eye, seemed to be inching down the bleachers, trying to get a closer look at what was going on in the center of the tent and the perverse display of the performers.

Urging Lucas along, I headed for the tent exit at a full run, clasping his hand tightly. We ran away from the grotesque display straight towards the canvas flaps that would lead us back outside. Upon reaching the black tent flaps, what I could only describe as a howl, rang out sharply behind us. Lucas and I both jumped, though we didn't slow our pace. We ran straight through the tent flaps, letting them flutter behind us as we ran through the carnival grounds, hand in hand, straight for the gates. Lucas was panting beside me as we ran, obviously scared out of his mind. I knew, without asking, that he had no plans to stop running until we were beyond the gates of CARNAVAL. Even then, we probably would keep running until we fell over from exhaustion.

We had nearly made our way to the gates, they were within my sight, when a sharp howl pierced the air behind us. Whatever had howled in the tent was now out in the carnival grounds. Somewhere behind us, muffled by thick canvas, were the horrified screams of teenagers. I gasped and ran faster, Lucas matching my pace. The unmistakable sound of something with more legs than a human running to catch up with us sounded from behind us.

"Run!" Lucas screamed.

I was gasping, my hands reaching for my throat, as I sat up in bed, woken suddenly from my deep slumber. My fingers clasped at my throat, as though I felt as if someone had been choking me as I slept. Jostling and thrashing as I sat there, it took several moments for me to realize where I was. If it hadn't been for Lucas' hands on my shoulders, trying to steady me as I fought to catch my breath, there was no telling what I might have done. Maybe I would have clawed at my throat until I gave myself a ragged tracheotomy just so I could feel like I was breathing again.

With Lucas' hands on my shoulders and my hands clutching at my throat, I was slowly brought out of the confusion that my dream had brought on. Incrementally, I was able to adjust to my new surroundings and remind myself that I was in bed at home, safe and sound. The things in my dream were not real, just imagined. Nothing was going to get me. The howls I heard were just my imagination playing tricks on me. The panic lessened, but my chest continued to heave as I forced myself to let go of my throat. Spastically, I turned my head, trying to find Lucas' eyes in the dark.

"Hey," He said gently, trying to soothe me as he held onto me. "Hey, babe. You just had a dream. It's okay. I'm here."

"*Oh. My. God.*" I gasped, finally able to catch a breath.

"It's okay." He chuckled warmly, pulling me into him. "Nothing's going to get you, babe."

Heaving against Lucas, my heavy, spastic breathing jostled us in the bed as I did my best to get my physical reactions to my dream under control. Other than the fading panic from such a dream, all I could think about was how ridiculous I felt. I was a grown man acting as if he didn't know the difference between a dream and reality. Luckily, my boyfriend obviously didn't judge me for being in such a state after such a vivid dream.

"It's okay, babe." He cooed in my ear. "I've got you. The big bad meanie things in your head won't get you."

"Har. Har." I managed to gasp breathily as my arms went around him.

He chuckled. "You okay?"

"I will be." I sighed, my breath finally slowing down as I squeezed him tightly and buried my face in his neck. "Thank you."

"It's okay." He said again, his hand reaching up to pat my hair as I nuzzled into him, reminding myself that everything was okay. "It was only a nightmare. I swear."

"I know," I mumbled into his neck. "It just felt so real."

"It wasn't." He reminded me. "I promise. Are you going to be okay?"

"Yeah." I nodded, my nose rubbing against his flesh.

He chuckled at the sensation.

I did it again.

"No." He admonished me, pulling away. "Don't get started. It's the middle of the night, and we need our sleep. You have a big day tomorr—today."

"Please?" I pulled back slightly to grin lasciviously at him.

"If you've recovered, we're going back to sleep." He tilted his head forward to put his forehead against mine, presenting an amused smile. "We need rest. Maybe when we wake up, though."

"You're worse than the big bad meanie in my dream."

"I do my best, babe." He gave me a quick kiss on the lips. "Come on. You wanna be big spoon or little spoon?"

I sighed. "Little spoon, please. Hold me."

Lucas chuckled. "All right."

Slowly, I slid back down into position on the bed and turned onto my side, facing away from Lucas. He inched up behind me, the length of his body pressed against the back of mine, which did nothing to squelch the desire I had for him at that moment. I did my best to not say anything else about that, though. Lucas was right. We had a big day, and we needed sleep more than anything. As Lucas' head laid down next to mine and he wrapped me up in his arms, I nestled my head in the crook of his arm with a sigh.

"I've got you, babe." He kissed the back of my head, tenderly.

"It was so real." I sighed sleepily. "You and I were kids again. At this circus or something. And there were weird clowns selling popcorn and cotton candy. And there was this bizarre guy named Richart who was the ringmaster...I think there were wolves or something?"

Lucas kissed the back of my head once more.

"That sounds like a great plot for a movie, Jacob." He teased.

"You should get into comedy." I rolled my eyes, though I wasn't unamused.

"Let's sleep," He said, another kiss to the back of my head. "There're no clowns or wolves here, babe."

"That's comforting." I yawned, nuzzling my head against his arm once more. "I love you.

"I love you, too." Lucas sighed dreamily.

Slowly, we both drifted back off to sleep, wrapped up in each other's bodies as thoughts of wolves and clowns fluttered away.

Jacob Michaels Is Dead

A Point Worth LGBTQ
Paranormal Romance
Book 6

Point Worth, OH
1975

Sitting atop the tree stump just inside the halo of light cast by the campfire, the man slowly opened the book, letting it come to rest upon his lap. The children gathered around the perimeter of the campfire sat in the lotus position, leaning forward expectantly. All of their parents had brought them to the old lands out by the lake to hear this story, just as parents had been doing for many generations past. Flames from the fire licked high into the night air, sending sparks and embers floating into the velvety blackness above. Skeletal arms and fingers of the trees in their deep autumn slumber flickered in and out of sight with each spout of flame from the fire. The man looked slowly around the circle of children sternly, solemnly, before suddenly clearing his throat, making the children twitch anxiously. Looking down at the book, his mouth opened, and his grave voice poured forth:
"Once upon a time..."

evil came to this land.
Its name...was Bloody Bones. Though, what it was, no one knows.
Where it came from, no one knows.
What it looks like, no one knows.
What is known is that it has almost always been here. Lurking. Waiting. Watching. From beneath us.
Rising from the depths of the water, it would drag wicked children into the depths, never to be seen again.
"Sass your parents...Bloody Bones will getcha!"
"If you don't clean up your mess...Bloody Bones will getcha!"
"Fight with your brothers and sisters...Bloody Bones will getcha!"
Parents would often say these things to their children, warning them that bad behavior would summon it. Bloody Bones would come for the wicked children. No one knew why everyone thought Bloody Bones only came for wicked children because, truth be told, he comes for all. Eventually, Bloody Bones comes for all of the wicked people, children and adults alike. No one is safe from it. It is everywhere at all times, waiting for its next wicked soul to claim. Though, no one really knows much else.
The one thing that is known is why it is here.
Many years ago...centuries...eons...who knows, really? Bloody Bones simply rose from the ground, given life by the very magic that permeates every inch of this Earth. But it wasn't just the magic of the land that gave life to it...it was also the evil that seems to fill the nooks and crannies where magic doesn't reach. Where there is good, there is always evil. You can't have one without the other. There must be balance.
Bloody Bones began its wrath of terror, claiming souls for its own. Ripping children from their beds and dragging them away, leaving tearful mummies and daddies wondering where their babes had gone. It killed livestock and family pets. Flying through the countryside, distorting the very magic which had begat it, attempting to create a new world in its vision.
Hell on Earth.

And if Bloody Bones had its way, that's precisely where we would be now. Instead of sitting around this campfire, safe and sound.

For many years...generations really...the people of this land lived in fear of and in servitude to Bloody Bones. Afraid to anger the master of the magic of this land. Parents clutched their children tightly to their bosoms as they put them to bed each night, wondering if Bloody Bones would come. Food and drink, sometimes pets and livestock, were left as offerings on the doorsteps of the homes as the sun went to meet the horizon each night.

Bloody Bones was satisfied...for a time.

It had magic.

Rule of this land.

Blood. Meat. Drink.

It was king.

But even kings grow weary and dissatisfied with their kingdom.

Bloody Bones wanted more.

More children were taken. More livestock destroyed. Houses were burned with families inside. His wolves terrorized the villages. Years of famine and illness cast a dark shadow over these lands. Bloody Bones cast these lands in darkness for many years.

But...as things usually go...where there is magic, there is hope.

Just as Bloody Bones appeared, so did The Guardian and The Oracle.

And, finally...The Witch.

The Witch knew that no one but she could release her people from bondage—to free them from Bloody Bones' reign of terror. Barely more than a child, the witch and Bloody Bones met on the field of battle. It was brutal, and it was not quick. The Guardian and The Oracle watched—as guardians and oracles often do—as Bloody Bones was sealed in the ground. Right here. Beneath us. Right where we sit at this moment.

It was obvious, as the witch collapsed to the ground, that the child might recover. However, instead of living to fight another day, the witch gave her life, the last of her power, to seal Bloody Bones away for good. As her blood spilled upon the Earth, she cast a wide net of magic with her final breath. As long as the magic of her family was in this land undisturbed, Bloody Bones would never return. It would stay sealed beneath us...forever.

Watching.

Waiting.

Plotting.

The Oracle and The Guardian watched as the land swallowed The Witch's body. A peculiar artifact sprouting from where she had laid.

They knew that with her spell, the witch had balanced the fate of these lands upon a razor's edge.

The magic would hold Bloody Bones.

But therey are those who would seek magic.

To claim it as their own.

To use it.

Even the witch's own family.

History becomes stories, and stories become legends, and legends become myth...and myths become nothing more than lies. Future generations of the witch's family would not believe that the magic truly held Bloody Bones within the Earth. They would attempt to use the magic as it suited them, to bring them their hearts' desires. Eventually, the magic that held Bloody Bones would be gone, squandered and perverted by the very people the witch had given her life to protect.

With a blood oath, The Oracle and The Guardian swore to watch over these lands, to ensure that if Bloody Bones were ever to return, they would be ready. They would find the most powerful witch in the family's bloodline, and—regardless the cost—get that witch to imprison Bloody Bones again.

With each witch's death over the eons—oh, yes, humans are weak and seek out the use of magic, and evil never rests—Bloody Bones grew stronger and stronger. The Oracle and The Guardian knew that...eventually...Bloody Bones would soon be too powerful for the same magics to keep it at bay. One day, it would rise from these lands a final time, no matter who stood against it, and Hell would come to Earth.

But...then, another witch was born.

And The Guardian and The Oracle recognized an opportunity to be rid of Bloody Bones forever...

"That's not true!" The boy doubled over with laughter, his arms slung across his tummy.

"True as we're sitting here!" The man's brow furrowed as he turned to glare at the boy who had distracted him from his storytelling.

"What a bunch of crap." Another kid, freshly in her teens, rolled her eyes as she jumped up from the ground. "You're crazy."

The man shrugged his shoulders as the children rose from the ground around the campfire. Chilly autumn air blew through their circle, making the firelight dance. Winter would come to Point Worth soon.

"You'll think crazy when Bloody Bones visits you tonight." The man cautioned her, pointing his finger brusquely at each of the kids in turn.

Mumbling about the "crazy man" and laughing amongst themselves, the children began to disperse, heading back up to the Old House, where their parents were waiting to drive them home. Every year, on the same day, the children of Point Worth came to these lands to hear the tale of Bloody Bones. At first, this was a sacred event, regarded with great solemnity by the children who were dropped off by their parents. Over the years, it became nothing more than one of the "crazy men" in town trying to scare the children with an ancient myth about their hometown, and, before that, the lands that belonged to the indigenous peoples.

The man sighed to himself as he closed the book and placed his hands on his knees, preparing to rise from the tree stump, when a child caught his eye. One of the younger boys had stayed seated by the campfire, watching the man. This boy lived on these lands with his family. Curious that he would be the only child not to heckle the man or his story. The man settled back on the tree stump, his eyes turning to the young boy, sitting there by the fire, captivated and terrified, his wide eyes affixed to the man.

"It's just a story." The man said.

It had been for the sake of the boy's comfort. No truth laced those words.

"Where did you hear that story?" The boy asked.

"Same as you." The man winked. "From an old man around a campfire. The last man to own this book."

"Is...is it tuh-true?"

"Don't let it bother ya' none." The man winked at the boy. "Bloody Bones ain't comin' for you, Robert. And, if he does, I'll fight him off for ya'."

Robert thought about this for a moment, and then a brilliant smile split his face. Leaping up, he gave the man a wave, and then he was running back towards his family home in the clearing in the woods, away from the shores of Lake Erie. The man watched as Robert ran gleefully towards home, allowing a passing smile to adorn his face. When the boy was swallowed up by the darkness and shadows of the woods, the man's smile disappeared, and his eyes went to the fire. Shadows danced all around him as the flames licked towards the canopy of trees overhead.

"Ya' know," The man started at the sound of a woman's voice, "no one really believes that story anymore. Which is a problem."

"Who's there?" The man's head whipped around, looking for the sound of the voice.

"The ground can be shakin', and the wolves can be prowlin'. The moon can turn to blood, and the lake can boil...but that story is no more than a myth anymore."

"Who's there?" The man repeated, clutching the book to his chest.

His eyes landed on the spot where little Robert Wagner, Jr. had been swallowed up by the shadows. A woman, old in visage but spry in body, stepped out into the light of the campfire. The man's eyes grew as the woman, a stranger to him, sauntered out of the shadows and towards the campfire, coming to stand on the other side of the flickering flames.

"Where'd you come from?" The man asked, unnerved by the sudden appearance of the woman he had never seen before.

"Here and there." The matronly woman shrugged as she peered into the man's sparkling eyes, not yet dulled by age. "Mostly here."

"Who are you?"

The corner of the woman's mouth turned upward slightly as her eyes lingered on the man's a moment longer. Then her eyes were on the book.

"That book doesn't belong to you." She said.

With a flick of the woman's hand, the book flew from the man's grasp into the waiting, outstretched hand of the woman. She smiled at the man and promptly tucked the book under her arm. Without another word, she turned and began to step away from the campfire.

"Huh-who are you?" The man demanded, rising from the tree stump.

"Well," The woman turned back to the man, "I'm Esther Jean Wagner. Or I will be. After a spell."

She winked.

Horrified, the man jabbed a shaky finger in her direction.

"You aren't Esther Jean Wagner." He demanded. "Esther Jean Wagner died in childbirth years ago."

Esther Jean Wagner smiled.

"What people don't know won't hurt 'em none." She winked again. "It's amazin' what people will believe with a little magic, ain't it?"

"What?"

For a few moments longer, the woman stared at the man. Suddenly, the man lowered himself to the tree stump again, his eyes slowly moving to the flickering flames of the fire.

"Esther...Jean...Wagner."

"That's right." The woman nodded. "That's who I am. You're good about tellin' stories. Tell anyone you want about me if it suits you fine."

The man's head nodded up and down like a balloon on a stick.

"But you ain't never heard this story before." She shook the book at the mesmerized man. *"That's one story you can stop tellin'. We don't need you goin' around, spoilin' the endin'."*

"Why?" The man asked robotically, his eyes still on the fire.

"These kids ain't the only folks listenin'." Esther Jean Wagner's brow furrowed as the ground rumbled underfoot for the briefest of moments. *"Tellin' stories is dangerous, Jackson Barkley. Some things are best left to be forgotten. For as long as they can."*

"Why?"

Esther Jean Wagner's eyes moved from the ground to the canopy of skeletal tree limbs overhead. The chilly autumn breeze blew through the woods once more, ruffling her hair and threatening to extinguish the fire.

"It might already be too late." She said, mostly to herself, before turning her eyes to Jackson Barkley. *"He's comin'. I don't doubt that you'll meet him."*

And, with that, Esther Jean Wagner disappeared back into the shadows, the book of stories tucked under her arm. Jackson Barkley sat before the fire, staring into its slowly dying flames.

Chapter 1

The ground was still shaking, maybe not as bad as it had been, but cracks had formed in the ground of the parking lot outside of the football stadium.

A pack of werewolves stood in a semi-circle, their leader at the center, a smirk on his face as the woman approached. Ancient and wise, confidence announced her arrival like perfume that had been applied far too liberally. Jason and his pack sneered and smirked, attempting to look menacing as the woman walked towards their half-circle of terror. Still the ground wasn't the only thing shaking. At least, it wasn't the reason that more than one werewolf's knees were wobbly. Whether something such as a werewolf would admit such a thing, every person in the pack knew that this woman was not to be trifled with, nor was she to be treated as harmless. With the snap of her fingers, she could easily incinerate any one—or all—of them.

Jason stepped forward as the woman stepped out of the dust and shadows, approaching the pack of werewolves as though they were bunny rabbits. She had nothing to fear from the wolves that comprised the pack, whether they were in wolf or human form. If it weren't the pack, one would think that the ground shaking underfoot would have unnerved the woman, yet it did not. She was unbothered by neither the werewolves nor the quaking underfoot. After all, this was the reason she existed. She had nothing to fear, for her destiny was tied to this moment. Just like it had been to every similar event spanning back to nearly the dawn of human existence.

Jason did his best to swallow down the lump in his throat and continue to smirk at the woman at the same time, though he knew that his fear would be palpable to her. Nearly anyone would fear this woman almost as much as they would the man in the black hooded cloak. Of course, no one was certain why such a seemingly harmless creature could be nearly as fearsome as the cloaked man, yet the fear was there. Perhaps it was because she had nothing to lose or gain, regardless of how events unfurled. Maybe it was because she had no fear herself. Or maybe it was because she was able to walk along on the shifting ground in a pair of high heels and not miss a step.

"Well," Carlita popped her tongue against the roof of her mouth as she stopped a few yards in front of Jason, "I guess today is as good as any other day for an apocalypse."

"You can't do anything now." Jason attempted a snarl, but to his chagrin, it came out as a wolf-y whimper.

Carlita looked across the expanse between them with a simple smile affixed to her face.

"As if I would." She said.

Jason nodded shakily.

"My allegiances have not changed, wolf," Carlita said, holding a hand up to examine her nails lazily. "Yet, I am quite surprised that we are seeing each other so soon."

"That's *her* fault." Jason spat.

Nearly a quarter of a million miles above them, the moon shone down, full and orange. Soon, it would be blood red, though darkness would mask it. Carlita glanced skyward and let her manicured hand fall to her side as she took in the hue of the moon, trying to mentally calculate how much longer they had. Suddenly, the ground stopped shifting. With a smile, her eyes landed upon Jason once again.

"They're no longer in Point Worth." She said. "For now."

Jason opened his mouth to speak, but a woman's voice came to Carlita's ears instead.

"They high-tailed it out of here, ya' bitch."

Carlita's smile widened as she turned her head to peer into the darkness at her right. Out of the shadows, Esther Jean Wagner stomped towards her. Clad in blue denim bib overalls, a plaid long-sleeve shirt, and gardening clogs, she looked as happy as she usually did, which was to say: *not at all.*

"Vieja loca blanca." Carlita snorted.

"Don't you talk that Spanish shit to me, Carlita." Esther Jean continued her march towards the woman in the red high heels. "You got somethin' to say, say it in a language I understand."

Jason took the opportunity to step back, slipping into the ranks of his pack, making himself a less likely target. At least a harder to hit target. Whether he would be a target for fire, a tongue lashing, or worse, he wasn't sure. He just knew that he did not want to be between the two women if they decided that they wanted to fight. It was unlikely that Carlita would allow violence to erupt during one of their meetings. Still, Esther Jean Wagner was a force all her own. She wasn't afraid of the woman in the red high heels. She had no reason to be.

"You crazy old white bitch." Carlita bobbed her head back and forth with a sneer as she took in the old woman who stopped merely a yard away. "That's not exactly what I said, Esther Jean. I added the 'bitch' because it felt right."

"How dare you talk to me like that?" Esther Jean's voice boomed.

A pack of werewolves, though in human form, cowered and whimpered. Destruction was upon them all. Whether it would come from these two women or the force that had caused the ground to shake, they weren't sure. But destruction was imminent.

"I wouldn't be talking to you at all right now if you had gotten Rob out of Point Worth sooner." Carlita examined her nails again. "Yet again, you just couldn't do your damn job."

"I did my job." Esther Jean snapped. "I got him out of this damn town before he came of age, didn't I?"

"And you did such a marvelous job."

"You look here, you bitch—"

Jason and his pack began to back up, thoughts of slinking away into the darkness crossing all of their minds.

"Don't even think about it, you sonsofbitches!" Esther Jean turned her head to snap at them.

The wolves froze in place. Carlita smiled, amused, though her eyes never left Esther Jean.

"I got him raised. I got him out of Point Worth when he was sixteen." Esther Jean jabbed a finger at Carlita's face, though she was smart enough to stay out of her reach. "I made him think everything was his own damn idea. I gave him those memories. I did everything we agreed upon. I. Did. My. Damn. Job."

"You," Carlita leaned forward, "did it poorly."

"Fuck you."

"Classy." Carlita moved back, her arms coming to rest over her chest. "You always were such a delight, Esther Jean. Oh, how I've cherished our millennia together. I'm kind of sad to see our time come to an end, even though it will mean never having to look at your face ever again."

"I did my job, damnit!"

"If you did your job, he wouldn't have come back."

"How the fuck was I supposed to know everything I did wouldn't be good enough to keep him away longer?" Esther Jean waggled her head at Carlita.

"Because I told you."

"You're always runnin' your damn mouth about something."

"That's what oracles do." Carlita turned her head to the wolves, who were, once again, trying to inch away. "If you boys don't stop being pesky, momma's gonna get mad."

Jason and his wolves flinched at the toothy smile Carlita flashed.

"Let 'em run." Esther Jean threw her hands in the air. "Where the hell are they gonna go anyway? I'm assuming they're goin' to turn tail whatever happens. Now that the arrival of their master is inevitable."

Carlita gave the wolves a stern look, then turned back to Esther Jean, all smiles once again.

"He took Lucas with him," Carlita said simply.

"Well, who the fuck saw that comin'? That was me. Some goddamn oracle you are! I told y'all pushin' them two together was gonna cause problems. I told y'all this whole goddamn plan was a bunch of cat turds hot-glued together, ya' old bitch."

"At least I've aged well." Carlita shrugged sweetly.

Esther Jean glowered at her.

"Meanness does nothing for the complexion, my dear." Carlita reached out as if to touch Esther Jean's cheek.

Her hand was slapped away sharply. Carlita shrugged again and crossed her arms over her chest once more.

"Look here." Esther Jean snarled, her finger jabbing at Carlita's face again. "I did what I was supposed to do. He left. It ain't my fault he came back. I acted put out just enough to not let on, but I never forced him to come back here. But even when he came back, I did all I could to confuse him, to make him think he was crazy, to scare him, to make him hate me. I pushed him and Lucas together again like we planned. I set him up on a date with a goddamn werewolf."

"I told him that werewolf was nothing more than a harmless pervert so he'd go on the date," Carlita interjected, unhappy with not getting her share of the credit.

"And I set up the whole scene the day after with Andrew. Hell," Esther Jean Wagner ignored her, "I had his ass jumpin' in the damn freezing lake to save a ghost. We got the werewolves after him—got assface over there to send three wolves out to the house to scare him. Even lured his ass outside in the middle of the night to be scared."

"You got Katie killed." Jason spat angrily before realizing who he was growling at, then corrected himself and calmed down.

"I got him interested in the cellar." Esther Jean Wagner continued. "I drew him down into that cellar over and over. I got him to jump in that damn well. Got more of assface's wolves to attack him and Lucas out on the Maumee after you sent 'em out there to *retrieve Lucas' memories*. Did better acting in these last few weeks than he ever did out in Hollywood. I gave him even more fake memories. I've lied my tail off and used every trick in my damn bag to get him to leave again. It ain't my damn fault he's made of sturdier shit than every other damn witch before him, is it? What kind of fuckin' moron—no matter how powerful—sticks around through all of that?"

"One who's in love."

"Oh, blow me." Esther Jean waved Carlita off. "That's the dumbest shit I've heard in my whole fuckin' life—and that's a long damn time. The bar is pretty fuckin' high."

Carlita chuckled. "I'll miss this."

"Yeah." Esther Jean shrugged. "Me, too. But it ain't my fault my magics wasn't strong enough for him not to see through, damnit. By mornin', he'll remember everything—even if I don't help him. And it won't be the shit we want him to think he remembers, either. Then we'll really be fucked, won't we?"

"What about Lucas?" Carlita asked, chewing at her lip thoughtfully.

"He ain't strong enough to see through shit. Not yet. Probably that damn vegetarian diet." Esther Jean sighed. "But Rob will help him."

"Lucas ain't meat starved. He's inexperienced." Carlita rolled her eyes. "And Rob will help him because he loves him."

Esther Jean threw her hands in the air.

"I didn't expect that to be real, all right?" She bellowed. Wolves cowered. "Who knew that's the magic they'd choose not to see through?"

"Sometimes, first love sticks."

"That's the dumbest shit I've ever heard."

"You may be powerful, Esther Jean," Carlita said. "But even you don't know everything. Maybe Rob and Lucas really were in love when they were kids. They weren't just going through the motions as most kids do. Your fake memories couldn't change true love."

Again, Esther Jean's hands were thrown in the air.

"No bother." Carlita waved her off. "Things will still go as they are supposed to go."

Esther Jean shook her head, a concerned look on her face.

"He may be strong, Carlita." She said. "But he ain't ready. Maybe if he'd stayed gone another ten years...but he'll do what he's supposed to do...because he's a good boy...but he ain't strong enough to stop *him*. This time, we ain't winnin'."

"Do we ever?" Carlita asked. "Really?"

"Well, no."

"Then," Carlita sighed, "this time will be no different."

"I suppose not." Esther Jean said with finality. "Our plans have gone to shit, damnit."

Carlita stepped back, as though ending their meeting, but her eyes landed on Esther Jean's once again.

"What?" Esther Jean snapped.

"It's a shame, really."

"An apocalypse is always a shame."

"No." Carlita shook her head. "You actually loved this one. He was special, wasn't he?"

Esther Jean just stared back at Carlita.

"I think you might have even believed he would end all of us." She added. "Eventually. If he had just stayed away long enough to mature more."

"Well," Esther Jean replied evenly, her eyes boring into Carlita's, "we'll never know now, will we?"

For several moments, Carlita and Esther Jean stared at each other, and a pack of confused werewolves cowered in the periphery. Finally, with an air of finality, Carlita shrugged.

"There's still time."

"Hours." Esther Jean scoffed. "We got hours."

"Rob will know sacrifice," Carlita said simply. "But maybe he won't be alone in that this time. Unlike you, I'm an oracle. I know when there's reason to hope."

Esther Jean didn't have a chance to respond. Carlita simply disappeared into the shadows, a plume of dust billowing into the air where she once stood. Esther Jean shook her head at the now empty spot that Carlita had once occupied. Sacrifice. Yes. Rob would know sacrifice. Just like every other witch before him, reaching back to the dawn of human existence. There was no way around that fact. Sighing to herself, Esther Jean turned on her heels to stride away from whence she came, the pack of wolves catching her eye.

"Well?" She snapped at them, making them all shiver. "Scat, ya' assholes! Go mark your territory or some shit! Tell your master I said to go fuck himself!"

Each wolf let out a yelp, as though having been kicked in the behind, then they all scattered, disappearing into the dark. They were not nearly as dramatic or graceful as the oracle had been. Esther Jean stood there in the now empty parking lot, the chilly early Spring breeze forcing her to wrap her arms around herself as she looked up at the orange moon. The ground had stopped shaking, but she knew that didn't mean anything had changed.

"*Why'd ya' have to take Lucas with ya', ya' damn fool?*" She said to no one. "*You would-a got out of here if you hadn't.*"

With a grumble and a "clop-clop" sound from her gardening clogs, she stomped back in the direction from which she came.

Chapter 2

Nelda Hammersmith wore glasses when I first arrived in Hollywood. Big spectacles that made her eyes look like they were staring out at me from behind fish bowls. Even then, as we had our first meeting, I knew that she didn't need the glasses. Mrs. Hammersmith, agent to some of the biggest and brightest stars in the universe that was Hollywood, liked to make statements. Sometimes those statements simply announced what an odd duck she was, but they were statements nonetheless. As I remember it, I don't recall how I found my way to Nelda's office in the heart of Los Angeles. I didn't remember much of my trip from Ohio to California. In fact, I couldn't even remember if I took a plane or rode in a car...I just knew that I had decided to leave Point Worth for Hollywood, and that was all there was to it.

Then I was in Nelda Hammersmith's office, telling her I wanted to be a star.

At first glance, she simply sniffed at me, appalled that some kid off of the street would be so brazen as to demand anything of an agent of her caliber. Seconds later, a cloud seemed to pass over Nelda's face...and then I was suddenly being proclaimed the Hot New Thing she had been waiting to discover.

You don't have anywhere to live in L.A.?

You can stay with me!

You're not old enough?

We'll lie!

Make up a backstory!

Change your name!

Suddenly, I was Nelda Hammersmith's new best friend who was going to help her become even richer—and hopefully, myself along the way. Even when she said my scene reads weren't all that great or my voice wasn't stellar, she looked hungry.

I had "IT."

That intangible, elusive thing that the biggest stars always possessed.

Nelda Hammersmith told me that if I "stuck with her," there wasn't anything I couldn't achieve in show business.

So...I stuck with her.

The Rolling Stones were playing on the radio when I was suddenly jolted awake in the passenger seat of my car. Lucas had obviously hit a pothole or speedbump because I was jostled in my seat, and my eyes flew open as the seatbelt bit into my chest. As one does in such situations, after the evening—and I guess proceeding weeks—we had endured, I looked around frantically, expecting an attack of some kind. Had Jason and his wolves caught up to us in their trucks, and were they now attempting to run us off the road? They were all dumbass country boys with pickup trucks, so I didn't feel that it was beyond them to attempt to spin us out, roleplaying their favorite NASCAR fantasies. They probably even had a wad of dip in their protruded lips with Gatorade bottles full of dip spit snuggled securely between their thighs as they slammed into my much smaller car. Or worse, cups filled with spit-soaked paper towels tucked between their legs. My mind raced, wondering if we had become complacent and hadn't expected them to come after us. I had fallen asleep so suddenly as Lucas drove that it was apparent I had let my guard down. A person who had gone through the day I just had would have to be stupid to just fall asleep and expect to be safe while they slumbered.

Of course, I had never claimed to be smart.

Lucas chuckled, though it was tense and slightly higher in pitch than normal as he glanced over at my worried expression and the crazy whipping around of my head as I looked all around. In my frenzy, it took a moment for me to realize that he was simply driving us east on the dark and deserted highway 2 towards Cleveland. We had just needed to get out of Point Worth and get to Hopkins airport so that we could fly to Los Angeles. Put as many miles between us and our former lives as we could, as quickly as we could. Of course, I didn't know how long I had been asleep or what had jostled me awake, so I had no idea how close to Cleveland we were when I awoke. Cleveland is no Los Angeles, but it is big enough that if we were nearby, I would at least see the lights in the distance. But the road and horizon ahead of us were dark.

"What's wrong, babe?" Lucas managed to mumble.

"Did you hit something?" I turned to him, trying to calm myself down. "I felt a bump."

"Must've been a big bump."

More nervous chuckling.

"So...you did hit something?"

"No." He turned his head to glance at me briefly, a worried expression chasing away the brief look of amusement. "You just startled awake, Rob. I didn't hit anything. You must have been having a bad dream."

"How long was I asleep?" I frowned to myself as my fingers found their way through my hair, pushing it off of my forehead.

"Um," Lucas frowned, "I don't remember when you fell asleep. But I've been driving for, like, maybe an hour?"

Turning my head briefly to glance out of the windshield, I looked out at the road before us. My eyes darted to either side of the road, taking in nothing but darkness around us.

"We should be getting kind of close to Cleveland," I said as I turned back to Lucas. "Right?"

"Right." He gave me a firm nod as his eyes stared out at the road before us. "We'll go straight to Hopkins, babe."

"Two one-way tickets." I smiled at him, but there was an uneasiness in my gut.

"We'll be in L.A. before the sun peeks over the ocean." He smiled happily as he steered.

"Maybe." I chuckled, trying to remind myself that we were safe. "I don't know when the next direct flight to L.A. is."

"Take anything." His eyes darted over to me nervously, though he tried to keep his focus on the darkness ahead of us. "I don't care if there are layovers or stops or anything."

"You're nervous." I reached over and laid my hand on his thigh, letting my fingers give him a reassuring squeeze. "I am, too."

"I—Rob, I just want out of this state. Ever since we drove out of Point Worth, I've wanted to throw up. I know if we can put some miles between us and that town, I'll feel better."

"I know what you mean." I nodded slowly, patting his leg. "Do you want to pull over and let me drive the rest of the way? So you can relax?"

"I'm not stopping this car unless it's in a parking spot at Hopkins." He chuckled, though he seemed less nervous.

"All right."

We sat in silence, my hand laid on his thigh as Lucas drove us down highway 2, trying to put further distance between us and our hometown.

"Hey," Lucas grumbled. "Talk to me. Give me something to think about besides...*everything else.*"

"You know," I began, "we could live really close to the ocean. We could get a place in Malibu or something, where we could step right out of our backdoor and...*boom*...ocean."

"That would be nice." He sighed dreamily.

"We could sit on our deck or in our backyard, sipping wine, snuggled up, listening to the ocean. Smelling and tasting the salt in the air. Watch the sunrise and sunset every day. Maybe we will get a dog."

Lucas was smiling widely out at the road before us, though I was worried his eyes were focused on something only he could see.

"Cook dinners together and read on the sofa with our new dog draped over our laps, and—"

"Big dog, eh?"

"You want a Pomeranian?"

"I like all dogs."

"Well, you can decide which dog we will adopt." I smiled at him. "And then we'll go upstairs when it's bedtime, lock the dog out of the bedroom, and do disrespectful things to each other. Every. Single. Night."

Lucas' smile was even brighter.

"After the disrespecting, we can let the dog in, though, right?" His eyes practically twinkled at the thought. "We don't want him to have to sleep alone."

"What do you have against girl dogs?" I teased.

"Him or her. Either or."

"Yes. He or she could still sleep with us once the disrespectful behavior is over, babe."

Lucas sighed happily.

"I love our life in L.A. already."

"I do, too." I squeezed his thigh. "Are you okay now?"

"Better."

"Are you going to be okay?"

"It'll take time." He replied. "But, yeah. I just...I mean...Point Worth is my home, Rob. Grandpa will—I'm going to miss some people. That's all."

"You can always call him when we get to L.A. He can come visit us."

"What about Mrs. Wagner?"

"No." I slid my hand from his thigh.

Lucas glanced over at me, nervously.

"What happened?"

"I don't want to talk about it." I shook my head.

"Babe..."

"She's not my grandmother, Lucas," I stated a little more sharply than I had intended. "I don't know how I know that...but I know it."

"How can you know something but not know how you know it?" He asked gently, obviously not wanting to fight, but also wanting answers he had a right to hear. "I mean, that's weird, right?"

"I guess."

"Rob, you forget that we have some of the same memories. If Mrs. Wagner wasn't your grandmother, don't you think that would be scratching around in my mind, too? I have no reason to think she's not, babe. That's weird, too, right?"

"Well, yes." I agreed. "I think maybe I'll figure things out once we have some time and distance between Point Worth and us."

"Why?"

"Lucas," I was chewing at my lip, "things haven't been right in my head, memory-wise, since I came back to that fucking shithole town. I thought I knew what my previous life was like, then I realized our memories were...I don't know? Fucked up?"

"But we have our memories back."

"Yeah. I mean. Yeah. We do."

Lucas gave me a suspicious look out of the corner of his eye.

"What?" I laughed a little too sharply.

"You don't seem convinced that we have all of our memories back."

"It's not that."

"Then what?"

"Just forget it." I turned my head, looking behind us. "I mean, I'm just all foggy from...everything. Right? Once we're out of Ohio, I'll feel differently about everything."

"*You've gotta be kidding me.*"

"I just need some distance. That's all." I could see lights off in the distance behind us.

That was odd.

"*No. No. No. No.*"

"Babe," I turned around to look at Lucas, "don't get all pissy with me, all right? I'm just all wonky in my head right now. That's all."

"*Fucking shit!*" Lucas growled, which made my eyes triple in size.

Lucas slammed on the brakes of my car, forcing me to turn and brace my hands against the dashboard to keep from being sent through the windshield. The sound of squealing tires against asphalt filled the interior of the car as I held onto the dashboard, and Lucas brought the car to a full stop. When we had come to a complete stop, I was still staring at Lucas, even more wide-eyed than before, and my fingers refused to be pried from the dash. Lucas' hands were no longer on the steering wheel and were slowly curling into fists, and his face had turned red with rage.

What the fuck was going on with him?

"*Fuck. Fuck. Fuck. FUCK!*" Lucas punctuated each curse with a slamming of his fist against the steering wheel, ratting it on the mount.

"What the hell is going on?" I gasped, finally pulling my hands away from the dashboard. "Lucas—"

"FUCK!"

Lucas ripped the driver's side door open and leapt from the car. Before I could react, he was stomping towards the front of the car. Quickly, I turned in my seat so that I could open my door and leap out of the car to chase after him. The last thing I wanted was for Lucas to march off into the darkness in a rage—for whatever reason—and then have to spend even more time in Ohio. When I turned to get at my door, my eyes darted to look out of the windshield once again. Lucas was standing in front of the car, his fists balled up in rage as he stared off at the side of the road.

What the fuck had caught his eye?

That's when I saw the sign.

"YOU'RE NOW LEAVING POINT WORTH, OHIO. THE SMALLEST TOWN WITH THE BIGGEST HEART. HOPE WE MEET AGAIN."

What the actual fuck?

When I was a young boy, my mother loved playing music whenever she did any chores around the house. Of course, her favorite bands and artists were from the 60s, 70s, and 80s. Sometimes she'd played some 90s rock and pop, but more often than not, bands like The Rolling Stones, The Beatles, Fleetwood Mac, Aretha Franklin, The Supremes, The Police, The Pretenders, The Mamas and the Papas, Bruce Springsteen, *and* John Cougar Mellencamp *would be heard coming from whatever device she was listening to music on at the time. From a very young age, I couldn't remember the house not being full of music, dancing, and laughing as my mom puttered around, doing everything she could to make it a happy and fun home for my dad and me.*

Mom would wash dishes as Don't Sleep in the Subway *by Petula Clark played in the background. Her hips would shimmy, and her feet would never stop moving as her head rolled around, and her hands washed and dried dishes. If it hadn't been for the fact that I grew up in the late 90s and early aughts, this wouldn't have been that odd. The fact that my mother was born in the late 60s—thus, had not been born, or at least, had not been that old when a lot of her favorite songs had been recorded—was odd, too, I suppose. However, my mother loved the music she loved, and there was no point in questioning it. Of course, I was very young when my mother was still around, so I didn't know at the time that her taste in music was unusual for her age. I just loved the happiness and dancing. I loved that, as a child, my mother encouraged me to dance and sing and prance around the house, carefree and happy.*

My mother encouraged my father to react with happiness and joy instead of anger and frustration when he was having a bad day. Instead of raising voices or complaining, we would eat and listen to music. Then we would dance and clean up as a family, though I was too small to really be of much help. Then I would groan as my parents shared a kiss at the sink, happy to be alive, married to their favorite person, and to have a home we all adored. My life with my parents was brief, but it was joyful.

It was the childhood everybody should have growing up.

But then my mother mostly disappeared from my memory after something...strange...rattled and shook our house. Every Little Thing She Does Is Magic *by* The Police *had been playing when it happened. I don't really remember the exact moment that was the last time I saw her, but I remember being in the kitchen with her when the house began shaking...then I was being put to bed by my father.*

The following morning, he was gone, too.

And a strange woman was there in his stead.

Why had my parents left me?

Where did they go?

Why would someone do that to such a young child?

"Fuck, fuck, fuck, fuck, fuck, fuck," Lucas chanted angrily as he stared at the sign and I slid out of the car in disbelief.

Instinctively, I wanted to go to Lucas and comfort him, to calm him down and keep him from getting more upset than he already was presently. I wanted to tell him that maybe he had just somehow driven in a circuitous route and brought us back to Point Worth. No big deal. We could get back into my car—maybe I would drive this time—and we could head out for Cincinnati again. Looking over my shoulder as I stood alongside my car, I knew that doing any of those things would be pointless. I could see the lights of Point Worth behind us—as if we had just left.

"Babe," I asked hurriedly. "Did you ever make any turns?"

Lucas was squatting down in front of the welcome side, his head in his hands as he rocked on the heels of his feet.

"No, no, no, no."

"Shit," I mumbled.

We had never left Highway 2, which ran straight through Point Worth. We would have been on a straight shot from Point Worth to

Cincinnati with barely any twists or turns. The only way we could have ended up where we were is if Lucas had taken a turn, driven south, back west, then in a northern direction before turning east back towards Cincinnati. And he would have had to drive through Point Worth again in order for us to see the sign indicating the city limit of Point Worth. We hadn't gone through Point Worth again. We weren't finding ourselves by the sign due to some mistake on his part.

Magic.

Not the good kind.

"Fuck, fuck, fuck, fuck." Lucas was kneeling now, his hands on his knees as he rocked and cursed. "Oh, fuck, Rob."

"Hey." I shook my head to clear my negative thoughts and overall sense of impending doom. My gut was sinking towards my ankles. "Babe."

Hustling over to Lucas before he had a complete nervous breakdown, I squatted down in front of him. His head was in his hands again as the headlights of my car partially illuminated us. I reached out and pulled Lucas towards me, and he practically fell against me, as if he had no strength left in his body. Whether or not he was freaked out by the fact that he had driven for over an hour and we never even got out of Point Worth or the fact that how screwed we were was suddenly dawning on him, I knew that I couldn't let him fall apart. I wasn't sure why my brain wasn't slowly turning to mush—I had every right to flip my lid—but I just wasn't surprised.

Somewhere in the back of my mind, I had known that we would never get out of Point Worth.

Above all things, I was mad that I had convinced myself that we could. That I had allowed myself to believe it.

"It's okay, babe." I held Lucas to me as my car idled, and Lucas shook, his arms violently grabbing ahold of me, as though he needed to be reminded what was real. "It's okay."

"How the fuck are we still in Point Worth, Rob?" He managed to choke out. "How the fuck is that possible?"

Lucas wasn't crying or falling into complete hysterics. Still, it was obvious that he wasn't holding himself together as well as he would have wanted under normal circumstances. The problem was—we hadn't found ourselves cast into a normal situation since we'd had coffee at the Sunny Side-Up Café right after I got back to Point Worth. Everything that had happened since I returned to Point Worth—to Oma's—had been a complete shit show. It was like riding a rollercoaster, my return to Point Worth. At first, things are fun and different, then the cars start to move, and you find yourself going uphill, slowly, slowly, *slowly*...you see the tip of the coaster that you will soon be cresting before the fall. And you start to dread the fall.

We had found ourselves at the top of the coaster. We were slowly inching our way into the fall. Soon...there'd be no stopping the downward journey.

"I don't know."

I knew.

Lucas knew.

"Why won't this fucking place just let us leave?" Lucas growled suddenly, making me jump, though I didn't let go of him. "I knew this place would never let me go, but fuck!"

Lucas pushed away from me gently and fell back against the asphalt, his knees rising so that he could wrap his arms around them. I fell to my knees in front of him, a great gust of breath escaping my throat as I shook my head. As I knelt there in front of Lucas, only the headlights of my car providing us with any light as the city limit sign loomed over us, what Lucas had said rang through my ears. Like a fly buzzing around my ear, his words were distracting me from any other thoughts.

"What do you mean?"

"What?" Lucas barked, though his anger wasn't directed at me.

"You said you *knew this place would never let you go?*" I frowned. "What did you mean, Lucas?"

Lucas looked up, his face no longer buried against his knees, and gave me a confused look, half of his face cast in shadow.

"You said," My brow furrowed, "that you *knew this place would never let you go.* That's what you said. What did you mean? It sounds like maybe you know something you're not sharing, Lucas."

He sighed. "No. Not really. Well, it's just—"

"—something that you knew."

Lucas stared into my eyes for a few breathless moments, then nodded.

"Why?"

"Because," He sighed, "I just know things, Rob. We've talked about this, and—"

"But you said this place would never let you go. You knew that. You've never mentioned *that* before."

Lucas was sighing again, and his legs shot out, leaving him sitting like a rag doll dropped right there in the middle of the highway.

"Because it's batshit crazy, Rob." He threw his hands up. "The fact that I know things is batshit crazy. That's bad enough, okay? But then to say something like: '*Ya' know, every time I drive over to Toledo, there's this inextricable force calling me back, as though I might be violently ill if I don't return to Point Worth?*' That's craziest of all, right? Look, I know you're special and everything, magic and all that jazz, but even you would have trouble with that. Who the hell am I going to tell something like that to? Who will understand it if I say that Point Worth—*a town*—has claws and they're buried in my fucking skin, Rob?"

"Calm down, babe." I reached out to touch the toe of his shoe gently. "I just want answers. We're sitting in front of this sign, and we passed a 'welcome' sign over an hour ago. I'm trying to understand. That's all."

"Baptizing the cat?" He grinned slightly, looking down at his lap.

"Hopefully not." I chuckled, though my heart wasn't in it.

"Rob." Lucas sighed. "When you found me at the football stadium...I knew that Jason and his pack weren't going to hurt me. I knew it. Not because I'm Mystic Meg or something, but because nothing was adding up. Why would they go to all that trouble? Especially since it was obvious that they wanted you to come get me. They wanted me with you, and they wanted to delay you leaving. They knew if they could waste time and also make sure you had me with you—you wouldn't be able to leave either. If I'm with you, you're stuck here—because this town won't let me leave. And they were delaying everything because..."

"He's coming." I nodded. "He's probably here."

"Who is he?" Lucas seemed to be pleading with the universe to give him answers.

"I don't know." I shook my head. "I mean...I know, and I don't. It's almost as if—"

"We don't really have our memories back?"

My eyes went to Lucas and were greeted with a raised, questioning brow.

"Yes."

"I've felt that, too." Lucas nodded. "You thought you went and got our memories, but I think that you only got what someone wanted you to get."

"Who?" I squinted.

"Your grandmother."

"She's not my grandmother," I replied, though it wasn't an admonishment, merely a reminder.

"Esther Jean Wagner." Lucas shrugged. "She's pulling our strings, Rob. I've known that, too."

I looked down at the asphalt, my hand still on the tip of Lucas' shoe.

"Fuck."

"Get in the car, Rob." Lucas' words drew my eyes upward to find him shaking his head solemnly. "I'll walk back into town. If you leave now, it might not be too late. Get in the car and drive as fast as—"

"You think I'd fucking leave you here?"

"You have to. I can't leave."

"Then I can't."

"Don't be ridiculous, Rob," Lucas grumbled. "Get in the fucking car and—"

"Hey," I gripped his foot tightly, "I'm not going anywhere without you. If you can't leave, I won't."

"You know that's the craziest thing you could decide, right? If you stay here, then...well, I don't know. That's one thing I don't know. My head feels cloudy. I can't see that far."

"Maybe a decision hasn't been made?" I suggested.

"Maybe. I wish..."

I couldn't help but smile.

"Be careful with wishes, babe."

Lucas smiled back. "I just wish we had the ending to the story in our hands. Then maybe...I don't know...maybe we could change it. If we knew what was coming, I mean."

"What?"

"If you know what's supposed to happen, sometimes you can change it."

"No, I mean, you said you wish you had the story in your hands?" I started to rise to my feet.

Lucas quickly followed, pushing himself up off of the ground to stand before me. Concern but also curiosity etched valleys in his face as he considered me.

"The book," I said, simply.

"Sure." He shrugged. "The book. What does that mean?"

"Books hold stories." I shook my head, trying to clear my thoughts as I marched towards the car, Lucas at my heels. "I mean, sometimes. Just, your thought about wanting to know the ending to the story. And books hold stories. I have a book."

"I have a ton of books at home." Lucas chuckled nervously from behind me as we approached the backdoor of the car. "But they're not going to do much to save us, Rob."

"This book will." I smiled to myself as I tore the car door open. "It's a spellbook."

"A spellbook?" Lucas snorted playfully. "Like a book that witches—"

I turned to him, a half-frown decorating my face. Lucas shifted on his feet.

"Sorry." He offered. "Obviously, you would have a spellbook."

"Right." I nodded as I bent down and reached into the backseat of the car to retrieve the book I had taken from Oma's—*my family's*—home. "Well, it's my family's book. I mean, I think. It's just been around as long as I can remember, and it might be able to help us. It won't give us the ending of the story, but maybe it can get us out of this fucking town. No matter who's trying to keep us here."

I lifted the heavy leather tome from the backseat and pulled it out of the car. Turning to Lucas, I smile widely as I handed it to him. Tentatively, as though he was afraid that it might bite him, Lucas took the book from me, cradling it gently in his own hands.

"Go on." I urged him. "You're the college graduate. Find us a spell that will get us out of here."

Lucas swallowed hard, steeling his resolve, before giving me a firm nod, then he fanned the book open. I watched eagerly as Lucas looked into the book, as though it would reveal the universe's secrets to him. Hell, maybe it would. I hadn't used the book in so many years, I had no idea what the book could do for us. I couldn't even remember what all was in it. All I could remember was a beautiful hand-drawn sketch of a skeletal tree in early Spring, a single flowering bud on one of the branches, near the end. It was the best hope we had for getting out of Point Worth, though. Anything that could help us cross the city lines and stay on the other side had to be a great thing. I watched as Lucas' curious expression turned to confusion as he stared down at the pages in the book. He flipped a page. Then another. Then another.

"What is it?" I asked. "Is there something that can help us?"

Lucas's brow furrowed even deeper, then he finally looked up at me.

"Rob." He shook his head. "This is, I don't know, a children's storybook? This doesn't have any, uh, spells, or anything. I mean, it literally starts with 'Once upon a time.' And there are children's drawings. Slightly morbid ones, but still."

He turned the book so I could look down at it.

"What?" I grumbled as my eyes met the pages.

As sure as Lucas had said it, the pages were filled with what looked like any ordinary children's story. Flipping pages as Lucas held the book, more writing—in a fancy script, but stories nonetheless—and pictures of ghosts and goblins leapt out to greet my eyes. The book was worthless.

The man and woman lay on the ground, unconscious and bleeding as the boy cowered in the corner, his hands held up defensively as the hooded figure bore down on him. For hours after leaving his room, the young boy had been at the mercy of the man in the black hooded cloak. Screamed at, threatened, forced to watch his parents squirm and plead as the menacing figure tortured them until they lay on the floor, nearly lifeless and unable to do anything to protect their son. The man in the black hooded cloak never stopped grinning as he subjected the young boy to the sights and sounds of his parents being punished for his stubbornness. Of course, the boy wasn't stubborn, he had been prepared. For his entire life, as short as it had been up until that moment, he had been warned that the man in the black hooded cloak would arrive one day.

And he was never to willingly accept anything the man gave him.

No matter how greatly he was tempted.

No matter what the man said.

No matter what the man did.

No power was great enough to pay the price that would be asked of him.

So, when the man arrived, in the boy's sixth year of life, the boy said:

"No."

For hours, the man in the black hooded cloak did all that he could, after rising from his throne of gleaming white bones, to convince the boy otherwise. Even as his parents screamed in agony and writhed on the floor, the boy kept saying:

"No."

To some, it may have seemed callous that a boy of such an age would allow his parents to endure such misery. But it had been his parents who made him promise to always say:

"No."

For they knew what it meant to say:

"Yes."

There is power in words.

There is power in:

"No."

Yet, as his parents lay on the floor of their home, beaten and nearly broken, barely hanging onto life, the boy still refusing the offerings of the man in the black hooded cloak, it became apparent that the boy would not be broken. Yes, he might cry and scream out with guilt and fear, but he would do exactly as he had been taught all of his life. He would say:

"No."

When the man in the black hooded cloak lifted his hand, not to strike the child physically, but to deliver another kind of punishment, the boy's grandfather intervened. He pleaded with the man to give him a moment with the boy, to talk sense into him. And, under the watchful eye of the man in the black hooded cloak, the grandfather convinced his grandson to say:

"Yes."

"No" became a "yes."

And the man in the black hooded cloak was appeased. He gave the boy what he had come to give him. As quickly as he arrived, so he departed. And the grandfather told his grandson that he now had a new task. He was never to use his gift. To do so would make him succumb to the will of the man in the black hooded cloak. So, no matter what, he was to bury his knowledge of his gift far into his subconscious. Forget that it was there. Never speak of it. Never even think of it. And he could still yet be saved from generations of bondage and imprisonment.

The young boy nodded, tears rolling down his cheeks.

In the morning, his parents would be worse for the wear, but they would be alive. And the boy had already begun building the walls in his mind that would trap his secret. He would speak of it to no one. One day, he would forget that he ever knew his secret.

The man in the black hooded cloak had been fooled.

He had achieved what he had come to do, but the boy had proved his will was stronger than even the man in the black hooded cloak knew.

Even if the day came that the gift was remembered, and he spoke of it to anyone, he knew what he would do.

And that would be anything but serve the man in the black hooded cloak.

Power unused has only one thing to do.

Grow.

What once was a seed delivered to the soil by a passing bird becomes a mighty Sequoia that shades the woodland creatures.

What once belonged to no one ends up belonging to everyone.

What once had a particular purpose ends up deciding its own fate.

There is power in stubbornness.

There is power in:

"No."

Lucas said nothing when I violently threw the book into the backseat floorboard of the car. He said nothing as I fell into the driver's seat of my car. Even as he climbed into the passenger seat, stoic and resigned, he said nothing. We sat at the Point Worth city limits for longer than necessary, since we knew there was only one way to go—nothing else to consider. When I sighed to myself, my hand reaching for the gearshift, Lucas' hand found mine. Together, we pulled the gearshift down to reverse. Lucas' eyes met mine:

"I love you." He said.

"I love you, too," I replied. "More than anything else."

A quick kiss, a lingering glance, and I slowly backed up, turned the car around, and pointed us towards Point Worth once more.

If we couldn't leave as one, we would stay together.

Maybe that upset Lucas, feeling as though he had conscripted me when my fate had been decided, but it wasn't his fault. I could have left if I wanted to go. But, without Lucas, my life in Hollywood would have slowly turned into the living nightmare it had been before. I would rather stay in Point Worth. Face whatever was to come. I knew what waited in Hollywood. At least in Point Worth, I knew there was a chance for something better. Even if we had to walk through Hell to get to it.

At least my hand would be holding his in this version of Hell.

Chapter 3

"Well," Carlita crossed her arms over her chest, "ain't that some shit?"

She stared down at the long crevice running along the middle of Main Street, steam rising in ribbons from the depths below. No wider than a man's foot, the crevice was still a concern, especially since there was no way to tell its depth. Of course, anytime such a crack appears in a road oft-traveled, people have reason to be concerned. The ground shifts, too much rain or too little rain, man-made disasters like fracking and drilling, anything can cause a road to develop the beginnings of a canyon. These types of things usually happen in states with frequent or powerful earthquakes, not in small towns in Ohio, though. There was no logical reason for the crack to be threading its way down Main Street, but logic had no home in Point Worth.

"It's some shit." Jackson Barkley gave a firm nod as he stood at Carlita's right. "It's a whole pile of evil horseshit."

"Mmm." Carlita agreed, her eyes not wandering from the steaming crack.

"I don't like this." Andrew piped up from her left. "I mean...this is fucked up, right? Even with all things considered, this is some end of days shit, right?"

Carlita slowly turned her head, her eyebrow rising as her eyes met his.

"Sorry." Andrew shrugged, then shivered.

"He's coming," Carlita said simply in Andrew's direction before turning to look at the gaping crack once again. "We all knew it was an inevitability."

"You've had a little longer to adjust to it than I have," Andrew muttered.

Jackson Barkley gave a dry chuckle.

"Well," Carlita fluttered a hand in the air like a butterfly's wings, "things still have a way of feeling like they creep up on you, baby."

"What do we do now, Carlita?" Jackson asked. "We could warn people, couldn't we?"

"They all know this is coming." She said.

"But," Mr. Barkley harrumphed, "it still ain't right to not warn them."

"They made their bed," Carlita answered sharply. "Let 'em lie in 'em."

"I suppose." Jackson sighed.

"We all know whose fault this is," Andrew grumbled. "The-fucking-Council. And Jason. His pack. Goddamn Esther Jean Wagner."

Carlita grinned.

"Goddamn Esther Jean Wagner." She repeated. "You forget Rob and Lucas."

"It's not their fault." Andrew shoved his hands into his pockets.

He had been shaking since he had met Carlita and Jackson on Main Street and had to do something to hide that fact.

"The bird learned a new song to sing." Jackson nudged Carlita impishly.

She chuckled.

"Shut up." Andrew rolled his eyes.

In unison, all of their eyes went back to the crack that ran down the middle of the street. The ground rumbled, and the crack spread wider.

"It's too late for warning or blame, kids." Carlita tossed her hands up in the air. "And we promised vieja loca that we would do what we could. So...let's do what we can."

"We're all gonna die." Andrew snorted.

"Maybe not." She said.

"Well," Jackson shrugged, "I'm older than most. Present company excluded."

Carlita patted his arm gently, smiling warmly at the old man.

"Ya' know," Jackson said, "I should really be mad at you and Esther Jean right now, Carlita—"

"Yeah?"

"—but I just can't bring myself to be mad. Y'all did your best, I suppose."

Carlita gave him a warm smile.

"Well, we'll see what the dawn brings before we claim it to be our best, shall we?"

He nodded, a smile coming to his lips.

The ground shook again, making all three of them step back as the crack in the street widened a few more inches.

"It's been nice knowing you fellas," Carlita said. "Just in case I don't get to tell you both later."

"Back atcha." Jackson croaked.

Andrew merely groaned.

The man in the black hooded cloak knew how to get his way. Promises and threats, torture if those methods did not produce results. Killing those who opposed him was a last resort, but one he gleefully indulged in whenever the mood struck. When the pack—only seven when they arrived—showed up in Point Worth, the man in the black hooded cloak saw his opportunity.

Add to his growing army.

Though he was unable to negotiate for himself, The Council met with the pack alpha. Offered them their greatest desires. The only price was allegiance to Bloody Bones.

The alpha responded swiftly. Courageously. For his pack was few in numbers compared to The Council.

Allegiance would be given to no one but his own.

No matter the offer.

His pack answered to themselves and the greater good.

The Council's answer was just as swift. At the behest of the man in the black hooded cloak, The Council, much greater in number than the new pack, quickly slaughtered six of the new wolves. The youngest, barely a teen, fled, a few cuts and bruises the only memory of the pack to which he once belonged.

Laughing and braying, the Council screamed at Andrew as he ran, announcing their plans to find those that would serve...him. If he wouldn't serve, he had no place with them. He was too young for The Council to expend any worry. If other packs wouldn't join...they'd make their own.

Andrew ran as fast and as far as he could.

He would never join The Council.

Or the man in the black hooded cloak.

But, if the time should come, that someone stood against either, he would answer the call to service.

Even if it meant his own death.

He vowed vengeance.

All he had to do was wait for a sign of hope.

And, when hope arrived, it arrived as a little old lady and a drag queen who were most definitely more than they seemed.

They offered nothing for Andrew's allegiance except hope. But hope is the greatest payment one can receive. So, Andrew pledged his allegiance. All he had to do for his payment, was lie.

"I'm sorry that I hurt Rob," Andrew stated blandly as he stood beside Carlita and Jackson on Main Street. "It is the only thing I regret."

"I know, baby," Carlita said. "But we've all done what we could. What we had to do. To end all of..."

She waved her hand at the crack, even wider than before, almost as wide as a man's foot is long.

"...this." Carlita finished. "Rob would forgive you if he understood."

"He would." Mr. Barkley gave a firm nod.

"I wish I'd been scarier." Andrew sighed. "Maybe he would have left the next day. Maybe I should have told him it wasn't primal instincts. I could have said that I would do it again if he was ever around when I was a wolf the next time."

"Could-a, should-a, would-a." Jackson chirped.

"He's a thick-headed one." Carlita grinned over at Andrew, though her smile was tight, fearful. "You did an excellent job, baby."

"Thank you," Andrew said softly.

"Him leaving would've just bought us more time." Carlita reached down and took Andrew's hand in hers. "That's all. Don't lose hope."

Andrew smiled down at his hand as Carlita's fingers laced through his.

"I never have." He said firmly.

"Good." Carlita sighed. "It's all we got."

The three of them stood and watched as the crack grew wider by another inch, and the ground rumbled once more. Carlita's other hand went to Jackson's, and she laced her fingers through his. Together, they all stood and watched. Waited. There was nothing they could really do but wait. They'd all played their parts—some with bigger roles than others—but now there was nothing left for them to do until he arrived. And there was only one way that would play out. Carlita knew what was to come, but she didn't dare tell her friends. Why scare them any more than was necessary?

Lucas sat rigidly upright in the passenger seat as I drove through the dark, the headlights off. We didn't want to draw any attention to ourselves unless it was necessary. Of course, it could be argued that driving down a country road in the middle of the night with your lights off will garner attention. However, in the little country town of Point Worth, Ohio, in bum-fuck-nowhere, there would be no one watching for cars with no headlights on driving down old country roads. From the city limits of Point Worth, I had driven twenty-miles-and-hour lower than the speed limit, not wanting to drive too fast so that I could react quickly if anything happened. I didn't know what we'd find as we entered back into Point Worth, but I wanted to be alert for it if something actually happened.

My mind raced with thoughts about what was going on in my hometown and what was going on with my life. When I had left Point Worth, I thought Oma was my...well, Oma. I thought I was rushing away to become a movie star because I was a wild teen who did what he wanted. I was chasing fame and glory and riches. As the years rolled by, it was apparent that the Hollywood lifestyle—being an international superstar—was not what I wanted. It did nothing to suit me or make me happy. Little by little, my life became a walking Hell where I didn't know what was real and what was fake. Fame can do that to a person. Having your memories fucked with makes it worse.

Memories.

What exactly from my past was real, and what was fake?

Why did my memories keep changing and shifting?

Why couldn't I stick a pin in them, tack them down so that I could tell what was really going on in my life? What had gone on in my past?

As I drove us further, I decided that I was going to assume everything I knew about myself and my past was a lie.

Then again, what good would that do? The only thing I could be certain of was that I had no way of knowing if the memories I had were true or not. Everything I thought I knew was up for debate, as far as I was concerned. Was anything I remembered from my childhood true—or was it all the things I was supposed to believe? Of course, I knew one thing for certain—Lucas wasn't wrong in saying that Oma had everything to do with our fucked-up memories. I didn't know how and I didn't know why—but she had done...*something*...to our memories. But, obviously, she had fucked with the memory of what it was she had done to our memories, too. If we had ever known what that was in the first place.

Because of that, there was no reason to not believe that everything I thought I knew was false. When Lucas slid his hand across the car and laced his fingers through mine, I realized something else. Not everything was a lie. Not every memory was false. I didn't have whatever gift my boyfriend had, but some things I knew for certain, too, because something deep inside me told me that they were true. Lucas and I did love each other. There was nothing inside of me that doubted that fact. Of course, I had no idea if our memories of falling in love were true, but we stilled loved each other. That was all that mattered. If we had really fallen in love as kids, that was fine. If we had only fallen in love once I moved to Point Worth and we had false memories about everything else, that was fine.

I loved Lucas.

Period.

And I knew he loved me.

Like Lucas, some things I just knew.

"Babe," Lucas exhaled heavily, "what are we going to do?"

"I don't know," I admitted, my fingers clenching his tightly for a moment. "But we'll figure it out, right?"

"Right."

"We can't go to Oma's." I shook my head. "That would...that's just a bad idea. I mean...I don't know what she's up to or why she's up to whatever she's doing, but without the Kobolds there—"

"Ernst and the other creatures?"

"Right." I nodded, one hand steering and the other clenching Lucas' hand. "Without them, it's a dangerous place."

"Yeah," Lucas whispered. "I don't really get what you mean by that."

I sighed.

"I don't know if this is true or not. Okay?" I glanced at Lucas. He nodded sharply. He understood. "But...the Kobolds were tied to, uh, magic that was, uh, tied to the land there. They're gone now. The magic is disappearing. If they're gone, and the magic is disappearing—or gone now—something bad is going to happen. I just don't know what."

"That's..."

"Batshit crazy?" I laughed nervously.

"Well, yes." Lucas chuckled with me. "But it's also not much to make a plan on, Rob. If we don't know what's going to happen, how do we decide what we should be doing?"

"We know that...*he*...is coming."

Lucas breathed out heavily, a moaning, hissing sound.

"What?"

"You said before that I met him, or might have met him, or that the Barkley's have something to do with him," Lucas mumbled. "I just don't remember. I mean...not everything."

"What do you remember?"

"Anytime you mention him, I can visualize him in his cloak. The hood. Red, glowing, piercing eyes. But I don't know why or what memory that comes from." Lucas shivered. "That has to mean that I have seen him before. Met him. Right? Otherwise, how would I be able to visualize him?"

"I don't know. Is that something maybe you just know so you can see him?"

"No."

"Then I assume that the Barkleys are just as involved as the Wagners, right?" I nodded. "You must have met him. I think you met him when you were a child. I had a dream...or vision...or something, Lucas. When you were a child."

I glanced over to find Lucas chewing frantically at his lip.

"We're close to it." Lucas looked up. "Let's just go to my house. Right there."

Lucas's hand slipped from mine so that he could point at the road up ahead. Sure enough, the turn to Lucas' house was coming up. Giving Lucas a nod, I eased my car into the turn and headed towards Lake Erie.

"Will we be safe there?" I asked nervously as the dirt road caused the car to bounce and shimmy. "I mean...a whole window is missing."

Lucas snorted.

"I just want to get my phone." He said. "We don't have to stay if you don't want to, babe."

"It's as safe as anywhere else, I guess." I shrugged. "But why do you need your phone?"

"Maybe I can call mom or dad." He explained. "Maybe they will—"

"Maybe they will what?" I turned my head to look at him, urging him on with my eyes.

"Shit." Lucas winced. "Rob. Look."

"What?" I turned my head to look out of the windshield.

Red and yellow light was what I saw before I realized I was looking at flames shooting into the sky ahead. Something big was on fire. And there was only one thing at the end of the dirt road that was big enough to create a fire massive enough to be seen that far away. Lucas' house was on fire. Surprisingly, Lucas didn't punch the dashboard or bang his head against his window. He didn't show any signs that what we were about to drive up on had affected him in any way. As we drew closer to his property, and we pushed past the line of trees, we could finally see the base of the fire. Lucas' beautiful home on the lake was an inferno.

"Oh, shit, Lucas." I moaned as I slowed the car to a stop, at least thirty yards from his house. "Oh, fuck. I'm so sorry. What—"

"Jason." Lucas' eyes were like daggers as he stared out of the windshield towards his burning home. "His fucking pack did this."

Fire danced and flickered in Lucas' eyes.

I wanted to tell Lucas that maybe he was overreacting or just making assumptions based on anger. Instead, I nodded firmly. He was right. We both knew that Jason's pack had done this. A knot in my stomach made me wonder if Oma's house wasn't also one big bonfire. For the briefest of moments, I felt guilty for being so angry with the woman who claimed to be my grandmother. Hopefully, she hadn't been in the house if it had been set ablaze. Something told me that if Jason or his pack snuck onto the property, though, the house wasn't what got set on fire. A devilish smile curled up the corner of my mouth as I stared out at the flames licking off of the roof of Lucas' home.

"Shit, Rob!" Lucas gasped. "Look."

"What?"

Lucas was pointing out at the scene before us, his finger nearly touching the windshield.

"They're still here!" Lucas announced in a panic.

Finally, my eyes landed on what Lucas had seen. Four men—conspicuously wearing only pants—were dancing jubilantly around the fire they had obviously started. The two of us watched as the four men danced around the house, howling up at the flames that licked towards the sky, proud of the destruction they had caused. They were far enough off that I had to focus my eyes, but I finally was able to see that Jason was not with them. It was just four members of his pack.

"Get us out of here, Rob." Lucas hissed. "Let's go."

"Okay." I nodded furiously. "Okay."

"Go, go, go!" Lucas urged me on. "If they see us—"

As I moved to put the car in reverse, so that I could creep away from the fiery scene on Lucas' property, two things happened. My hands slipped, and I simultaneously hit the horn, a brief, barking blast emanating from under the hood, and I accidentally flipped on the headlights.

"Jesus Christ, Rob." Lucas groaned.

"Sorry! Sorry!" I gasped, reached for the gearshift.

Once I had the car in reverse and had eased off the brake, about to give the car gas, my eyes shot up to look out of the windshield once more. All four of the pack members had spotted us—obviously—and were running at full speed towards the car.

"Oh, fuck." Lucas groaned. "Floor it, Rob!"

My foot hit the gas, and the car shot backward. There wasn't time to react in any other way, to devise any other plan. As I slammed on the gas and the car lurched backward like a slingshot, I felt, more than saw, the first of the wolves jump on the hood of the car. The passenger side window shattered inwards, and Lucas bellowed loudly.

Chapter 4

Screams reached Jason's ears as he stumbled out of the circus tent, clutching his bleeding arm, breathing raggedly, his eyes out of focus as he did his best to stay on his feet. CARNAVAL was in full swing, the rides—sans riders—swooped and swirled, their lights shooting a dazzling array of lights into the night sky. The screams of the two boys were getting further away. Freshly popped popcorn, fresh cotton candy, funnel cakes, corn dogs, and other carnival treats perfumed the air as Jason fells to his knees, his vision like that of a person underwater.

Why did he hurt so bad?

He'd just been bitten once.

Before he got away.

Jason gasped and clutched his chest as a sharp pain shot through his body like a lightning bolt. He bowed his head, trying to focus on the ground, doing anything he could to clear his vision.

What had happened? He suddenly couldn't remember.

Shaking his head and trying to clear his thoughts, he did his best to let his mind ride the waves of pain shooting through his chest.

Something was wrong.

He'd been bitten.

By a...wolf?

Where'd the wolf come from?

He'd been watching the circus performers. Why had there been a wolf in the freaking circus?

The posters.

On Main Street.

They'd been everywhere.

The carnival—CARNAVAL—had come to town. They had set up fences and rides and stands and tents out on the old Owens' land by the lake. The posters had invited all high school-age children to come participate in the carnival for free. Jason had gotten a few of his friends together, and they all decided to go check it out. They were the only students to show up...except for that Lucas kid who was just starting out in football. And that other kid...what was his name? Robbie. That was his name. He had shown up last. They were watching the acrobats and clowns...and...the ringmaster.

Something had happened. There were wolves suddenly. They had attacked everyone.

Jason coughed violently, holding his chest with both hands, doing his best to not topple headfirst onto the trampled down grass before him.

When his coughing fit past, he leaned back on his knees, looking up at the sky, watery stars and moon blurry in his vision. The screaming of *the two boys—Lucas and Robbie—had suddenly gone. Had a wolf gotten them? Jason panted heavily as another wave of pain, and also nausea, coursed through his body. He looked toward the gates that led out of CARNAVAL. Maybe he could get up...get help. Get away from the wolves. Fear shot through his body, realizing that any of the wolves might stray from the tent and the easier prey...and come after him again.*

As he looked toward the gates, even with his blurry, watery vision, he could see the figure coming towards him. He could just make out the red coat and black top hat. It was the ringmaster. Jason panted harder, clutched his chest tighter, as the man approached him at a leisurely stroll. When the ringmaster finally stopped before him, nearly close enough to reach out and touch, yet not quite, Jason looked up at him, his vision suddenly clear.

"Well," the ringmaster—Richart maybe?—said, "they were faster than they appeared, I'm afraid. Just disappeared. Strong magics, I assume."

The ringmaster laughed bitterly.

"Fucking Oracles and Guardians." He 'tsked.' "They always ruin a good time, you know?"

"What?" Jason gasped, his fingers clutching at his chest.

Richart bowed ever so slightly, his eyes boring into Jason's.

"No matter." Richart sniffed the air. "You'll do. I'm going to give you a choice, Jason Morris. You must make the right decision. And you must do it quickly."

Jason shivered at the sound of something with more than two legs sauntering out of the tent.

"I need your allegiance." Richart smiled wickedly.

Lucas yanked the sleeve of his shirt from the wolf's teeth as I spun the car around. I wanted to help him, but I couldn't drive the car and also fight the wolf who was trying to yank him out of the car. For once, I was going to have to trust that Lucas could handle himself. Besides, when I looked up, throwing the car into "Drive," my eyes locked on the red, glowing eyes of a wolf clinging to the hood of the car. *How the fuck was it holding on without human hands?* The screech of metal let me know that a werewolf's claws were good for finding purchase on almost anything. My lip turned up in a snarl as I hit the gas again, flinging us forward like a cannonball.

"Fuck you!" Lucas bellowed.

I saw him fling an elbow towards his window. A crunching sound let me know he had connected with the jaw of the wolf. The sound of a large animal rolling across the dirt road made me smile as we were propelled forward. The wolf clawing the hood and glaring through the windshield at me was a little tougher than the one who had tried to pull Lucas out through the window.

"Hold on!" I screamed before slamming on the brakes.

My car shuddered violently along the dirt road, skidding to a stop. The suddenness of our deceleration took the wolf by surprise, and it rolled from the hood of the car to land in a heap in the road before us.

"Seatbelt!" I screamed as I reached for mine and latched it quickly.

The second I heard Lucas' seatbelt click into place, I heard and felt something leap onto the back of the car. The wolf in the road before us was drunkenly stumbling to its...*paws?* Gunning the car again, I gripped the steering wheel until my knuckles were white, my teeth clenching as I aimed directly at the wolf before us. Lucas screamed out—either in fear or victory, I wasn't sure—as the front of my car plowed into the werewolf. A loud crunch and a strangled yelp reached my ears as blood splattered the windshield. I didn't take my foot off of the gas. As if going over the world's boniest, fleshiest speedbump, we were launched a few feet upwards before the car crashed down on the road once more.

"Flat meat," I stated simply as I kept my foot on the gas, urging the car away from Lucas' property.

"Rob!" Lucas gasped as he turned his head to look behind us. "There's one holding onto the trunk!"

"Why wouldn't there be?" I grumbled. "Hold on!"

Again, I slammed on the brakes. The wolf holding onto the back of the car with its claws smashed into the back window, splintering the glass, nearly sending it through and into the backseat. But its claws were pulled from the hood of the car as the stop jerked its body forward. Lucas yelped as I hit the gas again, sending the wolf rolling away. I was breathing heavily, my heart beating in my throat as I pushed my foot to the floor atop the gas pedal. Lucas had smashed one in the jaw. I had run one over. We had just seen another fly off of the back of the car, totally dazed and bloody.

Just as I expected, the fourth wolf made its presence known.

My window shattered as the wolf ran up alongside the car and threw its body against the moving vehicle. Lucas and I both screamed out in terror as glass shards rained inwards, and the car lurched up onto two wheels for a brief second.

Goddamnit, these guys are big.

And fast.

I had to keep my hands on the steering wheel to have any chance of keeping us on the bumpy dirt road, and the werewolf was running up alongside the car once more. Any second, I knew it was going to shove its jaws through the shattered window and bite me. Game over. I had no idea if I was immune to werewolf bites like Lucas—but we didn't have the time or desire to find out. Just as the werewolf came up alongside the car, panting and huffing, running at top speed—way too fast for any animal—it turned its head. I saw a flash of glowing red eyes as it lunged. Lucas' hand was suddenly on my forearm, and he was leaning across me, toward the window, one of his hands outstretched. He screamed out animalistically as magic coursed through my arm and into him, and fire erupted from his hand, a column of heat plowing into the werewolf, setting it ablaze and sending it tumbling away into the darkness.

My eyes shot over to Lucas as I thought of a burning pile of werewolf tumbling into the woods.

Fuck it. I thought. *Let the entire town burn down. I'm not turning into a werewolf today. If I can...*

"Go, Rob!" Lucas yelped as he positioned himself back in his seat. "Just go!"

"All right." I swallowed hard, keeping my foot pressed to the floor as I turned sharply off of the road to Lucas' house and onto the main road.

Pulling onto the main road that led out to Lucas' lands, I didn't let up off of the gas. Screaming down the road in the middle of the night in my busted-up car would surely attract the attention of any cop that might be out and about, looking for drunk drivers or someone else to ticket, but I didn't care. I wasn't going to stop until I was certain we were far enough away from the wolves. There was no point in keeping ourselves near an unsafe situation for fear that the cops might pull me over. With the mood I was in, and considering the adrenaline pumping through my veins, I would likely fight any cop that tried to stop us. Especially Sheriff Dennard.

"Damnit, Rob." Lucas bellowed to be heard over the wind whistling through the broken windows. "I'm bleeding."

Shooting a glance at Lucas, I mostly kept my eyes on the road ahead of us as I navigated the mostly straight, yet narrow two-lane road. There was no point in getting away from the wolves only to crash my car and have us out in the open like sitting ducks with no working vehicle.

"What?" I screamed back. "Did you cut yourself?"

"I guess one of 'em bit me." He returned. "Probably the one that I bashed in the face with my elbow."

He tried to twist his body so that he could show me that his right elbow was soaked in blood. I grimaced as I looked at his elbow, then realized his face was ashy-white. Nodding at him, I knew that we had to tend to his wound before we did anything else.

"Let me find a safe place, and we'll pull off, okay?"

"Okay."

For a few more miles, I skirted the northern perimeter of the Point Worth city limits, looking for somewhere secluded and hidden so that I could pull off of the road. A place where no one who might happen by and see the car easily. Finally, as I drove along, I noticed a break in the tree line. An old service road to one of the many unused boat docks that dotted the shore of Lake Erie. I eased the speed of the car and slowly turned onto the road, killing the headlights. Slowly, I eased off of the gas as we drifted down the road, disappearing amongst the trees that lined the old road. Finally, when we were far enough within the trees, and far enough away from the road, to where I felt that we were safe, I brought the car to a full stop and put it into park. It took quite a bit of willpower to force myself to turn the car off, but I finally flicked the key. Suddenly, we were greeted by silence and darkness.

Both of us took a moment to stare out into the inky darkness before us, our breaths ragged and sharp, filling the interior of the car with the sounds of sheer adrenaline. Briefly, I wondered if the wolves wouldn't happen by, hear the sounds of the thundering hearts in our chests and the sounds of our breaths floating from the broken windows of my car, and search us out. Of course, I knew that to be ridiculous. One, the wolves were not likely to regroup and follow us so quickly after Lucas set one of them ablaze, and I had run one over. Two, they would most likely be running, and they would never hear our breathing as they ran along the road. Though our breathing sounded thunderous to my ears in the confines of the car, outside of the car, it would be hard for anyone to hear. Paranormal or not.

"Okay." I unsnapped my seatbelt and turned gently in my seat, trying to get my breathing and heartbeat under control. "Let's see your boo-boo."

Lucas smiled pitifully as he unsnapped his seatbelt and turned towards me.

"Sorry, babe." He grumbled. "I know this isn't the best time, and—"

"If he had pulled you out of the car, I don't think he was going to tie you to a football field goal post, Lucas." I shook my head. "There's nothing to be sorry for, babe. You were defending yourself. And me. It's not your fault he got you. And, even if it was your fault, fuck it. The rules don't apply when you're fighting for your life. You're allowed to be clumsy."

"I know. I know." He shook his head as he fought to not smile as he stripped his button-down off. "That was intense."

Watching Lucas undress always had an effect on me. One that was not appreciated when we had just been fighting for our lives. So, I swallowed down those feelings and simply waited as he stripped off his shirt and turned his body so that he could present his elbow. Nearly in total darkness, there was still enough light for me to see the small gash on Lucas' elbow and the darker area that was seeping blood. I couldn't help but wince at the sight as I held his arm in mine, cradling his elbow.

"Well, okay." I shrugged, still holding his arm gently. "Do it."

"Do what?"

"The thing where you borrow some of my magic and heal yourself."

"Why don't we just find something to bandage it with?" Lucas suggested. "I'm not going to bleed out, babe."

"Why not heal it while we have a moment, ya' know?"

"I don't want to use your magic." Lucas shook his head.

"You just did." I chuckled. "To set furball ablaze?"

"That was life or death." He said. "This isn't."

"Why are you giving me crap here?" I teased him. "Just do your little trick, and we won't have to worry about this any—"

"Don't you feel that, Rob?" Lucas cut me off, his voice a whisper. "Haven't you been paying attention at all tonight?"

"To what?" I asked, still examining his wound in the dark.

Lucas looked around, as though expecting someone to jump out of the velvety black woods that surrounded the car and pounce on us.

"Can't you feel it all around?" He asked again, his voice even lower. "Something is changing. Shifting. Point Worth doesn't feel the same since we first tried to drive out of here last night. It feels...emptier or something."

"Emptier?"

"Like that thing that made Point Worth...*Point Worth*...is slowly draining away. I feel like..."

I waited for the space of several breaths until a shiver danced along the back of my neck, and I couldn't take the silence any longer.

"You feel like what?"

"Like something is draining all of the magic from Point Worth." He swallowed hard.

The words felt like a knife in my gut. I wasn't sure why, but those words meant something to me.

"Don't be ridiculous." I hid a shiver by letting go of Lucas' arm and snatching up his shirt.

Lucas watched me as I ripped one of the arms off of his shirt and began wrapping it around his elbow.

"You know it's not ridiculous," Lucas stated calmly. "I can tell. I saw it in your eyes just now. Something is majorly wrong. Things are changing."

For a few moments, I focused on tying the sleeve of Lucas' shirt around his wound, making sure it was secure. A makeshift bandage, but a bandage nonetheless. Finally, I let go of his arm and looked up at him once again. Lucas' eyes were placid, he wasn't fearful. But I could tell that all of his synapses were firing. He was thinking his problem out over and over, trying to figure out why he felt the way that he felt.

"Why are you immune to werewolf bites?" I asked suddenly. "Am I?"

"Well, I don't know if you are," Lucas answered automatically.

"Don't you just know things, damnit?" I barked, which hadn't been my intention at all.

Lucas just stared back at me.

"Sorry." I corrected myself.

"I don't know, Rob," Lucas stated evenly, controlling himself. "I feel that I should, but I don't. Okay? It's like a secret locked in a cage in my mind. I feel like...I don't know...maybe I don't know on purpose."

"What does that mean?"

"Like I intentionally forgot why I'm immune."

"Why would you do that?" I snapped, again without meaning to.

"That's something else I don't know." He bit the words off sharply. "If I forgot on purpose, I probably forgot why I forgot on purpose, too, right?"

I sighed.

"But...and you won't believe me...but I'm suddenly remembering something. Jason bit me in high school. After a football game one night. I had forgotten that, too. Until now."

"Why?" I barked, not caring if anyone heard. "Why did you forget that?"

"Why did you forget you could shoot lasers and fire from your hand, Rob?" Lucas was so calm I knew that he was controlling himself for my sake, so he wouldn't snap back at me and make our situation worse. We didn't need to fight. Not now. "You don't know either. So, kindly stop giving me the third degree. I already have a bite. I don't need a burn."

He smiled impishly.

I did my best not to do it, but a smile slowly formed on my face.

"Fine." I huffed, but my heart wasn't in it. "What happened when he bit you?"

"Same thing as now." He shrugged. "Didn't you wonder why Jason was so nonchalant that night out on the Maumee when I got bit? He was too blasé about the whole thing. He knew I wasn't going to turn, even though he said it would take a few moon cycles. I told grandpa about it happening—when Jason turned into a werewolf and bit me after the game way back when. He told me to pretend it never happened. So...I just did. I forgot about it. Something...I don't know what...made it easier to do."

My brow was practically a canyon as I frowned at my boyfriend.

"Okay." I held my hands up. "But wait. I found out that those guys at the Maumee were actually Jason's. Why would he send them to bite you if he knew it wouldn't turn you into one of his pack, huh? Why go to all that trouble and risk losing two of your pack members if it wouldn't get results, Lucas? Answer that."

"It was a scare tactic."

"What was he scaring you for?"

"He was trying to scare you." Lucas shrugged.

"What?"

"Haven't you wondered why things have gotten weirder and weirder the longer you've been here, Rob?" Lucas urged me on, his eyes pleading with me. "I really think...shit. I really think everything and everyone is trying to make you leave again. But you waited too long. And you decided to take me with you. We fucked up their plans, babe."

I couldn't help it. I rolled my eyes.

"That doesn't make any sense."

"Doesn't it?" Lucas snorted. "Weird shit at Esther Jean's house. The weird cloaked person in the back yard—that we know wasn't *him*? The guy on the cliff overlooking the lake? Weird sights and sounds. Sudden werewolf attacks. Andrew? Nothing odd happened while you were gone. And Point Worth is pretty fucking odd. Then you show back up...and it's like this town is putting on a show for you, Rob. Like everyone and everything is trying to remind you why you shouldn't be here. Once we got involved...well, I got pulled into this shitstorm."

"Sorry?"

"I don't mean this is your fault, babe." His expression softened. "I just mean that I'm collateral damage."

"Fine." I threw my hands up. "Why would Oma have been so upset about me leaving? Huh? She's done nothing but give me shit nonstop for a decade for leaving Point Worth. Explain that."

"Why would she be nice to you?" He shrugged. "That would make you want to stay more. And maybe she wanted you gone, but she also hated to see you go. Having to do something and liking what you have to do are two separate things. Besides...who has been messing with our memories, babe? Santa Claus?"

"I wouldn't be the least bit surprised if he landed on the hood of this car right this second," I mumbled. "With every single goddamn reindeer in tow."

Against our will, both Lucas and I turned our eyes to look out the windshield. Suddenly, we were looking at each other and having to slap our hands over our mouths to keep from laughing at the absurdity of such a thing. Santa Claus wasn't going to appear on the hood of the car. However, with all things considered, it wasn't completely crazy to imagine it.

"Look, Rob." Lucas shook his head. "I vaguely remember the man in the black hooded cloak. But I know I'm not supposed to remember. And for a good reason, I think. Something that happened when I met him...I'm not supposed to think about. Talk about. Or remember. For my own safety. Maybe other people's safety. I don't know. But I also don't know if I made myself forget or if this is Esther Jean Wagner's work at play. I...just...don't...know."

Slowly, I breathed out, unable to connect the dots as to what was going on in the little town of Point Worth, Ohio. Or what my life was even about. Just as I had been thinking before the wolves had attacked us, Lucas put into words what I knew to be true. We couldn't trust any of our memories.

"Jason said something to me." I sighed. "Last night. When I decapitated him."

"You're going to have to get better at that." Lucas teased.

"Next time, I'm taking his head with me." I snorted. "Or burning him until he's nothing but ashes. But...he said that my magic is the only magic in town that doesn't have anything to do with...him."

Lucas was nodding along, looking thoughtful.

"Do you think," I chewed at my lip, "do you think everything in this town that is some part magical has something to do with him?"

"Maybe?"

"He's coming," I said. "Maybe he's draining all of the magic he's put out there so he can use it?"

"For what, though?"

"Well, it ain't to pull a bunny out of a hat, babe."

Lucas chuckled ruefully.

"He's planning something big," I said. "I feel like he's been stocking away ammunition...waiting for the right time...and now, he's ready to use it."

"But for what?" Lucas repeated. "If we knew what he had planned, maybe we could figure out what the hell is going on. Make some sense out of all of this. Maybe we could actually freakin' remember things, and our memories wouldn't be a fog."

Lucas and I both slumped back in our respective seats. For several minutes, we sat there, just staring out of the windshield into the darkness. Lucas finally pulled his shirt on and buttoned it, looking slightly silly with one sleeve missing. However, the choice between looking silly and bleeding was an easy choice to make.

"We have to see Esther Jean," Lucas said with finality.

"No," I said. "I can't trust her."

Lucas slumped back in his seat, a harrumph escaping his lips.

Chapter 5

"Open up, Esther Jean Wagner!" Clancy Kelly pounded on the front door of the large house. "We know you're in there! You open up right this second!"

Clancy, Darby, and their son, Aiden, all stood on the front porch of Esther Jean Wagner's house, red-faced and angry, ready for a fight. They had allowed things to go on for as long as possible, but their patience was running thin. Robbie was nearly sixteen-years-old. Everyone was getting anxious, fearful that the day would come that it was too late to enact the plan. Esther Jean Wagner needed to do as she said and stop pussyfootin' around about it. The boy had to go—one way or another. The Kellys had a new plan of their own. They weren't going to wait for Robbie to go away. They'd take care of him themselves.

All three of the Kellys jumped back as the door finally swung wide, revealing Esther Jean Wagner, still in her bib overalls, plaid farmer's shirt, and gardening clogs, her arms crossed under her breast. The Kellys, filled with piss and vinegar only moments prior, found themselves inching backward on the porch, putting more space between the open door and themselves. Esther Jean Wagner merely glared out at the three of them and their shotguns, not looking the least bit concerned by the firepower they had brought with them.

"What are you fools doin' on my damn property?" Esther Jean Wagner barked. "Robbie's in bed. If you wake him up—"

"We're here for the boy." Clancy Kelly managed to choke out, though the crack in his voice betrayed him.

"That so?" Esther Jean's eyebrow raised precipitously.

"Give us the boy, Mrs. Wagner." The Kelly's eldest commanded in a voice no more authoritative or confident than his father's. "Give us Robbie, and we can have this all done with once and for all."

Esther Jean chuckled.

"You think that's gonna stop anything, ya' damn idjit?" She asked, her eyes boring into each of the Kellys eyes in turn. "You're just gonna do away with him, and then you ain't gotta worry no more?"

"That's about right." Mr. Kelly glanced at his wife, whose eyes were fixed on the floorboards of the porch, afraid to look up. "We're tired of this nonsense. We want to end it once and for all."

"He's the last." Esther Jean's eyes shot over to Clancy. "There ain't no more after him. You ain't even givin' him no chance to have any kids his own. There might be a distant relative, I supposed, but if you kill him—"

"Then we're rid of this curse!" The eldest son of the Kelly's barked, a little braver than he had been.

"You are the dumbest sonsabitches I ever had the bad fortune to look at in my life. Ugliest, too. If there was an award ceremony for stupid, you'd sweep the whole damn thing." Esther Jean leveled them with her eyes. *"He's comin' back one way or another. Somehow or some way. If you get rid of the boy, ain't no one savin' your sorry asses then. We'll all be up Shit Creek without a paddle in a glass-bottomed boat."*

"We got a chance to end this for good, Esther Jean." Mr. Kelly pled with her, no longer angry, simply lost for other solutions. *"I don't like it none—"*

"I think it's time for you, Clancy. Darby. Y'all need to retire down to Florida." Esther Jean stated evenly, her pupils dilating until her irises disappeared into a black hole. *"Get away from things."*

All three Kellys stiffened as their eyes locked onto Esther Jean Wagner's.

"And you should just forget this ever happened, Aiden." She addressed their eldest son. *"That'll get us right back on track."*

All three Kellys slowly nodded.

"We can't leave." Mr. Kelly seemed to have a thought, his voice pouring forth from his lips robotically. *"He'll never let us leave."*

"Well," Esther Jean fluttered a hand in the air as if this meant nothing to her, *"you're just goin' for an extended vacation. You ain't tryin' to escape, is ya'? So what if it's a really long damn vacation? You drive on out of town feeling like you plan on comin' back sometime in the future. But...don't."*

Again, all three of the Kellys nodded along.

"Now," Esther Jean Wagner's irises emerged from the black hole of their pupils, *"y'all get your pug-ugly asses off my porch, ya' hear?"*

The Kellys all shook their heads as if coming out of a dream.

"I don't want to see none of y'all on my property ever again!" Esther Jean warned them. *"If I do, I'll be the one using a shotgun, damnit. That's a damn promise."*

The door of the big house was slammed in the three adults' faces. Mr. and Mrs. Kelly looked at each other, confused for a moment, then turned to walk away. Aiden, their eldest, simply fell in behind them.

"All she's done is lie to me. To us." I muttered under my breath. "I can't trust her. She's not my grandmother."

"Babe," Lucas reached over, his hand landing on my thigh gently, his fingers giving the flesh there a squeeze, "no offense, but what other bright ideas do you have?"

"I don't."

"Exactly." He nodded firmly. "Who else is going to help us now?"

"How about," I searched my brain for the name of anyone other than the woman claiming to be my grandmother but wasn't, "Carlita?"

"We can't get out of Point Worth." Lucas frowned at me. "How are we going to get to Toledo to get help from her? And why did you think of her anyway, babe?"

"She's an oracle." I shrugged impishly.

"Good information to have had a while back." Lucas' frown deepened.

"Sorry."

Lucas shrugged. "Doesn't matter much now."

"How about Mr. Barkley?" I asked quickly. "Surely your grandfather knows something about—"

"Really?" Lucas snorted. "You think grandpa can protect us from anything? Can he fix our memories, babe?"

"Well, no..."

"Exactly. We have to see Esther Jean, Rob."

"No."

"Why not?" Lucas groaned. "I know you don't trust her, but it's not like we have any real friends left, Rob. We have to trust someone, even if it's a little foolish. Someone has to help us, and she's the only one I know with magic and maybe some information."

"I wish the book had been some kind of help."

"A storybook isn't going to help us, Rob."

"I know."

"So?"

"Look," I turned to look at Lucas, "Esther Jean Wagner—if that's even her real name—is a goddamn liar, Lucas. Suddenly, the other night, it just really sunk in. I didn't know her before my parents disappeared to...wherever they disappeared to, okay? Hell. She could have been the person who made them disappear for all I know. Especially with my lapse in memory here. Regardless of why my parents are gone, where they went to, if she had anything to do with it—I don't have any memories of her before they disappeared. It also makes me question everything about whether or not she has anything to do with our memory problems because..."

"Because what?"

"If she fucked with our memories, why didn't she just give me some fake memories about her when I was a small child?" I shrugged. "I mean, that's a real lapse of judgment on her part, right?"

"I suppose..."

"One day, some weird shit went down at the house. I was a small child. My mom was making breakfast in the kitchen, and shit...just went down. And she was gone. I don't know anything more than that to tell you. Then I remember my dad tucking me into bed that night. Then he was gone in the morning, and this...person...showed up and said she was my grandmother. I can remember that now. I came downstairs because someone was knocking on the door. It was that...*woman*...and when I asked her who she was, she said she was my grandmother. *I remember that now.* But I don't have any memory of her before that moment. If she was really my grandmother, I would have some sort of memory of her at Christmas or Thanksgiving...or a family reunion or talking to her on the phone during the holidays at the least. But...nothing, Lucas. She didn't exist to me before that moment."

"That's crazy."

"I'm not crazy!" I barked.

Lucas smiled gently at me.

"I meant that the situation is crazy." He squeezed my thigh again. "Not you, babe."

"Oh."

"I'm on your side, remember?" He reminded me. "We're a team."

"Yeah." I sighed as I laid my hand on his, letting our fingers intertwine. "Sorry. I'm kind of on edge here."

"I don't know why." Lucas teased.

Darkness was creeping in on all sides of the car. The woods around us were deathly silent, making our low voices sound like we were giving commencement speeches in a huge auditorium. At least, that's what it felt like. When a person is scared that they might be drawing attention to themselves, every little noise they make sounds amplified.

"Everything she has told me is a lie." I reiterated. "Well, maybe not every little thing. No one can lie about absolutely everything. But the important stuff was all lies. She knows what happened to my parents. She knows I'm not her grandson. She did something to our memories—just like you said—I believe that to be true. And she has something to do with all of this shit going on around us. We can't trust her."

"Do you think we can't trust her to tell the truth, or we can't trust her to keep us safe?"

"What's the difference?" I let go of Lucas' hand and turned to look out my window into the darkness. "Trust is trust. If you can't trust a person, you don't know if they'll sell you up the river the first chance they get. How do we know she won't help us until the man in the black hooded cloak shows up, Lucas? Then she just...tosses us to the wolves. No pun intended."

"Surely." Lucas snorted and pulled my hand back into his. "What other option do we have, though? That's my whole argument. We can drive around Point Worth until you run out of gas—which, by the way, we're running dangerously low on—or the sun comes up, whichever is first. Or we can go see if your—Esther Jean Wagner can help."

"How do we know she won't just attack us when we show up?"

"I don't."

"If she starts a fight, I'm not so sure I can take her, babe." I sighed. "She could easily kill us both. I mean, maybe. Sometimes she acts scared of me. Like she's afraid I'll blast her to smithereens or something...but other times...she's kind of formidable."

Lucas laughed.

"Yeah." He said. "I've seen those looks she gets."

I couldn't help but chuckle.

"Rob," He sighed, "just one last point I can make here. She kept you alive until you decided to leave town, and—"

"Which she probably put into my head!"

"—and if she wanted to do you harm, don't you think she would have done it when you were young and defenseless? When you didn't know how to use your magic?"

"I don't remember, Lucas," I grumbled. "Forget that part? Maybe she did try in the past and wasn't able? I don't have any idea what might have happened between us before I ran off. Which, I can't even remember why I really decided to do that."

"We decided that you should leave," Lucas said suddenly. "You and I."

"What?"

"You and I made that decision," Lucas stated, his eyes darting around as if trying to remember something. "Maybe Esther Jean had something to do with that, but—"

"Is that something you just know again?" I urged him on.

"No, Rob." Lucas turned to me, his eyes suddenly focused. "I just remembered that."

I just stared at him.

"Why are we getting glimpses of memories we didn't have before?" Lucas asked hurriedly. "Every now and then, I'm getting memories I didn't have...minutes ago. What is that about? Is Esther Jean still messing with us somehow? Is that a real memory? Is it fake? What's going on, babe?"

Chewing at my lip, I thought about that.

"You said something is draining magic out of Point Worth?" I began.

"Yeah?"

"Maybe whatever was keeping us in this...*fog*...is being stripped away, too." I suggested warily. "If we wait long enough..."

"We'll remember everything?" Lucas finished for me. "Like...remember the actual truth?"

"Maybe?"

Lucas continued to stare at me, as if processing that thought, working it over in his brain from beginning to end. Testing out the strength of such a theory before he settled on believing it to be true.

"Okay," I said. "Okay. Okay. So...I'm the only person in this town whose magic isn't tied to him, right?"

"Okay. Sure."

"Say the magic is tied to this land. To Point Worth. He's been siphoning off the land over the years...however many years he's been trapped—"

"I think he's been around a really long time, babe." Lucas shivered.

"Right." I nodded. "He's been siphoning it and parceling it out. Preparing for...I don't know. His return?"

"Okay. I can follow that."

"Now he's sucking it all back up. He's loading up for bear, Lucas."

"Are you the bear?" Lucas whispered.

"Obviously." I shrugged, then shivered involuntarily. "I just don't know why I'm a bear. I'm barely...*anything*. But, without my memories, I have no clue if I know the answer to that stuck somewhere in the deep corners of my mind or not. Maybe I do know...I just can't remember?"

"We have to see Esther Jean," Lucas stated firmly. "If she's losing her magic, too—"

"She said the other day that the Kobolds disappeared because..."

"Because why?"

"She made it sound like it was because I had jumped in the well and used up the magic that was left there," I said quickly. "Maybe that was a reservoir of some kind that only people in my family could get to...or maybe they disappeared because he's been draining magic for years now. The magic in the well was the only thing keeping them from being...*sucked up*...too?"

"That makes a little sense," Lucas said, then grumbled. "I wish I had my freaking memories. The real ones."

I nodded along. "But Oma—Esther Jean—said there was no point in planting the garden anymore. I'm not sure why she ever started planting it—I don't have a memory of the first time she planted it—but maybe she meant that the magic in the land was getting sucked up and the garden wouldn't thrive anyway. If that makes sense?"

"A little."

My eyes met Lucas'.

"He's definitely planning something big, babe."

"Let's see Esther Jean," Lucas repeated. "Let's go."

Sighing, I reached for the keys in the ignition. Pausing, I turned my head to look into Lucas' eyes again.

"If she kills me, you, or both of us, I'm going to be very pissed at you." I winked, though my stomach was like lead.

"Well, we can argue about it in Hell." Lucas chuckled nervously.

"Why wouldn't we go to Heaven?" I laughed as I started the car.

"No one is going to let two perverts like us past the Pearly Gates, babe," Lucas replied as he fastened his seatbelt.

"God loves the gays." I admonished him playfully as I put the car into reverse and eased up off of the brake. "He gave us Matt Bomer and Luke Evans."

"And another certain gay, hunky movie star." Lucas reached over to pinch my cheek as I laughed and started backing up.

Chapter 6

The Sunny Side-Up Café had flames licking up the north wall, inching towards the roof. The modest, yet beautiful, bushes out front were already skeletal candles, their flames licking towards the sky. Before long, the flames would be crawling over every inch of the café, devouring it from the outside in, until it was nothing more than a shell. The crack that ran down the center of Main Street was more than wide enough for a grown man to dive into, splitting the town of Point Worth from South to North. When the sun started to rise over the eastern horizon, night and day would meet at the center of town, and only one would win the battle.

Carlita held her hand out before her, focusing on the crack, doing her best to use what magics she had left to slow the widening of the chasm. Jackson Barkley still stood to her side, watching nervously as the ground rumbled beneath their feet, yet the crack didn't grow wider. Andrew was chewing at his lip on Carlita's other side, watching with the same level of anxiety as Jackson Barkley, wondering if Carlita could hold out long enough. Ever composed, Carlita's face was an impassive mask as she focused on the task before her. All she had to do was give Rob, Lucas, and Esther Jean just enough time to figure out a plan.

Deep in her mind, Carlita knew that Rob and Lucas had made a decision—one that neither of them quite understood yet. Carlita also knew that Esther Jean was aware and was preparing for their arrival. Beyond that, Carlita had no idea what was to come, which was a strange experience for an oracle. Carlita had lived her very long life always one step ahead of the game, knowing where she had to be, when she needed to be there, and why she needed to do the things she did. Aside from doing everything in her limited magical power to keep the crack in Main Street from spreading, she knew only one other thing.

And she was prepared for that if nothing else.

"Carlita," Jackson grumbled nervously.

"Yes, honey?" She responded simply, as though the work she was doing wasn't testing her down to her bones.

"There's no way you can hold it together forever." He said gently.

"Well," Carlita answered, "I don't have to, do I?"

"This is crazy." Andrew spat, though he didn't move to run away or abandon his friends.

"Well, if there was money in stating the obvious, you'd be able to take us all to the Bahamas, baby." Carlita turned her head to wink at him.

Beads of sweat were appearing on her brow, though her smile didn't falter. Andrew shook his head, but a smile came to his face. The ground stopped rumbling, but only for the briefest of moments, which took all three of them by surprise. Carlita frowned and turned to look at the crack in Main Street. Slowly, she pulled back on her magic and lowered her arm. Steam still continued to rise from the crack, but the ground was still, and the crack didn't suddenly split open before them. Jackson shifted nervously from foot to foot as Carlita and Andrew both stared down at the crevice before them.

"Well," Carlita mumbled, "I guess we just have to wait and—"

"Carlita!" Andrew gasped, his hand reaching out to squeeze her forearm.

"What?" She replied in unison with Jackson.

"Shit." Andrew hissed.

Carlita looked over at Andrew, to find him staring off towards the east end of Main Street. Jackson followed suit, his eyes traveling from the crack and over to Andrew. When they saw the fear in their friend's eyes, and where he was looking, their heads turned in unison to search out whatever he had seen. At the east end of Main Street, two wolves were standing shoulder to shoulder, red eyes glowing in the darkness at the end of the street that the flames—which were licking up the side of The Sunny Side-Up Café—did not cast light on yet. Both wolves' fangs were on display as they growled at the threesome at the other end of the crevice on Main Street.

"I'm surprised," Carlita stated blandly, turning her head to look at her friends in turn. "Are you surprised?"

"Carlita." Jackson whimpered, shifting more as he stood beside her.

"Goddamnit." Andrew hissed.

"Jackson Barkley," Carlita stated with finality. "I think it's time you go on into the hardware store, don't you? Give Esther Jean a call."

"Wuh-what?" Jackson stammered.

"Let her know she doesn't have much time, would you?" Carlita nudged him. "Go on now. Get out of the way. You got other things you need to be doing."

Jackson stared into Carlita's eyes for a few moments, as though unsure if he should listen or not. Would he be cowardly for abandoning his friends in their time of need—to make a phone call?

The ground began rumbling again, and the crack spread another inch. Steam exploded in bursts from deep within.

"Well?" Carlita nudged him harder. "Go. Tell Esther Jean to be ready, Jackson. Only you can do this."

"Right." Jackson nodded shakily. "Okay. Yeah."

When he showed no actual intention of moving, Carlita smiled warmly and reached for his hand. She gave it a gentle squeeze.

"My friend." She said. "You've done well. For your part."

A single tear slid down Jackson's cheek.

"I didn't really expect this to happen, ya' know?" Jackson shook his head.

"Well, I wish I could say I had your same confidence." Carlita chuckled. "Now go. Please."

Jackson nodded once, and then he was sprinting towards his hardware store as fast as his legs allowed. Carlita sighed as she watched him go, knowing she would never see the man again.

"Baby," Carlita turned to Andrew, "it's your time to shine."

"Right." Andrew didn't look at her.

His eyes were on the wolves at the other end of the street.

"Don't let me down," Carlita stated as she raised her hand towards the crack once more.

As magic poured forth in a column from Carlita's hand towards the growing crevice, and the ground shook underfoot, Andrew fell to all fours. A ripple of magic coursed through the air, and Andrew's body started to shift. The wolves at the end of the street leaned their heads back, fangs still showing as they howled up at the moon. The flames from The Sunny Side-Up Care shot into the air, roaring with fury as Andrew's skin violently split, sending fluids and sinew flying as he spontaneously turned. Carlita ignored the splatter of liquid against her side as she focused on the crack in the street.

Then two wolves charged west. Another wolf charged east to meet them.

The ground shook.

A low cackle carried on the wind.

"*That's what she said, Esther Jean.*" Jackson Barkley's voice was shaky over the static-y line.

Esther Jean stood in the kitchen, holding the large phone receiver to her ear. The only landline in the house had always hung just inside the kitchen next to the door that led to the cellar. Why Jackson Barkley hadn't bothered calling her on her cellphone was beyond her, but Esther Jean knew the call was important, regardless of the method of delivery. Cell service was probably down anyway. At least in Point Worth. She slid one hand into the pocket of her bib overalls and leaned her shoulder against the wall as she stared out at nothing.

"Well, I guess you'd have no reason to lie to me." She sighed into the receiver, wondering if the static would make it difficult for Jackson to understand her. "What's goin' on there?"

"*Are you fuckin' crazy, Esther Jean Wagner?*" Jackson barked, though humor slipped into his tone. "*Carlita's doin' all she can to keep this town from turnin' into one big sinkhole and Andrew's off fightin' pack. And you want to know how we're doin'? If my own long-departed wife rose from the grave, walked up in here, and took a shit on the check-out counter, I wouldn't be the least bit surprised. How's that for how we're doin'?*"

"That's about how I figured it was goin'." Esther Jean sighed. "All right. Well, y'all keep doin' the best you can. I got pots on every fire over here, too."

"*I'm sure you do,*" Jackson grumbled in disbelief. "*Probably sipping iced tea and waitin' on the boys to show up.*"

"Well, that's my lot in life, ya' old bastard."

"*I never did like you.*"

"Well," Esther Jean waggled her head, though there was no one to see it anymore, "you didn't have trouble liking me a few times after Betty Lynn died to get away from ya'."

Even with everything happening on Main Street, Jackson Barkley's laughter carried across the line to the receiver in her hand.

"*I'll miss the good times, that's for sure.*" Jackson sniffed. "*Esther Jean?*"

"What, bastard?"

"*Tell my grandson I love him. Might not get a chance myself.*"

"I'll do it. Twice." Esther Jean nodded firmly. "Tell Carlita, if you get the chance, that I'll make sure she didn't fight for nothin'. Ya' hear me?"

"*All right,*" Jackson answered. "*And Esther Jean?*"

"Yeah?" She barked, feigning annoyance.

But the line went dead.

The ground beneath the house rumbled gently, if "gentle" was ever a way to describe the movement from below. Sighing to herself, Esther Jean returned the receiver to its cradle smoothly. Just as quickly as it had started, the rumbling beneath the house stopped. She wanted to believe that maybe a miracle had occurred, but she knew better. It wouldn't be long before the ground was shaking again. When it did, it would be a shake to end all shakes. Esther Jean shuffled over wearily, her arms and legs feeling like lead, and grabbed her glass of tea off of the kitchen table. She looked around the kitchen one last time, then exited the kitchen, making her way to the front door.

When she exited the house, she didn't bother shutting the door behind herself. Anything that would want in the house would have no trouble finding its way in, closed doors and windows be damned. There was no protecting herself or her home any longer, so why bother pretending otherwise? Esther Jean shuffled out onto the porch, her legs pulling downwards, as if trying to send her into the Earth. She ignored the sensation, having felt it dozens, if not hundreds of times over the years—just never this strongly. Instead, she shuffled over to a chair and eased herself down.

Bringing the glass of tea to her lips, she took a sip. Licking her lips, she lowered the glass to the arm of the chair, cradling it in her hand there.

"Now," She looked out over her property into the thickening darkness that was slowly making the stars and moon blink out, "where the hell are them boys at?"

Lucas felt like a livewire next to me, the way he was shifting and shimmying in the passenger seat of the car as it idled at the opening to the driveway. The drive from the wooded area where we had parked, a few miles from Lucas' house on the shore of Lake Erie, to Oma's house had felt...different. Although I'd made the drive dozens of times over the last few weeks, the drive felt longer this time. But also, shorter. Lucas had remained silent the entire time, and I had nothing to distract me from the sense of impending doom permeating every fiber of my being. I both wanted to find someone to help us, yet I didn't want to see Oma. In my heart of hearts, I knew she wasn't my grandmother. I knew she had done nothing but lie and deceive me for my entire life. The reasons were completely unknown to me, and I wasn't sure I'd understand even if I had all of my memories back.

With the silence of Lucas making the ride tense, not wanting to see Oma, but also concerned about finding anyone who could help us with our problem, the ride felt both torturously slow and fretfully fast. As we sat at the end of the driveway, the car in Drive but my foot on the brake, I couldn't help but feel that it was darker outside than usual. The darkness that surrounded us out on the old road that led to the lake and Oma's house felt almost tangible. As if something was closing in around us, crushing down upon us.

Somewhere, in the furthest reaches of my brain, I knew that it wasn't just my imagination that the darkness was thicker and blacker than usual for no reason. The man in the black hooded cloak was coming, and that was affecting everything in Point Worth. If we were right in our hypothesis about what was going on in our little hometown, that made a lot of sense. He was draining everything from the land, all of the magic that made it what it was. He was siphoning off everything that was good and pure—even any source of light that chased away bad things.

Eventually, as the night wore on, I imagined Point Worth would look like *The Void* in *Stranger Things*. Nothing but inky blackness surrounding us, leaving us able to only see houses and people—no detail or light to the world. Just stuff. Stuff that the man in the black hooded cloak would eventually wipe away, just like he had done in my dreams. Nothing could prepare a person for what I knew he had in mind for Point Worth—and probably, eventually, the world—but I knew what those plans were. My mind couldn't even hold such an idea or wrap itself around an idea like that. Nothing but eternal dark and nothingness, with only him left. He would devour everything with his power, growing more and more hungry for power until he left the Earth nothing more than a black hole that no light escaped.

"What are we waiting on?" Lucas asked softly, his hand reaching for and squeezing my thigh once again. "Sitting here is just making this worse, babe."

"I know," I said, though my foot stayed on the brake pedal. "I'm just working myself up to doing this, ya' know."

"Rip the bandage off, Rob." He patted my thigh. "It'll be easier."

I looked over at him. He smiled.

"Promise." He reassured me. "And I'm here with you."

"No matter what?"

"No matter what." He leaned over and gave me a lingering kiss that never could have lasted long enough.

As Lucas pulled away, a smile on his face, I allowed myself a happy sigh, then I eased off of the brake and moved my foot to the gas. Inch by inch, we eased down the driveway, on our way to Oma's house. As we drove along, Lucas kept his hand on my thigh for reassurance, squeezing the flesh there to remind me that I wasn't alone. No matter what we found at Oma's house, we would find it together. Even though Oma's house was settled quite a way off of the road that led to the lake, we would have seen any flames if it had been on fire. A house as big as hers doesn't burn without letting the whole county know, so I knew that the wolves had not come and played pyromaniacs. However, the fact that the house was not on fire concerned me. Had they shown up but hadn't done anything to give it away? Were they lying in wait for us on Oma's property somewhere?

The thought made me nearly slam on the brake and throw the car into reverse, but my mind told me that there was nowhere to hide. If they were at Oma's, we might as well face the wolves, too. We'd eventually run into them somewhere. We couldn't leave Point Worth—not as a pair—and I wouldn't leave alone—and the darkness was closing in around us. There was no way we could luck out and not run into them before morning came. As we got to the far end of the driveway, Oma's house came into view in the clearing. It was funny to me that not even a month before, I had been elated to see the old house. Now, it made my stomach flip-flop in my gut.

Oma was on the porch, sitting there, drinking a glass of tea like the world wasn't burning down around her. That did nothing to make my gut feel better. Lucas gave my thigh another squeeze as I continued pulling up to the house, only stopping when I was within ten feet of it. I looked through the windshield at Oma, and she raised the glass in a salute and then took another sip, calm as you please. Of course, she had been waiting for us. Why should I have expected anything different?

Chapter 7

He was so strange, the boy with dark hair and eyes. Unlike the other boys in the Point Worth Regional Middle School, he didn't try to prove himself with bravado, bullying, or bragging behaviors. Carrying himself with confidence, or what could have been complete obliviousness in other's opinions, he was hard not to notice. He didn't pay attention to rude comments, nor did he seem to puff up when complimented. Like a self-sustaining organism found in the furthest reaches of the world, he needed no one and required nothing from anyone. He was an island. It made the other boys both angry and envious, emotions they were not mature enough to handle at such an age. It made the girls equally enamored and annoyed. The boy never took notice of either.

Lucas found himself staring at the boy during every class that they shared at the middle school. He'd watch the way the boy sat up, paying attention to the teachers, not caring if this made him look like a nerd. Lucas watched the way the boy sat back in his chair with ease and stared off at nothing when he was bored, unconcerned with teachers catching him. It wasn't rebellious behavior on the boy's part, the drifting off into daydreams—just starry-eyed childhood daydreaming to which all boys that age are prone. At lunch, the boy moved through the line with his tray, easily making conversation with other kids, even the ones he wasn't friends with, able to sit down and eat with any group he wished. Even if he sat down with a group of kids who didn't like him, by the end of their shared meal, the kids seemed to have changed their minds about him.

Robbie.

His name was Robbie. But he preferred "Rob."

Quick to make a joke that anyone could enjoy. Generous with compliments and positive words for all. Rob was one of Lucas' favorite people. But Rob had no idea. Just the sight of Rob passing in the hall and flashing his pearly whites made Lucas' tummy flip-flop, though he had no idea what that meant at such a young age.

Lucas could remember the first time he saw Rob walk into the first class they shared that year. He had already been in his seat, looking for someone he kind of knew in the class to become quick friends with, so he wouldn't feel like a nerd, when Rob entered, backpack slung over his shoulder in a Devil-may-care sort of way. When Lucas looked up, Rob's head slowly turned, as if from some slow-motion scene in a teen movie, and their eyes met.

Lightning.

Electricity shot through Lucas' body, and he had to avert his eyes from Rob's. Something had traveled through his body, shook him to his core, grabbed ahold of the innermost part of him that he didn't even have a name for, and turned his world upside down. When Lucas looked up again, Rob was looking away, seemingly unaware of what had just transpired in Lucas' soul. Finally, Rob made his way to a seat across the room from Lucas. However, before he sat down at his desk, his eyes flashed over to Lucas once more.

He looked...shaken.

Rob looked shaken. Someone like Rob could be unnerved.

It was then that Lucas knew something had been set in motion. He just didn't know what that thing was.

"Well," Oma swiped her hand over the arm of her chair, brushing away imaginary dust as we stood at the base of the steps up to the porch, "you boys took your time gettin' over here, didn't ya'?"

"Hi, Oma," I replied blandly.

She considered me for a moment as Lucas' head turned from mine to hers, then back again, watching our transaction with rapt attention.

"Couldn't get out, could ya'?"

"We're standing here, aren't we?" I snapped.

"Well," Oma sniffed haughtily, "maybe you just had a change of heart, smart ass. How the fuck would I know?"

"Because no one's been fucking with your brain." I tapped my temple with an index finger violently as I snarled up at her. "That's how, old woman."

"Wuh-hell. Someone's pissy." Oma waggled her head down at me before bringing the tea to her lips and taking a sip. "Someone tell ya' that even the gays don't look good in body glitter?"

Before I could snarl back some equally hateful retort, Lucas' fingers wrapped around my wrist, stopping me.

"Mrs. Wagner." Lucas piped up. "I've never been disrespectful to you."

"Ya' haven't." She nodded.

"But, we're here to tell you to stop messing with our memories," Lucas said. "Whatever you've done, we need you to undo it. Now. And we need answers."

"Ask wise ass over here." Oma gestured at me rudely. "He knows fuckin' everything, doesn't he? Speaking of which—you're so damn smart all of the damn sudden, why the hell did you not just stay gone, Robbie? Why didn't you leave as soon as Andrew tried attacking you? You're so damn smart, but every damn thing that's gone wrong has made you make one bad decision after another. Instead of runnin' tail and getting' away from danger, you just dive in headfirst like a grade-A village idiot. Point Worth's collective I.Q. went down a few digits since you came back. And it wasn't that high to begin with."

"You miserable old—" I began.

"Ya' just couldn't stay gone, could ya'?" She interjected. "You got out of town, and things was fine. Things would-a stayed fine a lot longer if you had just done as you was supposed to. But, like always, you had to do things your way. Here we are, Robbie. Good job!"

Lucas was squeezing my wrist tightly, so I kept my mouth shut.

"Why was he supposed to stay gone?" Lucas asked evenly, though I could hear in his voice, and feel in his grip, how tense he was.

"You boys may not got your memories," Oma crossed her arms over her chest as she turned her head to look at him, "but it doesn't take memories to figure out what's going on here, does it? This town is about to be swallowed up. He's comin' for ya'. And he shouldn't've been comin' for another few decades. That was the damn plan anyway—if wiseass over there had just stuck to the plan. I suppose it just is what it is. He's comin'. Bloody Bones is comin' for ya'."

As she said the last sentence, her eyes turned to me. A shiver ran up my spine as Oma said the name of the man in the black hooded cloak. A name we had sworn we would never say out loud again...unless it wouldn't matter either way. Her saying his name out loud confirmed my theory that he really was returning; otherwise she never would have said his name like that, out in the open, with not a care in the world. Lucas' hand fell away from my wrist immediately, and he gasped, obviously recognizing the name. In the deepest recesses of his mind, that name had been hidden away. Hearing it out loud had startled him.

"He's comin' for you, Robbie." Oma jabbed a finger at me. "Just like you've always known—when your head wasn't all clusterfucked. And he's going to pull Point Worth down to Hell in the process."

"There's access to Hell in Point Worth, Ohio," I stated blandly. "I'd like to say I'm shocked, but—"

"You can keep being a smartass all you want." Oma snapped. "But this is your damn fault."

"How?" I snapped back. "How is any of this my damn fault? I don't even remember everything except who he is and that he's trouble. Or the things you want me to think I remember. Well, that, and you're not my grandmother, you crazy old bitch!"

Oma's fists went to her hips, and her face turned up in a sneer as she leaned forward to launch in on me once more.

"Wait." Lucas jumped in before she could say another word. "You're not his grandmother. Buh-loody Bones is coming. We don't have our memories. You're blaming Rob for everything. Mrs. Wagner...you have explaining to do. None of this makes any sense whatsoever."

"Took the words out of my mouth!" I mumbled.

"Shut up, wise-ass!" Oma snapped.

"Are you going to help us or what?" I snapped back.

"Of course, I am, ya' damn fool!" Oma threw her hands up in the air. "That's what I'm here to do. I was just expecting to do it twenty years from now. When you wasn't such a damn pup and completely unprepared for what's to come. In all my years—"

"You'd think you'd have learned some patience and decorum?" I quipped.

"Rob," Lucas mumbled.

"Well, if you're going to keep bein' sassy with me, then I won't give a damn if—"

Before Oma could finish her sentence, the ground began to rumble beneath us. A low roar met our ears as the three of us did our best to not be knocked over. The rumbling and shaking turned into what I could only compare to all of the earthquakes I'd witnessed while in California. The only problem was, *we weren't in California.* We were smackdab in the middle of the buttcrack of Ohio. Earthquakes that can be felt like what we were experiencing was not common in Ohio. Lucas and I grabbed onto each other as the shaking under our feet intensified and off in the distance, a boom that was probably deafening if a person was nearby, sounded.

Just as quickly as the shaking started, it stopped. Glancing up at the porch as I held onto Lucas, just in case the ground started shaking once more, I saw that Oma had her hand braced against the porch railing, but she had remained on her feet. She looked drained. Not physically—something else. After a second, I realized that Bloody Bones siphoning off magic was doing a number on her as well. I couldn't help but wonder if that meant that she was losing her powers or if she was just experiencing side effects of such a perversion of nature. Slowly, Lucas and I slid our arms from around each other and stood tall, looking up at Oma as she let go of the railing and faced us.

"Well, shit." Oma spat. "I guess we gotta stop chewing each other new assholes and get down to business, don't we?"

"I'd say so," Lucas answered for us.

Chapter 8

Carlita was sprawled on the asphalt, legs splayed, and only her hands behind her holding her up into a half-seated position. Blood trickled from the corner of her mouth and from both nostrils, the result of the large pieces of shrapnel from the explosion. Bloody Bones had broken free. Smoke, almost like a dense, soup-like fog, hung lazily along the crack dividing Main Street, obscuring Carlita's view of what had risen. Smiling bitterly, Carlita turned her head to the side and spat, a rivulet of red splattering against the black road. She held herself up with one arm while she used the back of her other arm to wipe her mouth partially clean. Whether she liked it or not—and she hated admitting defeat—her end had come. She turned her eyes to look out at where the explosion had come from the crack in the street.

Bit by bit, the smoke laying like a haze on Main Street began to dissipate. At first, he was nothing more than a shadow in the haze, but as more of the smoke cleared away, Carlita could see him more clearly. The black of his cloak intensified, the outline of his hood became sharper. Bloody Bones stood next to the large hole in the center of Main Street, the large crack running in either direction away from it. Carlita didn't bother to rise to her feet since one only rises to greet someone they respect. She stayed there on the ground, watching as Bloody Bones raised his head and bright red eyes, and gleaming teeth peered out at her.

Carlita sighed, shaking her head at the sight.

She didn't want to be resigned to the fact that he had risen—yet again—but looking into the depths of his hood, her eyes meeting his, there was no denying the fact. He was back.

Bloody Bones walked casually towards her, the bottom of his cloak rustling in the breeze, sweeping away lingering smoke in wisps as he approached.

"We meet again, Oracle." Bloody Bones chuckled deeply, warmly, as if greeting an old friend. Of course, Carlita and Bloody Bones had known each other for a long time—but they were not friends. "You haven't aged a day."

He stopped before her, barely the length of a dining table between them.

"Well, you look like shit." Carlita shrugged, then coughed.

More blood.

Bloody Bones cackled.

At the far end of the street, Andrew stood on all fours next to a fallen, headless werewolf, the other werewolf's neck clasped tightly between his teeth.

"You did your very best for a very long time, old friend." Bloody Bones spoke. "But, inevitably, you failed."

"Friend?" Carlita snorted, blood dribbling from her nose as she ignored the pain in her side. "Honey, I give my friends rides to the airport. I wouldn't take you to the corner store."

Bloody Bones raised his arm.

A flash of light.

And Carlita fell back against the street, her skull making a sickening crunching noise against the asphalt.

Her eyes were open, but she saw nothing.

Andrew, in his wolf form, stared in horror as the werewolf in his grasp thrashed, trying to get away. With a quick jerk, Andrew tore the throat of the other werewolf, then let him drop to the street. He stared at the scene at the other end of Main Street, horrified at the death of Carlita. If she was dead...

There was only one thing to do.

He turned on all four legs and ran as quickly as he could, one of his legs hurt and refusing to work right.

There was only one place that was safe now.

If only he could get there on his hurt leg.

Bloody Bones smiled wickedly down at his first real kill since freeing himself from his prison, his red eyes and white fangs gleaming down at the oracle who was no more. Sharply, he tilted his head back and howled, summoning his wolves. He howled until he heard the answer of howls in the distance. Soon, they would come. And he could continue his quest. In the meantime...

Bloody Bones turned, his cloak dancing around him as he turned towards Barkley's Hardware. He had one more score to settle. Swiftly, without a second thought, he glided across the street and through the door of the old man's shop.

Moments later, Jackson Barkley's screams pealed through the air.

Then Main Street was silent.

Except for the howls of approaching wolves.

Ibiza was one of my favorite party destinations when I was in the middle of my (possibly—depending upon whom you ask) illustrious career as an international movie and rock star. Off the east coast of Spain, before one gets to Mallorca, Ibiza is a great place to get away from everything that a celebrity would want to get away from at times. There was the good food, the nightlife, other celebrities who understood my pain and troubles, the relaxation—though I did little of that—and the ability to just escape from what my life had become. It was on Ibiza, at a night club, off my head on Ecstasy, that I ran into Shepard Bachman. Horrible name, but also horribly famous.

Shepard Bachman, like myself, was an out and proud male actor from Hollywood, there to enjoy all of the hedonism the island had to offer. Possibly more famous than myself, Shepard had a few years on me, as far as careers go, so he'd had more time to work on his stock. He'd starred in more movies—even some of those superhero movies that make a billion dollars worldwide—and had the clout that made everyone desire him. When I had walked into the club with my "friends" and went to the VIP area to sit down at our reserved banquette, people noticed. When Shepard walked into the club, it was like a parting of the Red Sea. People didn't just notice—they were starstruck.

One way or another, he had ended up sitting next to me at my table, trading war stories, sipping obscenely expensive cocktails and champagne, laughing like he hadn't a care in the world. Maybe he didn't. I wasn't Shepard. I only knew the troubles of Jacob Michaels. For hours that night, we talked, laughed, drank too many drinks, popped a couple tabs of Ecstasy—the good stuff, none of that crap cut with meth—and danced like we expected the morning to bring about the end of the world. Within hours, pictures of us together would end up on blogs and tabloid sites, even some of the more reputable news sites. However, in those hours together, the world ceased to exist.

At the end of the night, in the wee morning hours, as everyone was leaving the club and my handlers were trying to shove me into my waiting vehicle, Shepard had proposed that we carry on the festivities. He could come to my hotel, or I could go to his. As soon as this suggestion met my ears, a vision of green eyes flashed through my mind, and I couldn't think of anything else but how nauseated the thought of sleeping with Shepard Bachman made me. Instead of answering, I merely stared at Shepard as though he was the most disgusting thing I had ever seen, and as the remnants of my Ecstasy induced euphoria coursed through my veins, I allowed my security to shove me into the waiting SUV.

As we drove away, Shepard staring after my car quizzically, all I could do was lower my head so that I wouldn't be sick.

"Fine." Oma shrugged, as though the world wasn't literally falling down around us. "Let's get down to business."

Oma turned to head into the house, as though this one sentence was enough to make us trust her enough to enter the house with her.

"Excuse me." I raised my hand, though her back was turned. "Crazy person? Yeah. You?"

Oma turned to glare at me, her hands going to her hips again.

"Last time I was in that house with you," I reminded her, "you tried to make sure I could never leave again. What on God's green Earth makes you think that I am going to step one foot in that house again?"

"Do ya' think you're safer out here, wise ass?" She asked sharply.

"Rob." Lucas grabbed my hand.

"Hold on, Lucas." I tried to stop him as nicely as possible. "Oma...*Lady*...how do we know that we're safe going in there with you? I don't trust you any further than I can throw you right now."

"Do you feel safe out here?" She barked.

"Absolutely not." I shrugged. "But at least I can see what's coming out here in the open. How do we know you don't have Jason and his wolves in there waiting to jump us? Or Bloody Bones himself."

I felt Lucas shiver next to me, his hand clenching mine tightly.

"Lord," Oma rolled her eyes, her neck rolling back so she could look up to the heavens for guidance, "you'd think with your memory gone, you'd still have common sense, Robbie."

Lucas squeezed my hand, stopping me from answering before he could.

"Meaning what?" He asked quickly.

"Meaning that if I wanted either one of you idiots dead," She waggled her head at us, "you'd be dead. I didn't protect y'all from them idiots of Jason's pack just to have them kill you tonight. And I didn't *fuck with your memories* just to prolong your sufferin'. But if you ain't gonna come in the house like a couple of sensible people, you ain't gonna know nothin' else than what you know right now. You can stand out here until Bloody Bones shows up and kills you both deader than shit. I'll stand here and watch. Might even make me happy to see it, the way you're treatin' me now."

"You just confessed to fucking with our memories, Oma." I snapped at her before Lucas could stop me. "How, exactly, are we the ones treating you poorly?"

"Let it go, Rob." Lucas shook his head.

"Listen to your boyfriend." Oma snorted.

"No." I stammered and pulled my hand out of Lucas'.

Oma watched me as I took a step closer towards the porch and looked up at her. To Lucas' credit, he didn't try to stop me from getting closer to Oma, nor did he tell me to watch what I said to her either. He knew that I had to do what I had to do, so he didn't try to intervene. Bonus points for Lucas. Oma just crossed her arms over her chest again and stared down the steps from her perch a few feet above me as I approached the porch.

"Tell me why you messed with our heads first." I jabbed a finger up at her, making her wince. "Tell me that first. I thought I understood what was going on with why we didn't have our memories—or we didn't have the right memories...or whatever—but now I don't know that I know anything that's correct. I need you to tell me why this is going on before I'll trust you enough to go in that house for even a second, Oma."

"I think that's fair." Lucas sighed from behind me. "And I'd really like to know myself."

Oma sighed, her arms dropping to her sides.

"Because, ya' damn fool," She tried to hiss, but her heart wasn't in it, "I was trying to keep you out of this fight until you had a real chance of winnin' it, wasn't I?"

"How would I know?"

"Well, that's the truth." She nodded firmly. "You forgot a lot of shit because of your own doin'. Not mine. Maybe I put the idea in your head, but it was still your own doin'. But, okay, so I've intervened since you got back. It was obvious that you being back here was undoin' your piddly ass magic and wishes, and something had to be done. I've done all I could to run you back out of this town. You shouldn't be standin' here right now lookin' up at me with all of this sass. You should be off gettin' stronger—just like I thought you would. I figured if we kept you alive a little bit longer, maybe if your magic developed a little bit more—you got a little more mature and less careless—you might live to end up in a nursing home before you hit the grave. But you came back—and it was obvious that threw a wrench in the works. So...I've done what I've had to do to try to get you back on the right path. The one that doesn't end in more death than necessary."

"Well," I shrugged, though I felt chastened for some reason, "Here we are. I'm back, and there's no leaving now. What does that mean?"

"Ask him." Oma jabbed a finger at Lucas. "He's seen it."

Turning to look at Lucas, I could see how pale he had gotten.

"Fire and death, right, Lucas?" Oma asked as I stared at my boyfriend. "You knew wise-ass here was comin' back, and you saw destruction. Tell him. Tell him he's an idiot for returning."

"Lucas?" I whispered.

He just looked up at me, all of the color drained from his face.

"Is that true?" I asked quietly.

"I saw a possibility, Rob." He stated softly. "That's all. I don't see absolutes. Anything can change, I guess."

Oma snorted, and a cackle erupted from her throat. Whipping my head around, I glared up at her.

"What's so funny, asshole?"

"You make wishes, and this one sees possibilities." She shook her head, ruefully. "Shit in one hand and wish in the other—see which one fills up first, why don'tcha?"

"What are you babbling on about now?" I barked.

"Your boyfriend there knows as well as I do that what he's seen is what's to come," Oma stated with finality. "Now it's just a matter of what all that fire and death means. How much fire? How much death? All we can do now is try to control how far it spreads. We can't stop it."

"Mrs. Wagner." Lucas sighed from behind me. "I didn't specifically see any of you dying. I didn't see anything particular on fire. You're assuming that the destruction I saw involved this town. And us. It could mean *his* destruction."

The fact that Lucas refused to say the name of the man in the black hooded cloak let me know how terrified he was.

"I can't argue that." She relented with a sniff. "But, I still call bullshit."

"Something up here," She tapped her finger against her temple, "told you that Rob was coming back—weeks before even I knew—and it told you that was bad. If the destruction and death you was seeing was Bloody Bones, it wouldn't have filled you with a sense of terror now, would it?"

"Maybe not." Lucas agreed. "But anytime I sense something bad is going to happen, I'm bound to not feel good one way or the other, right?"

"Suppose." She stated simply.

Looking back at Lucas was something I hadn't been able to do as they discussed what Lucas had seen—somewhere in the deep recesses of his mind where his magic worked. Knowing that Lucas knew things that I didn't and not knowing how he decided to interpret them made me uneasy.

How did I know if what he saw and how he felt about it was accurate? Even more importantly, I couldn't look and see if my boyfriend was still ashen-faced and uneasy. I didn't want to see the look on his face that told me that he expected doom for us all. Knowing that Bloody Bones was coming was bad enough. Having it painted all over Lucas' face and seeing how scared that made him was too much.

"So," Oma continued, "I answered your question. We goin' inside or we all gonna sit down for a spell and wait for Bloody Bones to show up and do what he's comin' to do? Y'all's choice."

My mouth desired to spit a few more expletives and insults back and forth with Oma before I even thought about going into her house once again. However, a gust of wind blew in from the direction of Point Worth proper, carrying what could only be the sound of a wolf howling with it. Shivering, I turned to look back at the town in the distance. Of course, all I could see was the vague lights that came from town. Lucas followed my lead, his head turning to look off toward town as well.

Lights, like we were used to seeing, were not what greeted us on the dark horizon. It wasn't large streetlights casting their hazy glow over Point Worth—it was red and yellow flickering light. Like fire. I gasped as Lucas began to shiver. I couldn't help but wonder if Oma hadn't already seen the fire behind us as we fought in front of her porch, yet refused to say anything. Maybe she hadn't wanted us to look back and see for ourselves that what Lucas had seen had come to pass. Was that her trying to distract us from finding out because she had something nefarious in mind...or did she just figure it didn't matter? Was she trying to hide more things from us, or unconcerned with everything now that everything was falling apart?

Why worry about fire when there're no firemen?

"Well?" Oma barked, causing Lucas and me to snap our heads back around to look at her.

"Point Worth is on fire," I said simply, my gut slowly traveling towards my knees as I stood there.

"Can't get nothin' past you, can we?" Oma rolled her eyes and turned towards the house.

"Oma?" I whispered.

"Ya' got two choices, Rob," Oma said over her shoulder, pausing for a moment. "Stay out here and watch your hometown burn—and not be able to do anything about it—or get in here, and maybe we can save *something.*"

Then she went into the house. Not another word about me being a wise-ass, no threats, no demands. Oma simply walked into the house, either confident we would follow as she wished, or simply not caring. Of course, with Point Worth on fire, there being no way for Lucas and me to leave Point Worth, and Bloody Bones coming...what else would we do? What else could be done? It truly didn't matter—as far as the town was concerned at that moment—whether or not Lucas and I followed her. So, she was willing to go inside and wait for us to make up our minds one way or another.

"Rob." Lucas sighed from behind me.

I turned to look at him. "Yeah?"

He wasn't ashen-faced or terrified anymore. He just looked sad.

"Get in the car." He said. "There's enough gas to get you out of town. Don't stay here. Maybe you can...I don't know...get far enough away that you'll have time to figure something out? Maybe you can figure out how to do something about...*him*...if you have time. But if you stay here, I'm afraid of what's going to happen."

For the space of several breaths, I stared at Lucas.

"What happens if I don't stay?" I stared into his eyes.

Those green eyes that held nothing but kindness. Now they looked defeated. Resigned. He had accepted something.

"The same thing," He shrugged, "except you won't be one of the casualties."

"Will you?" I asked. "And I can't believe I'm asking this, but will Oma?"

I jabbed a thumb over my shoulder at the house.

"Not that I care." I looked away.

"I only know how this ends if you stay." He whispered.

"Specifically?" My eyebrow raised precipitously.

"Well...I mean, no. Of course not. But there's already fire, and—"

I stepped up to Lucas, silencing him. Doing my best to be reassuring, I smiled and took his face in my hands.

"I'm a fireman," I whispered. "Remember?"

A small smile came to his face.

"Yeah." He nodded. "I said that. Somehow, at the time, I didn't really think this day would come, though, babe."

Looking past him, over his shoulder, I looked off toward town, the red and yellow light showing over the tops of the trees still. In fact, I was pretty sure that the fire was growing. Soon, it might even consume the whole town. Maybe it would work its way to Oma's. It didn't matter.

"The day came." I shrugged dismissively. "I say we go in there, find out what the crazy old lady has to say, and we face this together. Because if I leave—and you stay—and I lose you, there's no way I could face it alone. If I know my final day is coming, I want it to be with you. Okay?"

Lucas nodded. "Okay. I just want you to know that I wouldn't be upset if you ran away. Because you can."

"Oh, please." I gave him a quick kiss, then grabbed his hand, pulling him towards the house. "You'd hold it over me as long as you could."

"I would totally fight you in Hell." He agreed with a laugh.

"What?" I laughed as we began climbing the porch stairs. "You still don't think we'd get into Heaven?"

Lucas turned at the top of the stairs to look out at the fire raging in Point Worth.

"I think we're too used to Hell to ever do well in Heaven, babe."

"Fair enough." I kissed him quickly again. "You ready?"

"Yeah." He nodded.

"*Are you two gonna suck face out there all day or are we gonna do this?*" Oma bellowed from somewhere inside the house. "*I'm too old to be waitin' around this long for anybody—even you two.*"

I rolled my eyes, and Lucas laughed, but hand in hand, we entered Oma's house, prepared for whatever awaited. No matter what that thing was, we were going to meet it together.

Chapter 9

Oma was standing in the living room, hands on her hips, and though the lights were all out, I could see enough to know that she was alone. There was no one waiting with her, ready to jump out and attack Lucas and me as we entered the house. My first thought was to be a smart mouth and tell her to turn on a damn light so I could see all of her liver spots, but then I realized the lights might have been off for other reasons. With Point Worth on fire, Bloody Bones returning—and what was probably turning out to be the first stage of an apocalypse, lines were probably down all over town. Even if Oma wanted, the house might not have any power. For curiosity's sake, I reached over and flipped the switch on the wall. The darkness remained.

"I ain't standin' in the dark for my health," Oma said simply.

"Just checking," I replied.

"The power's out, genius."

"Got it."

"Rob." Lucas squeezed my hand. "Mrs. Wagner. Let's just stop fighting and being hateful. We're here so you can help us in any way that you can. But most of all, we need you to fix whatever you did to our memories. All of the fighting and insults are getting us nowhere."

"Fine." Oma threw her hands up in the air. "I guess I can keep from insulting smart mouth over here for a few minutes."

"Stop," I said.

Oma seemed to deflate, obviously unsure of what to do if she wasn't allowed to use her arsenal of hatred and insults.

"Well," Oma said, "I guess the best thing I can do is start with telling you about Bloody Bones. Well, reminding you, I guess."

"Why's that?" Lucas answered for us, causing me to glance over at him.

"Because that's where this all starts and ends." Oma waved him off. "Do the two of you remember the legend of Bloody Bones...or is that something your tiny little brains squeezed out when the genius over here made his wishes?"

"His wishes?" Lucas shook his head. "I don't really remember that."

"I don't either." I shrugged. "Not really. I mean...I remember that I made wishes...for some reason. But whatever you've done has made it hazy. I don't think I remember it for real."

"Well," Oma sighed, "old as I am, I don't know everything, but—"

"Imagine that," I mumbled.

Oma shot me a look, and Lucas gave me a disapproving, though amused look, but neither of them said anything.

"But," Oma glowered at me, "I know enough. Wish I had the book so I could tell it properly, but *someone* took it."

"The book?" Lucas perked up. "The book Rob had? It's in the car!"

Lucas started to move, as if to run for the car to retrieve the book, but Oma held a hand up.

"Why did you take the book?" She asked me. "I wanted to ask last night, but you was out of here like your ass was on fire."

"I thought it might help us get our memories back?" I shrugged as Lucas watched the two of us. "Maybe there was a spell or—"

"A spell!" Oma cackled. "That ain't no damn spellbook, you dumbass. That's the history of this damn land. It has the story of how Bloody Bones came to be. It's been passed down from villager to town folk, on and on, keeping the history of how this town came to be from generation to generation. For centuries—maybe longer—the elders would pass the story down to younger generations, reminding them of Bloody Bones and why we're here. They'd tell the story of The Oracle, The Guardian, and The Witch. Remind the younger generation that evil may sleep, but not for long. We must always be vigilant...in case he returns. And that asshole has popped up far too many damn times."

"What?" Lucas frowned.

"Yeah." Oma waved him off. "It's a storybook, really. But the story is real."

"I want to say that's all bullshit, but with what goes on in this town—this house—that just seems to be accurate. A storybook you kept hidden away under a damn bookcase for years. That checks out."

Oma just shrugged, agreeing with my assessment.

"Well," She continued, "once upon a time, as these stories always go, this land was filled with magic. People had barely even arrived, but they were thriving—best as people could in them days."

I glanced over at Lucas, and he just shrugged.

"No one knows why. No one knows how. No one even really remembers what might have caused it...but Bloody Bones used that magic to make himself corporeal. To give himself life. A body. What was he before? Hell if I know. Maybe he was a manifestation of people's bad thoughts, feelings, and intentions, but—"

"Big word for you," I mumbled.

Oma shot me a look.

"—**BUT**, he simply...came into being. Oh, at first, it was pretty harmless stuff. Grabbin' at the legs of people swimmin' in the lake. Mostly children. People started tellin' the story about '*Bloody Bones who lives in the lake and comes for bad children*,' thus, givin' this creature a name. Namin' somethin', givin' it recognition, gives it more power. Usin' his existence, givin' him a name, givin' him power over the minds of children, instillin' fear in someone with the knowledge of him—well, it just helped him become more powerful. He used the magic of this land to his advantage, makin' himself stronger. And, one day, he broke free from the power that held him to the land. A crack appeared one day. And it grew. And grew. From that crack, straight down to the pits of Hell, Bloody Bones rose."

"Again," I shrugged, "Ohio—portal to Hell—seems right."

Lucas hushed me, and Oma rolled her eyes.

"He began with simple mischief at first. Stealin' crops, saltin' fields so nothin' grew, fellin' trees, settin' fire to huts. Then he grew greedy.

As time went on and the people who lived here got more and more advanced, he began feastin' on chickens and stealin' food, snatchin' the occasional child. And like idiots, those people told greater stories about Bloody Bones and disobedient children, addin' to his legend, makin' him more powerful."

Lucas was suddenly holding my hand tightly.

"Things probably would have went on like that for a much longer time...but suddenly, The Oracle and The Guardian appeared. The Guardian was born from this land, like Bloody Bones, with one mission, to seek out The Witch. The Oracle was the same—though her mission was to watch over this town, these lands, to sense whenever Bloody Bones was coming. So...The Oracle and The Guardian worked together...and they found The Witch. The first of her kind. Not much more than a child, The Guardian and The Oracle found that she possessed control over the magic of her people, a magic that was separate from Bloody Bones. A power he had not been able to pervert to his whims and wishes. For many months, they worked with The Witch, hidin' her away, instructing her on what needed doin'...and then, The Oracle and The Guardian watched as The Witch met Bloody Bones in battle.

"In the end...The Witch cast Bloody Bones down, trapping him in the lands once more. She was worse for the wear, but The Guardian and The Oracle knew they could nurse her back to health. But The Witch knew somethin' that they didn't. She knew that if she let them heal her, she would only be livin' to face Bloody Bones in battle again one day. So, she used the rest of the power that resided in herself to strengthen the seal that held Bloody Bones in the ground, protectin' her people for as long as possible."

"What happened to her?" I asked.

"Well, she died, 'course." Oma shrugged, though her eyes looked dewy. "She sacrificed herself to give her people even longer to be free of ole Red Eyes. But, as they watched The Witch die and sink into the ground, The Oracle and The Guardian knew they hadn't seen the last of Bloody Bones. Maybe it would take a hundred or more years for him to find his way out to fight again, but he wasn't gone for good. Just as that thought occurred to them, where The Witch had once laid, something peculiar sprouted from the ground."

"What was it?" Lucas whispered in rapt attention.

"A well." Oma turned her eyes to me.

"Well, well, well," I stated blandly.

"It would contain all of the magic of her family. There in case it was ever needed to defeat Bloody Bones again. Just in case the next witch needed some help. She not only sacrificed herself for her family—and the people of this land—The Witch cast them a lifeline should they ever need it."

"I see," I replied evenly, and I could feel Lucas' eyes on the side of my head.

"But your damn family," Oma pointed a finger in my face, "down through the centuries have been reckless and ignorant with that power. They've used it on whims and wishes. And here we are with Bloody Bones back—at his strongest—and you done fucked everything up."

"Yeah." I shrugged. "It's easy to blame the last person who made the same mistake dozens of people made before, Oma."

"Well," Oma waved me off, "they're all dead, so you have to take the cussin' for all of 'em, ya' damn idiot."

"Fair enough." I relented. "But how the fuck was I supposed to know?"

"Because I've told you this damn story at least a hundred goddamn times, that's how!"

"Well, in my defense, I don't remember."

Lucas was shifting from one foot to the other.

"And I told you!" She jabbed a finger at him next, making him jump. "But you two thought you was smarter than me—than The Witch who knew what she was doing when she left that well of magic for this family. She knew that one day Bloody Bones would come back so powerful that y'all would need that little extra somethin'. And everyone just squanders it. Fuckin' humans. You're all worthless half the damn time—and the other half of the time you're diggin' in your own asses about one thing or another that don't matter."

"That's all well and good, Oma." I snapped. "But where does that leave us? That didn't make me remember anything—well, maybe I have a few flashes of the past working around in my head right now, but nothing concrete. What good does any of this do us?"

"Now," Oma glared at me, "we're goin' down to the cellar."

"I'm not going into any goddamn cellar with you."

"Rob." Lucas squeezed my hand.

"Damn-fuckin-right you are," Oma growled. "We need somewhere safe so I can lift the damn veil from you two. So you can remember everything."

"The...the veil?" Lucas peeped.

Oma fluttered her fingers in the air.

"Yeah," She grumbled, "the damn spell I did to make you both dumber than usual. I'll reverse what I done did; you'll remember everything...then wise ass over here can decide what he's going to do!"

"What I'm going to do?" I frowned.

"About Bloody Bones, of course!"

"Why do I have to do anything? Why is that my job?"

"Because you're the last damn ancestor of The Witch." Oma barked. "This is your job. Like it or not, that's what you was born to do, Rob."

I started to say something hateful back but stopped myself.

"Ya' know what?" I snapped at her. "If I could sink into the ground and get away from you, I'd do it, you old bitch."

"Good!" She snapped back.

Lucas just held my hand.

"Now, let's get down in the damn cellar where we got some protection if anyone comes nosin' around here, and we'll do this damn thing."

Lucas and I looked at each other, our fingers twining together as we considered the request—well, *demand*—from Oma. My instincts told me that we should follow Oma into the cellar, let her do whatever magic she felt she had to do, and then face Bloody Bones when he showed up. However, something kept pinging around in my head, some little voice telling me there was a question that needed to be asked. Just as I was about to take a step towards Oma, pulling Lucas with me, I realized what the voice was saying.

"Wait," I said, causing Oma to halt in her tracks and turn to look at me. "You said everyone talking about Bloody Bones, telling his legend, adding to his myth, gave him more power?"

"Yeah?" Oma shrugged.

"People stopped talking about him." I shook my head. "I do remember that people in this town stopped talking about him. In fact, people stopped believing altogether. So...how is he more powerful now."

"Because he stopped relying on the whims of humans and found a new way to get magic." Oma waggled her head. "Every time he's come back—up until the last time—he was using the magic humans give all their Gods, and—"

"All their Gods?" Lucas asked.

"What's any deity but the creation of humans brought to life by myth?" Oma said simply. "Humans have a very peculiar magic of their own. They tell stories. Those stories spread from mouth to mouth until the story is the truth. Stories have power, Lucas Barkley. Just as humans give God power, they give Bloody Bones power."

"Oddly," I turned to Lucas, "that's pretty logical."

Lucas shrugged. When I turned back to Oma, she was smiling, happy with herself.

"Still don't like you any." I shrugged at her.

She frowned. "Well, when you idiots—*humans*—stopped talkin', stopped givin' him power...he started takin' it from the land. I suppose he didn't know he could do that before. But desperate times call for desperate measures. And he didn't just take it. He used it. Not just to rise up and try to come back, but to gain allies. This town's full of 'em, too."

"He's been giving families around here power?" I nodded slowly.

"Damn right, he has." Oma nodded firmly. "Nearly every damn family in this town is connected to the power he stole from the land. Whatcha think's gonna happen when he takes it back?"

"Shit." I sighed.

"Grandpa!" Lucas gasped.

"Ole Jackson's probably already met his maker." Oma waved him off casually.

"Oma!" I growled.

Lucas gasped again.

"Well," She said, "it's just the truth. Carlita, too. Maybe even Andrew."

Lucas was looking at me desperately, his eyes welling with tears.

"Well, I don't really care about Andrew, but—"

"Ya' should." Oma snorted. "He's been tryin' to help me make you leave this town again to make it safer. S'why he was a douchebag to ya'. Why he attacked you. He could control his damn wolf—don't be ridiculous. He did that because I asked it of him."

"Then why'd he ask me out on a second date?" I growled.

"Because he probably figured you'd put out?" Oma threw her hands up. "That's none my damn concern! And, right now, it shouldn't be yours, either. Are we goin' down in this damn cellar so I can give you two idiots back your memories, or are we gonna stand up here in the world's most boring circle jerk until he shows up to kill us all?"

Lucas was holding my one hand with both of his, tears silently trailing down his cheeks as he thought of his grandfather, Jackson Barkley, possibly being dead. I gave him the most understanding, warmest look I could muster, and he just nodded at me. I turned to face Oma once more.

"Lead the way you insensitive old hag."

"Fine." She snapped, turned on her heels, and stomped towards the kitchen.

Turning to Lucas, he just shook his head, letting me know that it was not the right time to try to comfort him. Nothing I could say would have made him feel better about what Oma had just said anyway. Instead of saying anything, or trying to hug or kiss him, I stepped towards the kitchen, dragging Lucas behind me. As we made our way into the kitchen, Lucas shuffling his feet, Oma was swinging the cellar door wide and heading down the steps. I stopped for a moment as I looked at the dark opening that led down below and swallowed hard. The best I could hope was that we got into the cellar, and Oma removed...*the veil*...she had placed on Lucas and me. Then I could fight Bloody Bones.

What the actual fuck?

That was the best hope I could imagine? Some crazy scheme that seemed like a fever dream?

As Lucas and I descended the stairs cautiously, ours heads whipping around, trying to watch our backs, fronts, and sides at all times, I knew that the best-case scenario in this situation was still a shitstorm. No matter how the pie was sliced, it was still going to be bad. Oma was standing in the middle of the cellar, where the well had once stood, her arms crossed over her chest, waiting on us when we stepped down onto the dirt floor of the cellar.

"You look like the Cowardly Lion and The Scarecrow off to see the Great and Powerful Oz. Where's Dorothy, ya' assholes?"

I ignored her.

"Carlita was The Oracle." It wasn't a question. "Like *The Oracle*—from your little story."

"Wasn't a *little story*." She barked, her hands lowering to her sides.

"Whatever." I waved her off. "So...you're not my grandmother."

"I'm not." She said finally, her voice bland, as though she had to force herself to be emotionless.

"You're...The Guardian, I assume?"

She nodded. "Found the first witch, and I've been comin' back and dealin' with your dumbass family every time Carlita—*The Oracle*—sensed he was going to return."

Oma sighed, her eyes flashing to Lucas.

"Maybe," She stated wistfully, "if this night had any chance of turning out any other way than I know how it's gonna turn out, you could-a taken her spot, God rest her soul."

Lucas frowned as he chewed at his lip.

"Ya' got the gift." Oma shrugged. "Your foresight and all. I can kinda see her magics already trying to attach themselves to ya' now that their original vessel is gone."

"What?" Lucas whispered.

"If they had enough time, and I thought we'd make it through this night, I'd imagine I'd be helping a new oracle learn his craft. To help prepare us for the next battle."

"What does that mean?" I asked for Lucas.

"Your boyfriend has the gift." Oma waved a hand at him. "Came from the same magics that made me and Carlita. Now that Carlita's gone—*I know she's gone, I can't sense her anymore*—her magics will probably try to find a new oracle to inhabit. I imagine it would be Lucas. Ain't nobody else in this town got that kind of gift—or the wherewithal to use it as intended."

"So...Lucas would be your other half when this is all said and done?" I laughed bitterly. "And I'd just be the witch that gave his life so you could keep on watching Bloody Bones rise, and witches fall?"

"'Bout sums it up, yeah." Oma shrugged. "It's the way it's always been."

"I'm glad to see it pains you." I rolled my eyes.

Oma glared at me, though something in her eyes told me she wasn't mad. She was bitter.

"Just," Lucas interrupted before one of us could say something snarky to the other, "give us back our memories. Lift the veil...or whatever."

"Gladly." Oma nodded and stood up straight, squaring her shoulders.

Lucas and I kept our hands locked as Oma squared herself and planted her feet, her arms reaching out towards us, one hand pointed at Lucas, one at me. Then she smiled.

"This might sting a little." She chuckled.

Then there was a flash.

And a sting.

Oma didn't always lie about *everything*.

Chapter 10

"You will join us, goddamnit." Jason, barely decently covered in a pair of jeans, shoved a towel-clad Lucas into the locker. "It's your fate, you little asshole. I'm sick and tired of you giving me shit about it. This is who you're supposed to be."

Jason's forearm dug into Lucas' windpipe as Lucas' wet feet slipped and slid on the slick concrete floor of the locker room. The only thing keeping Lucas from falling and slipping all the way across the room and back into the shower—which he had just left—was Jason's forearm pinning him against the locker. If Jason pulled away suddenly, Lucas wasn't sure he could catch himself quickly enough to keep from busting his ass painfully on the floor. Or, maybe he would slide all the way across the room. Of course, the towel wrapped around his waist might have been enough to keep him from sliding too far.

Lucas had been so careful. Jason had been harassing him for months to join his pack, but Lucas had always been clever in avoiding Jason when he was alone. There was no way that Jason could fulfill his threats to turn Lucas into...one of them...if there were always witnesses to their exchanges. Even this night, only his third football game with the team, he had made sure he took an extra long shower. He waited until he was sure that all of the other guys had gotten showered, dressed, and left the locker room. The water in the showers had turned cold by the time Lucas finally twisted the knobs on the wall, and the water stopped cascading over his body. Shaking with cold, his fingers resembling prunes, Lucas had grabbed his towel, wrapped it around his waist, secured it, and headed to his locker to dress.

Of course, Jason was done being patient. He had been waiting for Lucas to emerge from the showers. At first, all Lucas could think was that he was grateful that Jason had not come into the showers after him. At least he had been patient enough to wait to have this exchange with him when they were both adequately covered up.

"I'm telling you, man." Jason laughed bitterly. "This isn't a choice. Eventually, we all gotta sign up."

"Sign up?" Lucas gasped, his hands clutching at Jason's forearm as he ground his teeth in pain.

"Bloody Bones, man." Jason grinned evilly, pushing his forearm harder into Lucas' throat.

Lucas' hands scratched at Jason's forearm, desperately trying to break free, or at least catch a breath of air.

"He's coming soon, man." Jason chuckled deeply. "And he needs us. You're either on his side...or you're against him."

"There are other ways." Lucas managed to gasp.

He didn't want to tell Jason what he felt in his gut, the things he just knew, but Lucas knew that Bloody Bones wasn't his only option. Somehow...he just knew it.

"Are you saying 'no'?" Jason growled, his jaw seemingly lengthening as Lucas struggled against the locker, his feet slipping and sliding on the floor.

Lucas' eyes bugged as Jason's forearm dug deeper into his throat, cutting off his oxygen. He watched through blurry eyes as Jason's jaw stretched, slight tufts of fur sprouting around what could only be described as a muzzle. Fang-like teeth slowly grew from Jason's mouth. The teeth of a wolf. Lucas struggled and slipped and slid as Jason's eyes turned red. Then his muzzle lowered to Lucas' arm.

Pain.

"Does it hurt?" Jackson Barkley asked as he knelt in front of Lucas, who was perched on the side of his bed rigidly. "Looks nasty."

"A little, I guess." Lucas' eyes were on the floor, by his grandfather's feet.

"That bruise 'round your neck is gonna be nasty." Lucas' grandfather sighed. "You gotta learned to stand up for yourself, Lukie."

Lucas looked up at his grandfather disdainfully.

"He's two years older, nearly a foot taller, and has fifty pounds on me, grandpa." Lucas snapped pitifully. "How am I supposed to stand up to him?"

Most people would expect a grandfather to bark back, to tell his grandson to 'be a man' or some other nonsense. Jackson Barkley was not that type of man—or grandfather.

"Lukie," Jackson reached out and laid a hand on Lucas' knee, "he's gonna see that you are immune. If you don't go changing into a wolf within a few moons, he's gonna know. That's all's I'm saying."

"I know." Lucas looked down.

Jackson rubbed Lucas' knee.

"He mentioned Bloody Bones," Lucas whispered.

"Don't say that name none," Jackson whispered back, but he was not cross with his grandson.

"I thought I had forgotten," Lucas said. "You told me to forget."

"I did."

"I remembered everything when he said that name." Lucas looked up into his father's eyes.

Jackson Barkley groaned and rose from his crouched position and sat down on the bed next to his grandson. He took Lucas' arm in hand and brought it closer to inspect.

"You'll just forget again," Jackson said.

"But maybe if I use—"

"No." Jackson snapped, and there was heat in his voice this time as he let Lucas' arm fall from his grip. "You forget everything you know again. Push it to the back of your mind. Never speak of it."

"But grandpa—"

"This conversation is over." Jackson Barkley stood from the bed abruptly and marched toward the door of Lucas' bedroom. "And another thing—"

Jackson turned to find Lucas looked down at his feet, his bitten arm cradled in his other.

"Aw, Christ." Jackson reached up to rub the back of his neck. "Look, Lukie..."

"What?"

"Your day is coming, son," Jackson stated lowly. "You aren't meant for what them powers was given to you for by...him. Your destiny is bigger than that. Better. Your destiny is good. I told you what you'd be one day if you just wait. Be patient. Forget."

"Jason will just keep trying, Grandpa." Lucas looked up. "I believe you. I trust you. But Jason won't give up. What am I supposed to do?"

For the longest of moments, Jackson Barkley stared at his grandson. Finally, as if he had made up his mind about something, he straightened up in the doorway of the bedroom.

"Maybe you need a friend?" Jackson suggested. "Then you won't be alone and worrying all the time?"

"Everyone at school sucks." Lucas groaned and kicked at the floorboards with the toe of his shoe. "I mean, the people I'm supposed to hang with suck. The guys in football...well, ya' know. They're like Jason. The girls are dumb, and everyone else has their own thing going on. No one seems to want to really like me unless it's about being on the football team."

Jackson Barkley smiled.

"Well, most teenagers...suck, I suppose." He chuckled. "Maybe you need to find a friend who has different interests than yourself then?"

"Like who?" Lucas rolled his eyes but smiled. "Justin McCafferty? He picks his nose and eats it. We're in high school for crying out loud."

Jackson Barkley laughed.

"Well," Jackson said as his laughter tapered off, "I got a friend out there on the lake. Maybe you'd like her grandson? You go to school together, anyway."

"Who?" Lucas perked up, though he was cautious about any suggestions his grandfather might have about how to make friends.

"Bobby...nah, Robbie Wagner?"

Lucas felt his breath leave his lungs.

"Rob?" He whispered.

"If that's what he goes by, sure." Jackson shrugged and leaned against the doorjamb. "Esther Jean—his grandmother—was tellin' me that he gets lonely out there on the far edge of town out by the lake. Guess he ain't got a lot of kids—ahem, young men—who live out by him either. Maybe you could make friends with him?"

"He's," Lucas felt his cheeks warm at the thought of Rob Wagner, "kind of...weird."

Lucas didn't mean "weird." He meant to say something entirely different that would have led to a discussion he wasn't ready to have with his parents or grandfather yet.

"Well, weird's okay." Jackson shrugged with a grin. "As long as it ain't the booger picking kind, right?"

Lucas grinned and looked down at his shoes so that his rosy cheeks would be hidden by the shadows.

"Well," Mrs. Wagner stood at the kitchen counter as Rob and Lucas sat across from each other at the kitchen table, "ain't this a cute little playdate?"

Rob smiled at Lucas and turned his eyes to his grandmother.

"What?" Mrs. Wagner shrugged as Lucas sank into his chair, completely out of his element and with nothing to say.

"Oma." Rob shook his head in a playfully reprimanding way. "Go away."

"It's my house." She demanded, though there was no power in her words. "Fine. Fine. I'll go dust the fuckin' bookcases or somethin', I spose."

"Thank you." Rob chuckled nervously as his grandmother marched out of the room, pretending to be upset.

Lucas frowned, noticing that Mrs. Wagner hadn't bothered to find a feather duster or cloth with which to do her chores. Of course, he had always heard that Esther Jean Wagner was...odd...so he decided to not let it bother him any. Instead, he picked up the can of soda—or "sodey pop" as Mrs. Wagner had called it—and brought it to his lips. Rob mimicked his actions. The two boys sat in silence, only the sounds of effervescent bubbles in the cans as a soundtrack.

"So," Rob finally spoke, luckily before the silence had grown too thick, "you're on the football team, right?"

"Yeah," Lucas answered eagerly, glad to have something, anything, to talk about. "Uh, yeah. Um, I tried out. I'm a running back."

"Kind of cool for a freshman to be on the team." Rob smiled, trying to think of a way to direct the conversation.

"I mean," Lucas blushed slightly, "I guess. I'm just small and fast, so..."

"Easy for you to sneak the ball by other players?" Rob smiled.

"Yeah." Lucas agreed. "Season's over, though, so we're just stuck in practices now. Maybe I can actually get off the bench next year."

"I feel like I know you." Rob blurted out suddenly, then looked down. "I mean, obviously that's stupid. We go to the same school, so of course, you'd seem, uh, familiar and stuff, right?"

"Right." Lucas' face was stuck between a smile and a frown. "But, I, uh, know what you mean. I feel like we've hung out before or something."

Rob shrugged.

"Did you go to CARNAVAL last year?" Rob asked. "I think I went to that. Around Halloween? It seems so long ago."

Rob gave a nervous chuckle as Lucas shrugged.

"I don't remember going," Lucas replied. *"I mean...it was such a big deal, right? It seems like I was there. Everyone was talking about it, anyway. Maybe that's why?"*

"Yeah." Rob agreed. *"Maybe."*

The two boys took sips of their sodas again, looking anywhere but at each other. Suddenly, Rob got a curious grin on his face, then leaned in conspiratorially.

"It's like I can remember the taste of the popcorn and cotton candy."

Lucas smiled. *"Right? All popcorn and cotton candy from carnivals tastes the same, though, right?"*

"Yeah." Rob relented. *"Wish I had gone. People wouldn't shut up about that for forever."*

Lucas laughed at the way Rob rolled his eyes and sunk down in his chair as though he had been through war.

"CARNAVAL this, CARNAVAL that." Rob groaned comically. *"I bet no one's parents let 'em go anyway. And it was gone the next day, so..."*

"Right?" Lucas laughed. *"I mean, Jason and—the guys on the team—they all probably went. I heard them talking about it a lot. But..."*

"What?" Rob leaned in, grinning. *"What were you going to say?"*

"Nothing." Lucas shook his head with a smile.

"Nah." Rob shook his head with an impish grin. *"You can't leave me hanging like that. You started a sentence; you have to finish it."*

"Is that how that works?" Lucas laughed.

"Yep." Rob nodded as he grabbed his soda. *"House rules."*

"Fine." Lucas rolled his eyes, though he was amused. *"Jason and the other guys on the team are kind of liars. That's all. They probably didn't go either. Just them wanting to be cool and stuff."*

Rob grinned widely.

"I don't really tell anybody anything worth hearing." He said. *"So, they'll never find out what you think of them."*

"Promise?"

"Promise." Rob made a cross over his heart with a fingertip. *"Not a word to a single person."*

"Cool." Lucas grabbed his soda.

Rob leaned in his chair so that he could look through the kitchen door to the other part of the house where, presumably, Mrs. Wagner was dusting.

"Do you want to see something cool?" Rob asked. *"A secret of mine?"*

Lucas chewed at his lip.

He wanted Rob to tell him or show him anything he wanted.

And he would take any secret to his grave if he had to.

"Yeah, man." Lucas nodded slowly.

"Come on." Rob stood from the table, grabbing his soda as he whispered. *"I want you to meet Ernst."*

"Ernst?" Lucas frowned as he followed Rob's lead.

"Shhh." Rob held a finger to his lips. *"It's a secret, remember?"*

Lucas laughed nervously, then turned his voice to a whisper. *"Okay."*

"Up in my room." Rob jerked his head towards the other part of the house. *"But you can't tell anyone. Promise?"*

"Promise."

"Like, for real." Rob turned to Lucas, still grinning, though he looked unsure.

Lucas' eyes met Rob's. Another flash of lightning in his gut.

And Lucas suddenly knew something else.

He knew why he had told Jason there were other ways besides Bloody Bones.

"Promise." Lucas breathed out.

Rob smiled. "Come on."

He winked and exited the kitchen. Lucas followed right at his heels.

Chapter 11

My mother was sprawled on the kitchen floor, the cast iron skillet, and the pancakes it once held on the stove was at her feet. Her eyes were wide open, and her mouth hung slack—she saw nothing and had no more words to say. Standing there, my small fists clenched at my sides, tears streaming down my face, I waited for my father to return. When the man in the dark hood had burst through the kitchen door and...did...what he did...to my mother...my dad had not been close behind him. Flashes of light had filled the kitchen and what I could only call "war screams" poured from my father's mouth as he...fought?...with the man who had hurt my mother.

As I waited for my father, I shuffled tentatively towards my mother, wondering if I should try to wake her up. Why wouldn't she get up off of the floor instead of lying there next to the ruined breakfast? Dad had chased off the scary man with the dark hood, so there was no reason for my mother not to move now. When I got close to my mother, I jerkily reached down, my hand slowly uncurling, reaching for her arm.

"Muh-mommy?" I had whispered.

My hand had barely had time to connect with her cooling flesh before my father had come soaring through the backdoor once again. Fury was painted his face. Until his eyes landed on mine, and he saw me touching my mother's arm. He came to me swiftly and scooped me up, burying my face in his chest, holding me to him. I didn't know how to ask him...was my mom dead?

What happened to my mom between the moment I touched her arm, and my dad put me to bed, I didn't know. We never went back into the kitchen. Dad and I spent the day in the house, refusing to turn on lights, even after the sun went down. He held me in his lap, his arms wrapped around me, not letting go unless I needed to eat or use the bathroom. Dad stayed by my side all day long, whispering to me how much he loved me, telling me stories about my birth, the first years of my life, what I meant to him and my mother. How I would be okay, and he would never let anyone harm me. His lips pressed against my forehead and top of my head more times than I could count in those hours between breakfast and bedtime.

Finally, when the moon was high in the sky, Dad took me upstairs and changed me into my pajamas. Then he tucked me into bed snuggly, the odd smile on his face illuminated by the sliver of moonlight that peeked through the blinds in my room. He whispered to me that he had to "take care of something," but if he wasn't able to come back, I would have someone to take care of me instead. Someone who would protect me just as fiercely as he and my mother had. So, no matter what, I shouldn't miss him if he didn't return. I was still too confused over what had happened to my mother and what he was telling me to really understand.

But he sat on the side of my bed, stroking my hair and back until I drifted off to sleep. I don't know when I fell asleep, or when Dad left my bedside, but when I woke the next morning, bright morning light was peeking through the blinds, and my dad was gone.

Knock.

Knock.

KnockKnockKnock.

Wearily, rubbing at my eyes, I stumbled down the steps into the living room, wondering why Dad or Mom hadn't answered the door. Why was someone allowed to knock so loudly and so much so early in the morning? A flash of my mom lying on the kitchen floor burst through my mind, and I frowned, trying to think of what that meant. As I stood at the base of the steps, the knocking still sounding, I remembered Dad saying that he had something to take care of, so I might have someone to watch over me for a while. Hesitantly, I shuffled over to the front door and grabbed the knob with both of my small hands. I swung the door wide, squinting at the bright early morning light as it burst through the door.

"Well," I heard a woman's voice, her figure haloed by the sun, "you're a lot smaller than I'm used to, that's for sure."

Slowly, my eyes adjusted, and I was able to open them a little wider to see who was speaking to me. A woman I had never seen before, maybe a little shorter than my mom was, gray hair, wrinkled face, stern expression, yet eyes that twinkled—imposing for a five-year-old—stood before me, arms folded over her chest. A large suitcase on wheels was sitting on the porch upright next to her, its handle extended, as though she had just dragged it up the steps.

"Who are you?" I had asked, my bottom lip jutting out in what I had hoped was a brave and defiant manner.

I was a man. This was my house. All five-year-old boys think that.

"I'm Esther Jean Wagner." The woman looked down at me sternly, though the warmth in her eyes was apparent. "You can call me Oma."

"What's an Oma?" My nose crinkled up.

"Grandmother." She waggled her head. "I'm your dad's mother."

Without further explanation, she grabbed the handle of her bag and swung it over the threshold into the house. I backed up quickly to avoid getting knocked over by the movement. The lady...Oma?...followed the bag, looking around the house. Once she was inside, she folded her arms over her chest once more and looked around, taking in her surroundings as her bag stood next to her once again. For a beat, I just stared at her back, wondering who this woman was who claimed to be my grandmother. Then, she turned her head and glanced over her shoulder at me. Our eyes met.

Oma.

Of course.

Dad's mom.

My grandmother.

"I've never met you before," I stated stupidly as I gently pushed the door shut, chewing at my lip.

"I've been gone for a spell, Robbie," Oma said. "But your dad said he had to take care of some things, so he needed me to look after you."

"Oh."

"I'm not as mean as I look." She winked down at me as I rounded her imposing figure. "Usually."

"You look pretty mean," I admitted though I wasn't sure if that was the right thing to say.

"I have my moments." She shrugged sharply. "But you don't give me no sass, and I won't sass back. That sound like a fair deal?"

Thinking about this, I slowly started to nod as I chewed at my lip.

"Good." She finally smiled down at me, her arms falling to her sides. "Have ya' had breakfast, Robbie?"

"No." I shook my head. "I just woke up and my mom...my mom..."

She waved me off, smiling, though her eyes were sad.

"Don't worry about all that." She said brightly. "Oma's here now. And I brought some friends."

"Friends?" I asked, my lip chewing intensifying.

"Wanna see what's in my suitcase?" She asked, a mischievous grin coming to her face as she bent down slightly.

"I don't know."

She stood up sharply, her nose hooking into the air haughtily, though she looked down at me through the corner of her eye. That twinkle never went away.

"Well, maybe I don't want to show you then." She waggled her head.

I couldn't help it. I giggled. She held her haughty pose a moment longer, then turned her head down to smile at me.

"It ain't nothin' that will bite ya' none." She said reassuringly. "Just some little helpers while your dad is gone."

"Okay." I was nodding slowly again.

"So," She asked once more, "you wanna see?"

"Okay." I agreed hesitantly. "You're not going to scare me, are you?"

"Not on purpose."

I shrugged. "Okay."

Oma smiled warmly and turned to her suitcase, bending over to reach for the zipper. I watched with fascination—and a bit of fear—as she pulled the zipper three-quarters of the way around the suitcase, slowly pulling back the flap. At first, nothing happened, but then, ever so slowly, a small humanoid hand peeked out. I gasped, and the hand froze. My eyes shot up to Oma, and she just winked at me. My eyes went back to the bag, and I watched as a hand became an arm, then a torso and head...and a small human-like...thing...stepped out of the suitcase. It was even shorter than me, wringing its hands and looking around, as though unsure of its surroundings. I gasped again as another creature stepped out of the bag, then another...eventually five of these...things...stood in the living room with Oma and me.

"How did they all fit in there?" I looked up at Oma with saucer-like eyes.

"Magic, of course." She winked.

My eyes met Oma's, and something passed between us.

I grinned.

"Goddamnit, Robbie." Oma cursed as she rolled her eyes. "Ya' gotta stop doin' that."

"Sorry." *My cheeks were warm as I winced down at the char marks on the tablecloth.*

"How many times have I told you that you have to control yourself?" *She barked, though her heart wasn't in it.* "If you keep doin' that, people are going to know about you."

"Sorry," *I repeated.*

Ernst scuttled under the table and stood up next to my chair, his hand reaching for mine. I did my best to smile at him as he gave me a reassuring look. Oma was snatching the cloth off of the table, yet another blunder of mine that caused damage to something in the house. Ever since she had been trying to teach me how to tap into my magic and control it, all I'd done was mess things up. It was a lot for an eight-year-old to figure out as quickly as she wanted me to do. Magic didn't like to have people telling it what to do. Sometimes it did whatever the hell it wanted.

"And you." *Oma's eyes shot over to land on Ernst, causing both Ernst and me to wince and shrink back, though he refused to let go of my hand.* "You ain't doin' him no favors treatin' him like a baby."

"Ain't mean nuffin' by it, Missus." *Ernst managed.* "He's jus' a boy."

"Just a boy?" *Oma rolled her eyes and wadded up the tablecloth.* "The two of you are a pair, aren'tcha?"

Oma gave us both once last withering look before she stood from the table, the bundled-up tablecloth in her arms, and then she marched out the back door. Obviously, she was going to pitch the ruined cloth in the outside garbage so that no one would ever see it and ask questions. Not that we had many visitors—and even if we did, they wouldn't be going through our garbage, inside or out. I looked down at Ernst, disgusted with myself as he gave my hand a squeeze.

"It's a'ight, Rob." *He reassured me, his other small hand coming up to pat the top of my hand while his other held it.* "You'll ge' the hang o' it."

"I'm awful." *I groaned.* "I don't even know why this matters. I mean...I'm going to end up dead anyway, right?"

Ernst's face turned up, and he thumped my hand.

"Now, don' go talkin' like all tha'." *He gave me a stern look.* "Ya' gonna end up 'owever you wan' to end up. And ya' will get the 'ang of this."

"Maybe." *I sighed.* "Thanks for...being my friend, Ernst."

Ernst's little cheeks turned pink.

"What?" *I asked, finally smiling at him.*

"Never 'ad no friend before." *He mumbled.* "'Specially with your kind. Nah supposed ta anyway."

"Well," I shrugged, a trait I had learned from Oma over the previous years, "I keep breaking every other rule she gives me. We can break that one, too."

Ernst grinned impishly up at me as we squeezed each other's hands.

"I'm honored ta be yer frien', Rob."

"Forever, Ernst." I nodded and leaned down to hug him. "Forever."

Like stepping out of a fog, things changed. I was no longer remembering my life as a series of memories or dreams, drifting overhead incorporeally, looking down at the events, but instead stepping up to a stage to watch them be acted out. It was almost like I was walking up to the front row of a theater and taking my seat, waiting for the show to start, but I was the only one with a ticket. I gazed out at the scenery before me as nothingness dissolved and was replaced with vague shapes and blurs, slowly coming into focus.

The play...*maybe movie?*...started with a view of a field of lush, green grass, and I immediately knew that I was looking at the land where Oma's—*my family home*—should have been. Except there was no house. But there were more trees. The grass looked more...*wild*. What would once be called Lake Erie was off in the distance. A young girl skipped into frame, but lazily, as if in slow motion. I stared up at the scene as I—*sat there, I guess?*—and watched the young girl, probably no more than ten-years-old enter the frame of my vision. In the middle of the field, the girl fell to her knees gleefully, then laid back in the grass, staring up at the brilliantly blue, sunny sky overhead.

Lying there in the grass, the girl's eyes closed, and she smiled, beatific in her innocence and happiness. I couldn't help but smile, though in the back of my mind, I remembered why I was experiencing these things. For several moments, I watched the girl in the grass, eyes closed, smiling at nothing...and everything...and then two people stepped into frame. Oma and Carlita. From the girl's garb and the clothing of the two people I knew already, I ascertained that this had happened so long ago that I had no way of putting a specific date to the events.

Carlita was the first to open her mouth, which startled the girl, though I couldn't hear what Carlita said, nor could I hear the girl shriek as she sat up quickly and scurried backward like a crab several feet. Oma stepped forward, her hands out as though to calm the girl, speaking mutely as the girl looked up at the two of them warily. For what seemed like forever, but was probably only seconds, I watched the three of them interact silently, not even one piano chord played to this silent movie, and then the girl rose to her feet. She took Oma's hand with a smile, which Oma returned, and then they walked away, my vision going black.

All I could hear was my heart in my chest, thuh-thumping for the space of a few breaths before the blackness started to fade away, revealing the same field once again, only at night this time. I gasped, though I couldn't hear that either, as Bloody Bones stood there in his black hooded cloak, fire shooting forth from an upraised hand at the girl. Oma and Carlita were standing several yards away, near the woods, watching as the girl returned her own magics in Bloody Bones direction. I watched in horror, seeing the toll this display was taking on the child, not much older than she had been in the first scene.

The fight wore on for several minutes, back and forth between Bloody Bones and the girl, but finally, with what I could only assume was a scream of rage, Bloody Bones was defeated. He reached towards the sky with fury and panic as the ground split open and he was pulled beneath, scratching and clawing, screaming silently at the girl. Once Bloody Bones had been sealed away, the ground swallowing him and sealing after him, the girl fell to her knees, exhausted and bleeding. Carlita and Oma stepped away from the woods, relieved smiles on their faces, as though they would approach the girl.

Disdainfully, the girl turned her head to glare at the two, making them stop in their tracks, suddenly afraid of this progeny of theirs. With a mouth twisted up in a howl, magic seemed to burst from the girl, spilling out and over the land, sliding over everything in its path. Without hearing a sound, or any narration, I knew this girl was imbuing the land with her magic, sealing Bloody Bones away as long as the magic could hold. I gasped, though still soundlessly, as the girl fell to the Earth. In direct contrast to how it had accepted Bloody Bones, the Earth accepted the girl, cradling her like a baby in a bassinet, as if lulling her to sleep, slowly absorbing her into the ground, then sealing shut behind her. Magic continued to glimmer, even as the ground sealed gently shut around her body, sparkling over the surface of the land, the trees, the lake in the distance.

Seconds ticked by as Carlita and Oma stared at where the girl had been, until suddenly, a well slowly sprouted from the ground, growing inch by inch until it was waist-high to a man and as wide as a human is tall. Oma and Carlita stared at this strange artifact, unsure of what to make of it. But when green light began emanating from its depths, bathing the ground around it in a sickly green halo, Oma and Carlita looked at each other with concern.

These scenes played over and over in front of me, fading to black, reappearing, disappearing, Bloody Bones fighting to his death. But always with a different opponent. Sometimes a young girl. Sometimes a boy. Sometimes a teenage boy or girl. The well stood watch as they met on this field. Then, after several versions of this fight, a house was the backdrop to the fight, with no well in sight, obviously tucked away in its cellar.

In between each fight, flashing scenes of people peering into the well, their faces illuminated by a sickly green glow, greedy smiles on their faces showed before my eyes. A fight, a different person staring into the well. A fight, a new person going to seek the magic in the well. Over and over, again and again, time passing as battles were fought, and people became greedier and more envious.

Finally, when the scene faded to black, then slowly faded back to show another fight, and I saw a moonlit night, with my father stepping into frame, I screamed.

And I finally heard sound.

"What is it?" I heard my voice.

Looking around, all I could see was darkness. But I had heard my own voice...well, my younger voice...so I knew that I should be seeing something in this vision.

"The source of your family's magic."

That was Oma's voice.

Slowly before me, like when the vision had started previously, a scene came into view. Barely breaking through the darkness at first, then gradually getting lighter and brighter until I could see what was going on. Oma and I were in the cellar of the house. I was on one side of the well, and she was on the other. Clearly, I remembered the day I had wandered down there—maybe thirteen-years-old—and found the strange structure right in the center of the room. Oma had always told me not to go in the cellar, going out of her way to remind me that I should never go down those stairs. One day, curiosity got the better of me. Though, when I had finally gone against her wishes and Oma had found me, my eyes had been on the well. I had never looked up at her when we spoke in the dank and dark room, instead looking into the depths of the well. Watching this scene replay, from the outside looking in, I was able to watch Oma instead of the well.

She was smiling.

Smirking.

Plotting. She had been plotting.

Of course, she had wanted me to go into the cellar eventually. That's why she had kept bringing it up for those many years. Now she had gotten me where she wanted me.

"Is it always here?" My younger self whispered.

She shrugged, only acting with part of her body. The smile never left her face as I stared down into the well.

"It comes and goes." She said, staring down at my younger self leaning over the edge of the well. "Shows itself when it wants to or needs to."

"Why's it here?"

"I done told you." She said. "It's the source of all your family's magic. It's here for you if you ever need it. Unfortunately, some of your kinfolk have been dippin' into it over the years and—"

"Dipping into it?"

She made a crude sound but never stopped smiling. Oma had gotten me exactly where she had needed me to begin moving the pieces on the chessboard.

"Yeah." She stated flippantly. "Idiots used some of the magic. Thinkin' it could give them money or power or some other nonsense that they wanted. They used it for wishes."

"Wishes?" My younger self breathed the word, fascinated.

"Wishes." Oma reiterated. "Thought the well could solve their problems instead of handlin' the problems themselves. But wishes are only as good as the person making 'em. Bunch of idiots. Now, we need to get out of here."

"Would it grant me a wish?" I had asked dreamily, staring down into the dark depths of the well.

There it was. Looking at this scene from the outside, I saw the grin on Oma's face widen. That's what she had wanted me to know—she wanted that thought in my head, chewing away at all of my other thoughts for as long as it could.

"I suppose." She said, then suddenly the grin was gone. "Now, get off that damn well. We're going back upstairs, and I never want you to come down here again. Don't even think about it. Don't talk about it to no one."

"Oma." My younger self pushed back from the well and looked up at her, my bottom lip jutting out.

"Don't 'Oma' me, mister." She jabbed a finger at the stairs. "I ain't got many rules around here, but this one I mean."

"Fine." My younger self rolled his eyes and started marching towards the stairs.

As my younger self disappeared out of frame, Oma's eyes followed him. When he was gone, Oma took one last look at the well, the grin returning to her face. She laid a hand on the edge of the well, giving it a soft pat as she smiled down at it, then she too was heading for the stairs.

'Everything Little Thing She Does Is Magic' by The Police was playing on the little radio on the kitchen counter when I walked into the room. Bright summer sunlight was pouring through the windows in the house, making everything look white and golden and nearly celestial. All of the curtains and drapes had been pushed back on their rods to help welcome the first day of summer. The house was sparkling clean and smelled of Oma's favorite lavender cleaner. I staggered down the stairs, all wonky elbows and joints, my hair surely sticking up in spikes all over my head, rubbing my fists into my eyes. My bare feet padded down the stairs and then across the floor of the living room towards the kitchen. It was my last summer before I started Big Boy School. Talks had been given to me over and over again about what to expect, the friends I'd make, the teachers I would love, the things I would learn. All I cared about that summer morning was getting some of the food in the kitchen that was scenting the house from top to bottom: bacon and eggs and butter and maple-y goodness.

When I entered the kitchen, I immediately saw her standing there, back turned to me, poking around in a skillet on top of the stove. My eyes lit up as an evil grin came to my face, and I tiptoed across the linoleum floor in the kitchen, sneaking up on her. I grabbed ahold of her sides, my head barely coming up past her butt, making her scream out in feigned shock. She had heard me walking up behind her, but it didn't matter. She let my five-year-old self pretend that I had snuck up and startled the daylights out of her. She spun around, hand to chest, gasping as she looked down at me with wide eyes. Then her face broke into a smile, and she dropped to kneel *before me. Her arms went around me immediately as she smothered my face with kisses.*

"Good morning, Robbie!" My mother managed to get out between my squealing and squirming as she smothered me with her kisses. "Good morning, my little ray of sunshine!"

"Mommy!" I squealed, pretending that I wanted to get away, but I was really wanting my mother's kisses to keep going until I was exhausted and collapsed in her arms.

I wanted to feel my mom's arms around me, comforting and loving me, leading me to the table for my breakfast. The smothering kisses and squeezing arms lasted for what was a very long time, but not to a five-year-old. Finally, my mom pulled back, her hands going to my shoulders so that she could get a good look at me. Immediately, one hand went to my head, to try and pat down the multitude of cow-licks in my hair. She smiled to herself as she gave up after a few seconds. My hair never wanted to do what she wanted it to do, and that was a battle she was slowly losing. Her hand went to my chin, pinching it between her fingers as she winked at me.

"Did you leave your appetite in bed, or is it here with you?"

I giggled. So silly.

"I'm so hungry, mommy!"

"What do you want for breakfast, baby?"

"What did you make?"

"What do you want?"

I giggled. This was our game.

"What did you make, mommy?"

She smiled widely.

"What do you want?"

"I want eggs and bacon and pancakes!" I crowed towards the ceiling, excited for a new day, full of endless possibilities and wonder.

The way a five-year-old lives each day...with possibility.

"Well," Mom kissed my forehead quickly, "you must have read my mind. That's exactly what I made."

Cheering, I headed over to the table, my mom patting me on the butt as I turned away from her. I sat down, yawning and rubbing my eyes again as my mom got a plate from the cabinet in Oma's kitchen and went over to the stove to serve my breakfast. That was probably the best thing about being so young—no real responsibility, all the wonders of the world, and your mom served you breakfast. As I sat there, listening to the spatula scrape against the cast iron skillet, I couldn't help but wonder where Oma and my father were. They always had breakfast with us in the morning. In fact, Oma was usually the first person down in the kitchen. She usually made our breakfast. Sometimes mom did...but not very often. Frowning to myself, I rubbed my eyes with my balled-up hands again, trying to chase the last of the sleep away.

Just as I was turning in my seat to peek at my mother over the chair back, I felt it. The rumbling in the floor. At first, it just felt like a train passing nearby, though there were absolutely no train tracks anywhere near Oma's house. My eyes grew wide as the rumbling turned into shaking, and the whole house seemed to shake with the movement. A low roar began, then louder and louder until it sounded like a tornado was about to rip the house apart. I looked at my mother in terror as she turned to me, the half-filled plate in her hand, her own eyes wide with concern. No...with absolute terror.

"Mommy?" I squealed as loudly as I could over the sound.

"Stay there, Robbie!" My mom replied desperately, her hand unsteady as she reached out to set the plate on the kitchen counter as the house shook.

The plate clattered to the floor, shattering, food flying everywhere as I grabbed onto the chair, trying not to fall off of my seat. Next, it was the small radio falling off of the kitchen counter, its crash to the floor muted by the roaring and shaking. The roaring and shaking increased until I knew that I would fall from my seat to the hard ground below. My mother held onto the kitchen counter, trying to stay on her feet and also not step on the broken plate shards or chunks of greasy food. Suddenly, as though it had never even started, the roaring and the shaking stopped. We were left in Oma's deathly quiet kitchen, me holding onto my chair, terrified, and my mother gripping the kitchen counter as though her life depended upon it. Slowly, she turned to look at me, her face ashen, concern etched all over it.

"Muh-mommy?" I peeped.

My mother's mouth moved, but whatever came out was muffled, as though she were speaking underwater.

Then the roaring and shaking were back, and green light filled the room.

"Robbie!" My mother screeched as someone in a black hooded cloak flew through the backdoor.

Oma had fucked with the only memory I had of my mother. But she hadn't done enough to make me completely forget it. She hadn't overlooked trying to inject herself into the memories I had before she appeared...she just hadn't done a good job. She wasn't as powerful as she thought.

Are you scared?

No. I'm just lost.

I'd be scared.

I have no reason to be scared. I just don't know what to do. Things are changing. She's worried.

What do you think we should do?

I don't know. I don't know anything right now.

I wish I could help you.

We could...run away.

Together?

Would you run away with me?
Of course, I...did you see that?
What?
Rob! Run!
Why? What did you see?
Rob!

"*Were you waiting for me?*"

Lucas was standing at the bottom of the bleachers, his letterman jacket on, making him look as sexy as he was. I was sitting in the bleachers, my boring coat pulled tightly around my torso to keep me warm. I had been waiting on Lucas. Just like I always did.

"*Of course, I was waiting on you,*" I replied, my voice not as deep as it now was. "*I'm always waiting for you.*"

He smiled.

"*I thought I was always waiting for you.*"

"*Well,*" I shrugged comically, "*one of us is always waiting. But...the wait is always worth it, right?*"

"*Abso-fucking-lutely,*" He replied. "*Don't you get scared out here all alone? What if someone tried to get you?*"

"*You'd protect me.*"

"*How can you be so sure?*"

I shrugged. "*I just know.*"

"*I'd argue,*" He said, "*but I'd be wrong. And I don't like being wrong.*"

"*You nearly fumbled the last pass.*"

"*I held on. For you.*"

"*For me?*" I chuckled.

"*So we'd have a reason to celebrate.*"

"*How do you think we should celebrate?*"

"*Maybe you can give me one of your amazing kisses?*" He said, glancing around, as though he thought we might not be alone.

"*You're the football star,*" I said as I lifted my legs to place my feet on the bleacher row below me. "*Show me your skills. Come get it. Make a play.*"

Lucas grinned wickedly then slowly stalked up the stairs, his eyes never leaving mine. When he got to my row, he stepped over my leg, then brought his other leg over it as well, positioning himself between my legs. He looked down at me as his hand came up to cup the side of my face as I looked up at him. I wanted him to kiss me so badly.

"*You're...beautiful.*"

I couldn't help but laugh. "*Is that a compliment for a guy?*"

"*I wasn't talking about your looks.*"

That made me swallow back any retort.

"*Do you want me to kiss you again?*"

"*Yes.*" I exhaled.

"Do you love me?" He asked.

"Yes." I breathed the word. "I love you."

Lucas sighed.

"I love you, too."

Then he leaned down, and his lips found mine. For several long seconds, our lips, no longer amateurish in their movements, pressed together passionately. When Lucas finally pulled away, he was smiling, his eyes dreamy, but there was also concern.

"Is tonight the night?" He asked gently, his fingers finding my hair.

"Yes." I nodded slowly, my eyes closing at the feel of his fingers in my hair.

"Are we still going to...ya' know?" He whispered his question.

"Yes." I tried to smile, but I was nervous. Not for the sex, but for the second part of our plan. "And then..."

"I don't want you to go." He swallowed hard, fighting his tears back.

"I don't want to go," I said. "But...I have to. You know that, right?"

"I wish I could go with you."

"Me, too."

"But you'll come back."

"Always."

"We'll always be together?"

"Even in death."

Oma was in the kitchen like she always was, preparing another breakfast, humming a tune to herself, cupboards suddenly slamming shut, and shadows shifting as I gamboled into the room. Bacon and biscuits and sausage gravy perfumed the air—the signature scent of Oma's house in the morning. Too hungry to entertain propriety, I plopped down into one of the kitchen chairs, prepared to eat. I was hungry. I was always hungry.

"What have I told you about flingin' your ass into my kitchen chairs?" Oma turned around; the large kitchen spoon in her hand was coated with gravy.

It made my mouth water.

"I'm sorry, Oma." I blushed. "Your cooking just always smells so good."

"I guess I can take that as an apology."

She cackled and turned back to the stove. Oma had rules in her house and a strict sense of what was and wasn't proper behavior. While she was quick to correct breaking the rules or displaying improper behavior, she was just as ready to laugh and forgive. Oma wasn't one to ever genuinely hold a grudge against anyone. Besides the Kelly family. As far as I knew, she'd never actually punished me for anything. Of course, Oma had a way with her looks and her words that let one know you would never want to suffer one of her punishments. So...I was a pretty good kid.

"Now," Oma said, the metal spoon scratching against the cast iron skillet, "what have you been up to the last few days?"

Summer sun was streaming through the window, making everything look soft and lazy and warm.

"Nothing." I shrugged.

"Nothin'." She snorted. "Nothin' my wrinkled ass, Robbie."

"Oma..."

She waggled her head. "Rob."

"Thank you." My pubescent voice cracked.

"I'll never get used to calling you that." She turned to me, putting her fists against her hips. "You're not a 'Rob.' You're too damn sweet to go by 'Rob.' I'm just goin' to call you 'Robbie' until you feel like a 'Rob,' and you can hate me if you want."

She gave me a wink and turned back to the stove. Since Oma's back was turned and she couldn't see it, I let myself smile.

"You've been stayin' away from the house from sun up to sun down the last few days." Oma teased over her shoulder. "To me, that spells out that you're sweet on some girl."

I shrugged, though Oma couldn't see it, as I sat at the table.

"You just gon' be quiet about it?" Oma chuckled to herself. "Ain't nothin' wrong with a fifteen-year-old boy catchin' sweet on a girl. All y'all go through it. Bunch of hormonal idiots just waiting for a chance to smooch...and do other things...with some willing girl."

My cheeks were red, and I was staring down at the table. Oma talking to me about the birds and the bees—such as it was—was bad enough. The fact that I didn't have a thing for any of the girls at school was another. Oma turned to me, her eyes locking onto mine.

"You're going to be a heartbreaker, Robbie," She sighed. "I mean, hell...just look atcha. Now that you're growing into yourself. You make sure you're bein' a gentleman until they tell you it's okay to act otherwise. Don't you let me hear a single word about you treatin' a girl wrong."

"You won't, Oma," I mumbled.

"Good."

She turned back to the stove.

"I don't have any crushes on any girls anyway." I found myself practically whispering.

"Well, that's okay, too." Oma nodded to herself. "Ain't nothin' wrong with bein' a late bloomer. Or never bloomin' at all. Keep you out of trouble as long as we can."

Oma laughed. I didn't.

There's a time in every young person's life where they decide the person they want to be with their parents—or their parental figure. Do they want to show their most authentic self and risk that it won't be good enough...or do they try on a persona so that they don't have to find out if the person they truly are is good enough to be loved? My teenage self chose the former.

"There's a boy I like, though." I felt the truth slide from my mouth.

The "skritch-skritch" of the spoon in the skillet stopped, and Oma seemed to freeze at the stove. My teenage heart palpitated within my chest as I waited for whatever was to come to...come. Thick, heavy silence grew between us in the kitchen as bacon sizzled in the other skillet, creating a soundtrack comprised of delicious sounds and smells. Just when I thought that I might scream out just to break the tension, the "skritch-skritch" of the spoon in the skillet started up again. Oma let the spoon rest against the side of the skillet and turned to me again, her hands on her hips once more.

"You know they got one them 'LGBT' centers over in Toledo?"

I shook my head nervously.

"Well, they do." She nodded. "I been thinkin' about goin' over there to volunteer while you was in school all week long. Help the boys and girls out. I guess that's just what I'll do."

Then she turned back to the stove and started stirring the gravy again. I allowed myself to give a wary smile.

"Maybe you can go with me?" She suggested gently.

"Maybe..."

"Who's this boy?" Oma didn't let my hesitance overtake the conversation. "Do I know him? I should. I know everybody around here. Better not be one them Kelly boys. Ugly, Irish assholes."

"Are you ever going to be nice to them?" I teased. "Besides, they're all a lot older than me, Oma."

"I'll sit up in my coffin to spit at them if they show up at the funeral." Oma waggled her head as she cooked. "Who's the boy, damnit?"

"Luc-Lucas Barkley?" I stammered, suddenly very nervous.

Oma turned to me again, the spoon in her hand dripping gravy onto the floor. She didn't notice.

"That Jackson Barkley's grandson?" She asked quickly. "The one who plays football?"

I nodded jerkily.

Oma cackled and then noticed the gravy on the floor.

"Shit." She admonished herself before retrieving a paper towel to clean up the mess she had made.

Oma bent down to wipe up the gravy.

"Well," She grunted as she wiped, "Lucas is a good kid. But Jackson Barkley will shit his britches knowin' that his grandson is..."

She glanced up at me, stopping herself from saying whatever it was she was going to say. I stared at her.

"I wasn't gonna say nothin' too bad." She waved me off as she stood up and deposited the soiled paper towel in the trashcan. "I don't even know if Jackson will give a shit, to be honest."

"Oma..."

"Well, I'm sorry." She snapped, but she didn't have the heart to put the full force of her sass behind it. "I was just gonna say he 'had a little sugar in his tank' is all."

"It's not the most offensive thing you've ever said," I mumbled, and Oma shot a squinty-eyed look over her shoulder, silencing me.

The cellar door creaked open suddenly, and I looked over to see Ernst come out, looking around as though to make sure that there were no visitors. Once it was clear to him that it was just the three of us, his eyes locked onto me.

"Good morning, Ernst." I beamed.

"Good-mornin', Rob." He smiled back.

Ernst exited the cellar and shut the door gently behind himself as Oma gave him a "good mornin'" over her shoulder. Ernst returned the sentiment and sauntered over to the table to stand beside me, his head barely higher than my lap in my seated position.

"Didja sleep well, Rob?"

I didn't respond verbally. Instead, I smiled and scooted my seat back, making the legs scrape against the linoleum unpleasantly. Ernst didn't hesitate as he climbed up and sat on my knee. Oma cast a disapproving glance over her shoulder and shook her head as she began piling a plate high with the heavenly concoction she had whipped up for breakfast. Doing her best to not slap the plate down on the table, Oma set the breakfast in front of Ernst and me before shaking her head once more. I picked up my fork while Ernst grabbed a strip of my bacon and began nibbling at it happily. It had taken a few years for him to sit at the table with me, under the watchful eye of Oma. He had become less fearful of showing impropriety when it became clear that Oma wouldn't say anything while I was around. Ernst was my friend. Oma let it slide.

"You two are thicker than thieves, ain'tcha?" Oma stated blandly as she made her own plate.

Ernst nibbled nervously and looked up at me, and I just gave him a wink.

Lucas never liked meeting anywhere we might be seen by the other kids we went to school with each day. Being a naïve, mostly sheltered country kid myself, I assumed it was because I was a theater kid, and he was a football player. It was a personal "head-slapping" moment for me when I realized the actual reason behind his secretive behavior. Of course, when Lucas and I had first started hanging out, I thought we were becoming just friends. I had known that I was gay...or, at least, I had a pretty good idea. Lucas hadn't indicated that he was gay when we started becoming friends, so it never crossed my mind that anything besides friendship was developing. Later, when we kissed for the first time, I had an Oprah "Ah-ha Moment." Obviously, he was gay—or gay-ish, which were the only LGBT terms I understood at the time—and wanted more than friendship. Knowing this, he wanted to keep the fact that we hung out a secret, even though I was not out of the closet to anyone except Oma at the time. I had just been too dense to understand what was unfolding before my very eyes. Lucas, of course, had been much quicker at figuring things out than I had been. He had always been smarter than me.

"We could go down to the bowling alley," I suggested as we walked along the shore of Lake Erie, beyond the woods bordering Oma's property. Lucas was skipping rocks sporadically, and I was collecting interesting pebbles in my pocket. We were fifteen and should have had more exciting things to do. "We could go see a movie or something. Ernst said he would show us some more tricks if you want."

Oma wasn't aware, but I had introduced Lucas to Ernst within the first days of becoming friends with him. I had known that he would be able to keep a secret. Just as I had suspected, and though Lucas had been gobsmacked by the appearance of a Kobold, he had kept his lips shut. He and Ernst had taken to each other after Lucas' initial shock wore off, and they always talked at least a little bit every time Lucas showed up to hang out. Lucas stayed clear of the house, though. He hadn't wanted Oma to see him. We always met at the edge of the yard or down by the lake. But Ernst would always at least say "hello" to Lucas before the two of us left to do...whatever it was we decided to do.

Lucas' reply was slow to come, "I like just being out here."

"Okay." I shrugged and bent down to grab a rock so black and shiny that it looked like obsidian.

Shoving the rock in my pocket, I turned to watch Lucas skip another one across the eerily calm surface of the lake.

"The play was really good," Lucas stated as he slid his hands into his pockets and stared out at the lake.

"Thanks." I smiled widely. "Oma took me to Toledo afterward last night. We got burgers and milkshakes and saw a movie and...it was kind of cool, I guess."

Lucas smiled, still looking out at the lake.

"I mean, it was kind of stupid, too." I backtracked. "I kind of just wanted to hang out with the cast. Grandmas, right?"

I sighed as though the weight of the world was on my world-weary fifteen-year-old shoulders. Cool kids don't feel happy about spending time with their parents or grandparents.

"I think it's cool."

Surveying Lucas' face for hints of a lie as he looked out at the lake, I found none.

"It was cool," I confirmed.

"Mrs. Wagner seems really nice."

"You never come inside..."

"I know. You were an amazing Professor Harold Hill."

"When in Rome."

"Ohio?"

"Close enough."

"Don't let an Iowan hear you say that." Lucas laughed. "They'll be fit to be tied over in I-Oh-Way."

"We're both going to be in trouble with a capital 'T.'" I teased.

Lucas smiled crookedly as he turned his gaze from the sun-sparkling water and looked at me. I did my best not to swallow down whatever it was that was making my belly feel the way it felt as he looked at me. His blonde hair seemed to practically glow in the spring sun. His eyes looked even more like jade than they usually did. Puberty was having its way with Lucas—in all the best ways. His jaw was becoming sharper, stronger. His baby fat was being shed, and days playing football was making him lean and muscular. But none of that accounted for what hid behind the jade of his eyes. Kindness can be exercised, but it can't be learned. Lucas was intimately familiar with the concept.

"You're really funny."

I shrugged.

"What does that mean?" Lucas mimicked my shrug with a small chuckle.

"I don't know." I had to keep myself from shrugging again.

Lucas stared at me for a moment before turning to walk along the shore of the lake again. I followed silently, my hands still in my pockets. Suggesting more activities we could do instead of nothing came to mind, but I let it go. Spending time with Lucas at the lake had actually become my favorite activity very quickly. I just didn't want him to get bored with it.

"Are you coming to the football game on Friday?"

"I guess," I said, "I mean, I always do, right? Everyone does."

We both chuckled.

"Do you usually watch the game…or do you ignore it like everyone else?"

"I watch."

He glanced out at the lake quickly then gave an upward nod.

"Do you…I mean, you cheer for me, right?"

I gave him a nudge with my shoulder as we walked.

"Obviously."

He smiled, his eyes down.

"Grandpa cheers really loudly, so if I can single anyone out in the crowd, it's usually him."

"I guess I'll have to cheer louder." I shrugged, regardless of my desires.

"You don't really like sports, do you?"

"Honestly?"

"Yeah."

"No," I said. "Not really."

"But you still go to the football games?"

"Something to do on a Friday night, right?"

"You could go to the 'bowling alley or the movies,'" He teased.

Again, I was shrugging.

"Why do you keep coming?"

How to respond to the question evaded me as we walked along the shore, the perfectly still water and lack of breeze making the silence palpable. Initially, I started going to football games because that's just what high school kids did. They went to football games and socialized and flirted and hung out. Sometimes they actually even cheered for the team. Over time, I realized that football was no more exciting than any other sport I despised. I enjoyed socializing with my friends…mostly…but I was also incredibly bored at the games, too. In sophomore year, when Lucas started playing, though, things changed.

The blonde, good-looking guy—though I wasn't entirely sure how I felt about that at the time—that I vaguely knew from classes and the hallways, caught my eye. It made the games more tolerable. After the very first game, I made sure to say "hello" to him in the hallways anytime I saw him. I'd smile at him in classes if I didn't actually talk to him. A friendship slowly began to form. And then Mr. Barkley had brought Lucas out to hang out that one day…and we became…friend? Lucas glanced at me as though he would add a follow-up question, so I knew that answering his first question was important; otherwise, he'd think of ten more.

"Well," I said, "I have to support you, don't I?"

"I guess."

"I guess?" I feigned a chuckle. "I don't have to come, do I?"

"No."

"Then show some gratitude, damnit." I genuinely laughed.

But the laugh was cut off when Lucas turned to me, took my face in his hands and pulled my face into his. My eyes opened wide in shock as his lips connected with mine. Lucas' eyes were closed firmly with concentration and determination. The kiss itself was too wet, too firm, too…perfect. After a moment, I let my eyes close as Lucas held his mouth to mine, though that was all the kiss really consisted of—two pairs of lips pressed together firmly and wetly. When Lucas finally pulled away, I let my eyes flutter open to find him staring fearfully at me. His hands didn't leave my face.

"You didn't pull away."

I shook my head.

"Oh, shit." He swallowed as his hands slid from my face, obviously concerned at my lack of verbal response. "I didn't...look, let's just...Rob, I didn't mean to—"

I ignored his sputtering and reached up to lay my hand against his cheek, letting my thumb jerkily brush over his cheek. His words, fortunately, ceased, which gave me the perfect opportunity to lean in and kiss him back. Lucas shut his eyes forcefully, eagerly, as I eased my face to his. The corner of my mouth turned up in amusement as I closed my eyes and gently pressed my lips to his. Lucas seemed to melt into me as I kissed him, my thumb learning to slide along his cheek more expertly as I did so. The kiss didn't last long—I didn't want to attempt more than a simple kiss. When I pulled away, Lucas' eyes stayed closed several moments longer than mine, as though he had lost himself in the moment, but when they finally opened, they looked greener than ever.

"You like me, too?"

I nodded.

"Was the kiss...okay?" He looked away but made no effort to pull his face away from my hand.

"The first one or the second one?"

"Either."

"They were both perfect."

Then Lucas was amateurishly pulling my face to his again right there on the shore of Lake Erie, pressing his lips against mine. It was perfect, too.

"Is that what you think?" I spun on my heels to growl at Oma.

"Of course, I do." She snapped back. "I think you're not thinkin' with your head. You're usin' another organ."

In case I was confused, she tapped a finger against her chest. At least she hadn't tapped her crotch. I rolled my eyes and turned back around, headed for the living room. Oma would never let me storm out on her, especially during an argument, but I was sixteen. What sixteen-year-old hasn't jumped on a huff and rode it away when the mood struck them? I hadn't even stepped from the kitchen into the living room when Oma snapped at me.

"Where the hell do you think you're goin'?"

"To my room!" I screamed over my shoulder.

"The day pigs fly!" She bellowed.

Chair legs scraping against linoleum sounded, and I picked up my pace slightly as I made my way to the stairs and started up them in a sturdy *march. If I could only get up the stairs, down the hall, and to my room, maybe I could lock the door and avoid Oma. Of course, if I thought a locked door would keep Oma from continuing the argument, I was dumber than dirt.*

"You swivel your ass and get back down here!" Oma shouted at me from the bottom of the stairs.

I turned on the landing to glower at her.

"No."

"Don't you sass me." *She put her hands on her hips and glared up at me.*

"It's my life!" *I snapped.* "And just like everything else, you're telling me how to do everything!"

"Robbie," *Oma looked at me through squinty eyes,* "this isn't about gettin' your driver's license or a curfew. This is about your damn life."

"Right." *I nodded firmly down at her.* "My life. Not yours. Not Lucas'. Just mine. I can do with it what I like."

Oma crossed her arms over her breast and cocked an eyebrow at me as she looked up at me standing on the landing.

"You're plannin' to do a damn fool thing, is what you're plannin'." *Oma waggled her head.* "You think you understand everything. Just like every other dumbass teenager. Well, you don't know shit, Robbie."

"What don't I know?" *I demanded.* "I know exactly what this means, and you're trying to convince me that I don't understand."

"You don't understand, damnit!" *She replied sharply.* "Your mother and father—"

"Where are mom and dad?" *I looked around dramatically.* "I think the only people who get to be involved in an argument are the ones here, don't you?"

"More fuckin' sass." *She rolled her eyes.*

"I've made my decision." *I crossed my own arms over my chest.*

"You're goin' to let yourself get kilt because—for what?" *Oma demanded.* "What's that gonna do for any-damn-one?"

"What's the alternative, Oma? Tell me that. You knew—**you knew**—this day was coming, and you just stayed silent. The only time you've ever stayed silent—"

"Don't you—"

"—and now I have exactly two choices, and you're telling me which one to make without even discussing it!" *I bellowed.* "This isn't about you. It's about me, Oma!"

"It's about everyone!"

"Why'd I have to be born?" *I screamed down the stairs at her.* "If I hadn't been born, I wouldn't have to deal with any of this!"

Oma's eyes grew wide as a hand went to her chest.

"I wish I didn't know any of this shit!" *I continued.* "I wish I wasn't here! I wish I didn't know what I know! I wish I didn't have to look at you! I wish I didn't have to worry about Lucas! I wish Ernst was safe! I wish I had more time—"

"Shut up, Robbie!" *Oma hissed, her foot rising to the first step of the stairs.*

My mouth stayed open, but I didn't say another word. Oma's hand was on the newel post cap and the other on her chest. She glanced down at the floor fearfully, then up at me desperately.

"Don't make wishes, Robbie. Not even in your own head," She pleaded. *"You know better."*

"Sorry." I snapped, but my heart wasn't in it. *"I'm still learning all the rules."*

"You think you're going to solve all of this with a wish?" She barked.

"It's better than your plan to feed me to the wolves." I barked back. *"Almost literally!"*

"It's only been eleven years since he was sent away last time, Robbie." Oma howled at me. *"Eleven goddamn years since your daddy put him in the ground. He's too powerful for you."*

"That's why I'm not going to face him!" I screamed, the glass panes in the front door shattering.

Oma jumped. I did not.

"I'll never face him," I added quietly, once the tinkling of broken glass tapered off. *"If I can avoid it."*

Oma just stared up at me in shock.

Then I stomped the rest of the way up the stairs. Once I'd made my way to my bedroom, I made sure to slam the door as hard as I could. The whole house shook.

"Stay down," Lucas whispered as we huddled behind the bleachers.

"Okay."

We had almost been seen. I managed to peek over my shoulder as I crouched there in the dirt under the bleachers in the football stadium. Jason and the other football players were walking through the bleachers, searching. I knew who they were searching for, but I wasn't sure why.

"Why are they looking for you?"

Lucas looked over at me, his eyes locking onto mine.

"They still want me to join them."

My eyes grew wide.

"But you're not—"

"It doesn't matter."

"Why would Jason-fucking-Morris think you'd want anything to do with them, Lucas?" I whispered. *"They're assholes."*

Lucas chewed at his lip.

"You're obviously so not."

He gave a nervous smile.

"You're not—you're not going to join them, are you?"

"I'd rather die."

"I don't want that either." I teased.

"They're going to make my life—our lives—really hard, Rob," Lucas sighed. *"I'm so sorry I got you into this."*

"We both cause trouble for each other." I gave him a crooked smile.

Lucas returned the look.

"Trouble won't stop us, though." He stared into my eyes. "Right?"

"If it does—it'll only be temporary."

I held out my pinkie.

It was a juvenile gesture.

Lucas stared down at my pinkie with a wicked smile. Then he pulled me into him and smothered my mouth with his. When he pulled back, he was still smiling.

"That's how I make promises."

"I like your method."

"LUCAS!"

Lucas was out of breath, and his fingers were laced through mine as we slid to a stop behind the tree. The moon was dark, and I could barely see any stars through the skeletal canopy above us. Somehow, I felt like the moon was watching us, tracking our movements through the woods. Hopefully, it knew how to keep its mouth shut. I pushed Lucas against the tree as he tried to control his breathing and not pant loudly so as to not give away where we were. How was I breathing normally, and the football player was out of breath after our jaunt through the cold, slumbering woods?

"ROBERT!"

"Oh, shit." Lucas hissed, his eyes fearful.

"It'll be okay." I grabbed his face between my hands and made him look at me. "I promise you it'll be okay."

Lucas looked into my eyes, the fear slowly melting away.

"You can run." I pleaded with him. "Run to the lake. Then keep running along the shore until you get to the road. Keep running until you get home."

"I won't leave you."

"This is only going to end one way, Lucas," I whispered desperately. "I don't want you to see it."

"I can't let you do this alone."

"I won't hate you if you run."

"You will eventually."

"Do you think I'll love you forever if you stay?" I managed to tease though I was terrified as the sound of crisp, cold leaves being stomped on sounded in the distance. "Is that why you're doing this?"

"I know you'll love me forever." He responded, then kissed me roughly.

It was a quick kiss, but perfect like every kiss that came before it. Lucas pulled back, his hands on the side of my face.

"Everything is temporary," Lucas stated firmly. "Everything."

"Everything." I nodded. "Are you sorry?"

"I'll never be sorry."

"Me either."

"Can we make it back to the house?" Lucas swallowed hard. "Before...will I just slow you down?"

"I want you with me." I grabbed his face in my hands. "I want you to be the last thing I see."

Lucas' eyes started to leak.

"I'm going to miss you."

"I'll miss you more."

"What if—what if it's not temporary?"

"Hey!" I whisper-hissed, holding his face firmly in my hands so he had to look at me. "Every-fucking-thing is temporary. Except us. Except us, Lucas. I promise you that."

Lucas stared into my eyes, two trails of tears winding down his face.

"I believe you."

I nodded.

"Are you ready?" I asked.

Lucas took a shaky breath, doing his best to stop the tears from escaping his eyes. Finally, he steadied himself, resolve settling on his face. He nodded.

"I can do this."

"I will do this."

"You'll come back."

A voice in the back of my head wasn't so sure.

"I will come back."

"Promise?"

"Yes." I nodded once. "I promise."

"I love you." Lucas whimpered. "Just in case I haven't told you enough. In case I never get to again."

"I love you, too."

I kissed Lucas again, then laced my fingers through his, and we raced away from the tree towards the house.

The room was cold.

Bitterly cold.

And I had no memory of the room.

But that didn't keep me from opening my eyes to find that I was lying on the bed in the middle of the room.

It wasn't apparent at first, due to my confusion at waking up in a strange room, chilled to my bones, but I wasn't even in Lucas' house. In fact, I wasn't sure whose house I was in, actually. The room did not look familiar—but it looked somewhat familiar at the same time. Maybe because it looked like a child's bedroom—the dark shape of an overflowing bookcase in the corner. A desk for homework along one wall. A toy chest that was overflowing. Cartoon sheets of some kind that I had kicked off in my sleep. With my child-sized feet.

I gazed down at my body only to find that I was not staring at my body but that of a child—or a very young teen. Maybe a tween? This revelation should have sent a shock of terror up my spine, but I was getting used to the odd things in my life. Instead of screaming out in shock or panicking in any way, I sat up cautiously and swiveled my hips to let my legs dangle off of the side of the bed. Giving a quick glance around the room, looking for any sign of danger, I lowered myself to the floor.

Icy cold floorboards slapped against my feet, and I winced, though I made no noise. It was dark, I had no idea where I was, and there was no way for me to know if there was anyone else in the house. Would someone come to investigate if they heard me? And if someone did come to investigate, would they be dangerous? Harm me in some way? I let my feet adjust to the cold of the floorboards as I scanned the room slowly with my eyes.

Just a typical tween's room.

Nothing unusual.

Other than the darkness.

Nothing looks normal in the dark.

As I stood there, my feet adjusting to the cold and my eyes adjusting to the darkness, my ears began to pick up the voices.

Beyond the door positioned at the opposite side of the room, someone was talking. Low and rumbly, the voices sounded muffled and hollow. My feet began to move without me willing it, and I found myself being drawn towards the bedroom door. The cold was pervasive, making my feet—well, the feet I now had—feel like blocks of ice. It pushed through the cotton of the pajamas I was wearing. It slid over and around my body, doing its best to compel me back into bed. To forget the voices and the door.

Suddenly, I found myself in front of the door, my hands reaching out to brace myself against it as my ear moved towards the cold, smooth wood. My ear connected with the icy surface, trying to hear the voices better. To try and figure out what it was they were saying.

The voices became louder with my ear pressed against the door, but I still couldn't make out what it was they were saying. After a few moments, listening to what sounded like two voices quarreling or, maybe, debating, I crouched down next to the doorknob. I leveled my eye to the keyhole and looked through into the room beyond.

What I saw...was I really seeing this?

In the room beyond, seemingly lit by fire or candlelight, was a pile of raw bones, gleaming white and splattered with blood. Sat upon what could only be described as the "throne" of bones was a hooded figure.

I knew that figure.

As if he knew I was watching, the hooded figure's head turned towards the door.

Red eyes peered out of the hood and into the keyhole.

Then I was falling backward.

"Why do you always read this book?" I asked, pointing at the book open in Oma's lap at my bedside.

I was snuggled down in the covers as snow fell outside of my bedroom window, blanketing the ground outside in knee-high fluff.

"I want you to remember this story, Robbie." She replied and shifted in her chair, trying not to lose her place in the book.

"Why do you keep it under the bookcase?" I asked.

"Well—"

"And why don't I ever get to read it myself?"

"Because—"

"Was that mom's and dad's book?"

"Why do you have so many questions?" Oma barked, though her eyes twinkled. "It's just a damn book. It only opens a certain way and only lets certain people tell its story. Yes. It belonged to your mom and dad. And I want to read it to you as often as possible, so you remember the story. Okay?"

I shrugged, smiling.

"Good." Oma nodded once. "Now, where were we?"

"You were telling me about the witch that The Oracle and The Guardian found who was going to defeat the bad guy," I replied.

"Right," Oma said. "Okay, so..."

"Are you Robbie, sugar?" I looked up from my plate of nachos at the Red Rooster Tavern.

It was only a little after three o'clock, and I was supposed to be meeting Lucas for a snack after school. As usual, football practice was causing him to run late, so I had started without him, happy to eat nachos, and wait until he was done. Mr. Kelly—the Kelly's son who had taken over the tavern when his parents left, and word had was about to sell the tavern to someone else at his father's behest—let the kids from the school come in for lunches and mid-afternoon snacks, but once six o'clock came, he shooed them all away. The cocktail hours had approached for the adults. When I looked up at the person who had asked me if I was Robbie, I saw a man I'd never seen before standing there. Catching sight of him immediately brought a smile to my face, though his appearance made me nervous.

Dark skinny jeans, fashionable, yet cheap, heels, a chunky burnt orange sweater that hung off one shoulder, a scarf in contrasting pink, and large Audrey Hepburn like glasses adorned his lithe frame. A purse big enough to hold A through F in the encyclopedia was slung over one forearm. He looked down at me, a broad smile that showed his immaculately bright, white teeth shined down at me.

'My people.' I had thought.

"That's me."

I had almost said it like it was a question.

"Oh, good." He threw his head back as if completely exhausted and slid into the booth across from me.

Immediately, I looked around, wondering what people would think if they saw my teenage self with a man...like this. He was definitely waving the Pride Flag with every ounce of his being. My eyes grew wide as I realized that everyone else in the Red Rooster Tavern seemed frozen in place. Immediately, I glanced over at the man sitting across from me.

"Wha—"

"Just a little magic." The man fluttered his fingers through the air with a cackle, then removed his sunglasses. "It won't hurt them none, baby."

I couldn't help but smile, though I was alarmed to hear someone besides Oma talk about magic in front of me.

"Who…"

"Carlos, baby." He held out his hand, palm down over the table towards me. "But I prefer 'Carlita' if you don't mind. I ain't got the wig on today, and the dress is at the dry cleaners, but that's just how these things happen."

I took her hand, giving it a gentle shake.

"Okay. Carlita." I slowly nodded. "I am Robbie."

"Good, good." She wriggled her fingers through the air again as though trying to remember something. "Now, listen, I don't want to be here any longer than I have to—I got my own matters to tend to, obviously."

"Okay?"

"Tell Esther Jean Wagner—"

I froze at the sound of my grandmother's name. This woman knew Oma? Why had she never mentioned her before?

"—that the man in the black hooded cloak is coming."

My eyes grew wide as I gasped.

"She told me that she had done talked to you about him."

"You mean Bloo—"

"No, child." Carlita hushed me. "Don't say his name this close to his return. Why speed things up, ya' know?"

A hand to my chest, I just nodded, my breathing increasing in speed as my heart thumped against my chest.

"He's comin', baby. It's time." Carlita reached out and patted my other hand that was atop the table. "I always hate this part, delivering the news to the next witch, but, well, that's what an oracle is for, isn't it?"

"Oracle?" I gasped again, then leaned forward, forgetting my rapid breathing and thumping heart. "The Oracle? From the story?"

"It's obviously not just a story." She leveled me with her eyes. "And everything Esther Jean Wagner's been preparing you for…well, it's time, baby. You tell Esther Jean that. Now. I gotta go. Things to see and people to do."

Carlita slid out of the booth and draped her purse handles over her forearm once again. Her sunglasses got pushed onto her face where they had been when she entered. Then she was stomping fashionably towards the door of the tavern as the people around me slowly started to come back to life.

"Wait!" I spun in the booth to look at her.

Carlita stopped just inside the tavern and turned her head to look at me, a smile coming to her face.

"If you're The Oracle…where's The Guardian?" I asked quickly.

Carlita just smiled.

"I have so many questions." I pleaded.

As if trying to think of something important, or trying to remember something, Carlita's head tilted back gently as she looked up at the ceiling, searching for words.

"You'll get a chance to ask them." She finally turned her head to answer me. "But it won't be for a while. This won't be the last time we meet, Robbie Wagner."

"Rob." I couldn't think of anything else to say.

"I'll try to remember that." She tapped her temple.

Then she was gone, the door swinging behind her and the people in the tavern coming to life like a snap.

"Are you sure you want to do this?" Lucas asked.

We were already naked, and he was on top of me, so I wanted to laugh at the timing of the question.

"Obviously." I nodded, my teeth biting into my lower lip.

The woods behind Oma's house were dark and creepy all around us. We had made our bed on a pile of leaves. It was so cold, especially naked.

"We don't have to." He whispered.

"I want to," I said eagerly. "I don't want to leave without doing this. Just in case—and as long as you want to, too."

"Just in case?" Lucas looked terrified. "You're coming back, Rob."

"I know." I nodded. "But this will make leaving easier."

Lucas kept himself propped over me with a hand on either side of my body digging into the cold ground. I could feel, against my thigh, that he wanted the same thing that I wanted.

"Say you'll come back."

"I'll come back."

"Promise?"

"Promise."

"We'll be together forever?"

"Even in death."

Lucas' body sank into mine. Under a nearly moonless sky, the stars already blotted out, we made love. And I wondered if I hadn't just lied to Lucas. What if I never came back?

"Fuck!" Lucas screamed as we slammed the door to the house behind us and threw both of our bodies against it. "They're right behind us, Rob!"

Lucas and I held ourselves against the door, digging our heels into the hardwood floor as the sound of wolves throwing themselves against the door sounded. We had passed Oma and Carlita as we ran through the woods towards the house. They had merely been standing there, watching us. Lucas had wanted to stop and scream for them to come help...but I had known that it would be pointless. They were meant to watch. Besides preparing me, those were their roles in this never-ending story. I had urged Lucas to continue running, to put as much distance between ourselves, Bloody Bones, and his wolves.

"I have to get to the cellar," I said, twisting the deadbolt, flipping the lock on the knob and sliding the chain in place. "Come on!"

"Rob." Lucas turned to look at me, his back still to the door.

"What?" I turned to look at him, my heart thundering, and my mind racing with the wish I had in my head. "What is it?"

"I don't want to watch you go." He said, his face a steel mask, though a single tear slid from his eye and over his cheek.

Simultaneously I hated and loved Lucas. I loved how much he didn't want me to go, but I hated how I would have to do what I had to do all on my own. When I saw a tear slide from his other cheek, I couldn't be mad any longer. I just wanted everything to be over.

"Okay." I nodded, trying to not shed any of my own tears.

Lucas stared at me, tears rolling down his cheeks, trying to figure out what to say. Suddenly, his eyes flicked away from mine, landing on something to my side.

"Ernst!" Lucas bellowed as the sound of more wolves throwing themselves against the door met our ears. "Ernst, we need your help!"

I turned to find my best friend at my side, looking up at me with wide, terrified eyes.

"Ernst." I sighed, no longer able to control my tears. "Hey."

"'Ello, Rob." He reached up to grab my hand.

"Ernst." Lucas continued. "Go with Rob. Don't let him be alone."

"Wha's 'appnin'?" Ernst looked up at me, the terror replaced by wonder.

"I'm going to make this all stop," I said, simply.

"I can't do it, Ernst," Lucas said, still bracing himself against the door as the chain rattled as the door was pounded on by wolves' bodies. "But I don't want him to be alone. Will you go with him?"

Ernst squeezed my hand, and a look of pride replaced all of the others.

"I'd be honored, Rob." He said.

I smiled down at him, trying to stop my tears but finding myself unable. I didn't want to leave Lucas, Ernst...I didn't want any of this.

"Go!" Lucas screamed as a green light started shining through the front windows of the house.

Gasping at the sight of the light and Lucas' form bathed in it, I pulled away from Ernst and ran over to my boyfriend. Quickly, I shoved my mouth over his. His lips accepted mine, and I felt the trail of tears on my cheek meld with the river of tears on his cheek. When I pulled back, Lucas looked more determined. I felt more determined.

"Even in death." He nodded.

"Even then." I nodded back.

"Go." He stated simply.

Pushing away from Lucas so that I couldn't second guess myself, I turned and ran towards the cellar door, grabbing Ernst's arm on the way. Together, we ran hand and hand through the living room into the kitchen, and I threw open the cellar door. The two of us dashed down the steps as more pounding sounded from above, and everything around us seemed to be glowing in a green light. Running directly to the edge of the well, I let go of Ernst's hand and climbed up on the wall of the well.

"Rob!" Ernst gasped. "Wha' are you doin'?"

I looked down at my friend.

"Stopping all of this," I said, simply.

"Don'!" He bellowed to be heard over the sounds upstairs. "Please, Rob!"

"I have to, Ernst." I felt tears flowing freely over my cheeks. "It's why I'm here. You know that."

Tears were flowing from Ernst's cheeks, too. I could see in his face that he wanted to say something, that he was trying to force himself to say something...but then his face turned into a steely mask like Lucas' had. He simply nodded at me.

"Thank you for making sure I wasn't alone," I said. "I love you, Ernst."

"I love you, too, Rob." He responded, his back straightening, bringing him to his full height—which wasn't that great. "An' I am proud to 'ave been yer friend.'"

"No prouder than I am to have been yours." I smiled as warmly as I could.

Then, before we could say anything else that would delay or stop me, I turned and gazed down at the well. The green light wasn't just coming from the windows upstairs...it was emanating out from the bottom of the well, too. I gazed down into its blinding depths and braced myself.

I wish...

I wish I could forget everything. I wish Bloody Bones was gone. I wish that Lucas, Ernst, and everyone I love could be safe again.

And then I was falling.

The world's largest lucky penny.

It was dark when my eyes opened once again. I was in my room, lying on my bed. I wasn't in my pajamas or under the covers. I was merely laying on top of the bed, fully clothed. The room was dark, and the moon and stars were twinkling in the sky outside of my window. A quick glance over to my bedside table let me know that it was well after midnight.

A flash of a memory—Oma's hand on my forehead.

Whispered words.

I shook my head to clear my thoughts.

Why was I in bed like this? How did I get in bed? I didn't remember ever walking up to my room and going to sleep. I had gone to have nachos at The Red Rooster Tavern and...then...I didn't know.

Sitting up in my bed, I could sense that the house was deadly quiet. Oma must have already gone to bed. A shadow in the corner of my room moved. My head jerked to the side.

Was that...

I thought I saw a...little person?

A smile formed on my face at the thought. That was the most ridiculous thing ever. I was too old to be creeping myself out.

It's time to go.

The thought entered my head like a bullet.

So...I slid off of the bed.

Next to where my feet landed was a suitcase on wheels, the handle extended, ready to be wheeled away.

And that's what I did. I crept down the stairs, carrying the suitcase carefully the whole way, even stopping at Oma's closed bedroom door to make sure she truly was asleep. Then I went out the front door, locking it behind myself, walked across the porch, and down into the yard. Turning to give the house one last look, I gave a sigh. Point Worth just wasn't for me. I was meant for bigger things.

Hollywood.

California.

Not Podunk, Ohio.

I turned, let the suitcase fall to the ground, and wheeled it behind me as I walked towards the main road.

Did you see that?

Chapter 12

Oma, Lucas, and I stood inside the fence that surrounded the garden, staring down at the ground as Oma jabbed at it with a stick. Lucas was holding my hand, his body slumped against mine, leaning against me for strength. The rush of our memories being returned to us—in no particular order—had done a number on him. In all honesty, my knees still felt like they were jelly, and there was a pretty intense throbbing at the lower base of my skull above my spine. Getting memories back—*real memories*—and so many at one time, well, the human body just isn't meant to handle such a thing. The walk up the stairs from the cellar and out to the garden had been challenging.

Of course, I really had no one to blame but myself. Oma might have fucked with our memories some, after I jumped in the well the first time, and since I'd been back, but we had lost a lot of our real memories in the first place thanks to me. I was the one who had made three wishes and jumped into the well in the cellar—when it was still there—to use the power to defeat Bloody Bones. But like every witch that had come before me, I had failed to understand that no magic would ever be strong enough to defeat him for good. He was just as big a part of the magic of the lands we stood upon as anyone else.

"Made sure they was buried properly," Oma said, jabbing at the ground and avoiding my eyes. "Respectful like. Me and the Kobolds saw to that, Rob."

"I'm sure you did your best." I had no fight in me now that I knew the truth.

"Your mom, well, she was really just collateral damage," Oma said quietly, staring at the ground. "Your daddy, he knew what was comin' for him. He just didn't realize it was comin' so soon. He met Carlita that mornin', while you was wakin' up and havin' breakfast...by the time he got to the house after talkin' to Carlita and bein' told he was comin', ole Red Eyes had done did what he did to your mother and was turnin' on you. Your daddy did his best to run Bloody Bones off...but he knew he had to face him in real battle. He knew he had to do what he was born to do."

"I see."

"Jesus in a gravy boat," Oma shook her head, "we had trained him like he was young. Just like all the others. But Bloody Bones never came when it was time. We thought maybe he was never comin'. Your daddy went on about his life. Got married. Had you...y'all was livin' pretty good. Then...poof. Bloody Bones decided to show up. It wasn't right. It wasn't fair. But it is what it is."

"It is that." I sighed, wrapping my arms around Lucas.

"So," I said, "I was born, and this ended up falling on me instead of some other distant relative simply because he decided to take a rest?"

"Essentially." Oma shrugged. "I suppose so. If he had come for your father when he should-a, well, we wouldn't be talkin' right now, Rob. But...well, you know the story of how Bloody Bones came to be. You know about the first witch. You know about how the magic to fight him was in her bloodline and the magic she used that made that well. You know your parents died that day—your mom protecting you—and your daddy doin' what he was born to do. You know I ain't your grandmother—"

"You're The Guardian," I said simply, unemotionally.

"Yes." She sighed and looked up at us. "By the time he came for your daddy, Carlita and I was about fed up with this shit. A witch defeats him, he goes away. Comes back, another witch defeats him. On and on and on. Ain't none of 'em ever been powerful enough to keep him in the ground for good or outright destroy him. Or send him straight back down to Hell."

"But—"

"Well," Oma interrupted me, "that ain't necessarily true. The first witch...well, she did it. He would-a stayed locked away for good, I imagine. If it weren't for that goddamn well. And then—"

"Why did the well just...pop up out of the round?"

"That I don't know." Oma shook her head. "Carlita and I have discussed that over...many, many years...and the best we can decide is that there was too much magic in The Witch—the first one—for these lands to contain. Or maybe she consciously did that knowing that there would be extra help in the future if he ever returned. But...like all humans...your ancestors was a greedy bunch. Usin' magic like Lake Erie is filled with it. They perverted and destroyed that well. By the time you came around, we knew there wasn't much left for you to use if the time came."

"Just enough to make things drag on a little longer." I nodded.

"Right." Oma nodded. "And I just lied to you."

"What?" Lucas whispered, standing up a little straighter next to me, though his hands stayed tightly around mine.

"I said the first witch was the only one that could've gotten rid of him for good," Oma explained. "That ain't necessarily true. When your daddy died putting that shitass back in the ground, and I came here to look after you, to train you, teach you...I saw a little of that first witch in you. I thought you could actually do what needed to be done—but in a more permanent way. We just had to keep you alive long enough for you to build up the strength to do it."

"So," I snorted, my eyes shutting as I smiled ruefully, "you taught me the story. You trained me how to use my magic, you told me about Bloody Bones. You let me find the well—put the idea in my head to wish things away so that Bloody Bones would get sealed away a bit longer, the pack of wolves he built with the help of The Council would back off once their leader wasn't there to lead...then you put the idea in my head to run away."

It wasn't asking questions. I was recounting my memories.

"That sums it up mostly." She agreed, letting the stick in her hand drop the ground so that she could cross her arms over her chest. "But then this one comes along."

Oma jabbed a finger at Lucas, and he actually twitched.

"While Bloody Bones was suckin' up magic out of the land and finding people to store it in until he was ready to rise and take it all back to use in his final attempt to stay in this world forever—to make it his...I don't know...*kingdom?*...he gave this one something special. Something he didn't mean to. He gave him the power to foresee things. Some folks around here ain't magical at all. Some is good with fire or levitating things. Some is good with potions or spells. But, Lucas here, he's special. I think he might have given him a bit of magic he didn't know enough about."

"What does that mean?" Lucas hissed his question.

"Well," Oma sighed, "your gift of foresight rivals that of Carlita—may she rest in peace. Way back when, when you two was becoming friends—"

"Which you and my grandfather arranged!" Lucas barked.

"Well, yeah." Oma shrugged again. "No sense in lyin'. When you two became friends—we saw a powerful witch and a powerful oracle. Carlita and I got to thinkin'...."

Lucas and I looked at each other, trying to figure things out. Finally, it dawned on me. I turned to Oma, an incredulous smile on my face.

"You thought that maybe I'd put this fucker in the ground for good, you and Carlita could, I don't know, *retire*, and Lucas and I could take over as guardian and oracle? Just in case he ever came back, and another witch needed to be found?"

Lucas snorted.

"That's about the size of it, yeah." Oma agreed, then her face turned angry. "But you was supposed to be gone *at least* another decade, damnit. You needed to mature and have your power grow. If you couldn't remember you had it, you wouldn't be usin' it for all them years. It could grow while he was stuck in the ground. But then you came back way before I expected it...and you started a whole chain of events, damnit. I tried runnin' you off. Made you think you was seein' things, hearin' things, savin' somethin' that looked like you form the lake, havin' Andrew attack you. Even negotiated with Jason and his pack to scare ya' a bit. They was more than happy to if it meant Bloody Bones would be destroyed, and maybe they could have their...*disease*...removed. Everyone worked together—except this one—since he didn't have his memories—to get you to leave."

"You pushed us together when I came back," I grumbled. "How did that serve your purpose?"

"Thought maybe you'd get scared off if you thought you was fallin' in love," Oma replied evenly. "You two was thick as thieves when you was young. I was quite impressed with the way you both worked together and put the dots together about the well and wishing things different. And, well, it brought me peace, knowing that when the time came—*ten years from now*—if you came back and banished Bloody Bones for good, and the two of you took over for me and Carlita—you'd have each other. You could spend the next millennia in each other's company. A love story for the ages."

I pulled my hand out of Lucas' and began a slow clap.

"Well done, asshole," I said to Oma.

"It wasn't a perfect plan." She hissed at me. "But we saw a chance to tip the tables in our favor. To get rid of this never-ending cycle of him comin' and goin'. We was tryin' to do right by you and your long family line, you asshole!"

"So, what now?" Lucas asked quickly, glancing over at me. "If Rob's here too early and Bloody Bones is off sucking up all the magic he pulled out of the land and stored away—"

"Yeah." Oma nodded. "I bet most the people in this town is dead already. He'll be heading this way soon, I spose."

"So, what do we do now?" Lucas demanded.

"He'll fight." Oma waved a hand at me. "He's gonna say he won't, but he will. It's what people like him do."

"People like him?" I grumbled.

"Witches." She spat. "Good people who do what they was born to do. Protect others. That's what people like you do. Because you was born to do it."

"Fuck you." I groaned.

She shrugged.

Something in my head, some tiny little voice was telling me something.

"So," I said, "he's been pulling magic out of the land and giving it to people. Giving them powers. Storing it away so one day, he could rise and take it all back and be more powerful than a witch could ever hope. Then he could squash that witch—me—easily and do what he's always wanted to do? Rule the world or some shit?"

"Spose."

"Where do you think he learned that idea?" I asked.

"What?" Oma and Lucas asked at the same time.

"People up here were using magic left by The Witch." I shrugged with a snort. "Maybe he got the idea of borrowing magic from that. Ya' think?"

"It's possible." She sniffed.

"But—" Lucas began.

"And did it ever occur to you," I interrupted him, "that maybe the first witch created the well to create balance?"

Lucas turned to me, a shocked expression on his face. Even Oma turned to me, concern etched all over her face.

"There's magic in the lands." I waved my arms around wildly. "Where he gets his power. Maybe the witch put the well full of magic there to create balance—that's what kept him in the ground. People siphoning from it, creating imbalance...he started siphoning and storing away his own. He knew the day would come that the well would run dry, and the scales would tip. You put the idea in my head to use the well—*my whole family had been doing it after all*—and wish him away. Then you confused me into using it a second time to implant more fake memories in my head when I got back. That was the last of it. There was no more balance. As soon as that well went dry, he's been digging his way up, lady."

Oma whispered something.

"What?" I barked.

"As above, so below," Oma repeated but not much louder or more clearly. "One of the first rules of magic."

"I don't know what that means," Lucas waved her off and turned to me, "Rob, what are we going to do?"

He took my face in his hands, turning my eyes from Oma to his.

"We know everything now." He said. "What are we going to do?"

"The only way to seal him back in the ground," I stared at Lucas for a moment, "would be to create another well. Create balance."

For several breaths, Lucas stared into my eyes.

"That would do it." Oma offered with a sigh.

Suddenly, a realization came to Lucas.

"No!" He demanded, his hands clenching at me. "You're not going to do that, Rob! No!"

"What other choice do we have?" I put my hands on his shoulders. "It's either all of us die, or...or..."

"That would leave me and her!" Lucas jabbed a finger at Oma, but his eyes stayed on mine. "You wouldn't be saving much, Rob. Everyone in this town is likely dead, having been drained by him. Taking the magic back will kill a person, right? Right?"

He was talking to Oma.

"I reckon so." She said, chewing at the side of her mouth. "But, I ain't goin' door to door to find out."

Lucas turned back to me.

"You can't sacrifice yourself just for us." Lucas shook his head. "I won't let you."

"I'm not sacrificing myself for the two of you," I said, placing a hand on his cheek. "I'm doing it for you. And the rest of the people in the world. I mean...do you think he's going to stop at Point Worth? That he'll be happy with that?"

"Rob..." Lucas groaned.

"Give me options." I offered to him. "Tell me what else can work. I'm willing to listen."

"There ain't no other way," Oma said sharply. "You meet him in battle, and you defeat him. Or he defeats you."

"Shut up!" Lucas barked at Oma, shocking me, but pleasantly. "What happens then, Rob? Huh? You seal him away; we get a new well...then someone else comes along and uses the power? Then another? And another? Until it's all gone in a few centuries, and he comes back? Then what?"

"Maybe someone in my bloodline will still be around..." I hadn't thought of that.

"If you can't destroy him, you can't let yourself be destroyed." Lucas shook his head. "This is an impossible problem."

"How can he be destroyed, Lucas?" I asked him, pleaded with him. "As long as there is magic up here, there's...Bloody Bones."

The ground shook. Oma gasped, and Lucas grimaced.

"That ain't supposed to happen," Oma mumbled. "Bastard already crawled up out of Hell."

"Again," I snorted, "totally shocked that the portal to Hell was in this town."

Lucas gave a tight smile as the ground settled. We looked into each other's eyes as Oma stood in the middle of the garden, looking around as though she might come up with a solution. Or maybe she was looking for a place to bury me if my plan didn't work. Who was to say? Lucas stared at me, different emotions flashing across his face in succession, as though he was trying to think of something to say—or maybe how to say it.

"What is it?" I asked softly.

"Rob," Lucas said, "I saw you coming."

"Point Worth was on fire," I replied. "And I'm a fireman."

"And I saw how this ends."

"I know."

"I don't know what comes after...but I didn't see you die." Lucas said. "I saw...I saw..."

"What?" I asked, leaning in and kissing his lips softly. "What is it, babe?"

"I saw myself die." Lucas swallowed hard. "Not you."

I'd never been a wordsmith or someone who could eloquently describe my feelings in a way that would sound poetic. So, I had no way to describe the feeling of my heart dropping from my chest like a rollercoaster towards my feet while it felt like someone punched me in the gut simultaneously. Lucas' revelation about what he had seen was a one-two assault on my body and mind. All I could do was stare at him dumbly as my entire body went numb, and my heart decided that it was going on vacation.

"I died," Lucas said. "Not you. That's how this ends. At least...that's part of it. I can't see past my death."

"That's not true." I shook my head. "You're lying. That serves no purpose in solving our problem. How do you even think telling me that is going to change my mind about this? You dying won't stop Bloody Bones."

The ground shivered beneath our feet again.

"Ooooh," Oma waggled her head, not caring about the words Lucas and I were sharing, "he is comin', and he is pissed."

"All I'm saying, Rob," Lucas ignored her, "is that you can't save me—if that's why you're choosing to do what you think you have to do. I'm going to die. So...if you're doing this, only do it if you're doing it for everyone else. Not me. It won't help me."

"Stop it." I shoved him gently, though I didn't let him fall out of my personal space. "Stop fucking saying that."

"Do you want me to lie?" He sniffled.

"No, I just—"

"There has to be another way, Rob." Lucas stopped me. "Nowhere in my vision did I see you die saving me. If you are supposed to do that, I would have seen it happen before my death. I didn't see that."

"That doesn't mean that I'm not supposed to fight him."

"Maybe there is still enough magic left in the lands." Lucas offered quickly as the ground shook again, but harder. "If he can do it, maybe you can take magic from the land, too? Use his own tricks to defeat him and lock him away? If you used everything that's left and stuff him back in the ground, send him to Hell permanently with all of that magic, maybe that will work?"

"Will that save you?"

He shrugged then shivered.

"How can I know what the right thing to do is now, damnit?" I winced. "How do I know what can save you? If I do what was in my head all along, obviously, you die. But how are we to know what will happen if I change my mind about how to defeat him?"

"Ya' can't change your mind," Oma stated.

"What?" Lucas and I both turned our heads to snap at her.

"Ya' can't use the magic in the land." She reiterated. "He's carrying it all with him. Do you think the grounds shakin' for fun? That sumbitch is stompin' this way and sendin' us a warnin'. He's loaded for bear, and there's nothin' you can do about it but do what's always been done."

I didn't like it, but Oma had a point. Turning back to Lucas, I took his face in my hands.

"There is only one way," I told him in a hushed tone. "How do you die? Maybe if I—"

As if knowing this was the most imperfect time, a wolf's howl filled the air, making Lucas and I both jump as I stopped talking immediately. Oma sighed and turned to us, giving us a look that said: "Well, shit." As a threesome, though Oma was standing a few yards away, we turned, looking off in the direction from which the sound came. Our eyes landed on the tree line of the woods, off in the direction of Lake Erie. At first, I saw nothing but darkness and the trees that helped to create that darkness.

Then there were a pair of red, glowing eyes peeking out of the tree line, about waist high. Then another pair. Another pair. Then another. And another. Five pairs of eyes stared out of the darkness of the woods in our direction. Finally, a new pair of glowing, red eyes joined the bunch, but much higher than the others. Lucas squeezed my hand as we all stared towards the glowing, red eyes in the distance. We watched as one wolf emerged from the darkness, then another...until five wolves were standing just outside of the tree line, staring us down, muzzles pulled back, fangs bared.

Without having to be told, I knew the wolf in the middle was Jason. The pairs on either side of him were what remained of his functioning pack. They all stood there on all fours, snarling at us, fangs bared and eyes glowing, ready to tear us limb from limb if they could. The three of us waited, just like them, as the sixth pair of glowing red eyes stepped out of the darkness of the woods. But they weren't shrouded by a hood any longer. Bloody Bones had pulled back his cloak, exposing himself finally. A gleaming white skull, smeared in rust-colored stains and dripping blood, bony teeth and fangs bared, red eyes staring out at us, Bloody Bones was no longer hiding himself away.

"Well," Oma looked over her shoulder us, "I'm completely shocked by this turn of events. Are y'all?"

Lucas gave a whimpering groan as I glared at her.

Then the wolves were charging at us.

Chapter 13

Three things began to happen simultaneously, but not at the same rate of speed as each other. Out of the corner of my eye, I saw Oma walking away, going to the far side of the fenced-in area of the garden, getting herself out of harm's away. Bloody Bones began walking in an arc towards the other side of the garden so that he would be out of this part of the fight and watch as well. If his wolves could do his work and save him the trouble, that was good enough for him. He just wanted me dead so that he could continue on with his plans to rule over the lands once again. Thirdly, I felt Lucas step a foot away from me, his hand tightening on mine. As the wolves charged us, getting closer and closer, Lucas raised his arm, pointing it directly at the wolves, and I felt a tingle start in my back, move over my shoulder blade, and down my arm.

A fireball shot from Lucas' palm and flew at the wolves just as they jumped in unison over the fence. Four wolves yipped and fumbled as the wolf on the left side of the pack burst into flames and fell to the ground, motionless. All four of the wolves seemed to be rethinking their tactic as their forward momentum halted so that they could glance at their fallen pack member. I wasn't going to give them an opportunity to regroup. Like Lucas, I held my hand up angrily and shot a fireball at the wolf on the right. The fire washed over him, and the other three wolves jumped back, yipping and howling.

Before that burning wolf even registered that he was burning alive and had fallen over, Lucas had used my magic once again to send a fireball in the direction of another wolf. More yipping from the remaining two reached my ears as I swiveled to launch a fireball at another wolf—the one I knew to be Jason. He was larger than the other four had been, so I knew that had to be him. As I raised my arm, Lucas' hand slipped from mine. I hadn't been paying attention when I had turned to aim at Jason, so I hadn't realized how loosely Lucas and I were holding onto each other.

As soon as my hand slipped from Lucas', and our connection to each other—his connection to a source of magic he could use to protect himself—slipped away, the Not Jason wolf jumped. I screamed out in horror as the wolf crashed into Lucas, and the two of them fell to the ground in a heap, the wolf on top of Lucas, its jaws snapping. Screaming out in rage, I turned back, intending to jump on the wolf that had leapt upon Lucas, knocking it away, but then my body was lifted off the ground. A bag of fur with four legs and snapping jaws followed me to the ground.

Jason came to rest on top of me as my back slammed into the hard earth of the garden, landing on all four of his paws. Disoriented and having had the breath knocked from my lungs, all I could do was grab wolf-Jason's neck and hold his head back as he attempted to snap at my face. Jason's glowing red eyes glared down at me as fangs snapped, and spittle dripped into my face. My hands couldn't even fit around his giant wolf neck, so choking him out wasn't an option. I could see the murderous look in his eyes, even though the eyes I was peering into weren't human. Lucas was screaming somewhere to my side, but I refused to turn my head to look for him, to see how he was doing, because it would have distracted me from protecting myself. I was no good to Lucas dead.

Wolf-Jason continued to snap his jaws, trying to get closer to my face as I screamed out in fear and rage and did my best to hold him back. While I never considered myself weak, my body wasn't at its best—and I was fighting a fucking wolf. Hardly any man is a match for a werewolf with human intelligence and preternatural strength. They'd have to be...

Special.

I knew magic.

Fuck, I was dumb.

And so was Jason.

My fear bled into my rage as I stopped screaming. I looked up into wolf-Jason's eyes angrily as I let my magic pour into my arms, down the length of them, and into my hands.

"Burn!" I growled, right before the fire burst from my palms.

Wolf-Jason was engulfed so quickly that I feared he might fall on me, trapping me beneath him, and sentence me to a fiery death as well. However, I couldn't even feel any heat from the fire, even as it burned away Jason's fur, and he leapt away, no longer trapping me beneath him. I watched just long enough to see him topple over onto his side, his legs kicking wildly, going nowhere, as he lay burning.

When I heard Lucas' screams again, the fury no longer impairing my focus, I leapt up from the ground and spun around, looking for Lucas and the wolf that had jumped on him. Less than a few yards away, Lucas was positioned in the same manner I had been with wolf-Jason on top of me. The last werewolf was standing over him, on all fours, effectively trapping him against the ground, snapping and snarling as Lucas did his best to push the beast's jaws away.

A few quick steps and my hand was against the side of the wolf as Lucas' hands stayed around its throat. The wolf had just enough time to glance at me out of the corner of its eye before I felt my magic rolling down my arm once again. Lucas looked up at me from the ground, relief flooding his face as I grinned evilly at the wolf I was about to kill.

"*And fuck you, too.*" I snapped.

Then the wolf burst into flames.

As I pulled Lucas to his feet, the wolf leaping away to collapse in a fiery ball, the first thing I noticed was the gash on Lucas' forehead, oozing viscous blood. Now that he had nothing to brace it against, his left arm hung limply at his side. Whether it was broken or dislocated, I had no idea, but something was definitely wrong with it. Fury rolled through me as Lucas stood there, bleeding and broken. I spun so that I could see all five burning heaps of wolf in the garden. With every ounce of energy I had in my body, and with my boyfriend bleeding and broken behind me, I summoned up my magic.

Sometimes, without being told, you just know some things to be true.

I knew that my eyes were glowing red.

Just like the wolves' eyes had.

Just like Bloody Bones.

Summoning every bit of rage I could, I focused that magic on the four burning heaps in the garden...and commanded my magic to do my bidding. Five different holes opened in the ground, swallowing the burning wolves, pulling them beneath the surface, dragging them down. Though I had no way of knowing for sure if they would end up where I wanted, I knew where I had told my magic to send them. And I hoped that my magic was powerful enough to do it. The holes in the ground were just beginning to fill back up, sealing away the wolves, the light from the fires being snuffed out, when I turned back to Lucas.

"Are you okay?" I asked, my eyes going to his.

Lucas looked...amazed.

"What did you do?" He asked, his good arm moving to cradle his hurt arm.

"Permanently solved a problem." I shrugged, stepping closer to him.

Lucas gave a brief smile, which was quickly replaced by a wince. I cringed and started to reach out to him. Unfortunately, as my body and arm moved as one, my eyes also moved. Black flashed in my vision, and my eyes were drawn over to the side of the garden fence where Bloody Bones now stood, his gleaming, bony smile and red eyes looking amused.

"Well done." He said as I stepped towards him, putting my body between him and Lucas. "Though I have to say, I am not shocked."

"You shouldn't be," I said as I felt Lucas' hand touch my shoulder for support. "You're next."

Bloody Bones' skull tilted back towards the heavens, and a long peal of laughter escaped his maw. In the corner of my eye, I could see Oma standing at her post, looking concerned. Obviously, no one had faith in what I had said.

"It's been eleven years since I've met a witch in battle." His coarse, gravelly voice met my ears. "I forgot how entertaining your kind can be."

"You want a show?" I snapped, my arm beginning to rise.

"I've learned from my mistakes in the past." Bloody Bones said. "And a few new tricks."

Before I could even blink, Bloody Bones' arm snapped up, and an orb of sickly green light burst forth. I didn't even have time to raise my arm. I certainly had no idea how to counter or block a spell. If I had a memory of being trained to do such a thing, it was failing me. All I had time to do was to realize that *this was it*. Maybe I had killed a few wolves...but I definitely was no match for Bloody Bones. Especially now that I didn't have a reservoir of magic the well had provided. I wasn't ready. And that was how I would die.

"*NO!*" Lucas screamed as magic flared in the air around us.

And then I was falling to the ground in a heap. The air was knocked from my lungs, and my vision blurred as a starless, moonless, black sky looked down on me. The world seemed to slow as my head swam from smacking against the ground so forcefully. Muffled sounds filled my ears.

Did you see that?

Shaking my head to clear the sounds and the confusion, I pushed off of the ground, rage filling me again as I came to my knees, my vision clearing, though I was still trying to catch my breath. Bloody Bones was still across from me at the garden fence...and he was smiling. Oma was standing a few yards away, a few feet within the fence perimeter, her mouth hung slack, her eyes wide and terrified.

All I could think was that, yes, Bloody Bones had knocked me on my ass...sent me reeling...but I was still alive.

But then I saw Lucas standing to my side. Looking up, I saw that he was looking down at his stomach, which he had his one good hand against. As I looked up, his head turned to me. His face was ashen, and a single tear was sliding down his cheek as his eyes met mine. Then he crumpled to his knees beside me. My voice caught in my throat as my face twisted in horror and disbelief when I saw the blood gushing out from between the fingers of the hand against his stomach.

My arms went out to catch Lucas as he fell into me, blood streaming down the front of him. Lucas' body was nearly dead weight in my arms as his body slumped against me, turning just enough so that he could look up at me, his face pasty white, his eyes looking dim, though they were wide open. His lips quivered, and his mouth opened as if to say something to me, but nothing came out, though another tear escaped his eye.

"Lucas." I gasped, holding him tightly, struggling to keep him off of the ground but also figure out what to do to help him.

Then Bloody Bones reeled back with an evil laugh, his arm held up aggressively. Another orb of sickly green light flew at us.

And nothing happened.

Bloody Bones jerked, and somehow, his skull-like face looked shocked.

"*I told him 'no.*'" Lucas croaked from his place in my arms, making me look back down at him.

Lucas' eyes searched my face as his blood oozed from his stomach and trickled between us, dripping onto my knees and the ground below. Reaching out with some part of my magic that was instinctive, something told me that there was nothing to be done. My boyfriend was dying right there in my arms as Oma watched—because that's what The Guardian does. It's what The Guardian has always done. And he had been killed by Bloody Bones. Because that's what Bloody Bones does. That's what he has always done. Tears welled in my eyes as I looked down at Lucas, trying to find the words to tell him how much I loved him. How sorry I was—*how everything in this moment was my fault and no one else's.*

Instead of my voice filling the space between us...faint green light did. And it wasn't coming from another offensive spell from Bloody Bones. It wasn't my magic. It was Lucas' eyes. They were glowing—like I had only seen them do once before. As if trying to communicate with me, and not having the use of his voice, Lucas' eyes searched my face, desperately trying to get me to understand something. For what seemed like hours, but was probably less than a second, I tried to understand what Lucas' eyes were telling me. Then, Lucas' fingers slithered across my forearm, smearing it with blood. Weaker than ever before, I felt Lucas draw my magic down my arm, almost like a trickle from a faucet...and his eyes glowed red.

A sudden realization went through me, and I gasped as I held my dying boyfriend.

As above, so below.

All things have to be equal.

And I was holding something that still contained part of Bloody Bones' stolen power. A piece that had refused to serve him. Someone who was going to die…*no matter what I did.* I could make things equal again. A tear slithered down my cheek as I looked down at Lucas in my arms, my lips slowly curling into a sad smile. Lucas somehow found the strength to give me a single nod, though no words escaped his lips.

"I love you," I said.

He nodded once more.

When I looked up from Lucas, my eyes settling on Bloody Bones, I knew that my eyes were glowing red once again. Underneath us all, the ground started to rumble and shake, and from the look that suddenly flooded Bloody Bones skull-like face, I knew that he knew someone else was the cause of it for once in his long life.

"Ohhhhhh, shit." I heard Oma crow, though I was too focused on the man made of bones in the black hooded cloak to search her out with my eyes. "You done pissed him off good, Red Eyes."

I want to say it was fury once again that filled me from the tips of my toes to the top of my head. But it wasn't. It wasn't a desire to make things equal due to altruism. It wasn't anger or rage.

It was vengeance.

And that would have to be good enough.

A howling scream emanated from my throat—a noise I never would have known I could make—as my head went back, and my face looked to the heavens. I drew all of the magic I could from my dying boyfriend, summoned up all of my own magic, and…

I made a wish.

The only wish that could make things right.

Put them back the way they ought to be.

The ground continued to shake as I screamed to the heavens, commanding anything that was listening to let me have my vengeance. A loud cracking sound filled the air, and the Earth split. Bloody Bones screamed in terror. When I stopped screaming to find him with my eyes, the ground was open beneath his feet, and what I could only describe as arms made of fire and melting flesh were pulling at him, dragging him down. A wicked grin split my face as my eyes continued to glow red, and I watched those…*things*…drag Bloody Bones into the ground.

Bloody Bones thrashed and fought, cast spells at the arm-like things attempting to drag him downwards, slowing their pull until he was no longer moving downward. In fact, he might have been reversing the pull, moving upwards infinitesimally. Desperately, I tried to search out more magic, trying to figure out what else I could put with my vengeance to finish the job…and my eyes landed on Oma. As soon as she saw that I had spotted her, standing by the fence, she rolled her eyes and sighed.

"Fine." She threw her hands up and began walking towards me and Lucas, who I couldn't bring myself to examine. "Ya' can't really create balance for good if you leave me behind, can ya'? Ain't got no damn oracle anyway."

My eyes met hers, and I smiled at her, unable to find words to say—not that my current state would have allowed me to speak eloquently. Bloody Bones saw Oma walking towards me and howled in rage, increasing his efforts to try and fight off the arms trying to pull him underneath. He fought harder and faster, but it didn't take Oma long enough to cross the distance between her and us. Coming to stand at my side, my shoulder even with her hip, she turned to face Bloody Bones as he struggled.

"Fuck you, Red Eyes." She cackled.

Then she placed her hand on my shoulder. I looked up at her.

"I only wish I'd eaten more donuts." I managed to say.

Oma continued to cackle as I smiled softly.

And I drew from her magic forcefully, grinning at Bloody Bones, looking him in the eyes as he was forcefully yanked down into the Earth by the arms that still held him. Fire shot from the crack in the ground, soaring into the sky in a pillar of fire as Bloody Bones' screams of agony descended further into the Earth until the sound of them could no longer reach my ears. Slowly, I crooked my head to look at Lucas. His eyes were closed, and I couldn't sense anything from him. Quickly, I crooked my neck to look up at Oma.

"Here comes the good part." She said, giving me a wink, though the smile on her face was sad.

I nodded at her, another tear rolling from my eye and over my cheek as I looked toward the house. The crack grew longer, reaching towards Oma, Lucas, and me. The three of us waiting for it to claim us as well. Just as the crack reached us, I saw movement at the corner of the house. Someone stumbling out of the decreasing shadows as the darkness dissolved from the sky, and the heralding dawn started to bathe the world in golden light once again.

Andrew?

Then the Earth was claiming the three of us.

Chapter 14

"*NO!!!!*" Andrew screamed and pushed off from the side of the house, still out of breath from his journey from Main Street to Esther Jean Wagner's on foot—of which he now only had two.

Andrew raced across the yard, limping and skipping, the crack in the ground slowly inching shut, closing off the space where Esther Jean, Lucas, and Rob had disappeared. The sun slowly rose in the east as he awkwardly leapt the garden fence and dove towards the narrow crack in the garden, landing over it just as the last bit of Earth sealed shut. For the briefest of moments, the ground shook underneath, and then all was silent and still.

Rising to his knees, Andrew brought his hands to his head, a look of agony twisting his face as he gazed down at the Earth that was as smooth as it had been before this night. Bird song suddenly met his ears as the world came to life around him. A gentle, cold breeze blew in off of Lake Erie, over the trees, and greeted Andrew's back. Andrew looked around frantically, wondering if anyone else was around, wondering if there was someone who could help him figure out what to do. Esther Jean was gone. Carlita was dead. Mr. Barkley was probably dead. Everyone he had been working towards this moment with was...no more.

There was no one around to reach out to, to ask for help or guidance. Andrew didn't even have a pack to run off to in order to be consoled. He was all alone in the backyard of a house that no longer had an owner and a garden that might never see planting again. With nothing more to do, Andrew pushed off of the ground in defeat and rose to his full height. Slowly, reaching up to wipe his nose with the back of his hand, Andrew turned on his heels. His feet began to move of his own accord as he walked towards the garden fence.

Barely at the perimeter of the garden, about to open the gate so that he could once again leave, find somewhere to go, someone to speak with, to help him forget this night, the ground shook briefly for another moment. Shocked and afraid, Andrew whipped around, expecting Bloody Bones to suddenly pop out of the ground.

But Bloody Bones did not suddenly appear out of the ground like he had on Main Street when the Earth had shaken. The ground didn't even crack. Instead, Andrew's eyes landed on a small green sprout that popped out of the ground like a thermometer on a roasted turkey. Andrew's eyes stayed on the sprout as it ever so slowly grew into a seedling. With ever-widening eyes, Andrew continued to watch as the seedling, nearly knee-high grew into a sapling. Though he didn't know why, Andrew began to smile as the sapling began to grow faster, picking up speed as its trunk widened, and its branches began to split and elongate, reaching towards the sky.

Bit by bit, the tree grew taller and broader as Andrew stood there in awe, backing up to give it room to grow without knocking him over. The trunk became wide than four men bundled together and the branches continued to split and thicken and reach into the sky. Then the process was complete. In under a minute, Andrew had been walking towards the garden fence, wondering what to do, and then he had watched a tiny sprout grow into a fully mature tree. One that would have taken decades— if not centuries—to grow.

Andrew looked up at the tree in wonder, examining its thick bark and gnarly roots that surely anchored it securely and deeply into the Earth. Hundreds of branches adorned the massive tree that towered over him in the garden, reaching out in an umbrella of brownish-black over Andrew's head. He continued to stare in awe as his eyes were drawn to one of the lower branches that seemed to shiver against the cool breeze coming off of the lake. Before his very eyes, a single bud appeared from a knot in the tree branch, slowly unfurling to show that the tree was announcing the coming Spring.

Smiling to himself, Andrew's eyes closed languidly. He sniffed the air, hoping he would smell Esther Jean, Lucas, or Rob on the air...but all he smelled was fresh air and dirt. Frowning to himself, Andrew wondered why his keen senses from being a werewolf did not pick up anything else...just as they always had. His eyes grew wide as an idea struck him. As he had done, many thousands of times before, Andrew willed himself into wolf form.

And nothing happened.

He was still human-Andrew, standing before a tree that hadn't existed just minutes before.

There was nothing for Andrew to do but smile and say his thanks as the warm, golden light of the sun kissed his skin.

It was the first time he'd ever had to thank a witch.

     "Thanks, Tom!" The field reporter spoke into her microphone as she looked into the camera.

     Behind her, the smoke and wreckage of Main Street created a harrowing scene with which to frame her story. Plumes of blackish, sooty smoke rose from Barkley's Hardware Store. The firefighters were still putting out small clusters of fire that were still burning in the First National Bank of Point Worth. The Sunny Side-Up Café was nothing but rubble. Men—naked for some reason—lay in the middle of the street, badly battered and bruised. A crack ran down the center of Main Street, nothing but darkness and cold below. A woman, partially covered by a sheet, was lying in the street, her heels with red soles sticking out from the bottom. The reporter gestured towards the scene behind her.

     "As you can see behind me here, Tom, and our viewers at home," She waved, shaking her head sadly, "the town of Point Worth, a small community within walking distance of the shores of Lake Erie, is in ruins. No one knows what caused these fires or many of these buildings to collapse, or what happened to these poor people behind me. The police are canvassing the town as we speak, looking for any citizen of Point Worth who might be able to shed some light on what happened in this little berg. The anonymous person who called the Toledo Police Department this morning merely said that there were problems in Point Worth, but failed to elaborate, give a name, or even stay on the line long enough for the dispatchers to thoroughly question him.

     "What we do know is that whatever happened here could possibly happen anywhere in this great state of ours. That is why the police are trying to put the pieces together and find anyone who might be able to let them know what happened. It's in all Ohioans' best interest to know if this was an isolated incident, or maybe even an act of terror. But—"

Chapter 15

"Did you see that?"

Rolling my eyes, I paused, stopping my pitch to look across the table. Three faces were huddled over the scripts I had provided at the beginning of the meeting, pointing and jabbing at the pages before them. Of course, I could've ignored yet another irritating statement in the middle of my pitch, but I was about done being polite with these three morons. Placing my hands on top of the table, I laced my fingers and stared at the people across from me. Letting a smile form on my face, I waited for them to notice I had stopped speaking.

"Did you see that?" The man on the right—Bob, I think—tapped his script again. "Right there. He wants to kill every damn character in this thing!"

"Thanks for the spoiler alert." The lady in the middle—Lucinda, I believe—rolled her eyes.

I liked her.

"Someone has to die, right?" The man on the other side of Lucinda shrugged.

His name was Ron. I had worked with him before.

"You can't really have this type of story and expect it to have a fairytale ending," Ron added.

"Why not?" Bob snipped. "Everyone loves a happy ending."

"Do they?" Lucinda gave him a saccharine sweet smile. "Do they really, Bob? People bitched for weeks and weeks about each death on *Game of Thrones,* but they kept tuning in, didn't they?"

"That's different!" Bob proclaimed.

"How?" Ron backed Lucinda up.

"They didn't kill the whole goddamn cast in one episode!"

"They killed *a lot of the cast* in single episodes. *The Red Wedding,* for example." Lucinda gestured vaguely. "You have had an issue on nearly every damn page of this script."

"This isn't *Game of Thrones!*" Bob added angrily.

"Bob, just look at it this way." Ron tried to play peacemaker. "If we—"

Before either Lucinda or Ron could stop him, Bob growled with frustration and pushed away from the table. My eyes tracked his movements as he jumped up from his chair and marched toward the door to the conference room, his chair still spinning lazily from the exertion. Once the door to the conference room had slammed shut behind him, I let my head turn back to Lucinda and Ron. They both looked apologetic—and frankly, embarrassed for their partner.

"Sorry." Lucinda winced.

"Don't apologize for a man." I raised an eyebrow. "Especially one like Bob."

Ron laughed as Lucinda let a smile come back to her face—we were obviously going to be friends. "This ain't your first rodeo with Bob, is it, Jacob?"

I shrugged.

"We have his opinion," I said, gesturing at the three scripts still open on the other side of the table. "What do you think of *Jacob Michaels Is...*? Think we can send it to series? Get the green light to at least fund a pilot?"

Lucinda chewed at her lip thoughtfully as Ron glanced over at her.

"Jacob." He sighed.

"Yes?"

"It is very dark. And everyone *does* die at the end." He gave me an apologetic look. "And, I mean, the Oma character. Love her, don't get me wrong. But this isn't going on network. We'd have to change her whole personality if we pitched to network. You know that, right?"

I laughed.

"Andrew didn't die," I said. "And I was thinking premium or Netflix."

"No one's going to give a shit about Andrew." Lucinda chuckled, though I could tell she hated breaking that news. "I mean, he's not a sympathetic character. He's kind of like the Severus Snape."

"Without a really good backstory." Ron helped her.

"Oma and Lucas." Lucinda brightened. "Those are your fan favorites. And you butchered one and sacrificed the other."

"Lucas and Oma?" I chuckled. I wasn't offended. "Rob gets no love, huh?"

They both laughed.

"Carlita." Ron performed a 'chef's kiss' type motion. "People will die for her. But you killed her off as well. Hell, even Lucas' grandfather got axed. In fact, it's pretty clear that most everyone in the town died—even ones you'd never know about. You left the one character no one will feel all that sympathetic towards. I mean...we live in the age of the internet, Jacob. They'll absolutely roast your ass on Twitter."

"I live to be dragged on Twitter." I shrugged.

Lucinda and Ron exchanged a look.

"Ron," I chuckled warmly, doing my best 'Nice Jacob Michaels' impersonation, "have I brought you anything that turned out to be bad before? Every movie we've worked on together has done well enough. Some have even done really well. Not a single stinker in the bunch."

Lucinda and Ron seemed to decide something telepathically, so Lucinda turned to me to speak whatever it was they had discussed subliminally.

"Jacob," She said, "this is very meta. It's cool. I mean, you're *Jacob Michaels*, your real name is Robert Wagner, and you're from Ohio, and you want to make a series where an actor with the stage name 'Jacob Michaels' goes home to Ohio to get away from the toxicity of Hollywood. I love that. But..."

"But what?"

"People might start to think this is really your life story," Ron explained.

"They'll think I really grew up in a house with a magical old lady and tiny little creatures that did household chores, and my hometown was full of people with magical abilities and werewolves? That I can shoot lasers and fire from my hands? That's crazy." I couldn't help but let a laugh escape my mouth.

Both Ron and Lucinda turned a pinkish color, but they laughed with me.

"Well, okay." Ron held his hands up. "Who do you see in the supporting roles? I mean...it sounds like..."

"Yeah." I nodded, stopping him. "Obviously Esther Jean Wagner for Oma. Lucas Barkley for Lucas Barkley...I found some new talent for Jason, Carlita, and Andrew, and—"

"You want your real grandmother and boyfriend to play your grandmother and boyfriend—and you want the characters to have the same names as the real people?" Lucinda's brow furrowed, thinking this over.

"Yeah." I shrugged as if this was the most natural thing in the world.

"Jacob." Ron gave a barking laugh. "Lucas has barely even managed to land supporting roles in the past...and now you want to give him a role in a project like this?"

"Talk about nepotism," Lucinda spoke out of the corner of her mouth to Ron.

They both laughed, but it wasn't at my expense.

"Sure." I shrugged. "He can do it. You said meta is good, right?"

"I just said it was cool. Not good." Lucinda teased.

"And your grandmother—God love her—" Ron began, "she's an incredible actress. But how long has it been since she's acted? The 70s?"

"She did some T.V. and a few movies in the 80s and 90s." I corrected him, though I knew he knew those things.

"Pardon me." He laughed.

"Come on, guys." I rolled my eyes with a smile, trying to be affable. "Jacob Michaels, his legendary actress grandmother—"

"That's pushing it." Lucinda mumbled.

"—his actor boyfriend. All from Ohio. All playing themselves in a T.V. show that pretends to be about their real life. It's like reality T.V. meets situational comedy meets dramedy. And it's full of magic and fantasy in my hometown in Ohio. Don't tell me people wouldn't eat that shit up if we do it right. People are dying for LGBTQ plus representation in their media. They want to see meaty roles for older women. Everyone loves drag queens—even Republicans. We could easily show the juxtaposition between the glamour of Hollywood and regular working-class Americans. It would be easy to show social issues and discuss them visually. But in a heightened reality, fantasy way that appeals to a broader audience than those just looking for something real. It's the best of both worlds. You could appeal to people out here and people in middle America. This is one of those shows that easily trends on social media every Sunday night and is discussed in workplaces across America on Monday. And the Kobolds? Ernst? Think of the action figures and stuffed dolls possibility. So...much...merch."

Again, Lucinda and Ron exchanged looks, seemed to have a telepathic discussion, and agreed on something quietly.

"We're not denying that it's intriguing—" Ron began.

"You, your grandmother, and Lucas are not getting paid well first season. Maybe the first two." Lucinda interjected.

"My feelings." I held a hand to my heart with a smile. "So...are we going to work on developing this?"

Another look between the two.

"Fine." Ron sighed.

"Don't sound too happy." I teased as I rose from my seat.

"I just don't know where we'll find little people to play the Kobolds." Ron ruminated. "I mean, there's always CGI, but that's expensive. Maybe forced perspective will work..."

"It's going to be a tough sell," Lucinda added a sigh and stood.

"I have a very inexpensive solution." I smiled warmly. "Don't worry."

"I guess we'll see what the studios say." Ron shrugged with a laugh.

"I have a feeling that when you take it to streaming, one of them will snatch it up. Easy three-seasons green light." I held a hand out towards her. "And then you can apologize for that comment."

Lucinda and Ron laughed, but ultimately, we all shook hands.

Then I was leaving the production office.

The drive out to Calabasas is too long when there's good news to be shared. It was a sunny day, though there is never a shortage of such a thing in southern California. For the first time in my life as a celebrity, I wished that I didn't have a Lincoln MKZ but something sportier, something the roof could be lowered on. Maybe a BMW 4 Series or a Corvette...hell, even a Jeep Wrangler would have been nice on such a wonderful day. To feel the sun on my face and neck and arms as I drove from the production office meeting back home, the wind whipping through my hair as *Scissor Sisters* blared from the radio would have made it the best day it possibly could have been.

Lucinda and Ron had been skeptical—or, more accurately, they had pretended to be skeptical—but they were going to help develop *Jacob Michaels Is...* into something we could sell to Netflix or Hulu. Maybe even Amazon Prime. Then, Oma, Lucas, and I would find ourselves on a studio lot—maybe even on location—shooting our first ever project as a family and team. I couldn't have been happier. Of course, I worked enough for all of us, there was no lack of money coming into our household, but I knew how desperately Oma wanted to get back to work on something substantial. Having a starring—or even co-starring—role in anything would make Lucas so happy. He had never been given a chance to show what a talented actor he was.

When I pulled into the driveway at home, easing the car into the garage next to Lucas' old pickup truck that had come with us from Point Worth a decade prior, I smiled. Oma's old Cadillac was on the far end of the garage, nearly permanently parked there since she always had someone to drive her anywhere. It was almost like yesterday that Oma had convinced the two of us two travel out to Hollywood to "give this acting thing a shot." Now...here we were...living in Calabasas, living the dream, and about to star in our first project as a family. Life couldn't possibly get better.

The garage closed quietly behind me as I entered the house. I didn't bother hollering out, trying to figure out where everyone was. Oma and Lucas had to be in the same place they always were when they had the day off. They'd both been waiting for me to get home from my meeting to tell them the outcome. I walked through the house, all floor-to-ceiling windows, granite, and steel, making my way to the back patio. Just as I had suspected, as I looked out through the glass doors that looked out over the patio, I saw Lucas and Oma seated at the table. Lucas had his nose in a book with a glass of lemonade on the table before him. Oma was staring out at the hills, a flute of champagne in her hand, held grandly before her. It was a nice contrast to the house dress and slippers she hadn't changed out of since breakfast.

Before I could make my way out to the patio to be with my boyfriend and grandmother, I felt my phone vibrate in my pocket. I extracted my phone, tapped the screen, and glanced down at the text message I'd received:

Ron: How about more of a murder mystery with fantasy or paranormal elements? We won't touch the characters or give you shit about who plays which character.

Smiling widely to myself, I realized that the script had hooked Ron and Lucinda more than they had been willing to let on in the meeting. No producer ever messaged so quickly after a pitch meeting. Quickly, but not so quickly as to seem desperate, I tapped out my short response.
Deal.

As I stepped out onto the patio, Oma turned her head to look at me, raising her champagne flute in a salute with a smile.

"Afternoon, assface." She quipped before bringing her drink to her lips.

"Good afternoon, you old bag." I nudged her shoulder with my hip as I went by. "How's the sauce?"

"Well," She sighed and smacked her lips, "I've had worse."

I laughed as I slid into the seat next to Lucas, who still had his nose in his book. A quick glance at the cover let me know that he was rereading *Interview with the Vampire* by Anne Rice. Using my forefinger, I thumped the cover, and Lucas jerked in his seat. Looking up from his book, as though he had been somewhere else entirely, he looked over the top of the book. For a second, he seemed disoriented, then his eyes met mine, and a smile bloomed on his face.

"Babe." He stated happily.

"Research?" I asked, nodding at the book.

Lucas set his book on the patio table, spine up, and leaned forward to give me a chaste, yet lingering kiss.

"Mmm." I winked as he pulled away.

"Not really research," He gestured at the book, "but, just in case they didn't like what you took to them today, maybe I could be inspired to come up with a better idea to tweak what we wrote."

"They liked it." I leaned in with a grin.

Lucas' eyes grew wide with joyful surprise, and his lips were on mine once again.

"Well, good," Oma grumbled from the other side of the table. "Y'all didn't have enough reasons to swap spit, did ya'?"

"Can it, old woman." I teased her as Lucas' arms went around my neck, giving me a celebratory hug. "This is good news."

"Yeah?" She turned in her seat to look at us as Lucas' arms slid from my neck, and he beamed at me. "Betcha dollars to donuts them sumbitches loved the idea of you in the lead, but where does that leave me and handsome over there?"

"Thank you, Mrs. Wagner." Lucas laughed.

"They probably told you that 'the old hag' and your 'boy toy' had to sit this one out, didn't they?" Oma waggled her head and slammed the rest of her champagne.

"I don't like that nickname nearly as much." Lucas turned up his nose.

"Ignore her." I patted his knee. "As a matter of fact, Oma, they are on board with all three of us. They said they want to change it to a murder mystery with paranormal and fantasy elements, but otherwise, they're going to move forward with all three of us."

Oma's brow raised.

"Well," The corner of her mouth turned up, "didn't think you had it in you to make that kind of deal. The washed-up old has-been and the professional extra get called up to the big leagues."

Lucas frowned at her, but he wasn't wholly unamused.

"Stuff it, Oma." I did my best not to chuckle.

"Oh, boy. It's true what they say. You don't buy champagne, ya' rent it." Oma stated simply before rising from her chair and scuttling toward the house.

Lucas watched her go, shaking his head amusedly.

"We should probably celebrate." He finally said once Oma was out of earshot. "Do you want to go out?"

"You hate going out." I leaned in with a grin and laid my forehead against his.

"I do."

"Maybe you'll be saying that phrase in a different context in the future?" I wiggled my eyebrows.

"Ya' never know." He winked.

"Time will tell." I sighed happily.

"I'll make us something special for dinner. Lots of wine." He slowly rose from his chair, so I sat back in mine to give him space. "Then, when the old lady goes to bed, we'll do disrespectful things."

"Obscenely disrespectful." I winked up at him.

Lucas grinned wickedly and made his way toward the house, just like Oma had. Of course, unlike Oma, he most likely wasn't going to attack the champagne after visiting the bathroom. I sat back in the patio chair and propped my elbows on the table, smiling to myself. Just thinking about developing a project with the two people I loved most in life would keep me happy for a long time. Unless things fell through, and the project just couldn't be brought to the small screen, I knew that I would be even happier in the months to come.

I nearly jumped out of my skin as a hand suddenly found my knee and had to stop myself from screaming out. Holding a hand to my chest, I laughed as the small man crept out from under the table. Ernst gave me an apologetic smile as he patted my knee and came to stand beside me.

"*I don' like California, Rob.*" He said in his high-pitched voice. "*Too much sun. I like shadows.*"

He squinted and held a hand over his eyes to block out some of the sunlight that threatened his senses.

I laid a hand on his shoulder. "I know. The others have said the same thing. Give it time. In a few months, maybe we'll all be back in Ohio."

Ernst's eyes lit up from underneath the visor made of his hand.

"*Did they like your ideas?*" He asked, hopefully.

"They did." I smiled down at him.

"*We've been 'ere so long.*" He sighed. "*I woul' love to be back 'ome.*"

I patted his shoulder and gave it a squeeze as I looked out at the sunlit hills around us.

"We'll see what the future brings, my friend." I smiled. "Only time will tell. Have faith."

And...scene.

A Point Worth LGBTQ+
Paranormal Romance Series
Will continue with Book 7 –
Murder at the Red Rooster Tavern

~Coming in 2021~

Jacob Michaels Is Tired

About the Author

Chase Connor currently lives in Des Moines, Iowa with his partner, his dog, Rimbaud, and spends his free time writing M/M Romance, LGBTQ YA novellas/novels, LGBTQ Paranormal Romance, as well as general LGBTQ fiction, when he's not busy being enthusiastic about naps and Pad Thai.

Chase can be reached at
chaseconnor@chaseconnor.com
Or on Twitter @ChaseConnor7
He can also be found on Chase Connor Books
https://chaseconnor.com
or on Goodreads
https://www.goodreads.com/author/show/18055910.Chase_Connor

He does his very best to respond to all DMs, emails, and Twitter comments from his reader friends and loves the interaction with them. Chase has several novellas/novels for sale on Amazon (and other sites) in ebook and paperback format.

Chase Connor's catalog can be read for free with Kindle Unlimited

Jacob Michaels Is Tired

www.ingramcontent.com/pod-product-compliance
Lightning Source LLC
Chambersburg PA
CBHW030838030726
47495CB00005B/1284